W9-CBA-015

An Outrageous Affair

ALSO BY THE SAME AUTHOR

No Angel

Something Dangerous

Into Temptation

Almost a Crime

The Dilemma

Sheer Abandon

An Outrageous Affair

Penny Vincenzi

THE OVERLOOK PRESS
Woodstock & New York

This edition first published in the United States in 2008 by
The Overlook Press, Peter Mayer Publishers, Inc.
Woodstock & New York

WOODSTOCK:
One Overlook Drive
Woodstock, NY 12498
www.overlookpress.com
[for individual orders, bulk and special sales, contact our Woodstock office]

NEW YORK:
141 Wooster Street
New York, NY 10012

Cataloging-in-Publication Datais available from the Library of Congress

Manufactured in the United States of America
ISBN 978-1-59020-101-5
10 9 8 7 6 5 4 3 2 1

For Polly, Sophie, Emily and Claudia,
who are all so outrageously good to me

Acknowledgments

Acknowledgments are a bit like Oscar speeches; corny, predictable but from the heart.

From my heart then, may I offer some predictable corn to the people who have helped me with *An Outrageous Affair*.

I could not have begun to write the chapters set in Hollywood without the help of my good friend in Los Angeles, Anita Alberts, who worked tirelessly to find me people to talk to about Tinseltown in the fifties: and wonderful Gabrielle Donnelly who did the same and took me to endless legendary eateries. It was all the best fun.

In New York, Nancy Alloggiamento gave up hours of her high-powered time to tell me about Madison Avenue and its attendant excitements, past and present; and so did Gregg Boekeloo who was wonderfully funny and informative on the same subject.

I would also like to thank Sally O'Sullivan, brilliant editor and friend, who has dispatched me over the years to interview countless actors, thereby providing me with a great deal of background and colour; and a special thak you to Angela Fox, who has not only given me lots of wonderful stories and gossip to weave into my story, but has advised me on such crucial points of detail as theatrical superstition and folk lore.

I would also like to thank my mother-in-law for the very valuable groundwork she put in for me into my research into wartime Suffolk, and all the people in Framlingham and Woodbridge (none of whom will remember me) who raked their memroies for G.I. stories for me, as I wandered through one dark January day two years ago.

I would like to thank Sue Stapely, legal whizz person, upon whose encyclopaediac knowledge of just about everything I increasingly rely and several other members of the legal profession who wish to remain anonymous but who have guided me through the quagmire of libel law and writs and the whole damn thing; to Caroleen Conquest, Morag Lyall and Katie Pope who have seemingly magical powers in transforming manuscripts into books; and to Carol Osborne without whom I would never finish any book because she sees to all the things that I should be doing at home. And, as always, a special thank you to Rosie Cheetham, without whose skill, inspiration and awe-inspiring patience as an editor I should be entirely lost; and to Desmond Elliott who, apart from his more conventional duties as my agent, makes me laugh and boosts my morale exactly when I need it most.

The Main Characters

ENGLAND

Caroline, Lady Hunterton, née Miller
Sir William Hunterton, *her husband*
Chloe, *their daughter, later Mrs/Lady Piers Windsor*
Toby and Jolyon, their sons
Jack Bamforth, *Caroline's groom*
Joe Payton, *arts journalist, later Caroline's partner*
Piers (later Sir Piers) Windsor, *Chloe's husband*
Flavia, *his mother*
Guinevere Davies, *his first wife*
Pandora, Edmund and Kitty, *children of Piers and Chloe*
Rosemary, *their nanny*
Jean Potts, *Piers's secretary*
Ludovic Ingram, *lawyer, friend of the Windsors*
Magnus Phillips, *journalist and biographer*

NEW YORK

Brendan FitzPatrick, *screen name* Byron Patrick
Kathleen, *his mother*
Edna, Kate and Maureen, *his sisters*
Kevin Clint, *a theatrical agent*
Hilton Berelman, *talent scout for Twentieth Century Fox*
Fleur FitzPatrick, *daughter of Brendan and Caroline Hunterton*
Poppy Blake, *a colleague of Fleur*
Reuben Blake, *her brother*

HOLLYWOOD

Yolande duGrath, *drama coach*
Rose Sharon, *friend of Brendan*
Naomi MacNeice, *studio executive*
Perry Browne, *Publicist*

Prologue

1972

From the *Daily Mail*, 10 July 1972
Final curtain comes down on Sir Piers Windsor

Sir Piers Windsor, who was knighted by the Queen yesterday, and has played all the great tragic heroes, was centre-stage in a dreadful real-life tragedy yesterday, when he was found dead by his secretary in the stables of his country home in Berkshire. Foul play is not suspected.

Sir Piers, who was 51, was at the peak of his profession. Only yesterday he was knighted by the Queen for services to the British theatre, and he had been earning huge critical acclaim for his production of *Othello* with the Royal Shakespeare Company in which he was playing Othello and Iago on alternate nights. His celebrated film of *A Midsummer Night's Dream* won three Oscars two years ago, and he was about to take a Shakespeare repertory company to New York. His innovatory musical version of *The Lady of Shalott* ran for five years in both London and New York and set entirely new standards for the genre.

An additional and dreadful irony was that he held a large party last night to celebrate both his investiture and the sixth anniversary of his idyllically happy marriage. Tributes have been pouring in all day from both the theatrical profession and the public. Lady Windsor, who is deeply distressed, is still at Stebbings Hall today with her three small children. She is expected to return to her London home shortly.

The meeting of Sir Piers and the Honourable Chloe Hunterton, as she then was, when she was only 18, has passed into theatrical folklore: after doing a course at Winkfield Place, Lady Windsor was working as a cook, and Sir Piers asked her to do a luncheon at his office. It was love at first sight, and they were married a few months later.

The writer and journalist Magnus Phillips, who has been working on a highly publicized book about Sir Piers, said last night, 'The theatre has lost a great talent and to his wife, family and friends his loss is immeasurable.'

The phone rang on Magnus Phillips's desk as he sat reading his own words. It was Chloe.

'I suppose you realize that you drove Piers to this,' she said. 'You and that vile book.'

'Oh Chloe,' said Magnus, 'there were any number of reasons your husband might have decided to kill himself. As you very well know. Anyway, it will be a while before it comes out now. I have to write the epilogue.'

The Tinsel Underneath
A Story of Hollywood
By Magnus Phillips
Published by Beaumans, 1972

The Tinsel Underneath is an extraordinary true story: of love and loyalty, good and evil, hope and despair – and above all of fierce, relentless ambition. It is a story that could perhaps have only taken place amidst the aristocracy of the acting world. The heart of the story lies in Hollywood, with all its glamour and promise – and attendant corruption and temptations; and yet it all began in the peace and beauty of the Suffolk countryside over twenty years ago.

Following on the success of his unique documentary-style bestsellers *Dancers* and *The House*, Magnus Phillips has written an enthralling study of the theatrical and film world. It is moving, scandalous, amusing: it reads at times like a thriller, at others like a love story. It is compulsive entertainment.

Dedication to *The Tinsel Underneath*.

For Fleur, in the hope she will forgive me.

'I'd like to tear down all this false tinsel to show the real tinsel underneath'.
Sam Goldwyn

Foreword to *The Tinsel Underneath*

There is a poem by Don Blanding (recited by Leo Carillo in the movie *Star Night at the Coconut Grove*) which describes Hollywood far better than I can.

Drama – a city-full,
Tragic and pitiful,
Bunk, junk and genius
Amazingly blended.

It goes on. It doesn't really need to; you get the idea.

The story told in this book is both tragic and pitiful; it contains a great deal of bunk, junk and genius; and (in another line from the poem) is both vicious and glamorous.

What is astonishing is the seemingly irresistible draw of Hollywood. It attracts the tacky, certainly; it also draws the talented, like lemmings to the cliff edge, lambs to the slaughter.

The two men in this book, equally ill equipped to cope with the city full of drama, for different reasons, both found their downfall within it. For one of them, the end came swiftly, for the other slowly, as tragedy pursued him down the years. But the roots were there for both of them, in the celluloid Babylon, put down in hope, torn up in despair; and not only for them. Other lives were sacrificed, other loves destroyed. All in the cause of greed, ambition, hope – and fear. And where the reality ends and the fantasy begins is something that perhaps only the next generation can tell.

1942

Caroline wasn't sure who was doing a better job at wrecking her life, her mother or Winston Churchill: her mother, she supposed, being clearly hell-bent on her personal downfall, on the destruction of her youth, although Winston was doing a pretty good job backing her up, removing any man under the age of forty-five from her orbit, enveloping the country in a funereal shroud of blackness and telling them all they had to look forward to was blood, sweat and tears. Of course such thoughts were near heresy, and she was frightened almost to express them herself, Mr Churchill being invested (probably quite justly) with Messiah-like qualities, worshipped and revered by the whole country; indeed when they all gathered round the wireless in the kitchen at the Moat House and listened to the majestic poetry of his voice, even Caroline stopped begrudging all that she was asked to give and give up. That was the whole trouble of course; it was all giving up, all negative. She would have rushed out tomorrow to join one of the forces, would have given her life gladly working in the Ops Room as a Wren, or as a mechanic in the ATS, would have personally toiled in the rubble of the bombed cities along with the fire services; would even have run a soup kitchen with the Red Cross, or trained as a nurse and volunteered for the most dangerous overseas postings. That was what she understood by the blood, sweat and tears Winston offered them, that was how she saw defending her island, whatever the cost might be, but her mother would have none of it, would not countenance her doing anything constructive, certainly not joining the services. 'Yes indeed,' she had said icily, when Caroline went and begged her permission to join the Wrens, proffering the famous poster: 'Free a Man to Serve the Fleet', 'and I think we can all imagine how you would be freeing men, Caroline. You can stay here and help at home, just as important to my mind, with Janey leaving us and going to work in the munitions factory, wretched girl, and Bob gone as well from the garden, and I can keep an eye on you.'

And so it was that Caroline found herself leading a life of sterile, barren misery; sometimes days would go past and the only person she would talk to was Cook, and that only to be asked if she could pull some onions or find some eggs. She felt quite literally sick with boredom much of the time; and almost frightened at the knowledge that at the age of twenty, in what she could see perfectly clearly was the prime of her life, she was leading the life of a middle-aged matron for months, years on end, with very little chance of escape. She was in effect a prisoner, and so desperate that she was seriously considering running away, locked up as she was (never mind that it was in a beautiful house) in the depths of Suffolk, miles from anywhere, too far from any of the towns to be able to make her own way there, and fraternize with the servicemen on leave. Woodbridge was an hour's drive in the trap and more than two hours' bike ride away and Ipswich an unimaginable journey, and while her mother could have driven her in occasionally, or even to one of the local village dances, she flatly refused.

Her mother indeed was her enemy and jailer: delighted to have the war as her ally in removing most of the pleasures of life from her daughter, deliberately placing obstacles in the way of any that might still be stealthily making themselves available to her. Her father, who might have helped her, might have spared at least an occasional gallon of precious petrol and his elderly chauffeur (replacing the dashing young one long since called up) to drive her to the odd party, but he was unaware of her predicament, working round the clock (and frequently sleeping) at his factory, on double time producing military uniforms. Caroline was thus entirely at her mother's mercy, living out day after day of aching, sick boredom – in the conviction that her life was more than half over, and without even any real blood and sweat to relieve it.

The Moat House, which was currently serving as Caroline's prison, was situated on the outskirts of Munsbrough, a tiny and charming Suffolk village halfway between Wickham Market and Framlingham; it had been in the Miller family for five generations when Caroline was born there. It was a beautiful, low, Elizabethan house, painted pink in the Suffolk manner, with heavy timbering and a small river running round three quarters of it which did duty as the moat of its name. There was a bridge over the moat which led into a small courtyard, with a high, curving wall, the same age as the house which, although small by regal standards, and having only eight bedrooms, was said to be one of the few where Queen Elizabeth had indeed actually slept. The hall of the house was flagstoned, leading on one side into a huge drawing room, and on the other an equally large dining room, and at the back the kitchen and utility rooms extended into an endless warren. There was a very fine rose garden, an orchard, and a walled vegetable garden greatly reminiscent of Mr McGregor's in *Peter Rabbit*, there was the large stable block, and beyond that four hundred acres of arable land (now leased out for the most part to a local farmer) grazed by the Millers' dozen or so horses.

Caroline's father, Stanley Miller, was a businessman, not a farmer, a big, burly, red-faced man, six feet three inches tall, and weighing at least seventeen stone, bullishly insensitive, good humoured and oddly patient, especially with children and animals; he had a big blanket factory just outside Ipswich which had made his father and his grandfather extremely rich and which made the shrewd Stanley even richer.

Jacqueline Miller had been the daughter of the modestly impoverished local solicitor, beautiful, with flaming red hair and dark green eyes; boys who had enjoyed her favours in the backs of cars and in cloakrooms during hunt balls testified to her almost voracious sexuality. It was said that she could come at least four times from every sexual penetration. However, sexy and beautiful as she was, by the time she was twenty her reputation was appalling, and no decent boy would have considered marrying her. But Stanley Miller, ten years her senior and desperately in search of a wife, had considerable problems with women; he was, despite his bluster, almost pathologically shy, incapable of talking about anything except the fluctuating price and future of the blanket industry, his exploits on the hunting field, and the weather. He was, moreover, to his immense embarrassment, a virgin. Jacqueline, equally desperate for a husband, and seeing him as an opportunity and a challenge, put to work not only her determination and charm, but what was known locally as her 'lobster grip' and lured him into bed, thus winning his heart, his fortune and his undying love.

They were married three months after their first coupling; everyone had said that Jacqueline must have been pregnant in her wild silk wedding dress, and beneath her huge bouquet of lilies, but she was not; it was over two years later, in 1922, that she finally produced Caroline and confounded local gossip. (There were those who said that Caroline was not Stanley's child, eager to extract every possible ounce of scandal from the relationship, but they were wrong, and if she had her mother's red hair, she had her father's blue eyes and height to prove it.)

But despite Stanley's great love for Jacqueline and her genuine fondness for him, the marriage was unhappy; his insensitivity, his almost total inability to communicate with her did not improve with the years, and she had finally grown lonely and hopelessly frustrated and even depressed. She was an intense, emotionally demanding woman; marriage to Stanley, she confided to her unusually sympathetic GP, was like marriage to some alien from another country who could neither speak to her nor understand what she said.

Caroline, being an only child, absorbed more of the odd, erratic tension in the house than she would have done had she had brothers and sisters. She observed her mother's swings of mood, heard her bright brittle voice on the telephone, watched her at breakfast on certain mornings, nervously shredding her toast into a mountain of crumbs, her face pale, her eyes heavy, looking blankly at *The Times* behind which her husband sat unusually silent, unwilling to meet anyone's eyes, even those of Janey the housemaid as she brought in the coffee.

Jacqueline kept Caroline at a distance; it was as if she was afraid to love her, to touch her, to hold her. Caroline could not ever remember her mother so much as coming to her room to kiss her goodnight except on the rare occasions in her childhood when she had been ill; she would get a graze of her mother's lips on her cheek, a pat on her hand, as she left the room to go up to bed; and when she had been smaller and tried to hug her, she had been gently put away from her, with the words 'Oh, darling, not now, Mama is tired.'

Her father was more affectionate, had allowed her to sit on his knee while he read her stories when she was tiny, had given her great big bear hugs when she hurt herself, and still did when he was especially proud of her – like when she had been blooded at her first hunt, or not cried when she had broken her collar-bone after falling off her swing – but she had grown up regarding physical contact as a rare, hard-won prize. And physical contact's grown-up sister, sex.

Caroline had discovered sex when she had been not quite eleven years old. She hadn't known it was sex of course, just a delicious explosion between her legs that had soared deep up into her body and slowly throbbed its way into nothingness. She had been in bed at the time, rather casually exploring her genitals with her hands, and wondering what the strange new hairiness she found there exactly signified, when she noticed that when she touched a certain place there was a fierce darting sensation. Not sure whether she liked it or not, she touched the place again . . . and then again . . .

From that night on she was hooked, a junkie, permanently hungry for the pleasures she could give herself. She was a little alarmed at first: the explosions were so violent, left her feeling so odd, at once peaceful and startled, that she was afraid there might be something wrong with her, that there was some strange condition in her body that she ought perhaps to tell someone about. She even pondered who for a time: Mama? No, Mama did not invite intimate disclosures; she would simply look at her rather distantly and say, 'Caroline, I really haven't got time to talk to you now. Talk to Nanny about it.' Nanny then? No, certainly not; Nanny's answer to anything physical that was not absolutely one hundred per cent normal and understood was a dose of syrup of figs, and a stern commandment to come and tell her if the dose didn't work. How could she tell Nanny about this odd thing that was half pleasure and half pain and only came when she herself brought it to being. Papa? Of course not, Papa was a man, and a very insensitive man at that; jolly and affectionate he might be, but not a person to listen quietly and attentively while you stumbled your way through something you didn't understand at all. A friend? Well yes, perhaps a friend, but then Caroline didn't really have any friends. Nobody liked her enough to be her friend, she was too bossy, too prickly, too selfish; she was an only child, hopeless at sharing, at playing even, and at ten was known as stuck-up, a loner, hostile to advances that she didn't know how to meet.

She was a pretty little girl, everyone agreed, with her shiny auburn hair and her big blue eyes, but she had, in those days, not an ounce of charm. An odd, difficult little girl, thought Caroline, who knew she was considered thus, with an odd, difficult little secret. She decided not to share it. It was after all one of the few nice things in her life.

She was twelve when she discovered what the secret was. Home for the holidays from Wycombe Abbey, which she hated even more than the little dame school in Framlingham, bored even with riding one long hot day, she went upstairs to her mother's room and began idly riffling through her drawers. She often did that, when her mother was out and she was bored; it was more interesting than reading or talking to Cook, exploring the endless piles of clothes, many of them never worn, or even taken out of their boxes. Jacqueline was a compulsive shopper, she found in it a comfort, an almost physical pleasure and she turned to it in her frustration rather as another woman would have turned to drink. At least three times a week, until the war and petrol rationing prevented her, she would take the car into Ipswich or the train to London and shop, and come back, easier, better tempered, great mounds of clothes emerging from the boot of the car.

Suddenly, as Caroline dug into a pile of silk chiffon slips she felt something hard. A box, she supposed, more goodies; but no, it wasn't a box, it was a book. How peculiar, she thought, what a funny place to keep a book when there was a small bookcase right by her mother's bed; maybe she didn't know it was there, had put it in by mistake, with some of the boxes.

Caroline pulled the book out, turned it over. It was obviously a novel, she thought, *Bodily Love* by Florence Graves. *Bodily Love*! What a hopelessly silly title. Probably her mother was ashamed to be reading such a thing, and that was why she kept it hidden. Then she opened it, started flicking through it, and discovered why her mother was ashamed – and also, in a huge rush of recognition, what her own strange, delicious sensations meant. She sat motionless, through the long afternoon, lost in a strange new territory, charted for her only by Florence Graves and her flowery prose, learning of 'the ebb and flow of natural desire', of the 'crest of the wave of passion', of the 'trembling release of climax'. Only half understanding, her heart thudding, her cheeks burning, she learnt of the nature of a sexual relationship between men and women; of the 'needs' of men; of Florence Graves's passionate affirmation that women felt such needs too. She had known, like all country children, the facts of birth, had seen calves and foals born, and had even once been an unseen witness to the mating of a bull and a cow, and had vaguely assumed that humans must follow roughly the same courses of action; what had seemed unthinkable, until that hot afternoon in her mother's bedroom, was that there might be any suggestion of pleasure in it.

Startled, she suddenly heard the car in the gravel drive, her mother's voice telling the chauffeur to take it back to Framlingham and meet her father off the train; she thrust the book back where it had been, carefully rearranging the underwear over and round it, fled to her own room and shut the door. She felt herself invaded with an intense sense of physical excitement, a need for release; she lay down on the bed, and slowly, sensuously, as if actually in the presence of a lover, pulled up her skirt, and stroked her own stomach tenderly for a few moments before deliberately, confidently, almost proudly, inserting her fingers into her wet vagina, seeking out what she now knew to be her clitoris and, with a sudden frantic urgency, brought herself to swift, violent orgasm.

Caroline's encounter with Florence Graves and her philosophies had a profound effect on her. Already acutely aware of her body and the pleasure she was able to extract from it herself, she had never before considered that she might be able to share that pleasure with somebody else. From that day on, as she lay in her bed masturbating, she conjured up visions of being held, kissed, entered; the thought did not disturb her, as it did so many young girls; it excited her, made her happy.

For a while, she was satisfied with fantasy; then, shortly after her fifteenth birthday, she began to long for reality. Her mother had made no attempt to educate her sexually; the whole of Caroline's year at school had been given a highly inadequate and confusing talk on reproduction in so far as it was accomplished by the rabbit, and told that if they had any questions about human biology, they should ask their parents. Consequently, to Caroline's straightforward mind, there were no moral issues, indeed no emotional ones to be confronted; simply the hurdle of finding someone willing to engage on what she now saw as a great adventure.

Adventure came in the form of Giles Dudley-Leicester, sixteen-year-old Etonian son of one of her mother's few friends. Giles was tall, skinny, and chinless; he had slightly watery blues eyes, a lisp and a serious lack of imagination. But he had two things in common with Caroline: he was a good horseman, and he was desperate for sex. After a Meet of the Harriers just after they both broke up for Christmas (for which Stanley had lent Giles a horse) they came back to the Moat House for tea and to wait for Sarah Dudley-Leicester to collect her son. Cook had laid out teacakes, buns, cucumber sandwiches, fruit and chocolate cake and a pile of gingerbread; they fell on it, ravenous, and ate the lot.

'Funny how hunting makes you so hungry,' said Giles, shovelling two sandwiches into his mouth at once. 'Can't understand it really, all you do is sit there.'

Caroline watched him with distaste. 'I'd have thought there was a bit more to it than that,' she said. 'You do have to concentrate rather. And we have been out for nearly five hours. I ache all over. I might have a bath. D'you want one?'

'Might be an idea,' said Giles. 'Can't think of anything I'd like better, as a matter of fact. Would that really be all right?'

'Yes, of course,' said Caroline. 'Mama's out, I'll use her bathroom, and you can use the nursery one. You know where it is, don't you?'

'What? Oh, yes, of course. I remember your nanny bathing me once when we were small and we all fell in the silage one afternoon. My ma will be relieved, she always complains about the filth in the car when I've been out.'

'But you're not going home naked, are you?' asked Caroline.

'What? No, of course not.' Giles was scarlet.

'Well then, I don't see how you having a bath can save her car.'

'Oh. Oh, no. Of course. You're right. Yes.'

'Follow me,' said Caroline wearily.

* * *

She was already getting into the bath when she remembered there were no towels in the nursery bathroom. She reluctantly put on her mother's bathrobe, collected a couple of towels from the linen cupboard and went up the stairs to the nursery floor. Giles was still lounging in the bathroom chair, reading *Horse and Hound*.

'Here. I brought you some towels.'

'What's that? Oh, right, fine, jolly good. Thanks, Caroline.'

She walked over to him and handed him the towels. As she bent towards him, the robe swung open just enough to show the top of her breasts; Giles looked up and found them confronting him. He went scarlet. Caroline smiled slightly contemptuously. 'Sorry,' she said. 'I'll leave you in peace.'

She was just turning away when she glanced down at him; beneath his muddied white breeches, the unmistakable line of his erection stood out. Caroline didn't hesitate. It was the situation, and the opportunity, she had been waiting for, in perfect and totally unexpected harmony. She bent down again, and laid her hand on the bulge.

'That looks nice,' she said matter-of-factly.

'Oh, my God,' said Giles. He looked earnestly terrified. But the bulge remained steadfast.

Caroline walked over to the door and locked it. 'Come on,' she said.

'Oh, Caroline, no,' said Giles.

'Why not? Don't you want to?'

'Yes. Yes, of course I do. But we shouldn't. And somebody might come.'

'I hope,' said Caroline giggling at her own wit, 'that we both will.'

'Oh, my God,' said Giles again.

'Never mind about Him. And Mama is out. Now then, Giles, have you ever done this before?'

'Er – well not exactly.'

'That makes two of us. But we should manage it. Now take your trousers off, and your shirt too. I believe nakedness is a help.'

Had Giles been more experienced, and less desperate for sex himself (his only experiences thus far having been homosexual activity at Eton), he might have refused. As it was, he felt he had no option. Half afraid, he removed his clothes; Caroline was lying on the floor, the discarded bathrobe serving as bedding; she patted it invitingly, smiling, while eyeing Giles's large erect penis with some trepidation. She had not expected it to be so large, and couldn't quite imagine how the small orifice which seemed to fit quite snugly round her own finger could possibly accommodate it. But she was nothing if not brave; and besides there was no going back now.

'Come on. I can see you want to,' she said conversationally. 'I think we're going to have a great time.'

Thinking about it in later life, she was always amazed it hadn't been worse. Giles was well endowed, totally without skill, and frantic; he plunged into her almost without warning, and it hurt dreadfully.

'Is that all right?' he whispered in her ear, in between tearing at her mouth with his.

'Oh, yes,' said Caroline, trying to sound matter-of-fact, anxious not to moan, and equally anxious not to move, lest the pain should get worse. 'Yes, that's fine.'

'Thank Christ.' He began to move up and down; she thought she might scream.

'Giles, could you –'

'Yes, what?'

'Could you just lie still for a bit. Just for a bit.'

'I'll try.'

He lay, remarkably still; Caroline lay beneath him, trying to distract herself from her pain, looking up at the peeling paint on the ceiling, and wondering idly whether her mother had ever even considered having it painted, and gradually began to experience a totally different sensation: a softening, a yielding, a desire to move somehow forwards, to go on and on into a new place, she knew not quite where. Tentatively she moved; at first very gently, then a little more strongly. It was a mistake; Giles felt it as a signal, and unable to control himself any longer, began to plunge in and out of her like a frightened horse, groaning and clutching at her hair. Caroline opened her eyes again, seeking the reassurance of the ceiling and saw his face, contorted, red, his eyes clenched shut. She thought she had never seen anything so hideous.

It was over in seconds after that; a huge, final plunge, a last groan that was almost a bellow, and Giles came shuddering into her. It hurt so much that Caroline had to bury her teeth in his shoulder to muffle her scream; and then, almost at once, just as she started to feel the softening again, his penis began to subside, and as she moved hopefully against him, slithered out of her altogether.

'I say,' said Giles, rolling off her, still panting. 'I say, that was all right, wasn't it?'

'Yes,' said Caroline, carefully, 'yes, it was all right. Um – Giles, I think I'll go and have my bath now.'

'Rightho,' said Giles.

Right through the Christmas holidays, on every possible occasion, they had sex. Once her body had recovered from its initial ordeal, Caroline began to enjoy it; she stopped shrinking from Giles's penis, stopped feeling any pain, and went forward to him, joyfully, hungrily. Giles, in his turn and at her request, moved a little more slowly and gently; and from a book he had found in his father's dressing room – 'What would we do without our parents' guilty secrets?' asked Caroline cheerfully when he told her about it – he learnt a little technique, and began to stroke Caroline's breasts (a little heavily to be sure, and rather as if he was petting the family labrador, but never mind, she said, it was still nice) and to kiss her rather more slowly and gently as he made love to her. They found themselves remarkably free to pursue their newfound pleasure: the hunting season was in full swing, and both sets of parents agreed it was a splendid way for them to spend their time, and how delighted they were that their two odd, rather difficult children had formed such a splendid friendship; after each day out, after they had had tea or lunch, and providing Jacqueline was out and Nanny well and truly asleep, they made their way up to the nursery bathroom, where Caroline had installed a pile of old linen from the cupboard, as being more comfortable than the bathmat, and tore off their clothes.

What neither of them gave a moment's thought to was contraception.

'She's what?' said Jacqueline, staring at Caroline's headmistress across her office. 'Caroline is what? What did you say?'

'Caroline is pregnant, Mrs Miller.'

'I assure you there must be some mistake. Moreover I shall consult my solicitor immediately, about what I can only term as slander. How dare you say such things about my daughter?'

'Mrs Miller, there is no mistake. Caroline is pregnant. Roughly three months. I have had her examined by the school doctor, and he has done a pregnancy test, just to make quite sure. I was naturally of precisely your opinion. That it could not be possible. But the fact remains that she is.'

'But – what does she say? Surely she denies it?'

'No, Mrs Miller, she doesn't.'

'Oh, my God.' Jacqueline rested her head on her hands for a moment. Then she looked at the headmistress. 'You'd better tell me about it.'

'I will. And I'll ask Matron to come in. She can tell you more than I can.'

Matron related the story in full. Soon after the start of term, Caroline had fainted in morning chapel. 'I assumed it was her period. I put her to bed for the morning, and asked if she was experiencing severe pain. She said she wasn't. I didn't think a great deal about it. Then two days later it happened again. She said she often fainted, and I shouldn't take any notice. I decided to keep an eye on her, and found her vomiting several times, usually in the morning. She said she'd eaten something and that she was sure it was nothing. About a week after that started she fainted again; it still never occurred to me of course that she might be pregnant. But I was worried and called the school doctor. She examined Caroline carefully, and then said she would like to talk to her in private. An hour later she came in and said she was very much afraid that Caroline was pregnant, but that of course she might be wrong, and before upsetting everybody, she would like to do a pregnancy test. That takes a few days, as you probably know. Anyway, I'm afraid it is positive. There is absolutely no doubt. Caroline is pregnant.'

'Oh God,' said Jacqueline.

'You had no idea, no idea at all that this might be – well, possible?' said the headmistress.

'Of course not. Of course I didn't.'

'I see.'

There was a long silence.

'What – what should I do?' said Jacqueline. 'What would you suggest?'

'Well, naturally, she must be removed from the school at once. That goes without saying.'

'You mean permanently?'

'I'm afraid I do.'

'But why?'

'Mrs Miller, do be reasonable. This is a highly respected, much sought-after school. You must be aware of what it would do to our reputation if it became known that a girl here was pregnant. Even had been pregnant.'

'I see. Suppose –'

'Yes?'

'Suppose it was a mistake. A hysterical pregnancy. They do happen.'

'Mrs Miller, she has had a pregnancy test, the Aschheim-Zondak test. It is highly accurate. Perhaps you don't know exactly what that involves,' said Matron carefully. 'Her urine has been injected into a mouse. The mouse, on biopsy, showed distinct ovarian changes. There can be no mistake.'

'Well, suppose she had a – a miscarriage?'

'Mrs Miller, I'm sorry. I know what you are saying. But the answer is no. Now shall I send for Caroline?'

'Yes, all right,' said Jacqueline.

Going home in the car, they were both silent. Caroline was white, and had to ask for the car to be stopped twice, so she could be sick; otherwise she said nothing at all. Jacqueline stared out of the window.

When they finally got home she went upstairs to her room. 'I'll talk to your father when he gets home,' was all she said.

They confronted her in the drawing room after dinner. They had discussed it carefully, they said, and had a long conversation with a friend of Jacqueline's who was a gynaecologist in London. He had contacts who might be able to help. It would mean going to a clinic somewhere in the country. Caroline had no idea what they meant. They asked who the father was, and when it had happened. She told them, and listened to them calling her a slut and a disgrace, and stood shaking while her father rang the Dudley-Leicesters and asked them to come over.

She felt very sick and very faint, and said so; they told her to go to her room and to stay there. She lay on the bed crying, and afraid, and listening to her parents shouting at the Dudley-Leicesters, and wondered whatever was to become of her.

Later that night her mother came to her room, looked at her distantly and merely told her that they would be going up to London with her the next day. Caroline did not dare ask why.

There were interviews with doctors, with psychiatrists, endless internal examinations that hurt, questioning about her last period, the last occasion intercourse had taken place. Finally she found herself in a small hard bed in a tiny white bright room in a clinic somewhere in the wilds of Northumberland, being given an enema by a hatchet-faced nurse, and then pushed roughly from the lavatory, where she was sitting at once vomiting and straining, on to the bed and given yet one more of the internal examinations, this time not even with a gloved hand, but a hard steel probe. It hurt horribly.

'All right,' said the doctor (she supposed he was a doctor), 'I think we can just about do it. Get her ready now.'

And they put her into a robe and shaved her pudendum and told her to climb on to a trolley, and without a word, pushed her, sick with fear, along the corridors and into another small room. There the same doctor was standing, sleeves rolled up, black rubber mask in hand.

'Now then,' he said, pushing the mask over her face, making her feel she would stifle, 'let's hope this is going to be a lesson to you.'

As she lost consciousness she felt him pushing her legs apart and saying, 'Put her in the stirrups . . .' and she tried to scream but the mask was smothering her, and the room was swimming and they were pushing her trolley into the brilliant lights next door.

When she woke up, she felt terribly sick; she moved, leant over from her bed and threw up into the basin beside her. Her stomach ached badly; feeling herself cautiously, tears streaming down her face, she found she was padded with cotton wool, and that in spite of it the sheet and her gown were soaked with blood. Terrified, she pressed the bell; the nurse who had given her the enema came in.

'What is it?'

'I'm bleeding. Terribly. And it hurts. Is it – is that all right?'

The nurse looked at her with distaste. 'You should be grateful you're bleeding. You girls are all the same. What do you expect?'

'I don't know,' said Caroline meekly.

And she didn't.

She didn't expect the pain, which was bad; the endless bleeding which was frightening; the internal examination she had to have next morning before she was allowed home; the weakness, the soreness that lasted for weeks; least of all she didn't expect the misery, the tearing, awful misery that went on day after day without relief. Her mother continued to ignore her, treating her like some unsatisfactory housemaid; her father was awkwardly more kind, and once took her in one of his bear hugs when he found her sobbing in the drawing room one morning, but never mentioned the matter either. Only Janey cared for her, held her as she wept, filled endless hot-water bottles, made her cups of hot tea, through the first few dreadful days, brought her books to read from the library, lent her her old wireless to listen to. But Janey didn't talk about it either.

About two weeks after it had all happened, when she was just beginning to feel better, she was sitting in the kitchen, drinking hot chocolate and reading Cook's *Daily Mail* when she heard the door open and Jack Bamforth came in.

* * *

Jack Bamforth was her father's groom; he had been with the family for most of Caroline's life. He'd taught her to ride, holding the fat little Shetland steady while she dug her small heels in and shouted, 'Giddyup.' He had carried her into the house when she had had her first bad fall and been concussed; he had taken her out hunting for the first time, reining his horse in patiently so as to be near her, urging her over the fences, steadying her nerve; he was, she often said, her best friend. When she discovered this annoyed her mother, she said it more frequently. Jack was thirty-five years old, small – about five feet seven inches tall – and very slightly built; he had a gloriously equable disposition, an eye for a horse that was legendary, and a face that would have sent Michelangelo into raptures: perfectly sculpted, classically beautiful bones, wide, innocent grey eyes and a mouth that said little but spoke volumes – mostly on the subject of carnal desire.

Jack had a wife, a big, sexy woman with a sharp tongue on her; but he also had a most awesome reputation for taking his pleasures elsewhere. All these elements set together, with his soft, flat Suffolk accent which gave his every utterance a kind of lazy charm, made him wonderfully easy to talk to, confronting any painful or difficult situation with a head-on gentleness that took any embarrassment out of it. Once when Caroline had been about fourteen and her period had started right in the middle of a day's hunting and her breeches had become horribly stained, and she just didn't know what to do, he had ridden up beside her and said, 'Best if we go home now, Miss Caroline, you look very tired and that horse is lathering horribly.' As she had sat riding back beside him across the peaceful fields, silent, near to tears with misery and embarrassment, even while grateful for the rescue, he had simply said, 'Nobody noticed, you know, nobody at all, only me because I was supposed to keep an eye on you,' and she had immediately felt eased and soothed. And another time, when she had been much younger at a gymkhana, and no one would pair up with her for the games, he had come over and put his arm round her and said, 'Silly lot of children round here, aren't they?' instead of pretending not to notice.

She looked up at him standing there, looking at her rather seriously, anxiously even, and wondered how much he knew, and how much she wanted him to know. What had happened to her had been the ultimate disgrace; best hidden, best buried. Even from Jack. Only – only burying it seemed to be making it worse.

'Morning, Miss Miller.'

'Good morning, Jack.'

'How are you?'

'I'm perfectly fine, thank you,' said Caroline crisply.

'Good. Are you sure?'

'Of course I'm sure. Why shouldn't I be?'

'Because you don't look fine. Not exactly.'

'Well I am,' said Caroline and burst into tears.

'Dear oh dear,' said Jack calmly. 'Dear oh dear.' He put his arm round her gently, and held her, like a father, like a brother; she could smell him, horsey, faintly sweaty. For the rest of her life those things were associated for Caroline with comfort. 'Here, have a hanky,' he said.

'Thank you. Thank you, Jack.' She blew her nose hard. 'I didn't mean to do that. It's just that – well I don't seem to be able to stop crying.'

'Want to tell me about it?' he asked carefully.

'What? Tell you about what?'

'Your illness. The virus you've had. I heard about it from your mama. I was very sorry.'

'Ah yes,' said Caroline, remembering her mother had told her that everybody knew she had had a strange virus which had necessitated a brief spell in an isolation hospital, but that she was hopefully clear of it now. She looked up at Jack and saw that not for a moment did he think she had had a virus, and that his grey eyes were very soft and concerned. 'Oh, no, Jack, it was nothing serious. I'm better now. I'm just – well a bit tired, that's all.'

'Well,' he said, gently careful, 'that's all right then.'

'Yes. Yes, I hope so. Anyway, it's over now. Well and truly over.'

'Good. Well I just wanted to let you know I was here if you needed me.'

'Thank you, Jack. Thank you very much.'

She was sent to another school, a morbidly depressing establishment in the Midlands. When she complained about its harsh regime, with its cold showers and daily hikes in all weathers, its terrible food, her mother told her she was lucky that any school would take her in.

But after only two terms, she had behaved so badly, been so rude and difficult to all the staff, so totally uncooperative when it came to doing any work, broke bounds, played truant, that they expelled her as well.

'You're seventeen now,' said her mother coldly when her trunk was unpacked for the last time, and she was lying on her bed, wondering what on earth was going to become of her. 'I see no reason to try to give you an education which you clearly have no interest in. You can stay at home and learn to be useful. Janey is leaving, to go and work in a factory in Framlingham, silly girl; all this war business has gone to her head, and Cook will need help as well. I suppose your father and I will need to find some sort of future for you, but I really cannot quite imagine what – unless it is on the pavements in Piccadilly.'

'I'd prefer that to helping Cook, thank you,' said Caroline.

Jacqueline lifted her hand and struck her across the face. 'I am at a loss to understand you,' she said.

'That's half the trouble,' said Caroline, and walked out of the room, refusing to let the tears start until she was safely out of her mother's hearing.

Jack Bamforth had said much the same thing as her mother, only more kindly. He made a special journey to the house one day, to ask her if she would like to come to the stables and talk to him.

'I don't know what about,' said Caroline rudely.

'Yes, you do. And it would do you good. Come on. You can help me with some tack at the same time.' He held out his hand; oddly moved, her eyes filled with the tears that always seemed to be at the back of them these days, Caroline took it.

Later, up to her elbows in warm soapy water, she said suddenly, 'I'm a bit of a case, aren't I, Jack?'

'Oh, I don't know,' he said. 'You seem all right to me. Miss Miller,' he added after a few moments.

Caroline hated him calling her Miss Miller; it made her feel distanced from him. 'Jack, I wish you'd still call me Caroline. I – I think you're my only friend. I don't want you to be so formal.'

'All right. But it'll have to be Miss Miller in front of your pa and your mama.'

'Of course.' She sounded almost meek.

'Why do you keep doing it then?' he said conversationally.

'Doing what?'

'Getting thrown out of these schools.'

Caroline sighed, and opened a tin of saddle soap. 'Maybe it's because I just desperately want to get a reaction out of someone. All my father ever says is, "Talk to your mother." About anything, anything at all. Good or bad. And my mother is so dreadfully distant and cold, I just want to shock her into some sort of emotion. Even anger. The other day she hit me, and I really felt good for a bit. Does that sound awfully weird to you?'

'No, not really. A bit extreme maybe, but not weird. You seem to be writing off your own future pretty sharpish though. Just to get a reaction from your parents.'

'I know.' She sighed, and looked at him, trying to smile. It didn't quite work.

There was a silence. Caroline reached out and took another bridle off its hook.

'This is filthy, Jack,' she said, and then started to cry again.

Jack put his arms round her and held her for a long time.

'Poor girl,' he said. 'Poor little girl.'

'I'm not really little. Old enough to know better. That's what everybody keeps saying.'

'Oh,' he said, letting her go and returning to the saddle he was polishing. 'Everybody is quite often wrong, in my experience. I don't think we're ever old enough for that. Any of us. Will they find you another school, do you think?'

'No. They've said they won't. I've got to stay here and help Cook. For now anyway. Maybe if there really is a war, I'll find something to do. Do you think there will be one? Papa doesn't.'

'Oh, yes. Oh, I certainly do,' said Jack. 'Your pa's wrong there. No doubt about it at all. We'll be at war in a very few months, I would say.'

'Oh, well, that'll give me something to look forward to,' she said.

* * *

By 1942, when she was twenty and had been leading the life of a middle-aged matron for three years, she was so desperate that she was seriously planning to run away. She had never really liked reading (although she had recently developed what was almost an addiction to women's magazines, her favourite being *Woman & Beauty*), she loathed sewing, and her only real pleasure was playing the piano. She had been considered quite a talented pianist at school, and had won several medals at classical music festivals, but it was not the music of Chopin and Bach and Brahms that filled the Moat House now, but songs from the hit parade, 'The White Cliffs of Dover', 'Blues in the Night', 'We'll Gather Lilacs' and the swing rhythms of Mr Glenn Miller. 'In the Mood' was to be heard particularly frequently coming from the music room, played sometimes briskly, sometimes as a morose dirge. Jacqueline had once remarked somewhat rashly that she was growing a little tired of the tune; Caroline would have had both hands cut off rather than stop playing it at length daily after that. She had very few opportunities for revenge.

Jacqueline was in any case seriously unwell herself: her headaches had worsened into a particularly vicious form of migraine, and she would lie in her room sometimes for days at a time, vomiting and in appalling pain, her vision so seriously affected that she was liable to fall downstairs or crash into furniture if she tried to move about. Caroline tried to feel sorry for her and failed almost entirely; and indeed, as the migraine did provide her with at least a few hours of freedom every so often, she would wake occasionally to hear her mother vomiting or groaning and experience a stab of positive pleasure.

There was a bus twice a week, and every so often, if it coincided with the migraine days, Caroline would catch it into Woodbridge, but it was no fun on her own. Although she did from time to time hang around one or other of the pubs, hoping to get chatted up by the local servicemen, they tended to be wary of someone so obviously out of their class, and to go for the local girls, hanging round the bar in giggling groups, and she would leave in time to catch the bus home again, feeling foolish and more lonely than ever. The only men to be found in the country were the prisoners of war, set to work on the land, and not even Caroline would have considered fraternizing with them.

'I really think,' she said to Jack one day as they rode across the fields, 'I might as well go and join a convent. It couldn't possibly be worse than this.'

'Oh, I think it could,' he said. 'A bit worse. You couldn't go riding for a start. Cheer up, Caroline. Something'll turn up soon. You see if I'm not wrong.'

'Jack, I know you're wrong,' said Caroline. 'Nothing is going to turn up. It can't.'

Chapter 2

1942–5

There were times, reflected Brendan FitzPatrick as he sat in the Crown in Woodbridge nursing his pint of lukewarm beer, when he felt quite sympathetic towards Adolf Hitler. Anyone who could force these cold, unfriendly, goddammned superior people into some kind of submission deserved a bit of support. He had been in the country for over three months now, three weeks of them stationed in the dank drear wastes of Martlesham Heath, and he had yet to meet a single one of them who seemed remotely worth helping across the road, never mind fighting and quite possibly dying for. He and around a thousand others had arrived in Ipswich from Glasgow where the US Air Force had deposited them, trainloads of nice friendly boys confidently expecting to be greeted most pleasantly, welcomed, quite possibly fêted, and they had been treated more as enemy than ally, met with hostility and suspicion almost everywhere they went.

They had been warned of course, indeed there was an official written document they had all been issued with on leaving home from the commander of the American armed forces. 'Two actions on your part', it had said, 'will slow up friendship with the Tommy: swiping his girl and not appreciating what his army is up against. Yes, and rubbing it in that you're better paid than he is.'

Balls, Brendan had thought, real balls, what kind of schmuck would do any of those things; but a few days' close proximity with the Tommy had left him for one positively itching not only to swipe as many girls as possible from under his upturned nose, but to wave a fistful of dollars in his face while he did it.

Even worse than the Tommy were the civilians: the people in the shops, in the pubs, on the streets who appeared to consider the smiles and the Howdys of the boys as a natural prelude to large-scale rape and pillage. They had tried to be polite and friendly to all of them, addressing all the ladies as ma'am and any gentleman over the age of around twenty-five as sir, always ready to buy drinks for anyone in earshot in the pubs – and godawful places they were, most of them – and passing around gum and Lucky Strikes and offering lifts to anyone they passed on the road, although that was officially not allowed, but they might as well have goose-stepped through the streets and daubed swastikas on the walls for all the good it did them.

Only the children were friendly, running up behind them and saying, 'Got any gum, chum?' and trying to copy their casual salutes. But the children knew the soldiers were out of bounds and that they would get called swiftly to heel if their mothers were around, 'as if they were in danger of being kidnapped or molested,' said Brendan disgustedly to his crew chief in the mess one night. The crew chief had laughed and patted Brendan on the back and told him to be patient. 'Not all the boys have been behaving entirely well. You have to try and put yourself in these people's place. Most of them have men in France or the mid East, they're lonesome and fearful and very hard up; it's hard to see us arrive with apparently not too much to do and apparently also in not too much danger. Give 'em time; they'll come round.'

'Are we talking years here,' asked Brendan, 'or decades?'

Even the countryside was a disappointment; Brendan, who knew his Old Masters, had expected something closely resembling a Constable painting (particularly as they were in Constable country), all small golden fields, stiles and, yes, goddamnit, haywains, and he had found merely a flat grey landscape under a flat grey sky, that echoed his sagging spirits exactly. The joke was that there were only two seasons in England: winter and July. It didn't seem very funny to Brendan.

In the normal way of things, his spirits did not sag easily; he was sanguine, sunny, easy-tempered. He came right in the middle of a family of five, from Brooklyn in New York City, with two sisters above him and two below, adored by them all, and by his mother as well; but the adoration had never done him any harm, merely fuelled a natural self-confidence, an easy, extrovert charm in an entirely positive way. Brendan was an actor, or rather he was about to be an actor; he had majored in drama at high school, done a summer school at Juillard in between working in various food markets and gas stations, and had just got the understudy of Stanley in *Streetcar* in a small but highly respected company in the Village when he had been hauled off the stage, into the air force, and thence to England. Even then he had remained cheerful: he would get a chance to see Stratford-upon-Avon, he said to his sisters as they commiserated and wept over him, and breathe Shakespeare's air; might even, when the war was over, get a chance to study at RADA. Some of the finest actors in the world were English moreover, look at Laurence Olivier, John Gielgud, Ralph Richardson. His sisters, who had seen *Wuthering Heights* but had not heard of the others, all pronounced Brendan as greatly resembling Olivier, but better looking and felt that the English stage would be enormously enriched by his arrival. The nearest he had actually got to the English stage was the one constructed in a hangar on the base where a terrible band and a worse singer had performed twice; they had been promised visits from real stars, such as Vivien Leigh, Bing Crosby and Bob Hope, but that seemed about as likely to happen as the Suffolk folk taking them to their hearts and asking them home for supper after church.

In time both things happened; in the meantime, Brendan was almost literally homesick. He was a New Yorker; the noise and trouble and energy of a city, any city, but particularly that city, were what fuelled him, mobilized him; as day after day of quiet, stultifying rural England settled upon him, he became more and more morose. In the first few weeks he had gone out in the evening with the other boys to try to pull a girl, not even to pull one, just to talk; but he was a sensitive lad, he found it hard to take the general hostility in the pubs, and to accept that the girls who finally came over to talk to him, dance with him, were regarded, in their own community at any rate, as little better than tarts. He even scored once or twice, but they had been joyless occasions; Brendan liked a woman to talk to him, to joke with him, as well as to screw him, and all he achieved from these girls was a wham, bang, thank you ma'am in reverse, and being given the impression he was a mighty fortunate fellow. And so he gave up, went out less and less; he was still training, there was no proper flying yet, so he didn't even have the excitement, the release of danger and the raids to lift his depression. And so it was at the end of three months that he found himself sitting in the bar at the Crown, dragged there reluctantly by some of his more pragmatic companions, cold, depressed, and achingly randy, with a sense of nothing, absolutely nothing to look forward to.

At precisely the same time, Caroline Miller was walking up Quay Street towards the Crown, with a sense of desperation and hunger that was equal to, indeed greater than, his own.

She had heard about the GIs of course; everyone had. They were the talk of the countryside.

'Have you met any of them yet?' Mrs Blake in the Co-op at Wickham Market had asked her only the week before, wrapping up the week's cheese ration carefully.

'Met who, Mrs Blake?'

'The Americans. Now there's just about a half-ounce extra in there, tell Cook. I had to give her a bit less last week, and promised to make it up. Tea did you want?'

'Yes, please,' said Caroline. 'And tell me about the Americans, Mrs Blake.'

'Well, there's a whole lot of them arrived,' said Mrs Blake, 'over at Martlesham.'

'What sort of Americans?'

'Well, airmen, I suppose, as it's Martlesham. Come to help, or that's the idea. I can't see it myself; they won't know where they're going or what they're doing, will they? I mean it's a long way away from America here, isn't it? They won't know which way they're meant to be flying their aeroplanes, will they? More of a hindrance than a help I'd have thought they'd be.'

'Well, I suppose someone will tell them what to do,' said Caroline carefully.

'Yes, well maybe they will. I don't like the idea of it myself. Filling the English countryside with a lot of strangers. Bad enough having the prisoners of war. At least they're under lock and key most of the time. Those Americans certainly aren't that, from what I've heard. Heaven knows what they'll be getting up to. Well, of course we can all imagine, can't we? Got your points, Caroline?'

'Yes. Here you are,' said Caroline, fishing in her bag for the family ration books. 'Er – when did they actually arrive, these Americans?'

'Two weeks ago. And they've been into Ipswich every night, I heard. And Woodbridge. They have all the petrol they need or so it seems. Well that can't be right, can it? And they've got plenty of money too. Five times what our soldiers earn, they do. And they've brought all sorts of stuff with them.'

'What sort of stuff?' said Caroline curiously.

'Oh, nylon stockings. Sweets, or candy as they call it. And chewing gum. Stuff like that,' said Mrs Blake darkly. 'I hear they've been trying to get friendly with our girls as well,' she added, as if the American soldiers were committing some unspeakable crime. 'Offering them drinks and cigarettes and asking them out for dinner, and that sort of thing. Well, no nice girl is going to fall for that, is she?'

'Of course not,' said Caroline.

She had been walking down the village street when the liberty truck arrived. A big jeep, full of men: young, laughing, healthy, noisy men. Caroline tried not to look at them and failed; she felt exactly as if she had been starving for years and someone had just offered her a plate of delectable food. They saw her watching them and laughed; she tossed her head and walked quickly away from them. They parked the truck, and got out; and then followed her, walking at exactly her pace, so that if she hurried they hurried and if she slowed they slowed. The whole length of the village she walked, into the post office and out again, and then turned, and went slowly back towards the Moat House; still they followed.

Finally, irritated now, rather than flattered, even slightly embarrassed, she turned on them. 'Is this the sort of thing you do at home?' she said.

They stopped at once, plainly disconcerted; the one in front, assuming the position of spokesman, gave her a loose salute. 'Oh no, ma'am,' he said, 'no we wouldn't, not at all. No offence, ma'am.'

'Yes, well I suggest you get back to your barracks,' said Caroline, 'and find something more useful to do.'

They shambled off down the street, muttering to one another, looking over their shoulders once or twice; she felt ashamed all of a sudden for being so unfriendly, and sorry for them being so far away from their own country. She also, for the first time for what seemed like years, felt the stabbing intrusion of sexual desire.

'Mama, I absolutely have to go into Woodbridge tomorrow.'

'Really. Why?'

'Well, I just can't manage without a pair of shoes any longer. I've been saving up coupons. And it's Friday. There's the bus. All right?'

'I suppose so. Don't miss the bus back though. I certainly haven't got enough petrol to come and fetch you.'

'I won't. Actually, on second thoughts, I might cycle. Then I'll have more time.'

'More time for what?'

'Mama, I am so tired of this.'

'I do assure you, Caroline, so am I. Now I do not want you cycling into Woodbridge, it's much too far, and before you start making any devious plans I had in any case told Cook she could borrow your bike tomorrow. And I shall need the trap.'

Caroline didn't believe her.

But God was on her side: she woke up to hear the now-familiar groans of pain and her father on the telephone to the doctor, and smiled to herself in the darkness. Not only would she now be able to escape, her mother would be quite incapable of noticing and her father would have taken refuge in his bedroom at the factory.

'Yes. I'll take those,' said Caroline, looking rather unenthusiastically at a pair of lace-up brown shoes, the only ones in her size, in the Woodbridge shoe shop. 'They'll do. Now what about stockings?' She spoke casually; she had planned this piece of dialogue with care.

'Stockings,' said the girl. 'You'll be lucky. The only people got stockings are the Yanks. Sweet-talk them into giving you a pair. That's your best bet. Isn't hard,' she added. 'And they're real nylons.'

'I just might,' said Caroline with a grin. 'If I can find any of them.'

'Well, that isn't difficult. Problem's avoiding them.'

'Really? I heard they didn't come to Woodbridge. Prefer Ipswich.'

'Don't know who you've been talking to. They love it here. Come every night to the cinema. And the Crown of course.'

'Really? Well I'm surprised. I've never seen them.'

'Well maybe you go home too early. They don't arrive till about eight.'

'Oh well, that explains it,' said Caroline. 'That's much too late for me.'

Brendan FitzPatrick was not shy, but he was nevertheless hopelessly tongue-tied just at the sight of her. He had never seen anyone so indisputably a lady, just walking into a bar, quite plainly looking for a pick-up. Twice he cleared his throat and tried to galvanize his long limbs into moving towards her and twice he found himself rooted to the spot. He decided he would have to have at least another pint of their disgusting, warm, bitter-tasting beer before he tried again.

Caroline knew Brendan was watching her and she liked it. He was extremely good-looking, she thought to herself, hardly able to believe her good fortune in almost immediately finding so glorious an example of her prey. He was tall, about six foot two, with broad shoulders and large hands (giving her cause to wonder pleasurably about the size of other segments of his anatomy), dark curly hair, and bright blue eyes, with very long eyelashes; he had slightly tanned skin and a heavily freckled nose and forehead, and a mouth that was almost girlishly soft and sensitive.

She watched him for all of sixty seconds before deciding to take positive action; terrified that if she didn't, he would turn his attentions to one of the large number of pretty girls thronging into the Crown. She stood up, paused for a moment, almost faltering and then, with an almost visible rush of courage, walked towards him.

'Good evening,' she said. 'I wonder if you could possibly give me a cigarette.'

And Brendan FitzPatrick had taken her thirstily in, all her tall, English well-bredness, her massing red hair, her high forehead, her clear, light skin; her blue eyes, her straight nose, her neat, full mouth; had looked at her rangy body in its rather severe brown tweed suit, relieved by a sweater that clung to her full, high breasts; glanced briefly even at the long, slender legs, and then, clinging to his self-control along with his warm remaining quarter-pint, fumbled in his breast pocket for a pack of Lucky Strikes and handed it to her in total silence. Caroline took one out, and then another one for him, and in a gesture of odd intimacy, replaced the pack in his pocket. She smiled. 'Thank you. Here –' She produced her own lighter, a Dunhill, from her bag. 'Light?'

'Thanks,' said Brendan, taking the cigarette and putting it in his mouth, allowing her to light it, watching her light her own, and then remove the cigarette and take a tiny shred of tobacco off her tongue with the tip of her finger, all without taking her eyes from his. 'Can I buy you a drink?'

'Yes, you can. Thank you. Gin and French.'

'Ice?'

'Oh – no, thank you.' She smiled. 'In any case, I don't think ice has reached Woodbridge. Not its pubs anyway.'

'You know I just don't understand that,' he said, realizing with a rush of relief he would be able to talk easily to her. 'What it is about ice here. Or rather what it isn't. It's not a hard thing to manufacture after all. The ingredients aren't too tricky.'

'No, but people just don't like it. They think it spoils the taste of things. You should hear my father on the subject.'

'What's your father's drink?'

'Scotch.'

'Scotch what?'

'Scotch whisky of course,' said Caroline, amused.

'As in bourbon?'

'I believe it's a bit the same. I've never tasted bourbon.'

'Well you should. Before you are even the slightest bit older.'

'Not with the gin,' she said, laughing. 'I should be drunk.'

'That's perfectly fine by me. Barman, a bourbon please.'

But bourbon, mercifully for Caroline, had not reached Woodbridge either.

They left the Crown at half past nine. 'I have to go home,' said Caroline desperately.

'And how do you get home?'

'Well, I have my bicycle. But I have to make a start.'

'How far is home?'

'About eight miles.'

'Jesus. You're going to ride eight miles on a bicycle? You'll never get there. Besides, you might get raped or something.'

'Not very likely,' said Caroline, resisting the temptation to say 'no such luck' with difficulty. 'And anyway, the bicycle has become standard transport down here.'

'I know. But for girls? After dark?'

'Of course,' she said, laughing. 'There's a war on. And I know every inch of the way. I grew up here.'

'Well, it doesn't sound too good to me. Would you allow me to drive you? I just happen to have a Jeep outside.'

Caroline looked at him, up and down, her eyes lingering just momentarily on his crutch.

'I think I would. That would be very kind.'

Kindness was not the sensation Sergeant FitzPatrick was primarily experiencing.

The Jeep was parked at the bottom of the hill, near the station and the estuary; Brendan looked longingly at the water, with the moonlight glancing off it, the masts of the boats knocking gently against one another as they rocked in the tide. 'I've yet to see this place by daylight. It seems really nice-looking to me. Real pretty. Real old too.'

'You could call it quite old I suppose,' said Caroline. 'The shire hall is medieval. Now look, you can just take me as far as Wickham Market which is fairly straightforward; you shouldn't get lost and then I'll cycle the rest and you can get back.'

'I won't want to get back,' said Brendan, his eyes flicking over her as she stood by the Jeep. 'I'll want to be with you.'

'Don't be silly. You can't possibly come home with me. My mother would horsewhip us. First you, then me.'

'Sounds kind of fun.'

'I'm not joking.'

'Nor was I.'

'Well anyway,' said Caroline, trying to ignore the throbbing that was going on somewhere deep within her, 'more to the point you'd get lost. It's utterly dark and there aren't any roadsigns and, even more to the point, I'm supposed to be with a friend. I can't turn up in a Jeep.'

'Couldn't I be your friend?'

'Not tonight.'

In the event, they were friends before they were lovers. Frantic as she was for sex, and more frantic still for sex with Brendan, Caroline had learnt at least a little caution.

'No,' she said, pushing him away from her in the back of the Jeep where they had climbed, on the second time Brendan drove her home. 'No, I'm sorry, you can't.'

'Why not?'

'Because I'm a nicely brought-up girl, that's why not.'

'Nonsense,' he said, laughing. 'Well brought up you are not. That's why I like you.'

'How do you know I'm not well brought up?'

'Well-brought-up girls don't ask strange men for cigarettes. Not where I come from at any rate. Or take lifts from them. Or kiss them in a fairly forward manner before saying goodnight, on the very first date. Or ask them when they might be around again. Your father may own half the land in Suffolk and your mother may be no end of a lady, but you are not well brought up. Not in the way you mean.'

'OK. I'm not well brought up,' said Caroline. 'But I'm still not going to sleep with you.'

'Why not?'

'I don't want to.'

'That's not true.'

'Of course it's true.'

'You feel as if you want to,' he said, moving his hand gently up under her skirt, feeling the wetness of her pants, the tender, eager trembling of her, the shudder that went through her as he touched her.

'Well I don't. And don't do that.'

'All right,' he said suddenly, surprisingly. 'I won't. Now here's the phone box, are you going to call your pop?'

'No, I'll cycle.' She sighed. 'Papa's not there, just my mother and she's not well. I don't want to wake her up.'

'But I thought you got clearance to see a film with a girlfriend?'

'I did. But that was this afternoon. And she doesn't believe me anyway. If she wasn't ill she'd have been over to fetch me.'

'What's the matter with her?'

'She suffers from terrible migraine. Brought on by – oh, a miserable nature.'

'Why does she have a miserable nature?'

'I don't know.'

'Well anyway, surely you could tell her all about the film? Since we just saw it? Every detail of the plot? And the newsreel?'

'No. She has a very suspicious nature. As well as miserable.'

'Why suspicious?'

'Oh,' she said lightly, 'I'll tell you one day.'

She did tell him. She told him a few weeks later, when, weary of talking, he tried to force her to have sex with him; stabbing at her through her pants, clinging to her, almost shouting, 'Please, Caroline, please,' over and over again.

'Oh, just stop it,' she said, dragging her skirt down, pushing him away. 'I can't. All right? I just can't.'

'Is there something wrong with you?'

'Yes,' she said, tears beginning to flow, 'yes, I think there is.'

Falteringly, diffidently, she told him about the baby.

So it was they became friends, talking endlessly; he heard about her parents, her schooling, her odd solitary childhood and the screaming boredom of her war. And she heard about him, about the large Irish family he came from in Brooklyn, about his mother Kathleen ('She can't be called Kathleen, it's a cliché.' 'My family is one big cliché, Caroline, and don't knock it'), about his four sisters, Edna and Maureen and Patricia and Kate, and the small house near Fulton Street in Brooklyn where they lived, and about how Brendan was going to be the Gary Cooper of the forties or, well, maybe now the fifties and how his agent was confident, really confident, that he could make Hollywood; about his father who had died of a heart attack the day Brendan got his first ever part, before he could even hear of it, and about Kathleen, so warm and loyal and proud you could get a hold of the love in her ('You don't know how lucky, how terribly lucky you are, Brendan') and so determined he was going to make it she was practically packed, ready to go with him to Hollywood.

Caroline, listening enthralled, as much of her mind on Brendan's future as she could detach from a growing obsession with his penis, felt that she too could be as lovingly convinced of his potential success as the devoted Kathleen.

'I've been to town,' he said, beaming, producing a packet of Durex from his breast pocket the next time he drove her home (two weeks later, Caroline having been curfewed after failing to catch the bus home twice). 'From now on, you're quite safe with me. In more ways than one. Now will you come on and get into the back with me?'

'Oh, Brendan,' said Caroline, 'I still don't think I can.'

'Caroline,' said Brendan, 'next week I start flying. Daytime raids on Germany. I may never come back. Don't you think you owe me a few happy memories?'

Caroline climbed into the back.

Sex with Brendan was wonderful. Even in the back of a Jeep. He was experienced, skilful, gentle; he led her all the way, and then waited while she came, over and over again, crying out, clinging to him, her head thrown back, her hands clawing the air, her entire being absorbed in her passion and her pleasure, before he would release himself.

'How old are you, Brendan?' she asked, as she lay finally stilled in his arms, the first night. 'Are you really only twenty-three?'

'I'm really only twenty-three.'

'You're very clever,' was all she said, 'for only twenty-three.'

* * *

She crept into the house that night, high with happiness and sex. It was totally silent. She went and got herself a drink of water, then slowly inched her way up the stairs. She had just, she thought, reached safety, when the door of her mother's room shot open and her mother appeared, the light behind her snapped sharply on.

'Where have you been?'

'Out. I told you. To a film with a girlfriend.'

'That was this afternoon.'

'It wasn't. It was this evening.'

'Caroline,' said Jacqueline, 'I may be stuffed with drugs, but I am still capable of telling day from night. Now will you kindly tell me what you have actually been doing.'

'Seeing a film.'

'What film?'

'Oh, Mama, the one that's on in Woodbridge, of course. *Casablanca*. Do you want me to run through the plot with you?'

'No, thank you. I can't be taken in by that old trick. I don't believe you.'

Caroline shrugged. 'Believe what you like. I'm tired, can I go to bed please?'

'How did you get home?'

'I cycled.'

'From Woodbridge?'

'Well of course.'

'I don't believe that either.'

'Mama,' said Caroline suddenly, 'if you treated me with a little more respect, and – and affection – you might learn a lot more about me.'

'I'm afraid I'd find that very difficult,' said Jacqueline. 'Oh, just go to bed, Caroline, for God's sake. But please don't think we'll bale you out of difficulty again.'

'I wouldn't ask you again,' said Caroline.

For some reason after that, probably her own increasing ill-health, and what was undoubtedly a quite severe clinical depression, Jacqueline began to leave Caroline alone. She spent more and more time in her room, ceased cross-questioning Caroline, and gradually appeared to lose all interest in what she was doing. Stanley spent most of his time in Ipswich; consequently Caroline spent all of her time, or all the time that the United States Air Force would allow, with Brendan: and fell helplessly and promptly in love with him. They had a lyrically perfect year; he had a great deal of freedom (the USAF being more generous in that department than its British counterpart) and almost unlimited access to a Jeep. Most evenings, and many days, he would drive over to Wickham Market, or sometimes, if Jacqueline was sufficiently unwell, right up to the house (although she would never allow him through the gates, saying their luck would run out, that it would be pushing things, that he would get gunned down, that she would get pregnant, that he would find someone else, and he said of all those things, the only one that was totally unthinkable was the last).

If they were together during the day, they would go off into the Suffolk countryside. Determined he should learn to appreciate it, Caroline took him on a painstakingly thorough inch by inch guided tour of it, down the lanes, across tracks, through villages. They looked at the beautiful houses that studded the breadth of the county; stood in the small but oddly grand churches in the tiny perfect villages, such as Earls Soham and Hartest and Grundisburgh; walked across the wide just-rolling fields, in the thick, fairytale forests of Rendlesham and Tunstall, and through the wild, windy marshes at Aldeburgh, and Orford, where the sea-birds cried and the grasses moaned and soughed in their relentlessly sad melody. The beaches were all ravaged with rolls of barbed wire, but the cliffs at Southwold and at Minsmere were still sharply, freely beautiful, the Alde and the Deben flowed placidly along, and the peace of the countryside seemed oddly undisturbed. Caroline made him learn the strange, rather grand names of the towns and villages, with their French and even Latin connotations: Walsham Le Willows, Thornham Magna and Boulge and the almost Chaucerian notes of Walberswick and Saxmundham, Culpho and Hoxne. She insisted he saw the perfection of Lavenham, of Long Melford, of Chelsworth; she made him visit the abbey at Letheringham, took him to Melford Hall, Sutton Hoo; and in nearly all those places, sacred ones apart, they had sex, endlessly joyful, inventive, loving sex, in woods and fields and ditches, in stables and barns and ruined cottages, on clifftops, in marshes and, most of all, in the safe haven of the Jeep.

But they were not always alone: Brendan took Caroline to dances in the mess, and she took him to hops and barn dances in the villages, they met his buddies in the pubs, and for the first time in her entire life, Caroline realized, she was happy.

There were only two things that came between her and her contentment: one was the chilling, choking terror she had to live through every time Brendan was on a raid, which was frequently two or three times a week, and the other was a hot sweating fear that she might become pregnant. But as the months went by and the first year became the second and 1942 became 1943 and the Battle of the Atlantic had been virtually won, and the Allies had invaded Italy, Brendan survived again and yet again, piloting his stubby little Thunderbolt – more commonly known as a jug – through the hazardous skies, and her period continued to arrive with an almost fearsome regularity, she began to relax, to trust in her happiness, to think that the God who had done so little for her up to now had decided to smile on her after all.

And then with a stark, dark cruelty, He abandoned her again.

She found it almost impossible to believe, the three events that so totally changed her life, all happening at once, early in 1944: Brendan taking her hand in his and telling her he had to move, that he was being sent to Beaulieu in Hampshire, but that he would be back, and when he was back he wanted to marry her; and then her father, her huge, kindly, useless father, dying quite suddenly, of a heart attack, and then her mother, having quite genuinely mourned his death, taking off to London with a squadron leader in the air force with almost indecent haste; and then her period stubbornly, determinedly failing to start. She told herself it was emotion, nerves, that once Brendan had gone, the funeral was over, her mother had returned, she had sorted out the worst of the dreadful bleak post-death administration, it would be all right, but time went by, weeks and months of sad occupation, and she found herself quite, quite alone and indisputably pregnant.

She had no idea what to do; her mother had, if nothing else, at least seen to the organization of her abortion. She went to the doctor; he shook his head, said yes, she was undoubtedly pregnant, about four and a half months, maybe more; he could suggest nothing really except putting her in touch with an adoption society. What about an abortion? she said to him, tears of terror running down her face, but he had looked at her coldly and said did she not realize abortion was illegal and besides it was too late, far too late for such a course.

Sick with fright, as much as from her condition, she tried to be calm, to think what to do, but she couldn't begin; finally, oddly reluctant, driven to it by her utter despair, fearful of seeming to put pressure on him, she wrote to Brendan, asking for help. Brendan did not reply.

Sir William Hunterton asked Caroline to marry him on 31 December, the night she went into labour, and weary of loneliness, wounded almost beyond endurance by Brendan's silence, fearful of what was to become of her, she accepted.

William had been a great friend of her father's; he was forty-three years old, and had never married. He was a shy, very quiet man, he lived alone in a very beautiful small house in Woodbridge from which he ran an extremely unsuccessful antiques business. He was tall, very thin and stooped considerably; he had grey, slightly thinning hair, pale blue eyes, a long slightly hooked nose and a chin which one of his small nephews had once described with masterly tact as 'a little bit not there'. He was only ever to be seen wearing shabby tweeds, and a shabbier British warm, which was replaced in the summer by a series of crumpled linen jackets; he was kindly, learned, and much respected in Suffolk circles, and his friendship with the bluff, ebullient Stanley Miller was generally regarded as totally inexplicable. When Suffolk circles heard he was engaged to be married to Stanley Miller's daughter, they pronounced it not just inexplicable but outrageous. Had anyone actually stopped to think, they would have realized both relationships had their roots in the same thing: William's need to be with a stronger, tougher, more outgoing personality which would overcome his own shyness and inability to communicate; and at the same time, a knowledge that there were very real things he was bringing to the partnership – a calm, steady outlook, an orderliness of mind, and a surprisingly quirky sense of the ridiculous. It was this in particular which gave him the courage to propose to Caroline.

He had of course attended the funeral, and had stayed after the small gathering of friends and neighbours had left Moat House, ostensibly helping her clear up (Jacqueline having taken to her room with a more than usually appalling migraine), but actually keeping her company in the nightmare post-funeral let-down.

'We shall miss him,' he said, 'you and I. He was the best friend I ever had.'

'Yes,' said Caroline. 'William, would you like a drink?'

'I would, my dear, yes. A very large whisky I think. Why don't you have one too? You look a bit peaky.'

'I feel it,' said Caroline, sitting down suddenly.

'You've got a lot to cope with,' he said. 'Look, I'll get the drinks. How do you like yours?'

'With ice,' she said and, reminded forcibly why she liked her whisky iced, started to cry.

'There there,' he said, patting her hand awkwardly. 'Don't cry.'

'Why not?' she said, sniffing hopelessly. 'Why shouldn't I cry?'

'I don't know, my dear. I really don't. You've got a lot to cope with. You must let me help you. With the arrangements and all that sort of thing. Have you seen the will yet?'

'Yes, I have, and he's left everything to Mama. Quite rightly of course.'

'Of course. Well, you must let me know if there's anything I can do. Now or in the future.'

'Thank you, William. I will.' She looked up at him and smiled suddenly. 'What did you admire about my father, as a matter of interest? You never seemed – well, kindred spirits exactly.'

'Oh, well there you're wrong. We were, in our own way. We both liked houses, and nice things to put in them, and we both loved the countryside round here, although I did find it hard to watch him massacring the wildlife. And I enjoyed talking to him; we both had a great love of jokes, you know. We were – relaxed together. And I admired all sorts of things about him. His quickness. His courage. His ability to take risks. I have none of those things.' He looked at her. 'I think you do, though.'

'Maybe,' said Caroline, smiling up at him. She wondered how he would feel if he knew exactly what risks she had been taking.

William took to coming in once a week, to help her with the mountains of paperwork, and she would invite him to supper, and they would sit chatting for hours. Jacqueline had gone now, with her squadron leader, and he made her feel peaceful and less alone, and quite often he would manage to make her laugh, telling her some ridiculous joke or other.

One night, about two months after Stanley's death, when she was feeling particularly low, she drank far too much claret (her father's cellar was still extremely well stocked) and suddenly, in the middle of one of William's stories, felt faint and very sick; she excused herself and just made the lavatory in time.

She came back, some time later, pale and shaken and sat down, looking at William very directly. 'I think I ought to tell you,' she said, 'that I'm pregnant.'

'I thought you were,' he said.

She told him everything: about Brendan, about their enchanted time together, about how she had written not once but twice and he had not replied, about the doctor's hostility, about how she didn't know how she was going to cope, didn't even know where she was going to have the baby. William sat calmly listening to her, occasionally taking a sip of his brandy; when she had finished she looked at him defiantly and said, 'Well, go on, aren't you going to tell me what a bad girl I am?'

'Of course not,' he said. 'There's a war on.'

He was even more helpful after that; his shyness prevented him from actually accompanying her to the doctor or the hospital, but he made sure she went for check-ups, discussed which hospital would be best (a private room at Ipswich they finally decided), helped her write to adoption agencies. Quite early on, she said to him, 'You don't think, do you . . .' and he had said very firmly, 'No I don't,' and that was as far as they went in any discussion that the baby might be kept. Caroline regarded its loss with apparent total equanimity. She agreed with William that there was no possible way she could offer it a satisfactory home, however much money she had (and she had a great deal), and she would be doing the best possible thing for it in giving it away. The baby would be taken away at birth, before she had time to become involved with it, and first fostered and then adopted; it would be placed with a nice suitable family who would love it and give it a safe secure home. It was all very neat and tidy and was clearly the very best thing for everybody. Any doubts or conflicting emotions she experienced on the subject she crushed mercilessly; if Brendan had written, showed himself even halfway prepared to support her, then things might have been different; but as he had abandoned them both, then she had to do the best she could. William told her it would be far better for the baby to be with a family, to have a proper status in the world and, more and more these days, she did what William told her.

Three months after Stanley's death, news came from London: Jacqueline and the squadron leader were dead; his flat, in Kensington, had received a direct hit from a German bomber. Caroline's only real emotion, to her own great surprise, was a purely unselfish pleasure that her mother should have had at least three months of happiness at the end of a sad, conspicuously joyless life.

She did not know what she would have done without William after that: he became father, husband, mother and friend to her. His weekly visits became almost daily, and he never arrived at the Moat House without some sort of small present for her: a book he had bought at a sale, a few tomatoes from his greenhouse, a bunch of wild flowers he had picked on the way. The baby was due in January; by October he was fussing over her, telephoning her twice a day to make sure she was resting, making sure that the doctor had been for her check-ups. He had put by two gallons of petrol, he told her, just in case of emergencies; she was to phone him at the shop if she ever needed him, if the promised ambulance was unable to come. Caroline was touched, warmed, comforted by his devotion; she looked forward to his visits, had Cook save up the rations for when he was coming to supper, made her increasingly hazardous journey down the steep cellar steps to fetch a bottle of wine for him, even began to read the books she knew he would like to discuss. It was agony, the reading; but when she saw his pale, rather mournful eyes sparkle as she said she had quite fallen in love with Phineas Finn, or that she considered Marianne Dashwood the most interesting of Miss Austen's heroines, she felt she had repaid him just a little for his kindness.

She felt increasingly fond of him, and she knew he was very fond of her; but never in her wildest dreams did she imagine he was planning to ask her to marry him.

When he did, when he finally managed, over a New Year's Eve dinner, after asking for a second brandy after a second bottle of wine, and he had paced the room, looking at her anguishedly at each turn, and she had sat, her hands folded neatly on her huge stomach, watching him amusedly, imagining he was perhaps going to ask her some kind of favour, some money loaned perhaps, or the use of one of the greenhouses, when he said suddenly, desperately, all in a rush, 'Caroline, I would like you to marry me,' she felt physically faint with shock, she closed her eyes and leant her head on her hands.

'I'm sorry,' he said quickly, 'I shouldn't have, not now, I should have waited. I've upset you, forgive me.'

And no, no, she said, not at all, she was not in the least upset, it was nice of him, so very nice of him to ask her, under the circumstances, and she was very honoured and flattered, but . . .

And he had said, yes, no doubt, but, he imagined, she did not want to marry him, she did not love him, he had been a fool to think she might, to have embarrassed both of them by asking her, and poured himself yet another brandy; and Caroline had stood up and put her hand on his arm, and said, 'William, I can't tell you how glad I am you asked me. And how fond of you I am, but . . .'

And before she could voice the next phrase she felt a sudden rush of water between her legs, and she looked down at the small pool on the floor and said, with no embarrassment whatsoever, 'Oh, God, I've wet myself.'

'No', he said, suddenly surprisingly in command. 'I think your waters have broken. Now we must phone the hospital at once; there is a danger of infection from now on.'

'William,' said Caroline, staring at him in as much astonishment as if he had declared himself a secret transvestite, or had an ambition to be a high-wire artist, 'how on earth do you know that?'

'Well,' he said, hurrying out to the hall, 'I've been mugging up on it all. Just in case, you know. The first stage of labour will follow quite quickly now. You may begin to feel contractions any moment. But they shouldn't be too severe for a while.'

'William,' said Caroline, quite overcome by this as proof of his love for her, as nothing else could have done, and following him, with some difficulty, into the hall, and putting her hand in his as he stood waiting for the operator to answer, 'William, I think I would like to marry you very much. If you really meant what you said.'

She had not expected it to hurt so much. Somehow she had thought it would be like the abortion and she would wake up and it would all be over. She had not been prepared, and no one had troubled to try to prepare her, for the wrenching, howling agony of the contractions, hour after hour, of the fear that her body would break with the violence of them, that they would grow so much worse that not even screaming would be a release; but somehow, through it all, the quiet, calm face of William Hunterton stayed in her head, and made some sort of a sanity for her to cling to.

They gave her gas, but she hated it, it frightened her even more than the pain, the swimming, swirling suffocation of it, and she begged for something else, anything, to help her; but the midwife, who was kindly, albeit brisk, said it was gas or nothing, and that she really should try to get along with it, as she would certainly need it when she was pushing baby out. No one had told Caroline she would have to push baby out; she had imagined it would simply, eventually find its own way.

She looked at the midwife in terror, panting in between her pains, with fear as much as exhaustion, eighteen hours into her labour, and said, 'I don't know what you mean, push. I can't, I can't do anything.'

'You'll find out,' said the midwife briskly. 'You'll know what to do. Now do try to relax a little bit more, and let's have another go with the gas with the next pain. You've got quite a long way to go yet, and you're wearing yourself out like this.'

'A long way to go?' said Caroline, her voice rising to a scream, as the pain started rising in her once more. 'How long, how long?'

'Oh, a good hour or two yet,' said the midwife. 'Now come on, there's a good girl, and let's breathe this in, shall we?'

'I don't want it, I just want to die,' moaned Caroline, pushing the mask away. 'I just want to die, now, before it goes on any longer.'

'Oh, they all say that,' said the midwife. 'You'll feel differently when baby's here. You won't be able to remember any of this.'

She had been born, her daughter, swiftly in the end, in a great rush (too late, they told her severely now, for pain relief), and she had lain there, looking into her great dark blue eyes, stroking her tiny, damp head, kissing her helplessly frond-like fingers, and wept with love.

'You're lucky it's a girl,' said the midwife, lips pursed, swift to remind her troublesome patient of her punishment to come. 'Most adoptive parents want a girl.'

And Caroline, aching with the love of her baby, and the dark dread that she must lose her again so soon, put both arms protectively round her, and rested her cheek on the small dark head, and wondered how it was possible to experience such joy and such unhappiness at precisely the same moment.

She was holding the baby when they came; she had sat up sleepless all night, unwilling to waste even a moment of the time she had left with her. She had stroked her silky skin, outlined the small, squashed profile, unfolded the tiny hands a dozen, a hundred times. She had rocked her when she cried, holding her close to her breast, had refused to let them take her away, insisting they brought her the bottle so that she could feed her. She had undressed her, examining, studying every inch of the tiny body, smiling at the little dangling, helpless legs, frowning anxiously at the sore-looking umbilicus. She had changed her nappy, her nightdress, wrapped her again in her shawl. She had managed to get out of the bed and stood at the window, holding the baby, showing her the darkness, the stars; and when she had felt she might sleep, she had walked softly up and down the room, fighting it away, learning how the baby felt in her arms. She knew what she was doing; she was trying to encase a lifetime in one night, storing the feel, the smell, the sound, the warmth of her child away, so that she could have it with her always; and when the morning came, and she knew the lifetime was over, she could hardly bear it. She heard their steps outside, their voices, and a chill took hold of her, a dreadful primitive fear. She would have run if she could, and when they came in, she was shrinking back on the pillows, her eyes wide with fear.

'Good morning, Mrs Miller.' It was Matron. 'And what a nice morning it is too. How are you? I hear you had a little bit of a struggle yesterday. Never mind, all over now. Now then, Mrs Jackson from the Adoption Society is here to take the baby. I'll leave you together, Mrs Jackson, for a while. You see, it's a beautiful baby, and a girl too. That was lucky wasn't it, Mrs Miller?'

'Yes,' said Caroline, obediently zombie-like.

'Right then. Well, just ring if you need me.'

'All right.' She lay there and looked at Mrs Jackson; the baby moved slightly in her shawl. 'I want to know where she's going,' she said.

'Oh, I can't tell you that,' said Mrs Jackson. 'We find it best for the mother not to know.'

'Really? Best for who?'

'Why for both of you. Mother and baby. Much better just to let go altogether. It's sad of course,' she added brightly, 'but it's so much for the best, and you must think of baby.'

'Yes of course,' said Caroline. 'Yes of course. What about the papers?'

'Well, you have to sign one set now. The baby will be placed with her foster parents. In a few months, when we are satisfied that we have found the right adoptive parents, there will be more legal formalities naturally. I did explain all this to you before,' she added severely.

'So until then I can change my mind?' said Caroline, with a wild stab of hope that was half fear.

'Of course not,' said Mrs Jackson, looking warily at her, hoping that the brisk sensible young woman she had interviewed before was not going to turn into one of the neurotic difficult ones who made life a nightmare for the adoptive parents. 'You can't just wander in one day and take the baby back.'

'No,' said Caroline humbly. 'No, of course not. But . . .'

Mrs Jackson sighed. 'So, if you would just like to sign here . . .'

Caroline looked at the form, but she could see nothing, it might as well have been written in hieroglyphics for all it meant to her; she took the pen, and held it very still above the line where her signature should go. She looked down at the baby and then up at Mrs Jackson, in an odd, appealing gesture. 'Please help me,' she said. Mrs Jackson chose to misunderstand. 'I'll hold the baby,' she said, 'that will make it easier for you.'

'No,' said Caroline sharply. 'No, I want her.'

Mrs Jackson looked at her warily. 'I hope you're not going to change your mind,' she said.

For a long moment, Caroline hesitated, wondering how she had the strength to do what had to be done, whether if, in spite of everything, she should keep the baby, bring it up alone. She could move away, go and live somewhere else, pretend she had been widowed; the country would be full of women on their own. She had plenty of money, she could give the baby a good life. What she was doing was madness, unnecessary.

'I don't think . . .' she said, summoning her greatly depleted strength. 'I really don't think . . .'

And then the door opened and a nurse came in, looking slightly less hostile, almost friendly in fact, with a huge bunch of white roses, and said, 'These are for you. Sir William Hunterton just brought them in and said he would visit you when you felt ready.'

Caroline looked at the card on the flowers which said, 'From William, with my love' and she thought of the promise she had made to William the night before, to marry him, and her assurance that he would not have to accept another man's baby; she saw his face, William's face, kind, concerned, loyal, before her blurred eyes, his gentle courage stretched to breaking point as he drove her to the hospital through the total darkness when no ambulance could be found, and she was already groaning with a pain that terrified him more than her; the grip of his hand as they wheeled her down the corridor towards the labour ward, the kiss he gave her on her forehead as he said goodbye, his promise that he would stay and wait for however long it took, and she knew it had to be done, for all their sakes. She thought of all the months of care William had lavished upon her, the daily phone calls, the funny little gifts, the awkwardly careful questions; she thought of his struggle to make his proposal, and the way his whole face exploded in happiness when she had said she would like to accept; and she knew that she could not fail him, that he deserved that she should keep her promise. And she also recognized something else, something which surprised her, almost shocked her: how totally she had come to depend on William, his counsel, his support, his companionship, and how she found it impossible now to contemplate managing on her own. There could be other babies, lots of other babies; she had no trouble having babies, that was one thing she did know about herself; she could have another baby straight away, she could be back here in less than a year with a new baby, one that would make William and her both happy. All she had to do now was be brave and it would soon be over, and then she could begin again. She was always beginning again.

She took a deep breath, and suddenly, almost brutally, as if she were inflicting some physical injury upon herself, handed the baby over to Mrs Jackson. 'Take her,' she said, 'take her quickly. Look, I've signed. Now go away.'

'Thank you, Mrs Miller. I know you've made the right decision. Can I do anything for you?'

'No,' said Caroline, her teeth clenched in an effort to keep from crying out. 'Nothing. Just go. Go, go, go.'

The pain she had felt as the baby had been pulled from her body the night before was nothing compared with the wrenching agony of seeing her carried out through the door.

In a German hospital near Munich that very same day, after months in coma, surgery and intensive care, Flight-Lieutenant FitzPatrick was finally deemed well enough to be given the unread letter from Caroline Miller that had been in his pocket the day he was shot down.

Interview with Kate FitzPatrick for Two Childhoods chapter of *The Tinsel Underneath*.

Brendan was more of a pet in this household, I tell you, than a little boy. We all spoilt him, us four girls and our mother. He was always so good-natured and so loving. 'You have a perfect boy there,' Father Mitchell used to say to her. He was a good friend to us, Father Mitchell, always in the house after our father died. And for some reason we never felt jealous of Brendan, just adored him. Ridiculous really.

He didn't do at all well at school. He was just so dreadfully lazy. And he always got bad grades; but when our mother went to the school somehow all the teachers had something good to say about him all the same. That he was kind, thoughtful, helpful, always nice to talk to. He had charm, Brendan did, even when he was just a little boy.

We were very poor, and none of us had much; but Brendan did get more than the rest of us. The second helping of dessert, the new jacket. 'Well, he's a growing boy,' Mother used to say, 'he needs more food,' or 'he can't wear your hand-me-downs.' We used to resent that a bit, but then again, I think we thought she was right. We didn't often argue about it. Like I told you, he was more like a pet than a child in the house.

Of course, he could learn things when he had to. When it was a play he wanted to be in, the words went into that head of his easy as anything. 'Hear my words,' he'd say after sitting with the book for half an hour, and we all would say, 'You can't know them, not yet,' but he did, every time, word perfect.

He was very good indeed at his acting. He made you believe in him. After a bit you just forgot he was your naughty brother and thought he was – well, whoever.

I remember once they did a little thing, a kind of history of America, and he was Lincoln, making the speech at Gettysburg. Well and there we were, all of us Yankees, dabbing our eyes with our handkerchiefs. We almost had to take our mother out of the hall, she was sobbing so loudly.

If he had a fault, it was that he was just a little bit conceited. He knew all about his looks and what he could do with them. The girls all fell in love with him, and he certainly knew how to keep a half-dozen of them going at a time. He could be a terrible liar when it suited him. I used to feel ashamed, listening to him at the door. 'I've to help my mother this evening,' he'd say to one of them, and then he'd be off for a walk with another one, as soon as the coast was clear. When he was only fifteen he had girls coming round all the time. He was really quite precocious.

Further notes for Two Childhoods chapter of The Tinsel Underneath.

Interview with Peter Gregson, psychiatrist. Head boy at Abbots Park Preparatory School during Piers Windsor's first year there. Wishes to be anonymous.

Well, I liked Piers Windsor very much. He was a nice little chap. He seemed very young, even to me. I was thirteen, in my last year. Just moving on to Winchester. So he looked like a baby to me. He was very good-looking, pretty almost. Boys who looked like him were more at risk. Poor little buggers. Sorry, unfortunate choice of words. This is anonymous, isn't it? I'd hate to upset anyone.

Anyway, he had a bad time at first, being bullied, but that seemed to get sorted out after a bit. Some big boy took it upon him to protect him. Or so we thought. It was in his second term, and there was an end-of-term concert. The youngest ones were doing a scene from *Peter Rabbit*. Windsor was going to be Mr McGregor. He was absolutely marvellous apparently. He seemed a bit happier and more confident.

Then the scandal broke. Poor little tyke was caught in bed with this bigger boy. I honestly don't think they were doing anything much. It's more comfort, when you're that age, you know. It's a bit of warmth and cuddling, feels like home. Nobody realizes how alone, how desperately abandoned you feel in that situation. I would no more send a child of mine away to school than shoot my right hand off. I heard about it in my position as head boy. Not officially of course; it was kept completely hushed up. But one had quite a lot of dealing with the staff on a day-to-day level. The parents were not to be told, because of the scandal. Piers and the other boy were beaten, and told if they were ever seen even speaking together again, they would both be expelled. Barbaric. I have my doubts about this beating business too. In my experience, sadistic masters got some kind of a thrill out of beating small boys.

Anyway, that was that. Or so they all thought. But then Piers was found in one of the lavatories, vomiting. He'd taken half a bottle of aspirin. God knows how he got them. He was rushed off to hospital and stomach-pumped, and again, it was agreed his parents should not be told. And as a punishment, he was stripped of his part in *Peter Rabbit*.

I tell you, it has haunted me to this day that I just let all this drift on under my nose and didn't try to do anything about it. I'd find it a bit hard to face him now, to be honest with you. Talk about the Nazis. The English public school system is almost as evil in my view.

Chapter 3

1945

Caroline and William were married at Easter in St Mary's Church, Woodbridge. They had planned a small wedding, but in the end the church looked quite full, and at least saved the organist from the embarrassment, as she put it, of drowning out the voices. William had a large family: three sisters, all married, who came with their husbands and the ten children they had between them, and a brother, and two elderly aunts plus the large family of his best man, Jonathan Dunstan, with whom he had been at Eton. There was nobody on Caroline's side of the church except Cook and Janey, who had come at Caroline's express invitation, and Jack Bamforth and his wife and children. There was also the small problem of who should give her away, and she ran through her circle of acquaintances, even considering Jack and, in a moment of wild mischief, Giles Dudley-Leicester, whose constipated-looking wife Angela she had taken a great dislike to, but in the end it was agreed that William's brother Robert should do it, and she gave in, thankful not to have to worry about it any more.

William wore his morning suit, and Caroline wore an extremely beautiful dress from Worth in ice-blue lace, quite long, almost to her ankles, cut low at the neck, with a tight, full waist, and a great taffeta bow, rather like a bustle, at the back; and a wide-brimmed straw hat, trimmed with blue and white flowers and a half veil which she said made her feel at least a bit like a bride.

The service was quite simple, but Caroline walked into the church in a stream of sunlight to the glorious waterfalls of Bach's Fugue in B Minor and everyone agreed, however grudgingly, that she did look not only lovely, but happy, and they sang 'Love Divine' and 'Dear Lord and Father of Mankind' (which Betty Baxter-Browne, née Hunterton, hissed to her husband was a very strange choice of hymn for such an occasion) and the vicar gave a very nice address about love healing hurts both large and small, and the hope that any new marriage must give to everybody after the war. As they walked back down the aisle to the Wedding March, Caroline on William's arm, she looked not at the congregation (most of whom she did not know) but up at him with an expression of such unmistakable affection that all three of William's sisters suddenly found they could not meet each other's eyes, in the light of all the deeply unpleasant things they had been saying about her and the marriage over the past few weeks.

The reception was held at the Moat House; Mrs Bamforth and Jack took some extremely good champagne round from Stanley's apparently inexhaustible cellar and two girls from the village followed them with trays of canapés, and there was a very impressive cake which Cook had spent the last two months baking and icing. After they had cut the cake, Jonathan Dunstan got up and made a short and highly embarrassing speech about how long it had taken William to make up his mind to go to the altar, and that he had always had trouble getting himself together over anything, even at school, except for cricket, but now he had decided to bowl this maiden over ('Some maiden,' hissed Betty, dangerously audibly to her younger sister, Joyce) and they were clearly going to make a lot of runs together. He went on to say that if ever William was to retire, he would be there to pick up the bat, at which Barbara Dunstan had a coughing fit and had to be given an extra glass of champagne, which mercifully cut the speech short. Then Jack Bamforth quite unexpectedly stood up and said he would like to say a few words.

'How extraordinary,' whispered Betty to Barbara Dunstan who she had gone over to join, 'he was serving the drinks a few minutes ago.' There was an odd buzz in the room, a ripple of general unease, which Jack ignored, just stood there totally relaxed in the spring sunshine, with his handsome face politely patient, and his grey eyes fixed rather distantly on Caroline.

'I thought that as Caroline had no one much to speak about her, I should,' he said in his soft, rolling Suffolk voice. 'She's had a very sad time just lately, and I think we all greatly admire the way she's managed to take care of everything since her father's death and the subsequent one of her mother.' A couple of the ladies looked meaningfully at one another at this point, but most of the room was standing listening to him carefully and courteously. He had always had that effect on everyone, Caroline thought, listening to him with something very closely akin to love.

'All I wanted to say then,' said Jack, smiling at her, 'was that all of us who have known Caroline all her life, we all know what a very special person she is, and how lucky Sir William here is to be marrying her. She's brave and kind and a fine horsewoman, what's more important,' he added, grinning at them all, 'and those of us who have worked for her have never known anything but the greatest consideration and care from her. I hope she won't mind me telling you that all of us here at the Moat House held a little party of our own when we heard she and Sir William were going to stay here and keep it as their home. I hope she and Sir William will be very happy, and I ask you all to raise your glasses to wish them well.'

'Hear, hear!' cried Robert, and the room took up the toast, raising their glasses, smiling most benignly, and Caroline, flushed and with her eyes soft with pleasure and tears, went over to Jack and kissed him gently on the cheek.

'I don't think I ever liked anything more than that in my whole life,' she said. 'Thank you.'

'That's all right,' he said, 'you deserved it, and it needed saying. Are you all right?'

'Oh yes,' said Caroline, with a sigh, knowing exactly what he meant. 'You seem to be always asking me that, Jack. Yes, I'm quite all right, thank you.'

But she wasn't.

They went to Edinburgh for their honeymoon; for no other reason than that it was totally removed from the experience of either of them, and seemed far enough away for them to relax into their new selves. The war was not quite over, but peace was sufficiently nearly there for people to be totally relaxed; they went up by train (petrol still being severely rationed), booked into the Royal Scottish Hotel, and hired a car when they got there so that they could explore the surrounding countryside as much as their petrol coupons would allow.

They had a big room with an even bigger bathroom on the first floor; William had said to Caroline rather bashfully that he did not feel able to ask for the bridal suite, but that the rooms they had were the very next best, and he hoped they would be all right for her. Caroline had kissed him tenderly and said she would have stayed with him in a boarding house in Clacton had he so wished. William's rather pale blue eyes softened with pleasure as he looked at her.

'I do realize how very fortunate I am,' he said. 'I hope I will not be a – well – a disappointment to you.'

'Dear William,' said Caroline, 'you couldn't possibly be a disappointment to me. I know you far too well for there to be any nasty surprises.'

'That is not absolutely true,' said William, carefully, 'but perhaps we can work together through any difficulties.'

Oh, my heavens, thought Caroline, looking at his face flushed with the effort of confronting such a subject, he's talking about sex. It had been something she had carefully not confronted herself; during her pregnancy her usual voracious appetite had been dulled, by misery and loneliness, and since the birth of her baby she had kept her entire consciousness carefully fixed on anything, anything at all that was not to do with her body, its functions and, most dreadful of all, its capacity to reproduce. Nevertheless, confronted it had to be; William was clearly not marrying her for her cooking, or even her company alone; and he had told her several times he hoped they would have children. Nevertheless, until such time as she was forced to consider it, she knew she couldn't; when that time came, she presumed, her body would see her through.

'William,' she said, very gently, 'I know what you mean, and I'm sure it will be quite all right.'

'I hope so,' he said, 'the situation will be a little irregular, to put it mildly.'

They had arrived at the Royal at tea-time the day after the wedding (having spent their actual wedding night in chaste exhaustion on a series of trains); unpacked, went and looked at the castle and strolled round the town, and then came in for dinner. 'Early, I think,' said Caroline briskly. 'We're both tired.'

They ate well: smoked salmon and venison ('They have obviously been ducking the war up here,' said William), drank a bottle of excellent claret, took a further stroll round the hotel garden, and went up to bed.

'Oh, William,' said Caroline, turning to him as she walked into the room. 'Champagne! How romantic. And how luxurious. How did you manage that?'

'I'm afraid,' he said, his pale face flushed, 'I smuggled it in from your father's cellar. I hope you don't mind. I really felt we had to have one, and when I made enquiries, they told me of course that they had none. But at least they were able to provide the ice bucket.'

Caroline kissed him gently on the lips. 'You're a wonderful husband. I'm very lucky.'

Undressing in the bathroom (having left the bedroom to the ferociously embarrassed William) she reflected on the task ahead of her. Unless she was greatly mistaken, William was virtually inexperienced; he would need careful and infinitely tactful initiation. It was going to be very difficult; she shrank from it. Apart from anything else, fond of him as she was, she did not find him in the least physically attractive: not repellent, not even unattractive, but simply not attractive. However, it had to be done; it was her penance, the price she must pay for having someone to love and care for her, someone kind and gentle and good, and there was no way out. Caroline took a deep breath and walked out into the bedroom.

He had poured the champagne; they sat in bed side by side and drank it, slowly, relievedly relaxing. By the third glass William was blessedly giggly. 'I shall have to be careful,' he said to her, 'I believe this can lead to disaster in this sort of situation.'

'Darling William, you are obviously a man of great worldliness,' said Caroline, leaning to kiss him and then turning out the light. 'You've been deceiving me.'

'I'm afraid not,' he said, rather sadly, taking her in his arms, 'I have only – well – made love three times in my life, and in each case it was somewhat disastrous.'

'Why?' said Caroline, genuinely interested.

'Oh, I suppose because I was not able to give the ladies in question any pleasure.'

'How old were they, these ladies?'

'Oh, I really couldn't say. I suppose between thirty and forty.'

'Who were they, William?'

'Two of them were prostitutes, I'm afraid,' he said, sadder than ever. 'I was out in France, just after the First War, with some undergraduate friends and they – we – thought it would be fun. It wasn't.'

'And the third?'

'Oh,' he said, and she could hear the desperation combined with amusement in his voice, 'she was a friend of my mother's. She seduced me one afternoon, when my mother was out. I was only sixteen at the time. I was very shocked. It wasn't a – well – a success. She told me that.'

'And since then?'

'Since then I've just – well, tried not to think about it, and – well, you know . . .' His voice trailed away.

'I know. And nobody else ever tempted you?'

'Well of course I did think about marriage from time to time. But someone always asked the person in question first. And I'm very old fashioned, you see, I could never have – well, had a relationship with someone I respected and wasn't married to.'

'Poor William,' said Caroline tenderly, stroking his face, 'what a lonely life you've had.'

'In some ways, yes.'

'But you really can't blame yourself for not giving pleasure, as you put it, to two prostitutes. They're not too capable of it, I believe. As for some old bat, coming on at you when you were only sixteen, it's enough to put anyone off for life. Or was she beautiful and sexy?'

'No,' he said, horrified. 'Fat and plain, as I recall.'

'Oh well. There you are then.'

There was a long silence; they lay holding one another. Caroline waited for some feeling to come into her body, some gesture from him, but there was nothing. She felt herself slipping dangerously, senselessly, into sleep and roused herself. It was no use putting it off.

'Now look, my darling,' she said, 'the first thing we have to do is take our clothes off. We're not going to get very far with your pyjamas and my nightdress between us.'

'Oh, no, no of course not,' said William. He got out of bed, removed his pyjamas and slithered hurriedly back in. Caroline, also naked by now, took him in her arms again. He was still stiff, awkward; she turned his head and began to kiss him, slowly and very deliberately. For a long time nothing happened; then slowly, nearly fearfully, he began to kiss her back, and she felt with a sense of almost awed relief his penis hardening against her, and sensations within her own body going out to meet it. Perhaps, she thought, blanking out her mind to everything except the immediate physical present, perhaps it would after all be all right.

It was, in some ways. William proved, after a short time, to be a competent lover: tender, careful, inevitably inhibited, but competent. He did not want sex very often, for a bridegroom; days would pass, sometimes a week or even two, between encounters. But when he did approach her, gently, almost apologetically, kissing and caressing her in a kind of formal ritual, entering her slowly and cautiously, his excitement and his climax rising suddenly and swiftly at the end, she managed to respond, to go out to him, to move with him, sometimes even to climax herself. And afterwards, as they lay together, William smiling with infinite happiness, stroking her hair, saying he loved her and thanking her over and over again, she would relax in his arms, and thank him too and somehow manage to keep her thoughts with him, in this bed, this room, this moment, and never, never for an instant to wander into a pair of stronger, rougher arms, a younger, hungrier body, and a voice that cried out with her own in exultation and joy. And she also managed, with even greater effort of will, to keep her mind away from a tiny tender body, a soft, floppy head, a set of frond-like fingers and a pair of dark blue eyes that looked into her own with squinting serenity and which filled her dreams night after night. It wasn't easy, especially when she woke crying, sobbing aloud, finding the pillow wet, her face flushed, and William holding her, patting her shoulders awkwardly, asking her if there was anything he could do; but she did manage it.

Until she got pregnant. And then she fell apart.

'Yes, there's no doubt about it, Lady Hunterton.' The doctor smiled at her. 'You're about eight weeks pregnant. Everything is very satisfactory. How do you feel?'

'Fine,' said Caroline. 'Absolutely fine.' But her mind was flailing about, sucking her down into a whirlpool of confusion. Pregnant! A baby! Another baby, another body fluttering and turning inside her, growing, invading her thoughts, her mind and her heart, another birth, another person, another object and another source of love. She expected to feel joy and she felt nothing but sadness; expected to forget the first baby and remembered her more and more vividly. This was betrayal, rejection; she felt ugly, cheating, dishonest. William was beside himself with joy and pride; seeing her obvious distress he imagined its source was physical, thought she was feeling sick and tired, and insisted she rest, put her feet up, go to bed early, stop worrying about the house, stop doing everything. Caroline stood it for a couple of weeks, during which time she hardly spoke without the greatest effort, could not sleep, saw the baby's face before her wherever she went and whatever she did; and then, finally, frantic with misery, she went to the one person she knew she could always talk to: Jack Bamforth.

Jack listened to her carefully, sitting in his little office he had made in the stable yard, tut-tutted a few times, looked at her drawn, thin face and said, 'Maybe you should get her back.'

'I can't, Jack, William won't have her. I know he won't. It's the one thing I can't ask of him.'

'Have you actually?'

'Have I actually what?'

'Asked him?'

'Well, no.'

'Well then.'

'Jack, you don't understand. The night she was born, when he came to see me afterwards, and he'd stayed there all the time you know, twenty-four hours nearly, just to be near me, I promised him then. I can't go back on it now. It would break his heart.'

'Oh, I don't know,' said Jack, 'tough things, hearts. They don't break that easy, Caroline.'

'William's would.'

'Well, but you're giving him a baby of his own. That would help surely.'

'No, I know it wouldn't. Really it wouldn't.'

'Well then, I don't see what you can do.'

'No.'

He looked at her carefully again. 'Do you know where she is?'

'No. No, I don't.'

'It's all settled and done with then?'

'Yes. No. Oh, I don't know. She's still with her foster parents.'

'So you've got – room for manoeuvre?'

'Yes. No. Jack, don't talk like this, please.'

'I'm trying to help you.'

'Well you're not,' she cried, standing up and walking away from him towards the door. 'You're hurting me, that's all you're doing. You don't understand. You couldn't. Just leave me alone, will you?'

'All right,' he said placidly.

'Mrs Jackson, this is Lady Hunterton.'

'Lady Hunterton? I'm afraid I don't know –'

'Yes you do, Mrs Jackson. I was Caroline Miller.'

'Oh yes.' The polite voice iced over. 'Is there anything I can do for you, Lady Hunterton?'

'Yes. Yes, there is. I want to see the baby.'

'I'm afraid you can't do that, Mrs Hunterton.'

'Why not?'

'Because you agreed that you wouldn't, when you handed her over. I explained that to you.'

'Yes, I know you did. But I've been talking to a solicitor. And I do know I can change my mind. And get the baby back if I want to.'

'I don't think,' said Mrs Jackson, her voice more icy still, 'that your solicitor knows quite what he is talking about.'

'Oh, yes he does, Mrs Jackson. He's a very good solicitor.'

'I see. I can't begin to tell you, Lady Hunterton, what a lot of heartache you will be creating for yourself and your baby. Her foster parents wish to adopt her, things can be finalized shortly.'

'I haven't signed any adoption papers.'

'Lady Hunterton. You would be greatly damaging your baby to interfere at this stage.'

'Possibly. Well anyway, let me tell you, I have no intention of signing any adoption papers. Not yet. And I may very well want the baby back.'

'William.'

'Yes, my darling.'

'William, you really are happy about this baby, aren't you?'

'Caroline darling, you know I am. So happy. It's more than I could ever have hoped for. I feel so infinitely fortunate.'

'Good. Because . . .'

'Yes?'

'Well, because I feel – well, not quite, quite so perfectly happy.'

'Oh, my dear, that's because you've been so unwell.' William's pale blue eyes were anxious, compassionate. 'I feel so bad that you have to endure all this sickness. So guilty that I can't help. But when it passes, I'm sure you'll be perfectly happy. And I can try and make it up to you.'

'William, it isn't just the sickness, I'm afraid.'

'Then what is it? Is it me? Am I doing something – something to upset you?'

His face was so distraught Caroline had to smile. She reached out her hand and patted his. 'No, William, it's nothing to do with you. You've been wonderful to me. No, it's – well the thing is, William, this is all rather reminding me of the other baby. I'm finding it rather painful.'

'Of course you are.' His voice was gentle.

Caroline looked at him, startled; she had expected hostility. 'You understand?'

'Yes, of course I understand. I would be some kind of monster if didn't. I'm very sympathetic.'

'Oh, William,' said Caroline, going up to him, and putting her arms round him. 'What a remarkable man you are.'

'Not really.'

'Well, William, what I wondered was, whether we could – well, at least talk about it.'

'We are, my dear, surely. We can talk about it whenever you like. You're not, after all, on your own.'

'No, William, I don't mean just talk about how I'm feeling. I mean talk about maybe, just possibly, my – well, my seeing the baby again. Just to find out how she is. And –'

'No, Caroline.' His voice was bleak, strangely cold, final.

'But, William, I only wanted to –'

'No, Caroline. I'm sorry, but it's the one thing you just cannot ask of me. I love you very much, and I have always totally put out of my mind anything that has happened to you before we met. But you cannot, and you must not ask me even to consider having that baby here. I simply couldn't stand it.'

'Why not? Why not, if you love me? William, I think about her all the time. I dream about her, and it's been worse since I've been pregnant. It's terrible, it's like a sickness. I'm finding it almost impossible to stand it. Please help me, William, please.'

'Caroline, as I just said I will help you all I can. But I cannot and will not have that child here. You did agree.'

'It's my house,' said Caroline, her pain making her cruel. 'I can do what I like in it.'

'Yes, you can of course,' he said very quietly, 'but I should not be able to stay.'

He walked out of the room.

Passing his study door a short while later Caroline, with a rush of horror at her own cruelty, heard him weeping.

'William, I'm sorry,' said Caroline, for the hundredth time that night, as she lay in his arms, 'so terribly sorry. I love you so much and you've been so good to me, I should never have said that. Please forgive me.'

'I forgive you,' he said, gently polite, 'but I meant what I said. Let us have that quite clear between us. I cannot let you even begin to hope that you can have the other baby here. Not if I am here. I'm sorry.'

'I understand,' said Caroline. 'I do understand. Hold me, William, please, and let me show you how much I love you.'

'Lady Hunterton, of course you are within your rights to take the baby back. But I would not advise it. She is – what – ten months old. She has settled. She is extremely happy. Why upset her, and her parents?'

'They're not her parents.'

'They have worked hard at being her parents.'

'You're a solicitor, could we confine ourselves to legal matters please, not moral ones?'

'Yes, Lady Hunterton.'

'Now then, I am not proposing I actually take the baby back. Not yet. But I do not want to sign the papers. I want more time to think.'

'Yes, Lady Hunterton. Well of course, you are certainly under no legal obligation to sign the papers.'

'Good.'

'Jack, I told you it wouldn't do any good,' said Caroline, one golden autumn day, when she had forced herself to face for what seemed like the hundredth, the thousandth time, the need to let her daughter, Brendan's daughter, go. 'I suggested it and it nearly broke his heart. I've delayed signing the adoption papers, but honestly I don't know why. It's just upsetting everyone. Me most of all. I think I should just pull myself together and get on with it, and enjoy this baby. Don't you?'

'Caroline, you came to me for advice and I gave it to you. You don't have to take it. It might not have been very good, but I can't change what I think.'

'No, I know. I'm sorry. But I think maybe I should agree. It's the only way out, I think. Everyone's right, I should think of the baby.'

'Maybe.'

'Well, of course I should, there's no maybe about it. Yes, I'll sign the adoption papers. I'll go in next week and do it. Get it settled. Don't you think I should, don't you think that would be best?'

'Maybe.'

She went back into the house and called the Adoption Society.

'Mrs Jackson, it's Lady Hunterton. Look, I've been thinking. Best to get this settled. I'll come in next week, Tuesday – I have to see my gynaecologist – and sign the papers then.'

'Very well, Lady Hunterton. I'm sure you've made a very wise decision.'

'I'm sorry, sir, Lady Hunterton is not at home.' John Morgan, who worked as butler, valet and gardener at the Moat House, spoke with a combination of firmness and regret to the wild-eyed and patently distraught young man on the doorstep. 'She has gone into Ipswich to see her doctor.'

'Her doctor? Is she ill?'

'No, sir, she is perfectly well.'

'Then why does she have to see a doctor? And how long has she been called Lady Hunterton?'

'Since her marriage, sir.'

'When was her marriage, for crying out loud?'

'I'm sorry, sir, I really don't think I have to endure this cross-examination. You are very welcome to come back later, if you are really a friend of Lady Hunterton's. When Sir William is here.'

'Look, my friend, I need to find Lady Hunterton and I need to find her fast. Where is this doctor that she doesn't need to see?'

'I really do have to ask you to leave, sir.' John Morgan was beginning to feel almost panicky. He was young, had been employed by the Huntertons when he was demobbed, and had found it difficult to adjust to taking the initiative after years of being Gunner Morgan and doing exactly what he was told. He saw Jack Bamforth approaching the house with great relief. 'Oh, Mr Bamforth, I'm rather glad you're here. Could you please try and persuade this gentleman to leave? He is very anxious to contact Lady Hunterton.'

'Really?' Jack looked the tall figure up and down, taking in the gaunt features, the black hair, the desperation in the dark blue eyes. 'Who are you?'

'My name's FitzPatrick. Brendan FitzPatrick. And I want to see Caroline and my baby.'

'About time too,' said Jack. 'Where have you been for the past almost two years?'

'In a German military hospital.'

'I see.' Jack's voice was its soft, level self; only those who knew him best would have recognized something approaching panic beneath it. 'Do you have a car? Because if it's your baby you want to see, we probably have to get into it and move rather quickly.'

'You're talking like an Irishman,' said Brendan, 'but I forgive you. My car's over here.'

'Let's go.'

No, said the gynaecologist's head girl of a receptionist, Lady Hunterton had left. She was going on somewhere else, but she really couldn't say where.

'Well, can you find out, for Christ's sake?' asked Brendan.

The receptionist looked at him as if he was in kindergarten, and said no she really couldn't, it was none of her business to ascertain where Mr Berkeley's patients were and certainly not to pass the information on.

'I just have to find her,' said Brendan. 'Quickly. It's life and death.'

'Well, I'm sorry. I really don't think I can tell you anything.' She turned away into her pile of letters.

Jack leant forward on the desk. 'We need your help,' he said.

'I've told you both I can't . . .' said the receptionist, turning irritably towards him; she found herself gazing into a pair of exquisitely sad grey eyes, felt a soft gentle lurch somewhere in the location of where she supposed her heart to be, and said, 'Well, perhaps if you told me a little more . . .'

'We can't tell you very much,' said Jack, 'but this gentleman is a very old friend of Lady Hunterton and he has news for her of the utmost importance. News that he has to give to her quickly. Before he goes away again. He has to leave the country tonight. I know Lady Hunterton very well, I work for her, I know she would want to hear this news. Please could you just ask Mr Berkeley if he knows where Lady Hunterton might be? It could make all the difference to all of us.'

The receptionist picked up the phone; her eyes never left Jack's face.

'So you see,' said Caroline, biting resolutely into her rather tough bread roll, 'I am going to let her go. I feel sort of much better now I've decided. Terrible but better. It's the awful indecision that's been worst. And I can't bear to see William looking so hurt. He loves me so much and I owe him such a lot. I'm sure once I've done it, once I know she's gone for ever, I shall settle down; it will be like coming to terms with a death or something. So I just don't want to wait any longer. In fact I – oh, my God. My God.'

Caroline Hunterton's friend Jessica Capel, with whom she was having lunch, watched in fascinated horror as Caroline's face turned a ghastly grey and thence to greenish white, before she slumped off her chair and fell slowly to the rather worn carpet of Miller's restaurant. Looking over her shoulder to see what on earth might have caused this dramatic chain of events, she saw Jack Bamforth, Caroline's groom, walking towards the table, in the company of an extremely tall and thin young man with wild, dark blue eyes, dressed in a rather shabby jersey and the unmistakable pale khaki trousers of the United States Air Force.

Caroline sat holding Brendan's hands in both hers, her eyes fixed helplessly and hopelessly on his face. 'It's terrible,' she kept saying, 'it's so terrible. First I lost you and then I lost the baby and now I'm going to have to lose you both all over again. It's terrible.'

Brendan lifted their bundle of hands, turned it and kissed one of Caroline's; he smiled gently into her eyes. 'You don't have to lose me,' he said, 'you don't ever have to lose me again. I shall take you back with me, to New York, you and the baby, and we'll all live happy ever after.'

'Which baby?'

'Well, our baby of course.'

'And – this baby?' She gestured at her burgeoning stomach.

'Oh, well, she can come too,' he said easily. 'Plenty of room. And then we can have another if you like, to kind of tidy things up. She looks like a big girl, that one in there. I'm sure she'll be very nice.' He removed his hand and stroked the stomach tenderly; a great wave of heat ran through Caroline, warming and confusing her.

'Oh Brendan,' she said, 'I love you so terribly much. This is so dreadful.'

'I don't see why. It seems perfectly fine to me. I think we can work things out all right. Better than all right. I love you too,' he added, placing his other hand on the bulge also, and moving them together very slightly, gently, and with infinite tenderness.

Caroline closed her eyes; the room swam. 'Don't,' she said.

'Why not? Don't you like it?'

'Of course I like it. I love it. I love you. I want you. So just don't do it. All right?'

'All right.' His face was puzzled, but perfectly good-natured. 'Let me get you another drink.'

'No. No, really. I shouldn't.'

'Well an orange juice then?'

'No, really. I have to get home.'

'Nonsense,' he said. 'You are home. Your home is with me. Wherever I am.'

'No, Brendan, I'm afraid it isn't.'

They were sitting in the bar of the Grand Hotel; Jack had gone back to the Moat House in Caroline's car (which he had garaged at his own cottage) with a carefully constructed story about Caroline spending the evening with Jessica (which Caroline was to confirm, telephoning apparently from Jessica's house) and Jessica, overcome with the romance of the situation, eager to get involved and to claim some vicarious excitement from it herself, had agreed to cooperate should William phone. 'But he won't,' said Caroline sadly, 'he'll be too afraid and too much of a gentleman.'

'So where is home then?' Brendan was saying. 'It's where the heart is, or so my dear old mother always says. Which makes things pretty simple for you and me, I'd say.'

'No, Brendan, I'm afraid it doesn't.'

'Honey baby, I don't get all this,' said Brendan, his handsome, easy-to-read face rumpled in its puzzlement. 'Here we are, terribly in love, and together at last, just like in the movies, and with a beautiful baby not so far away who we can take with us, and OK, so you're married to some old guy you certainly don't love, but I don't see why we can't just iron out all the creases.'

'Brendan, I do love him. I love him very much. Not like I love you, of course, of course not, but I do love him. He's been terribly kind to me, and patient and unbelievably loyal, and he loves me very much indeed, and he's been here all this time that you weren't . . .'

'Now come on, baby. That wasn't my fault.'

'I know. But nor was it his. And he was, anyway. With me. Even while I was having – having the baby, he was there all the time, just waiting, in the hospital, and somehow that helped get me through. And –'

'What about screwing? Do you enjoy that? With him?'

Caroline met his eyes steadily. 'Yes. Yes, I do.'

'You're lying.'

'I'm not.'

'OK. Well, we'll leave that one. Christ, I cannot believe I have actually found you again, and you're talking about leaving.'

'I'm sorry, Brendan. But it's too late. It's just too late. All the time I was pregnant, all the time you were away, I fantasized about this, about how you'd turn up, just walk up the drive, and we would be together again, and there'd be gorgeous music and a sunset, and we'd walk off into it, to have our baby. But now, everything's changed. I've changed, and I dare say you've changed.'

'I haven't.'

'All right. You haven't.'

'Caroline, can you honestly look me in the eyes and say you don't love me, you don't want me?'

She looked him in the eyes. 'No. I can't.'

'OK. Let's go back to my place. I'm staying in a hotel just down the road.'

'Brendan, no,' she said, but her eyes were huge and dark, and she was breathing faster. 'No, no, no.'

'Yes. Yes, yes, yes.'

'Brendan, I really do mean what I just said.'

'I know you don't, but just in case you do, I have to put it all right, say goodbye to you properly. And try and change your mind.'

'Brendan,' she said, and she was standing up now, spirals of desire twisting in her body, 'Brendan, I'm pregnant. Five months pregnant. We can't do this.'

'Yes, we can. I like pregnant ladies.'

'No, it's terribly wrong.'

'It isn't.'

'It is.'

'Come on. I've been dreaming about this for a long time. I don't care if you have twins right in the middle of it. And nor do you.'

'No. I'm not coming.'

He undressed her slowly, tenderly, as if he was afraid she might break. He kissed her already swollen breasts, moved down and caressed and kissed her stomach. 'It's beautiful,' he said, 'you're beautiful.'

'So are you,' she said, gazing with a frantic hunger at a body that was young, hard, strong. 'Really beautiful.'

'How does it feel? To be pregnant? Is it sexy? Is it scary? What is it?'

'Not sexy. Not really. You do feel sort of – ripe. Ready. It's hard to describe. But I've never been happy and pregnant. I don't know. To me it means, always, sadness, loneliness, loss.'

'Come with me and you can be happily pregnant.'

'No, Brendan. I'm not coming with you.'

'You said you weren't coming here. And here you are.'

'Oh, for Christ's sake,' she said, and for the first time it was the old Caroline who lay there, looking up at him, her eyes enormous, molten with longing for him. 'Just please, please, Brendan, make love to me, I can't stand it any longer.'

After that it was all confusion, and she could not have told you where she was, or why, nor even her name; only that there was a bright hot need in her that needed cooling, quenching, and as he sank into her, infinitely gentle, she felt her entire being go into the great dark depths of him, her hunger at once increased and eased. He led at first, and she followed, opening and folding, rising and falling, and then suddenly she could feel the fierceness growing, a snarling explosion that blanked out thought, emotion, time, space, and she climbed, rose, struggled on the waves of it, reaching, clutching for release and relief and then, at last, it broke, broke in great dark, endlessly extending curves, and as at last they began to ease, to soothe, to die away, she clung to him, saying over and over again, no, no, make it go on, go on. And when finally he came too, and she felt him shudder slowly and sweetly into her, she knew that whatever she had meant by love before, she had not known, had not understood it at all.

'Are you all right?' he said after a long time. 'Is the baby all right, is this really all right?'

Yes, she said, yes, of course it was, everyone had sex when they were pregnant, once the first few weeks were over, although not, she added, smiling at him, kissing him in between each word, with someone other than their husbands, and he smiled too, and said I love you, and Caroline, weak suddenly, with emotion and anxiety, fell suddenly and easily asleep.

It was late when she woke: almost ten o'clock. He was sitting on the bed, smiling at her, watching her. 'Brendan,' she said, strengthened by the sleep, the happiness, 'Brendan, I have to go. Ask them to send up some tea or something, and I'll have a bath, and I must go. You know that, don't you?'

'No,' he said, full of bravado, like a small boy who won't admit he's frightened by someone bigger and stronger than he is. 'No, I don't. I can't lose you again, Caroline, I just can't.'

'I'm afraid,' she said, 'I'm afraid you have to.'

Brendan started to cry; clinging to her, his head on her breast, sobbing. 'Caroline, you don't know what you're doing to me. You just don't. All the time I was in that hospital, my legs broken, my lungs punctured, in terrible, terrible pain, I thought about you. You got me through, kept me sane, kept me safe. If you hadn't been there I would have died. Given up and died. And then, when – when I was better and they put me in prison camp, and I was hungry and utterly lonely, and still in pain, and afraid, I just hung on, on and on, because I knew at the end of it, you were there. By then I knew about the baby, and that made me brave too. Ever since I was released, and I've been travelling, to find you, I knew that once I was here and with you it would all be wiped out and life would be sane again, good again. And now you tell me it isn't. Caroline, I can't stand it, I really can't. You've been with me all this time, you can't leave me now.'

'I have to,' she said, and the effort of saying it, of staying loyal to William, and to herself, made her physically weak. 'I have to.'

'Caroline, no.'

'Brendan, yes.'

He began to cry again, his head buried in his hands. Caroline looked at him, and her heart ached with such love and such sadness that she wondered how she was possibly going to bear it: not just then, not just for that hour, that night, but for whole of the rest of her life.

'Brendan,' she said, 'don't. Please don't.'

'I have to,' he said, suddenly angry. 'Why shouldn't I? Why should I make it easy for you, to leave me, to go to him? What right have you to tell me what to do, to ask anything of me, anything at all?'

'None,' she said, sadly, 'none at all, I suppose.'

And then, in a great blinding shot of brilliance, she realized what she could do for him, and for herself as well, and what would make sense of the whole sad, dreadful story and put at least some of the wrong to right.

'Brendan,' she said, 'Brendan, you must take the baby. Our daughter. You must have her, and take her home with you.'

All the way back to Jack's cottage, she talked about the baby. She told Brendan everything she knew, and everything she remembered, which was painfully, dreadfully little; about her black hair, her dark blue eyes, her waving little flower-like fingers, her small, perfect head. She told him where he should go to set about reclaiming her, promised to phone Mrs Jackson first thing, and her solicitor too – 'You're on her birth certificate, as her father. I insisted, thank God' – made him promise to do it, to take her, to care for her, to make her his own.

She got out of the car quickly, brutally, snatching even her hand away from him, knowing if he held her again, she would weaken, give in to him, to his arguments and his love; and knowing too that if he could not have her, he would certainly want to have the baby.

Brendan watched her as she tore open the door of her car, started the engine, drove manically, recklessly fast, away from him down the lane, and felt as if some vital part of him had been wrenched away.

He sat there for many hours, all night, until the winter sky began to lighten and he became aware of the cold, of his own physical discomfort and weariness; and then, slowly, like an old man, and aware of every action he made, he began to move. He turned the key in the ignition, let in the brake, moved forward, turning the steering wheel stiffly, rather erratically, as if he had never done any of it in his life before. He moved jerkily, awkwardly down the lane, dimly conscious of the beauty of the misty morning unfolding before him, of the almost flat rolling countryside, the neatly irregular hedges and toy-like clumps of trees in the distance, the panoramic stretch of sky with the sun a great golden mass striking through the mist. It reminded him fiercely, horribly, this landscape, of the magically happy time with Caroline in the war, when they had travelled it together and she had showed him its quirky beauty, taught him of its rather reluctant charm; and he had indeed learnt to see it, had grown to love it even, but that had been because of her, her vision, her presence beside him, and without her the beauty was fraudulent, the charm hollow.

He stopped again, finding the pain in him too harsh to bear, and sank his head on his hands on the steering wheel; when he looked up he realized he was in Easton, the picture-postcard village next to Caroline's, where the harriers were kennelled, and that just beside his car was the lych gate and the church.

Almost in a trance, Brendan got out of the car, and walked up the path; the door was open and he went in. The church was tiny, stone-walled, a blend of modest country charm and an odd grandness, with big carved wooden pews bearing family names, ornate memorial plaques in marble with gilt carving, and wild country flowers set in great jugs below the high vaulted windows. Brendan sank on to his knees in one of the pews at the front, near the tiny altar, and tried to pray, thinking with a touch of wryness even in his misery how horrified his mother would have been to see him there in an Anglican church, and became slowly aware above his pain and his thudding heart of an odd, loud howling; he wondered in the madness of his pain if it was the hounds of hell, and then realized it was not, it was merely the hounds of Easton, demanding their breakfast. The noise was horrifying, on and on; he wondered how the villagers could stand it, but he was actually grateful for it: it suited his mood, they were howling for him, he felt, expressing his agony, and it was almost cathartic, oddly comforting. Then, unbidden, into the noise and the silence around it, he began to hear, as if for the first time, Caroline's voice talking about the baby, and he remembered and made sense of what she had said: 'You must have her and take her home with you.' He heard the other things she had said about the baby; how pretty she had been, how she had had his eyes, his black hair, and what else had she said? A little stalk-like neck, frond-like fingers, and a head like a little flower. Brendan sat and thought, and imagined her, and thought about having her with him, being with him, growing with him; as the sun rose, and filled the church, he relaxed and grew warmer, and in spite of himself he smiled. 'A little flower,' he said aloud, 'my little flower. That's what I shall call her, Fleur. Fleur FitzPatrick. It's a fine name.'

He liked children; he would make, he thought, rather a good father. He would go and find the dreadful Mrs Jackson, and thence the lovely Fleur, and start organizing it all straight away. Make the arrangements and take her away with him home to New York, and they would be together always.

If he couldn't have her mother, at least he would have his daughter. It would be some kind of a comfort.

Brendan stood up and walked out of the church and down the path towards the car.

None of it was quite that easy of course: in fact it was horrendously difficult, a nightmare of complex legalities, of appalling officialdom. Several times, as the battle raged, he was tempted to abandon the whole idea. Then he thought of her, his daughter, with Caroline's blood in her veins, and knew he had to go on and have her.

Finally, on a dark, foggy day early in January she was his; he sat in Caroline's solicitor's office, his heart beating so hard and so high he really felt he might choke from it. He heard a car draw up outside, heard the door open, footsteps on the pavement, the front door open, and more footsteps walking nearer and nearer to him, and in an endless age, time suspended, he saw the door open, slowly, silently, and Mrs Jackson herself walked in with a child in her arms.

So this was Fleur, this was his daughter; a little, tense, wiry thing, with loose ringleted curls, lovingly dressed for the last time by the mother who was losing her, her big dark blue eyes and long black lashes wet with tears and bewilderment at what was happening to her. She was struggling in Mrs Jackson's arms, sobbing almost silently, her small chest heaving; instinctively Brendan held out his own arms, but she looked at him blankly and buried her head silently in Mrs Jackson's shoulder, pushing him away when he tried to take her.

'Come along, darling,' he said gently, 'come along, my little one, little Fleur. Come to your daddy. I've come to take you home.'

'Her name is Angela,' said Mrs Jackson fiercely, her face white and contorted with pain and rage, 'not Fleur, and she knows another daddy and another home. I do hope you know what you are doing, Mr FitzPatrick, for the child certainly does not.'

'I do,' he said, taking the child, ignoring her struggles and her cries, 'I most certainly do. She is mine and she belongs with me.'

But as he sat in the hotel room that evening, listening to Fleur's endless crying, and watching her later as she tossed fitfully in the little cot he had bought so confidently for her, he did not feel quite so sure.

Chapter 4

1952–4

'I don't want to be Mary,' said Fleur. 'Not if I have to wear that silly blue dress. Why can't I be Joseph?'

Sister Frances looked at her curiously. In all her years of teaching First Grade, she had never known a little girl turn down the chance of playing Mary in the Nativity Play.

'But, dear, why not?' she said. 'It's so lovely to be Our Lady, and sit holding the baby in the stable with all the shepherds and the three kings and . . .' Her voice trailed away as she realized she was in danger of overselling the role. Which was ridiculous; there were plenty of other little girls dying to play it. It was just that Fleur FitzPatrick, with her dark curls and extraordinary blue eyes, her rather grave, pale, oval-shaped face, would have made such a beautiful Virgin Mother. Still, if it was not to be, it was not to be, and Sally Thompson, she of the blonde waistlength hair and deceptively angelic little face, would do just as well; certainly she did not want a reluctant Mary in the play.

'I told you why not,' said Fleur. 'I don't want to wear a dress. I hate dresses. I'll be Joseph.'

'Fleur, you'll be who I say or no one,' said Sister Frances firmly. 'You do not go picking and choosing what you'll do in my class. Besides, Joseph wears a sort of dress as well. That is to say, he wears a robe. Am I right in thinking you would object to that as well?'

'Oh, no, that'd be OK,' said Fleur. 'If that's what all the men wore then. Well it's up to you, I guess, Sister. Can I go now, please?'

'Yes, dear, you can go.' She looked at Fleur shrewdly. 'Your father will be very disappointed,' she said, playing her trump card. 'I told him I was going to choose you and he was, oh, extremely proud.' Fleur's love affair with her father was well known in the neighbourhood.

Fleur turned and looked at Sister Frances.

Now, the old nun thought, now I have got her.

But the little girl's voice was cool. 'You shouldn't have told him without asking me first. You're right, he will be disappointed. Very disappointed. Good afternoon, Sister.'

'Good afternoon, Fleur.'

* * *

That night at supper, Fleur decided she should get the bad news over. 'I'm very sorry to be a disappointment to you, Daddy,' she said, 'but I am not going to be Mary in the Nativity.'

'That is a disappointment, Fleur.' Brendan's dark blue eyes, so exactly like his daughter's, were concerned and puzzled over his forkful of chicken. 'Sister Frances told me she was going to ask you. What went wrong? Were you naughty or something?'

'No, I was not. I turned it down, that's what happened.'

'Turned it down? Fleur, why? A girl doesn't turn that role down. It's a classic.'

Fleur smiled and went over to him and started to climb on his knee; she loved it when her father talked theatre to her in that grown-up way.

'Fleur, you're to go and sit down again this instant and finish your dinner.'

'Yes, Aunt Kate.' Fleur returned to her chair, her small shoulders drooping.

'Oh, Kate, leave the child be.' Kathleen FitzPatrick spoke from the head of the table where she was picking extra bits of chicken out of the pot and ladling them on to Brendan's plate. 'She sees little enough of her father, it's nice for them to have a bit of a cuddle when they can. Eat that up now, Brendan, you're too thin, by a long way.'

'She sees plenty of her father,' said Kate coolly. She was jealous of her mother's devotion to Fleur, and of Brendan's intense love for her. 'He hasn't had a job for months.'

'He has too!' said Fleur indignantly. 'He did all those radio commercials the other week, and he had that understudy in the Village, and he's . . . well, I just can't count them all,' she said, her voice trailing away.

'Be quiet all of you,' said Brendan easily. 'Kate's right, and Fleur should not be climbing on my knee at mealtimes, much as I would like it. Now, Fleur, you can tell me just as well from over there why you have decided not to be Mary.'

'It's the clothes,' said Fleur plaintively. 'You know how I hate wearing dresses when I don't have to. And that is one drippy dress.'

'Oh, Fleur, my darling, you can't choose not to be Our Lady just because you don't like the dress,' said Kathleen. 'That is nonsense. Besides, it's a lovely dress, and a lovely colour, and it would go with your eyes. Now of course you must play the part. You will be doing both me and your father out of a great treat if you don't.'

'Well, I'm sorry,' said Fleur, 'but I just can't. That Sally Thompson can do it, she's been praying for the chance. I told Sister Frances I'd be Joseph, but she didn't seem to like that idea too much. Can I go and play now, please?'

'You stay and help me clear away,' said Kate, 'and let Mother and Brendan go and sit down.'

'Oh, for heaven's sake,' said Kathleen, 'let the child go. What should I be wanting to sit down for? Run off, Fleur darling, and play. Tracy was looking for you earlier. Will I walk you down to her house now, or will you stay at home?'

'I'll stay at home,' said Fleur. 'I have things to do. Thank you for my dinner.'

'You're welcome,' said Kathleen automatically. She looked at Brendan and winked. 'That child will rule the world one day,' she said, 'you see if she doesn't. Turning down Our Lady indeed. What willpower.'

'I think it's ridiculous,' said Kate, 'quite ridiculous. She should be made to do it.'

'Why, for heaven's sake?' said Brendan. 'If she doesn't want to.'

'But, Brendan, it's such a stupid reason. And she's such a little girl.'

'It's not such a stupid reason. You know how Fleur is about wearing clothes and trying to make-believe she's a boy. I think we should respect that. And she's not such a little girl either, she's seven. She knows her own mind.'

'Ridiculous,' said Kate again. 'Well, since neither of you mind letting Fleur off helping with the dishes, perhaps you could let me off as well. I have things to do also. Thank you, Mother.'

'You're welcome,' said Kathleen again, but this time she did not smile and she did not wink. 'Your sister is turning into a regular old maid,' she said to Brendan. 'The other three all married, and two of them mothers, and here she is still living at home and not a beau in sight. It's a pity.'

'Well, she never got over Danny Mitchell, did she?' said Brendan. 'That was a tragedy. To think I survived being shot down and prison camp, and Danny had to die of pneumonia before he ever went up in the sky. It doesn't make sense.'

'Not a lot in this life makes sense,' said Kathleen.

She was much given to such philosophies.

Brendan walked Fleur to school next morning; she loved that, walking the whole length almost of Avenue Z, down to PS209, her hand in his, and all the mothers staring at him because he was so handsome; there weren't many handsome men in Sheepshead Bay, well, certainly not as handsome as her father. Most of them were either swarthy and Italian, or Jewish. Brendan didn't really like Sheepshead Bay, and kept promising Kathleen and Fleur that when he was famous and rich, he would move them up to the Heights, into one of the narrow rowhouses; quite often on Sunday afternoons he would take Fleur up there and pick out a house for them, mostly from Willow or Poplar Street, with their iron railings and stained-glass windows. Fleur could see they were very grand and very nice, but she loved Sheepshead Bay, she thought it was more fun. It was near the beach, and all the houses were so pretty, with their clapboard fronts and peaked roofs; their house was painted blue, and it had quite a big yard where she could play, and she could ride her little red bike along the street, and there was a nice feel about the neighbourhood. Grandma didn't really like it too much either; not enough Irish, she said, only about ten per cent, and she would have preferred the Flatbush area. Kate wanted to get out of Brooklyn altogether and go and live in New Jersey, but meanwhile they were all stuck in Sheepshead Bay and Fleur didn't mind one bit.

Walking out with her father was even worth having to wear the awful clothes Grandma dressed her in for school: little pinafore dresses with full skirts and sashes, blouses with puff sleeves, black patent Mary Jane shoes with ankle straps, and socks with little lace cuffs. She and Grandma had worked out a kind of trade-off and when she was not in school or in polite company, she was allowed to wear blue jeans and sneakers, and take the ribbons out of her curls; when she was ten, Grandma had promised, she should have her hair cut short, but until then it hung almost to her waist, and drove her half mad, with all the time and attention it needed.

'Now, darling, don't you take any notice of Sister Frances. If you don't want to play Mary, don't you play her, whatever she says. And I want you to hold your thumbs for me this afternoon, because there is a part I want to play and I'm going for it.'

'Will it make you rich and famous?'

'A little bit famous, and not so very rich. But it would get people noticing me. At last,' added Brendan and sighed. The seven years since the war had been most notable for him by a lack of success. He had done a bit of repertory, a lot of radio commercials, a few radio dramas, but most of the time he had been resting.

'So what is the play called? So I can think very very hard about you.'

'It's called *Dial M for Murder*. It's a new play about a man who manages to get his wife declared guilty of a murder.'

'That she didn't do?'

'Yes, that's right.'

'That sounds really exciting.'

'It is.'

They had reached the school, a big ugly building on the corner of Coney Island and Avenue Z, which Brendan had always thought looked more like a prison than a school, but Fleur loved it. She loved work and learning and doing better than everybody else; she was already flying high, miles ahead of everyone else in her class in both reading and maths, and she was popular too, she wasn't rearded as a swot or a bore. She was successful in the playground where she could run as fast as any of the boys, no one ever caught her in games of tag, she could beat any of the girls at hopscotch, she could do double turns on the skipping rope and catch anything, however high or awkward the throw. One of her many ambitions was to play baseball, and she had already tried to get into the Little League, but so far Mr Hammond had said no, girls just didn't play baseball, and he couldn't consider it, but Fleur was working on him. She spent quite a lot of time working on people.

What she really really wanted of course was to be a boy; Fleur had looked around her at what women got out of life and what men got out of it, and there was no doubt in her mind which of them had the better deal. She had no intention of getting married and having babies and spending her time washing and baking and changing diapers; she was going out there into the world to make her fortune. She wasn't absolutely certain how just yet, but that did not alter her basic intention. And when the other little girls talked about marrying rich men and having fur coats and big houses and massive cars, Fleur would always say she was going to have the fur coat and the big house and the massive car, but she wasn't going to marry a rich man, she was going to be a rich woman.

Brendan had not told her a great deal about her mother yet. He thought she was too young. Later on, when she might be able to understand, he planned to take her through the whole story, but for now he had simply explained that she had been a girl he had met in the war, and they had fallen terribly in love, and got married, but that before Fleur had been born Brendan had been taken prisoner and when he got back, Caroline had assumed him dead and had remarried. Her new husband didn't want Fleur nearly as much as Brendan did and it had been difficult for Caroline to handle that, so he had been able to bring her home with him. Fleur had been too small to spot any anomalies in this story, either legal or emotional, when he first told her; she had simply said that it was a good thing they had each other and left it at that. The story only served to reinforce her passion for her father, and her deep conviction that they were more important to one another than anyone else in the world.

Occasionally these days she would ask what her mother looked like, and Brendan had told her, and once she had said she wondered if they would ever meet; she had also remarked recently that she didn't think she would like her very much, but that it didn't really matter one way or the other. Brendan had assured her that she would like Caroline, and that it was hard for her to understand what a difficult time she had had. Fleur had been silent for a bit and then nodded and said 'Maybe.' Kathleen had thought the whole thing terribly wrong and had wanted Brendan to say he had adopted Fleur, but he said he had too much respect for the truth generally to bring up his daughter on a pack of lies. 'One day she'll want to find her mother and it will be far better for her not to have to find out the real truth all of a sudden. She's a happy child, she can cope with what I've told her.'

This was true; Fleur was happy and well adjusted, and oddly mature for her age. She saw herself as not quite her father's contemporary, but certainly not far behind him; he was to her entirely perfect in every way, above and beyond criticism, her best friend, her confidant, her chosen companion at all possible times. To be Brendan's friend was to be Fleur's also, and without question, and to be anything less than that was to meet with disdain and mistrust. Brendan tried not to think about Caroline too much; it was pointless and painful. She had refused to let him tell her where they lived, saying she would not be able to stand it, that sooner or later she would just turn up on the doorstep. Mostly now he was able to think of her fondly and dispassionately, but when he was very low, or alternatively very happy, he longed to see her and hold her and talk to her with a yearning so strong it made him feel physically sick. He had had many girlfriends since, mild flirtatious affairs, and a few more serious; pretty, fun girls in the theatre, or the stores and restaurants he worked in from time to time to make some money. A girl always knew when Brendan FitzPatrick was getting serious about her in two ways: first she was told about Caroline Miller, and then she was taken home to meet Fleur. Most of them could handle the first, but the second was a different matter. That was a relationship that required real courage to take on. As a consequence, no one had ever come near forming an association with him that was anything approaching permanent. One day, Brendan supposed, he might really fall in love again, and want to get married; in the meantime, he was perfectly content with the way things were.

The audition went well; Brendan felt it in his bones. When he was called back later in the afternoon to read again, he knew he had the part; and when the director said, 'Could you let me have your agent's number right away, Mr FitzPatrick,' he knew it was only a formality. He stood waiting on the subway for his train, smiling foolishly into space like a young boy in love.

When he got to Sheepshead Bay he bought some beer at the market just by the station and a big bag of candy for Fleur; by some happy chance, Edna and Maureen had come to spend the day with their mother, and had waited to see him, and to hear how he had done, and they had only to look at his face as he stood there in the doorway to know. Edna fished in her bag for some money and told Brendan to go and buy some more beer; Fleur said she would come with him, and could they maybe go to Wiesens and buy some pastries for dessert, which they did. They were all sitting laughing and drinking and stealing from Fleur's candy when the phone rang and it was Brendan's agent saying yes, he had definitely got the part, and rehearsals started straight after Christmas and he was to be paid one hundred dollars a week.

'Jesus Christ,' said Brendan, putting down the phone. He was white and shaking.

'For the love of God, Brendan, whatever is it?' said Kathleen. 'Have you not got the part after all?'

'I've got it,' said Brendan, 'I certainly have got it. And they're going to pay me one hundred bucks a week. I'm on my way.'

The family fell into an awestruck silence.

The play was successful; it ran for three months. They tried to transfer to Broadway, but that didn't quite come off. Brendan got good reviews: not brilliant, not raves, but good. Good enough to get another part, in a revival of *The Man Who Came to Dinner* at the Circle on the Square; this time, the reviews of Brendan's acting were less good, but his 'film-star looks' were remarked upon with varying degrees of patronage and unkindness in almost all the papers. Brendan squirmed, and contemplated spending some of his precious salary (otherwise almost entirely dedicated to paying Kathleen back for all the years she had supported him) on acting lessons at Lee Strasberg's studio, and told his agent that in future he only wanted to go for character roles where his looks were irrelevant. His agent told him not to be a dickhead and to be grateful for what little he did have to offer the theatre and made him accept a spread in *Mademoiselle* magazine featuring the new heart-throbs of the fifties. Brendan squirmed further, but did it, and when *The Man Who Came to Dinner* closed, auditioned for seven parts in a row and didn't get one of them.

'I guess I wasn't on my way after all,' he said to Kathleen one afternoon in October. 'I haven't worked for months. So much for our house on the Heights.'

'Oh, well, my darling, I suppose that's what you would call show business,' said Kathleen, 'and we can do without the house. We have a house. But Fleur needs some new clothes. Can you give me any money for those?'

'I can't,' said Brendan, speaking with great difficulty. 'I don't have a dime. My own shoes are worn through. Look. I'll take a job in one of the stores, it's nearly Christmas. That will help.'

He got a job selling jewellery in Macy's and then got offered double overtime if he would play Santa two nights a week in the Christmas Grotto. Biting his lip, and thinking of Fleur and her clothes, and the new bike she had set her heart on for Christmas, he did it.

After Christmas things got worse. He got turned down relentlessly for everything: large parts, small parts, TV commercials, even some modelling jobs. The only work he got was another modelling job in *Mademoiselle*, and that was as replacement for someone else, which the fashion editor made abundantly clear. Fleur's feet grew again; he went back to Macy's and sold some more jewellery.

Then Kathleen fell ill. It was her chest, really, always her Achilles' heel, she told the doctor. He said, smiling at her tenderly, that only the Irish could call their chests their heels, and told her she must go into hospital, that she had double pneumonia, and if she didn't she would be joining the angels faster than she'd planned.

Brendan, summoned home from work to see the doctor, said she was not to go into the state hospital, he wanted her in the nice private Catholic one near the Heights. Yes, they had medical insurance, of course they did; but when he was asked to produce the policy, it was out of date. Kathleen had been economizing on the premium payments, among other things.

Brendan saw her into the state hospital, settled her in the huge, stark ward, told her he'd be back later and went home. Fleur found him at the kitchen table in tears.

And then, just like in the movies, as Fleur excitedly told Kate later that night, the phone rang. It was a theatrical agent in uptown Manhattan; his name was Kevin Clint, and he would like to see Brendan right away.

Brendan left Fleur with a neighbour, made Kate promise to visit Kathleen that evening, put on his best, least shiny suit, cut out fresh cardboard soles to line his shoes, and got on the D train uptown.

Kevin Clint's office was on 57th Street, between 6th and 7th. He had a small but very lush suite on the fourth floor actually over Carnegie Hall; as the elevator stopped in between each floor, Brendan could hear musicians playing. A girl with extremely long red nails and a spectacular bosom looked at him coolly as he walked in.

'Yes?' she said.

'I'm Brendan FitzPatrick. Mr Clint asked to see me.'

'He did?' she said, implying that this was excessively unlikely, her eyes skimming with only mild interest over Brendan's face and body, lingering briefly but pointedly on his crotch.

'He did,' said Brendan firmly, resisting with difficulty a strong urge to fold his hands over his fly.

'OK. I'll see if he's in.'

She disappeared. Brendan sat down on the black leather couch, and waited. After about ten minutes she came back looking mildly flustered.

'He says he won't be too long.'

'Thank you,' said Brendan.

She went and fetched herself a coffee from another room; she didn't offer him one. Brendan sat and watched her drink it; there was nothing else to do. There were a few certificates on the red fake silk walls telling anyone who cared to know it that Kevin Clint was an accredited member of the Association of Stage and Screen Agents (Brendan greatly doubted if such an association existed) and several photographs of a man he could only assume was Kevin with people such as Tony Curtis, Frank Sinatra, Debbie Reynolds and Stewart Granger. Brendan wondered how easy it might be to fake such pictures and then asked the girl if he could go to the men's room.

'Sure,' she said, with another meaning look at his fly, 'down the corridor, second left. Here's the key.'

Brendan took the key and went along to the men's room. It was already locked. He waited. After ten minutes no one came out and he went back to Kevin Clint's office.

'There seems to be someone in there,' he said, feeling foolish; he would like to have left it, but his bladder was almost unbearably full.

'There often is,' she said, and went back to her typing.

Brendan went back to the men's room; after about another ten minutes the door opened and two men came out. They were both giggling; they stopped when they saw Brendan, looked him up and down and then at each other and broke into fresh fits of laughter. Brendan, who knew the effects of marijuana when he saw them, looked at them tolerantly, smiled, and went in. 'Hey, he's pretty,' said one of them as the door swung behind them.

Kevin Clint finally saw Brendan after two and a half hours. He sat, behind a vast white desk bearing three white and gilt telephones, on a black swivel chair; the room was otherwise bare, apart from two white leather couches, and a low black and chrome coffee table. There were several more photographs on the walls.

He gestured at one of the sofas. 'Hi, I'm Kevin,' he said. 'Sit down.'

Brendan sat.

Kevin Clint was small and neat; he had dark eyes, rather pale, soft skin, and very shiny black hair. He was dressed in a dark suit with a light grey waistcoat, a purple and white striped shirt, a purple tie, and a pearl tie-pin;

he wore a gold watch, pearl cufflinks, a heavy gold bracelet, and smelt strongly of aftershave. He was very patently homosexual.

'I'm sorry to have kept you waiting,' he said, with a smile that showed very even, neat white teeth. 'I've been on the phone to LA.'

Brendan didn't believe this, but he smiled politely back and sat down on the couch.

'About you,' went on Kevin Clint.

Brendan believed this still less; he didn't even bother to extend his smile.

'Drink?' said Kevin Clint.

'Yes, please.'

'What do you like? Bourbon? Martini?'

'Do you have a beer?' said Brendan.

'I do,' said Kevin with a just audible sigh that spelt out his disapproval, and poured Brendan a Budweiser. He made himself an elaborate martini, and took a cigarette from a gold cigarette-box on his desk. He offered one to Brendan.

'Now then,' said Kevin Clint, inhaling deeply, sucking his cheeks in, 'let's talk about you.'

'That would be good,' said Brendan.

'I had a call about you. Yesterday.'

'From?' said Brendan.

'From a talent scout at Fox.'

'Fox?' said Brendan.

'Yeah. As in Twentieth Century.' Clint smiled; he liked seeing these new young guys stupefied.

'Can't have been,' said Brendan. 'Not about me.'

'Sure was. The New York guy, that is. He'd seen you in *The Man Who Came to Dinner*, didn't think much of you, then saw that spread in *Seventeen*. He says you have an interesting look. I think so too,' he added, his eyes lingering briefly on Brendan's. Brendan looked hastily away. 'He thinks you should maybe test.'

'Test?'

'Yeah, you know, a screen test. For the movies. You know?' He was beginning to grow impatient; Brendan was proving dumber than most.

The room spun briefly round Brendan. He gripped the arm of the couch to steady it. 'Yeah. Sure. Sorry. I must sound stupid.'

'A little.' Clint smiled slightly coolly.

Brendan pulled himself together. Alongside the fear of looking a fool, a greater one that the whole thing might be pie in the sky had shot into his consciousness. He met Kevin's cool with ice. 'Well I'd naturally like to know who your colleague from Fox is. Before we go any further with any of this. I mean I have heard this kind of thing before. It's kind of turned out disappointing.'

'Really?' said Kevin. He was clearly not remotely deceived by this. 'Well, yes, of course I'll tell you. It's Hilton Berelman. Does that reassure you? About any disappointment that might be coming your way?'

Hilton Berelman. Jesus H. Christ. Brendan remained silent with an effort. Hilton Berelman was just about the best-known talent scout in New York. Agents sent photographs and résumés to him endlessly, automatically, hopelessly. He had a great deal of power and influence; he was also one of the best-known homosexuals in New York. He managed to look steadily back at Kevin.

'Yes. Yes, of course it does.'

'Naturally,' said Kevin, lighting another cigarette and gazing through the smoke at Brendan with a mixture of amusement and disdain, 'you may still be in for a great deal of disappointment. Mr Berelman may not find you quite as promising as he had hoped. There are a lot of young actors trying to get to Hollywood you know. You have a long way to travel before you even get on the plane. Perhaps,' he added, with just a flicker of the mean little smile, 'perhaps you would like to call him. Just to check I'm on the level. Do. Feel free.' He pushed the phone towards Brendan, and sat back in his chair.

Brendan felt his bowels begin to melt; he also felt he might be sick. 'No,' he said, 'no, of course I don't want to call him. Thank you. And I do realize that – well, I'm very fortunate that Mr Berelman wants to see me.' He could hear himself beginning to sound humble again; he swallowed.

Kevin suddenly took pity on him. 'Anyway,' he said, with a broader smile, a pat of Brendan's hand, 'what he wants is for you to go along to this studio, and have some shots done. Then he'll send them down to LA.'

Brendan felt a strong urge to withdraw his hand; he resisted it, left it on the desk. Kevin Clint's settled just slightly more firmly over it.

'Right, then,' he said, fighting to keep a tremble out of his voice, 'of course I'm terribly interested, and of course I must go and get these shots done. Now? Today?'

'No time like the present,' said Kevin Clint, brisk and suddenly warmer again. 'I'll just give him a call. Then you can go and see the guy from Fox on Monday. OK?'

'OK,' said Brendan. He smiled again.

Clint made the call. 'Bernie? Yeah, it's Kevin. I'd like to send someone over right away. For some shots. You can't? Why not?' There was a silence. Kevin smiled into the phone. 'I see. Well of course not. Sorry to interrupt. No, sure. Well when can you? In the morning. OK, fine. I'll tell him. Good. Bye, Bernie. Bye.'

He smiled at Brendan. 'He's busy right now. But he'll do the shots in the morning. Here's the address. Now take along a few changes of clothes. Casual, smart, maybe a tux. OK?'

Brendan looked at him blankly. Panic was setting in again. He was wearing the only change of clothes he had. The most his bank balance could stand was probably a new pair of socks. 'I don't think . . .' he began.

Kevin looked at him, recognized the panic, and smiled rather distantly. 'Sorry,' he said, 'maybe you don't have that many clothes. If it's a problem, take what you can and just hire a tux from somewhere.'

'OK,' said Brendan, wondering how he was even going to find the money for hiring. He was beginning to feel rather odd.

'Holy shit!' said Kevin Clint. 'Holy fucking shit. Florence, get Hilton on the line, would you?'

He was holding Brendan's pictures, just delivered by hand from Bernie's studio. There were three: one of Brendan in a dinner jacket, looking extremely serious and smooth; one of Brendan in a dark suit (belonging to Edna's husband) lighting a cigarette, his eyes coolly amused through the haze of smoke; and a third of Brendan in a pair of Levi's and a white cotton shirt open at the neck, sleeves turned up, smiling his impressive smile. In all of them, something was going on between Brendan and the camera; something had interceded, something charming, attractive, and yet not entirely respectable. It was, together with spectacular good looks, precisely what Kevin and Hilton Berelman devoted their working hours to finding.

Brendan had been visiting Kathleen in the hospital when Kevin Clint phoned. Fleur, who was well trained, took the message carefully.

'Mr Clint called,' she said. 'You're to go and see him tomorrow morning. At ten. He sounded real creepy,' she added.

'He is,' said Brendan. 'Did he say anything else?'

'Nope. Nothing.'

'Oh, well, I suppose it's good news he wants to see me.'

'Yeah, I guess. How was Grandma?'

'Not very well,' said Brendan briefly, trying to dispel the memory of Kathleen breathing fast and lightly, with the high colour of fever in her face, reaching constantly for the oxygen mask; and of the old women in the beds around her, many of them plainly senile, and the strong stench of incontinence in the air.

'I wrote her a poem. Could you take it when you go over tomorrow? And I thought I'd get her some flowers.'

'Fleur, you don't have any money for flowers.'

'I know, but there's lots in the park.'

'You mustn't take flowers from the park.'

'I don't see why not. Grandma needs them more than any of the people who go there and don't look at them.'

'Well don't let anyone see you picking them,' said Brendan, He didn't have the heart to chastise her any more.

'OK. Daddy?'

'Yeah, what is it, honey?'

'Daddy, could I maybe go to summer camp this year?'

'Summer camp? Fleur, I don't know, it's very expensive.'

'It is? Oh, OK, forget it then.' She smiled at him bravely, but he could see she minded badly.

'Do you want to go particularly?'

'Well yes, but it doesn't matter.'

'Tell me why.'

'There's one in New Jersey where you can do baseball all day and every day. I thought it might help with Mr Hammond and the Little League.'

'I'm sorry, darling, I can't afford it. Not at the moment.'

'OK.' She smiled again, an odd little twisty smile. 'I think I'll go up and do some reading for a bit.'

'All right, Fleur.'

When she came down to supper, she was very cheerful, but he could see she had been crying.

'The pictures weren't bad,' said Kevin Clint carefully. 'Hilton wants to see you.'

'Sure.' Brendan was being equally careful.

'Of course there's a lot of guys with not bad pictures.'

'Of course.'

'But maybe if Hilton likes you . . .'

'Yes.' Brendan's direct blue eyes met Kevin's veiled brown ones. 'Should I maybe talk to my agent now?'

Kevin looked at him blankly. 'I'm sorry?'

'I mean shouldn't I tell my agent what's going on?'

'Why? What does he need to know?'

'Well, clearly he'll need to be involved. Looking over the contract, talking terms, all that sort of thing.'

'Brendan,' Kevin spoke very slowly and patiently, 'as from now I am your agent. I thought that was understood.'

'No,' said Brendan. 'Not understood at all.'

'Ah. Well, clearly we have been talking at cross-purposes.'

'We haven't been talking at all.' Brendan felt panicky, he wasn't sure why. 'So what did you think?'

'I thought – well I thought, I suppose, that you and my agent would work together.'

'You did?' Kevin smiled his most economical smile; his mouth broadened slightly, his eyes remained cold. 'Then I had better explain. If you are to' – he paused – 'if you want to go this route with Hilton and myself, then you sever any contact you have with any current agents. I imagined you would have realized that.'

'No,' said Brendan. 'No, I didn't.'

'Brendan! Really! You surprise me. What do you think I've been doing all this for?'

Brendan was silent.

Kevin gave him a slightly menacing look. 'No, from now on – providing, that is, that all goes well – I am your agent.'

'And if you're not? If I don't agree? John Freeman has been very good to me.'

'Oh, I have no doubt. And he's done a lot for you, hasn't he? Two radio commercials and a lead part in the Christmas Grotto at Macy's. Quite a year's work.'

Brendan didn't realize how much they knew about him. 'Well, it's been a bad year. I don't want to walk out on him.'

'Well then, perhaps we should forget the whole thing. I'll call Hilton now.' He looked at Brendan coldly. 'It's a pity.'

'I still don't see why John can't deal with Hilton Berelman,' said Brendan stubbornly.

'Because,' said Kevin Clint, very patiently, smiling again, 'because Hilton wouldn't like John Freeman. In fact he doesn't like him. He's met him already.'

'And you're saying there's no way I can get this screen test without Hilton? And you?'

'That is correct. The three of us would be working very closely together. Very closely. I thought you realized that.' He looked at Brendan thoughtfully, his eyes skimming over his body; lingering on his mouth, his crutch. He walked over to the couch, sat down beside Brendan, his thigh against Brendan's, and put his hand gently on his shoulder. 'I think it could be quite a partnership,' he said, 'the three of us. Now I shouldn't be telling you this, but Hilton is quite certain that he actually wants to test you. Quite certain.'

Brendan swallowed. He tried to move his leg without appearing too aggressive. Kevin's leg followed. 'I'll have to – think about it,' he said.

'Of course,' said Kevin. 'But not for too long. They want you over there next week.' He smiled again, slightly less economically, moved his hand to cover Brendan's, clasped together in his lap. 'Oh, dear, I shouldn't have told you that either. How indiscreet I'm being today. Now you go and have a think, and maybe a chat with your mother. I believe she's in hospital?'

'Yes, she is. How did you know that?'

'Oh, this is a tiny little world, Brendan. Of course I knew. How is she?'

'Not very well,' said Brendan.

'And which hospital?'

'The state hospital. In Brooklyn.'

'Now that can't be very nice. Not for an old lady. If you were working with us, you'd have the money for a private hospital. Think about that.'

'The hospital is all right.'

'Oh good. I'm glad.'

'Well, I'd like to think about it. For a bit.'

'Of course. I certainly don't want to rush you.'

Kevin's mouth was now rather near Brendan's. The smell of his aftershave was very strong. Brendan felt sick. He stood up suddenly and looked down at Kevin. 'I'll – I'll call you then.'

'All right, Brendan.' Kevin looked up at him, confidently, almost trustingly. 'No rush. There are plenty of others queuing up for screen tests. You must do what you think best.'

Brendan reached the street still feeling sick. All his life he had told himself there were certain things he could not, would not do. However great his need, however intense his desire. There were some prices that were too high. He must hang on to that. He had to. There was no way, no way on God's earth he was going to act as whore to a pair of gays. Not to get star billing in Hollywood; not even for his mother; not even, no, not even for Fleur. In the long run it just wasn't going to be worth it. He saw Fleur suddenly, vividly, her thoughtful dark blue eyes looking at him from her candid, slightly tough little face, and thought how she would feel if she found out, later on, that her father had prostituted himself, betrayed her adoration of him, and knew that he could never, ever fail her. In that particular way. He might not be able to send her to summer camp, or keep her in blue jeans and baseball jackets, but he could stay the person she thought he was, that she loved. He could give at least that to her.

He made for the nearest bar, bought a can of beer, and stood there staring into it. He began to steady, to feel better, to see the nightmare recede. He looked at his watch: nearly two. He could go and see Kathleen if he hurried, before Fleur came home from school. Or he could take Fleur with him and they could go together. Kathleen would love that. But – no, maybe not. It would upset Fleur. He'd go right away. Then he realized the train fare downtown had just gone down his throat. Did he have to walk, right to Brooklyn? It was impossible. Completely impossible. God, he was a disaster. How did he get into this kind of mess? How was he going to explain to Fleur he couldn't even pay his fare to visit her grandmother? After all the hope and excitement of the last few days. What would she think, what would Kate think? Shit, how did he get out of this one? There had to be something he could do. Was he mad, completely mad, turning down Clint and Berelman, looking their gift horse right in the mouth? Maybe he could handle the whole thing. String them along. They obviously wanted him pretty badly. It could all be a case of double bluff. And then possibly, just possibly, he'd been overreacting to Kevin Clint's innuendoes. Maybe the guy was just a flirt. Testing him for his reactions. Yeah, that was probably it. Brendan drained the can, and decided that, actually, he'd been a fool to think otherwise. A complete fool. Thank God he hadn't over-reacted, hadn't gone rushing out of Clint's office. What a fool he'd have looked. And tomorrow he'd tell him that sure, he'd be glad to have Berelman represent him in Hollywood, but that John Freeman was his agent, and he knew they were all going to have a great time working together. If they really wanted him, they'd buy that one, and if they didn't he didn't want to know.

None of which actually got him home. Well, he'd have to pawn his watch – again. At least it would be for the last time. The very last time.

He went to a call-box, called Clint collect. Clint was surprisingly easy about that, asked him to go back and sign some papers. And said he'd lend him some money. And when he was able to tell Fleur and Kathleen that that was what had been arranged, he felt really deep-down good about it.

He arrived in Los Angeles in the late afternoon a month later; Brendan stepped out of the plane, felt the warmth fill him to his bones, looked up at the intense blue sky, and the palm trees carved into it, and knew he was going to be happy. Not even the thought of Hilton Berelman waiting for him, not even the memory of Kathleen sitting up in bed in her room in the private hospital, very bright-eyed, making him promise to come back soon, no, not even the creases on his shirt left by Fleur as she clung to him sobbing at the airport, finally having to be prised off by Kate and Edna, to the accompaniment of promises of visits, of presents, of a home prepared for them both in Los Angeles and the reminder of the summer camp she was booked into, none of it damaged the pleasure of that moment.

The studio had sent a car; Hilton had been promised a limo and a limo it was not, he explained slightly petulantly, but it was a big shiny Studebaker with a driver in a grey suit which seemed pretty impressive to Brendan. All the way into town, along the freeway, Hilton who was also big and shiny with oddly pale skin, slicked back black hair and a sprayed-on smile, was making notes in his diary; he kept asking the driver things, hopefully, whether he had any messages for him from the studio, or whether a dinner had been fixed for the evening, and the driver just said 'No, sir,' in a very flat voice which implied he didn't think it was worth making any kind of effort for Hilton. The drive seemed rather dreamlike to Brendan; it was early evening by then and they were driving straight into the sunset which dazzled him, so he could hardly make out anything ahead except rows of bouncing, lurching cars and the great fluorescent stretch of blue sky. Then they turned in off the freeway, and everything shot back into focus: the wide, straight boulevards, the lines of palm trees by them, the mass of huge, shiny cars, the dazzle of white, surprisingly low buildings.

Hilton had said he would be put up at the Chateau Marmont; Brendan had expected some crummy motel with fancy windows, and was amazed at the sight of it, set high above the street, and built in stone, with high towers and leaded windows, high iron gates and huge oak doors. Brendan, who had flown extensively over France, had no difficulty acknowledging the style; the whole thing, it seemed to him, was like a film set in itself.

His room was not at the front of the Chateau which disappointed him, but what it lacked in view it made up for in style; it was large and lavish, with its own bathroom, and a couch, desk and chair all in the same odd Louis Quatorze style, so it had pretensions almost to being a suite. And he could always sit in the bar, and look out over the city, he told himself, as he showered and changed, and ate some of the fruit which was in a large basket in his room. He expected to have quite a lot of time sitting in the bar; he was still deeply suspicious as to the outcome of this adventure.

He and Hilton dined that night with a young, highly enthusiastic press agent who had been assigned Brendan as his task of the week; his name was Tyrone Prentice, and he had a lot of ideas. He kept calling Brendan Byron and smiling at him rather contemplatively. Brendan said he couldn't see what point there was dreaming up publicity for him when he hadn't even done a test, but Tyrone said in a shocked voice that publicity was what Hollywood was all about, and you couldn't begin too early. 'Then if your test goes well, even if you don't work for a while, we can start turning you into someone. Now I'm wondering here, this name of yours, Byron, I really like that. Do you have a great knowledge of the poet's work? Or maybe did your mother read some of his verse while she was pregnant, which is why she gave you the name?'

Brendan said it wasn't his name at all, but Tyrone said well, that was hardly the point, it had a great ring to it, it was a lot more memorable than Brendan and the Fitz must go as well. 'This is make-believe town, Byron, and we don't have too much time for the truth. Not when we're working anyway.'

Brendan sighed and said well, yes sure, his mother had always been a great admirer of Byron, and that his younger brother was called Childe Harolde. This was entirely wasted on his audience.

Next day Tyrone and Hilton took him down to the studios. Theatrical was near RKO on Melrose. Hilton insisted they made a detour to show him Goldwyn on Santa Monica, and stopped the car so he could get a really good view of the Hollywood sign.

Brendan was disappointed in the studios. He had somehow expected, against all logic he knew, a cross between the New York Opera House and the set for Atlanta with a yellow brick road snaking through it somewhere, and Lana Turner and Joan Crawford wafting about in white fox wraps; not an endless stretch of huge windowless buildings interspersed with smaller ones, and perfectly ordinary-looking people walking about apparently doing perfectly ordinary things. Later, as Tyrone took him on a lightning tour of some of the lots, and he walked from a nineteenth-century street into a medieval market place, and thence into a contemporary courtroom, he felt oddly comforted.

'Byron, this is Yolande duGrath. Yolande, Byron. Byron Patrick. Hilton said to knock Byron into shape for his test. OK?'

Yolande duGrath was head drama coach at Theatrical Studios; she was sixtyish, tiny, sliver-thin, with a Louise Brooke style, bright red bob, and huge brown eyes with long black, very fake eyelashes. She was vital and expansive, and she had a smile that made arc lights unnecessary. She had once been an actress herself, but had discovered she liked teaching others better; she had never married, but was rumoured to have had love affairs with most of the great stars. There was no one she did not know: she had been a guest at Pickfair, dined with Garbo, sailed with Errol Flynn. Cary Grant took her regularly to tea in the Polo Lounge; Clark Gable had been one of her dearest friends. She was perhaps most famous for her definition of the quality that separated the actors from the stars: it was larceny. 'Larceny is sexual,' she would say, 'larceny is "hey who is this?" Larceny is up to mischief. It's the first quality I look for when I'm given someone new.' Betty Bacall, she was much quoted as saying, was larceny on legs.

Brendan took one look at her and loved her.

'OK,' she said, 'yes, I heard about you. You're the pin-up from New York. We had another like you, not so long ago. He did OK. Tony Curtis, you heard of him I dare say?'

Brendan said yes, he had heard of him.

'OK. Let's have a look at you. Tyrone, honey, you can just get lost. I'll let you know when I'm through.'

Tyrone left the theatre reluctantly.

Yolande sat down on the edge of her stage and patted the place beside her. 'Come and sit down. We can talk for a bit. Did they tell you why you were here?'

'Here in Hollywood, or here in your theatre?'

'In my theatre. You know why you're in Hollywood. Whether you stay or not is up to you.'

'It is?'

'It is. Well, to an extent. If you have what it takes in other departments that is. I'll tell you about that in a minute. But if you do, then all you need is will. It's perfectly simple. You've got to want to succeed so much that nothing else matters. Nothing and nobody. You'll have to think dirty and act dirty, and not give a damn when people do dirty to you. This is a tough town to be in and you need to be tough. It's also very phoney. It's full of tinsel and beneath the tinsel there's more tinsel. You have to see that, and not let it destroy you.'

'Do you give this little lecture to everyone?' asked Brendan.

'No,' said Yolande briefly. 'Only the ones I like. The other thing is that Theatrical is a very quixotic studio. All the studios in this town follow the style of their chief executive. At Columbia everybody talks dirty, because Harry Cohn talks dirty. At Warners they're all mean, because Jack Warner's mean. Dick Maynard who rules over us is temperamental and difficult, so everyone tries to be more temperamental and difficult than the next man. Except for me. So you aren't in with an easy deal. I really think you should know that.' She smiled at him. 'Now then. Let's see your pictures. Oh, yes, yes, that's good. I like that. You could just about have it. Just.'

'Have what?'

'A quality.'

'What sort of quality?'

'Hard to describe. What's your real name?'

'Brendan. Brendan FitzPatrick.'

'Well, Byron is certainly better. Not good, but better.'

'Thanks.' Brendan sounded nettled.

She smiled at him, her great brown eyes dancing. 'Darling, you have to learn to take a lot of shit here. That was nothing. That was a rabbit turd. Wait till the horse manure descends. OK?'

'OK,' said Brendan.

'Now, they're testing you in a couple of days. Just a perfectly basic test. No real acting. They don't have any particular role to test you in.'

'No acting? So what do I do?'

'I'll tell you. It isn't hard. It's the way you do it that matters. They'll tell you to walk into a room. Look to the left, look to the right, show off the profile. Well at least that's OK. Then they may ask you to start talking. Say your name and so on. It's all to see how you react with the camera. The one thing you must not do, Byron, is try and be like another actor. Just do what they ask. If you've got what they're looking for, they'll see it, and if you haven't you can't fake it. OK?'

'OK,' said Brendan again.

'Now then, let's see a little acting. Go get on that stage and tell me you love me.'

'That's easy,' said Brendan, laughing. He climbed up on to the stage, walked to the front and said, 'Miss duGrath, I love you.'

'No, not like that, not charmingly, not socially. You love me carnally. Let's have that.'

'OK. Miss duGrath, I love you. I really love you. I'm obsessed with you.'

'Uh-huh. Now tell me you loathe me.'

'Jesus Christ, Miss duGrath, I loathe you. Utterly utterly loathe you.' Brendan was beginning to enjoy himself.

'And now you're scared shitless of me.'

'There's something about you, Miss duGrath, that frightens me.'

'Not so bad. Let's see how you move. Walk off, walk on, sit down, stand around. OK. Off you go.'

Later, when Brendan had gone off with Tyrone, she went into the tiny office she had backstage and picked up the phone. 'I've seen your boy,' she said. 'He looks quite good, but I'm not so sure about the acting.'

Nor were the talent agents. They put him through more than just saying his name and showing the profile: they gave him some lines from a love scene. Brendan felt as if he had never acted in his life, standing there on the tiny set, the lights hammering down on him, saying he had never felt this way before. When they looked at the test, it looked as if he had never acted in his life.

After he had been in Hollywood for two and a half weeks, he did get a part. It was a waiter in a nightclub, and he had to say 'Martini or bourbon?' The scene took three days to get right, and Brendan thought he had never been so bored in his life. A week after that he got a walk-on in a musical, and then a bit part in a Chandler-style thriller. Tyrone was working hard on him, sending endless publicity stills and releases to the magazines, bombarding Louella Parsons and Hedda Hopper's offices with phone calls (all unreturned) and making him run the gamut of set-up incidents in restaurants and nightclubs. Twice he brought him into Romanoff's with a starlet, early in the evening, when it was only half full, set them both down at a table, mussed it up a bit, put down a half-empty bottle of wine and two glasses in their hands, took a few shots and then hustled them out of a side door. They didn't even have time to drink the wine. He wrote a caption, saying here was Theatrical's hottest new property Byron Patrick, fresh from the New York stage, dining with Tina Tyrell, newly signed with RKO. Tyrone, who knew his stuff, had managed to get one shot with Romanoff himself standing behind the table. Brendan was astonished by this performance, but Yolande told him it happened all the time.

'They do it with the big stars too. Half those pictures in the fan magazines of them all drinking champagne with each other are faked; they work too hard and get up too early to nightclub. Mostly they just go home and go to bed. But that makes boring reading. So they do these set-up jobs. Even Louella and Hedda are fooled by some of them. These are good shots, darling, let's hope someone uses them.' They didn't.

For two weeks after that Brendan didn't work at all; then he got another waiter part, and the week after that Hilton, who had come back across from New York to see how things were shaping up, came into his room at the Chateau and told him his contract was not being renewed, and that he had to move out. 'Maynard says we've wasted enough money on you. I told him I agreed. He's fired Tyrone as well. So that's it. You've shot your bolt, Byron. Best get on the other side of the door.'

Brendan had been expecting this all along, but it was still a shock. He sat down on the bed. 'So what happens next?'

'Not a lot. You can either stay here, or go back to New York.' Hilton looked at him coldly; he had backed a loser and he was anxious not to expend any further time or emotion on him, to dissociate himself from him as soon as possible.

That was the good news from Brendan's point of view; the rest was bad. He thought quickly. Returning to New York would be painful. Kathleen would be ashamed, Fleur would be disappointed. There was enough money for a few weeks, in both places. He had conserved his assets carefully. If he stayed in Hollywood he at least had a chance; he was getting to know his way around, he had made a few contacts, there were plenty of other agents in town and there were the cattle calls every day. There was no need to starve.

'I'll stay,' he said.

'OK,' said Hilton. 'Pack up those clothes we bought you, will you?'

Brendan stared at him. Then he pulled the suitcase they had also bought him from the closet and jammed all the clothes and shoes he had brought to Hollywood into it.

'Cigarette case,' said Hilton. 'And lighter.'

Brendan threw them in. 'Would you like a pint of blood?' he asked.

Hilton walked out of the door without another word. Watching him get into the car outside and then checking out of the Chateau Marmont later himself, Brendan felt more cheerful than he had for weeks.

Interview with Edna Desmond, Brendan's eldest sister, for Young Lions chapter of *The Tinsel Underneath*.

It was so truly terrible when Brendan was sent to England in the war. I don't think our mother slept properly until he came home again. I don't think any of us did. We all missed him so. Oh, of course he was spoilt, indulged, but he was such a light in the house. A day without Brendan was duller, longer. And we were so afraid,

afraid something would happen to him. We lit candles for him, every Sunday, every Friday; maybe it helped. He survived a lot. 'He is one of God's favourites,' said Mother one night, as we waited to hear, after he had been taken prisoner. 'God will take care of him.' I think we honestly thought he was that important, that God would keep a special watch for him. Well, maybe He did. And then he came home, so much older and more serious, hardened, toughened, bringing Fleur with him. Well, that was hard for our mother to cope with. Hard for all of us, but more for her. She was shocked, at first, and ashamed of him. Then she got to understand and she forgave him, but I don't think we ever felt quite the same. She was so good to Fleur: a mother. We all got to love Fleur of course; she was easy to love in those days. A pretty, sparky little thing, very bright and sweet. Although even when she was tiny, she was tough. Brave and – what can I say – kept everyone, except her father, at arm's length. It was as if she didn't quite trust us.

Oh, but she loved him so. It was a love affair. They were all the world to one another. If she could be with Brendan, she certainly didn't want to be anywhere else. Not playing, not at a party even. And he was a bit the same. He never really had any serious girlfriends. If anything looked like it was getting serious, Fleur saw it off. I'm not joking.

I never shall forget the day he left to go to Hollywood. It makes me cry still, just thinking about it. That child just broke her heart. We all saw him to the airport, and she sat there, quite silent in the car, white-faced, her eyes huge, clinging on to his hand. And when it was time to say goodbye, she had to be prised off him. It took two of us to drag her free. She wasn't screaming, just sobbing, terrible, grievous sobs. 'I love you, Daddy, I love you,' that was all she said, over and over. She knew she couldn't go with him, she'd accepted that, but she just couldn't stand the pain. It was an awful thing to see.

When he'd gone, finally, and I shall never forget, the front of his shirt was just drenched with her tears, she just stood there, staring at the barrier, at where he had gone, quite motionless, for a long time. And finally she agreed to come, and she walked alone, she wouldn't take our hands, very slowly, her little head held high, in front of us. And when we got home she went upstairs to her room, and wouldn't come out for, oh, twelve hours.

She was calm when she did, but a lot of the fight had gone out of her. It didn't come back for a long long time.

Brendan used to talk to us for hours about Caroline, Fleur's mother. How much he had loved her, how much he had been hurt. It was a terrible story, but I suppose we should try not to blame her. It was all a series of dreadful coincidences, but we all felt that surely, surely if she had loved him, she would have waited for him. We all saw her, in spite of everything Brendan said, as a hard, selfish woman. I mean who could part with that tiny beautiful little thing? Brendan tried to explain, to excuse her; but it made little sense. And then she married, so quickly, some English lord or other, and had more children. You cannot tell me she could have loved either of them, Brendan or the lord. As she grew up, it was so hard for Fleur to understand, to cope with.

And the other thing of course, Brendan being so hurt by what Caroline did, it excused, for us, much of what came later. We forgave him because of the damage Caroline had done.

Chapter 5

1954–6

Brendan was getting desperate. He went to the cattle calls every day, trying for extra work, but the studios were cutting back altogether with the new competition from television. It was a favourite film business statistic at that time that in the five years between 1946 and 1951 the number of people owning TV sets had increased from ten thousand to twelve million. Another favourite was that by 1952 movie profits had dropped five hundred million dollars. Warner Brothers led the way in closing down studios; contract players were being cut from the payrolls, and a large number of the old back lots had fallen into total disrepair. Expensive and spectacular gimmicks such as Cinemascope and 3D didn't seem to be working quite the magic everyone had hoped for. Howard Hughes had quit, and Zanuck was on the way out. The golden days of Hollywood (everyone said) were over. There was also the horror of the McCarthy era to deal with; as stars were bullied and pressured into betraying friends and declaring them as having communist sympathies, questioned and then cross-questioned in front of the committees, many of them cracked. Others who held out found themselves swiftly dropped by their studios. Brendan was warned repeatedly not to express the most mildly socialist or even liberal view, and thus get branded a 'Tinsel Town Pink'; if he did, he was told, he would find himself under serious suspicion. It was a time for testing characters; the news that his greatest heroine, the larcenous Betty Bacall, was amongst the courageous who stood up and were counted as friends of some of the accused merely served to set her on a higher pedestal still for Brendan.

Brendan, worried, hard up, missing Fleur, wondered why he stayed. Probably the main reason, he said one night to his girlfriend, Rose Sharon ('No, of course it's not my real name, you dummy, they put the Sharon bit in to give me a biblical ring for *The Robe*'), was because in spite of everything they all had fun. There was a great sense of companionship amongst the swarms of unsuccessful young actors; they earned their livings pumping gas or carrying groceries out of the markets, or the more fortunate worked in one of the innumerable restaurants and bars. Rose, who after her minute part in *The Robe* had not worked at all, was a waitress at the Garden of Allah, on Sunset Boulevard, where the stars lived in gilded luxury in their poolside bungalows. Brendan had a job at Musso and Frank, the writers' favourite hangout on Hollywood Boulevard, which he loved because it felt more like New York than LA with its dark deep interior and long straight bar and wooden panelling and waiters with long white aprons; William Faulkner and Raymond Chandler and reputedly Hemingway sat and drank and talked in the back room there from lunch through to long after dark.

He got fired from Musso and Frank in the end for chatting up his favourite customers and keeping the others waiting too long for their orders, and after that it was the gas stations, and occasionally washing up at Schwab's. Schwab's was the famous drugstore on Sunset where Harold Arlen had written *Over the Rainbow* and Lana Turner was supposed to have been discovered and actually hadn't been at all. It was a great hangout for young actors, and if they weren't at the Rain-check Room or Barney's Beanery, they were there, sitting around in the back room, playing gin rummy and gossiping. If anyone wanted to find someone really badly, they would begin at Schwab's.

He and Rose were very fond of one another; like him, she was ambitious to be a real actress, 'not just a Hollywood doll', and they spent long hours over a shared beer, planning how they would achieve success. Brendan would not have told her so in a thousand years, but he did not really rate Rose's chances too highly; he thought she was pretty, but not spectacularly so, with golden-brown hair rather than the peroxide blonde favoured by the Misses Turner, Grable and Monroe, and a neatly charming little face; he could certainly see no larceny about her. Her greatest asset in Brendan's view was her singing voice which was remarkable, deep and slightly harsh, with a tender quality on certain notes and phrases which was reminiscent of the young Judy Garland's. Brendan was always urging her to go to the calls for singers, but Rose said no, she wasn't going to be a song and dance girl, that wasn't what she was in Hollywood for. Brendan said if she really wanted to be a real actress she was in the wrong place anyway, she should head for Broadway, but Rose said she couldn't afford to get there, and she knew Hollywood, she had grown up in California and the thought of cold, distant New York didn't seem any more promising.

After a bit they moved in together, into a tiny walk-up apartment over a garage on La Brea; at first the idea was simply to cut down on their outgoings, but they got very drunk one night, and Rose was in despair over ever getting so much as a one-line part, and Brendan took her into his arms to comfort her and dry her tears and, slightly to their surprise, they suddenly found themselves enjoying some excellent sex. Rose was remorseful in the morning and said she had never done anything like that in her life before, and Brendan, deliberately misunderstanding, said she was clearly lying, and pointed out that it had been the best fun, they were very fond of one another and it also meant they no longer had to take turns for the camp bed and that was that. He told her all about Fleur and Caroline and she told him all about her long-term affair with a married man which she had finally managed to end six months earlier, and after that they became inseparable.

* * *

Meanwhile Brendan's money was running out. It was five months since he had been signed off from the studio, and apart from the occasional extra work, he was earning nothing except what he made at the gas stations and Schwab's. It was enough to live on, but it wasn't enough to send home to Fleur and Kathleen.

'You should get yourself a job as a gigolo,' said Rose one night, half seriously, as they sat thumbing rather desperately through the *Hollywood Reporter*, looking for calls they might conceivably have not heard about. 'It would help a lot. Just for the odd day here and there. This town is full of sex-starved ladies who'd pay good money for you.'

'Don't be silly,' said Brendan, kissing her slightly absentmindedly. 'I wouldn't do anything like that. I'd rather give in altogether. And I can't stand older women anyway. I like fresh-faced young ones like you.'

'Good,' said Rose. 'But don't write it out completely. You might get desperate.'

'Not that desperate,' said Brendan. He knew he was lying.

Naomi MacNeice was one of the very few women with any power in Hollywood. She was a studio executive at ACI (frequently compared to RKO in its size and stature) and was, amongst other things, in charge of new talent. ACI was an interesting studio, best known for its ability to be second with any trend, a commercial, clever, well-thought-out second. Let Columbia and Warner pioneer and make the mistakes, was the philosophy at ACI, we'll watch the successes and be right on their tail. It was headed up by a man called Stephen Sarandon, an icy cool, shrewd businessman who told his chief executives every day that they were in Hollywood to make money above all else. 'Anything else is icing on the cake.'

True to Yolande duGrath's observations, the entire studio style followed Sarandon's: everybody tried to be cooler, shrewder, more obsessed with making money than everybody else. Naomi MacNeice fitted the mould very neatly. She had also great talent; in the three years she had held the job, she had been personally responsible for signing up (amongst others) the new young actress, Janey Chamberlain, already twice nominated for an Oscar, the brilliant dancer Brett Durante, who was said to have Gene Kelly practising for an extra hour a day for fear of being moved out of a job, and the dark sultry Mimi de Leon, who couldn't act for nuts, but whose presence in a film would guarantee a line right around the block to watch it. Naomi was consequently extremely powerful.

She was forty-five, owned to thirty-seven, and looked like an older Grace Kelly, with ice-blonde hair immaculately coiffed, equally icy blue eyes, a perfect, pale porcelain skin and a figure that owed its twenty-year-old shape to a regime in the gymnasium every day that was so harsh her own instructor urged her to ease it off otherwise she'd kill herself. Naomi told him she would far rather die than get fat, and continued to rise at six every morning and work out until eight, when she breakfasted on a slice of lemon in warm water and went to work. She was too busy there to think about being hungry.

She was famous in Hollywood: her entrance into Ciro's or the Mocambo would result not in a silence, as Betty Bacall's might, or Lana Turner's or Yvonne de Carlo's, but in a buzz of chatter; the people who knew her would stand up to greet her as she passed their tables (to be greeted with her gracious cool smile), and the ones who didn't would remark on her arrival, wonder what she was doing there and who with, and relate some well-worn anecdote about her.

She lived in a Spanish-style mansion on San Ysedro Drive, with a series of lovers and a quartet of Siamese cats; anyone enjoying the favours of her skinny body had to do so with the cats roaming the bedroom and often the bed. She had been married several times, but was currently and ostentatiously single; Hedda and Louella and Sheila Graham all devoted regular space in their columns to a debate as to when and indeed whether this might change once more. There were rumours (much fuelled by rejected lovers) that she was a lesbian, but nobody had any direct experience or proof of this; Naomi seemed in no hurry to set the record straight one way or the other.

All the unsuccessful young actors in Hollywood dreamed of being discovered by Naomi MacNeice; but Brendan, having served her the wrong dressing on her salad once at Musso and Frank, had decided it would be more like a nightmare and said so. Yolande duGrath, who was one of the people he said it to, had enjoyed the remark and indeed the accompanying anecdote so much she repeated it a few times to a few people, including Naomi herself over lunch at Trader Vic's. Naomi had smiled coolly and asked what the inefficient young waiter was doing now. 'Washing dishes? Or pumping gas?'

'Both,' said Yolande.

'Does he have any talent?'

'Very little. But he looks OK. His face works with the camera.'

'Larceny?' asked Naomi. Yolande's yardstick was well known.

'A little larceny.'

'Did Theatrical try him out?'

'Yes. He was on sixty days. He tested badly.'

'He sounds like a no-no altogether,' said Naomi.

'Not altogether,' said Yolande. 'He has great charm, Irish charm.'

Naomi had an Irish great-grandfather. 'Maybe I should have a look at him,' she said. 'We need a new juvenile lead very badly.'

Yolande's eyes met hers in frank amusement. 'You could,' she said. 'Olivier he isn't.'

'I'm not looking for Olivier.'

When Brendan got the message that Naomi MacNeice had called him at Schwab's, he assumed it was a hoax and didn't call back. Naomi, who was not used to not being called back, told her secretary to call again. This time, shaking with a mixture of excitement and terror, he phoned the number. It was not her direct line, nor even her private secretary, but the general switchboard at ACI and he had to put ten quarters in before he was put through.

'Is Miss MacNeice there please?'

'She's engaged right now. May I help you?' Janet Jones, Naomi's private secretary, had initially got the job on the strength of her voice which would have frozen out the entire Palm Desert.

Brendan took a deep breath. 'She – uh, asked me to call.'

'She did?' Miss Jones's voice implied that God Himself was rather more likely to have invited a phone call than Naomi MacNeice. 'What name is it?'

'Brendan FitzPatrick. That is – no, it's Byron Patrick.'

'Which?'

'I beg your pardon?'

'Which of you is calling?'

'Uh – Byron. Byron Patrick.'

'Are you quite sure of that?'

'I think so.'

'Very well. If you'd like to hold on.'

Eight more quarters later, she said, 'If you'd like to come in this afternoon, Mr Patrick. At three thirty.'

'But – I – how –'

'Goodbye, Mr Patrick.'

The phone went dead.

'It has to be one huge hoax,' said Brendan. He had invaded the lush poolside dining area at the Garden of Allah to tell Rose, who was lining up knives with military precision.

'Only one way to find out.'

'I can't.'

'Why not?'

'I shall look such a fool. Turning up there.'

'More of a fool if you don't. Brendan, will you please get out of here, I shall lose my job.'

'OK, OK, I'm going. I'll see you tonight.'

'Fine. Good luck.'

'I still think it's a hoax,' said Brendan. But it wasn't.

'Yolande duGrath tells me you have no talent,' said Naomi. She was sitting behind her massive mahogany desk, her back to the window, the thick curtains behind her blotting out the Californian sunshine. The air-conditioning and a huge fire roared in unison; the room was chilly. Brendan looked at her blankly, too upset to try to appear cool.

'I'm sorry?'

Naomi sounded mildly impatient. 'I said Miss duGrath tells me you have no talent.'

'She did? She can't have. She's my friend.'

'Perhaps that's why she said it. Friends have a duty to be honest.'

'Then she should have said it to me. Not you.'

'I expect,' said Naomi with an infinitesimal smile, 'she imagined that not having your contract renewed would give you a clue.'

'A lot of talented people don't have their contracts renewed,' said Brendan bravely.

'Really? You must let me have a list.'

There was a silence.

'Would you like to read for me?'

'What?' said Brendan. He couldn't help it.

'Mr Patrick, I think you must have a little trouble with your hearing. It can't be helping your rather dismal career. I said, would you like to read for me?'

Brendan looked at her. 'Yes,' he said finally. 'Yes, of course I would.'

Naomi looked at him for a long time. 'Well,' she said, 'I am casting for a thriller next week. I need a detective. He's something of a – what shall we say – a fool. I think you might play him rather well. The casting stage at eight thirty on Tuesday. Good afternoon, Mr Patrick.'

She didn't even come to the casting; nor was Brendan tested. There were forty-two actors in front of him, and after the forty-first they were all told to go home, Brendan was almost in tears.

'I told you she was a no-good bitch,' he said to Rose that evening. 'She's vile. I loathe her.'

'She sounds disgusting,' said Rose. 'Coffee?'

'Do we have any left?'

'Just about one spoonful. We could share it.'

'You have it. I just decided I need something stronger. I'm going out to get a beer. I'll be back in a minute.'

'OK.'

Out on the street he met a friend, a fellow gin rummy player.

'There was a call for you this afternoon. Latish.'

'There was?'

'Yes. From some dame called Janet Jones. Ring a bell?'

'A dismal one. A death knell. What she say?'

'You've to call her. First thing.'

'Can't think why. Maybe I left something at the studio.'

'Maybe you did.'

'Mr Patrick?'

'Yes.'

'Miss MacNeice has asked me to call you. She wants to see your publicity pictures. She says you're to bring them to the Brown Derby at twelve. And have lunch with her.'

'I – can't,' said Brendan, speaking with great difficulty.

'Why not, Mr Patrick?'

'I – uh – have another engagement.'

'Mr Patrick.' The freezing voice sounded almost kindly. 'Don't be such a fucking idiot.'

'Sit down,' said Naomi MacNeice. 'Do you have the pictures?'

'Yes.'

'Can I see them, please? Thank you. What are you going to have?'

'A Cobb's salad. That's what everyone has here, isn't it? De rigueur. Once a week, regular as clockwork. That and a few fake calls brought to your table, and then you're safe to leave again.'

She looked at him, her ice-blue eyes touched with amusement for the first time. 'Quite correct,' she said. 'Although some of the calls are genuine of course.'

'Oh really?'

'Really.' She was looking through the pictures. 'These are quite good. Who took them? Bernie Foster? I thought so. Tell me, is Mr Berelman still – what shall we say – hand in glove with Mr Clint these days?'

'I think so,' said Brendan carefully. A sense of danger had suddenly settled in him.

'Oh well.' She looked at him amusedly and then back at the pictures. 'Obviously you didn't get to see very much of them. Which is very fortunate.'

It was a statement, not a question. Brendan swallowed.

'Anyway, let's not waste valuable time on them. I'm sorry about yesterday. But we had no choice; a fast decision was essential.'

'Really?'

'Yes,' she said, sounding almost patient. 'Really. Now then, I do have a possible part for you. It's an eastern.'

'Oh,' said Brendan. His heart sank. Easterns were films in the *Thief of Baghdad* genre and meant fooling around in boleros and baggy trousers swinging from the rigging of ships, or off the side of Arab horses, holding cutlasses.

'Don't sound so enthusiastic. They're good box-office. I'd have thought it would beat pumping gas.'

'Maybe.'

'It's a nice neat little part. The princess's childhood sweetheart. Before she meets the thief.'

'Who turns out to be a good guy?'

'Of course. How perceptive you are. Well, if it doesn't interest you, Mr Patrick, I must ask you to excuse me. I have a great deal to do.'

'No,' said Brendan, 'no, I'm sorry. Of course it interests me. Of course I'd like to test.'

'Oh, I don't want you to test,' she said, looking at him amusedly.

'You don't?'

'Oh, no.'

'I see.'

He sank back into his corner, totally deflated, putting down his glass. Naomi continued to eat her salad. The waiter suddenly appeared with a phone.

'For you, Miss MacNeice.'

'Thank you. Hallo. Yes, Janet. Yes of course. No, I'll be back. About two. I've nearly finished. Yes, I've spoken to him. Yes, of course I'll see them. I'm sending Mr Patrick up to wardrobe this afternoon incidentally. Let them know, please. We don't have much time. Goodbye, Janet.'

She put down the phone and met Brendan's eyes. She smiled at him for the first time; and for the first time he realized what a beautiful woman she was.

'I told you,' she said, 'some of the phone calls are perfectly genuine. Or did you perhaps think that one was a fake?'

'No,' said Brendan, swallowing a very large mouthful of wine. 'No, I didn't. I do hope,' he added, returning her smile a little nervously, 'that I was right.'

'Yes, you were,' she said. 'Now I must go. The bankers are in town, it seems. Good afternoon, Mr Patrick.'

Brendan sat there for some time, staring after her, and wondering if he had imagined the strong steady pressure of her leg against his during most of the lunch.

He had not. Two days later, after he had been measured endlessly by costume, had his hair cut, been told to grow his sideburns, and to take some riding and fencing lessons, done a tint test (to see how he looked in colour film), been photographed by publicity and even finally been given a script to study, a call came through to make-up from Janet Jones. Would Mr Patrick please come straight up to Miss MacNeice's office?

Brendan walked through the vast back lot and found his way with some difficulty to Naomi MacNeice's office; she was sitting in one of the large leather chairs that flanked her fireplace. A tall blond man with an absurdly tanned face sat in the other; he stood up as Brendan came into the room and walked over to him, holding out his hand.

'Byron!' he said in a voice that dripped honey, with a smile that revealed two rows of the most perfect teeth Brendan had ever seen. 'I am so glad to meet you. Miss MacNeice has been telling me about you. I'm Perry Browne, spelt with an "e" ' – he paused and showed a few more teeth – 'and I'm your press agent. Well, not solely yours, of course, I'm working on this film generally, but I have a special brief as of now to make your name b-i-g.' More teeth.

Brendan blinked, dazzled.

'Naomi, can I get Byron a drink? And another for you? What is it to be, Naomi, another pink gin? Byron, what do you like to drink? I think Naomi has just about everything.'

'Uh – a glass of white wine, please,' said Brendan.

'White wine!' cried Perry, sounding enraptured. 'White wine, wonderful! Californian Chardonnay, Byron, or let me see, Naomi has a lovely white Bordeaux, or there's a gorgeous Chablis. Which would you think?'

'The Chardonnay, please,' said Brendan, who would have preferred beer, but didn't think he could possibly drink beer in Naomi's office.

'The Chardonnay!' cried Perry in triumphant tones. 'Of course! Here we are, then, a glass of very delicious Chardonnay. I think I might join you, if you don't mind.'

'Oh, Perry, of course he doesn't mind,' said Naomi impatiently. 'Now then, Byron, what we've got you here for is to discuss basic publicity strategy.'

'Yes,' said Perry, 'background, training, all that sort of thing. Interests, ambitions, special skills and talents. You know, Byron, as well as I do, of course you do.'

'OK,' said Brendan, disliking Perry more with every moment, 'how much do you want to know?'

'Oh, everything, every little tiny thing. Then we can work out a really nice story.'

'Born in New York. Grew up in Brooklyn –'

'The Heights?' said Perry hopefully.

'No, Sheepshead Bay.'

'Sheepshead Bay! Charming!'

'Majored in drama at high school. Summer school at Juillard. Off Broadway in Tennessee Williams.'

'Off Broadway! Wonderful! Byron, you're a publicist's dream –'

'Then went to England in the war. USAF. Flew bombers. Shot down. Eighteen months in German hospital and prison-of-war camp –'

'Oh my!' said Perry. 'A war hero! Go on, Byron.'

'Back to New York, back to Sheepshead Bay with my daughter.'

There was a silence so intense it almost hurt. Brendan looked from one to another; they were staring at him, Perry looking almost frightened, Naomi colder than ever.

'The dream becomes a nightmare,' she said distantly. 'Are we to understand then that you're married? Or have been?'

'No,' said Brendan cheerfully, feeling in command of the situation for the first time since he had met Naomi. 'No, I'm not and I haven't been. The mother of my child is an English girl. She's now married to someone else. She – couldn't keep Fleur.' He watched Perry and Naomi visibly relax.

'Ah!' said Perry. 'Just a little wartime romance. A bit of war effort. And Fleur! What a lovely name. I'm sure she's a very lovely child too, Byron. But I think perhaps we shouldn't mention her in your release. We are billing you as a new young romantic lead after all. A child would be – well, not ideal. Would she, Naomi?'

'Not ideal,' said Naomi.

'Well, I wouldn't have wanted her mentioned anyway,' said Brendan. 'And she wouldn't want it either,' he added firmly, lest they should think Fleur was merely an adjunct to him, not a force in her own right. 'I think she's best left out of all this.'

'Of course! How wise you are, Byron. Nothing worse than the Hollywood brat, is there, Naomi? Who cares for her, Byron? A nurse?'

'No,' said Brendan, 'my mother.'

'You have a mother?' cried Perry. 'How wonderful!' He spoke as if a mother was an esoteric rarity, a prize orchid or a fine piece of sculpture.

'Most people have a mother,' said Brendan.

'Yes, but not when they are your age, devoted, supportive mothers. That would be a great story – but then we would have to mention the little girl perhaps. So no, maybe not. Now, Byron, how did you come to Hollywood?'

'Via Kevin Clint and Hilton Berelman,' said Naomi. She sounded almost rattled.

'Uh-uh,' said Perry, 'least said soonest mended there. I don't see why that has to come out, Naomi. I mean Byron hasn't been exactly making waves up till now.'

'Let's hope not,' said Naomi.

'Well now, perhaps, Byron, you might have come anyway? Maybe your wonderful mother suggested it? Saved up the fare herself perhaps? I mean if Clint and Berelman hadn't sent you? What do you think?'

'Whatever you think,' said Brendan wearily. He was beginning to feel sick. Tyrone was looking like a regular guy compared with this creep.

'Well, we can work on that one. Now, what are your hobbies? Do you ride, or play baseball or surf, or play the piano? What can we find there?'

'I can't ride,' said Brendan, 'not properly. Although I have to have some lessons for this film. I hate the sea. I'm bad at baseball. I'm tone-deaf. I can't think what you can say.'

'Wine!' said Perry suddenly. 'Wine! I have a wonderful idea, Naomi. Byron obviously knows about wine. He can win an award. Or be elected to a fellowship of wine buffs. So civilized, so urbane. So right for his looks. What do you think?'

'Nice idea,' said Naomi. 'I like it.'

'Good. Byron, you're looking puzzled. It's really very simple. We arrange for you to be photographed receiving a crate of wine – something a little bit special – at your door, and announce that you've been elected a golden vintage member of the fellowship of the Californian Vine. Something like that.'

'I couldn't be,' said Brendan, 'I hardly know red from white.'

'Oh, that won't matter. Not one bit. Not at first and you can mug up very quickly. Of course it won't be a real award. But, in no time, you'll be known as the star who knows about wine. You can give little tastings, maybe even have your own vineyard somewhere, oh, it will be charming. Charming.'

'OK,' said Brendan, trying to sound authoritative, and hearing himself failing, 'if you think so.'

'Now, what about clothes and things? Do you have some really nice clothes?'

'Not any more,' said Brendan, thinking of the bulging suitcase Hilton had taken back to New York.

'That's no problem,' said Naomi. 'We can get him some clothes.'

'Of course. Where do you live, Byron?'

'On La Brea at third.'

'Oh, dear. On your own or do you share with some other young actors?'

'One actress.'

'Who's that?' asked Naomi. Her voice was colder than ever.

'Her name is Rose Sharon.'

'Indeed! What an interesting name.' Perry's teeth were widely bared again. 'Does she have a lot of work?'

'Enough.'

'Oh, good. But you see, Byron, you really can't go on living there. Or with her. The fans won't like it. You're a bachelor. A young lead. Incidentally, Byron, how old are you?'

'Thirty-five.'

'Too old,' said Perry. 'What do you think, Naomi? Twenty-seven?'

'Twenty-six,' said Naomi.

'Twenty-six it is. Well, you've given me lots to think about, Byron.'

'Good,' said Naomi. 'I think that's all for now, Perry. Come back to me with your proposals, will you?'

'Of course! *Tout de suite*. Byron, it's been lovely meeting you. I just know we're going to enjoy working together. I'll call you in a day or so.'

'Fine. Thanks,' said Brendan.

Perry withdrew, almost genuflecting at Naomi. She smiled a trifle less coldly and poured Brendan another glass of wine.

'He's a little excessive,' she said, 'but very good at his job.'

She drove him up to her house herself in her car, a silver-blue Pontiac.

'No driver?' said Brendan, surprised.

'I like driving,' said Naomi. 'My driver has a very easy life.'

The house was vast, with an elaborately tiled roof and high Moorish windows, set above the obligatory well-sprinkled lawns; great banks of azaleas and bougainvillaeas lined the drive, and led to a vast vaulted front door. Naomi parked the car and the redundant driver appeared as if from nowhere to take it away again; the door swung open as they approached and the butler saw them in with an almost-bow. He was English and tail-coated: 'Good evening, madam, sir.'

'Good evening, Crossman. Drinks by the pool, please.'

'Yes, madam.'

Brendan, fascinated, followed Naomi through a dark panelled hall, a vaulted library, walls lined with enough books to service a small university, and out the other side on to a terrace by the pool. Naomi led the way to some chairs and a table and waved Crossman towards them. He carried an ice bucket and some glasses in his white-gloved hands; his expression as he looked briefly in Brendan's direction was blank.

'Thank you, Crossman.'

'Will you be dining here, madam?'

'Possibly.'

'Very good, madam.'

Another almost-bow; a gracious withdrawal.

'He's – uh – very nice,' said Brendan. Crossman reminded him of the Moat House and Caroline; the knowledge that he had seen the real thing in operation gave him an odd confidence.

'Yes,' said Naomi shortly, dismissing Crossman from their consciousnesses. 'Champagne, Byron?'

'I'd rather have a beer,' said Brendan.

Naomi looked at him coldly. 'Byron, if you are to be the Hollywood wine buff, you will have to stop drinking beer. I'm sorry.'

Brendan held out his hand for the glass. 'OK,' he said, 'if you say so.'

'I think you'll like it,' said Naomi. 'You probably haven't had a great deal of good champagne.' Her expression was patronizing, almost contemptuous.

Brendan felt anger rising in his throat like bile, physical, sour-tasting. He sipped the champagne, hoping it would help; it didn't.

'Now, then,' said Naomi, 'your domestic life. We have to take a look at it.'

'I don't think,' said Brendan, very slowly and carefully, 'I don't think I want to look at it. Not in that way.'

'Then,' said Naomi, 'I'm afraid this part will almost certainly be your last. Incidentally, has anyone talked to you about money?'

'No,' said Brendan, 'no, they all said you would take care of that. As I don't have an agent, I thought I'd wait.'

'Quite correct,' said Naomi, 'and I have said two hundred and fifty dollars a week.'

Brendan was silent. It sounded OK to him. It sounded fine, in fact, but he wasn't going to say so; the fact that Naomi had not seen fit to discuss it with him in any way increased his anger.

'You don't have any comment on that?' She sounded amused again, over-confident.

'You haven't asked for any.'

'I didn't imagine we'd have a discussion about it.'

'Why not? Was I supposed to be so grateful there would be no more to be said?'

'Frankly, yes.'

'I realize,' said Brendan, speaking with difficulty, 'that I don't have a great deal of influence in all this. But it might have been a courtesy.'

'My dear Byron,' said Naomi, 'this is not a very courteous business. However –'

'So I am discovering.'

'However, we can certainly renegotiate your next picture. If there is a next picture, of course.'

'Yes,' said Brendan, 'yes, I think we should.'

'Right. Now then, your domestic life. First of all, I have to stress that you must move out of your little love-nest. Straight away. You can see this girl, if you must. But you are not to continue living with her. It would do your image no good at all.'

'I see.'

'And then the child. Your daughter. I think the best thing there –'

'Miss MacNeice, I really will not discuss my daughter with you. She is my business.'

'Byron, if you are to work for me, everything to do with you is my business.

I appreciate that you feel protective about your daughter, but I have to be the judge of whether or not we talk about her, and how we handle her existence.'

Brendan stood up suddenly. 'Miss MacNeice,' he said, 'I really have had enough of this. My daughter is mine, and I shall decide exactly what happens to her. She will not become some promotional toy for you and Mr Browne to play with. And if anything about her finds its way into a press release I shall personally break your neck, and wind Mr Browne's balls very tightly round his cock and stuff the lot up his own well-licked arse. Do I make myself clear?'

Naomi sat looking up at him, her face blank. 'Perfectly,' she said. She put down her glass of champagne, and stood up suddenly. 'Well,' she said, 'now I know where I stand, let us get on with other matters. Please come with me.'

She turned and walked round the pool towards the pink poolhouse; as she walked she kicked off her high-heeled shoes. Brendan followed her.

She walked into the house, waited until he was inside with her and then shut the door. Brendan watched her mesmerized as she undid her pale blue shirt and slid it off her shoulders; her breasts were tiny, but very brown, the nipples large and dark. She undid her skirt and let it fall to the floor; she wore a pair of very diminutive black panties and nothing else. Then she reached up and undid the tightly bound pleat of her hair; a great fall of silver blonde cascaded round her shoulders, making her look suddenly ten, even fifteen years younger. Slowly, casually, as if she was simply walking across her office, she went over to the corner of the room and pressed a button; a large bed descended from the wall, covered in white linen and a heap of pale blue cushions. Naomi lay down on it, and with her eyes fixed still on Brendan's face, removed her panties and lay back on the cushions, her legs slightly spreadeagled.

'Byron,' she said, sounding a trifle impatient, 'come along for heaven's sake. Surely you didn't think I was doing all this for the satisfaction of seeing your career develop, did you?'

He did it of course; he went over to the bed and took off his clothes and made love to her, not once, but twice; it was an extraordinary experience, exciting, gratifying, yet utterly without tenderness. He felt himself in thrall, possessed. Her body was neat, hard, voracious; she took command of him, controlling his every movement. He felt at once resentful and oddly charmed; he followed where she led him, waiting, moving, still, released. Naomi came not once but three times; hard, strong, careful orgasms; after the last time, she threw back her head, arched her body, and pulled him down deeper and deeper into her, and said, 'Now, Byron, now, now quickly,' and with surprising, almost shocking, ease he felt his body rise, tip, fall into orgasm.

Afterwards, she was brisk, organized, organizing; she smiled at him briefly, approvingly, lifted the house phone, and said, 'Dinner by the pool, Crossman, half an hour,' and then, rising from the bed and walking to the bar, poured two large brandies, and brought them over to where he lay. 'Let us drink,' she said, 'to our partnership,' and drank deeply from her own glass; she did not hand Brendan his, but sat looking at him with an expression of deep amusement in her eyes. He raised himself on to his elbows and watched almost detachedly as she picked up his penis, dipped it carefully in the brandy, and then, bending, began to sip at him, tenderly, carefully, efficiently like a cat with some cream.

He did everything she said: he told Rose that he had to move out, that it was part of his new contract, and endured quite silently her scorn, her amused distaste as she watched him pack, pausing painfully over their joint possessions – 'Do leave everything, Brendan, I'm sure Miss MacNeice will have a clock, and possibly even a flower vase' – her deliberate disinterest in where he was going.

Naomi moved him into a penthouse apartment just off Doheny Drive at Sunset and had it decorated by someone called Damian Drake, who Perry Browne had recommended: all white and silver, with mirrored ceilings and black blinds and white carpets and hardly any furniture at all, beyond a very large circular bed, a pair of black leather couches and a sunken bath so big it would have washed half Hollywood, as Brendan remarked to an unamused Naomi. The only other feature of the apartment was a cellar, which as Hollywood's first Master of Wine he clearly had to have, but which was a minor logistical problem in a penthouse. In the end, Damian constructed a small mezzanine floor shut behind a cellar door on the way up to the roof garden; inside, several hundred empty wine bottles, with cobwebs supplied by the props department, lay and waited for the next photographic session.

Brendan took to his role of wine expert with some difficulty. It was all very well, he pointed out, for Naomi to say it was a great deal safer than surfing, and easier than riding, but at least surfers only had to know a wave from a flat sea, and riders to recognize an Arab from a piebald; he was required to discourse authoritatively on sweets and dries, clarets and burgundies, vintages and vineyards until he felt as confused as if he had drunk his own cellar dry. Nevertheless it was a clever idea of Perry's and it worked, bestowing upon him exactly the right degree of sophistication and urbanity. Since only a small handful of people in Hollywood had the faintest idea that wine began life anywhere other than in a bottle or that there was more to distinguish/differentiate between champagne and claret than that opening champagne was noisier, he got along very well. He was constantly being photographed with this or that starlet drawing the cork of that or this wine at public dinners or private parties, or even at the door to his cellar, pronouncing a wine here amusing and a wine there a trifle unenterprising, so that quite quickly no serious gastronomic occasion was considered complete without the attendance of Grand Vintner Byron Patrick, whose career as young male lead at ACI was escalating as satisfactorily and rewardingly as his own cellar.

After the eastern, Brendan progressed to a swashbuckle drama, where he played second lead, that of an eighteenth-century English lord (dressed, he complained, like a complete fool, in claret-coloured velvet breeches, with a fountain of white lace frills at his throat; but the fans loved it, and the magazines compared him to a young Stewart Granger), and thence to what he pronounced to Naomi was a proper part, that of an adulterous charmer in a modern comedy of manners. Naomi told him tartly that a proper part was one which paid the bills: as his contracted salary was now a thousand dollars a week, of which five hundred went winging its way to New York, a great many bills were being paid.

Brendan was perfectly aware of his shortcomings: his talent was modest (as the critics were invariably swift to point out) but Naomi knew what she was doing; his style was exactly right for the time, and his looks were exactly of the style and form that the camera flattered and fawned upon (as his burgeoning fan mail testified). Nevertheless he knew there were at least two dozen other young men, possibly even two hundred, just as handsome, just as photogenic; he owed all his success to Naomi and in return he had to supply certain commodities whenever she wanted them – his company at her side at parties, his charm on tap when she felt low, and his body to assuage her apparently ceaseless sexual appetite. He found, to his own interest and with a degree of self-distaste, that it was quite easy to perform for her, in whatever way she wished, both in and out of bed. He expected to feel worse about it than he did; in the event he looked at the person he was becoming: a plastic pastiche of himself, with an easy, bogus charm and a set of entirely expedient values, and then at what it was accomplishing for him, and shrugged his concern off. There was nobody in the world to care what he was really like, except for Kathleen and Fleur and they were benefiting greatly anyway. He did not even let his thoughts stray in the direction of Caroline: she belonged far into his past now, literally another country, another life. Kathleen wrote to say Fleur was in the school baseball team, and that she had grown about six inches and was turning into a real beauty; Fleur wrote to say she missed him and when was he coming home. Brendan, who was a lousy correspondent, communicated with postcards of Hollywood and told them he'd be home soon. Any thought of having them over to live with him (as he had once imagined he might) was totally out of the question. They would not be able to come to terms with his new life and, besides, Naomi would not have countenanced it. And what Naomi said went.

As he got to know Naomi he did not exactly like her more, but he admired her and found her increasingly interesting; she was quixotic, authoritative, intensely domineering, but she was also emotionally insecure, prone to depression and a chronic insomniac. The only cure for the insomnia was sex: Brendan grew accustomed to being summoned from his bed at two or three in the morning when he slept at the apartment, falling into Naomi's waiting car and being driven to the house on San Ysedro, where she would be waiting for him, tense, hungry, pacing the library or the pool deck. She would greet him without a smile, without warmth, but would lead him impatiently, imperiously to her room; she was always at her most demanding of him at these times, requiring only speed, a swift release. He would enter her fast, almost brutally, and feel her orgasm rising equally fast and violently. She came swiftly, noisily, tearing at his back with her long red nails, and then lay, panting, her face contorted still, wet with sweat and tears. After a moment or two she began to breathe more evenly and easily; five minutes later she would fall asleep and he was required no more. He found it degrading initially to be used as something little more than a sedative; then as it all became part of the price he paid for success, and security, for himself and Kathleen and Fleur, he adjusted to it as he had to everything else, with his mind firmly away from any moral and emotional implications of any kind.

Naomi did not always want him with her; she had a small posse of men friends but Brendan was young and good-looking and his star was rising, so increasingly he was required to be at her side at the more public and well-attended parties. At first he was nervous and ill at ease, particularly at the more orgiastic gatherings; he did not know quite where to look and how to behave as actresses with faces as familiar to him as his own family's stripped off and swam naked in swimming pools, daring one, two or three men to join them in what was patently sex under the water, or stood on dinner tables, throwing their skirts up over their heads, revealing how true the rumours were that they wore no panties; he was nervous when first confronted by the small anterooms or cloakrooms off many of the ballrooms, dining rooms and halls of the great mansions of Beverly Hills where cocaine was discreetly but freely available, supplied complete with silver straws to anyone who happened to feel a need for it; and he grew positively frightened when at one party (where Naomi was not) he found himself led into a bedroom by two young actresses who removed first his clothes and then their own and proceeded to seduce him while half the rest of the party watched through a two-way mirror.

But he learnt and he learnt fast: he grew to know which actresses were lesbians, and which actors were homosexuals, which ones were likely to wish him to indulge in group perversions, who took cocaine, who smoked marijuana, and therefore the predictable form of many of the parties he was required to attend – and how to handle them. He could look down now on the rather pathetic ranks of the young actors and actresses who were part of the slave system – and whose role was the gratification of the stars and directors, particularly on rainy days, when shooting was limited and slow – but he found himself, with a degree of pleasure, on the other hand, at the receiving end of endless propositioning from young hopeful actresses who would come to his dressing room or would telephone his apartment, offering their services in return for a helpful word in the ear of the director.

He got to know how Hollywood worked, who dined where and commanded the best tables; how Clark Gable always got the number one table at Romanoff's (an honour previously accorded to the gangster Bugsy Siegel, gunned down nearly ten years earlier, but still a big Hollywood legend); Jack Benny and Lena Horne at the Luau; how James Dean could almost always be found at the Yucca and Gable and Bogey would never miss a big fight at the Legion Stadium on Friday nights. He watched Hollywood genuflect at Louella Parsons and Hedda Hopper and fawn at the feet of Elsa Maxwell. He learnt where the women went for their abortions (to one Dr Killkare, he was affectionately known), and for their amphetamine and slimming shots, and which doctors would supply drugs on prescription, and which intensely virile actors were impotent or transvestite or both and which women were nymphomaniacs and which little more than prostitutes. And after a while he loved it all; it was a heady, rich mishmash of a recipe and it was addictive.

Naomi bought him a silver blue Oldsmobile and a mass of clothes from Syvedore's, on Sunset; she took him for weekends to the Racquet Club at Palm Springs and to stay with friends in the huge mansions on Hope Ranch at Santa Barbara, where he rode the trails (which he thought looked more like film scenery than a lot of film scenery) and dined at Ronald Colman's one-time restaurant, the San Ysedro Inn, or to Ojai, with its orange and avocado groves which had been used as the background for *Lost Horizon*. He was popular, petted and praised; he could choose who he wanted to be with and who not, could afford to discard people who seemed disagreeable or tedious, along with his fine clothes and expensive toys; and whenever he felt depressed after going through the dailies, and seeing his acting growing, it seemed to him, increasingly mediocre, he could cheer himself considerably by looking at his photographs and reading the fawning articles about him in either *Photoplay* or *Motion Picture* almost every week.

He didn't exactly believe the articles; but they entered his consciousness none the less.

But there was one lesson he never quite learnt, try though he might, and that was that he should trust no one, and disbelieve everybody. It was against his nature, he couldn't quite do it. It was all right while he was sober, he could be the smooth sophisticate of the PR handouts, the stories in the papers; but a few glasses of wine, a smoke of marijuana, and he was his old self, the boy from Brooklyn: an easy touch for a loan, a sympathetic ear for a sob story, a helping hand out of a mess. It won him many friends; but it was a danger. It made him vulnerable.

Introduction to chapter on Kirstie Fairfax for Lost Years section of *The Tinsel Underneath*.

Hollywood destroys many more people than it creates. It may be a cradle of creativity, but it is also a graveyard of hope and innocence.

Kirstie Fairfax, like Brendan FitzPatrick, was lured to Hollywood by an unscrupulous agent, a set of false hopes, a wardrobe full of cheap clothes. She was a beautiful young girl of sixteen when she arrived in Hollywood, with blonde hair, blue eyes and a thirty-eight-inch bust, who had done well at dance classes in downtown Chicago. Not enough to see her on to the silver screen; but she was not to know that.

The agent, one Rod Selway, told her she could make it there and make it big; if she would pay him a mere five hundred dollars to cover his expenses he could ensure her a screen test. Kirstie cashed in all her savings, paid him the money, bought an air ticket, and arrived in Los Angeles late in 1956 with twenty dollars left in the world and an introductory letter to a number of studios. None of whom had heard of Selway, none of whom wished to test Kirstie.

Three weeks later, the twenty dollars all spent, Kirstie found herself sitting in an all-night café, trying to face up to the humiliation of returning home to Chicago, when she was picked up by a talent scout. Or someone she thought was a talent scout. Yes, sure, he said in answer to her question, he'd heard of Rod Selway, he was a good guy, but lacked the contacts. He could get her a test, no trouble at all; and he could offer her temporary work in his club while she waited. Her reputation and her self-esteem rescued, Kirstie went along with him. The club was little more than a brothel; the screen tests few and far between. But she at least had a roof over her head, money, and a good time. For a while she was satisfied.

But she still wanted to be a film star. She knew she could dance, she was sure she could act; she was convinced she had the looks. She took acting and dance classes; and she clawed her way on to the outermost reaches of the Hollywood network. And in a bedroom at a party one night, where she was exercising her considerable talents for oral sex, she met Brendan FitzPatrick.

Chapter 6

1960

Bad news does not always come efficiently, rushed over the airwaves, borne by officials, imparted by grave-faced, heavy-voiced authorities; it can arrive hopelessly, messily, in painful disorder, late, distorted, and so doubly shocking. The bad, the terrible news came thus to Caroline; she sat, one early September day, thinking herself to be perfectly happy, believing herself entirely safe, sewing name tapes on to her sons' clothes, packing them neatly into their school trunks, occasionally glancing out of the window to see her daughter riding (rather nervously and badly she noticed) in the paddock nearest to the house, waiting slightly impatiently through the two o'clock news bulletin for *Woman's Hour* to begin. There was an item on it that promised to be interesting, trailered the day before: an interview with a journalist who had written a book about scandals in Hollywood. She always listened to *Woman's Hour* when she could; she found it stimulating and amusing, an upturn, a flash of colour in her often monotone day. She was particularly looking forward to the Hollywood item; she had given up hope of hearing anything about Brendan, but her interest in the whole industry had been sparked by her following of his career.

The first time she had encountered Brendan in the pages of *Picturegoer* she had certainly not been looking for him; but there he had been, on the kitchen table where Cook had left him, smiling, posing with a beach ball and a blonde starlet on an upturned boat, looking a little more solid than she remembered him, and with a haircut that Caroline could only describe to herself as common, but otherwise exactly the same, and she had sat down, weak, shaken, trying to make sense of the caption, which read, 'Latest heart-throb arrival in Hollywood, Byron Patrick, working out on Muscle Beach helped along by Stella Stewart, currently under contract to Universal.' 'Byron!' she said aloud to the picture. 'Byron? Can't be. What nonsense,' but it was so unmistakably him that she waited every fortnight for *Picturegoer* with a sense of illicit excitement; there was no news of Byron for months after the first time, but then she saw his name at the bottom of a long cast list for a thriller. In the issue after that, there was a picture of him at a restaurant with a starlet called Tina Tyrell, followed by a silence and then quite a lot for a while; indeed he had seemed to be doing rather well and was what the magazines called a box-office draw. She hadn't been sure what she had felt about that: very little in an odd way; it had all seemed rather impersonal, and she found it hard to equate the handsome, glossy creature with a ridiculous name, playing on the beach with starlets or arriving at premières wearing a white dinner jacket, with the Brendan she had been in love with, the father of her child. She didn't even feel jealous of, or even interested in, the starlets; they engendered no more emotion in her than if they had been cardboard cutouts – which she supposed they were in a way.

She worried about Fleur, and whether Hollywood was a suitable place for her; but clearly Brendan was earning plenty of money and was providing for her well. She wondered if she might see a picture of Fleur in one of the magazines; they did sometimes show the families of stars and for a while she became rather obsessed with that idea, leafing through them feverishly in search of a little girl with Brendan or Byron (ten, eleven, older than that) with dark hair and wide blue eyes, but of course she never found one. Then she relaxed about that too, relieved even, telling herself it was foolish, that Brendan would have had more sense than to expose Fleur to any kind of Hollywood publicity. But she had become, in a very modest way, quite knowledgeable about the place, which restaurants were where, and who went to them, who was with which studio and so on. Hollywood scandals sounded intriguing and fun.

She had sat through an earlier item about budget meals slightly impatiently and had just turned the volume up when Cook came in with some menus. Even without looking at them it still took time to dismiss her, by which time the journalist, Joe Payton (who had, she at least managed to take in, a very sexy voice, throaty, slightly raw-sounding and with an accent that was certainly not public school, but not what Jacqueline had called C-O-M either), was halfway through his item.

'There are so many different types of scandal,' he was saying to the interviewer when Caroline finally managed to give him her attention. 'Marital scandals, like those of Lana Turner, six or maybe seven husbands, all little better than one-night stands; alcoholic scandals, think of Frances Farmer, who put drink in everything, including her porridge, and ended up for ten years in the Snake Pit, the famous Hollywood asylum, for want of a little compassion; crime scandals like the ones surrounding gangster Bugsy Siegel who was one of the kings of Tinsel Town until he got gunned down in his own living room; drug dependency scandals, and we all know about Judy Garland who was given uppers, downers and God knows what else just to get her through each day until the poor kid didn't know what time it was.

'Then there are what I call manipulation scandals, where young actors are taken to Hollywood, asked to deliver, used by just about everybody in just about every way, and then when they fail get dumped, often literally on the street. There was a young man about three years ago, called Byron Patrick, a truly tragic case, who was sent to Hollywood, got taken up by some casting director and set up in a nice apartment, expensive car, nice clothes, all that sort of thing, and then some unfavourable story about him was published in one of the scandal sheets. She turned him out of the studio and the apartment and presumably her bed, and he ended up a down and out on the beach at Santa Monica. Now he was actually killed on the Pacific Coast Highway by a passing car, but of course really it was Hollywood who killed him. And then . . .'

Caroline switched off the radio. She shut her eyes, bent her head over her sewing and started to shake. She felt very cold, and very sick; after a while she got up and went up to her bedroom and lay down on the bed. She didn't feel very much, only a terrible deadness and a complete lassitude; hours passed; she knew there were people talking downstairs, she heard the boys come in from riding, and then later, much later, William's car draw up in front of the house, and his voice calling her.

After a while he came up, walked into her room; she looked at him, and it was as if she didn't have the faintest idea who he was.

'Caroline, my dear, are you ill? What is it?' he said, and yes, she said, yes she did feel a little odd, a terrible headache, and sickness, probably a bug, she would just stay in bed if he would forgive her, Nanny could see to the boys, Chloe had gone to tea and to stay the night with a friend. 'Please go, William, please,' she added, a rising hysteria in her voice, 'I just need to be alone.' Alarmed and frightened, but anxious not to upset her further, he went out and closed the door.

Many hours later, he came in quietly. 'Are you all right, Caroline?' he whispered and she was silent, pretending to be asleep, and he went away again, relieved not to have to do any more for her, and slept in his dressing room.

All night she lay there, fully dressed, her eyes wide open: thinking, remembering, raging, and the worst thing of all, it seemed to her, was that she had had no idea, she had thought simply, and quite cheerfully even, of Brendan alive and doing, if not well, all right, taking care of Fleur who would be growing up happily, fifteen on her last birthday, and all the time – how much of the time, dear God, how long ago had it happened? – he was dead, cold, run over like a dog on the highway. And what story had there been, in the – what had the man called it, the scandal sheet? – was it about her, possibly, her and Brendan? At that thought, that her past, her sad, literally shocking past was to reach out at her from what she had thought its safe hiding place, she felt a rise of such panic she had to bite her fists to stop herself from screaming. But no, she thought, no, that couldn't possibly have been. If it had been, then surely she would have heard of it: William would have heard of it, she would have known. Although, if it was in these articles that this man was writing, then maybe the story had yet to reach her. But then again, surely, the journalist would have contacted her. Yes. Yes, of course he would. Obviously it was something quite different, it had to be, something horrible and undoubtedly ugly, but at least that would leave her and William and her children safe. But then she thought on, through the long night, and reflected on the awful fact that Fleur was alone, with no one in the whole world to care for her and love her and see that she was safe and had what she needed. Fleur, whom she had imagined to be so perfectly safe, with the one person apart from herself she should be with.

As the hours passed, the pain got worse; she remembered Brendan as he had been, laughing and tender and funny and handsome, sitting beside him in the truck, showing him the countryside, teaching him about English life. She remembered sex with him, wild, strong, wonderful sex, her body arching, rising, reaching out for him; and she remembered love with him, gentle, all-reaching, all-embracing love. She remembered the pain of losing him once, and of losing their daughter; she remembered the last time she had been with him, living a lifetime with him in just a few hours, remembered his voice saying, 'I can't lose you again, Caroline, I just can't,' heard her own voice saying, 'I'm afraid you have to,' and then remembered his tears, and her own mingled with the memory; and then she remembered most forcibly, most painfully, saying to him, 'You must have our daughter, Brendan, and take her home with you.'

And now their daughter was alone, not being cared for, not home with him at all; and where was she now, her Fleur, her lovely, long, slender, dark-haired daughter, who was she with and how could she find her?

At that thought Caroline sat up; the urgency of the emotion gave her strength, eased her pain. Whatever else she did, she had to find Fleur, and make sure she was safe. No matter what it cost her, or William, or her other children, she had to find Fleur.

But how was she to do it? How could she begin to find one little girl in the whole of the United States of America? She could be anywhere: probably New York, possibly Hollywood, conceivably somewhere else altogether. She might not even be in the United States of America at all. 'Oh, God,' said Caroline aloud, lying down again, tossing her head fretfully from side to side, 'oh, dear God, help me.'

It was not God, however, who helped her. It was, as it so often had been in her life, Jack Bamforth.

She went to the stables as soon as she knew he would be there. He was heaving manure out of one of the boxes, and he looked up and smiled at her.

'Morning, Lady Hunterton.'

'Good morning, Jack. Jack, could we – could we talk?'

'Talk?' he said with his gentle, carnal smile.

'Yes, talk. Really talk.'

He put down his fork. 'You look terrible.'

'I feel terrible,' she said.

'Look, come into my office. I've got a flask of coffee there. Come on. You're frozen.'

He poured her a lidful of coffee from his thermos, and offered her a biscuit from the old tin with the Queen's photograph on it that was kept permanently filled by Cook for the stable staff.

She shook her head and smiled faintly. 'No, thank you.'

'So what is it? Tell me.'

She told him. She sat there, dry-eyed, very composed, and told him, and when she had finished, he shook his head and said, 'What a dreadful business,' and patted her hand and then sat quietly thinking.

'You'll be wanting to find her, I expect? To see if she's all right?'

'Oh, Jack, yes, I will. I have to. Don't you think so?'

'Yes. Yes, I do. It may be – painful, but I do think so. Will you tell Sir William?'

'I'm afraid I have to, yes. Well, what do you think?'

'I think he's not a fool, Sir William. I think you can't do anything else. Not really.'

'But, Jack, how do you think I should go about it? I mean I just don't know where to start. I don't have an address in New York. I don't have an address anywhere.'

'Didn't he give you one?'

'No. No, I wouldn't let him. I knew if I had one, I'd never be able to stay away from them. Well, from Fleur anyway.'

'Well I can see that. What about the adoption people?'

'Maybe. I could ask. I could explain, couldn't I? They might help. It's a long time ago though. She's fifteen now, Jack. She was fifteen on New Year's Day. Can you imagine?'

'Just about,' he said. 'It seems to have gone pretty quick to me.'

'Anyway, yes, I will try the adoption people. Do you have any other ideas?'

'Well,' he said, 'what about this journalist person? He might have a trail or two you could pick up. Worth a try.'

Caroline stared at him in silence for a moment or two. 'Jack, you are extremely clever,' she said, 'really very ingenious indeed.'

'You have to be,' he said, smiling at her, 'working with horses.'

* * *

The conversation with William was painful. He was very thin and looking very old these days, she realized, looking at him properly for the first time for ages. Well, he was fifty-eight. No longer young. And he smoked too much and ate too little. It was showing. I'm not young either, she said to herself, thirty-seven years old, with two teenage daughters; well past my prime, whatever and whenever that was. She forced her mind back to the conversation with William.

'I cannot tell you,' he was saying, 'how unhappy about this I am. You know you promised me you would never have anything to do with that child again. Our marriage has been built on that premise.'

'Yes, William, I understand, and I have kept my word to you totally, but surely you must see everything has changed. Brendan is dead, and Fleur may be all alone in the world.'

'Please don't use her name,' he said. 'I don't like it.'

'William, I'm sorry. But please, please, try to understand.'

He was silent for a while, looking out of the window.

'I very much doubt,' he said, 'if she is all alone in the world. Most people have families. Her father undoubtedly had a family. A large Irish one, I believe. I cannot believe they would have abandoned her. Besides she is – what – a little older than Chloe. Not a baby. Not totally vulnerable. I feel sure she is perfectly all right. I think you should leave things be. Besides, it may be years since – since her father died. I cannot see the sense in chasing all over the States for her. She probably wouldn't welcome you at all, even if you found her.'

'I know,' said Caroline very quietly. Then she looked at him again, her blue eyes pleading. 'William, think if it was Chloe. Think if you heard that I had died, and you didn't know where she was and who was looking after her. Wouldn't you have to know, need to find out? Please, William, think.'

He thought, silently, drawing heavily on his cigarette. Then finally he looked at her. 'I have to be honest,' he said, 'and yes, yes I would. Or I would think so. But if you were as unhappy about it as I am, I would try very hard to dissuade myself.'

'Oh, William,' said Caroline, her voice half a sob, 'William, I can't. I'm sorry but I can't.'

'Then,' he said, standing up and looking at her, his face heavy and infinitely sad, 'then you must clearly go ahead. Now if you will excuse me, I have to go to work.'

The woman at the Adoption Society was very clipped, very brisk. She was not empowered to hand over addresses of adoptive parents, under any circumstances. Yes, she realized the circumstances were rather extraordinary, but those were the facts. She would ask her superiors, but she was quite sure they would agree with her. She made a phone call, and said that her superiors had said if Caroline liked to write and put her case they would consider her letter carefully. She was sorry but there was no more she could do.

Caroline stormed out of her office, drove home very fast, poured herself a very strong Scotch and went down to the stables.

'Well,' said Jack, 'it looks like the writer fellow, doesn't it?'

'Yes. How do I find him, though?'

'You could phone the people at the wireless programme.'

'Jack, I know I've said this before, but I really don't know what I'd do without you.'

The people at *Woman's Hour* were sympathetic and helpful. They said they couldn't give Caroline Joe Payton's number, but they would pass her name on to him, and ask him to ring her; they also gave her the number of his agent in case he didn't ring.

She rang the agent anyway and spoke to a very superior-sounding girl who said she would see if she could contact Mr Payton, in tones that implied it was about as likely as contacting the Angel Gabriel.

Three days later, when Caroline had given up all hope of ever hearing from him, the phone rang just before lunch: it was the girl from *Woman's*

Hour. 'Lady Hunterton? Sorry to have been so long. Look, I've tracked Mr Payton down for you, but I'm afraid he's away for a couple of weeks. He's on holiday apparently. I'm sure he'll ring you when he gets back. I have left a message.'

'Oh,' said Caroline, feeling suddenly hopeless and chill. 'Oh, thank you. Er – do you know where he is?'

'I'm afraid not,' said the girl, sounding faintly amused.

'What paper does he work on?'

'The *Herald*.'

'Thank you. And thank you for taking so much trouble.'

'That's all right, Lady Hunterton.'

She dialled the *Herald*, asked for the film department.

The man on the switchboard chuckled. 'We don't have one of those. Who was it you wanted?'

'Er – Mr Payton.'

'Oh, Joe. Just a minute.'

There were a lot of clicks; then a girl picked up the phone. 'Show pages.'

'Er – could I possibly speak to Mr Payton?' said Caroline.

'I'm afraid not. He's on holiday.'

'And when will he be back?'

'In a fortnight.'

'Oh, God.' The news was not really particularly crushing, but to Caroline it seemed that way. She felt tears rising into her eyes, heard her voice quiver. 'Well – well, thank you.'

'Are you all right? Is it urgent in some way?' The girl sounded concerned.

'Well – yes. In some way. Yes, it is.'

'Well, look. He's only at home. I'm not allowed to give you his number, but he's in the book. He lives in St John's Wood.'

'Oh,' said Caroline, 'oh, thank you very much.'

'One of Joe's young ladies from the sound of it,' said his secretary, putting down the phone. 'When will he ever learn?'

Joe Payton's voice sounded different on the phone: just as sexy, but lazier, less businesslike. 'Yes?' he said. 'Yes, this is Joe Payton. What can I do for you?'

'Well basically,' said Caroline, 'you can listen to me.'

'I'm listening.'

'But it's a bit difficult on the phone.'

'I always thought that's what phones were for.'

'Well – this is very complicated. And personal. We couldn't – meet, could we?'

'I don't know. I'm a very busy man. Are you beautiful?'

'Not very,' said Caroline, smiling in spite of herself. 'But I could do my best. Brush my hair and put on some make-up, that sort of thing.'

'What's your name, and just, briefly, what is this about?'

'My name is Caroline Hunterton, and just briefly, I once – well, I knew Byron Patrick. I heard you on the radio the other day.'

'And . . .?'

'And, I didn't know he'd died.'

'And . . .?'

'And – well, I need to find his – his daughter.'

'His daughter! Did you say his daughter?'

'Yes. Yes, I did.'

'Miss Hunterton, this sounds like a wonderful story. Of course I'll meet you. Do you want to come round?'

'Well, I can't exactly come round.'

'Why not?'

'Because I'm not in London. I'm in Suffolk.'

'Oh. Oh, I see. Well, what about tomorrow? Shall I meet you somewhere? Shall we have lunch?'

'That would be nice. Yes, thank you.'

'OK. Let's see, there's a funny old place in Fleet Street called the Coffee House Club. Just opposite the law courts. I'll meet you there at one, if that's OK.'

'All right. Thank you. Thank you very much indeed.'

'But, Mummy, you did say you'd take me to Ipswich tomorrow. To look for a dress for Sarah's party. You promised.' Chloe looked up at her mother from the breakfast table, her brown eyes large with misery, and in her anguish knocked the jug of orange juice over. 'Oh, sorry. Sorry.' She started dabbing at it frantically with her napkin.

'Chloe, leave that, you're just making things worse. Get Mrs Jarvis to do it in a minute. I'm sorry about tomorrow, but I can't. Something very important has come up and I have to go to London. We can go to Ipswich the next day.'

'But I'm going to stay with her the next day, and then it's the party. Mummy, please can't we go? Or couldn't I come to London with you, and wait while you do this important thing, and then we could go and find a dress, in Harrods or somewhere?'

'No, Chloe, it's out of the question. You've got plenty of dresses, you'll have to wear one of them.'

'They're all too small for me. And it's such an important party.'

'Nonsense. They're fine. And you're only thirteen, it can't possibly be an important party.'

'I'm nearly fourteen and it is. There are going to be boys.'

'Boys! Oh, my God.' Toby clasped his hands together and rolled his eyes towards the ceiling. 'Better be careful, Chloe, you might get raped.' He was twelve and in his last year at prep school: large for his age, good-looking, arrogant. His mother spoilt him disastrously.

'Not likely,' said Jolyon, 'none of them would even look at her, never mind rape her. They'll go for the pretty girls. Or at least the less ugly ones.' Jolyon was two years younger than Toby, gentler, nicer, still badly behaved, still spoilt.

'Be quiet both of you,' said Caroline. 'Chloe, I'm sorry, but I really can't take you. Maybe we could go into Colchester early on Wednesday morning, before you go to Sarah's.'

'No, it's all right,' said Chloe. 'Don't worry, Mummy. I'll wear one of the ones I've got. I'll breathe in a bit.'

'It'll have to be a lot with that stomach,' said Toby.

'Well if you're sure . . .' said Caroline.

'Of course,' said Chloe.

Caroline looked at her and thought that Toby had struck home. Chloe was pretty, in an English rose kind of way with her dark red hair and her creamy skin, but she was definitely overweight. She really must try to get her to do something about it. 'All right, darling. That's very nice of you. I'll make it up to you some other time.'

'Fine.' Chloe smiled at her mother and went in search of Mrs Jarvis to enlist her help with clearing up the orange juice. But she knew her mother wouldn't. Caroline didn't put a great deal of effort into making things up to her.

Caroline didn't have the faintest idea what Joe Payton was going to be like. She had somehow expected someone slightly middle-aged, wearing a suit; not a tall, rangy, attractive creature, clearly several years younger than she was, with rather long, floppy blond-streaked brown hair, piercing green eyes, and a peculiarly soft shy smile, wearing a big shaggy grey jumper and blue jeans. She immediately felt rather silly in the smart going-to-London outfit she had chosen from her crowded wardrobe with great care that morning (mindful of Joe Payton's interest in her appearance): a cream bouclé wool suit, just covering her knees, and very high-heeled, very pointed-toed shoes. She felt at once over-dressed and country bumpkinish, and her hair, flicked up neatly at the sides, seemed suddenly stiff and formal, her eye make-up black and heavy and clearly ageing.

Nevertheless Joe Payton stood up as she approached the table and smiled appreciatively. He didn't see a formal suit or a stiff hairstyle, he saw a tall woman with a perfect oval face, creamy skin, oddly hungry blue eyes, hair of a ravishing dark red, and a great length of very good leg ending in particularly slender feet. Joe was a connoisseur of beautiful women; he also knew a class act when he saw one.

He held out his hand. 'Mrs Hunterton, I presume?'

Caroline hesitated briefly. 'Well – yes.'

'You don't seem too sure.'

'Well – no – that is, yes. But please call me Caroline.'

'OK, Caroline. Call me Joe.'

'This really is very kind of you – Joe.'

'My pleasure. Now this is a funny old place, but it's quiet and the steak's great and the wine is wonderful. And although it's full of journalists, they're the quiet kind. Quiet drunks.' He smiled at her again. 'What would you like to drink?'

Caroline looked round the room, an odd blend of café and grill room, with its yellow-brown walls and its old-style waiters, and at Joe's reassuring, ravishing smile, and felt her nervousness leave her. 'A gin and tonic please.'

'Ah. That's what I like. A real lunch-time drinker. None of this small sherry nonsense. Michael, two gin and tonics please. And then we'll order quickly. As we have very important business to attend to, don't we, Caroline?'

'Yes, yes, we do.'

'Do you like steak?'

'Yes. Or cutlets if they have them.'

'They do. Good idea. Pink, I presume? Thought so. Michael, lamb cutlets, rare for two and some veg, and a bottle of the '57 Beaune. Now then, fire away.'

'Well, it's –' She was suddenly tongue-tied, not knowing where to begin. 'Oh, dear, I don't know where to start.'

'Let me ask you some questions, like a good journalist. How did you meet Byron Patrick?'

'He was a GI. He came to Suffolk, where I live, in the war. Only he wasn't called Byron Patrick. He was called Brendan FitzPatrick.'

'Jesus, what a wonderful name. Only Hollywood could change that. OK. So what happened next?'

She was silent.

'Sorry, not a leading enough question. So you got along really well? You must have been – what? Twelve? Did he give you chewing gum?'

She laughed. 'He did actually. But I was a little more than twelve. I was twenty when I met him.'

'Living with Mummy and Daddy?'

'Well – yes.'

'And, forgive the blunt Fleet Street question, but did you have an affair with him?'

'Yes. Yes, I did. Look, this isn't going to be published, is it?'

'Of course not. Don't be ridiculous. Caroline, you don't have to tell me anything. You can ask all the questions if you like. I just started because you didn't. I'm not very subtle, I'm afraid.'

She took a large mouthful of the gin and tonic. It tasted very strong. She felt herself relaxing. 'All right. Let me ask. Did you ever meet him?'

'Oh, no. He died in 1957, long before I wrote the book.'

'Nineteen fifty-seven?' She was silent again. So Fleur had been twelve. Just twelve.

'You didn't know that?'

'No. No, I didn't. Until I heard you on the radio, I thought he was still alive.'

'But you'd lost touch?'

'Yes. Oh, yes.'

To her horror she felt tears stinging her eyes, a lump in her throat; she looked down, away from Joe. He caught the flash of tears, studied her bent head, and felt an overpowering urge to caress her slender, suddenly vulnerable neck. He put his hand over hers instead.

'Look, don't be embarrassed crying in front of me. I cry a lot myself. I cry in films. I cry at weddings. I even cry on Christmas Day. If I were you I'd be blubbing my head off.'

She looked up at him and smiled shakily. 'You're being awfully nice to me.'

'Well, I like pretty ladies.'

'Oh.'

'Now let's get on. Ask me some more questions.'

'How did you find out about Brendan?'

'Well, like I said, I was researching this book. Looking out for scandal. I looked up all the old columns Hedda Hopper and Louella Parsons wrote – you know they were – are – the Hollywood gossip queens. And got out all the back files of *Confidential* – you know about *Confidential*?'

She shook her head. 'Not really.'

'You haven't missed much really. It was the most powerful and the most feared publication in Hollywood at that time. It claimed to "tell the facts and name the names" which made it sound more as if it conducted a fearless search after truth, rather than the filth-peddling it actually was. They used hidden mikes and telephoto lenses and infra-red film, and sent private detectives and hookers in pursuit of the people they were trying to nail. Nasty stuff. They made the terrible twins look like innocent cub reporters by comparison. I came across Byron – Brendan – quite late in my investigations. There was just a small paragraph about him. It was actually something they'd picked up from another rag, something very small and a great deal tackier. If that's possible. And less accurate,' he added hastily.

She looked at him intently, almost frightened. 'What did it say?'

'Oh,' said Joe easily, 'it said, you know, he was living with this woman, this studio head, and she'd, well, got tired of him.'

'That's not what you said on the radio.'

'Wasn't it?' He looked at her wide-eyed, and drained his glass.

'No. You know it wasn't. You said there'd been some dirt.'

'Yes, well there was, but I don't remember quite what.'

'You're a liar.'

'Yes, I am.'

'Please tell me.'

He looked at her anxiously. 'Look, Caroline, it wasn't very nice – dirt.'

'Dirt isn't often nice.'

'Oh, I don't know,' said Joe cheerfully. 'There's dirt and dirt. But this was dirty dirt.'

'I want to know what it was.'

'Really? You sure?'

'Yes, of course I'm sure,' said Caroline irritably. 'I wasn't born yesterday. As you can very well see,' she added inconsequentially. The gin was making her head spin slightly.

'I can indeed see that. I can see you are a very worldly, very sexy and probably very wise woman. The kind I like. How's that?'

'Flattering,' said Caroline, laughing.

'Good. Have another gin.'

'No, thank you. But they could pour that wine.'

'I think it's breathing or something.'

'Well, let's suffocate it.'

'You're really fun,' he said. 'I like you.'

'Now tell me the dirt.'

'Well,' he said carefully, watching her face, 'it seems there had been implications of homosexuality.'

Caroline felt the table rock slightly beneath her. She stared at Joe, trying to sort his words into sense. 'But – but that's ridiculous. Really.'

'Yes, of course it is,' said Joe, relieved at her reaction. 'Most of what those rags print is ridiculous. Was. They've gone now, the worst of them.'

'So how could it hurt him? Saying he was homosexual when he clearly wasn't.'

'Well, mud sticks. And Hollywood's a sticky place.'

'Is this – this part of the story in your book?'

'Yes, it is,' said Joe simply. 'But no details, just that there had been these stories about him, implying that he was homosexual.'

'Pretty irresponsible,' said Caroline coldly, 'when you didn't know if it was true.'

'I saw the cuttings. And whether they were true or not, that was not the point of my story. The point is that lies in Hollywood get to be believed. If they're interesting enough.'

'I see. So you think this woman he was living with believed it?'

'I imagine so, yes.'

'And drummed him out of the studio?'

'Something like that. Well, actually yes, she did. Literally. Turned him out of his apartment. Like I said, he was sleeping on the beach.'

'And – and he was killed by a car?'

'Yes,' said Joe Payton, very quietly, watching her. 'He was. While – while he was drunk apparently.'

'Who told you that?'

'A wonderful old dame called Yolande duGrath. She was Byron's – Brendan's – drama coach. And a good friend to him. She really tried to help him. She was very fond of him. She said he was one of the good guys.'

'Yes,' said Caroline, hearing the catch in her voice, trying to control it, 'yes, he was. Definitely.' She waited, struggling to control herself. 'And – and is he buried there?'

'Yes, he is. Over in the valley. At the back of the Hills. Yolande went to his funeral.'

'Was there anyone else there?'

'Well, his mother and his sisters. And his – his girlfriend, she said.'

'Ah.' Well, there would have been a girlfriend, Caroline Hunterton, what do you expect, you silly cow. You have a husband and three more children. Naturally he would have a girlfriend. Caroline stood up suddenly. 'I – just have to find the Ladies,' she said. 'Excuse me.'

In the Ladies she sat and cried quite hard for about two minutes and then felt calm again. She washed her face, repaired her make-up and went back to the table, with a bright smile. 'Sorry about that.'

'That's all right.' Joe Payton looked at her thoughtfully, almost tenderly, and then he said, 'Don't mind me. Nobody does. Look, your cutlets have arrived. Pink and pretty. *Bon appétit*. Have some more wine.'

'Thank you.'

'Whereabouts in Suffolk do you live?' he said, clearly anxious to change the subject.

'Quite near Framlingham. Do you know it?'

'A bit. My second wife lived in Ipswich.'

'Do you have a third wife?'

'No. I'm not fit for marriage.'

'What went wrong?' she said, genuinely curious.

'I suppose I haven't grown up yet.'

'And how old is not grown up?'

'Oh, I'm twenty-eight.'

'That's young to be a film critic and have written a book.'

'Yes, well, I didn't waste time going to university or any of that nonsense. What about you?'

'Oh, I didn't waste time going to university either.'

'No, you silly woman, I mean are you married? Still? Not divorced or anything?'

'Oh, yes,' said Caroline. 'Yes, I'm married.'

'Children?'

'Three. A girl and two boys.'

'How old?'

'Chloe is nearly fourteen, Toby's twelve, Jolyon's ten.'

'You must have heard it a hundred times, but you really don't look old enough. Chloe, Toby and Jolyon. Very upmarket. And what does Mr Hunterton do?'

'He's an antique dealer.'

'And do you live in a grand house? And have ancient retainers and ride to hounds?'

'Quite grand, I suppose.' She smiled at him, enjoying herself, suddenly willing to play the part he was casting her in, that of a glamorous older woman. 'The retainers are quite young and I do ride to hounds.'

'And have a passionate affair with your groom, I dare say.'

'Fairly passionate,' said Caroline. 'Certainly we're very close.'

'Well it all sounds like a film script to me. You don't have a title as well, do you?'

'Actually,' said Caroline, slightly shamefaced, 'yes, I do.'

'I knew it. I knew you were a high-class bird. So you're – what? Lady Hunterton?'

'Yes.'

'Wow.' He looked at her, smiling, appreciating her heightened colour, her widened smile. 'You know I really am enjoying this.'

'So am I,' said Caroline, 'and I was dreading it. Now – could we get back to Brendan?'

'If we have to. I was rather hoping we'd get on to me.'

'In time, maybe. So there wasn't a – little girl at the funeral?'

'No. Well, not as far as I know.'

'And Yolande – this drama coach – she didn't tell you about her?'

'Absolutely not, no.'

'Honestly?'

'Honestly.'

'Oh.' She was silent again. Then she looked up and met his eyes very directly. 'I have to find her. I simply have to. Do you think I could write to the drama coach? Or the girlfriend?'

'You could. If you like. Er – who exactly is this little girl?'

'I told you. Brendan's daughter.'

'Ah, yes. But – but who's her mother?'

She looked at him, her eyes wounded and afraid.

He took a deep breath, covered her hand with his. 'You?'

'Yes.'

'Ah.'

'Let me tell you about it.'

'You don't have to.'

'I want to.'

'Go on then. Have some more wine.'

She had some more wine and told him. It took a long time.

'But I gave him the baby,' she finished. 'I'd never signed the adoption papers, you see, so I arranged for him to have her, to take her home to America. And that made sort of sense of it all, him having our baby, taking care of her, loving her. And that was the last time I saw him.'

She looked up; Joe was staring at her, his green eyes full of tears; one rolled down his face and splashed on to his brown wrist. He wiped it away and got out his handkerchief, blew his nose.

'I told you I cried easily,' he said.

Caroline smiled at him shakily. 'I thought journalists were supposed to be tough, thick-skinned, cynical people.'

'They are. I just haven't been trained properly.'

'I see.'

'Christ,' he said, 'what a story! What a fucking awful thing to happen. It must have been very – painful.'

'Yes,' she said, 'it was. But you see why I have to find her. I have to know who's looking after her. If anyone is.'

Chapter 7

1960

Joe sat down at his desk as soon as he got back to his flat, and wrote a long letter to Yolande duGrath. He told her everything he had learnt from Caroline that day, explaining why she needed to find Fleur; he said he assumed Yolande might well have known about the child, but hadn't mentioned her in order to protect her. He said he respected Yolande's loyalty, but he felt if she could now help Caroline, she should. He added that he swore on his mother's bible (women, particularly older women, were always impressed by mothers and their bibles) he wouldn't write about any of it, and he asked Yolande to write back to him as soon as possible. He added that Caroline was a really nice woman and was obviously acting with the best possible intentions. 'There is no way she's a stringer for *Confidential* or the *Screws of the World*.'

He went out and posted the letter, picked up a packet of fish and chips and went home and thought about Caroline.

He had really liked Caroline. He had been disturbed by Caroline. Sexually and emotionally she was strong stuff. She was also rather beautiful, with her pale skin and that glorious hair, and her racehorse-like body. And those legs . . . Joe gave up some time to contemplating Caroline's legs. It wasn't just their length. It was the way they moved. She somehow seemed to glide on them; they propelled her forward in one smooth easy movement, rather than in a series of steps. She should have been a model: she'd have made a fortune. Only clearly she didn't need a fortune: had one already. Lady Hunterton! God. Joe had never had an affair with a real lady. He liked the idea. She was also clearly a mass of pent-up emotion, the lady; there was a tension about her, a sense of agitation. OK, it had been an emotive occasion, and a bloody awful shock, and in fact she had handled it well, taken the story on the chin. Poor cow. What a hideous filthy business. But he had the feeling that she brought intensity with her, to everything. Particularly to bed. And she was obviously frustrated. Probably hadn't had a good old bang since her Brendan had left her. Poor woman, poor poor woman. Well, maybe he should regard her as a cause, see it as his duty to relieve her from her frustration. It would certainly be no hardship. But then it could all get a bit heavy. Partly the intensity and partly the old boy. Joe presumed he was old; he sounded old from the way she had talked about him. Maybe he should steer clear. He had got into terrible trouble with over-intense married ladies before. On the other hand, she had clearly found him sexy too . . .

Most women found Joe sexy. It had led him into trouble, that fact, all his life: the first time when he had been only fifteen years old. Joe was the much loved younger son of rather elderly parents; his brother was nineteen years older than he was, and Joe had come as a considerable shock to his mother, Patricia, who had been serenely confident that the five months that had passed since her last period had signified the start of the menopause rather than the conception of Joe. It was only when her middle-age spread began to seem rather concentrated on her stomach and she noticed an increasing sensation of what felt like wind in her lower abdomen that she went rather nervously to her doctor and learnt that in a little less than four months she would be a mother again.

Mrs Payton was delighted; Mr Payton, less so, and young Master Payton, about to go to university to read engineering, was embarrassed and appalled. From the moment he learnt of Joe's existence Nigel hated him; he hated his mother's swollen body, he hated her increasing ill-health, he hated the labour pains he was forced to witness (being alone in the house with her) until the ambulance arrived, and most of all he hated the thought of what his parents must have been doing to result in all this.

Then Joe was a most beautiful child, everyone said so, with his blond hair and his most unusual green eyes, where Nigel was and always had been plain; Joe had charm where Nigel was shy; he was sunny where Nigel was dour. His parents doted on him, and Nigel's steady but modest successes at university were totally eclipsed by Joe's progress through sitting, crawling, walking and talking. The day Nigel brought the news home of his first job, the excitement was entirely pre-empted by Joe being able to ride his tricycle; his engagement to his long-term girlfriend was as nothing to Joe writing his name in joined-up writing; and the purchase of his first house was completely swallowed up by Joe passing his eleven-plus to the grammar school.

Mr Payton was a clerk with the local council; the little family lived in a small, immaculately kept house in Croydon. They were hard up, but careful, and they could afford such essentials for Joe as his uniform and a bike, so that he could keep up with the other boys at the grammar school, although they never had a car or went away on holiday; sometimes in the summer Mr Payton would hire a car for a week, and they would go out for days. Joe never minded sitting in the back of the car while they drove slowly and carefully round the leafy lanes of Surrey, or out on to the Hog's Back, picnicking on the running board and then climbing back in again; most boys of his age would have been wild with boredom, but he was perfectly happy, chatting to his parents, and looking out of the window, spotting car numbers and making a careful study of his particular passion which was motorbikes. He could tell you not only the make and the year of every motorbike that passed, but where it had been built, its engine capacity and the fuel most suited to its running.

Joe was usually perfectly happy; he had a sunny, outgoing nature and nothing ruffled him. He didn't much like his elder brother, but that was the only cloud in his sky. He worked hard at school, did well, was polite to his parents and their friends, and was constantly held up to other boys as an example of how they should behave. If he hadn't been so patently normal and good in a fight, he would have been wildly unpopular.

And then he discovered girls.

By the time he was thirteen he was taking them to the pictures, and at fourteen delving into their knickers at parties or behind the bushes in the park. At fifteen he was relieved of his virginity in the bus shelter, by Denise Decker from the launderette; the experience of real sex seemed to him so wonderful it was all he could do not to burst into the front room and shout about it to his parents.

Shortly after that he fell in love: the object of his passion was one Michelle Humphries and she was in the corresponding form to his at the girls' grammar school. Michelle was very pretty with blonde hair and blue eyes; she was a hot-blooded young person, with a reputation for being something of a tease, but she was also known to have Done It on occasions with the right person and under the right circumstances. Joe Payton, already considered very much the heart-throb of the fourth and the fifth, could clearly be seen to Michelle to be the right person; unfortunately the right circumstances – the absence of Michelle's parents at the cinema – changed to the wrong when the film was so popular and the rain so heavy that Mr and Mrs Humphries decided to return home again, and found their daughter in flagrante with Joe in her pink and white very virginal-looking bedroom. Once it was clearly established that Michelle was not pregnant, she was forbidden ever to see Joe again, and for their part the Paytons told Joe that should the incident repeat itself, he would have to leave school forthwith and forgo university.

Joe's sex drive and his outstanding looks being what they were, he was out of school, married with a pregnant wife and working for the local branch of Sainsbury's within six months. He accepted this with good nature; he really hadn't wanted to marry Sonia Rees, only daughter of Mr and Mrs Rees who kept the King's Head, but he was prepared to meet his responsibilities, she was fun and they had a wonderful time in bed.

They had a couple of rooms at the King's Head which they could call their own, Sonia was still working at the hairdresser's, and they were perfectly happy until she fell down the stairs one night and lost the baby.

After that things deteriorated swiftly: Sonia became deeply depressed, Mrs Rees's dislike of Joe became a pathological hatred, and a year after the marriage they were applying for a divorce. Joe was twenty when the divorce came through (having obligingly supplied the adulterous grounds), and had got a job in the accounts department of the *Daily Mail*. While there, he studied how the newspaper worked, made friends with some of the journalists, and in due course applied for and got a job as a junior reporter on the *Sunday Dispatch*.

'And the rest,' as he was fond of saying to anyone (usually female) who would care to listen, 'is history. Moved on to the sports pages, had an affair with one of the show-business reporters, started reviewing films when someone else was too drunk to write it up one night.'

He also got married again, under the misapprehension that his second wife was as enthusiastic about sex and him as she purported to be; when she proved to be equally disinterested in both subjects he returned (but not before putting considerable effort into his marriage) to his bachelor existence. He was divorced for the second time on his twenty-sixth birthday. In and around his marriages, women continued to fall helplessly in love with him.

Joe's success with women was due for the most part to one simple fact: he liked them. The other factors in his personal equation: his considerable good looks, the sense of ease he carried about with him, his untidy, slightly shaggy appearance, and his tendency to cry at any moment of high, or even low, emotion, while all guaranteed to make any female want to be with him and take care of him for the rest of their lives, were as nothing compared with his patent pleasure in their company. Joe did not simply flatter women by telling them they were beautiful or sexy or clever, he did so by appreciating them. In an age where most men were still intent on hanging on to their superior positions in society, and treating most women like chattels or vessels or both, to find one who actually asked women their advice and took it, listened intently to their views on things, encouraged them to pursue their own careers, read their magazines, sat and watched them while they got dressed and made up their faces and did their hair with a kind of serious interest, sympathized with their PMT and their period pains, looked at babies in prams, and actually enjoyed going shopping and comparing this dress and what it might do for its owner with that one, was totally, seriously, and overwhelmingly irresistible.

Joe switched on his television and opened another bottle of beer. He'd have a snooze in front of *Perry Mason*, and then go out. He'd heard there was to be a big party in Chelsea that night; he'd go down to Finch's in the King's Road and see if he could find it. Caroline Hunterton had aroused him; he felt in need of sex. And he plainly couldn't have it with her. Or not yet . . .

'Can I go up to a matinée this Saturday?' Fleur looked up from *I Love Lucy* at her grandmother. 'I'd really really love to go.'

'Do you have any money? Because I certainly can't afford to give you any.' Kathleen sounded weary; it had been a long day. She really was too old to be standing serving in a shop, and the customers at the M & B clothing store in Sheepshead Bay weren't exactly the most courteous or considerate.

'Yes, I do. I got a whole lot babysitting last night for that putrid little creep of a child of Mary Donetti's. First he screamed, then he ate, then he puked, then he filled his diapers, then he screamed some more. God, how I hate babies! I never, ever intend to have any babies.'

'I'll remind you of that,' said Kathleen, 'when you're married and mooning over cribs.'

'I do not intend to go mooning over a man, let alone a crib.'

'Well, we'll see. What is it you want to see on Saturday?'

'*Luther*, I've heard it's just wonderful. So would that be OK?'

'I suppose so. Yes, of course. But I think you might switch that rubbish off now and go and do some studying.'

'OK, Grandma. I will. And I'll come and help you with dinner just as soon as you're ready.'

'You're a good girl, Fleur.'

'I try to be. Hey, did you hear about Clark Gable?'

'What in particular about Clark Gable?'

'He just died.'

'He died! Well for heaven's sake. And it only seems like yesterday he was carrying Scarlett O'Hara up the stairs in *Gone with the Wind*.'

'Yes, Grandma, I know, but it was twenty years ago. Well, I don't suppose he'll be having some tacky funeral at the Wee Kirk of the Heather.'

'Fleur, that was not a tacky funeral. It was – well, just how they do things over there.'

'It was tacky.'

'Well,' said Kathleen with a sigh, 'I don't suppose it made any difference to your father.'

'No. Which reminds me, I must write a letter to Miss duGrath. She sent me a really nice card for my birthday.'

'Fleur, that was months ago.'

'I know. I'm sorry. I'll do it after dinner, I promise.'

Fleur went up to her room slowly, her thoughts half occupied with Saturday's matinée and half with her father. She liked thinking about him, and talking about him; it kept him alive in her. The violent, passionate grief had long gone, but she still ached in a small, sad place for him every day of her life.

She paused in the middle of getting her books out, gazing out of the window, remembering the funeral. It had been tacky, it had, it had, standing there in the chapel, just her and Grandma and the aunts, a couple of people she didn't know, and kind, lovely Miss duGrath holding her hand as tightly one side as her grandmother was the other, watching the coffin go through the curtains, and vowing, fiercely, wildly, savagely, that somehow, some day, she would get even with whoever had been responsible for his death.

She still had only the haziest idea how it had all happened: he had been run over, she had been told, killed by a car on the highway, but she knew, she felt in every fibre of her aching body, as she stood with her head bent, holding back the tears with sheer willpower, that there was much more to it than that. She had heard people talking about it, had listened while Miss duGrath talked quietly to her grandmother in the next room while she was supposed to be asleep, heard her saying, 'Well, of course, it was the story really, the story and the system, that was what killed him.'

She hadn't understood what they meant by either, the story or the system, and when she had asked her grandmother the next day on the plane home, she had told her she must have misunderstood, that her father had been knocked down by a car, and that was that; ever since, whenever she had broached the subject, it had been firmly closed again.

And so she had had to wait; there was nothing she could do, she could see, until she was grown up, and when she was grown up she could find out what had really happened. Fleur was a pragmatic person; she could come to terms with anything providing it was clearly necessary. So she just concentrated on first getting over, and then remembering her father, and on doing well enough at school to be sure of getting into college and then getting the kind of job that would convert her from being a helpless, moneyless schoolgirl into a powerful rich woman. Powerful rich women could do anything, Fleur knew: and anything included wreaking revenge on whoever needed it wreaking on them.

Fleur at fifteen was clever, ambitious and talented: she looked extraordinarily like her father, with his almost black curly hair, his dark blue eyes, his slender build, his considerable height. She was already five foot nine and rising, as Kathleen was fond of saying, and her height was largely in her legs, long, slender, colt-like legs. At the moment, the height was a disadvantage, for she towered over the boys, and they all went for little neat girls like Susie Coltretti and Maria Fendi, with their great breasts and tiny waists; but Fleur didn't mind, she could see, simply by looking at their mothers, that in the fullness of time Susie and Maria would be fat instead of charmingly plump, their olive complexions adorned with already just-discernible moustaches, their rounded, swaying hips descended helplessly into great solid plateaux, and she would still be thin, lithe, rangily sexy, and she was content to wait.

She was always top of every class, every subject; she excelled in maths, she had a grasp of physics and Latin that awed her classmates into silence, and she had never got below an A minus for English, but nobody minded, nobody taunted her with being a swot, because she was also brilliant at games; she could run faster and jump higher than most of the boys, and she could wield a baseball bat more ferociously and more effectively than most of them too. And then there was her power of mimicry: Fleur FitzPatrick, it was well known, could not just take off Mr Lowell the music master, she became him, with his careful, over-light walk, his waving hands, his slightly manic gaze, while her impression of Mr Hicks, the head, with his awkward, self-conscious air, his rather desperate way of looking round a room, was so exact that even the staff, confronted by it, would delay rebuking her (having found her, in flagrante, so to speak) for as long as they dared in order to savour its delights. Everyone said she should be an actress; but Fleur had seen enough, in her short life, of the problems, the deprivations, the heartaches of the theatre, and she had no stomach for any of it. She wanted to shine on a different stage: one where there was less competition and more opportunity. She wasn't sure of the exact nature of the stage yet, but she knew she would find it.

Luther was wonderful; Fleur came out of the theatre her head spinning with Osborne's prose, Finney's mastery of the role and the stage. Sitting on the D train, heading back for Sheepshead Bay, mindful of her promise to Kathleen not to be roaming New York after dark, she pondered on its Englishness and how much she had liked it, appreciated it. Well, she was half English: occasionally she allowed her mind to drift towards that fact, even explored it. She didn't know much about her mother; her father had been economical, to put it mildly, in his description of her, promising to tell her more when she was older. And now she needed so desperately to know, needed to understand, to find out about what this mysterious, cold (for she must have been cold), unloving (and certainly she must have been unloving) person who had borne her and then rejected her, given her away because she was inconvenient, an unsuitable accessory to her life, and, all right, given her to her father, but what kind of mother gave her child away to anybody, particularly allowed her to be taken thousands of miles away from her caring and her love? Now she needed so badly to know what she looked like, sounded like, what sort of life she led, how she passed her time, what amused her, interested her, bored her, what she liked doing, eating, reading: and did she have other children and who was their father, and did they know, and what did they want to know about her? All these questions occupied Fleur's attention to an increasingly considerable degree; and she could not see how she was ever going to find an answer to them. Normally, she didn't even talk to her grandmother about it; she knew it distressed her, knew moreover that there was very little that even she could put into the rather fragile equation. But tonight, her head filled with English history and English language, an odd sense of estrangement somewhere in her heart, she felt she must confront Kathleen with it all, yet again, force her attention on to it.

Over supper (pizza from Wiesens, bought as a present for just the two of them, to save Kathleen cooking), she looked at her with her father's eyes and said, 'Grandma, do you really know nothing about my mother?'

And Kathleen, recognizing that the time had come for Fleur to learn as much as she was able to tell her, took a deep breath, opened the bottle of Irish whiskey that she kept in the sideboard for occasions of great importance, and began to talk.

At much the same time, in her small, messy appartment, the walls of every room including the bathroom peppered with signed photographs of virtually every great name and famous face that had appeared on the cinema screen over the past twenty years, Yolande duGrath read and reread the letter from the charming young English journalist to whom she had rather rashly (she could now see) talked at such great length a year or so previously and wondered how much she should trust him, and whether she had any right to break the confidence of another young man who had placed his sad and extremely intricate history within her care.

'Could I speak with Lady Hunterton please?'

'One moment please. Who can I say is calling?'

'This is Joe Payton.'

'Please hold on, Mr Payton.'

There was a silence; Joe tried to imagine what the scene at the other end might be: what kind of a house and a set-up Caroline inhabited, who would be answering her phone in that prehistoric way. She was an interesting project, that was for sure.

'Lady Hunterton is down at the stables with the children at the moment, sir. Can I ask her to call you?'

'Yes, please. She has my number.'

'Very good, sir.'

The phone rang quite soon; Caroline sounded nervy, impatient. 'Joe? Yes? What news?'

'Er – Caroline.' He wasn't liking this. 'Caroline, I'm really sorry, but Yolande wrote back. She doesn't have any idea where Fleur might be. She doesn't really know anything about her. She said Byron – Brendan – never talked about her. I'm terribly sorry.'

'Oh.' It was a small, sad sound. 'Oh well. I suppose it was hoping too much.'

'Not really. I mean it wasn't hoping too much. She just can't help. She would if she could, I'm sure. She was terribly fond of Brendan. She ended up his only friend really.'

'Yes. Well, maybe she was.' The voice was chilly suddenly, hostile.

'Caroline, believe me, she was. She really tried to help him through those last awful months.'

'Joe, Brendan was a talker. He talked to everybody about everything. If this Yolande person had been his friend, he would have told her about Fleur and about me, and about – well, everything. I know he would. I don't think she can have been a friend at all. Not a real friend.'

'Well, I don't know, Caroline. I can only tell you what she said to me. And I'm sorry. You're obviously upset.'

'Oh, I'm not upset,' she said, the words heavy and harsh down the phone. 'Just a daughter, lost, out there somewhere, a daughter who probably thinks I abandoned her at birth. Of course I'm upset. Goodbye, Joe.'

She put the phone down. It rang again at once.

'Caroline, listen. I don't know what I can say to make you feel better, obviously nothing at all really. But I'm terribly sorry you feel so bad. And I want to help. What can I do? I don't know.' He paused. Then, 'I could buy you another lunch. I'd like that.'

'No,' she said and he could hear her smiling, relaxing into the phone, 'no, you have better things to do than buy expensive lunches for neurotic women.'

'I can't think,' he said, 'of anything better in the world than buying expensive lunches for women, neurotic or otherwise. I love eating and I love women. Go on, let me. Maybe we can come up with something.'

'You're very sweet,' said Caroline, 'and I'm sorry I got cross with you. It's not your fault. Any of it. And you've been terribly kind. But honestly, I don't think it would serve any purpose.'

'Yes, it would. It would give me pleasure. That's a very worthy purpose.'

'No, Joe. But thank you anyway. Goodbye.'

'Goodbye,' he said and put the phone down, feeling bleak.

'Is that Joe?'

'It is.'

'Joe, it's Caroline.'

'I knew you'd come round to the idea in the end. It's a bit short notice for today, but I could manage tomorrow.'

'No, you fool. I'm not ringing about lunch.'

'Pity. What then?'

'I've been thinking. Putting what I know of Brendan with what you know of Yolande. It doesn't add up. I bet she does know about Fleur. I bet she even knows exactly where she is. I think she just didn't want to tell you.'

'Why not?'

'Because she doesn't trust you. I wouldn't.'

'That's a very offensive thing to say. All forthcoming invitations to lunch hereby cancelled.'

'Joe, you're a journalist. It was a journalist who killed her friend.'

'No, it wasn't. You haven't read my book. It was the Hollywood system.'

'I have read your book, and I loved it –'

'You did? Really?'

'Really.'

'Invitation to lunch reinstated. Immediately. If there's one thing no author can resist it's someone loving what they write. It's a real turn-on.'

'Well I'm glad I just turned you on. But –'

'Are you really? Did you mean that?'

'Joe, please listen to me.'

'I am listening to you. It's wonderful.'

'Joe, please! Listen, I'm quite sure that if this Yolande person had been Brendan's friend, she would have known about Fleur. But I also think she'd want to protect her. So I think she does know and she won't tell you.'

'So?'

'So I thought I'd write to her. And explain. Ask her to help me. That is, if you give me her address. What do you think?'

'I don't know, Caroline. I really don't know.' He sounded guarded.

'But, Joe, why? What harm can it do?'

There was a silence. Then, 'It could harm you. Hurt you.'

'So?'

'So I wouldn't like that.'

'Oh.'

'Because I like you.'

'Oh.' Caroline was silent for a moment, trying to analyse the emotion that was surfacing in her, over her frustration and pain. She realized with a pang of recognition that it was sexual in origin and an odd combination of delight and desire. She crushed it hastily.

'Well, that's really kind of you and I do appreciate it, but honestly, Joe, I'll risk it. If you'll only let me. Give me the address, please.'

'Well, I'll think about it.'

'Oh, for God's sake,' said Caroline. 'Joe, this is my daughter we're talking about. Not some silly story. Now will you or will you not give me Yolande duGrath's address?'

'On one condition.'

'All right,' she said, smiling into the telephone, trying to ignore the delicious warmth melting into her body, focused primarily somewhere in the region of her belly, 'all right, I'll have lunch with you.'

'Good. Tomorrow at one.'

'Same place?'

'No. Not the same place. Come to the Guinea. It's in Bruton Lane, just off Berkeley Square. Best wine list in London. See you there at one.'

'Oh, my God,' said Fleur. 'Oh, my God.'

'Fleur, whatever is it? You look as if you've seen a ghost.'

'What? Oh, sorry, Grandma. No, I'm just fine. I – just remembered I had an exam this morning, and I didn't revise the right stuff. I – just have to go up to my room and find the books. Excuse me.'

Back in her room, she sat on her bed; she felt sick and shaken, her body somehow bereft of substance. She took the letter out of the envelope and began to read it again.

My dear Fleur,

It was really good to get your very nice letter, and I'm glad you liked the card. I envy you seeing Luther; we don't get enough serious drama over here.

I was so pleased to have news from you; it sounds as if you are going to make a real stir in New York in the next few years. Scriptwriting sounds a wonderful idea, although maybe a little difficult to get a foothold in initially. Certainly majoring in literature is the right first step. When the time comes, then, yes, of course you must get in touch with me and I will do what I can.

Fleur, I have some news for you. I have thought very carefully about telling you this, and I have decided you are old enough to make your own decision about pursuing it. When I was your age I was married, and I would have thought ill of anyone who ventured to entrust the major decisions of my life to an adult. Also, your grandmother must be getting on now and I dare say still regards you as a small girl. I did not think we should trouble her.

I have had a letter from your mother. She sounds a very nice person. She lives in England as of course you know, and is married and has a daughter only a little younger than you, and two little boys. Her husband is called Sir William Hunterton. I don't understand all those English titles, but I guess that makes her Lady something or other. Anyway, she had no idea your father had died until she heard a programme on what she calls the wireless the other day. She imagined until then that the two of you were still safely together. I expect this might explain her silence all these years. She tells me that she and your father agreed that she must never see either of you, certainly until you were quite grown up. Now she is anxious about your welfare, has no idea where you are, and wants to see you and make sure you are all right.

Anyway, I didn't want to do anything that you felt you would not welcome. You may want to see her very badly and you may not. I am therefore giving you her address, and you can make your own mind up, and get in touch with her or not as you wish. I think it would be courteous at the very least to reassure her that you are well and not living on the streets of New York as she seems to imagine.

Please write to me if you want to or have any queries that I might be able to answer, and in any case let me know what you decide to do. I have written to her and told her you have her address and that you may or may not be in touch.

I know you will do the right thing.

Your friend,

Yolande duGrath

Fleur wished she could be as certain that she would do the right thing. She felt fairly confident of doing the wrong. She felt confused, frightened, exhilarated, lost, all at once. Pleasure and happiness that her mother was concerned for her mingled with outrage that she should have dared to agree with her father that she would never see her. What kind of a mother could form such an agreement? How could anyone just hand over her child with so cool a detachment? Or be able to hold herself to it? How could she, all these years, have remained so distant? OK, so it was nice she was bothered in case her father had left her alone in the world; but if she had really loved her, really cared, she would have made sure she had some way of checking anyway, all along the way. Why hadn't she known about Kathleen, been sure to know where she and her father lived, just in case of some problem or other? It all seemed quite horribly casual: as if she, Fleur, were some package, to be handed over and got rid of with as little bother as possible.

Just the same, it would be – oh, wonderful, marvellous, to meet her mother. To see her, hear her, talk to her, know how she moved and walked and sat and ate; to feel, at last, that she had proper roots, like everybody else, was a balanced piece of creation instead of an odd hybrid born of a faceless, voiceless, impersonal creature. But then – would it? Suppose she was as detached, as cold, as unloving as Fleur had always imagined? Wouldn't that be worse even than having no one, knowing nothing?

Wouldn't it make her feel as if she too must be lacking in the most basic, crucial emotions, like warmth and tenderness? And then suppose they hated one another? Or had nothing in common, nothing to say? And had to make some excuse to part, never to meet again, a baffling blank become an unpleasant fact? Nothing, surely, would be worse than that.

But then, again, they might really get along; they might enjoy the same things, laugh at the same jokes, share the same emotions. Who could help her, and how could she know? There was no one in the world, no one at all that she knew, could dredge up from anywhere, who had the faintest knowledge of her mother, who could say, well, OK, Fleur, yes she did give you away, but she was fun and warm and concerned for you. Or, no, Fleur, she might have written now, but believe me, she is one tough proposition, and if she wasn't, she'd have got in touch with you before.

She had to make her own decision, based on no evidence of any kind, except Miss duGrath's own opinion (based on one letter), whether or not to go and find her.

It all seemed too much for Fleur; she watched the view from her window blur before her tears; and then, as she had learnt to do so many times, ever since her father had first gone away from her to Hollywood, she took a deep breath, buried the hurt and the uncertainty deep inside her, and just got on with the rest of the day. She would decide what to do later. When she had had time to think.

'Caroline, this is Joe. I was just wondering if you'd had any news?'

'No, Joe, not yet I'm afraid. You know I'd let you know if I had. I suppose – well, she must be half scared of writing. I expect it'll take her a while to get round to it.'

'Do you want to have lunch?'

'Joe, I'd love to, but I have to get Toby off to school this week. And Chloe is going back next week. There's such a lot to do.'

'Caroline, let me buy you a Christmas lunch. I'd really like that. Cheer you up, and it would certainly be fun for me.'

'Um – well, yes, all right. Yes, I'd really love to. I must say I did think I would have heard by Christmas. At the very latest. I am very much afraid she just doesn't want to have anything to do with me.'

'I don't suppose it's that, Caroline. I expect she's just scared. She is only a kid.'

'I suppose so. Joe, do you think if I sent Fleur a Christmas card to Yolande duGrath that would be a good idea? Then she could forward it. And I thought maybe I could send her a birthday present too. She'll be sixteen on New Year's Day. What do you think?'

'If you need to buy the card and the present in London, I think it would be a wonderful idea. No, seriously, why not?'

'All right then, I will. Thank you.'

* * *

'Caroline, this is Joe. I thought you might be feeling a bit blue. As it's Fleur's birthday. Happy New Year.'

'Happy New Year, Joe. And yes, I was. Am. So thank you. You're a good friend.'

'I keep hoping to be a bit less of a friend.'

'I know you do.'

'Caroline, have you heard anything yet?'

'Oh, no, Joe. I don't suppose I ever will. I don't think I even want to any more. I think she must be a rather horrid child. Not to write and thank me for the Christmas present. I mean real pearl earrings. I mean if she didn't like them, she should have had the courtesy to send them back. I mean –'

'Caroline, are you crying?'

'No, of course I'm not crying.'

'Caroline, my paper has asked me to do a series on what they call the old order. You know, class and all that. Could I come and interview you and Sir William?'

'No, of course you couldn't. You know you couldn't. Anyway, I thought you were supposed to be a film reviewer.'

'Just been promoted to features editor.'

'Congratulations, Joe. That's really good. I'm pleased for you.'

'Well, could I let you take me out for a celebration lunch?'

'Oh – I don't know. Tell you what, someone has given me and William tickets for the Centre Court at Wimbledon next week. He hates tennis, and anyway, he isn't terribly well. Why don't I take you instead? Maria Bueno is playing. Would you like that? Or does tennis bore you to tears?'

'Tennis suddenly is the thing that interests me more than anything in the world.'

'Good. Wednesday. All right?'

'All right. No news, I suppose?'

'No, Joe, no news. I won't get any news. Not now.'

It was August when the letter came. A hot, dry-as-dust day. Caroline was sitting in the garden. Chloe was playing tennis rather badly with a friend, and Jolyon and Toby were alternately mocking her and kicking a tin can round the lawn.

Dear Lady Hunterton,

You wrote to me last year. I got raped on the subway last month and now I think I might be pregnant. I don't want to tell my grandmother. Please could you send me $500 for an abortion. I imagine you must have the money.

Yours sincerely,

Fleur FitzPatrick

Chapter 8

1961–2

'I'm going to come with you,' said Joe.

'No, Joe, really you can't. What on earth would William say?'

'William doesn't have to know. I'll just meet you on the plane. Honestly, darling, I couldn't let you go through this thing on your own.'

'I'm perfectly capable of going on my own,' said Caroline, trying to suppress the warmth and sense of pleasure that was invading her at the thought of spending several days with Joe.

'I know you're capable of it, but I don't want you to. You're going to have a foul time, and I want to be able to help you through it.'

'Joe, you're so nice to me. I really don't know why you should be.'

'Two reasons. One, I like you very much indeed and feel responsible for you, and for getting you into this. Two, I live in hope of persuading you to get into bed with me. It seems to me there's a little more chance of that if we're together in New York than if you're in Suffolk and I'm in London. Just slightly more practical.'

'Joe, I am not going to go to bed with you. So you'd better not come.'

'Caroline, I'm going to come. Apart from anything else you don't know New York and I do. A bit. I can help you. Now, when are you going?'

'The day after Boxing Day,' said Caroline, seeing, welcoming defeat. 'The plane leaves at ten a.m.'

'I'll be on it. And what does William have to say about it?'

'Not a lot,' said Caroline, putting away from her the wretched memory of William's cold, bleak face, his distant voice as he listened to what she had to say and then nodded and said, 'Very well, if you must. Please let me know what you will be telling the children,' before walking out of the room.

'And the children?'

'I – haven't told them yet. I'm going to talk to Chloe now.'

'What will you tell her?'

'Oh, not very much. Some soothing lie.'

'Are you sure that's wise? She is nearly sixteen.'

'Joe, I think I know my own daughter.'

Chloe looked up from wrapping Christmas presents as her mother came into the room.

'Yes, Mummy?'

'Chloe, I'm very sorry indeed, but I have to go away for a few days after Christmas. Look, I'm sorry to interfere, but you've got that wrapping paper the wrong way round.'

'Have I? Oh, yes. Why do you have to go away?'

'An – old friend of mine is dying. She lives in America. In New York. I really do have to visit her – be with her.'

'America! That's a long way. Who is she?'

'Oh – a friend of my mother's actually. She was at school with her. She has cancer. She has only a few weeks to live.'

'You never mentioned her before.'

'No, I know. I wasn't particularly close to her.'

'Well then, why are you going all the way to America to visit her?'

'She was very good to me when I was young. Now, Chloe, let's not waste any more time discussing why I'm going, it isn't very important –'

'It is to me.'

Caroline looked at Chloe, and wished she didn't find her so irritating when she was patently such a nice child, very kind and caring and loving. She sometimes wished she wasn't so nice; she felt she could handle her hostile emotions better if Chloe occasionally rounded on her, or flew into sulks or rages like most teenage girls. But she continued to be patient, eager to please and polite and, worse than all those things, caring and loving, rather like a puppy. She was endlessly nice to her mother, bringing her cups of tea in bed in the morning, offering to help her with this and that, asking if she could go shopping or dog-walking with her; and all Caroline could feel for her in return was not exactly dislike, but a sort of withdrawal, a distaste for her company and certainly her physical presence. If she hadn't been away at school two-thirds of the year, she wouldn't have been able to stand the situation; as it was she struggled through the holidays and counted the days until the beginning of term. This trip to New York would at least relieve her of Chloe's company for much of the rest of the holidays.

'Well, it's very nice of you to be so concerned. But it really isn't worth you worrying about. Now, will you be all right for a week or so? Daddy will be here, of course, and I've arranged for Nanny to come and stay –'

'Oh, Mummy, not Nanny. She treats me as if I was six.'

'Well, maybe she does, but I feel easier when she's here.'

Chloe sighed. 'Oh all right. Mummy, I'm sorry to sound selfish but will I have to miss the Junior Hunt Ball? The New Year's Eve one?'

'Not as long as your father can take you. Although I can't imagine why you want to go, you never go hunting and you'll feel out of it.'

'Well, I do want to go. The others are all my friends. They don't mind me not going hunting. It's only you who does actually.'

'Well I do, I suppose, but only because you're missing out on something that I think you'd enjoy. However, we've been over all that far too often. Have you got anything to wear? Because if not that could be difficult. Darling, do be careful, you're getting that sellotape in a most appalling tangle. Look, it's stuck on to the wrapping paper.'

'Oh, damn. Oh, I wish I could do really lovely parcels like you. Yes, I've got that dress I made at school last term. It's really nice. Even though I say it myself.'

This was quite true; Chloe was, rather oddly, given her clumsiness, a superb needlewoman, and had made herself an evening dress in silver taffeta, with a swirling ballerina-length skirt and an off-the-shoulder neckline. When she had tried it on to show her mother, Caroline had for the first time in her life admitted that Chloe did look very pretty; her dark red hair and clear skin set off by the silver, her slightly plump shoulders flattered by the swathed neck, her waist looking suddenly more slender above the full skirt.

'Yes, it is nice. And you look lovely in it. Yes, well, you can wear that.'

'But I haven't got any shoes. That's the only thing. Could I maybe get some shoes?'

'Chloe, there's no time to get shoes. Not before I go. The shops are all shut.'

'But I've only got my school shoes. Could I borrow a pair of – of yours?'

'They'll be too big. And too high-heeled.'

'Oh, Mummy, please. Not much too big. And I am nearly sixteen.'

'Oh, all right. Have a rummage through my wardrobe. See what you can find. But you're not to drag Nanny round Ipswich. She's too old.'

'No, Mummy.'

'And I rely on you to keep an eye on the boys.'

'Mummy, I can't do anything with those boys. Honestly. They're totally out of everyone's control and specially mine.'

'Nonsense. They're just high-spirited. All teenage boys are like that. Now I have to go and get organized. Oh and Chloe –' She hesitated, searching painfully for the right, tactful words. 'Look after Daddy. He isn't very well.'

'What's the matter with him?'

'I'm not sure,' said Caroline truthfully. 'When I get back I'm going to make him see the doctor.'

'Mummy?'

'Chloe, what is it now? I really do have a lot to do.'

'Did you – have you read my report yet?'

'Yes,' said Caroline absently, 'yes, it was very good. Well done.'

'Thank you.' Chloe knew her mother hadn't read it; if she had, she would have known she had been nominated for Head of House next term, and that she was to be swimming captain of the whole school, before even going into the sixth.

Well, her father would be pleased. She would show it to him later while her mother packed. She wondered who this old friend was and how she could possibly merit her mother leaving the family in the middle of Christmas.

'Can I see the letter?' Joe settled himself into the seat beside Caroline. 'Got enough room?'

'Yes, thank you. Plenty.'

'It won't seem like that in ten hours' time. Now look, let's order a drink – you need to be completely plastered to cope with this flight – and then let's work out what we're going to do.'

'All right. Here's the letter anyway.' She handed it to him. It had come a week ago, and she had hardly slept since.

Joe read it in silence and then covered her hand with his. 'Poor you.'

'Yes. Well, as I said, she doesn't seem a very nice child.'

'I suppose she's a very hurt and angry child.'

'And frightened, I suppose.' The gin and tonic was already seeping into Caroline's weary tense senses; she felt warmer, softer suddenly. She moved her hand under Joe's; he took it in his, and began massaging her palm gently with his fingers. She looked at him, her face suddenly raw and open with emotion; he smiled back at her and stroked her cheek lightly with his other hand.

'I think it's only fair to tell you,' he said, 'that this is only the beginning of an intense assault on your very determined fidelity to your husband.'

'Not on the plane!' said Caroline, laughing.

'There are the toilets. Have you not heard of the mile-high club?'

'No,' said Caroline.

'Membership is earned by having sex during the flight. I'm not quite sure how you prove it. Shall we join?'

'No.'

'Well, on the way back maybe.'

'Maybe.' She smiled again.

Joe got his flight bag out from under the seat and pulled a set of papers out. 'I'll be working on it. Now I have some work to do. I was telling the paper the truth when I said I was going to do some interviews in New York.'

'Who are you going to see?'

'Bobby Kennedy – I hope. Shirley Maclaine. Joe DiMaggio.'

'What a marvellous time you're going to have.'

'I hope so. But my main purpose is to see your time isn't too terribly bad.'

'You're a nice man, Joe.'

'I know.'

Caroline studied him as he sat totally engrossed in the newspaper cuttings he had brought with him. Her tiredness and the second gin and tonic the stewardess had served her had brought her emotions very near the surface. She found it little short of miraculous (she now dared admit to herself) that she had resisted him for so long. It wasn't just that he was extremely attractive: and he looked particularly so at this moment, his shaggy fair hair looking more in need of a comb and a cut than usual, his long rangy body – dressed rather scruffily as always in jeans and an over-large, rather geriatric-looking sweater – sprawled across two seats, his thin, sculptured face unusually intent and unusually serious; it was that he was so good to her, so caring and thoughtful, so persistently flattering and appreciative. There was also his ridiculous way of crying whenever anything touched him: he cried over films, books, newspaper reports, stories of friends' fortunes, both good and bad; he cried, he assured Caroline, at weddings, he cried when friends had babies – and he quite often cried when Caroline was upset. He was a highly emotional man, and it added to his sexiness. And then he made her laugh, he infected her with his own high spirits, made everything seem oddly and intensely pleasurable. But most of all, and this was where the real miracle of resistance came in, he was inordinately sexy. He had a way of looking at her, of flicking his lazy green eyes over her, moving from her eyes to her mouth and then on to her breasts and then her stomach and her thighs: he could reduce her to almost helpless desire simply by sitting there and studying her. And then he was a great exponent of the art of talking dirty, talking sex; he had never done more than kiss her, but he had discussed what he would like to do to her, would indeed do to her, with such infinite humour, hunger and grace she quite often had the greatest difficulty in not removing her knickers there and then and thrusting herself at him under the table, or in the taxi – which was as near to privacy as she allowed herself or him. Caroline was still intensely highly sexed; she was married to a man who had no idea how to satisfy her, and she felt as if she had a huge spring coiled somewhere in the depths of her body; she could feel it physically, its stirring and its pressure, endlessly trying to unwind, and prevented only by the boundaries of her body itself. One day, some time, the spring would be properly unleashed; and the thought of that, when she allowed herself to dwell on it, was almost beyond her own imaginings.

Caroline wrenched her thoughts away from her body, and returned to the ordeal in front of her, reading and rereading the letter from Fleur until it seemed to her it would melt under her own intense emotion.

Dear Caroline Hunterton,
I was hoping not to have to write to you ever again but my grandmother has insisted.

She is very ill, in fact dying, of cancer of the liver. The doctors say she has only a few weeks to live. For some reason, she wanted to meet you before she died; she feels she has to talk to you.

I suspect she wants to ask you to look after me, but of course this is out of the question. Clearly neither of us would wish it. I am almost seventeen and quite able to earn my own living, and my aunts will take care of me.

She is in the state hospital in Brooklyn, which is adequate. It would be nice if she could be somewhere better, but none of us has any money. You, I imagine, have plenty; I don't know if you could help in this particular way.

I had originally thought it better if we did not meet, but I know my grandmother would die happier if she thought we had become friends. So I think you should come to the hospital with me.

Please let me know if you can come, and also where you will be staying. Perhaps you could phone me when you get to New York.

Yours,

Fleur FitzPatrick

It was a strange, heartbreaking letter to receive from a daughter who had occupied your thoughts obsessively for seventeen years, Caroline thought, but better perhaps, less shocking than the earlier one, announcing her rape and pregnancy. She had longed to go to New York then, to try to help Fleur, to take care of her, to ease her pain, and when she sent the cheque had offered to do so, but a terse note from Fleur by return, saying that she would be fine now, that everything was fixed, and telling her to stay in England, had arrived and Joe had warned her strongly against going, simply turning up.

'You would simply add to her trauma. She couldn't handle it. She's obviously OK. She's a tough little nut. This is not the correspondence of an emotional cripple. She wouldn't have written to you unless she had got it all together. Leave her alone. She'll survive.'

'But, Joe, she's been raped. The worst thing that can happen to a woman. And she's only sixteen. She needs comforting, caring for, and I'm her mother.'

'Yes, and she's never met you and she obviously thinks you're the most uncaring person in the world. I know that's tough, but forcing yourself on her now would be tougher. How can she talk about it to someone who isn't just a stranger, but the one person who should be closer to her than anyone else? It would be impossible. You'd both of you just get badly hurt. Please, darling, I can see it's really difficult, but please leave her be.'

Leaving Fleur be then had been the most difficult thing she had ever done, with the possible exception of handing her over that first morning, but somehow she had done it. She had written twice more, asking her if she was all right, and had received one laconic postcard saying, 'Everything is OK now. Fleur FitzPatrick.'

Now she was actually going to meet her. Almost seventeen years to the very day after Fleur had been born, she was to look at her across a room, meet her eyes, hear her voice, hold out her hand to her, speak to her, touch her, discover precisely at long last what she was like. And she was terribly afraid . . .

'May I speak to Fleur, please?'

'Who is this?' The voice was guarded, cautious: a light, cool voice, with a strong American accent. Caroline closed her eyes, clutched Joe's hand tighter.

'It's – Caroline Hunterton.'

'Ah.' She could hear the withdrawal, the coldness. 'Well, this is Fleur FitzPatrick. Was – was your flight OK?'

'Fine, thank you,' said Caroline, disproportionately touched by this attempt at politeness. 'Yes, very good indeed.'

'Where are you staying?'

'At the St Regis.'

'Where's that?'

'It's on East 55th Street,' said Caroline.

'Oh yes. Well look, I think the best thing would be if you came to the hospital. I could meet you in the foyer. It's near Flatbush. I don't suppose you'll want to risk the subway –' the voice held a tinge of contempt, and something else – amusement? – 'so just tell your driver to come to St Margaret's Hospital, near Lafayette Street.'

'When? When is visiting time?'

'Oh, we can see her any time. They're pretty liberal here when you're dying.'

'All right. Well, this evening? Six o'clock?'

'Sure.' The phone went down.

Caroline felt so sick as the cab driver lurched across Brooklyn Bridge, alongside and apparently perilously close to one of the trains, that she thought she was actually going to throw up. She wound down the window and tried to lean out but the driver snarled at her. 'Lady, don't do that. Want to get your head knocked off?'

'I'm sorry,' said Caroline, 'I don't feel terribly well.'

'Well, hang on to it. I don't want anyone throwing up all over my cab. You spew in my cab, you clean it out. OK?'

'OK,' said Caroline humbly. Sheer terror kept her from vomiting. It was a long journey; far longer than she had expected. The trip down through Manhattan and the financial district had been slow, with the rush-hour traffic; but she had been distracted by the excitement, the beauty of New York in darkness; she kept looking back at the skyline, etched out in lights against the sky, and even in her anguish, marvelling at it and the fact that she was actually seeing it.

Now, as they lurched through endless streets for what seemed like hours, she felt as if she was on some nightmare pilgrim's progress, a trial of endurance and fear, that was destined never to end, and that for all eternity she would be sitting, lurching from side to side in this cab, feeling ill, fearful, vulnerable. She wished more passionately than she had ever wished anything that she had accepted Joe's offer to accompany her, but it had seemed cowardly at the time; she had felt Fleur would regard it with contempt, and besides she needed to be as alone with Fleur as the workings of a great hospital and the needs of a dying woman would allow. But now, she longed for him, for a friendly hand, a supporting voice, a kindly spirit. And she was late too: it was already nearly a quarter to seven; she had never expected it to take so long; suppose Fleur thought she wasn't coming, didn't wait for her. She would never find her again.

Suddenly the taxi flung to a halt. Caroline was practically thrown on to her knees; she put out a hand to save herself and bruised her wrist badly. It didn't seem to matter.

'Here we are, lady. St Margaret's Hospital. That'll be twenty-two dollars.'

Twenty-two dollars! Almost eight pounds. He must be ripping her off. Well, it didn't matter. Caroline pulled out a wad of notes with her bruised aching hand. 'Could you – take what I owe you?'

'Lady, I ain't a nursemaid. Just find me a twenty and a five. That'll do.'

'Oh, a twenty and a five. Yes. Yes, here you are.'

'OK.'

No thank you, no goodnight. He just pulled away into the darkness, her only human contact in this utterly solitary journey; slowly, carefully, as if she were treading a minefield, Caroline walked into the foyer.

She realized suddenly that Fleur would not know her, would have no idea what she looked like. She at least had some idea what she was to find. It gave her an advantage, a sudden sense of confidence as she stood looking round. The place was packed, filled with people, with families, with small children, crying babies, some of them waiting apparently for nothing, some of them talking, a few obviously greatly distressed, most of them standing in a long line at the reception desk. She stood there, her heart beating so hard it made her breathless, her eyes desperately roving over the crowd, searching for a tall slender girl with dark hair and blue eyes. A girl she had borne and then been parted from seventeen long years ago, and who now, at last, she was to be with again. But she was not there. After five minutes of looking, of walking round, of peering into corners, of looking outside again on the steps, even in the lavatories, Caroline knew Fleur was not there. And she didn't know how to bear it. She sat down suddenly on a newly vacated seat, weak, sickened with sadness, nursing her aching wrist, wondering how Fleur could be so cruel and how she could ever have believed that she would find her. Dimly through her own misery, the crying babies and the thick, strange, different accents, not just the American, but the Italian, the Spanish, the Indian, she could hear the Tannoy, endlessly giving out messages, incomprehensible, irrelevant, intrusive. At the end of each one there would be a bleep, then a moment's merciful silence, then a second bleep and another one. And then suddenly Caroline recognized a word: a name. Her name. Sounding strange, the stress coming singsong-like on the first and last syllable Hun-ter-ton, but unmistakable. She stood up and pushed her way to the front of the queue at the desk, careless of hostility. 'Excuse me,' she kept saying, 'excuse me, there's a call for me, excuse me, excuse me.' And – as much, she realized afterwards, because of her expensive fur coat, her tall Englishness, the aura of money and authority she carried about with her, as her own desperation, the crowd parted and let her through. These people had learnt to make way for authority. Certainly in a situation like this one.

'Yes, ma'am?' She was at the desk now. A black, impatient face confronted her. 'Can I help you?'

'My name is Hunterton. There's a message for me. On the Tannoy.'

'Ah, yes. Yes, you're to go right on up to Ward 7B. Miss FitzPatrick will be up there with her grandmother.'

'Ward 7B. Yes, yes of course. Er – where – how do I find it?'

'Over to the elevator. Seventh floor. Turn right.' The voice was more impatient now. 'Next?'

'Er – is everything all right?'

'Ma'am, nothin' is all right in this hospital. Certainly not in Ward 7B. Why don't you go on up there, and you can find out for yourself. Next!'

Caroline went over to the elevators; they were slow, grindingly noisy, packed. They stopped at every floor; by the time she reached the seventh she was alone apart from a little old black woman and her granddaughter. 'Now you listen to me,' she was hissing in the little girl's ear, 'you just be good tonight, and no cryin'. Your mother don't want to be visited by a child who cries. It don't help her any to get better. You just smile at her and be good.'

The child was silent; she appeared to be in the grip of an overwhelming terror.

'Are you going to 7B?' asked Caroline.

'Yes, we are. Follow me, honey, we'll show you the way. Come along, Aurelia, now remember what I said.'

Ward 7B was down the corridor, quite a long way; the old woman walked slowly, but Caroline didn't like to run, it seemed rude. At the ward, huge, neat, awesome, she halted; Aurelia and her grandmother made for the bed nearest the door, where a young woman clearly in the most appalling pain lay twisting and turning on her pillow. Caroline winced and looked down the beds, and then started very slowly walking towards the other end of the room.

And then she saw her, straight away, sitting facing her, but looking at the person in the bed, holding her hand, and stroking it, smiling very sweetly, and then, as Caroline watched her, she leant forward and whispered something into the pillow. Caroline had not known quite what to expect, but it had not been this: this tangible, visible tenderness. She felt a stab of tears behind her eyes, a harsh roughness in her throat. She could still not see who was in the bed, shielded as she was by the curtains and the pillows propped round her; so she moved forward again, and Fleur looked up across the bed at her, with her great dark blue eyes smudged with weariness and grief, and just for a moment, before the defences went up, Caroline saw in those eyes not just curiosity, desperation, fear, but a flash of greeting, and of relief that she was actually there.

'Fleur?' she said, stepping forward, right up to the bed, and the girl nodded, and put her finger to her lips and gesticulated at the pillow. Caroline had not seen anyone near to death before, but she recognized it now; Kathleen lay back, her grey hair spread about her, her face pinched and waxy, her lips slack, moving occasionally, her hands clawing gently but constantly at the sheets. She was emaciated, except for the huge extended abdomen; her arms were like small sticks with skin hung on them, her neck so thin it seemed scarcely possible it could support her head. Caroline looked at her for a long time, Brendan's mother, and felt a genuine aching grief of her own, having never known her, never spoken to her, but known her son so well; and then she turned to Fleur, Brendan's daughter, looking up at her with an oddly trusting expression, and found that in the great white heat of emotion she was experiencing, the predominant one was entirely maternal and tender, a sense that this child had had enough, and needed respite.

'Come along,' she said gently, 'she will sleep for a while. We can stay nearby and ask the nurse to call us. Come along, Fleur, come with me.'

And, childlike, obedient, utterly unlike the harsh, hostile young woman Caroline had been expecting to find, Fleur stood up and followed her out of the ward.

At the end, by the nursing office, they paused. 'We are relatives of Mrs FitzPatrick,' said Caroline firmly. 'She is asleep at the moment. We shall be just along the corridor. Please call us if she wakes.'

And the young nurse, as awed by the authority of the fur coat, the English accent, the air of confidence as the people downstairs had been, nodded and said she certainly would, and directed them towards the drinks machine.

They walked towards it in silence; when they got there, Caroline got out her purse and said, 'What would you like, Fleur, tea or – or coffee? It seems quite wrong that I don't know even what you like to drink.'

But this was too big a step forward to Fleur, she was not prepared to make such concessions to friendliness; she shrugged and said, 'I don't care,' and then sat huddled on the bench seat, watching Caroline struggle with the unfamiliar coins, the temperamental machine.

'Here,' said Caroline. 'Tea. With sugar. Great English remedy for shock. Drink it.'

'Thank you,' said Fleur. She would not look at Caroline; she sat looking at her feet, her long, slender feet, on which she wore rather expensive-looking brown leather low-heeled pumps, Caroline noticed rather irrelevantly. She was dressed all in shades of brown, a brown coat pulled round her against the world and the cold, a brown skirt, a beige sweater. Her legs were long and very slim, her hands long-fingered and graceful. Caroline had expected, possibly, beauty; she had not expected grace. She sat looking at her, drinking her in, much as she had seventeen years before, when she had been committing her to memory; now, finding her again, having her restored to her, there was as much to see, to explore.

Finally Fleur spoke. 'She probably won't go through the night,' she said. 'She suddenly, just this afternoon, got much worse. She – she hemorrhaged. The pain was so bad, I was afraid. I – well, they've given her so much stuff now, she doesn't know anything any more.' She turned to Caroline, and the blue eyes were full of tears; she pushed her heavy dark hair back with a gesture of immense weariness. 'I'm sorry,' she said, more formal, less friendly all of a sudden, 'I'm sorry I wasn't downstairs. You were very late, and I didn't want to leave her. What happened?'

'I'm sorry,' said Caroline, 'I didn't think it would be so far, take so long. And it was the rush hour, I suppose.'

'Yes.'

'Did she – does she know I'm coming?'

'Oh yes. I told her. I told her we'd already met. She wanted to know all about you. I told her some lies. I don't think she took much of it in. It made her really happy. I can't imagine why.' She looked at Caroline coldly; more the girl of the letters, the phone call.

'Well,' said Caroline, 'it doesn't really matter, does it? Why, I mean.'

'No. No, I suppose not. I was going to ask you if we could move her, but it's not worth it now.'

'No, I'm afraid not. Where are your aunts?'

'Well, one of them has been here all afternoon and gone home to her kids. One died, oh, about five, six years ago. One will be here quite soon. And the last one, Edna, is flying over from California tonight. I don't know if she'll make it.'

'Miss FitzPatrick! Can you come quickly, please. Your grandmother is asking for you.'

Fleur stood up, dropped the cardboard cup and ran along the corridor. Caroline followed her. They reached the bed together; Kathleen was awake, looking confused, frightened. She reached out for Fleur's hands, clung on to them. 'You naughty child. Where did you go? I need you here with me.'

'Is the pain bad, Grandma?'

'The pain is nothing compared with worrying about you.' She was half lucid, half drifting in and out of hallucination. 'Now did you bring Caroline with you this time?'

'Yes I did, Grandma, and she is here. Look, here, take her hand.'

She placed Caroline's hand in the frail, dry one; Caroline held it gently, smiled into the fierce blue eyes. Those eyes. So that was where they came from. Irish eyes.

'You're very pretty. I knew you would be. Brendan only liked pretty girls.'

'Thank you.'

'Now I want you to promise, promise me to look after Fleur. She has no money, I have no money. She is a clever child, she has to finish her education. She must not be wasted. Brendan would not have – not have . . .' The voice, initially urgent and hurried, weakened, trailed away.

'I will. I will look after her. I promise. I will take her home with me and care for her. She will be safe and she will be loved.'

'Safe and loved. Yes. The girls, they can't do anything for her. None of them. You must. Fleur, you will be safe and you will be loved. With your mother.' The voice was exhausted, so faint it was scarcely there. Then a new sound came from the thin throat: a wail of pain, of agony.

Fleur looked frightened, she pressed the bell on the bed frantically. 'Nurse, nurse, come quickly, please, give her more morphine quickly, for God's sake.'

Death, Caroline told Joe much much later, when she arrived back exhausted at the hotel, was not swift, was not easy, was not peaceful; it was, as she had seen it that night and the following day, hard, as hard a struggle as birth, the pain as intense, the drama every bit as great. They stayed, she and Fleur and Brendan's sisters, they sat and endured as Kathleen endured, they forced themselves to listen as she cried out in pain, they felt her relief as the morphine lifted the pain away, they waited afraid of its return. And each time, as she drifted away from them into the half peace, they looked at each other, Caroline made entirely one of them by the drama, by her willingness, her courage, to share it with them, and said, although not in words, this time she is gone, she has left us; and each time, Kathleen clung on, desperately, bravely, fearfully to life. The priest came, administered the last rites; Fleur and Caroline, who had never witnessed the ritual, watched him in something close to terror as he anointed Kathleen, blessed her, and as she went through the awesome act of accepting the gift, the extreme unction, pronounced her sins forgiven. The night passed, morning came, around them the life and death of the ward went on, the nurses aroused Kathleen, washed her, changed her bed, administered her drugs; at one point Fleur slept, sitting next to Caroline, her head falling heavily on to her shoulder, and Caroline thought that despite the horror, the grief, the ugliness she was witnessing, she had not in all the long years since Fleur's birth felt so at peace, so happy.

When Kathleen finally died, with no fuss, no drama, just a slowly decreasing series of breaths, her eyes wide open, but calm, almost humorous, Fleur and Caroline were alone with her: Edna, worn out with her journey, was asleep in a chair in the day room, Kate had gone to telephone, and Maureen was at home briefly, necessarily, with her husband and children. Fleur looked at Kathleen, then at Caroline, her eyes big and afraid, and Caroline nodded gently and went for the nurse; when she came back Fleur was holding Kathleen's hand again, quite calm, but with great tears rolling down her white face. They closed Kathleen's eyes, the nurses, straightened her sheets, and then asked Caroline and Fleur to leave; they could come back later, they said, when they had done what had to be done. Fleur walked quite quickly down the ward, out into the corridor and then leant against the wall, shaking, her eyes closed; Caroline, without conscious thought, without self-consciousness, put her arms round her and said, 'It's all right, Fleur, she's all right now,' over and over again. And Fleur, briefly allowing herself to accept the comfort, leant against her, put her head on Caroline's shoulder and wept: peacefully, easily, almost happily.

'She was always there,' she kept saying, 'always there. She was my mother, my father, my family, all I had,' and Caroline did not find this hurtful or hard to accept, she just kept saying, 'I know, I know,' and thinking that Kathleen's death, however painful, however fearful, had accomplished a wonderful thing for her and her child.

Later, much later, when they had all seen Kathleen again, quite peaceful now, and Fleur, oddly grown up and in command, had thanked the nurses, and they had the death certificate, they discussed, briefly, the funeral arrangements, and Maureen said she must get back again to her family, and Kate announced she must go to work, and Edna phoned her family and asked her husband to come up with their children for the funeral.

Then finally Caroline said, and they could all see how true it was, that she was tired, that she would like to go back to her hotel. Kate said she would help her find a cab, and thanked her for staying and walked out into the suddenly bright sunshine with her.

'It was good of you to come,' she said again, on the hospital steps, 'very good. My mother became obsessed with meeting you, with knowing Fleur would be in good hands. Of course, she saw her as a child. Fleur is quite able to care for herself. But she could never see that. To her, Fleur was a baby. Brendan's baby, and she had to take care of her.'

'Yes,' said Caroline, 'yes, I can see that.'

'And now did she just write to you? Out of the blue?'

'She did,' said Caroline carefully, anxious not to reveal Fleur's earlier letter, lest they had not known any of it.

'It must have been a great surprise,' said Kate, awkwardly, not sure how to handle the situation, not sure how much Caroline would have wished her to know, 'not having seen Fleur for so many years.'

Caroline said yes, it had indeed been a surprise, but that Fleur was a beautiful girl, and clearly a brave and loving one, and a daughter such as she could be proud of.

'Indeed,' said Kate, 'and she is clever too, very clever. You will enjoy getting to know her. Now here is a cab. Please come and see us again, tomorrow perhaps, and we will be looking for you at the funeral. It will be good to have you there.'

None of them seemed remotely hostile, or even aware that she had had no part in Kathleen's life until the time of leaving it; her sharing of the trauma had made her part of them, part of the family, the one night worth months, years of closeness.

She fell asleep immediately she had settled into the cab and given the driver the address, waking to find him shaking her and looking in through the door at her in an oddly kindly way.

'Lady, we're back. Twenty dollars. OK?'

'OK.'

Joe wasn't there when she called his room; he had left a message to say he would be back at tea-time. She was relieved: she couldn't face yet describing what had happened or sharing her emotions about Fleur with anyone. Not even Joe. She went up to her room. She lay in the bath for a long time, ordered some tea and a sandwich from room service and climbed into bed; she had thought she might not be able to sleep again, but she did, easily and dreamlessly, and woke to hear the telephone ringing. For a moment she thought she was at home: 'Caroline Hunterton,' she said, picking up the receiver.

'Hallo, this is Fleur.'

'Fleur, how are you feeling?'

'I'm OK. I just called to let you have the time and place of the funeral. My aunts would like you to be there.'

'I see.' Fleur was obviously anxious that she should not think it was any wish of hers.

'Yeah, well, it's at the Catholic Church of Our Lady of the Sorrows, in Sheepshead Bay. Just off Avenue Z. The day after tomorrow, two o'clock.'

'All right, Fleur. I'll be there.'

'Yeah, OK.'

The phone went dead. Oh well, thought Caroline, what did I expect, gratitude, friendliness? Yes, she thought, yes, I suppose I did, a word of thanks might have been nice. She sighed; she and Fleur obviously had a long way to go.

* * *

The funeral took a long time; a full requiem mass. Caroline, who was not familiar with the Catholic Church, was surprised; Church of England funerals were swift, easy affairs compared with this. And yet she liked it, liked the sense of there being more to the ceremony than just dispatching someone with the greatest possible speed and ease; this was more like death itself, difficult, drawn out, but important and meaningful. Afterwards they went and stood round the grave while Kathleen's coffin was lowered into it; she stood in between Kate and Edna, with no sense that she was not part of the family, tears in her eyes. Fleur stood apart from them all, her face tight and closed. She did not cry.

Afterwards Caroline went up to her.

Fleur looked at her, hostile, rude. 'Yes?'

'Fleur, we have to talk.'

'I don't see why.'

'I see why, Fleur.' It was amazing how easy it was to keep her temper with this awkward rude child, when her other daughter, so gently, so compliantly polite, drove her into a fury of irritation. 'Because of my promise to your grandmother. Because I want to see you are looked after.'

'My grandmother is dead. She won't know.'

'No, but I will know. And I don't like breaking promises.'

'Oh, really. Well I'm surprised.' The tense white face was working suddenly, the voice shaky with unshed tears. 'I would have thought a mother who could just hand over her baby, never see her again, never want to know where she was even, I would have thought that sort of person would be real good at breaking promises. I'll be fine, Lady Hunterton, just fine; I'd rather go on the streets than start taking anything from you now.'

'Fleur!' It was Kate, who had heard the end of this speech, and come over to them, looking shocked. 'Fleur, how dare you speak to Mrs – Lady – Hunterton like that? When she has been so good to you. To your grandmother –'

'Good! You call sitting by a bed for twelve hours good, when there have been seventeen years of absolutely nothing, no letters, no visits, no nothing. Well, I'm not going to be taken in by her, even if you are. She's one big sham. Standing there crying when a little bit of help might have kept Grandma alive. I have to get home now. I have schoolwork to do.'

She went running off, almost blindly, through the graves; Caroline looked after her, white-faced, her hand over her mouth, trying to stop crying out.

'I'm sorry. I'm so sorry.' Kate's face was gentle. 'She's terribly upset. She loved our mother so much. She's done everything for her, all her life.'

'I know,' said Caroline. 'I understand. Just. Could you – could you tell her something from me, please? So that she feels a little – well, just a very little less hostile towards me. Could you tell her a day hasn't passed since she was born that I haven't thought about her, and that her father and I made a pact that he should never tell me where she was, or I would have come after her to find her and take her back.'

'Yes.' Kate's rather peevish face was oddly gentle. 'Yes, I will. I'll tell her. I don't know how much she'll understand but I will tell her. And in time I do know she'll come round. She's a nice child really. Very nice.'

'I believe you,' said Caroline with a shaky smile.

She was alone in the hotel when the message came. It was the day after the funeral. Joe had gone to Washington for two days to see Bobby Kennedy; he would get back next morning and then they were to go home. Caroline was tired and depressed. She had given up hope of getting through to Fleur; she had phoned the house in Sheepshead Bay and Kate had answered the phone and said she would go and get Fleur and had then come back, clearly embarrassed, and said that Fleur was out, and she would try and get her to call.

Joe had been patient, gentle, undemanding; he had done a great deal of listening, about Kathleen's death and the funeral and Fleur, and some counselling (mostly in favour of doing nothing, nothing at all and waiting for Fleur to come round). Apart from that he had left her alone, had not once tried to pressure her into any kind of commitment to him. Caroline was touched and relieved by this, and felt illogically guilty at the same time; when she said as much (her judgement just slightly impaired by the double brandy he had insisted she drank before she went to bed) he had laughed and said there was plenty of time for her to think about him, when she began to feel better. Caroline told him she wasn't going to feel better and he said that was against human nature and that she would. Caroline said that unless Fleur came round just a little, made a move towards her, however, slight, she would never feel better again.

'Now listen, my darling. That child has had a dreadful – what – six months. She holds you in some way personally responsible for some of it. At the same time she wants you and she needs you and she simply can't let herself admit it. Or let you know it either. She's fighting a huge battle with herself. With life. Just be patient.'

'I'm not a patient person,' said Caroline.

She had phoned twice and spoken to Nanny. Everyone was fine, Nanny said, although Sir William was very tired, and Chloe was looking forward to the ball. Would she like to speak to Chloe?

Caroline felt that of all the people in the world she would not like to speak to, Chloe was the leader by a long head. She made an excuse and rang off.

'Lady Hunterton?'

'Yes.'

'I have a message for you. From Miss FitzPatrick. She didn't want to speak to you. She says could you meet her in the foyer here in half an hour.'

'Yes,' said Caroline, 'yes, thank you. Thank you very much. I'll be there.'

'I just wanted to apologize.' Fleur's eyes were wary, but brave. 'I shouldn't have spoken to you like that. You were very – kind to me at the hospital. And it was good of you to come.'

She had obviously been rehearsing this speech; Caroline found it slightly difficult not to smile.

'That's all right, Fleur. I hope I helped a bit.'

'Yes, you did. A bit.'

'Good. Shall we have tea?'

'Oh well, I'm busy. I don't have a lot of time.'

'Really? What are you so busy with?'

'Oh – schoolwork. I have exams soon.'

'Do you like school?'

'Yes, I suppose so.'

Caroline looked at her carefully. 'Look, there are a few things we have to sort out. Don't you think? It's all right, I don't have the slightest intention of taking you home to England with me and sending you off to boarding school –'

'Does your daughter go to boarding school?' The use of the word 'daughter' was clearly deliberate: making it plain that Fleur did not regard herself in that light.

'Yes, she does. She likes it. Who told you I had a daughter?'

'Miss duGrath.'

'Ah.'

'Yes, well all right. Maybe I could spare a little time. But I do have to get back.'

'Come on then. There's something actually called the Tea Room here. They serve the most delicious cakes and hot buttered toast.'

'I'm not hungry.'

'Well, I am.

'Now then,' said Caroline, when Fleur was sitting opposite her, drinking her tea and resisting (clearly with some difficulty) the pile of gateaux confronting her, 'now then, what is it best for us to do?'

'I don't know what you mean.'

'Well, I want to help you. Make sure you go to college, have a chance of a good career. I do have – money, you know.'

'Yes, I realize that. I – well, that is –'

'Yes?'

'I'm sorry I didn't write you more before. When you sent the money for the abortion.'

'That's all right. I understand.' Caroline was silent, terrified of taking a wrong step. 'Are you – all right now?'

'Oh, sure.'

'No, I can see you're all right physically. But it must have been very traumatic.'

'Oh, no. No, not really.' She was looking down, crumbling a pastry into dust; Caroline tried to take her hand. Fleur snatched it away. 'I told you. I'm all right.' She turned her head, looked round the restaurant rather wildly; Caroline saw her eyes were full of tears.

'Look,' she said, 'look, you don't have to talk about it now. But I had an abortion, when I was younger than you. Oh, physically I was all right, it was – well, properly done. But I've never got over it, and I never will. I needed to talk about it, and for a long time I couldn't. When I finally found someone who would listen it all seemed better. Not all right but better.'

Fleur looked at her with frank curiosity. 'Why did you have to have an abortion?'

'Oh, because I was stupid. But what happened to you was far worse. Surely.'

'Yes,' said Fleur, oddly awkward, 'yes, it was bad. Really bad.'

'Tell me about it.'

'I'd rather not.'

'All right.'

There was a long silence.

'Did you really love my father?' said Fleur suddenly.

'Oh yes,' said Caroline and her eyes were soft, cloudy, far away. 'I really loved him. More than I've ever loved anyone. Before or since. It was so terribly, terribly sad, what happened to us.'

'What did happen?'

'Don't you know?'

'A little. Grandma told me a little. But maybe I should hear some more of it from you.'

'Oh. Dear God, no wonder you hate me. Well, I'll tell you.'

She began to talk; she told Fleur about how happy she and Brendan had been, how much they had loved one another, how they had planned to get married. How she had become pregnant and how Brendan had never known; how she had married William and then how Brendan had come back.

'It was impossible, quite impossible, that I could go with him. I couldn't. I couldn't leave William. Not by then. It was too late. But I could give your father something. I could give him you. That seemed to make things better.'

'I just don't know,' said Fleur, staring at her, digesting all this with difficulty, 'I just still don't know how you could give me away. As if I was a package or something.'

'I don't know either,' said Caroline. 'But you have to remember I was very young and very alone, and it seemed the only thing to do. I thought it was best. And I was terribly wrong. I'm so sorry, so very sorry. As I said to your Aunt Kate, not a day has passed since then that I haven't thought about you and longed for you.' She looked up, her eyes bright with tears.

Fleur was still staring at her, silent. Then she smiled, a quick, odd little smile. 'Maybe we should try to get to know each a little,' was all she said.

'Oh, God, I don't want to go home,' said Caroline. 'I just don't want to go home. I just love New York so much. I feel happy here. It feels like home.'

'Well, it isn't home, as you'd soon find out,' said Joe. 'It's a tough, hard, unfriendly place, and not for the likes of you. Besides, you're only happy because you got your daughter back. It's got nothing to do with New York. If she'd been in Indochina you'd have felt you wanted to stay there.'

'I suppose so. What a wise man you are, Joe. Thank you for everything. Everything. I don't know what I'd have done, how I'd have got through it without you.'

'Oh, you'd have got through,' he said, looking at her with a rather odd expression in his green eyes. 'You were born getting through. You don't really need anybody, Caroline, anybody at all.'

They were sitting having dinner; their plane left in the morning. Caroline, uneasily aware it was the last night in the hotel, the last night with Joe, released at last from tension, fear, grief, knew she was in an awkward, potentially dangerous situation and didn't know how to deal with it. Joe was in an uncharacteristically awkward mood: silent, uncommunicative, contradicting almost everything she said.

She looked at him and decided she had to confront the situation head on, force it to a conclusion. 'Joe,' she said, refilling her glass. 'Joe, we have to talk.'

'Oh,' he said, 'I think we've done quite enough of that. We've talked an entire week away.'

'Yes, I know, but not about us.'

'No, just about you. You and Fleur and her aunts and her grandmother and her father, and her birthday, and how wonderful it was that you'd been able to celebrate her birthday for the first time and take her out to lunch, and whether she'd rather have a bracelet or a necklace for a present. It's taken up a great deal of time.'

'I'm sorry.'

'Oh, it's all right. I should have realized. I guess I'm not quite as unselfish as I thought. I imagined I could get through this week like some sort of cross between a guardian angel and Sir Galahad and there just hasn't been quite enough in it for me.'

'No. No, I can see that. Well' – Caroline took a deep breath, tried to sound light-hearted, amusing, amused – 'well it's all over now. We have tonight. We can talk about you all night. Tell me about Kennedy. You never really –'

'Caroline, for fuck's sake, I don't want to talk about Kennedy. I don't want to talk at all. I want to go to bed with you and screw you into the ground.'

Caroline looked at him; a shaft of physical longing shot through her, so strong, so hard, she moved in her seat, swallowed, looked away. Then she looked back at Joe. Her eyes were very clear, very candid. 'Well –' she said, and the invitation hung in the air, waiting to be taken.

'No, Caroline,' he said, and the words were literally shocking; she sat staring at him, feeling cold, slightly sick, 'no, I don't want to do it on your terms. I don't want to be told that now you've finished everything else you had to do, and you're feeling much better and your daughter is on her way to forgiving you, and before you get home to your husband and your other commitments, you could fit me into your schedule, spare me a little time even, and open your elegant long legs for me. That's all a bit too orderly, a bit too pragmatic for me. Frankly, Caroline, I find it a turn-off. Now, if you'll excuse me, I'm going up to my room. I have work to do.'

* * *

They ate breakfast together but in silence. Joe was polite, distracted, dividing his attention between the *New York Times* and some typewritten pages he was correcting. Caroline sat watching him, half angry, half remorseful. Then she finished her coffee and stood up.

'I'm going to finish packing,' she said, 'We have to leave in about half an hour.'

'Fine.' He didn't even look up. She went over to the lift, up to her room, moved about it, putting last-minute things into her case. She ached, throbbed with sexual energy and frustration. It was a physical pain, and the only way to bear it was to keep moving around. The thought of Joe and what she had not had with him was almost unbearable. And now there was no chance, no chance at all; she had blown it. She had taken no more trouble over him, given him no more time, than one of the doormen at the hotel; she had used him relentlessly for more than a week, and now she was getting what she deserved.

The fact he hadn't had to come with her was irrelevant really. He had come, he had wanted to help her, he had helped her, and he had been helping her for weeks and months, more than a year. She did not necessarily owe him any sexual favours, indeed they seemed a total irrelevance, but she certainly owed him some gratitude and some grace.

She looked at her watch. Twenty minutes before they left. He was probably back in his room. She owed him an apology at the very least, an acknowledgement that she understood what he had been saying. She went along the corridor and knocked on his door.

'Joe? It's me. Can I come in?'

'Sure. It's unlocked.'

She went in and looked at him; he was staring out of the window, his back to her.

'Joe, I'm sorry.'

'It's OK,' he said, turning to face her, infinitely weary. 'I didn't have to come.'

'No, but you did. And in spite of what you said I couldn't have managed without you. I've been very selfish and you're right to be angry. It was just that Fleur needed my time –'

'Fleur! Yes, Fleur, and Chloe and the boys, and that ever so aristocratic, broken reed of a husband of yours –'

'Don't say that about William. How dare you!'

'I dare, because I'm sorry for him. For all of them. I see what you do to them. Exactly what you do to me. Give them some rationed aspect of your time and attention, and all the time holding yourself back. You don't ever give, Caroline, not properly. Only with a very careful eye on your life and your commitments and the clock.'

'Joe, this is just not fair.'

'It's perfectly fair. Everybody around you gets short-changed. No wonder Fleur feels the way she does about you. I would too.'

'You bastard!' Caroline went over to him and hit him hard across the face. 'How could you say that, how could you! You don't understand me or any of it. I never, ever want to have anything to do with you again.'

Tears of grief and rage had begun to flow down her face; Joe looked at her and his expression softened suddenly. 'I'm sorry, Caroline, that was totally out of order. I shouldn't have said that. I just wanted to hurt you. Look, sit down and I'll get you a drink –'

'I don't want a drink,' she said, 'and anyway it's time we left. We have' – she looked at her watch – 'precisely seven minutes before the taxi comes.'

'Seven minutes!' he said, angry again. 'Seven minutes. How precise. Yes, well, you can't do much in seven minutes, can you, Lady Hunterton? Not without getting seriously behind schedule.'

He turned away from her again. Caroline brushed her tears irritably away, and then suddenly looked at him, seeing him as if for the first time, and thought she had never, in her whole life, not even on Brendan, seen such a sexy back: it was not just the narrow hips, the surprisingly rounded, almost girlish bottom, the long, rangy legs, it was the slight stoop of his shoulders, the oddly vulnerable bend of his neck, the way his shaggy fair hair fell thickly on to his collar. Contemplating it, and her own desire, newly heated by raw emotion and rage, she suddenly knew what she had to do, that if she did not she would regret it for the rest of her life, and that even if she was rejected, she would deem it better than walking out on him now. She took a deep breath, stepped forward and put her arms tightly round his waist, rubbing her head gently against his back, moving one hand down over his stomach, reaching, searching, finding the rising hardening penis.

'I think actually we could do quite a lot in seven minutes,' she said.

She came in little more than seconds, so charged was she with frustration and longing and delight at him. He pulled her down on to the bed, pushed up her skirt, tearing at her pants; Caroline, shivering violently, found his fly, unzipped it, thrust herself upwards, upwards, and as he entered her, as she received him into her hungry, empty, aching self, as she closed around him, in a great tumbling shower of pleasure, she shrieked aloud, and moved, just twice, and then it was there, she had found it, a white-hot, tender violence, and she clung to him, kissing him frantically, crying at the same time, and she heard his voice, felt his hands on her, and then felt him coming too, deeply, rhythmically, endlessly into her; then she tipped back her head and smiled at him, smiled into his extraordinary green eyes, and said, 'Perhaps we should join the mile-high club.'

'Perhaps we should,' said Joe, and she saw that he was crying.

Her phone rang just as she was leaving the room, tearing round desperately, checking things, trying to tidy her hair, to change her clothes, all at the same time.

It was Fleur. 'I just rang to tell you goodbye,' she said, 'and to say that I plan on going to California as soon as I can. To visit Miss duGrath and see if I can find out some more about why my father died.'

'Why? Suddenly?' Caroline was playing for time.

'I always intended to. But I couldn't before. Not while Grandma was alive. She wouldn't have let me. I have to go. I have to know what happened.'

'Fleur –'

'What?'

'Fleur, I don't know that it would do any good.'

'Why not?'

'Well – maybe it isn't a very nice story.'

'You know what happened, don't you?' said Fleur, her voice icy, detached suddenly, the rift between them widening hideously again. 'Why can't you tell me?'

'No, I don't know. Not really,' said Caroline firmly, glad this conversation was taking place on the telephone. 'I don't think any of us do.'

'I don't believe you.'

'Fleur, listen. I have to go. I have a plane to catch. I'll write to you. Tell you what I know. I promise. All right?'

'Oh, don't bother. I'll find out by myself, go alone.'

'Fleur, you can't. You couldn't cope. Not by yourself.'

'Caroline,' said the voice, half amused, half hostile, 'I'm used to coping by myself.'

Newspaper clippings, background to the Lost Years section of *The Tinsel Underneath*.

From the *Los Angeles Times*, 19 August 1957

The body of a young girl was found washed up on the beach at Santa Monica early this morning. The autopsy revealed that she was four months pregnant. So far no one has come forward to claim kinship with her. Foul play is not suspected.

From the *Los Angeles Times*, 4 September 1957

The inquest on the young woman who was found dead on the beach at Santa Monica on 19 August was held today. She has been identified as Kirstie Fairfax, an actress. She had not worked for some time, it was stated, and was very depressed. Michelle Zwirn, a neighbour and close friend of Miss Fairfax, said that she had been led to believe she could have a part in a new film being cast at ACI, starring Byron Patrick, but had heard on the day of her death that she had not got it. She said she had had no idea that Miss Fairfax had been pregnant. Miss Zwirn appeared very distraught at the inquest; later it was revealed that her brother, Gerard, has sustained terrible injuries in a recent accident, and is unlikely ever to walk again.

The verdict on Miss Fairfax was of suicide while the balance of the mind was disturbed.

Chapter 9

1961–2

Chloe wasn't at all sure now about the silver dress. Her brothers had fallen about, clutching each other and hooting with laughter when they had found her trying it on, telling her she looked like a Christmas parcel, 'a jolly lumpy one,' added Jolyon. 'Don't suppose you could get a long enough bit of string to go round you,' said Toby, and Nanny had said, having come down the corridor to see what the noise was about, that it was very pretty, and it was nice to see a dress that had been made at home for a change, which had worried Chloe in case the dress was so obviously home-made that everyone would know and despise her for it. Her father had told her she looked lovely, but then he would have said that if she had been dressed up in one of the sacks Jack used to store the horses' feed. So here she was, looking at herself worriedly and wondering what else she could wear, and indeed if she ought to go to the ball at all. Not for the first, or even the hundred and first, time in her life did she think wistfully of having the kind of mother who was so interested, so concerned that her daughter should look right at parties, she would spend days helping her find exactly the perfect dress. Lots of the girls at school had mothers like that: they would tell of days shopping, lunching, gossiping, giggling with their mothers – not in her wildest dreams could Chloe imagine giggling with her mother – of dress rehearsals in bedrooms, of harmless deceptions perpetrated upon the fathers who were paying for the dresses, of mothers waiting up until they got home, dying to hear every detail of the party or the dance. The very most Chloe ever got from Caroline was a 'Very nice, darling', as she went in to say goodbye, and then she always had to ask her if she looked all right, the information was never volunteered.

Oh well, at least she wouldn't lose anything by her mother being in New York. Chloe told herself she was silly even to think about not going to the dance, that the dress was perfectly all right really, she was just being silly, and went into her mother's room to try on some shoes.

The ones in the wardrobe were useless: too high-heeled, as Caroline had said. It wasn't just that they were too sophisticated for her, she could hardly walk in them, let alone dance. She looked round the room. Her mother was orderly; she had a rack of shoes in another cupboard, ranged in colours; they were more low-heeled certainly, but a bit old-fashioned. Still, they would probably do; the black suede ones were quite pretty, and fitted her. She swirled this way and that in the dress, her courage and confidence growing, managing to field a small ornament on her mother's bedside table that her dress had knocked flying. Yes, they would be all right. Not perfect but all right.

And then she saw a big box just sticking out by a corner under the bed. Mrs Jarvis had been spring-cleaning in her mother's absence and hadn't put anything back quite right. The pictures had been put back on all the wrong walls, and the collection of Battersea boxes on the dressing-table were all higgledy-piggledy. Caroline would be cross about it when she came home; she liked everything to be absolutely perfect. Well, never mind. That was not Chloe's problem. But the box might just have shoes in it. Caroline never threw things away. She pulled it out.

No, not shoes, just a lot of old photographs. Oh, but what photographs! Chloe settled down happily and started leafing through them. Her mother as a child, sitting straight and brave on a lively-looking little pony, with a very young-looking Jack Bamforth holding on to the reins. A formal study of Caroline and her parents, Jacqueline looking a little stern but ravishingly beautiful, and Stanley beaming roguishly down at his little daughter. Caroline jumping at a gymkhana. Caroline sitting on a rather big black horse at a meet at the Moat House with Stanley beside her on a huge grey and Jacqueline, looking gorgeous, holding a tray with glasses on it, smiling up at the Master. Caroline blowing out the candles on her birthday cake when she was about eight or nine, surrounded by her friends. And then some school photographs, standard groups, and a few of games teams, Caroline captaining some of them, much less interesting. Chloe was about to push the box back under the bed when she noticed that under the photographs was a brown paper bag and under the brown paper bag there were some magazines.

Intrigued – for she liked magazines – she pulled them out. They were old, yellowing copies of something called *Picture-goer*; she smiled as she recognized her idol, Rock Hudson, looking dashingly boyish on the cover of one, and started flipping through it. It hardly seemed the sort of magazine her mother would keep or even read; one of the pages was a bit blotchy as if it had been wet. It was a gossipy page, covered in small pictures of film stars in Hollywood, out at parties, playing tennis or posing on the beach; there was one picture slightly bigger than all the others of a very good-looking man, a bit like Tony Curtis, holding out a big beach ball to a very pretty girl: Byron Patrick, said the caption, new heart-throb in Hollywood. Well, she'd never heard of him. Whoever he was, he hadn't made it. She got out the rest; this was fun. She didn't see anything familiar in the next one, not even Cary Grant, but in the third, on a page entitled Hollywood Round-Up, there was quite a big picture of the same man, Byron Patrick, all dressed up like Ali Baba, with a knife between his teeth. Underneath that were two copies of the magazine folded open at pages with pictures of Byron Patrick.

Chloe was amused and slightly puzzled; obviously her mother had had a bit of a thing about Mr Patrick. But if she had, why on earth should she keep the magazines with pictures of him hidden under her bed, under a whole lot of school photographs? Oh, well, they probably reminded her of her youth.

She flipped through all the magazines again, all five of them; the common link was, without doubt, Byron Patrick. He was in every single one. Tucked inside the very last one was a big shiny print of him, just head and shoulders, smiling into the camera, smoking a cigarette, with what was obviously supposed to be a real signature, but actually printed on, in that funny scrawly American writing, in the corner. Her mother must have sent for it: how funny. For the very first time in her life Chloe felt mildly superior to her.

Underneath the magazines there were the letters. In a biggish brown envelope. She looked inside, saw them and tried to make herself put the whole lot back. She was an honourable child and a truthful one, and not given to poking and prying into other people's things. But her curiosity had been aroused by Mr Patrick, and this new, strange side to her mother, a reader of film magazines and a fan of young Hollywood actors; the letters might explain a little more. And if, she thought, with a rare flash of irritation and self-pity, her mother had been there with her, buying her some new shoes instead of forcing her to rummage through her bedroom in search of her old ones, she would not have been in this odd, tempting situation. Looking around her cautiously, as if she might be observed, Chloe pulled the letters out of the envelope.

There were only three: innocent ordinary-looking letters, just words on paper. It seemed incredible to Chloe that they could have the power to do her such harm, hurt her so badly.

The first was from a Mrs Jackson from an adoption agency, in Ipswich, dated 6 May 1945.

Dear Lady Hunterton,
I would be very grateful if you could see your way to signing the adoption papers for your daughter. Her adoptive parents are naturally anxious to have the matter settled. Perhaps you would call into my office one day shortly and attend to it.

May I congratulate you on your recent marriage.
Yours sincerely,
Irene Jackson

The second was also from Mrs Jackson and it was angry, almost vituperative.

Dear Lady Hunterton,
I would urge you very strongly not to go ahead with your dangerously ill-considered decision to place your daughter in her father's care. I do assure you that if you feel she will be happier with her natural father, this is a

misapprehension. No doubt you feel that, as the child's mother, you know what is best for her. I regret to have to inform you that you do not. Not only will you be causing great distress to her prospective adoptive parents, which may be of little interest or concern to you, but also to the child herself, who will find herself with total strangers. I would have thought that the maternal bond of which you speak so eloquently might have been expected to give you a little more insight into the needs of your own child.

If, however, you are determined to go ahead, please ask your solicitor to contact me immediately.

Yours sincerely,

Irene Jackson

The last letter, which was rather crinkly and splotchy, was on airmail paper. There was no address.

My darling, darling Caroline,

I know we agreed that you should never know where I live and where Fleur is living also, and I am not breaking that pledge. I also know we agreed I should never contact you again.

Nevertheless, I wished you to know two things.

One is that Fleur is happy, settled and good; she is bright and beautiful, and my mother adores her. So do her aunts. She is saying a few words (in a good, strong American accent), and scuttling around fast on her skinny little knees. She eats and sleeps in an exemplary manner and plays a great deal with sundry pieces of paper, string, and other contents of the waste-bins, ignoring the expensive toys I have bought her in a most determined way. Everyone says (of course) that she looks like me, but when I see her looking at me, in an oddly intent concerned way, or she throws back her head and laughs, and when she falls asleep in my arms, with her small head settled in the crook of my elbow, I know I am with you, or at least a small part of you, again.

The second thing is that I love you and I always will. And I can only contemplate the knowledge that I shall never see you again, and find the strength to live with that knowledge, when I am close to and loving and caring for Fleur.

We both send you our best, our dearest, our most tender love.

Brendan

Chloe sat for a long time in her mother's room. She did not notice that it was dark, she did not hear Nanny calling her, she did not hear the boys fighting and yelling on the stairs. She simply sat (having put the letters and the magazines and the photographs back), as if turned to stone, looking into nothingness, and wondering if the strange pain in her heart would ever go away again.

She wasn't even sure what she felt: confused, yes, shocked, yes, but beyond that – what? How much did she mind? That she had a sister, a sister little more than a year older than herself? That her mother had been in love with, borne a child to another man, not Chloe's own kind, gentle father, a child she had never mentioned. How had it happened, how could her mother have done such a thing, and how was she ever going to be able to face her mother, be even polite to her again? And did it explain her mother's near indifference towards her, that sometimes seemed almost dislike, and did this person, Fleur, was she the recipient of all the maternal love, the tenderness, the interest, that Chloe had never known? All these things she probed, cautiously, carefully, as if exploring the extent of a wound, an aching tooth; and she could not begin to find any answers.

She went to the dance, surprising herself with what a good time she had; came home, slept for a few hours; and then woke up very early with a horrible headache and a raw feeling all over. She got up and dressed, and went down to the kitchen; Fortnum and Mason, the yellow labradors, and their mother Fenwick gave their usual impression of dogs who had not seen any human being of any kind in the last ten years, and followed her outside. It was raining, but Chloe didn't care; she walked a long way, over the fields, and round the lanes, and as she got back near the house, she saw Jack Bamforth's old Standard Vanguard pulling in to the stables. Chloe liked Jack, he always seemed to understand that she didn't like riding and moreover didn't behave as if it was a rather serious personality defect she suffered from; he waved to her now and walked towards her.

'You're up early, Chloe. Happy New Year.'

'Happy New Year,' said Chloe and burst into tears.

'Oh now, this won't do,' he said, smiling at her and producing a large spotlessly clean hanky from the pocket of his rather dirty breeches. 'What's the matter, fallen out with the boyfriend?'

'I haven't got a boyfriend,' said Chloe, sniffing and trying to smile at the same time, 'to fall out with.'

'Just as well. Load of trouble, boyfriends.'

'Are they?'

He looked at her, at the smudged brown eyes, the drawn white face, the helpless droop of the mouth, and wondered what was wrong. She could hardly be missing her mother: Caroline gave her less love and attention than a cat its kittens. 'Is your papa all right?' he asked sharply, for Sir William's health had been giving cause for concerned gossip all over the county.

'Yes, I think so. Yes, he's fine.'

'Your brothers been torturing you? Little buggers,' he added conversationally.

'No worse than usual.'

'Would you like a cup of tea? I've one in the flask.'

'Oh yes, Jack. I'd love one.'

'Come on then. Into the office. I've some biscuits too.'

'I'm not hungry.'

'Please yourself. Well now,' he went on as she settled herself into the tattered leather chair in front of his desk, 'are you going to tell me what's the matter or not?'

'I – I don't think I can.'

'Is it something to do with your mother?' he asked carefully.

'Yes. No. Oh, Jack, I don't think I ought to talk about it. It's – well, it's family.'

'Why not talk to your papa?'

'Oh, no!' She looked at him, horror filling her eyes. 'No, I couldn't. He'd be so – well, no, I couldn't. It would upset him even more than me.'

She looked at Jack and his grey eyes were very tender, very thoughtful, and there was a long silence before he spoke. Then he said, 'Chloe, this may seem strange to you, but I've known your mother for a very long time. Since she was a lot smaller than you. We're – well, we're as close as two people could be, coming from different classes and backgrounds, and me working for her. And when she's needed a friend – which she has from time to time, especially when she was younger, your grandmother not being much use to her, and before she was married to Sir William – I've tried to be that friend. I even made a speech at her wedding. I'm very fond of her, and I think she is of me.'

Chloe was sitting speechless, staring at him.

'There hasn't been much happened to her over the years that I haven't known about. I've never told a soul, of course. I wouldn't dream of it, you don't have to worry. Now you don't have to say anything, anything at all, and certainly not now. But if you do need someone to talk to, or have any questions, you could try me. It would never go any further. All right?'

Chloe nodded. She still didn't say anything.

'Well now,' he said more briskly, 'I've work to do. Your brothers are hunting today and there'll be trouble if their horses aren't ready. Your grandfather used to make your mother tack her own horses up. Much better really. But they can do no wrong, those boys, not in your mother's eyes, can they?'

Chloe shook her head.

'So if you'll excuse me now, I must get on. I should go and get some breakfast if I were you. I'll be here later on if you need anything.'

'Thank you, Jack.'

By mid morning the rain had stopped and a watery silvery sunshine was washing over the drenched fields; Jack was just getting Caroline's horse ready to take him out and exercise him before he kicked the entire loose-box to bits when Chloe arrived in the yard, very pale and composed, with a determined look in her eyes.

'Jack,' she said, rather quickly, as if fearing she might change her mind before she had finished speaking, 'Jack, do you know who Brendan is, and is it him my mother's gone to see in New York?'

Chapter 10

1963

'You're fired. As of now. Just get your coat and go. OK?'

'But –'

'But nothing. You were rude to that lady, and nobody in this diner is rude to anyone. OK. Now go. Scram.'

Fleur scrammed. She walked along the road, furiously swinging her bag. It just wasn't fair. No one was nice to her, no one would help her. Aunt Kate treated her like she was six, her teachers at high school all hated her and criticized her constantly, her own mother was refusing to send her any more money. And now just because some old woman had complained when she slopped just a tiny bit of coffee in her saucer, and she had answered her back, quite mildly really, she'd been fired from her night job at the diner, which was her only hope of getting together enough money to go to Los Angeles.

Over a year she'd been waiting now; it was driving her mad. And she had to go, had to know what had happened.

She didn't believe one word of the letter her mother had written. Well, she believed it, but it just wasn't sufficient explanation. Her father had been a sensible, strong person; he just wouldn't have got so drunk he didn't know what he was doing and wandered on to the freeway and been run down. She'd written back saying as much, and saying she could remember Miss duGrath herself saying it was the story that had killed him, the story and the system, and she wanted to know what story and what system. If Caroline wouldn't tell her, she would find out some other way. If it meant going to Los Angeles, she would go. Perhaps Caroline would send her the money for her fare.

Caroline then wrote back (desperately playing for time), and said Fleur was not to go on her own, and that there was no question of her sending her the money; if she was really determined to go, then she would go with her. She said in any case they had only just begun to get to know each other and needed more time together. Fleur had got terribly excited about this, and had even drafted a letter to Miss duGrath, telling her they were coming but then Caroline had written again (and this had made Fleur really angry,) and said she couldn't come just now because her husband was ill. Not merely ill, he was dying, he had a brain tumour, and because of the nature of his illness, he was subject to very violent mood swings, and she knew that not only would he not be able to cope with her absence, but the family would not either. Fleur wrote back as politely as she could and said that of course her mother must stay with her husband, she could wait. Unless Caroline would send her the money for her trip and she could go on her own.

Caroline had then replied to say that she was not prepared to send Fleur the money to go to Hollywood on her own (although she would on the other hand very much like to make available the money to send her to college) and she would just have to wait, for a great many reasons, not least of which was that she wanted to be with her when and if she began to make some discoveries. Whereupon Fleur decided that if she was ever to get to Hollywood, she would have to forget about Caroline and raise the money herself.

She had got the job at the diner quite easily; she was pretty and personable and had seemed an ideal waitress. Which she was in some ways: she was quick and neat, could run the bills up in her head, and never forgot a side order or whether or not a coffee was to be white or regular. The only problem was the customers. Fleur was finding everybody pretty enraging these days, she couldn't get along with anybody, not even her friends; all her teachers and her aunts had a down on her, and she spent a large part of every day in a furious bate. But the customers were something else: demanding, stupid, ungrateful, mean with their thanks, meaner with their tips. She found it harder and harder to smile, and almost impossible to be polite. And this evening she hadn't managed it, and now she'd got the sack; and only seventeen dollars saved towards her fare.

It just wasn't fair; why did she have to have such a hard time? Other girls had mothers who looked after them and cared for them; she had no one except scratchedy old Aunt Kate, who got worse-tempered every day. She missed her grandmother horribly; although Kathleen had been old, she had been much younger at heart than her daughters, always ready to hear about what Fleur was doing, the clothes she wanted to buy, the films she went to, the music she liked. Living with Kate was awful; and there was no hope of college, no hope at all. There was no money. Caroline had offered to send her, but she didn't believe anything Caroline said any more. No doubt she would need all her money sending her crappy daughter to some expensive school or other. Anyway, she didn't want any of Caroline's money. She was still only a very little way down the road of forgiving her; the last thing she wanted was to be any more beholden to her than she already was. One day, when she was a person in her own right, when she could meet her mother on equal terms, then perhaps they could become friends. But not before.

Although how on earth she was to be a person in her own right, Fleur had no idea. Without college, without a proper education. She was just going to have to be a stenographer somewhere, for some crabby old man, her brains wasted, and would probably die an old maid. Life was awful. She wished she was dead.

By the time she got home she was actually crying; great tears of self-pity and rage rolling down her cheeks. She went in, ignored Kate, poured herself a cup of coffee from the pot on the stove, and went up to her room. She hardly heard the phone ringing.

'Fleur, you don't know me, but my name is Joe Payton. I'm a friend of your mother's. I'm in New York and she's asked me to see you.'

'You don't have to see me.'

'I know I don't have to. But I want to. I'm very fond of your mother and I think you ought to know you're causing her a lot of anxiety.'

'Oh, is that right? Well, why doesn't she just cut me out of her life again? Then she wouldn't have to experience any anxiety at all.'

'You,' said the English, slightly drawly voice, 'need your bottom smacked.'

Fleur put the phone down. It rang again immediately.

'I don't know who's brought you up, but they should have told you that was an extremely unpleasant and alienating thing to do. Not to mention the height of rudeness. I had planned to try and help you. Even tell you a few things which might make you feel better. I really don't think I can be bothered. Now if you feel like apologizing, and making an appointment to see me, you can ring me at the St Regis. Otherwise, you can climb back into your self-pitying little shell and stay there.'

Fleur sat, looking at the phone, tears of self-pity and outrage stinging at her eyes. What did he know, sitting there in his ritzy hotel, what did he know about being lonely and scared and needing money and no way, it seemed, of getting any, and how dared he slag her off as if he had some claim over her? Stupid bastard. God, she hated them all. All of them. Well, there was no way she was going to apologize. No way. She didn't need his help. And no doubt now he'd report back to Caroline that she had rejected him and been rude into the bargain and they would compare her with the mealy-mouthed Chloe and that would be the last she'd hear from any of them. Well, good. She didn't need them. She didn't need anyone. She was managing perfectly well on her own, and . . .

'No, you're not, you silly bitch,' she said aloud, 'you're not managing at all.'

'What was that, Fleur?' said Kate who was passing through the hall.

Fleur said, 'Nothing,' and went and sat on the stairs and reflected how badly she was managing, how much she did need help and that it had been really kind of Joe Payton, whoever he was, to offer it, and she certainly needed it, could probably use him if she put her mind to it. After a strong cup of coffee and several false starts she managed to psych herself up to pick up the phone and ring the St Regis.

'Is this Mr Payton? This is Fleur FitzPatrick. I'm very sorry I was rude. I guess it was pretty inexcusable. I – I got fired today, from my job. I was upset. But I'd really like to see you. Please?'

There was a long silence. Then Joe Payton said, 'OK. I'm sorry about the job.'

'Yeah, well, I guess it wasn't much of one. At a diner.'

'A job's a job. Never mind, I'm sure you'll get another. How about lunch tomorrow?'

'Sure. That'd be good. Where shall I come?'

'To the hotel. You know where it is?'

'Yes, I do. Thanks.'

Joe was sitting waiting for her in the lobby. Fleur looked at him, long and lanky and somehow too big for himself, holding *The Times* in large bony hands, unmistakably English, with his slightly shabby sports jacket, extraordinarily long legs crossed in well-worn grey flannels, a large hole in the sole of one of his brown brogue shoes, a button hanging perilously at the end of a long thread on a very frayed cuff, his blond-streaked brown hair flopping untidily over his forehead, and all her hostility, her suspiciousness had gone: she fell in love with him, just like that. She was not properly familiar with the emotion at the time, had only known pale shadows of it before, crushes on masters, on boys at school, but she recognized it none the less for what it was, strong, tender, sweeping, afflicting her mind, her body and her heart in equal intensities.

'Mr Payton? Fleur FitzPatrick,' she said.

He stood up and a pair of green eyes in a thin, freckled face looked at her with interest and amusement, and he gave her his hand in return, a strong, very warm hand, and that first touch affected her with such strength, such force that she was to remember it for the rest of her life. 'How do you do,' he said and the voice was the usual English drawliness, but with a funny slightly gravelly quality.

'I hope I'm not late,' she said, 'I missed the Express.'

'No, it's fine. I've been nursing a martini, which I only drink in New York, and reading yesterday's *Times*. You look very smart. I'm afraid I don't quite compete with you.'

'Oh,' said Fleur, pleased and surprised he had noticed: she was in her very best clothes, a short kilt over black tights, with a grey turtle-neck sweater and loafers, and Kate's black blazer which wasn't quite right, but better than her own kicked-about donkey jacket. 'Oh well, I don't go out to lunch every day.'

'Me neither,' he said. 'Let's go in.'

They ordered. Fleur, only slightly daunted by the menu, ordered steak, and avocado.

'Shall we share a tournedos?' said Joe. 'They're very good here.'

'Yeah, OK.'

Joe smiled at her, a wide, friendly smile; her heart turned over. God, what was happening to her? This was strong stuff. She hauled herself back into line. Sexy, altogether gorgeous he might be, but he was one of them, one of the other side; she had to be careful.

'Right. Do you drink?' he said.

'Yes. Of course.'

'Sorry. Didn't mean to insult you. Let's have a bottle of the Sancerre. It's delicious. Now then. Where shall we begin?'

'I don't know. How is my mother?'

'She's extremely – upset. And exhausted. With nursing her husband. You know he's died? She's been wonderful. She never left him for more than an hour or so. It's a particularly horrible thing, that.'

'Yes,' said Fleur, carefully sober, 'yes, I know it must have been very difficult for her. I do try and remember. It just – gets hard sometimes.'

'I expect it does. And your – that is, Chloe, she was terribly devoted to him you know, she's been horribly upset. That's been hard for Caroline too.'

'What's she like?' said Fleur, unable to suppress her genuine curiosity.

'I haven't met her. But I believe she's sweet: an old-fashioned girl.'

'No wonder my mother likes her so much,' said Fleur sourly.

'No wonder,' said Joe Payton easily. He looked at her consideringly. 'But Fleur, she – she likes you very much too. You have to believe that.'

'Oh, really?'

'Yes, really. And she'd like you more if she knew you better.'

'Yeah, well, that's her fault isn't it? Sending me and my dad away, for ever.'

'She didn't have a lot of choice,' said Joe and his voice was gentle.

'Yeah, she told me,' said Fleur. She could hear her voice hardening. 'I'm afraid I still find that a little hard to believe.'

'And there's something else,' said Joe. 'She really wants to pay for you to go to college. Why won't you let her?'

'I don't know,' said Fleur, although she did, quite clearly: she didn't want three or four years of being beholden to Caroline, being grateful, being nice. 'I just don't.' She was silent; then her natural pragmatism spoke: 'But I might like to go to secretarial school. Get a good job that way.'

'I'll pass that message on,' said Joe, smiling at her with an odd complicity.

He understands, she thought, with a thud of her heart; he really does understand. 'Does my old-fashioned sister know about me?' she asked, her voice more than usually truculent.

'Yes, she does. She found out while your mother was here with you. She was very shaken. But I think she's survived.'

'Oh.' She was silent, digesting this information. 'So what's your relationship with my mother? Platonic? Or what?' She knew it was an impertinent question, that she was not handling this well, but it seemed desperately important. She needed to establish just where Joe stood in this complex business and how she could and should react to him.

'I don't know,' he said easily, 'that it has a great deal to do with you.'

'I disagree,' said Fleur. She felt irritation rising up in her. 'She's my mother. She's supposed to be devoted to her husband, so devoted she couldn't leave him. Here's you, knowing everything about her, obviously real close to her. The row of beans doesn't totally add up.'

Joe looked at her and grinned again. 'I suppose you deserve some honesty. Yes, I'm close to her. I've tried to be a good friend to her through all this.'

'A friend?'

'Well – a loving friend. Fleur, maybe I could start by telling you how I know your mother. It's relevant. You see I wrote a book, and there was a section in it about your father. I was talking about him on the radio and she heard me. Got in touch with me.'

'Really? So you know what actually did happen?'

'Well – some of it. Not everything.'

Fleur felt as if she had been struggling along a very long tunnel, and that suddenly at the end of it was a faint pinprick of light. She raced, half frightened, towards it. 'Tell me what you know. Please.'

'Fleur,' he said and his voice was gentle, the green eyes carefully exploring hers. 'I will tell you. But are you sure about wanting to hear? It's not an entirely nice story.'

'Of course I'm sure.'

'All right. But have some of that wine.'

She took a sip, a careful sip. She didn't need wine, didn't need cushioning, she needed the truth. 'Go on.'

'Well, there was a scandal. With your father. It – it had received a lot of publicity, and he was dropped by the studio.'

'What kind of scandal? With some woman?'

'Yes.'

'Who was it? Some film star? He was very handsome, you know,' she said, anxious that Joe should be fully aware of how wonderful her father had been. 'Girls always did love him. But when he was here, in New York, he never really got involved with anyone. Not seriously. I guess it was different over there.'

'I guess it was. No, not a film star. A casting director. But then there was some other – problem.'

'Oh really? What?'

Joe was clearly embarrassed. He took another large drink of wine, and said, 'Well, there was a scandal over someone else. It was in some rather unsavoury magazines. Someone less suitable, as far as I can make out. You have to remember I only saw a lot of very old cuttings. It was a while ago, after all.'

'Yes, it was,' said Fleur. Her heart was thumping painfully. She felt there was quite a lot here she wasn't being told, but at least it was something.

'And this casting director, her name was Naomi MacNeice, was very angry. He was dropped by the studio. They are terrible prima donnas, these people, you know. He didn't get any more parts, and he had no money. He was living – well, with some friends, when he was knocked down by the car.'

'And it was as simple as that?'

'Well – yes,' said Joe carefully.

She didn't believe him. Well, she believed him: as far as the story had gone. But there was more and she knew it, and she needed to know, and he wasn't going to tell her. Just the same, it had been kind of him to try to help, to answer some of her questions. And he was clearly trying to shield her from something out of kindness, however misplaced. He had certainly done more than anyone else to try to help. She smiled at him, and said, and meant it, 'Thank you. Thank you so much for telling me. I needed to know so badly.'

The small speech had an extraordinary effect on Joe; he stared at her and swallowed and tears appeared unmistakably in the green eyes. He got out his handkerchief and wiped them, and smiled at her. 'Sorry. Don't mind me. I cry all the time. Can't help it. I'm an old softie.'

Fleur stared at him, profoundly affected, touched by the tears. 'I like it that you cry,' she said finally. 'My father used to cry. Men ought to cry, he said, they shouldn't be afraid to feel.'

'No. Mind you, it can be embarrassing at times.'

'That doesn't matter. Who cares what other people think?'

'Well – occasionally I do.'

'Well I don't think you should.'

'Do you cry?' he asked her.

'Oh yes, quite often. Mostly with temper,' she added. 'I have a terrible temper.'

'Like your mother,' said Joe, smiling at her. 'Those remarkable legs of yours are obviously not all you inherited from her.'

'No,' said Fleur, blushing, feeling foolish, but still wildly delighted that he had noticed, had liked her legs. There was a silence; then more to ease her own embarrassment than anything she said, 'Anyway, I'm glad to know what happened. It's so much less terrible than I expected. It's like – like when you learn the facts of life. Adults get all squirmy and can hardly meet your eye, and then the worst it sounds is kind of tacky.'

'Yes, I suppose it does. And I'm afraid your father's story does sound kind of tacky, too. As you put it.'

'The worst thing,' she said, determinedly not dwelling on the tackiness, 'the worst thing is the waste. The awful waste. It just need not have happened. If he had stayed in New York with us; if he hadn't met this woman; if – well, there are a lot of ifs. Aren't there?'

'I'm afraid so,' said Joe, carefully, clearly recognizing another enormous, unspoken if hanging in the air: 'If my mother hadn't sent him away.'

'So,' she said, 'so, now I know what Miss duGrath meant about the story killing him. I suppose it did.'

'In a way, I suppose so too.'

'And this magazine. What was it called? *Confidential*?'

'No, the original story was in something called *Inside Story*. Even tackier.'

'Who was the editor? And who wrote the story? Do you know?'

'Fleur, I have no idea. It's long since folded. Why, are you going to go and murder them both in their beds?'

'No,' said Fleur, 'that would be too quick and easy for them. But it might be nice to make them suffer rather slowly, for a long time. Don't you think?'

She did feel better. Much better. The state of rage she had been in ever since her grandmother had died and she had met her mother had cooled, eased right down. Hearing the story from Joe Payton, incomplete as it had been, had helped a lot. It was an awful, sad, sordid story, and clearly it was actually sadder still, but at least it was no longer a total mystery. She could begin to face it head-on and meet it in the eye, and get to know it.

She needed to know more, though. She needed to know what this woman was like, who had so casually picked her father up and used him and then discarded him again, like a Kleenex; she needed to find out who these people were, putting out these filthy lies; and she needed to try and see the actual article that had been written. She wondered if Miss duGrath had it; she could ask her to show it to her. And she longed almost unbearably to visit her father's grave.

And of course there was Joe to think about: beautiful, kind, tender, sexy Joe.

She waited for news from Caroline in a fury of impatience, her hostility growing; her tolerance and forgiveness for her mother hung on a fragile thread, and she could feel it stretching, near to snapping.

When she got the letter saying that Caroline simply couldn't get away, not until the autumn at the earliest (although promising that yes, of course she could go to secretarial college), that her children were still upset at the death of their father, that she had to stay with them, she tore it into shreds, flung it into the lavatory and pulled the chain over and over again, weeping with rage. 'Bitch,' she kept saying, 'bitch, bitch.' She had been mad to trust her, mad to listen to her. Caroline was simply not interested in her, she was too wrapped up, totally wrapped up, in her other hateful goody-goody daughter and her disgusting, arrogant sons – well, they had to be, all boys were disgusting and arrogant – to give any of her precious life to her.

Then another letter arrived, a few days later.

Dear Fleur,

I know you will be very upset that your mother cannot take you to Los Angeles in the foreseeable future. I would like you to try and believe that she is upset too. Things are very difficult for her. And I'm glad that you are going to accept her offer of secretarial school. She wants to do this for you very much.

I do think, though, it would be good for you to go to Los Angeles. I wonder if you would like to go with me? I have to go there in July anyway, to research a book I am writing about the new-wave heroes in Hollywood, and it would be nice for me to have your company. We could go and see Yolande, and I could show you around, and of course we could visit your father's grave. I should warn you I shall be busy and not able to be with you all the time.

Let me know what you think.

Joe Payton

Fleur read the letter several times. Then she raised her hands above her head and whooped very loudly for sheer joy. LA. With Joe. Days and days of him. Near him, able really to study him, to get to know him. The offer was wonderful. She sat down and wrote her reply.

Dear Joe,
I think it is really kind of you to offer to take me to LA. I would very much like to accept. I promise to try not to be a nuisance or to get in the way while you are working. Please tell Caroline I quite understand that she is too busy to take me herself, and that I would like to go to secretarial school this autumn.
Yours,
Fleur FitzPatrick

Fleur and Joe stayed at the Chateau Marmont. It was Yolande's idea.

You'll really love it [she wrote to Fleur]. Your father stayed there when he first came to Hollywood. I'd love to put you up, but I don't have the room. Fleur, I don't know how much I can help you in other ways. Naomi MacNeice has fallen from grace and has been mixing her drugs rather too much. She isn't well, and lives in a tiny beach house out at Malibu. She certainly won't see you, unless you say something very clever. I'm glad you and Mr Payton have become such good friends. He is a very wise and kind man. I knew I was right to trust him!
Yr affec friend,
Yolande duGrath

They touched down in LA at lunch-time, in a shimmery, blue-skied haze; Fleur was childishly and, she feared, foolishly excited. 'Oh, wow,' she kept saying. 'Oh, wow.'

Joe didn't seem to mind; he smiled at her and patted her hand. He did it quite a lot. Fleur wondered rather hopelessly if physical contact between them would ever be any closer than that.

He had arranged to pick up a car at the airport. He took Fleur on a quick tour of LA on the way to the hotel. 'There's the Hollywood sign. Did you know it used to say Hollywood-land? They tore the last letters off in 1949. Now, this is Sunset Boulevard, where all the ritzy restaurants were, the Mocambo, and the famous Garden of Allah, and Schwab's, where all the out-of-work actors used to hang out –'

'Like my dad?'

'Like your dad, I dare say, yes.' He put his hand over hers again. 'You OK?'

She nodded. 'Yes, I'm fine,' she said, looking down at the hand.

'Good. Well, I think we'll maybe cut the tour short now, get settled in. Have a drink and then do some more sightseeing after that.'

'Yes, all right.'

Later, just before dinner, they drove up to Griffith Park and looked down from the Observatory; the neatly defined sprawling grid of Los Angeles, softened by the dusk, sparkled below them. Beyond it was the ocean, converted into mist by the evening light. The sun sank steadily, heavily into it. Fleur sighed. It was horribly, painfully romantic.

'It's really beautiful here,' she said. 'I'd like to stay for a long long time.'

'Don't you remember it at all?'

'Not much. I was only twelve.'

'Of course you were. A baby.'

'No,' said Fleur, feeling a stab of irritation. 'Quite grown up actually.'

Next morning they drove down towards Venice; Yolande duGrath was waiting for them with iced tea.

'It's so very nice to see you again,' she said to Joe. 'And Fleur! My goodness, you've grown. And you look so like your father.'

'Do I really? Grandma always said that, but I thought she was just, you know, making it up.'

'Oh, no. You have his eyes, his hair, his height. Just look at those legs.'

'Her mother has long legs too,' said Joe. He obviously felt he had to stake a claim for Caroline somewhere in all this.

'Does she?' said Yolande. 'I'm sorry I didn't get to meet her. Brendan told me so much about her. She sounded a lovely person. You must be very happy to have found her.'

Yolande smiled at Fleur. She felt her face closing in, her eyes hardening. 'Yes, it's nice,' was all she said.

'Joe, what's the new book about? Anything I can help with this time?'

'It's about the new young Hollywood heroes. Know any of them?'

'Not many. I'm better on the old ones. Montgomery Clift, he's interesting. Are you doing him?'

'Yes. And Anthony Perkins.'

'Oh. Now there's a lovely man.'

'Larceny too,' said Joe and laughed.

'Yes, plenty of larceny. I'm glad you remembered that.'

'Yolande, everyone in this town knows about you and your larceny.'

'Could I see the article about my father?' said Fleur. She didn't know what they were talking about, and she felt very on edge suddenly.

'My darling child, I'm afraid I don't have it.'

'Where did you see it, Joe?'

'In the *Sunday Times* cuttings library,' said Joe. 'Great place. But they don't let you take things out. Sorry, poppet.'

Fleur glared at them both. 'I think you're keeping it from me. It's not fair.'

'Honeybunch,' said Joe, 'we're doing nothing of the kind. You have to believe me.'

She didn't believe them, but there was nothing she could do about it. At least he had called her honeybunch. She felt quite weak with delight.

Yolande proposed lunch: 'There's a perfectly lovely Chinese restaurant I know you'd like. If you don't mind driving us there, Joe. Called the Formosa. It's just off Santa Monica at Formosa. It was a great little place in the fifties. Then I thought we could head off to Forest Hills in the Valley and look at Byron's headstone. Pardon me, my darling, I still think of him as Byron. He was Brendan to you, wasn't he?'

'Yes, he was,' said Fleur.

She felt very subdued that night. She had coped with seeing the headstone, had stood there for a long time, while Yolande held her arm, looking at it, reading the still-fresh inscription: 'Brendan FitzPatrick, 1919–1957. Beloved Father and Son.'

'Shall we go into the chapel?' said Yolande gently.

'Yes,' said Fleur, 'yes, I'd like that.'

And then she was twelve years old again, and she was standing between her grandmother and Yolande, holding both their hands, and trying, trying so hard not to cry, digging her nails into her palms to distract herself from the other, dreadful pain, watching her father's coffin, huge and dark and dreadful, disappearing through the double doors, with the small posy of white roses she had placed on it, with a card that read, 'Daddy, with all my best love, Fleur'. When she came out into the brilliant sunshine, she looked at Yolande with the same despair and bewilderment as she had felt then, and discovered it had hardly eased at all.

'I guess I need to get a good night's sleep,' she said to Joe after dinner.

'I guess you do. Want to talk first? About anything?'

'I don't think so. No. But thank you. You're being very kind.'

'I like you, Fleur. I find it easy to be kind. And besides, you deserve kindness.'

The next day he had work to do, people to see; Fleur said she would amuse herself. 'Please don't worry about me. I'll be fine.'

'Sure?'

'I'm sure.'

When he had gone, she looked up the number of ACI Studios and, her heart beating rather fast, picked up the phone.

'I'm going to see Naomi MacNeice tomorrow,' she said, as they ate dinner.

'Fleur, you really are a remarkable young lady. How on earth did you manage that?'

'Oh, told them I was a long-lost relative,' said Fleur, her heart leaping at the tribute. 'They gave me her number in the end, and then I got the maid.

I said to ask if Naomi would speak with Miss FitzPatrick. She said she'd ask. And then she came on the phone.'

'Naomi did?'

'Yeah. She said who was I and I said I was Brendan FitzPatrick's daughter, or maybe she remembered him as Byron. And she said, "Oh, so you're the little girl and how old are you now, eleven or twelve?" And then she said what could she do for me. She went on for a bit about how my dad couldn't act, but had such a wonderful face. That was a bit hard to take, but I took it.'

'And then?'

'And then I said could I go and see her. And she said yes, but she couldn't tell me where he was. So I said that was OK, I'd just like to meet her anyway. And she said yes, I could go tomorrow afternoon. She lives at Malibu Colony.'

'Fleur,' said Joe, 'you really are something else. As they say in your country.' He hesitated. 'Could I come with you? I think you just might need the moral support. I promise I won't get in the way.'

There was a long silence.

'No,' said Fleur. 'No, I really would rather go on my own.'

'OK,' said Joe, and she could see he was concerned. 'At least let me chauffeur you. The Colony is a way away from here.'

Naomi MacNeice was clearly very ill. She was stick thin, so thin it seemed her skin could not contain her sharp bones. Her face was wizened, her hair sparse. She was wearing a trouser suit of aquamarine silk, which hung off her bones like washing on a line. When she smiled, her tiny, thin face could scarcely accommodate the width. And this was the lady who had been so powerful in Hollywood she could pick people up and drop them again like discarded Kleenex: well, thought Fleur, the mighty certainly did fall.

'Miss MacNeice. I'm Fleur FitzPatrick. It's so kind of you to see me.'

'Come along in, dear. Come right in and have some tea. You don't mind if we sit inside, do you?'

'No,' said Fleur. 'No, of course not.' The house was hot and dark, and smelt stale; she felt slightly queasy.

'Good. Only I don't like the sunlight these days. It's awfully bad for the skin, you know.'

She led her into a dark, sunken room, the walls lined with leather-bound books. A fire, the inevitable accompaniment to Californian luxury life, roared in the grate. It was unbearably hot. The chairs were all black leather; chinoiserie-style cabinets and cupboards stood against all the walls. There were photographs everywhere: Tony Curtis and Janet Leigh, Burton and Taylor, Mike Todd and Taylor, Gable, Bogey and Bacall. All grinning, all signed, 'To Naomi' or to 'Dear Naomi' or even 'Dearest Naomi'. Fleur's eyes ranged over them, looking, hoping, to see one of her father. It was impossible and in any case the room was terribly dark; the few lights were fringed and dim. She began to feel she was in some kind of nightmare.

'Now then, what can I do for you?' said Naomi. 'If you want news of your father I have no idea where he is. He left straight away, you know. I should try that agent of his if I were you. The one in New York. The one there was all the trouble about.'

'What a good idea,' said Fleur. 'You don't – you don't have his number, do you?'

'Oh yes, dear.' The reply was almost shocking in its crispness and efficiency. 'Never mislay a number. Just a moment. Mappy! Mappy! Bring me my address file, will you?'

A Hispanic maid appeared with a huge black file; Naomi MacNeice took it.

'Right. Both in New York. Can you get to New York, dear?'

'Yes, I think so,' said Fleur.

'Good. Do be careful there, won't you? Such a frightening place these days. Now then, Clint. Kevin Clint. Nasty piece of work. Yes, here we are, look, write them down, here's a pad. What a disagreeable pair. Do be careful, dear, don't let them sign you up for anything, will you? Hand in glove I'm afraid. They've brought a great deal of trouble to this town over the years.'

'I won't,' said Fleur. 'Er – what kind of trouble?'

'Oh, the usual trouble. They didn't waste their time with anyone who wouldn't play ball. No, I'm afraid no smoke without fire and all that kind of thing. That was why the article was so damaging.'

'Miss MacNeice,' said Fleur, very quietly and gently, 'do you have a copy of the article?'

'Oh no, dear. I had every copy I could get hold of shredded.'

'And you don't know who wrote it?'

'I really don't want to go into all the details,' said Naomi MacNeice and she looked oddly sad suddenly. 'Oh, it was such a waste. So stupid of him. All he had to do was keep his mouth shut. But we did have fun while it lasted. And he was doing well. I handled him very cleverly. Everything Tony Curtis did, I found something similar. He was Tony's style, you see. And it did work.'

'Miss MacNeice, my father was living with you, wasn't he? When – when he was doing so well?'

'Yes, dear, of course. Well, some of the time. Of course I kept him in an apartment of his own as well. It doesn't do to have one's actors too much in one's pocket. But yes, we were together. But that wouldn't have meant he wouldn't have been with Clint and Berelman as well. Nothing means anything very much, dear, not in that way, not in Hollywood. You do what you have to do. Byron did what he felt he had to do. But it was unfortunate they found out.'

'Found out what, Miss MacNeice?' Fleur's voice trembled slightly. 'Please tell me.'

'Oh no, dear, you're much too young to understand. Although you're a big girl for ten, aren't you? But I had to ask him to leave. Of course I did.'

'Of course,' said Fleur automatically. 'Of course you did.'

'But he's a nice boy. A charming boy. I was very fond of him. So many people were. That was half his trouble. And then he'd get so involved with people. There was that terribly handsome English boy, for one. I never trusted him. Although I'd like to sign him now. You don't know where he is, do you, dear?'

'Who?' said Fleur. She was getting increasingly confused, panic illogically rising in her.

'Oh, I forget his name. He was in *Town Cousins*. It'll come back to me. Now where was I?'

'You were saying my father got – got too involved with people.'

'Yes, he did. He couldn't cope, you see, he wasn't bright enough for them all. Just couldn't cope.' She was silent for a long time; Fleur began to think she must have gone to sleep. She shifted in her chair, and coughed. Naomi sat up with a start and looked at her. 'Oh, I'm sorry. I do get so tired. It's these terrible migraines. I wonder, dear, would you mind going? Now if you see Clint or Berelman, they might be able to help. And ask them if they've got anyone exciting to send over to me while you're about it. I need a big star, to get back on the circuit, you know. Tell them I don't mind if he's fucking chickens as long as he's good in front of the camera. Will you remember that, dear?'

'Yes,' said Fleur, 'yes, I'll remember.'

'And if you find your father, dear, do give him my regards.'

'Yes,' said Fleur, 'yes I will.'

Fleur walked out to the car in silence; the sudden sunshine hurt her eyes. She got in without a word, and sat looking away from Joe out of the window.

'You OK?' he said.

'Yeah, I think so. She was gaga. Absolutely gaga. Let's go and get a drink.'

'All right. What about going to Alice's restaurant? On Malibu Pier. You'd like it.'

Fleur shrugged. 'If you like.'

The restaurant was pretty; they sat and watched the surfers. Joe bought her a Bacardi and Coke and himself a beer.

'Fleur, you mustn't –'

'Oh Joe, don't worry, don't start fussing. I told you. She was gaga. She didn't make any sense at all. She thought I was still ten.'

'Ah.'

'She did give me his agent's address, though. And the talent scout. In New York.'

'Fleur, I really don't see why you want those.'

'Well I do. I need to find them. To know what Miss MacNeice was talking about. She – oh, it doesn't matter.' Her voice shook slightly; she turned away again. Joe caught the flash of tears in her eyes.

'Fleur, look at me. What is it?'

'Nothing.' She sounded irritable. 'I keep telling you she's gaga. There's no more.'

'Then why are you crying?' he said gently.

'I'm not. Well, not really. Oh, she upset me. That's all.'

'All right. Don't tell me. Do you want anything to eat?'

'No.'

'Fine.'

Much later that night she was crying; she thought quietly, but Joe knocked on the door. 'You all right? Bad dream?'

'It wasn't a dream.' Fleur sat up, sniffing, wiping her eyes. 'It was awful, Joe. Awful there with Miss MacNeice.'

'Want to tell me now?'

'Yes, maybe I do.' She sniffed loudly. Joe handed her a handkerchief. 'Thank you,' said Fleur, handing it back to him.

'Keep it. I always have dozens. Ready for when I cry.'

'Oh – all right. Well anyway, she seemed to imply that – well, my dad was doing something terrible. With those guys. Clint and Berelman. What could it have been, Joe? Drugs, maybe? Or – oh, shit, Joe, something – something else. Something horrible. What do you think? What do you know?' Her face was working, panic in her eyes; she looked like a small, scared child.

'Oh Fleur, I don't know,' said Joe, carefully baffled. 'Really I don't. You said she was gaga. Obviously she is. Don't cry, Fleur, don't take any notice. Nothing she said, nothing, could possibly be worth taking seriously. You mustn't be upset.'

'No,' said Fleur. 'No of course it couldn't. But I need to find those guys. I really do. Oh and Joe, she said something about some English guy. A boy, she called him. Does that mean anything to you?'

'No,' said Joe, intrigued, 'no, it doesn't. Did she say a name?'

'No, she'd forgotten. He was in some film called – what was it? *Cousin* something.'

'Not Burton, surely?' said Joe, incredulous. '*My Cousin Rachel*?'

'No. No, that wasn't it. Oh, I don't know. It doesn't matter.' She was silent for a while. Then she said, her face utterly bleak and white, her fierce blue eyes dead and blank, 'Joe, I don't know if I can bear this. Supposing – well supposing –'

'Don't suppose,' he said and opened his arms, and drew her into them. She lay against him, quite silent; his closeness, the wonderfulness of being held by him meaning nothing, nothing at all but comfort, peace. He stroked her, her back, her hair, her neck, saying her name, over and over again, quietly, tender.

After a bit she sat back and looked up at him, smiling shakily. 'I'm sorry. I just suddenly couldn't stand any more.'

'You've stood a lot,' he said, 'such a lot,' and as he spoke, she saw the familiar tears in his eyes. It restored her to normality, to courage.

'Now you are not to cry,' she said, smiling. 'That's just not fair. You'll start me off again. What a good good friend you are, Joe. Even crying for me. Nobody ever cried for me before. Except maybe Grandma.'

Joe lay awake for much of the night, thinking about the increasingly labyrinthine puzzle of Brendan FitzPatrick, and wondering what he had truly been like, this man, who Caroline and Fleur had loved so much and who seemed so unworthy of either of them.

Background to Lost Years section of *The Tinsel Underneath*. Transcript of telephone conversation with Michael Williams, porter at Santa Monica Hospital, August 1957.

I remember Gerard Zwirn being brought in. I wish I didn't. I wish I could forget it. Fifteen years later, I can still hear him screaming. I never saw a man in such pain. He'd fallen off the pier. It was a miracle he hadn't died. Better he did. His spine was completely wrecked – broken in three, four places. He couldn't speak, just this godawful screaming every time he hit consciousness.

I really couldn't tell you who brought him in. I didn't take much notice. It was a man, that's all I know, a tall man. He'd put him in his car; it was the worst thing he could have done. Made the injuries worse. He seemed very upset. Then I got a trolley and we took Zwirn into Emergency, and that was all I can tell you. I asked how Zwirn was from time to time, because I couldn't get him out of my head; he was there for months, not getting better; then he went off to Rehab and I never saw him again.

1963–4

'But – would it were not so – you are my mother.'

The sorrow, the wretchedness in the voice reached out and touched Joe: touched everyone who heard it. He put out his hand to take Caroline's, feeling, fearing she must have felt it more than most; she did not respond, she was far from him, caught up, entirely engrossed in the scene in front of her.

What have I done, that thou dar'st wag thy tongue,
In noise so rude against me?

Gertrude's face, sensually foolish, looked at her son; her son, distant with distaste, stared back at her.

They must have prayed for this, thought Joe, all of them, to do this, to be on this stage, tonight, one of the most glorious nights in theatrical history, the debut of the National Theatre at the Old Vic: Peter O'Toole, as Hamlet, with all his tense emotional passion, his hair dyed white in the Olivier tradition; Diana Wynyard, as Gertrude, Michael Redgrave, Rosemary Harris, Max Adrian; on and on it read, a roll-call of theatrical aristocracy, the programme bearing for the first time the words the National Theatre. It was a great privilege, he felt, to be there at all, part of it; worth even climbing into his dinner jacket, even worth sewing two buttons on to his dress shirt, listening to Caroline's reproaches in the taxi as she noticed that he wore brown shoes with his suit. 'Caroline, who is going to look at me amongst that lot –'

They had had a lottery in the office of the *Mail*, one of the papers Joe worked for: four tickets had arrived, a pair for the theatre critic and his wife, the other two won by Joe. Joe had a reputation for luck.

He had wondered about taking Caroline: not because he didn't want to, but there were uncomfortable echoes in the play for her, he felt: a dead husband, a new love, a critical hostile child. Well, two critical hostile children, two daughters, but the one on this side of the Atlantic was currently causing her the greater grief. Distanced from her mother ever since she had found the letters from Brendan, had discovered the existence of Fleur, Chloe had become further estranged since the death of her beloved father. She had been overtly antagonistic at first, coldly polite later, and avoided contact whenever she could. She had gone straight back to school after the funeral, and had arranged to be away for much of the holidays. Caroline was finding it hard: she was accustomed to being easily able to dominate Chloe, and now suddenly she was helpless, powerless in the face of her dislike.

As Gertrude was: Joe switched his attention back to the stage.

'Good night, Mother,' said Hamlet with exquisite courteous irony, dragging Polonius off the stage in his wake; the curtain came down, to a sudden silence and then wave on wave of applause. Seats snapped up, people rose, pushed their way to the bar. Joe hated this part of theatre-going: the battle to get a drink, the struggle to find something relevant to say, the crush in the bars.

'Want to go out?' he said to Caroline, and she shook her head, still half lost in Elsinore, in the play, and they stood aside to let people out and then sat down again.

There was scarcely a face that was not famous in the stalls: everyone was there, Olivier himself of course, beamingly benevolent, the Redgrave family, Kenneth Tynan exotic as always – Joe wondered whether the rumours about his homosexual relationship with Olivier were true, and decided, looking at the pair of them, quite possibly so – George Devine, Peter Hall, Peter Brook, the Grades, Robert Morley, Rex Harrison, dozens of pretty girls, scores of famous faces from the gossip columns, David Bailey, Jean Shrimpton, Terence Stamp. Joe sat back contentedly, eating his way through the box of chocolates he had bought Caroline, looking at them all, at their faces, all locked into the smooth unruffled smiles of first-nighters and wondering if it was just another thing they learnt at drama school.

'Excuse me,' said a voice in his ear, and Joe stood up to let its owner past: a male face of extraordinary beauty, remarkable even in such company; that face had never grown, he felt, it had been carved, sculptured out of bone and flesh and blood, the wide high cheekbones, the fine jaw, the poetic mouth. The hair was light brown, almost golden, the eyes grey and absurdly long-lashed; he was only saved from perfection – and thus effeminacy – by a nose that was just a fraction too long, not quite straight enough, but was still remarkable, a pleasure simply to see.

He smiled at Joe and said thank you, ushering a girl before him; she was tall and slim and arresting-looking, with a mass of wild red hair, and looked somehow familiar, and then Joe, looking after them both, realized who the man was: Piers Windsor, the new, great white hope of the British theatre, whose Henry V had caused such a stir, whose Romeo currently had women swooning in the aisles, who was turning his hand now to directing, and wasn't there talk of a musical? He was strongly tipped to take over the Olivier mantle in maybe ten, fifteen years' time.

They settled now, three seats on from Caroline, and Windsor's head was bent towards the girl who was smiling at him, whispering something in his ear; Caroline had recognized him now and was flushed with pleasure.

'He is just amazing-looking,' she said in a hiss to Joe. 'I never thought he'd look that good.'

'Why shouldn't he?' said Joe, mildly nettled by her obvious admiration.

'Because usually they don't. He looks marvellous. As good as in that film.'

'What film?'

'*Kiss and Don't Tell*. It was wonderful. And the other one. *Country* something. Can't remember.'

'I didn't know you went to the cinema so much,' said Joe, laughing at her.

'I don't usually. But I take the children in the holidays.'

'Ah.'

'What was it, the other one? It's annoying me. *Country Wife*? *Country Girl*? Joe, you must know.'

'I don't. Sorry. Oh, thank God, they're all coming back, it's going to start again. There's a long way to go yet. It's the full length you know, this one, all five hours of it.'

'I know,' said Caroline.

The lights were just going down when she turned to Joe and hissed in his ear, '*Town*. Not *Country*. *Town Cousins*.'

'What was? What are you talking about?'

'Piers Windsor's film. It was called *Town Cousins*. I can settle down now.'

Joe shook his head, smiling at her indulgently, settled into his seat. And then saw Piers Windsor's perfect profile etched against the light from an exit and reflected on what a bastard he probably was, a complacent, conceited bastard; and then thought what a silly name *Town Cousins* was for a film; and then, unbidden, idly tracing its way through his head, he heard Fleur's voice, after she had left Naomi MacNeice: 'She said something about some English guy . . . a film called *Cousin* something . . .'

He thought no more about it, nothing at all; put it out of his head, gave himself up to pleasure.

That weekend, for the first time, he went to the Moat House and met Chloe. He thought she was lovely: with her dark red hair and hurt-looking brown eyes, and her quiet, pretty manners. She clearly didn't feel particularly friendly towards him; she sat in near silence through lunch, and was about to disappear up to her room when he asked her if she would take him for a walk.

'I've eaten far too much, and I need to digest. As my old gran used to say. And I know your mother wants to ride, and I'm terrified of horses, and – well, would you walk with me, Miss Hunterton?'

Nothing could have endeared him more to Chloe than the information he was terrified of horses.

'Yes,' she said, 'yes, of course.'

Chloe realized with something near to irritation, merging with relief, that she was enjoying her walk. Joe's shaggy, smiling friendliness, his contentment to be quiet, soothed her hostility. She did not feel embarrassed by the silence, or even obliged to chatter mindlessly in order to fill the vacuum. They wandered out of the garden and up the lane and then out into a field; it was cold, and Joe pulled his rather shabby, threadbare-looking jacket round him.

'I should get one of those,' he said, nodding at her Barbour. 'This is no good in a wind.'

'We could have lent you one,' she said.

'Next time, maybe.'

She found she quite liked the idea of next time.

'This is a beautiful place,' he said, looking across the gentle seesaw of land that passes for hills in Suffolk. 'I don't usually like the country, it frightens me. But this is so gentle, somehow.'

Chloe looked at him curiously. 'What do you mean it frightens you?'

'Oh, I'm a townie. I like to be able to disappear if I feel like it. To be anonymous. You're awfully visible in the country.'

'Oh,' said Chloe. She wasn't quite sure what he meant, but she liked the way he kept revealing his insecurities. Most adults pretended they could cope with anything. Except maybe Jack Bamforth. She felt a bit the same with Joe, she realized, as she did with Jack Bamforth. Comfortable, confident. She smiled at him. 'Well, I like it here. Perhaps I don't have any need to disappear.'

'Perhaps. That was a wonderful lunch. Your mother tells me you're her live-in cook.'

'Well, in the holidays. I do love it. We did have a cook, but she got old, and it's hard to find young ones.'

'Well, you're the best young cook I've ever met.'

'Thank you. I want to do a cooking course, but Mummy won't let me.'

'Whyever not?'

'She says it's silly. She says I should go to university. Did you go to university?'

'I did not. Too busy supporting a couple of wives. And getting on with what I really wanted to do.'

'A couple of wives?'

'Well, not at the same time.'

'Oh.'

He smiled. 'Sorry. Your mother obviously hasn't told you much about me.'

'No. She doesn't tell me much about anything.'

'Well,' said Joe, 'I always tell everybody a great deal about everything. It gets very boring for them, but I enjoy it. I was married at seventeen, and then again at twenty. So I'm a man of the world, you see.'

'What went wrong?'

'Oh, undoubtedly me. I was very immature.'

'I suppose most people are at seventeen,' said Chloe and sighed.

'No, not at all. You seem rather mature to me. But I wasn't. Anyway, I'm not married at the moment.'

'Are you thinking of marrying Mummy?'

She surprised herself by the directness of her question; but she felt so hurt, so rawly angry still at her father's death, she had to know, had to find out where he stood in her new, difficult world.

'Good Lord, no,' he said carefully. 'She's just a good friend. I've been trying to help her through this awful time. That's all. I'm very fond of her though,' he added. 'She's a very special person.'

'Is she?'

'Oh, yes. She's one of the bravest people I've ever known.'

'My father was very brave,' said Chloe, slightly hostile.

'Yes, I know. Very very brave. I wish I'd known him.' He looked at her carefully. 'You were very close, you two, weren't you?'

'Yes, we were. I miss him terribly,' she said and burst into tears.

Joe stood still and looked at her, at her grief and loneliness and loyalty and felt his own eyes beginning to fill. He wiped them with the back of his hand and cleared his throat. This was no time for self-indulgence.

'Tell me about your dad,' he said, taking her hand, passing her his own rather grubby handkerchief. 'Tell me about you and him.'

Chloe told him. She told him about how her father had always loved her best, always taken her side against her brothers; how he had always had time for her, how he had watched her endlessly swimming in galas, appreciated the meals she had cooked, told her she was pretty, pretended not to notice when she knocked things over: 'I'm terribly clumsy,' she said, and 'Me too,' said Joe; how she had felt happy and safe with him; how she no longer seemed to have anyone at all she could call her own.

'He just loved me I suppose,' she said, sniffing and smiling shakily at Joe. 'Mummy doesn't, you know.'

'Oh, I think she does,' he said carefully. 'She seems to love you to me.'

'No, she doesn't. Not properly. She finds me clumsy and cowardly and irritating. She always has. I try so hard, or I used to, to please her. I've given up a bit lately.'

Joe's eyes began to prick again. He sniffed, reached out for the very damp handkerchief and smiled at her, slightly embarrassed. 'When you get to know me a bit better, which I hope you will, you'll find I cry rather easily. Bit awkward for a man. But I can't help it. Anyway, I'm also clumsy and cowardly and irritating, and it doesn't seem to stop your mother liking me. I don't think those kind of things matter. I'm sure she loves you very much. You seem a lot more lovable to me than those brothers of yours,' he added.

'They're awful,' said Chloe simply. 'I hate them.'

'I think I might too. Anyway, all I was going to say was that I hope I can be your friend. But I don't want you feeling you've got to like me, and accept me, because you don't have to do anything of the sort. You can hate me if you want to. I mean I hope you won't, but I can see why you could. OK?'

'OK,' said Chloe. She smiled at him. 'I don't think I'll hate you.'

'Well, that's a promising start. But if you feel it coming on, just let me know and I'll get the hell out of it for a while.'

'Thank you,' she said simply. 'I will.'

Chloe began to feel better from that moment. Over the next few months Joe visited more frequently: sometimes he even stayed the night. He slept in the guest room and she had never seen him and Caroline doing anything more intimate than kissing briefly as he arrived and left; nevertheless, her instincts told her that they were very close, and if she had not liked Joe so much, found him so gentle, so easy, so thoughtful, she would have found it very difficult to handle. He did a lot for her, and her fragile confidence; he talked to her, canvassed her opinion on everything, even showed her articles he was writing. He told her she was pretty, and that she was clever and talented; perhaps the most important thing he did was persuade Caroline that she should be allowed to go to Winkfield. When Caroline told her she had arranged an interview there, Chloe looked at her and said quietly, 'Joe talked you into this, didn't he?'

'In a way,' said Caroline carefully. 'Let's say he made me understand how badly you wanted to do it. I still don't quite understand, but you certainly seem to have a flair for it. And if you really don't want to go to university –'

'I really don't,' said Chloe.

'What do you want to do?' said Caroline. She sounded genuinely baffled.

'Well, for now, cook. Directors' lunches, that sort of thing. But what I really want to do is get married and have babies.'

'Chloe! How very old fashioned,' said Caroline with a small laugh.

'Yes,' said Chloe, aware that her voice was very cool. 'Yes, well, that's the way I am.'

'I got it! I got the job.'

'Fleur, that is wonderful! I'm so pleased for you.' Margie Anderson's plain face was awed as she looked at her friend. 'How much are they going to pay you?'

'Loads.'

'How much is loads?'

'Fifty bucks a week.'

'Wow!'

Fleur had been saying for a while that she wanted to work in advertising, ever since a careers talk at secretarial school, but what had clinched it for her was seeing a Rock Hudson-Doris Day movie the year before; Doris Day had been working at an advertising agency on Madison Avenue, and Rock Hudson had been one of the clients, and although Fleur could see the real thing might be just a little different, she had watched Doris Day coming out of the agency and walking down Madison and she had known that was the kind of glamorous lifestyle she wanted. Glamour was in Fleur's bones; she craved it, and she would roam Fifth Avenue and peer into the Plaza and the Pierre and explore Bonwits and Tiffany's, studying the particular form of glamour to be found there; she would read voraciously about glamorous people and what they did and where they went and what they wore, people like Jacqueline Kennedy and her sister Lee Radziwill, and Baby Jane Holzer and Maria Callas and Truman Capote, so that she did most assuredly know glamour when she saw it. And she saw it in the advertising profession. 'I walked in there,' she said to her best friend of the time, Margie Anderson, 'and there were all these gorgeous people who looked like they were having a good time. It just blew me away.'

Advertising is really just a branch of show business. All the elements are there: the shows, the stars, the critics, the audience. As an industry, it is not noted for its quiet, retiring introverts. The great figures in advertising are showmen: fiercely professional, highly polished, well rehearsed. There are exceptions to this rule: Tom Wolsey, of Lennen Newell Wolsey in London was one, Kenneth Roman of Ogilvy's in New York was arguably another. But on the whole, the born-to-advertise man is only truly happy performing. The audience does not have to be appreciative; rather the reverse. Nothing will give the true advertising person more pleasure than winning round a combative peer group on the creative floor, a cynical account director, a critical difficult client, or a hostile sales force to the view that the campaign he has just presented to them is the best, indeed the only one worthy of their consideration. Agency people get up every morning with a clear mission in life: to create better advertisements than the next man – or woman – and they dress, eat, drink, and talk with that mission in mind. It is a religious fervour; and nothing, not love, not sex, not the maternal instinct can be allowed to interfere with it, stunt its growth, halt its footsteps. And in the sixties, when life was so infinitely showy, when style was God, the industry moved into a new era of brilliance, originality and self-obsession.

Silk diMaggio, a medium-sized agency (for which read billings of sixty million dollars), possessed all three qualities to an excessive degree. Nigel Silk was old money, charming, deceptively languid, blond – 'by Harvard out of Brooks Brothers' as some wag had once labelled him – who provided the agency with its business acumen, and Mick diMaggio was no money at all, eighth child of an Italian immigrant who ran a deli off Broadway. Mick (so another wag had said) talked like Italian ice-cream spiked with bourbon; he wrote fluid, beautiful, witty copy that haunted the public consciousness. He was one of the first examples of the big breakaway in advertising from the WASP culture – Gerry della Femina was perhaps its most famous example – spearheading an invasion of rougher, tougher, brasher people, seeing, saying and doing things in an entirely different way. Silk diMaggio had got their big break when the entrepreneur tycoon Julian Morell had given them his New York store Circe to launch, and subsequently his cosmetic range Juliana; now their client list incorporated Pinski's Diners, upon whom Mick had bestowed immortality by tagging them with the line 'Meals not food', R-S-T-shirts ('the only T you could take to the opera'), Bechstein's

Beds ('every night a masterpiece'), a slice of Oldsmobile, and Chapman's Chocolate Peanuts ('try the willpower test').

Silk diMaggio were clever, confident and highly visible ('People want to work here so badly they crawl on their hands and knees through this door,' said Poppy Blake, administrative PA to the creative department, to Fleur, as she showed her round on the first morning of her job as junior secretary in the creative department). They won at least three major creative awards every year, and Silk and diMaggio were both paper millionaires several times over. The agency was actually on Madison, about halfway between Brooks Brothers and Condé Nast; it occupied the second and third floors of a new building. It had a reception that was all white and chrome, with walls peppered with awards certificates and huge examples of the agency's work; it had a creative department that was one huge, buzzing, hyped-up workshop where the junior art directors and copywriters sat around a vast drawing-board and drew and wrote and shouted and threw paper aeroplanes and made up silly jokey campaigns and gossiped and got excited and bad-tempered and rejoiced and worried and produced very often superb work; and it had side rooms off it where the copy heads and senior art directors did much the same in a very slightly quieter, more ordered style. Mick diMaggio's office was on a gallery, approached by a spiral staircase in the very centre of the creative floor; he could be seen there (and he could see all his staff from it) from very early in the morning until very late at night. His office furniture consisted of a large drawing-board, a high swivel stool, a fridge and a stereo, on which he played classical music all day long. His mood could be gauged by the style: opera heralded triumph and excitement, orchestral music meant intense cerebral activity, reedy esoteric sounds indicated depression or even despair. The rare occasions when Mozart was actually replaced by Puccini or even Wagner were heady: they meant a problem had been cracked, a copyline created, a new campaign born. On really good days when the volume level was turned up high, he would appear on his spiral staircase, his broad swarthy face beaming, a champagne bottle clasped in one brown hairy hand and several glasses slung upon the fingers of the other.

'Gather round,' he would cry, 'we have it here. Listen, listen and look,' and they would stand there, the young ones, sipping the champagne, looking at his roughs, reading the honeyed, funny, charming, totally relevant words and learning what advertising was all about. The senior art directors and copywriters didn't join in this adulation; they thought it was self-indulgent and unnecessary, and would pretend they weren't noticing all the hubbub and shouting and even the popping of the corks, but sooner or later they would get drawn out. Mick would put his head round first this door and then that, beckoning, saying, 'Come along, come along, join in the fun, we have something to celebrate here I think,' and in the end they would all come out and there would be a brief, noisy party while everyone told him how wonderful he was and then they would all go back to work. Mick would go and find Nigel Silk, who worked on the floor above in a great

Japanese-style room with a black door and black blinds and a white-tiled floor, and endeavour to sell the new campaign to him.

Nigel was not easy to sell work to; like all the best advertising account men he was totally unimpressed by creative work for its own sake; there had to be a rationale, a totally straightforward, commercial reason for saying what was being said. It was no use, he said, an ad being funny, or clever, or charming, or beautiful if it wasn't going to persuade the public to put money down on the counter and ask for the product by name. He and Mick had some terrible fights, and Mick would threaten to resign and go and work for Doyle Dane or Ogilvy's or Wells Rich Greene, who were all constantly making him offers, and Nigel would say fine, off you go, I'll help you clear out your desk, but Mick never went and Nigel nearly always won.

Seeing which of Mick's campaigns got through Nigel's black door and were released to the clients for their delectation and hopefully their approval probably taught the rest of the agency more about advertising than anything else.

Fleur felt as if she had died and gone straight to heaven in her first few weeks at Silk diMaggio; she was in a state of total enchantment from the moment she walked through the door in the morning until she had to be dragged out of it at night. She sensed an instinct in herself about advertising: she could see how it worked and why; she felt serene in what she was doing, and she felt at home. She had a sense of being absolutely in the right place, that she had been born to do what she was doing. She woke up in the morning and felt a thrill of pure pleasure going through her at the prospect of what lay ahead; it seemed to her better than anything, better than going to the movies, going to parties, shopping, gossiping. Indeed as she said to Margie quite frequently, working at Silk diMaggio was exactly like going to the movies and a party and shopping and gossiping, all rolled into one, it was that heady, that much fun. She had been lucky to get the job, and she knew she was lucky, coming as she was from a year's temping in tedious jobs in downtown New York and with no more qualifications to her name than graduating from Brooklyn High School and completing a secretarial course in an admittedly excellent college and with the highest marks in the class; but she also knew that the creative department in general, and Poppy Blake in particular, had seen off six secretaries in as many months, and that she was earning every cent of the fifty dollars a week they paid her. In fact, she told herself firmly, as she set out from what was now her Aunt Kate's house in Sheepshead Bay, a little over an hour before she needed to on her first morning, they were lucky to get her.

By the end of the first month, Poppy and the rest of the department were immensely impressed by her. Fleur was a worker. She didn't mind how late she worked, or how menial the job she was asked to do. As well as typing with formidable speed and accuracy, filing with awe-inspiring discipline, turning a stash of tatty, half-destroyed bills for sandwiches and Cokes and cigarettes into neat petty cash accounts, and getting everybody off to meetings with all the right notes, roughs and copylines, she would do other things too that were no way in her job description. She would come in at six a.m. if she was asked, or even if she wasn't, to tidy up the studio or to sort out sheets of contacts and boxes of transparencies, she would stand in patiently for models on photographic sessions for hours, while perfectionist art directors fiddled with reflector boards and fill-in flash and wide-angle lenses; she would book and cancel and rebook studios and locations; she would organize sandwiches and coffee and wine and cigarettes for meetings, and always remember that Poppy only liked rye bread and Will Wingstein, the copy chief, only drank Sanka and that Mick diMaggio didn't like ice with his bourbon; she had even been known to wash the studio windows one morning when there had been no time to get the contractors organized, and Nigel Silk had said the chairman of RST was coming in and could they get the goddamned things clean, he had never seen anything quite so filthy outside the Bronx.

Everybody liked her and all the men – or at least all the men who were not homosexual – fancied her; she was so pretty and coolly sexy, with her dark blue eyes and her nearly black hair, carved into the neat, geometric bob that the English hairdresser Vidal Sassoon had made famous, her long long legs, ever more gloriously visible as skirts rose and rose, her narrow, slender body with its oddly voluptuous breasts. She was funny too, and in spite of being a touch spiky, she was very good-natured, she didn't mind being teased, or even shouted at, and if she did feel cross when the older and more lecherous members of the staff patted her neat, firm little buttocks in the corridors or the lifts, she never showed it, merely smiled patiently and tolerantly at them and hurried on her way. And yet she had no particular friend at the agency; she was not to be seen gossiping with the other girls in the sandwich bar at lunch-time or in the evening, she did not go out with them on hen nights, and never accepted invitations from the men in the agency either. She remained just slightly alone, slightly aloof; never involved in quarrels, feuds, petty politics. She simply went to the agency every day and worked, and got to know how everyone else worked; from the very beginning it seemed very clear to her that if you were going to succeed in life you succeeded on your own terms, in your own style, you capitalized on your own strengths, you learnt to camouflage your own weaknesses and you didn't get caught up in anyone else's. And Fleur was going to succeed: and when she was successful, she had a very clear agenda.

At the top of it, way above her own apartment, a walk-in closet full of clothes and a series of love affairs with men over whom she had total control, was the clearing of her father's name, and revenge on whoever it was who had sullied it – and caused his death. That was still, through all her new happiness, her growing confidence, her increasing awareness of her considerable personal assets, the force that drove her. It was one of her first thoughts every morning and one of her last every night. She seemed to be no nearer achieving it: she had visited the addresses given her by Naomi MacNeice for

Clint and Berelman and found them long gone; she had trawled the phone directories, *Variety*, the theatre listings, all in vain. Clint and Berelman, it seemed, might have never existed, so efficiently, so thoroughly had they disappeared. She had even considered putting a notice in the Missing Persons columns, but had drawn back from that one on the advice of Poppy (in whom she had confided some fragments of her story) who said she would get a thousand letters from nuts, all hoping for some money, and none from the guys she was looking for. She had written to Yolande, in the hope that maybe they were still in Hollywood, and Yolande had written back to say they were not, but that she would keep an eye out for them; and so for the time being she was forced to abandon her quest. But not for long: she was not going to allow them to elude her for ever. She couldn't.

When she had been at Silk diMaggio for six months, she was working late one night, filing a mass of contact sheets and negatives that had been left on her desk several hours earlier, when the door opened and Nigel Silk walked in.

Fleur was a little in awe of Nigel; Mick was a known entity, he often patted her head as he went past, winked at her as she took his coffee or his Coca-Cola into meetings, asked her how she was. But Nigel was, she felt, truly the boss: remote, authoritative, powerful. She had also never known anyone like him in her life; embryonic diMaggios – clever, emotional, volatile – she had gone to school with, lived next door to, all her life, but tall cool blond men in suits from J. Press and pink button-down shirts from Brooks Bros and Gucci shoes and briefcases, they were creatures from another country altogether, an alien race, one whose language and customs and lifestyles were almost unintelligible to her.

Almost, but not quite.

'It's Miss FitzPatrick, isn't it?' he said, smiling his slightly remote, cool smile.

'Yes. Fleur FitzPatrick.'

'What a pretty name. It sounds as if you made it up.'

'I didn't.'

'No, I'm sure you didn't. It's very late, Fleur FitzPatrick. Very late indeed.'

'I know, Mr Silk. I just wanted to get this done.'

'Can't you do it in the morning?'

'I've got a session in the morning. And lunch for twenty-two to get in by midday.'

'Really? What a hard-working girl you are! I hope you enjoy yourself enough to justify all this endeavour.'

'Oh, I do,' said Fleur, sitting back in her chair and smiling up at him. 'I just absolutely love it here.'

There was such pleasure, such pure, undisguised honeyed conviction in her voice that Nigel was startled. 'Do you? Good. That's how you need to feel about it, you know, that's how we all make the business work.'

'I know it,' said Fleur, smiling up at him.

'Well, Miss FitzPatrick, I'm going home now. I don't like to think of you alone in the building. Can I give you a lift anywhere? Where do you live?'

'Brooklyn.'

'Ah. Well, what about the nearest subway?'

'No, really,' said Fleur, 'I'd rather finish this. I'll be fine.'

'And I'd rather you didn't. Come on. Look . . .' He hesitated. 'I live quite near here. In Sutton Place. My driver is terribly under-employed. And I'm not going out tonight. My wife has invited eight extremely boring people to dinner. If you don't mind making a detour, I'll have him drop you home.'

Fleur looked at him, at his grey eyes, his perfectly cut fair hair, his beautiful clothes, his tall slight frame, and thought she had never before this moment known quite what a gentleman was. She decided she liked the breed. He wasn't gorgeous like – well, like Joe was gorgeous – but he was very attractive.

'I don't mind doing a detour at all,' she said. 'Thank you very much.'

Later that night Mr Perkins told Mrs Perkins that Mr Silk seemed to have his eye on a new young lady, and Mrs Perkins should just remember what he'd said and he'd watch the situation very closely, it was going to be interesting, and if he knew anything at all, it was that the young lady in question would be more than a match for Mr Silk any day of the week.

Within a month she had gone to bed with Nigel Silk. Looking back afterwards, wondering why she had broken all her rules for him, she could see it was because he was going to help her towards one of the ultimate goals she had set herself. Not a brilliant career, she could see to that for herself, on the back of her own talent and drive and guts, but towards a glamorous, glitzy lifestyle. Nigel Silk was a crash course in glamour.

'He's married of course,' said Fleur to Margie Anderson, because she was the only person she could tell, 'to someone absolutely gorgeous. She's friends with Jackie Kennedy. I was reading about her in *Vogue* the other day. She's terribly terribly rich, much richer than him, and they have an apartment in Sutton Place and a house at Bar Harbor, and a yacht, and she's on the best-dressed list, well, the *Woman's Wear Daily* one anyway. She's blonde and very tall.'

'Well, why should he be interested in you?' said Margie, who was slightly sceptical about Fleur's new conquest.

'Because she bought him, and he's bored with her.'

'How do you know?'

'Agency gossip.'

'You shouldn't believe gossip.'

'I always believe gossip,' said Fleur. 'It's usually at least partly true.'

It was partly true; Serena Silk treated Nigel rather like some well-trained dog. She had set him up in business, she owned both their homes, she ran their lives and in particular their social lives, and the whole arrangement suited him as well as it suited her. The one bit of real estate that Nigel owned was a studio apartment in a warehouse downtown, near the financial district; it was a place, he explained to Fleur over their second (or was it their third?) after-work drink together, where he could work in complete peace, when he needed to get away from the hubbub of the agency, the phones, the incessant interruptions. Fleur had nodded politely, and accepted his offer to show it to her; it had housed, apart from a desk and a light-box, and a few other office accessories, a very large bed.

Fleur had not had a great deal of sex; she had been to bed with a couple of boys at high school, and with a young waiter at a diner at Sheepshead Bay, and she had had an affair with a teacher (which had resulted in the pregnancy, and the abortion which Caroline had paid for: she sometimes felt bad about that these days, but then told herself that it was the very least her mother could do for her, having abandoned her and neglected her all her life). But she had had enough sex to know that Nigel Silk was absolutely no good at it. On the other hand, everything else to do with the affair was fun: after the sex, for instance, they always showered together and standing there in the steaming, fragrant water (lathering one another with Chanel No 5 soap) was much better and more exciting than the sex because it was glamorous and fun, and the sort of thing that happened in the movies. He had given her a huge white bathrobe and they would sit for hours, talking and drinking champagne and watching the skies and sometimes having a picnic which he brought with him, lobster or salmon and wonderful exotic salads and peaches or raspberries, and gorgeous soft, runny cheeses, Brie and Roquefort; that was all fun. Sometimes she stayed the night there in the studio (telling her Aunt Kate that she was staying with Margie) and in the morning they would have breakfast, coffee and croissants and orange juice, watching the sunrise on the waterfront.

He called the shots, named the days; he never took her anywhere, the studio was their territory and that was that. Serena had no idea it was there, he said, but if she did it wouldn't matter, she wouldn't care.

He would spend week nights in the studio with Fleur, but never weekends; he brought her presents which she had to keep in the studio and never wear to the office. It was frustrating, but it was nice to know they were there, and fun to use them when she was there; she now had a Gucci watch, and a Gucci ring, a Tiffany key chain, a big leather Gladstone from Mark Cross, several shirts and cashmeres from Brooks Brothers, a sweater from the Bermuda Shop, and a great deal of very expensive lingerie from Saks and Bonwits. She was learning and she was learning fast. Nigel had also given her the money to get her hair really well cut at Kenneth, and although she was not allowed to wear the clothes he bought her, she had a vast stock of Chanel No 5 perfume, so she smelt expensive all the time, which made her feel good about herself, and he did let her buy some expensive shoes from time to time, because she managed to persuade him that no one would notice. He also paid for her to have driving lessons, and even took her on a long weekend to Miami, which was a disappointment because instead of going to Palm Beach which she would have loved, they stayed at Miami Beach, which she hated, despite having the largest suite in the Alexander Hotel. She supposed he was frightened of meeting people he knew at Palm Beach.

The whole arrangement suited Fleur very well; she was not remotely in love with Nigel, she had no other claims on her leisure time, and she felt she was gaining a great deal from the relationship. She was, she told herself, getting a college course in glamour, and she was going to graduate summa cum laude. And all she had to do by way of payment was listen to and sympathize with Nigel, and tell him he was wonderful in bed.

Nigel had told her one lie: that Serena would not care if she found out. Fleur was sitting in the studio late one evening, wondering what had kept Nigel, when the door opened and Serena walked in. She was very polite, almost charming, told Fleur that it was time for her to leave, that enough was enough, that she had told Nigel the same thing, and asked her for the key to the apartment and her charge cards. Discomfited for the first time, Fleur said she had no charge cards, but handed over the key.

'I hope,' said Serena, smiling at her sweetly, 'you don't imagine he was in love with you.'

'Oh no,' said Fleur, smiling equally sweetly back, 'anyone can see Nigel is only in love with himself.'

After Serena had gone, she took the leather Gladstone and packed it carefully, with all the lingerie and shirts and sweaters and Bermudas and polos; the jewellery, and the bags. As a final stroke of inspiration, she took the bathrobe.

She didn't quite know whether to laugh or be angry; she certainly wasn't upset. Only her pride was hurt, and that didn't really matter, nobody had ever known about it. Except for Margie of course, and she would just admire the way Fleur had handled it all. She wouldn't look down on her, just because it was over. And she had learnt a lot about glamour and gained a lot of nice clothes. But it would still be nice to upset Nigel, to worry him, to leave him with a legacy of pain. Stupid bastard.

Inspiration suddenly came to Fleur. She sat down at the big desk and wrote a note to Nigel at the agency, marked it personal, and mailed it on the way out.

Miss Delmont handed it to him, lips pursed, the following morning, and watched him carefully as he read it, while appearing to be busy at her filing. She observed that he was quite white, and clearly shaken; he tore it into tiny pieces and then sat looking out of the window in silence for a long time. Finally he got up and poured himself a neat bourbon.

'So what did it say, this note?' asked Margie, looking at her friend in awe over an espresso the following evening.

'Oh,' said Fleur coolly, with a funny little smile, 'I told him I hadn't been taking the pill since Christmas and that my period was late. I said I'd let him know as soon as I was certain, but that of course as a good Catholic girl, I wouldn't be able to consider having an abortion.'

'Oh, Fleur,' said Margie. 'You are clever.'

'I know,' said Fleur.

Background to early Hollywood chapters, *The Tinsel Underneath*. Interview with Estelle Mapleton, maid to Naomi MacNeice.

I liked Mr Patrick very much. He was always so kind to me. He was a genuine person. You don't meet too many genuine people in this town. He once lent me a hundred dollars. He said, 'I know you may not be able to give it back for a long time, Mappy – that was what Miss MacNeice called me, Mappy, I hated it – but don't worry about it.'

But he was a silly boy. No match for the system really. He trusted people, that was his problem. He even trusted Miss MacNeice. There was always someone, someone he had around his neck, someone he was trying to help. He used to say, 'I've been lucky, Mappy, I feel I should pass some of it on.'

I never heard him talking about anyone called Zwirn, but that doesn't mean a thing. I do remember something about Kirstie Fairfax though. It was very sad that. She was a lovely girl, Byron had met her somewhere, tried to persuade Miss MacNeice to give her a tiny part in a movie. They had a row about it. She was very jealous. He had only to look at a girl, and she went ape-shit. And then there we were being told he'd been looking at boys.

It was very bad, the scandal. I was ashamed of Miss MacNeice. I never saw anyone kicked out faster. He had no chance to explain, to disprove anything. One day he was in his apartment, with his car and his fancy clothes; the next he was out on the street in the things he stood up in. I said to her, Miss MacNeice, 'What will become of Mr Patrick?' and she said she never wanted to hear his name again, that as far as she was concerned, he didn't exist. He phoned a couple of times; I tried to get her to speak to him, but she wouldn't. One awful day he turned up outside the house on San Ysedro. He stood outside the gate all day ringing on the bell; I kept going down, saying go home, Mr Patrick, just go along home, you know she won't see you. 'I don't have a home, Mappy,' he said, 'unless you count the beach.' That was just before the accident. When she got home she just drove past him and in. Parsons said she could have killed him, the wheels were so close. I think, you see, she was really fond of him. I think she was very hurt.

Parsons, Miss MacNeice's driver, thought the same. But we both liked Mr FitzPatrick. His trouble was, you know, he was too honest. And he trusted people. You can't trust people in this town.

That's what killed him in the end. Trusting people.

I'm sorry I haven't been more help.

Chapter 12

1965

'Chloe, I love you. Will you marry me?'

Joe Payton licked his fingers carefully one by one and looked across the kitchen table at her. 'I cannot allow any woman who can make a chocolate mousse like this one to get away from me. Be mine, and I'll keep you in squalor for the rest of your life.'

Chloe giggled. 'All right. I accept. Will you tell Mummy, or shall I?'

'Oh, you can. Definitely.'

'Fine. Here, give me that bowl back, there's still much too much in there to waste.'

'It's not wasted if it's going into me.'

'It can go into you later. Now look, you've got chocolate all over your sleeve.'

'Oh, my God. And I was looking so immaculate.'

He rubbed the mousse rather half-heartedly with his handkerchief; it spread it slightly more evenly on to the shirt sleeve, but had no other effect at all. As the sleeve already had a hole in it at the elbow, and the collar was frayed almost into nothingness, the general effect was not markedly worse.

He sighed. 'It says here' – he indicated the *Daily Mail* which he was reading in between licking Chloe's various cooking utensils – 'that David Frost always looks svelte. I'd love to look svelte, wouldn't you?'

'Yes, but I don't think either of us are very likely to,' said Chloe.

'Oh, I don't know. When you went off to London the other day in that white coat thingy and those white boots, I thought you looked wonderfully svelte.'

'Thank you, Joe. But I didn't tell you what happened: I spilt my British Rail coffee on the coat and when I got to London I had to hotfoot it to Fenwicks and get something else to wear.'

'Well, never mind. At least you started out looking svelte. I never even begin. And you've got your honours degree, haven't you? I haven't got anything like that.'

'Yes, I've got my degree.' She smiled at him; it was one of the many jokes they shared, she and Joe, which annoyed Caroline and which they knew annoyed her, about her honours degree in cookery, in actual fact her diploma from Winkfield Place.

'Now look, my darling,' said Joe, standing up, 'I have to go up to town now; your mother said she'd be back from her ride before now, but she isn't as we can both plainly see, so can you tell her I've gone and I don't know when on earth I'll be back. It's all down to when this preview ends, and whether the divine Miss Christie is there or not. Now you'd better not present that piece of information quite like that to your mother, she might get the wrong idea.'

'All right. See you later.'

'Bye, darling.'

'Bye, Joe. Oh, Joe –'

'Yes, darling?'

'Don't you think you might stand more of a chance with Miss Christie in a clean shirt?'

'Maybe. Yes, OK. I'll take one with me and change on the train. I'm awfully late.'

'All right.'

Chloe looked tenderly at his departing E Type, screeching out of the gates. She adored Joe.

Just over a year after her father died he had moved into the Moat House 'on a part-time basis' as he put it; he still kept his shabby flat in Primrose Hill, since he could never, he explained to Chloe, become a country lover. She had not felt in the least that her father had been set aside for someone else, but simply that there was another person in the family, a successor of sorts, who he would have found it easy to like and accept himself.

The arrival of Joe in her life had eased her relationship with her mother too; they had talked quite a lot about Caroline's past, about her relationship with Fleur's father, although hardly at all about Fleur, that really was too painful, and Joe had managed to explain how it might have happened, and to soothe her hurt – to a degree. They were polite to each other, these days, she and Caroline, kissed each other at Christmas and on birthdays, and tried to be considerate of one another, but that was the full extent of their relationship. Certainly, she did not feel her mother loved her. Joe was right about an awful lot of things, but not that. Caroline tolerated her, Chloe felt, appreciated her good nature and her helpfulness, was grateful that she liked Joe, and didn't give her any trouble, and that was about the full extent of her emotions towards her. Chloe felt more or less normal about life again, except when she thought about Fleur; and most of the time she fought off such thoughts by sheer willpower. But when the willpower failed, she was consumed with a white, blistering heat of jealousy. She supposed this was what it must be like to feel jealousy over some man. Only it couldn't be worse. This was agony.

She knew Joe had met Fleur, indeed he had tried to tell her she would like Fleur; but she had politely but very firmly shut him up on the subject.

'I don't want to hear anything about her, Joe, good or bad. I'd rather just think she wasn't there at all. If you don't mind.'

And Joe had shrugged and given her his sweetest smile, and said he didn't mind at all, but if she changed her mind, he was around. Chloe told him she wouldn't change her mind. She simply closed her mind to her, in a way that was half fierce, half frightened. She was sure that Fleur was amusing, confident, pretty and thin, that she didn't knock things over, and that Caroline and she had long, easy, close conversations with one another; just the knowledge that she was there, on the other side of the world, was a permanent, almost physical pain in her life; but she had to live with it, it wasn't going to go away, and it was like being overweight and clumsy, something she had to endure and to try to cope with.

She had once, after a solitary dinner and two glasses of wine with Joe, when Caroline had been taking the boys somewhere, said as much to him; he had looked at her in astonishment and instead of talking about Fleur, had said yes, sure she was clumsy, it was one of the most endearing things about her, but she wasn't overweight, surely she knew that, she was a knockout these days, and the sooner she realized that the better.

Chloe had gone upstairs after that, and studied herself in the mirror, seeing herself clearly for the first time for years, and she could see to her great amazement that he was right: well, perhaps not knockout, but she had lost a lot of weight, and although she wasn't sliver thin, for she had her grandfather's slightly heavy build, there was no fat on her body at all, she was slender, and looked much taller too; her face had taken shape, she had cheekbones there all of a sudden, and an extremely pretty curving jaw, and her brown eyes looked larger and her mouth wider and more expressive. Her hair was a bit wild; it was a nice colour, that dark red, but maybe she should get a decent haircut? A bob maybe? Her legs had lost weight too, got more shapely; they weren't her mother's legs, thoroughbred legs, Jack had called them once, but they weren't bad, and she could probably get away with the new short skirts now. Chloe stood there for a long time, hitching up her pink tweed skirt, turning from left to right, sucking in her cheekbones, pouting into the mirror the way models did into the camera, and felt a wild, heady excitement. She was pretty! It was true. Actually pretty! And more than pretty, she was almost thin. It was amazing. Astonishing! Why hadn't she realized? Why had it taken Joe Payton to point it out to her?

And then she thought that once again, if her mother had had more time, more attention to spare for her, she might have known; if she had said, come on, you look really good (or even you could look really good), let's go and buy you some nice clothes, you deserve them, and it'll be fun, we'll have a nice day; but she hadn't. She seemed to give no more thought to Chloe than to the paper on the drawing-room wall, something that was there, to be glanced at occasionally, and checked for signs of wear and tear, and a great deal less than she did to her horse. Not to mention the boys. And probably to her. Her, over there in America. Had her mother taken her shopping, pronounced on what suited her, insisted on getting her this dress, that sweater, make her have her hair cut, or helped her with her make-up? Laughing, chatting, joking with her?

Chloe had switched her thoughts from her with a great effort, went downstairs again to the kitchen, where Joe was engrossed in the *Sunday Times*, and kissed him on the top of his shaggy blond head.

'You're such a good friend to me,' she said simply.

Joe blew his nose hard.

Chloe had got a job with Browne and Lowe, freelance caterers, shortly after she had left Winkfield. Jenny Brownlowe, who was both Browne and Lowe, had taken one look at her, at her smiling face, her neat clothes, her pretty manners, and had known she hardly had to look at Chloe's diploma or the letters from her principal; within weeks Chloe had graduated from number three in the team, designated primarily to chopping vegetables and shopping, to number two, and within months to helping plan menus. Chloe's clumsiness and shyness vanished in the kitchen; she became competent, calm, deft. She had a great feeling for food: she could tell what something was going to taste like before she had even finished reading a recipe; she could time the preparation of three very disparate dishes so that all of them were at the same stage at precisely the same moment, ready to pack up and drive off to their destination (or alternatively to pass over to waiters and waitresses to serve); she had a flair for presentation, using flowers and chopped vegetables and even grasses as adornments for plates and trays and baskets of food (Mrs Brownlowe had once said she thought Chloe would be able to make a plate of tripe look chic), and she was thoughtful and innovative with her combinations of vegetables and fruits, serving such unexpected combinations as aubergines with carrots, grapefruit with raspberries with great success.

Her personality suited Jenny Brownlowe as well; despite being one of the most successful small concerns in London, and having a vast list of clients for whom she did weddings, parties, shoots and debutante balls, as well as the inevitable lunches, she still became neurotically anxious about every single job. Chloe's calm, and her ability to create it in the room where she worked, was invaluable to her.

After a year with Mrs Brownlowe, Chloe was happier than she would ever have believed: and she knew she looked lovely. She had lost still more weight, she had grown her red hair quite long (rather than cutting it short as she had planned at first) and wore it with a heavy fringe that emphasized her brown eyes; and she had learnt to dress. The clothes that filled the shops, Bazaar and the 21 Room at Woollands and of course magical, wonderful Biba in Kensington Church Street, little short shifts in fine wool and cotton and lacy crochet, suited her perfectly, as did the slightly exaggerated make-up all the girls wore with such aplomb: the long false eyelashes, the complex eye-shading, the dark blushers, the light, pearly lipstick. For the first time in her life, she liked looking in the mirror.

What Chloe dreamed about was to be the most important person in the world to someone, someone who loved her and cared for her and appreciated her, someone who had time for her, someone who thought she was worth listening to. A bit like Joe, she supposed; but Joe wasn't her type. Much as she loved Joe, sexy as she could see he was, even, she didn't personally find him attractive. Chloe liked men who were more formal-looking than Joe, and probably rather serious, really well dressed, sophisticated: and dark-haired. Her hero was Cary Grant.

She had never had a boyfriend; not a real one. Boys had danced with her, bought her drinks, asked her to make up parties for race meetings and tennis afternoons, kissed her almost dutifully when they were drunk, or taken her home, but not fancied her, tried to persuade her to go to bed with them. Chloe knew she wasn't very sexy. Her mother was sexy, she could see that, and she could see which of her friends were sexy (and no doubt Fleur was sexy). But maybe love, when it came, would make her sexy, or maybe make it less important; certainly it would do something. It had to. She just hoped it was going to come soon.

After Joe had gone, she made herself another cup of coffee and contemplated the day ahead. She would not normally have been at the Moat House on a weekday; but she had worked the previous Sunday and Mrs Brownlowe had insisted she took the day off.

'See if you can find that flat you're always talking about.'

'Oh – yes,' said Chloe, trying to sound enthusiastic. Her flat-hunting was more than a little half-hearted; she didn't actually like the idea of living alone, and of sharing with a load of other girls even less. When she had to stay in town, she used the tiny boxroom in Joe's flat; it suited both of them. It had initially irritated Caroline, who was jealous of their friendship, but Joe had said he liked having her there, she was company, and she kept the place tidy, which was very nice for him.

Anyway, it was a lovely day, far too nice to go trailing round the endless streets of Earl's Court and Kensington; she was cultivating a large and ambitious herb garden at the Moat House, the fruits of which she trailed up to work with her, to Mrs Brownlowe's delight. She decided to work on that.

She stopped at lunch-time, achingly but happily tired, and sat down to a piece of toast and Marmite (her favoured diet at all meals, left to herself) when the phone rang. It was Joe.

'Darling, I've done something seriously stupid. Locked myself out of the flat. Everything I need's in there. Wallet, car keys, the lot. I can get by until after this bloody preview, but then I need to get in. I seem to remember, or maybe it was wishful thinking, you were coming up tonight?'

'It was wishful thinking,' said Chloe. 'But I have an early start tomorrow. It would actually be better for me to be in town tonight. I'll be your fairy godmother, Joe, don't worry.'

'Chloe, I love you. Listen, you can come and see this film if you like. As a reward, mingle with the mighty afterwards. How does that sound?'

'Terrifying,' said Chloe. 'You'll have to hold my hand all the time. OK, Joe, I'll meet you there. What's the address?'

'Seventy-nine Wardour Street. Basement. Follow the noise of clinking glasses. I'll be waiting for you.'

'Now you're not to be frightened,' said Joe, 'and I will hold your hand. Come on in.'

He had been waiting for her at the bottom of the slightly grubby flight of stairs down into the preview theatre. It was not at all what Chloe had expected: no famous faces, no flashbulbs, no champagne, just a lot of people talking loudly in a very small cinema. Joe found them two seats near the back, introduced her to the man next to her who was a journalist from the *Daily Express* and spent a lot of time trying to tuck his long legs under first his own seat and then the one in front.

'For God's sake, Payton, keep still,' said a small smiling man in front of him. 'You'll be eating popcorn next.'

'Sorry, Donald,' said Joe apologetically. 'Donald Zec,' he said to Chloe. 'From the *Daily Mirror*. Very important person. Aren't you, Donald?'

'Very. Who's this gorgeous creature you've got with you? Thought you were a happily married man, near as dammit, Joe. You really are disgusting.'

'This is my almost-stepdaughter,' said Joe. 'Chloe Hunterton.'

'Stepdaughter!' said Zec. 'Go tell that one to the marines. You stay close to me, my dear. I'll look after you. Why don't you come and sit with me now? This man is as close to totally amoral as it's possible to be. I can't bear to see you in such danger.'

'It's all right,' said Chloe, smiling at him, wriggling out of her coat. 'He almost is my stepfather, and I can handle him.'

'Good. This is going to be a terrible film, Joe. I've written the review already.'

'Is she coming?'

'I believe so. Complete with retinue.'

'Does that mean Julie Christie?' said Chloe.

'No, darling, it means the star. But I'm more interested in one of the supporting cast. Big new hope for the cinema. Name of Tabitha Levine. She has a small but meaningful part. Everyone's watching her.'

'Oh,' said Chloe humbly and settled down to do the same.

Donald Zec was right and it was, if not a terrible movie, a mediocre one, a much hyped tragi-comedy in which Margaret Lamont, who played the lead, married a young man half her age who then left her for her daughter (Tabitha Levine's part). At the end there was some half-hearted applause followed by a stampede for the bar. Joe led Chloe over.

'Julie is managing to tear herself away from me tonight,' he said. 'I just got a message from her agent. I might try to have a word with Tabitha though. She's over there now. Can you hang on?'

'Yes, of course,' said Chloe.

She looked at Tabitha curiously; she was tall and immensely pale, with a lot of dark red hair, not unlike her own, except that Tabitha's was riotously curly. She was wearing an elaborate embroidered Indian dress, several rings on each finger, a squaw band round her forehead, and small round spectacles with bright blue frames. She was smoking and fiddling with her hair, and looked bored and rather intense, quite incapable of putting in the kind of sparkling performance that had just been on the screen. She was surrounded by a large crowd of people all laughing uproariously at her every utterance.

'Bit of a dog I'd say.' It was Donald Zec. 'Got everything you want, sweetie?'

'Oh – yes, thank you,' said Chloe. 'I'm really enjoying myself. Is Margaret Lamont coming?'

'Should be. They all drift in, casually, as if they hadn't expected to find anyone here. Pathetic really. Look, there's Sam Brixton, the director. And oh, yes, here comes Margaret now.'

Margaret Lamont bore more than a passing resemblance to Zsa Zsa Gabor; she came into the room smiling radiantly from behind a large pair of dark glasses, and held out her arms to Sam Brixton.

'Here she is!' said Sam. 'You missed it. Marvellous, darling. Rave reviews already spewing out of typewriters. Come and have a drink, and say hallo to a few people.'

'God spare me,' said Zec. 'Stay there, sweetie, I'm going to get us a bottle before it all disapears.'

Chloe turned round to take another look at Tabitha and put her hand up to push her hair out of her eyes: a voice said, 'Christ!' under its breath and she realized she had knocked its owner's arm and made him spill his wine.

'Oh dear,' she said, blushing helplessly, 'oh, I'm so terribly sorry, let me –'

'No. No, it's perfectly all right,' said the voice, carefully under control now. 'Don't worry, always a crush these things. It was only white, fortunately, no harm done.'

Chloe forced herself to look up and meet her victim's eyes: he was a tall man, very slim, very stylish-looking; he had thick golden brown hair, beautifully cut, and a face that could only be described as chiselled, with high cheekbones and a mouth that was almost girlish. His eyes were large and a very distinctive grey, and when he smiled at her, he revealed teeth of almost alarming whiteness. He was wearing a light grey suit, the entire left side of which was splashed with the wine, and a silk shirt of palest turquoise, and he was smoking through a long cigarette-holder. Chloe thought she had never in her life seen anyone quite so perfect; it was as if he had been made up.

'I'm so sorry,' she said again, 'so terribly sorry. Let me get you some more.'

'No, really, I've had far too much already. We had a bottle hidden under the seat.'

'Good Lord,' said Donald Zec, who had returned with a three-quarter-full bottle of wine. 'Piers Windsor. To what do we owe this honour, good sir?'

'I'm here to pick up Tabitha,' said Piers.

'Oh really? How interesting. I shall tell the gossip column people the minute I get back to the office. Have you two met? Chloe Hunterton, Piers Windsor.'

'I'm afraid we have,' said Chloe humbly. 'I made him spill his wine.'

'Oh, do him good. Humble him a bit. This man has more suits, Chloe, than most of us have pocket handkerchiefs. He discards them when they're used like Kleenex. What's the next project, Piers? Or will this run never end?'

'I hope so,' said Piers Windsor. '*Romeo and Juliet* is a very exhausting play. I have a little scheme, Donald. I'll let you know when it's solidified a bit.'

'Do, do,' said Zec. 'Now Chloe, my dear, there is your escort looking for you, and I have to get back to the office. Lovely to have met you. And you, Piers. Joe, she's all yours. You're a lucky man.'

Then he was gone, and Piers Windsor turned back to his friends with another brief flashing smile at Chloe, and Joe took her arm and said, 'Let's go and get a Chinese.' They sat in a Chinese restaurant in Gerrard Street in silence while Joe wrote his article about Tabitha Levine on a series of paper napkins, and Chloe toyed with some rather unappetizing spring rolls.

'How on earth did you get to be talking to Piers Windsor?' said Joe, finally putting the napkins into his pocket.

'I made him spill his wine,' said Chloe. 'I'm so sorry, Joe. Letting you down in front of your famous friends.'

'No need to be sorry,' said Joe. 'I'm delighted. Man needs wine spilt over him.'

'Well, he seemed quite nice to me,' said Chloe, 'and terribly good-looking. What does he do?'

'You really are an innocent, aren't you?' said Joe. 'He's an actor, honeybunch. A very famous actor.'

'Oh yes, of course,' said Chloe. 'I remember now. I read something about him the other day. He's doing *Hamlet* or something, isn't he, at the moment?'

'Romeo actually,' said Joe. 'With the RSC. Rather too old for the part, but brilliant apparently.'

'Oh, well, I knew it was Shakespeare at least. I don't have a very good memory for names,' she added apologetically.

'Or faces it seems. Didn't you see his most famous film, *Town Cousins*? Made him.'

'No,' said Chloe humbly. 'I didn't.'

'Well, don't worry about it,' said Joe, 'and anyway, it was before your time of course. He's only done stage things recently, and rather serious ones at that. He takes himself too seriously altogether, for my liking. But he is clever. And extremely talented. And he knows it. Anyway, poppet, let's go back to the flat now, I have things to do.'

The last thing Chloe thought of as she fell asleep that night was Piers Windsor's chiselled beauty, and the awful sight of the spreading stain on his immaculate grey suit, for which she had been entirely responsible. She hoped fervently she would never see him again.

Joe had forgotten all about Piers Windsor and the strange, almost non-thought he had had at the Old Vic that night: he didn't even remember when he was talking to him at the preview. It was only afterwards, chatting absent-mindedly to Chloe in the Chinese restaurant, talking about *Town Cousins*, that it came back to him. And even then he couldn't quite remember the form of it: only a half-reported conversation that Fleur had had with Naomi MacNeice. Something about an Englishman, and a film called *Cousins*. Well, he thought, as he tried to get comfortable on his rather lumpy bed – Caroline threatened to burn it every time she came to the flat – it probably didn't, almost certainly didn't, mean a thing. Tiny slivers of coincidence: no more. Naomi was crazed, Fleur had been upset and incoherent and there must have been a thousand English actors in Hollywood at the time whom Naomi would have known. Only not all of them in a film called *Town Cousins*. No, not even *Town Cousins, Something Cousins*, Fleur had said. He wondered what Naomi had said. Maybe he should ask Fleur. Then he thought of where that particular course of action might lead and shuddered. Fleur would be over here on the next jet, loaded gun in her handbag.

No, any idea there might have been any connection with Brendan was a nonsense, and he should just put it out of his mind. Of course the man was ghastly enough to have done anything. Slimy bastard: Joe really hadn't liked him at all.

He looked at his watch: shit, four o'clock. He'd never sleep at this rate. He got up, poured himself a large Scotch, and settled down to read his prized early proof copy of *In Cold Blood*, Truman Capote's latest, the shock true story of two psychopaths who murdered a family in a farmhouse in the middle of nowhere just for the hell of it. He finally fell asleep and dreamed Fleur was in a farmhouse in the middle of nowhere and Piers Windsor was advancing on her with a broken wine glass. He woke up, sweating, to hear the phone ringing.

'Joe Payton? Harry Oliver. *Evening News*.'

'Oh – Harry. Morning.'

'You OK, Joe? You sound a bit rough.'

'I'm OK,' said Joe, shaking his head, rubbing his eyes. 'Bit of a heavy night.'

'Lucky sod. You available for a quick job?'

'Yeah. Probably. What is it?'

'I want a profile of this Windsor guy. He suddenly seems to be news.'

'Piers Windsor?' said Joe, his brain suddenly and magically clear.

'That one. I'd want it fairly quickly. Say in about three days.'

'I'm not sure,' said Joe, knowing he was going to do it, feeling a sharp stab of intrigue. 'It depends how in-depth.'

'Very in-depth. I want him at home; he's got a big place somewhere in Berkshire, where he's got some horses. And a boyfriend I wouldn't wonder.'

Interest grew sharply in Joe's head, to join the other drifting tracery. 'A boyfriend? Is he that way?'

'Don't know. Probably. They mostly are. And he looks it, doesn't he? He's never married again, since the early days. Lots of starlets on arms at premières. Devoted to his old mother. What would you think?'

'I'd think you had a filthy mind,' said Joe cheerfully. 'Any gossip about it?'

'No, nothing tangible. I'm just rambling really. But he's an interesting guy, and very much in the news at the moment. This thing he's doing, this musical, have you heard about it?'

'Er – no,' said Joe.

'Well, it's going to be big. Original. Some poem by someone. Can't remember who.'

'Oh,' said Joe, '*The Lady of Shalott*. Yeah, sure, I do remember.' He felt a stab of something more than just interest. Maybe it was having sat almost next to Windsor at the theatre, maybe it was because it looked like an interesting story, a high-profile one – absolutely not anything to do with that tiny drifting thought – but he wanted to do it. To find out more about Piers Windsor. 'Yeah, OK,' he said, 'but it'll depend on when I can see him. He's quite a difficult guy.'

'Do it when you can. As long as it doesn't take more than three days. A hundred quid, OK?'

'One twenty-five,' said Joe.

'OK. If you can turn it in in two days.'

'Go fuck yourself,' said Joe cheerfully. He put the phone down and started making notes.

Piers Windsor's agent was very unhelpful. Mr Windsor was exhausted with doing *Romeo*, and extremely busy with work on *The Lady of Shalott*. He had done several interviews, and indeed he was surprised the *News* hadn't wanted to do it earlier. If Mr Payton cared to put his request in writing, he would see what he could do . . .

Joe rang the RSC. The stage door manager said he really didn't know when Mr Windsor would be getting to the theatre that evening, but he would certainly leave Mr Payton's name and a note that he had called. He thought it was very unlikely that Mr Windsor would be able to see him.

Who's Who gave Piers Windsor's address: Stebbings, Drewford, Nr Coleshill, Berkshire, and another in Sloane Street, but no phone number. Joe tried Directory Enquiries without success (ex-directory both), wrote and mailed two postcards to the private addresses requesting interviews and then returned to *Who's Who*. Clubs, the Garrick (that was worth a try; he left a message there) and the RAC.

Then on an impulse he called the RSC again: did they have any seats for that evening? They did: a return, second row stalls. Hideously expensive: well, the *News* would pay. Joe reserved it and then set off for Fleet Street and the *Evening News*.

'File on Piers Windsor, please,' he said to the librarian.

'Which one? We have three.'

'Oh – early life. Up to – let's see, 1960.'

'Childhood?'

'Might as well.'

He sat down with the files. The early ones were always the most interesting. There was very little on Windsor's childhood. Born 1921. A few charming photographs of a small boy with golden curls. Father banker, devoted mother, prep school at eight, poor little sod, St Luke's, Worcester, at thirteen, where he'd won the drama prize for playing Juliet; now there was something to blight a young life. Into the air force in 1939, based on ground staff at Plymouth through the war, working in the radar unit – Lucky that, thought Joe cynically; if ever a man had seemed cut out for a safe war it was Piers Windsor – then RADA where he'd met his first wife Guinevere Davies. And then rep and marriage to Guinevere Davies, divorced in 1954, followed by a very long stint doing more rep until 1958 when he did Mercutio at the Old Vic, and then the film *Town Cousins*, which had made him famous. Which took him up to 1960. And no mention of Hollywood, until then, which was much too late for him to have crossed Brendan's path, not even a short stay, no connection with Naomi MacNeice or any of the other names.

Joe felt a sharp stab of disappointment: and then common sense intervened. What an absurd idea: what a flock of wild geese to be chasing. As if it was even imaginable that Piers Windsor would have had any connection with Brendan FitzPatrick and his sordid, sorry end. How had he even begun to entertain the idea? He must be cracking up. Mid-life crisis, he thought, and felt depressed; he took the file back to the desk.

'Thanks,' he said. 'I'd better have the later ones now.'

Piers Windsor (Joe read in several reports) was engaged in a unique project, to stage Tennyson's *Lady of Shalott* as a musical (providing he could get the backing), destined to hit the West End stage some time the following year. He had bought the rights, had spent months working on the concept and was currently engaged in discussions with writers, lyricists, composers and casting agencies – and backers.

'It will be something unique and very wonderful,' he was quoted as saying to a reporter from the *Express*. 'I am more excited about it than anything I can ever remember.'

'Well, bully for you,' said Joe aloud to the radiantly smiling photograph of Piers, and then realized it was seven and he'd be late for the real thing.

There was no doubt, Windsor was a bloody fine actor. He took hold of the imagination and did what he would with it. Romeo's tender, passionate, half-fearful love was a tangible thing; he acted everyone, including Melanie Welsh, who was playing Juliet, off the stage. The criticism, accurate and some of it heavily bitchy, that he was far too old for the part, seemed suddenly irrelevant; his physical beauty, his slight build, and something he had done with his voice – made it lighter, more sensitive – made him entirely credible. The tremble of pain in his voice at 'Night's candles are burnt out' made the house catch its breath, and as he bent over Juliet, said, 'Thus with a kiss I die,' strong men found themselves swallowing hard, their womenfolk fumbling for their handkerchiefs. Joe watched it through a blur of tears, felt genuine pain.

He said as much in a note that he handed in at the stage door; it worked. Five minutes later, Piers sent a message to come to his dressing room. He was sitting removing his make-up, smiling, charming, gracious; Joe half wished he had not come, so effectively did it wreck his pleasure in *Romeo and Juliet*. But he smiled and went forwards, holding out his hand.

'Mr Windsor, that was wonderful. Wonderful. I had tears in my eyes.' Shit, he was as bad as Windsor himself.

'How nice of you. Coming from you, Mr Payton, it means a great deal. To what do I owe the honour of this visit? Drink?' Joe nodded. 'Viv, open us a bottle of the Sancerre, would you?'

Viv, a plump middle-aged and patently homosexual man (a clue? wondered Joe. No, most of them were) who was pressing clothes in a corner of the dressing room, produced a bottle of wine from an ice bucket, opened it and poured out two glasses.

'Very nice,' said Joe. 'Thank you.'

'Not quite cold enough, I'm afraid,' said Piers Windsor, sipping it. 'I always bring one in ice-cold from the fridge and we keep it on ice, don't we, Viv, but it does warm up a bit. Viv, do have a glass yourself.'

'Thank you, Mr Windsor, but I won't.'

'I keep trying to tempt him,' said Piers, laughing, 'but he signed the pledge ten years ago and it's hopeless. Now, you were going to tell me why you were here?'

'You'll find out in the morning. Or if you go to the Garrick tonight,' said Joe. 'I've written you several cards, left lots of messages, requesting an interview.'

'How nice. Who for?'

'The *Evening News*.'

'Well – I don't know.' Piers was peeling off false eyelashes now, looking at Joe warily in the mirror. 'I've done so many lately. Everyone is so interested in the *Lady*. And I'm not mad about the *Evening News*. You're not staff are you?'

'No,' said Joe hastily. 'Freelance.'

'I mean, if it was the *Sunday Times* magazine . . .'

Joe thought fast. He was very well in at the *Sunday Times*. They would probably like a piece. He would get more out of Windsor. And for some reason, he still felt intrigued, unsatisfied. He gambled wildly (and unethically). 'If it was for the *Sunday Times*, would you do it?'

'Absolutely, my dear chap.'

'Could we do some shots at your house? At Stebbings?'

'Well – I don't know. I do value my privacy enormously. Wouldn't the flat do, in Sloane Street? It doesn't feel so much like home. More of a hotel. That would be all right.'

'Well, look,' said Joe, 'I'm pretty sure I could do this piece for the mag. I'll call them in the morning. But I know they'll want the country place. We could do a deal.' He drained his glass, watching Piers Windsor carefully in the mirror. The other eyelashes were being tugged off now; they pulled the whole eye out of shape, which looked faintly obscene. Windsor looked at him and Joe could read the absolute complicity in the look.

'OK,' he said. 'You get me the *Sunday Times* and I'll think about letting you come to Stebbings.'

In the morning Joe called the *Sunday Times* and offered them Piers Windsor at home in Berkshire; they said (as he had known they would) they'd be delighted. Then he called the *News* and (hating himself just a little) told them Piers Windsor wouldn't see him. Then he called Piers Windsor. It was arranged he should go down on Sunday morning with a photographer.

Stebbings was a very nice house: Queen Anne, redbrick, with fine rooms, beautiful grounds, and a wonderful view from the back over the Berkshire Downs. Joe and the photographer were shown into the drawing room, were served coffee and waited three quarters of an hour until Windsor arrived, looking carefully casual in jeans and a cream polo-necked sweater.

'So sorry,' he said smiling, holding out his hand, 'endless call to my bankers about the *Lady*. I think, fingers crossed, we're quite a little further on. So it's celebration time. Now then, where shall we start?'

'In here, I think,' said the photographer, 'and then some in your study, Mr Windsor. I presume you have a study, and maybe a few at the stables.'

'Fine. Providing I can have a few prints. I have a beautiful new mare, bought just last week. I'd like to have a couple of good photographs of her.'

'Sure,' said Joe, giving the photographer a warning wink. 'And I wondered if a couple of shots in the kitchen? I read that you like cooking.'

'I do. Good idea. I have a girlfriend coming down a little later for Sunday lunch. Wouldn't that be rather cosy?'

'Very,' said Joe. And very cosmetic, he thought. God, he didn't like this man.

The pictures took over an hour to do; the photographer was just loading up his car when a dark green Mini Cooper roared into the drive and a very pretty girl with wild red hair climbed out. Aha, thought Joe, Tabitha Levine. The Lady of Shalott herself. Even more cosmetic.

Tabitha hugged Piers, and kissed him on both cheeks. 'Darling, you didn't tell me the press were coming.'

'I didn't know,' said Piers. 'Want to be in a piccy or two?'

'Oh – well, I don't know. . .' Her reluctance was charming, transparently phoney.

'Oh Miss Levine, please do.' Joe smiled at her. 'It would make my article. Make the feature.'

'Yes, darling, do,' said Piers. 'Then we can just mention, you know, that you are being considered – only considered, mind – for the Lady. It's all absolutely marvellous publicity. And it is for the *Sunday Times* magazine. Nothing tacky.'

'Oh – oh, well all right,' said Tabitha Levine. 'I'll just go and do my face a bit. Can you wait?' she said to the photographer.

'Of course. As long as it takes.'

It took over three quarters of an hour. Piers started talking to Joe, dishing out the well-rehearsed details of his early life.

'I had the most marvellously happy childhood: just the three of us. Father died when I was fourteen, which was tragic of course, but until then it was just perfect; lovely summer holidays in Cornwall, and we had such a pretty house in London, in Kensington, near the gardens. I used to sail my boat in the Round Pond, and Mummy and I used to go and chat to Peter Pan. Of course there were dark times, I had to go away to school at eight, which I didn't like so very much, but I really don't think it did me any harm, and the holidays were even more wonderfully happy. And I adored St Luke's of course; you know I won the acting cup for Juliet, a source of great amusement to everyone.'

'Yes, I expect so,' said Joe, making notes: check out prep school for quotes, where is Mummy now, contemporaries at St Luke's. 'Was that the trigger for your acting ambitions?'

'Oh, no, not really, I did little plays at prep school, that sort of thing. I always loved it. I suppose I liked being the centre of attention,' he said and laughed modestly.

Too right, thought Joe.

On and on it went: the days in the RAF ('I was so disappointed never to get any action, but I just had this flair for radar'), RADA (runner-up for the gold medal) and then into rep.

'And then you met your first wife?'

'Yes,' said Piers easily, his grey eyes wide and candid, 'Guinevere Davies. She was the most wonderful actress and a truly lovely person. We were very much in love. But – well, you know as a profession its success rate is not high in the marriage business. After two years our careers began to clash; parting seemed inevitable.'

'What was the biggest clash?' said Joe carefully, raking over dates in his head.

'Oh, she was offered a wonderful part: Jennifer Dubedat in the *Doctor's Dilemma* at the Bristol Old Vic. I had just got a six-month run in Edinburgh. I suppose – selfishly – I thought she should come with me. Although I didn't say so, didn't try to press her.'

'No, of course not,' said Joe.

'And – well, after that it was downhill all the way. We divorced in – oh, 1956, something like that.'

'And you were on the rep circuit all this time? From 1950 to 1958, when you got the famous Mercutio? Quite a long time.'

'Mr Payton, some actors never leave the rep circuit,' said Piers. 'But yes, that's right. The companies got better of course: finally I followed Guinevere down to Bristol.'

'Never tried your luck in Hollywood?' Joe was trying so hard to sound casual, he was afraid it came out rather leadenly.

'No. Never.' Was the voice just a touch too quick, too firm? Or was it imagination, distorting it? He looked up at Piers; the smile was boyishly rueful. 'I should have done, perhaps. But I didn't. Then, tremendously luckily, Hollywood came to me, with *Town Cousins*. And you know the rest.'

'Yes, indeed.' He listened, as Windsor talked about his roles, his interpretations, his ambitions, his theories of acting. It was one of the great hazards of doing an interview: cutting them off too soon. Nobody really wanted to read all that stuff (except the actor himself) but if you didn't give them a good run at it, you never got close enough to them to ask them the tough ones.

Like: why have you never married again; how upset were you by Guinevere's departure; how much money are you looking for to put on *The Lady of Shalott*?

He edged towards that one carefully now: 'How close are you to getting backing for *The Lady of Shalott*?'

'Oh – very near, I think.' Windsor's smile was neat, controlled. 'The thing about this business is, you get the money if you can get the names. I've been wonderfully lucky with my names. David Montague is conducting. Damian Lutyens is doing the lyrics, he's young but wonderfully talented and high profile; he did the score for *Pretty Lady* last year, you might just remember. Lydia Wintour is doing the costumes and the set design and Julius Hovatch has provisionally signed to play the Knight. That was the big breakthrough, really, getting Julius. "Tell the others I'll do it for scale," he said, and that was the most wonderful gesture of course; you know what scale is, Joe, the Equity rate, because then everyone else tumbles in on that and you save thousands.'

'Yes of course,' said Joe. They were impressive names: David Montague frequently conducted at the Royal Opera House (where his wife was a diva), Damian Lutyens was the current darling of the critics, and Julius Hovatch had played in hit after hit both on the legitimate stage and in musicals. Of course they all played follow my leader, these guys. And Tabitha Levine, with her haunting beauty, her glorious voice, her short but dazzling chain of successes, most recently a glorious revival of *Guys and Dolls* in a limited run (orchestrated by David Montague). Piers Windsor was clearly as talented an impresario as he was an actor.

'Why the switch from acting?' asked Joe, suddenly, genuinely interested.

'Oh, but it isn't really a switch,' said Piers, just slightly reproachful. 'I've been directing for years, of course. I directed this *Romeo* you know, and *As You Like It* last year. Musicals are a new venture, but they fascinate me, I've wanted to do one for years. Pulling all the elements together is just a very exciting experience. But I remain an actor, Joe. Even when I'm directing, I act.'

'Yes, of course,' said Joe, carefully humble.

Tabitha Levine appeared in the doorway, looking only very slightly more glamorous than when she had arrived. 'Piers darling, the photographer wants us in the kitchen. Can you come?'

'Yes, of course. Joe, help yourself to a drink, over there, look; I won't be long.'

'Thanks,' said Joe. He poured himself a tonic water, and wandered over to the window: the garden was beautiful, but perfect, overdone, even the spring blossom looked as if it had been painted on. He turned back into the room; also pin-neat, unlived in. Well, the guy couldn't possibly spend much time here. It was a backdrop, like all the others he commissioned. Joe went over to the bookshelves and studied the books: all predictable stuff, theatrical biographies, art books, rows of Dickens, of Trollope. Then he noticed, right on the very top shelf, a familiar cover: *Scandals* by Joe Payton.

Intrigued, he pulled it down; it looked scarcely opened. He flicked to the flyleaf: Piers Windsor, it said, June 1960. Joe turned to the chapter about Byron and a card fell out; in a sloping, rather fanciful script was written, 'Piers. Aren't you glad you escaped all this? It's a good read. Enjoy! Happy birthday. Best love, Guinevere.'

Now, thought Joe, I wonder exactly what that might mean.

Mrs Guinevere Windsor seemed an interesting person to talk to suddenly.

He tracked her down through Equity; she was living near Cardiff and fronting an arts programme on regional TV. He called the station, asked if they could ask her to ring him.

Nothing happened for nearly a week, while he wrestled with the piece, tried to make it sound less bland and predictable; he had given up all hope when the phone rang one afternoon, and a lovely deep lilting voice said, 'Mr Payton? Guinevere Davies.'

'Miss Davies!' said Joe. 'How very kind of you to ring me.'

'I can never resist an opportunity to talk,' she said. 'I can tire the sun with talking.'

Joe grinned into the phone. 'Sounds like – let me see, Dylan Thomas?'

'No, no. Hopeless. Someone called W.J. Cory. Bet you haven't heard of him.'

'I haven't,' said Joe.

'I tend to talk in quotations. What can I do for you?'

'I'm a journalist. As you know. Two things. First I'm doing a round-up of all the arts programmes for a piece in the *Guardian*.' God, the lies he told in the course of a working day. 'So I'd like to talk to you about yours. Second, and this is really cheeky, I'm writing a profile of your ex-husband in the *Sunday Times*. I'm getting background on him, you know, filling in colour so to speak. I wondered if you had any anecdotes of your life together that you would share with me?' There was a silence: she's going to ring off, he thought, and braced himself for the click. It didn't come.

'I'm not giving you any dirt,' she said, 'I'm fond of the old bugger, really. We stayed good friends. I value friendship. Love without its wings.'

'Byron.'

'Good. We could get along well, I think, Mr Payton. I liked your book about scandal, by the way. In fact I gave it to Piers for his birthday once.'

'Really? How very nice of you.' Joe's heart began to thump rather hard. 'Why did you think he would like it?'

'Oh, I thought all that early Hollywood stuff would amuse him. He was – shit, I have to go to the studio right now. Excuse me. I'll ring you when I've had time to think a bit.'

'Please do. And I'm not looking for dirt,' said Joe earnestly.

'All journalists are looking for dirt,' said Guinevere, laughing. 'Is this arts programme stuff on the level?'

'No,' said Joe humbly. He liked her too much to lie to her.

'I thought not. I'll ring you anyway.'

The prep school Piers had attended, Abbots Park, was still open. The headmaster sounded young and enthusiastic; he said Mr Windsor's headmaster had been at least three before him, a Mr Jeffries who had sadly passed away. 'But I tell you who might be interesting for you to talk to, Matron. Her mother was matron here, at that time, and she would have stories to tell, perhaps. How would that be?'

'It would be great,' said Joe.

Matron's mother was a formidable lady called Mrs Gregson with a shelf of a bosom and a stern mouth. Joe couldn't imagine she would have been a great comfort to any small boy who was homesick. Yes, she remembered Piers Windsor; she remembered all her boys. It was clearly a point of pride with her. 'He was a nice little boy, although he was not a good mixer. And not sporty, of course, which never helps. He had a lot of trouble settling down. Even after the first year, we still had tears. He was teased, I'm afraid. Well, it's part of growing up, isn't it? A good preparation for life. They all settle in the end. It just takes some longer than others.'

'Of course,' said Joe, his heart going out, albeit reluctantly, to the small, tearful Piers Windsor, being teased, crying still, in his second year. 'Er – was he in school plays that you can remember? Early promise?'

'Yes, he was very good indeed. In his last year, they did *Toad of Toad Hall* and he was Toad. Quite out of character, and remarkable. I remember some upset in an earlier year when he was going to be Mr McGregor in *Peter Rabbit*, but he had to be pulled out. Had trouble learning his lines. And – well, these things pass.'

'Oh, that was a shame. Er – what things?' said Joe carefully.

'Oh, you know, ups and downs of school life,' said Mrs Gregson rather too quickly. 'But yes, Mr Toad, wonderful. His mother was such a charming woman, and so pretty. She used to worry about him, being homesick, but of course we all reassured her. No point parents being worried, is there?'

'No, of course not,' said Joe. 'And his father?'

'Oh, I don't remember his father. He never came, as far as I can recall.'

'Didn't he even come to plays and things?'

'Oh, I really wouldn't know that, Mr Payton. I think I've done quite well for you already.' She stood up, and smiled rather sternly; the interview was clearly over.

The head of St Luke's was less helpful; he said he would consider Joe's request and come back to him: three days later Piers called Joe.

'Look, Joe, I'd rather you didn't go raking around my past, without checking with me first. It's a tiny bit intrusive, I feel. I've told St Luke's I'd rather they didn't talk to you, but if you want more information, then ask me. I'm at your disposal.'

'I'm so sorry,' said Joe. 'I really didn't mean –'

'Of course not. And I know it's standard practice with these things. I'm just a bit stupidly sensitive, I suppose. A private person. Look, you obviously want more. Let me buy you lunch. What about the Garrick one day next week? Thursday?'

'Sure,' said Joe. 'Thanks.'

He rang Guinevere; she was slightly defensive. 'I've had a think,' she said, 'and I don't think I should start talking. I can never stop, you know.'

'That sounds wonderful to me,' said Joe. 'But –'

'No, really. I don't think I should. I'm so sorry, Joe. I think it would have been fun, meeting you.'

'OK. I think the same,' said Joe. 'Maybe I'll find another pretext for that. Er – you were in the middle of telling me why you thought he'd like my book when you had to go on air. You wouldn't like to finish that sentence even, would you?'

'I would have thought that was perfectly obvious,' said Guinevere, increasingly cool. 'Hollywood at that time was so intensely glamorous and shocking. I knew he would like it.'

'That was the only reason?'

'Yes, of course.'

'Fine. Well, hail and farewell, Miss Davies.'

He knew when he was beaten. He had a strong feeling Piers had been on to Guinevere.

Lunch at the Garrick was actually very pleasant. Piers was a good raconteur; he told wonderful stories of actors, of first-night horrors, last-minute rescue operations and spoke with genuine passion and intense seriousness of his work. Warmed by the bottle and a half of claret they shared, and the new small knowledge of what had clearly been a sad childhood, Joe warmed to him. He also decided the man was if not homosexual, then certainly with very strong inclinations in that direction: it was not simply the theatrical dialect, the intensely showy behaviour, the phoney intimacy that gave the impression. They in themselves meant nothing; it was something much more subtle, more delicate, more refined. Joe rather prided himself on his sexual instincts; he would have staked a year's salary on this one.

'Tell me about your father,' he said suddenly.

Piers, caught unawares, looked at him sharply and then down at his plate; there had been a strong flash of anger in his eyes. Joe thought it was directed at him, and braced himself for further castigation, but when Piers looked up again, he was smiling carefully.

'He was what would now be called an absentee father,' he said, 'always working, always away. But very generous. I suppose he was just making a life for my mother and me.'

'Were you close to him?'

'Well – not really. No, not at all.' That was almost too quick. There was something here all right. 'It's hard to be close to someone you never see. But when he died, I was desperately upset. To have missed out on so much. So obviously I did – love – him.' The words came out with difficulty.

'And your mother?'

'Well, of course I loved her – oh so much. She was wonderful. So brave and – gay. Always such fun. Always there when I needed her. I had an ear abscess at school once, and she came down, sat with me all night. I think Matron was a little disapproving.' He laughed. 'And of course always at plays and everything. She's very frail now, poor darling. Lives in a nursing home. Angina.'

'How sad. I'm sorry.'

'Yes, well. I would hate her troubled in any way.' The meaning of his remark was very clear.

'Of course not. Er –' Joe didn't want to let on he'd been down to Abbots Park. 'What plays did you do at your prep school?'

'Oh – well, my moment of greatest glory was Toad in *Toad of Toad Hall*. Gave me my first real taste of applause. Three curtain calls.'

'Did you like it that much?' said Joe, grinning at him.

' 'Fraid so,' said Piers, slightly (but carefully) shamefaced. 'It was wonderful. Dreadful lot, we actors.'

'Nice to meet an honest one,' said Joe. 'Anything else?'

'Oh, let me see. No, nothing much. Joseph in the Nativity Play. Walk-on part in *Peter Rabbit*, I seem to remember. It was early on, the younger ones didn't get to be in the plays.'

Joe didn't ask him about Mr McGregor. Maybe Mrs Gregson had confused him with someone else.

'Well, thanks very much for lunch,' said Joe as they walked out of the door of the Garrick Club. 'I think I've got everything I need now. Would you object to my talking to Tabitha?'

'No, not at all. About the *Lady*, you mean? It's very important, Joe, that you do make it clear that all these people are only signing up provisionally. And the search for the Lady is a very good publicity stunt. I still haven't got the go-ahead from the backers. If it comes through while you're writing the article, I'll let you know. How long can I have?'

'Oh – about a week,' said Joe. 'Maybe two. They'll be subbing it for a day or so as well. We can always drop a sentence in. Look, I'm going along to Moss Bros. Have to hire a penguin suit for some do. My last one's dropped to pieces. Thanks again.'

'I'll come with you,' said Piers. 'I want to order a new hunting coat.'

'Do you hunt?' said Joe, surprised. Piers didn't seem tough enough or insensitive enough to enjoy such an activity.

'Sometimes, yes. I don't exactly like it, but I don't want the neighbours in Berkshire thinking I'm a weekend woofter.' He laughed just slightly too long.

Joe looked at him thoughtfully. He was an odd mixture this man: the light charm of manner, the intense seriousness and steely attention he gave his work – and clearly immense physical courage. Joe would have been deprived of food and water for a week before going on to the hunting field. And the courage extended to his attitude to his work: he would attempt any obstacle, storm any citadel if he believed truly it was right. It must have been a tough decision to play Romeo at his age, to risk critical derision, and the possible loss of public esteem – but he had done it. He might be no nicer than Joe had imagined – but he was certainly more interesting.

Coming out of the door of Moss Bros as they turned into it was Chloe. She was looking very pretty, in a dusty pink angora shift, but she was clearly flustered.

'Darling!' said Joe. 'What on earth are you doing here? Your mother's not making you wear a DJ to the ball as well, is she?'

'No,' said Chloe, 'but we have to produce some uniformed waiters next week at a huge dance, and Mrs Brownlowe sent me in to reserve some jackets.'

'I see. Piers, you've met Chloe, haven't you?'

'Indeed I have,' said Piers, bowing slightly over Chloe's hand, and smiling into her eyes. 'We met under rather – exciting circumstances, did we not, Miss Hunterton?'

Chloe blushed.

'And what are you doing getting jackets for waiters, Miss Hunterton?'

'Oh, it's for my work,' said Chloe. She still appeared paralysed with unease.

Joe took pity on her, explained what she did.

'How charming,' said Piers Windsor. 'Do you ever do business lunches, anything like that?'

'Oh, yes,' said Chloe, 'that's one of our main things.'

'Well, I could find that very useful. My agent is always giving lunches, and we are always being let down by caterers. Do you have a card or anything like that?'

'I – think so,' said Chloe, rummaging in her bag and producing a rather crumbled, dirty card. 'I'm sorry, this is all I can find.'

'Thank you. I may well call on you.'

'Well – good. Now if you'll excuse me, I must go,' said Chloe. 'Goodbye, Mr Windsor. Goodbye, Joe.'

'Charming,' said Piers Windsor, looking after her as she disappeared down the street. 'Simply charming.'

'Yes, she is,' said Joe and wondered why he felt such a strong sense of unease.

Tabitha added very little to his knowledge of Piers (except by confirming without saying anything at all that she clearly considered him to be homosexual). She added very little to his knowledge of anything except herself. She was beautiful, sexy, funny and entirely self-absorbed. Joe found her very attractive, and they had an extremely long lunch at the Caprice (at her instigation); it cost him a great deal of money as he was refused entry in his rather shabby sports jacket and baggy flannels and had to hurtle into Simpsons and buy a new suit. Well, it had a bit of class, and it would impress the famous Miss Levine. He decided it had been well worth it, as they emerged rather unsteadily into the sunshine at quarter past four.

'That was such fun,' said Tabitha. 'I didn't think I'd enjoy it nearly so much. Can I just say one thing though? You're really nice and really fun and really sexy, but I think I preferred you in your frayed jeans to that rather spivvy suit.'

'Thanks,' said Joe.

He was quite pleased with his article, although he felt it was a touch empty. He had thought it very fair to Piers without being sycophantic, but the lawyers phoned him and said there were a couple of sentences which they felt dodgy and asked him to rewrite; amazed, Joe said in what way were they dodgy?

The lawyers said he implied, albeit with infinite subtlety, that Piers was a homosexual, and that it just might be actionable; Joe, still more amazed, said he had intended to imply nothing of the kind. Reading the piece again, though, he could see what they meant; he rewrote the offending sentences carefully, reflecting that he might not have established that Piers Windsor had been in Hollywood with Brendan FitzPatrick, but that he was certainly likely to have had intimate knowledge of his sexual inclinations if he had been. He thanked God he had absolutely nothing that he need report to Fleur, and added a small thankful postscript to the prayer to the effect that Piers had now left his life for good.

Chapter 13

1965–6

'I'm afraid I'm going to have to make some changes,' said Mick diMaggio.

His expression as he looked at Fleur was sombre; she felt very sick suddenly. Obviously she was going to be fired. Nigel would have said something; someone else would have said something; or maybe they'd found out she'd left early that night in August to go the Beatles concert at the Shea Stadium; or, no, Poppy would have reported her for borrowing five dollars from petty cash the night she was working late and missed the bank. That was definitely it. Bitch. That was a really lousy thing to do; she'd put it back straight away next morning. Poppy was supposed to be her friend. She met Mick's eyes very steadily; best to go down fighting.

'Suzy is leaving,' he said. 'Very sadly. For an extremely unimportant job at Bates. Copy Group Head. What a waste.' He shook his head, his eyes mournful. 'Well, you see, I need to replace her. And I thought I'd put Hank Barr in her job. Which would leave me a junior copywriter short. And I thought you might like to do a copy test. We're impressed with you, Fleur. We'd like to see you progress.'

'Shit,' said Fleur. She couldn't help it. Her language was always very bad when she was excited. 'Shit.'

'I'm afraid,' said Mick, 'you'll have to do better than that.'

Fleur passed the copy test; she hoped very much it wasn't all because of Nigel Silk, that he might have told Mick to give her a job, to buy her off. She didn't think so: for Mick to appoint a creative person he had no time for would have been akin to – well, to Dior working with Crimplene rather than silk.

She hardly ever saw Nigel these days; apart from an anguished, quiet 'are you all right' several weeks after Serena had found her, and she had delivered her pregnancy note, and she had been forced to say, with great reluctance that yes, she was all right, he had avoided her with great skill. Fleur was relieved; she had feared reprisals, and she felt in any case, and despite herself, hurt. The very least he owed her, she felt, was a little honesty, and possibly even an apology. Well, she had quite a few mementoes from the relationship; the Gladstone and the watch would see her through a very long time, and the cashmeres would come in pretty useful too. The whole episode had merely served to reinforce her view of men as selfish, dishonest egocentrics. There were exceptions of course: her father, Joe, and quite possibly Mick; otherwise, forget it. She had better things to think about than love in any case. Her career. Which looked like it was on its way.

The first copyline of hers that appeared in the press was only a tiny ad in health sections of the mass-circulation women's magazines, but it was hers and it was unchanged. She felt as if she had posters up all over New York. It was for a cure for premenstrual fluid retention called Pre-P; it was not a glamorous product, even Fleur had to admit, but she didn't care.

'Take Pre-P,' she wrote, 'and feel all-over tension just draining away.'

'That's very good, Fleur,' said Mick. 'I like it. Is that really how it feels?' He was endlessly fascinated by the mechanics of the female body; nothing made him happier than an in-depth discussion on the menstrual cycle, or hormonal changes affecting the libido.

'Well – yes. Yes, of course it is,' said Fleur, 'that's why I wrote it.'

'Well, it's a good line. And a good concept. Clever girl.'

A few weeks later she had got her really big break: working as assistant copywriter on a new account, T. & J. Stores. T. & J. was a small chain of grocery stores, looking for a new strong image; Fleur's immediate boss, Hank Barr, had been set to work on it; he had already put three strategies up to Mick who had turned them all down. Hank, who was anyway feeling insecure, was in despair; he had failed in his last two projects as well, and he could see his future at Silk diMaggio, as well as his dreams of a new agency called Hank Barr Associates, vanishing into nothingness if he did not come up with something soon. Fleur, who was fond of Hank (probably because he was tall and gangly and reminded her of Joe), found him at his desk with his head in his hands one lunch-time, and said would he like to talk to her about it. Hanks said no, not really, although he appreciated her sympathy, and then proceeded to talk about it for some time

'Mick said give the thing a personality,' he said. 'I've been down the efficient road, the good-to-your-pocketbook road, even tried the "we stock more than you'd believe" road. Mick quite liked that, but Nigel said that wasn't strategy, and since then I've been going in a downward spiral.'

Fleur looked at him thoughtfully. She had learnt a lot just listening to Nigel in the studio overlooking the river; and she knew exactly what he meant about strategy. Nobody would want a store just because it was efficient or even economical: they all tried to be that. It had to have a real personality, one that would be remembered. There must be something they could find, something different about it: even that it was untidier than anywhere else. 'The answer's in the product,' Nigel had said. 'It's always there, if you look hard enough.' Hank obviously hadn't looked hard enough.

'I have it,' said Fleur. She felt quite sick she was so excited.

Hank looked at her slightly warily. 'Have what?'

'The strategy. Maybe even the copyline. For T. & J.'

'You do? Well, I certainly need it. Mick was on my back all yesterday afternoon.'

'Well, we can get him off it. Listen. "The store that's smaller than it looks." '

'What? Fleur, that doesn't sound very clever to me.'

'Well you're dumb then,' said Fleur impatiently. 'Hank, I spent yesterday afternoon in a T. & J. and this woman came in and the man told her her little boy had been going too fast on his skateboard and she said he was doing the job of a small neighbourhood shop.'

'Well?' said Hank, looking at her blankly.

'Well – can't you see how exciting that is? A real concept. It gives T. & J. a story to tell. Behind the supermarket façade there's still a real old-fashioned store. It's pure Norman Rockwell stuff, Hank, you must see that.'

Hank looked at her thoughtfully. Then he suddenly picked up his pen and started scribbling. 'Fleur, you just might have given me an idea. Get me a coffee, will you?'

'Don't mention it,' said Fleur, slamming out of the room.

The presentation was fixed for a week later. Four of T. & J.'s big guns were coming in: Mick diMaggio would be there, Nigel Silk would be there, Hank would be there, Bobby Wilson, the executive on the account, would be there, and Fleur would be there in her capacity as Hank's assistant. She was excited, nervous; she spent hours the night before working out what to wear. She finally settled on a black suit she had just bought, with a short slightly flared skirt and a grey cashmere sweater, one of the trophies from her liaison with Nigel. She liked wearing the clothes he had given her in meetings; it discomfited him, made him slightly nervous. She always wore the Gucci watch as well. It was revenge of a kind: small, but meaningful. One day, she told herself, one day she would have a larger one.

She sat listening to Mick as he did the presentation in a state of near awe. It was like being at the movies, the theatre; she wanted him never to stop.

'Personality,' he said. 'It's so indefinable, isn't it? We all want it. To have that quality that makes people remember you, notice you, know you're there. I certainly want that.'

As if he didn't, thought Fleur, sitting staring at him transfixed.

'Certainly every company wants it. Every company dreams of being the next Hathaway, the next Schweppes, the next Volkswagen. And you know why? Yeah, of course you do. Not just to have their profits, although that'd be nice. But also to have people say, oh yeah, I know about those shirts, they're great, but do I have to wear the eye-patch, and sure, I'd love a drink, with you-know-who, and gee, I'd certainly like to own the car that gets the snowplough driver to work. That is a seriously good ambition, isn't it? To have a share in the national psyche, to be a household name, to mean something to almost everybody. That'd be something. That'd be fame. That'd be a kind of an immortality. Well, we think you can have that with your stores. We have that strong a concept for you. Something that's going to get a hold of people's imaginations, send them scuttling into your stores, going out of their way to get to one. Go with this one, and you'll say goodbye to anonymity for ever. Hank, would you like to take over from here.'

Hank took over from there. He presented Fleur's thinking, Fleur's concept, Fleur's copyline; T. & J., after an initial resistance, bought it. Silk diMaggio got the account. Hank Barr took everyone out and got them drunk.

Fleur was sitting at her desk late that night, wounded almost beyond endurance at the fact that Hank had not so much as given a nod of recognition in her direction, when Mick diMaggio came back, gave her a hug and told her to dry her eyes.

'I think Hank behaved more than a little shabbily today, and when his euphoria has worn off I intend to tell him so. You have to remember he is fairly untalented. It makes people very insecure. He was one of my mistakes, I'm afraid. You, on the other hand, have a great deal of talent – and a nice way with the clients as well. I'm sorry I didn't say anything before, Fleur. I wrongly and rather unimaginatively thought you were tough enough to take it. Now dry your eyes, I have a proposition to put to you. I want someone of the right sex and in the right age range to work on the Juliana account. Obviously we are a large team already, but with this youth cult raging, I really think your input could be valuable. I'm not promising you the autumn campaign, mind you: just a say in things here and there. How would you like that?'

'Shit!' said Fleur. It was all she could manage, she was so astounded and excited.

'You'll have to come up with something better than that, darling,' said Mick, standing up and grinning down at her. 'We have a big meeting with Julian Morell next Monday, mostly to discuss spring promotions. Come to that, and wear that most distractingly short skirt you wore today. Julian likes beautiful young ladies.'

Fleur thought Julian Morell was the most exciting man she had met in her entire life. He was upper-class English, she realized, being just slightly aware of such a quality, with all Nigel's sophistication, his charm, his patently well-bred assurance, but with a warmth, a sensuousness that Nigel entirely lacked. He was tall and slim, with dark hair and very dark eyes, and when she was introduced to him as the latest recruit to the Juliana team, he took her hand and bowed over it very slightly and said, 'How delightful, and how valuable I am sure you are going to be,' and the eyes were warm and probing and somehow inviting, all at the same time. Fleur would have allowed herself to fantasize over him quite extensively had she not known of his extremely well-documented and colourful private life: divorced from his first wife, running an on-off relationship with the dauntingly beautiful Camilla North, who was the creative director of his company, and linked endlessly with a long succession of the models who appeared in his advertisements. He was a wonderful client ('They're rare, darling, as you know,' Mick said) and a great bonus in her life.

* * *

Working on the Juliana account occupied a great deal of her time; as with all cosmetic companies, there were launches of products right through the year, and the team were constantly being sent early samples of products to try, to become familiar with, to comment on, to work with. She had started on it in November, when there were major summer campaigns planned, colours for the following autumn being discussed, fragrances being developed for the Christmas after that. She met Camilla and once she had got over her early terror, came not exactly to like her, but to respect her. Camilla was beautiful, red-haired, immensely elegant, stick-thin and always the same: icy cool, gracious, totally in control – and enormously talented.

'She is our biggest danger,' said Mick. 'One of these days, she's going to leave Julian, and set up on her own, and then we shall lose the account.'

'Surely not,' said Fleur. 'She's not an advertising person. She's – well, a cosmetic person. Isn't she?'

'Oh, no, she's much more than that,' said Mick soberly. 'She began her association with Julian designing the interior of that exquisite store of his. And then moved into the company. She's creative director of the whole thing, not just Juliana, and advertising director. She may not be quite an advertising person, but I'd hate to pitch against her on that account.'

'But doesn't she work for him because – well, she and he have this weird relationship?'

'No, not really. It really, believe it or not, has very little to do with that. She's brilliantly clever, powerful in that company in her own right and more than capable of telling Julian to fuck off every now and again. It's a very volatile relationship, I tell you, baby. Anyway, we have to keep her sweet. Now what did you think of those new lip colours?'

Most of the time of course she didn't work on the ads herself, but wrote endless pack and counter display copy; but she could feel her confidence and her skills growing almost physically. And her pleasure, her excitement in what she did never faltered.

'I don't often say this, darling,' said Mick, 'but you seem to have a slight flair for this.'

'How about something else you don't often say?' said Fleur. 'Like take a raise?'

Mick laughed and said too right, he didn't often say it and wasn't about to now; two weeks later he gave her a raise, and she was able to start looking for her own apartment. She was tired of living with Kate; she wanted independence.

She found it six weeks later, after tramping up what seemed like a hundred flights of stairs, jumping up and down on a thousand creaking, dodgy floorboards, haggling with dozens of hatchet-faced, wall-eyed landlords and ladies. It was a tiny top floor of a brownstone on the Upper West Side, running between Amsterdam and Columbus and within walking distance of Zabars Deli. It was really not an apartment at all, just a large room, with a tiny bathroom off one side of it, and a tinier kitchen off the other; it had no heating or air-conditioning, and the hot water system was primitive to put it mildly and either came out so hot it scalded, or so cool it was hardly worth the bother. But the ceiling was not covered with polystyrene tiles, and the walls were not coated in embossed paper, and the sash window was tall and had a wooden curtain rail and looked over the yard which actually had a tree in it, albeit slightly dusty, and there was a small, pretty iron grate which, though clearly no use at all for containing a fire, was a charming accessory to the room. The apartment was extremely cold when she looked at it, and she could see it would be extremely hot a few months later. The neighbourhood was colourful, noisy, ethnic, full of crying babies, fighting kids, loud, late music, a fair amount of crime – and friendly faces. Her landlady was the distracted mother of five children under seven, whose husband was a professional saxophonist working on average two days out of every month. Their name was Steinberg, and they took a great fancy to Fleur, making her welcome at their Friday night family feasts, apologizing endlessly for the crying babies and the saxophone noise. Fleur could not have cared less about any of it, it was her home, her own small castle, and she had never been so happy.

She spent the first weekend sanding the floor, and then varnishing it, with the help of Edna's husband, and Kate, who was genuinely sad to lose her, got out Kathleen's old sewing machine and made her some fine muslin curtains for the summer, and some heavy woollen weave ones for the winter. She went to the flea markets down in the Village and bought rag rugs for her floor, a small pine chest, an oval mirror on a stand and a Victorian china jug and washbowl. She acquired a clothes rail from a bankrupt fashion house for her clothes, and hung the walls with discarded agency roughs, fished from the waste-bins or snatched from desks en route to the wastebins (with Poppy's blessing). Her only concession to extravagance was her bed, which she bought new from Macy's; Fleur was a bad sleeper, and her only hope of a reasonable amount of oblivion lay in thick, firm mattresses. She found a tattered patchwork quilt in one of the markets, and asked Maureen, who was clever with her needle, to show her how to repair it. She had set herself a target of a patch a week, but it was slow, painstaking work, and she grew impatient with it, and three months after moving in, she had still only replaced two.

It didn't seem to matter; it still looked wonderful. The whole place looked wonderful; she was immensely proud of it.

'Can I bring my brother to your little gathering on Saturday?' asked Poppy. 'He's dying of a broken heart and I'm sure you could cheer him up.'

'Of course,' said Fleur. 'It will mean the walls will entirely give way under the pressure, and the floor as well I dare say, but he's extremely welcome. I didn't know you had a brother, Poppy. What's his name?'

'His name is Reuben, I'm afraid,' said Poppy. 'Our parents had most colourful ideas about names. We would both much rather have been called Mary and Mike or some such but I suppose it makes us memorable.'

'Well anyway, bring him,' said Fleur, smiling pleasedly. She was looking forward to her party, which was by way of a housewarming.

'He's not very talkative,' said Poppy. 'I warn you.'

'I like quiet people,' said Fleur and there was a sudden wistfulness in her voice. Joe was quiet.

She had asked far too many people; twenty-two jammed into her hot, overcrowded room. The floorboards did creak ominously, and everyone kept spilling drinks over everyone because it was so difficult to move. But it was still fun, and Saul Steinberg came up and played his saxophone for a while, outside the door so they wouldn't be quite deafened – 'Live music, my dear, how smart,' said Poppy – and then Saul said why didn't they come down and sit in the kitchen and have some coffee, Mary had just made a huge jug. They went down and Fleur found herself sitting on the kitchen floor next to Reuben Blake, whom she had not yet managed to say more than five words to. He was devastatingly attractive; she had taken one look at him and decided that the solution to one of her lesser, if pressing problems, one of acute sexual frustration, could lie most agreeably in his hands. Literally, she thought to herself, with a grin.

He was very tall, and almost too thin; he had very long, gangly arms and legs, with huge bony hands. His hair was dark sandy blond, and his eyes were what she could only describe as mud-coloured; he had freckles all over his face, and when he smiled, which was seldom, his teeth were rather crooked.

'What do you do?' she said to him, passing him a tin mug of steaming coffee, and he sighed and said he worked at Bloomingdale's, as a display designer; he added after a very long time that it was horrible. Why was it so horrible? Fleur said, and he said he didn't really know. After that he lapsed back into a gloomy silence, which he did not again break; he left with Poppy soon after twelve with a mournful smile, shook Fleur's hand and thanked her and said it had been an interesting evening.

'I'm afraid your brother didn't like me,' she said to Poppy on Monday morning, and Poppy said not at all, he had said he'd found her very nice to talk to.

'But he didn't talk to me,' said Fleur, slightly irritably. 'He said, let me see, about two dozen words at the most, the whole evening.'

'Fleur,' said Poppy, 'two dozen is an enormous number for Reuben.'

'Even when he's not broken-hearted?'

'Even when he's not broken-hearted. He's even worse today. The girl finally absolutely finished things off, he spent the whole of yesterday just lying on his bed, staring at the ceiling. He's very emotional.'

'Good,' said Fleur. Emotional in her very limited experience meant good in bed.

'Is that Fleur?'

'Yes, this is she.'

'Ah.'

A long silence followed. Fleur waited, coughed, said, 'Yes?'

She was just about to ring off when the voice said, 'This is Reuben Blake.'

There was another very long silence; Fleur smiled into the telephone. 'Yes, Reuben?' she said finally.

'I have tickets for an art exhibition in the Village,' he said.

'How nice,' said Fleur. She was determined not to make this easy for him.

After another very long pause he said, 'Would you like to go?'

'Oh, yes,' said Fleur, smiling even more radiantly into the phone, 'yes, Reuben, I would.'

He met her in the Village Square; he was ten minutes late and he came shambling along, his disjointed-looking limbs somehow all out of step, his dark gold hair ruffled and untidy. Fleur realized with a pang of pain why she had so instantly liked him: he reminded her of Joe.

Not that he was in the least like Joe to be with; Joe talked, joked, listened, empathized. Reuben simply was there. He didn't even greet her properly; merely nodded, smiled and said, 'Sorry' (short for 'sorry I'm late' she supposed), and indicated towards a small gallery just along on 7th. Fleur, amused and determined not to talk until he did, walked beside him, and followed him into the gallery. It was an exhibition of early twentieth-century primitives; Fleur was enchanted by them. She moved slowly around them, Reuben half forgotten, spellbound by their charm, their innocence; she lingered for a particularly long time by a prairie scene, all yellows and blues with a tiny red house set in the middle distance, walking backwards and forwards, enjoying it. Reuben, who had long completed the circuit and was slightly desultorily doing it again, suddenly appeared beside her. 'Like it?'

'I love it,' said Fleur. 'It's – well, it's so happy somehow.'

'I suppose it is,' said Reuben and disappeared again; when she had finished looking at the pictures she saw him outside, standing in the evening sunshine. She followed him out and looked up at him smiling, slightly challenging; after at least sixty seconds her resolve weakened and she said, 'What now?'

'I expect you're hungry,' said Reuben and yes, she said, yes she was. 'Like pizza?' he said, and yes, she said again, yes very much, and so they went to Ray's Pizza and bought two huge Americans and stood there eating them, and Fleur kept thinking, any moment now he will say something, surely, and still he was silent.

'I'll take you home,' he said, when finally they had finished, and she said no, no, she would be fine, but he insisted, and they took the F train right uptown, and he sat next to her, smiling at her every so often, rather vaguely. When they got out at 79th and turned into her street, it was full of people in spite of the cold, and Saul's saxophone was throbbing somewhere in the air, and he smiled suddenly and said, 'Hey, this is a really nice place,' and then he said, 'Well, goodnight,' and ambled off before she could even thank him.

She went to sleep upset, sure that the whole thing had been a disaster; and in the morning not even Poppy's reassurances – that he was always like that, always quiet, hopelessly shy – could comfort her and she sat staring at the paper in her typewriter trying to write something amusing and interesting about liquid eyeliner, quite convinced that she was doomed for the rest of her life not to have anything more to do with men. And then her phone rang. It was the gallery they had been at the night before, 'Just checking, Miss FitzPatrick, that we do have the right picture here for you.' She said there must be some mistake, she hadn't reserved or paid for any pictures and they said yes, yes, there was one here, *Prairie* it was called, paid for in her name, and the agency number as the contact, and was that correct, because there was another one called *Prayer*, and they would hate to get it wrong.

Fleur said they hadn't got it wrong and walked very slowly over to Poppy's desk and told her what Reuben had done, and Poppy said this had clearly been quite an evening; and then Fleur's phone rang again, and it was Reuben, who said he had so enjoyed talking to her the night before, and it was so rare that he met a girl he could talk to, that he would like to see her again, and was she busy that evening?

Fleur said she wasn't.

Love, she supposed: of a sort. Certainly sex, and sexual desire; in the long silences of those evenings, she would sit and look at him, and he would sit and look at her, and the hunger between them was almost tangible. He kissed her for the first time after their third date; they had been to the cinema, to see *Dr Zhivago* (the third time, for Fleur, but she still managed to express pleasure and delight), and then out to supper in a restaurant in Little Italy, and as they sat there, he suddenly said, 'She's beautiful, Julie Christie,' and yes, said Fleur, adding with some asperity that so was Omar Sharif, and he smiled at her and said, 'You're beautiful too, I think,' and went back into his plate of *tagliatelli al forno*. Fleur was so stunned she was unable to eat anything more. As usual he escorted her home in almost total silence, and on the steps of number 33, he turned her face up to his and said, 'I meant it, you're beautiful,' and bent down and kissed her. It was a kiss such as she had not experienced before: it reached into every corner, every area of her; she felt it in her throat and her breasts, and her back and, dear God, she felt it in her pelvis, and she felt it in her legs and she felt it in her head and she felt it in her heart. And when it was over, she pulled back and looked up at him and said, 'Thank you so much, so very much for the picture, I didn't know whether to thank you before,' and he said damn, the gallery wasn't meant to tell her, just deliver it to the agency when the show was over, and she was so overwhelmed by this long speech that she smiled and kissed him again.

Well,' he said, 'I must get back,' and he was gone, ambling down the street without a look back, leaving her throbbing, longing for more of him, and her heart alight with pleasure and triumph.

She had been entrusted with all the pack copy for Juliana. Not earth-shattering, not the stuff awards were made of, but still important. She had asked Julian if she could work for a couple of days behind one of the Juliana counters, so she could get a clearer idea of what women were interested in when they bought cosmetics; he had been pleased and fixed for her to work at Bergdorf's. Standing there, confronted by rich, demanding, vain women, to whom she had to be not just polite but deferential, she learnt that above all they wanted to be flattered, to be told that the cosmetics they were buying were merely adornments, improvements on an already pleasing image. She worked that into every piece of copy: 'Second Look foundation flatters and enhances the fine skin you were born with'; 'Skimon eye shadow takes on the smooth texture of your own lids'.

Julian was very pleased with it; it was such a simple idea, he said, but it contained a great truth, and he asked Mick to look at working it up into a full campaign.

'Sure,' said Mick. 'Bella, darling, what do you think about that?'

Bella Buchanan was the art director on the account; she was a baby-blue-eyed blonde, with a face like an angel, ferociously hostile to Fleur. Fleur couldn't make out why.

'Well, obviously I think it would be great,' said Bella, smiling her perfect smile at Julian. 'I mean, it was a concept I actually put to Fleur when she was telling me about her days at the Juliana counter. I'm just pleased you like it.'

'You –' said Fleur and then stopped again, biting her lip, 'you did, didn't you.'

Later that night, Mick came down to see her. 'That was very nice copy,' he said. 'Did Bella really think of that line?'

'What do you think?' said Fleur.

'Good girl,' he said and went back up into his eyrie. Five minutes later, some Stravinsky filled the office; he was evidently in the very painful early throes of some campaign or other.

'Do you know why Bella hates me so much?' Fleur asked Poppy that night. They were sorting transparencies after the presentation.

'Jealousy, I suppose,' said Poppy. 'And not just professional either.'

'Pardon me?'

'Fleur, she was Nigel's little friend. Before you. And consequently very jealous of you.'

'I – don't know what you mean.'

'Yes, you do, Fleur.'

'Oh,' said Fleur. 'Oh, I see. Er – does everyone else know?'

'No, not everyone. I guess the woman who cleans the toilets might not.'

'Oh, shit,' said Fleur.

'I'm kidding you,' said Poppy. 'Hardly anyone knows. I do because I know everything. I kind of think Mick does. But not many people. Nigel is very discreet. Listen, it doesn't matter. It was tough and you handled it well. But anyway, Bella was the one before you. She lasted a long time. I thought and Mick thought that it might even be serious, be coming to something, you know? But – well, Serena knows her stuff. They still have – what should I say – well, a certain closeness.'

'Are there really that many?'

'There are that many. Although since you there hasn't been anyone. You should enjoy that. Nearly a year, and Nigel still celibate.'

'Hardly,' said Fleur bitterly.

'Well, if you were married to Serena wouldn't you be celibate?'

Fleur laughed. 'Maybe. I wish I'd known you knew. I could have talked, got over it quicker.'

'You did better your way. Better not to talk. Anyway, that's why Bella hates you. Plus you're young and pretty and even a bit talented.'

'I bet you say that to all the girls,' said Fleur and giggled.

She was beginning to yearn for Reuben. 'Is he always so slow off the mark?' she said to Poppy.

'Sometimes,' said Poppy noncommittally. There were times when she could say as little as Reuben.

It was another silent man, Buster Keaton to be precise, who was indirectly the catalyst in the situation, who brought them together. They had been sitting on the subway, she and Reuben, travelling uptown to her apartment, and she had seen in someone's paper that Keaton had died.

'Oh, wow, that's sad,' she said. 'I loved him so much. I bet you did too.'

'Never knew him,' said Reuben with one of his lugubrious smiles.

'Oh, Reuben, you know what I mean. My dad used to take me to see all his movies.'

'You still miss your dad?' he said, looking at her thoughtfully.

'Yes, I do. Terribly. And one day –' She spoke without thinking, stopped herself.

'What?'

'Oh – nothing.' She was silent, withdrawn from him suddenly. She had told him a little about her father, that he had been an actor, that he had died in Hollywood when she had been a little girl, but that was enough, as much as she wanted to give. It was painful territory; she didn't like entering it with someone new. It hurt all over again. She had been so busy, so happy lately, she had set aside her real ambition, the one beside which being rich and famous and setting up her own agency and getting even with Bella Buchanan all paled into significance: but she knew she would return to it, knew it was what mattered; it was her guiding force, her inspiration, it was what drove her, made her what she was. She supposed it could be most truly defined as an obsession.

'OK. So why should I like Buster Keaton?' he said, breaking into her thoughts.

'He never said anything either,' said Fleur, and smiled at him, and then: 'Joe loves him too,' she added, thoughtlessly careless, remembering Joe imparting this piece of information on their tour of Hollywood.

'Who's Joe?'

'Oh,' said Fleur quickly, afraid of the explanation, of the complexity, 'oh, just someone I know.'

'Is that all?'

'Yes,' she said, and buried herself in the paper, not noticing the expression on Reuben's face.

When they got to Amsterdam, he walked her to the house, said, 'Goodnight,' and walked away again.

'Reuben!' she called, startled. 'Reuben, what is it?'

'Nothing,' he said, and continued to walk.

Fleur ran after him. 'Reuben, please! What did I say?'

'There's obviously someone else, and I don't want to share you,' he said simply, and turned away again. It was the longest sentence he had ever spoken.

'Oh!' said Fleur, and she looked at his back, and the droop of his head, and a great shoot of joy and longing went through her, so harsh and strong it was almost a pain; she could feel its progress from her head to where she imagined her heart must be, and then down it travelled to her loins, swiftly and surely, moving her, melting her; and she put out her hand and touched him, very gently, on his back, his tall, bony back, and said, 'Reuben, don't go. It isn't – like that. Honestly. And I'd like you to stay.'

He turned, and looked at her, and all she could read in his face, in his eyes was sex, raw, greedy; and he moved towards her and took her face in his hands and kissed her, very hard, differently from all the other times.

'Oh, God,' was all he said, and she took his hand and they ran, as if escaping some dreadful danger, ran back up the street and into the house and up the stairs and into her apartment and she stood against the door, staring at him, breathing heavily. He slipped her coat off her shoulders and pushed his hands up beneath her sweater, and stood there, cupping her breasts, and she felt his thumbs massaging her nipples and she moaned quite quietly, and started walking backwards, very slowly and carefully, until she reached the bed; she lay down on it, and swiftly, joyfully, in almost one movement, tore off her sweater, and lay there, her arms open to him.

'Shit,' he said. 'Shit, you're so beautiful,' and he put one hand down and touched her face, and with the other he was tearing at his fly, struggling out of his jeans, and then he was kneeling at the foot of the bed, kissing her breasts, teasing the nipples with his tongue, and she moaned again, and said, 'Wait, wait,' and pulled off her skirt and her pants; he sat up and looked at her and pushed her legs tenderly, gently apart and began kissing her there, tonguing her, probing within her bush for her clitoris, his hands beneath her, holding her buttocks, and she felt him find it, felt herself heat, become molten, thrusting at him softly, achingly hungry. He went on and on working at her; she felt a climax growing, growing and didn't want it, didn't want the first time this way, and she pushed his head back and said, 'Please, please, in me, now,' and he stood up, and looked down at her, and then settled on her, very gently, and she felt his penis on her vulva and then making its journey inwards, on and on, to her innermost depths. Huge he was, reaching and reaching within her; she felt, and seemed almost to see, new places, new boundaries unfolding within her, and she did not move, did not stir, just lay and discovered him and he was discovering her. Suddenly he said, 'Look at me. Now. Quickly,' and she opened her eyes and stared into his, a new nakedness, one she had not known before, had not wished to know, one of absolute abandon, total vulnerability; as she looked, she felt her climax begin, and she moved, gently, drawing on him, adding his heat to her own, and he said, 'Be still, be quite still,' and he began to move himself, so slowly, so tenderly at first she scarcely felt it and then faster, harder, and he seemed to light upon some new place altogether in her, and she climbed, higher and higher in a blinding, sweet pleasure that went on and on, each beating of it stronger than the last, and she was crying out, she could hear herself, the strange wild cries of sex, and he was there with her, and he said quite loudly, 'Christ, you're beautiful,' and began to come, strong rhythmic spasms, and she lay arched, her head thrown back, gripping the sides of the bed, almost afraid of the pleasure he was giving, and her capacity to take it.

Afterwards they lay in silence for a long time; he pulled the torn quilt over them both and cradled her, her head on his shoulder, kissing her hair, and she said nothing, nothing at all, just smiled at him, and then suddenly he sat up and said, 'I need to pee,' and she laughed and said, 'In there.'

When he came back, looking much more the Reuben she knew, awkward and angular and smiling his crooked smile, she said, 'How funny you are.'

'Why?'

'Most people don't say anything when they're making love. You talk more than when you're not.'

'I know,' he said. 'There seems a bit more to say.' He settled down beside her.

'Do you not like talking?' she said curiously. 'Or do you just see no need for it?'

'No,' he said, 'I can see the need. I just can't find the words.'

'That's because you don't get any practice,' she said briskly. 'Maybe I can give you some lessons.'

'I've liked it that you haven't tried to make me talk,' he said slightly warily.

'Oh, really? It hasn't been entirely easy.'

'Well, I'm glad you managed it. Most girls keep asking me questions. It makes me nervous.'

'Are you easily made nervous, Reuben?'

'Very.' He looked at her again, and then said, 'Are you going to tell me now? Who Joe is?'

'No. Well – a friend. It's rather – complex. But it wasn't what you think. Do you mind my not telling you?'

'Not really,' he said after a long silence. 'The only thing I really mind is lies. I'm phobic about lies. Lies and unkindness.'

'Oh,' said Fleur. She looked at him thoughtfully. If they were going to get much closer she was going to have to tell him at least some of it.

Chapter 14

1966

'Well, that's the end of civilization as we know it,' said Caroline, throwing the *Daily Telegraph* down on to the table. 'Dreadful little man. This is your fault,' she added to Joe.

'Sorry,' said Joe. 'Won't do it again.'

'Yes, you will.'

'Yes, I will.'

'Do what?' said Chloe, looking up from her porridge.

'Vote Labour,' said Caroline. 'I must say I never thought to find myself intimately involved with a socialist.'

'I never thought to find myself with a blue-rinse Tory either,' said Joe. 'You could throw me out. But I don't think my one vote could actually have granted Mr Wilson a ninety-eight-seat majority.'

'I don't have a blue rinse,' said Caroline crossly.

'Ideologically you do.'

'Well, it's a disaster for the country. And the economy. I wouldn't be surprised if it doesn't lead to a total collapse of the pound. My father always said a large Labour majority . . .'

Chloe heard, with some relief, the phone ringing. She went to answer it.

'Is Miss Hunterton there?'

Now, thought Chloe, now, how do I know that voice? 'Yes, Chloe Hunterton speaking.'

'Chloe, this is Piers Windsor. Do you remember me?'

'Oh – yes, of course. How are you?'

'A little harassed. I'm sorry to ring you there, but a nice young lady in your office gave me your number. I want a lunch done for tomorrow. At my agent's offices. We've been let down. Could you do that, do you think?'

'Well –' Chloe paused. 'Well, how many for?'

'Ten.'

'Oh, I see. Very small. Well – the thing is, Mr Windsor, Mrs Brownlowe is away in Scotland, doing a deb's dance.'

'Well, what about you? I'm sure you must be capable of doing something?'

He must be mad, thought Chloe, after I spilt wine down his suit. 'Me? But –'

'Yes?'

Courage suddenly came to her; of course she could do it. She had done several now. And he was so nice, so charming, it would be fun. 'Well, yes, I suppose I could,' she said, feeling an empty space where her stomach had been as if she was going down too fast in a lift. 'I'd have to get Mrs Brownlowe's go-ahead of course, and clear the menus and everything with her, but I have done small lunches once or twice before.'

'Good. I have total faith in you. Your stepfather tells me you are a genius. And that I should be sure to ask for your chocolate mousse.'

'Oh.' So he'd checked her out; well, she supposed that was only sensible. 'Um – what sort of a lunch did you want?'

'Oh, something cold. That would be fine. Salmon or something. We're entertaining some potential investors.'

The lift seemed to be gathering speed: Chloe closed her eyes briefly, a habit of hers when she needed to be calm. 'Right,' was all she said.

She was in the kitchen at six in the morning with Sarah, the new girl. Minty, the more experienced assistant, was still in the country with Mrs Brownlowe. She had hardly slept, and her hands had been shaking so badly while she got dressed that she'd ripped a nail and broken a zip, but as always, the minute she got into the kitchen, she felt calm and in control. Sarah looked at her admiringly as she ticked the menu off on her fingers.

'Now then. Cold curried chicken, I thought. That's easy. And for starters we might have vegetable tartlets. Lots of interesting salads, and then chocolate mousse. Special request. Nothing difficult, nothing that can go wrong between here and there. You start on the pastry, I'll do the mousse. Thank goodness we had too much chicken for Mrs B's dance.'

'Um – Chloe.'

'Yes?'

'I think the chicken's off.'

'Oh, it can't be.'

'Well it is. Smell it.'

'Oh, God. I'll just have to go to Smithfield straight away.'

'You'd better hurry. The rush is about to start.'

'Oh dear,' said Chloe. 'This isn't going to be funny.'

That was only the beginning: Chloe found herself in a snarling, fuming traffic jam; then Sarah knocked the tartlets she had made on to the floor; the cream for the mousse curdled; and when they went out finally to Chloe's car she had a puncture.

They finally got into a taxi with, Chloe calculated, a precarious twenty-nine minutes to spare, the food in boxes and aluminium containers. The taxi driver was good-natured but doomy. 'There's some state visit today. Middle of town's jammed. Never make it, not in thirty minutes.'

'We've got to,' said Chloe. 'We've just got to.'

'You could pray,' said the taxi driver.

'He isn't on our side today, He wouldn't be any good at all.'

'Well you'd be far quicker on the tube. Pick up a cab at Holborn.'

'But – oh, all right. Thanks anyway.'

They staggered down the escalator, on to the tube. 'If we fall over and drop this,' said Chloe, 'I'm going to run away.'

'I'll come with you.'

The train roared along: Earl's Court became Knightsbridge, Hyde Park Corner. 'Green Park next,' said Chloe happily. 'Holborn four stops.' The train stopped. It sat in total silence for a minute or two, then made its revving noise, shook itself and settled into immobility again. The silence was shatterproof; people fidgeted, cleared their throats nervously, read their papers. Chloe felt beads of sweat breaking out on her forehead; panic formed in a great knot in her throat. She thought she might scream; she gripped her boxes more tightly and closed her eyes. It was nearly ten to twelve; nothing could save her now.

A guard came wandering along the train, swinging his bag and whistling: Chloe looked up at him, her soul in her eyes.

'What's happening?'

'Trouble on the line, love. Shouldn't be too long. Not more than ten minutes.'

'That's too long,' said Chloe faintly.

'What's the trouble?' He looked at her, concerned. She was grey and trembling.

'Oh, I have something terribly urgent to do.'

'How urgent?'

'Oh – as urgent as anything could be. My job, my whole life, depends on it.' Her brown eyes were enormous and wet with panicky tears.

'Dear oh dear,' said the guard. 'Nothing's as bad as that. You'd better come with me. Up to my phone.' He motioned to them to follow him up the train; they picked up their boxes and aluminium urns and went.

Out of earshot of the other passengers he said, 'The front of this train's in the station. I could take you up to the driver's van and let you out. Only nobody has to know, OK?'

Chloe nodded. 'OK.'

They walked the length of the train. The driver's cab just reached the end of Green Park station. Their benefactor stepped into it, whispered in the man's ear; he listened and then spoke in an unintelligible Scottish accent. The guard turned round.

'He says it's more than his job's worth to let you out.'

'Oh,' said Chloe bleaky.

The guard looked at her and his lips twitched slightly. 'But he says he don't rate the job too much. Come on, quick, while no one's looking.'

'Oh, thank you. You're an angel.' She reached up and kissed his cheek.

'That'll do,' he said, smiling embarrassedly, rubbing the place she had kissed. 'Come on now, buck up. I don't want to lose *my* job, even if *he* doesn't mind.'

'Now, what's the address? We have exactly one minute,' she said to the cab driver in Piccadilly, 'to get to – let me see – Smithfield. We'll give you double fare.'

'Could be difficult.'

'Treble?'

'Easy,' said the driver. He took U-turns where it said no U-turn, he overtook on the wrong side of the road, he shot lights, he even went down a one-way street the wrong way; he did it in six minutes. The fare was three pounds; Chloe gave him a ten-pound note.

'Keep the change,' she said and ran into the building.

Piers's agent was called Geoffrey Nichols and he was clearly very grand and successful: the guests, Chloe realized, were not actors, but money men, being courted for backing Piers's production of *The Lady of Shalott*. It was evidently an important lunch; and the talk was not really about the theatre at all, nor actors, nor musicians (except as commodities, expensive precious commodities), but money, money with which to mount the musical, to hire a theatre, to pay actors, to make costumes, to advertise and promote the play. His guests, initially watchful, almost antagonistic towards him, changed in mood as the meal went on, the wine went down. By three o'clock they were noisy, cheerful, telling increasingly filthy stories, exchanging ever more malicious gossip (Chloe noticed with interest that from time to time Piers Windsor's eyes flicked towards her and Sarah, as if to make sure they were not offended, or indeed listening too closely), assuring Piers that they were on the brink of making their decision, that the answer was quite likely to be yes. Piers's accountant was there; he had prepared financial documents, cash flow, profit forecasts. The bankers studied them, suddenly silent, alarmingly sober; Chloe found herself caught up in the drama, the tension, wanting, willing them to agree. At half past three her task was done, the table cleared, except for brandy, cigars, ashtrays, coffee, the plates stacked neatly on the side, and she and Sarah sat quietly, reading, while the noise in the background ebbed and flowed. And then it happened.

One of the men came into the kitchen, cigar dangling dangerously from his hand, in search of a cloth; he'd spilt some wine.

'Here,' said Chloe, 'let me do it.'

'No,' he said, 'no, of course not, I can't allow you to clear up after me, a pretty girl like you,' and waved his cigar expansively around while reaching for a cloth on the sink. Its brilliantly glowing end caught Chloe on the cheek; the pain seemed to arrive from a long way away, slowly settling into her, harsh, searing pain. She first flinched and then cried out; she couldn't help it.

'Oh, my God,' he said. 'Christ, I'm so sorry, stupid, clumsy oaf. Here, let me see.'

'No,' said Chloe, clutching her face, her teeth clenched, 'no, really, it's nothing.'

'What is it?' Piers Windsor was in the kitchen, his face taut with concern.

'It's nothing,' she said, 'really.'

'Please let me see.'

His hand removed hers very gently from her face; it was warm, his hand, very dry, she noticed, careful, tender. For a second she was distracted from her suffering by a new emotion, she knew not what; she stood there, her brown eyes dilated with pain, fixed on his, as if trusting him in some way to ease it, make it better.

'That's extremely nasty. I think perhaps we should get you to Casualty.'

'Oh, no,' said Chloe. 'No, honestly. I'll be all right. If maybe I could go to my doctor, leave the washing-up; well, Sarah could do it.'

'I think,' he said and there was just a flash of amusement in the large grey eyes, 'I think we can let you off the washing-up. But I don't think a doctor. I think you need Casualty. It's quite a big burn. It could get infected. I'll come with you. Try to be brave.'

She was brave; very brave. The pain was very bad; she had a burn the size of a shilling piece on her cheek, just above the jawline. The registrar who saw it (after what seemed like hours) said she was lucky it hadn't been higher; it was bound to scar a little, but wouldn't mar her beauty. He grinned at her and was clearly put out that she didn't smile back.

'Now we have to dress it, and you must come back every day for three days for me to see.'

'Could I please have something for the pain?' Chloe's teeth were clenched to stop them chattering.

'Hurt that much, does it?' He seemed surprised. 'Yes, we'll give you a shot of Valium. That'll do it.'

Finally she was driven home, in Piers's car, to Joe's flat, with Sarah moved in for the night – for of course, inevitably under the circumstances, Joe had gone away for a few days with Caroline; they hardly ever went away together, it was so unfair. Fretful with pain, the Valium hardly taking the edge off it any longer, she tossed endlessly on the pillow, and occasionally got up and paced round the room.

She woke to hear the door bell ringing; surfacing to slightly more ease, she staggered to open the door. A boy stood there with a bouquet of flowers so enormous he was almost invisible; huge white gracefully leaning lilies, white roses, white freesias, tied with a massive white bow.

'Thank you,' she said and took them in, sat down weakly on the sofa and, with her fingers shaking, opened the card.

'With sympathy and every possible apology, Piers Windsor.'

* * *

'Good God,' said Joe, coming into the flat, dumping his bags on the floor, 'where on earth did those flowers come from?'

'Piers Windsor,' said Chloe.

'Piers Windsor sent you flowers! What on earth for?'

'It's a bit of a long story,' said Chloe, finding herself oddly near to tears.

'Tell me. And, darling, what on earth is that on your face?'

'It's a burn,' said Chloe and then the tears did come, tears of relief at seeing Joe, of being able to talk at last about her trauma: five days ago now, and still the burn hurt, still she felt shocked by it. 'But it was worth it,' she said, hiccuping slightly after she had explained. 'He got the money for his play.'

'Well, that makes it quite all right,' said Joe, his voice heavy with sarcasm. 'Stupid bastard.'

'Oh, Joe, it wasn't his fault. And he's been so kind. I can't tell you. So terribly kind.'

'So he bloody well should have been,' said Joe. He looked very upset.

Piers phoned every day; she was amazed and charmed by the calls which became proper and quite lengthy conversations, rather than terse How are yous? After a week, he insisted on taking her to see a consultant to get advice on plastic surgery.

'It's only a tiny scar I know,' he said, 'but it's on your face, and such a very pretty face.'

After they had left the consultant (who had advised leaving well alone for at least a year) Piers took her out to tea at Fortnum and Mason, and talked to her at great length about her life. He seemed totally fascinated by what she felt were excruciatingly boring answers; and at one point when she said slightly desperately, 'I must seem very dull to you,' he said, 'Chloe, I cannot tell you how extremely interesting I find you, how very much I am enjoying your company. I could sit here all night talking to you, I really could.'

Chloe felt herself blushing, and feeling at the same time rather light-headed; she wondered if she was falling in love with him, and if it was the reason she suddenly found herself quite unable to swallow the mouthful of teacake she had just taken, when a girl suddenly appeared at the table. She had long straight dark hair, a white face, and heavily made-up dark eyes, with thick fake lashes stuck on both top and bottom, and then a heavy line of them painted in as well; she was wearing a red lace trouser suit and carrying a small dog under one arm.

'Piers! It is! I couldn't believe it. Taking tea in Fortnum's. How lovely to see you.' She bent and kissed him, and then, ignoring Chloe totally, sat down on a sliver of his chair, and started biting into one of his sandwiches. 'You don't mind, darling, do you? I'm starving, and Geoffrey hasn't arrived yet.'

'No,' said Piers, smiling back at her. 'Chloe, this is Annunciata Fallon. Annunciata, Chloe Hunterton.'

Annunciata gave Chloe a smile so brief, so cool it scarcely altered the shape of her mouth, and then turned her attention back to Piers. Chloe sat quietly, watching her, hoping the white-hot rage and sense of dismay that filled her did not show.

'What news, my darling? I was so sad not to see you at the *Hair* party last week. It was such fun.'

'Yes, well, I had hoped to go, but I couldn't make it in the end. I heard it was quite – wild.'

'It was, absolutely wild. Everyone was there. Except you – and Suzy of course.'

'Yes, well, Suzy is in Los Angeles.'

'Oh, of course. Is she well?'

'Very well,' said Piers carefully, his eyes on Chloe. 'She's going to be there for a few months. It's not a big part, but it's a gem. She's very happy with it.'

'And you're not going over there too?'

'Of course not,' said Piers, and his voice was edgy suddenly. 'Apart from anything else *The Lady of Shalott* is keeping me very occupied at the moment.'

'Ah yes, the *Lady*. Well, the rest of us are all going to get very jealous of her, I can see. What news of her, Piers?'

'Oh – hopeful, I think,' said Piers. 'I have most of the money now. And Dominic has definitely signed. But –'

'Don't tell me, no actual Lady yet?'

'No actual Lady yet, no.'

'I heard Tabitha –'

'Well, possibly.'

Chloe was puzzled by this; she had heard at the lunch that Tabitha was definitely to play the Lady. She sat carefully silent; this was not a conversation she should or could possibly enter.

'I wanted Vanessa originally,' Piers was saying. 'But she turned it down. Or rather she'd just signed to do the film version of *Camelot*. Such a pity.'

'Such.'

'And then I thought about Julie, but she's too current-looking.'

'Oh much. Susannah York? I've heard some talk about her.'

'Well – possibly. She may not be available . . .'

'You could consider an unknown,' said Annunciata. She smiled at him, the dark eyes under the lashes full of such helpless, naked greed that Chloe was startled.

'Sweetheart, I'd love to. Especially if the unknown was you. But I can't afford to. I need a name. To get the backing.'

'Oh well.' She stood up immediately, all pretence at charm gone. 'Well, I must leave you to enjoy your tea. There's Geoffrey now. See you around, Piers.'

Piers looked at Chloe slightly apologetically as Annunciata swept off across the room. 'I'm sorry about that. She was rather rude.'

'I didn't notice,' said Chloe untruthfully, wretched that he had called Annunciata sweetheart.

'She's a very talented, but rather difficult actress. Hell to work with. She never seems to realize that's why she doesn't get the parts.'

'Couldn't someone just tell her?' said Chloe wonderingly.

'They do. But she's very neurotic. She's taken an overdose twice. It's easier to opt out.'

'Goodness,' said Chloe. She looked across the room at Annunciata's back which was very pointedly turned to their table. 'I suppose your profession is full of – of – well, neurotic people.'

'I'm afraid so,' said Piers with his gentle, charming smile. 'It's a neurotic business. It's very nice to meet someone like you, who so patently isn't.'

'Oh, I don't know,' said Chloe. 'I can be quite emotional. You'd be surprised.'

'Yes, I would,' he said, looking at her very seriously. 'You seem the essence of stability to me. And courage,' he added.

'Oh,' said Chloe, 'not a lot of choice, if you mean my face.'

'On the contrary, I think there was a lot of choice. I can think of a great many people who would have screamed the place down, threatened to sue, all sorts of unpleasant things.'

'Well,' she said and was silent. She felt disturbed and disconcerted by the interlude with Annunciata, demoted abruptly from being Piers's friend to being someone who had no business to be with him, no part of his world.

Piers looked at her for a moment thoughtfully, then said, 'Now what about you? Are you a wildly ambitious young woman? Do you plan to run a business with a cast of thousands? Your own hotel chain perhaps?'

'Oh, good gracious, no,' said Chloe. 'I'm not ambitious at all. Well I am, but not in that way.'

'In what way then?'

'My ambition,' she said, looking down at her plate because she was always slightly embarrassed at telling people about it, but at the same time wanting him very much to know, 'my ambition is to have a happy family. That's all, really. I want to be married to someone I love, and to have a lot of children, and a house that's full of people laughing and having fun. I want my children to feel I'm always there for them, and that they are the most important thing in the world to me.' She paused, and looked up at him, half embarrassed, half defiant, and said, 'I expect that sounds very boring to you. Not very swinging sixties at all.'

Piers looked at her and suddenly put out his hand and touched her cheek, pushing back her heavy hair. 'It sounds lovely,' he said. 'Not boring at all. I think perhaps, Miss Hunterton, you had better marry me.'

He had not meant it of course, and she had known he had not meant it; but she still found it a profoundly affecting remark. She sat there, looking down at her plate, crumbling her biscuit to pieces, and wondering what on earth she could say next, when he said, 'Are you free tomorrow night? Because if you are I would really like you to have dinner with me.'

Chloe sat and stared at him and felt the most extraordinary things happening to her. She was wildly, wonderfully happy, excited, filled with energy and confidence and pleasure. She was dimly aware that the pianist was playing 'Some Enchanted Evening' which she had always hated, but which suddenly seemed to her one of the nicest tunes she had ever heard. And the whole room suddenly seemed very bright, and very beautiful; and everyone in it seemed to be smiling, warm, friendly. She was also aware of an entirely new sensation in the depths of her body, a warmth, a quickening, that reached outwards into every corner of herself, and at the same time she wondered at it she knew somehow precisely what it was.

'You don't have to,' she said finally. 'You really don't have to.'

Piers Windsor smiled at her. 'I know I don't have to,' he said, 'but I want to.'

He took her to the Ritz. She supposed it was inevitable. It was a flashy, showbizzy place, and he probably went there all the time. Nevertheless it was exciting. Exciting and flattering that he should take her there. Her main worry was that they would meet lots more Annunciatas.

He offered to send the car to pick her up in Primrose Hill, but she said she would rather make her own way; he was waiting for her in the cocktail lounge when she walked in. She had spent most of the day looking for something to wear and had finally fallen in love with a black crepe ankle-length dress, by Ossie Clark, with long tight sleeves; it was very plain, skimming over her body, cut low at the bosom (and she was proud of her bosom; it was, despite the fact she had lost so much weight, still quite impressive) and buttoning right through to the hem. She had pulled her hair back from her face, and pinned it in a waterfall of curls on top of her head; she made herself up extravagantly, with (taking her cue from Annunciata) rows of false eyelashes, and a lot of dark brown eyeshadow. She looked stunning, she knew, and more stunning than he had clearly expected; he sat staring at her for a moment or two, before standing up and bending to kiss her cheek.

'You look – older.'

'I know,' she said, her words totally belying the sophistication of her appearance. 'I thought I should try. Try and look older. My mother says I look as if I'm still at school.'

'You don't look,' he said, 'in the least like any schoolgirl I have ever known. What would you like to drink?'

'Oh, dear,' she said, 'I can't drink. Not yet. Not till I've eaten something. I get drunk terribly easily. Could I have some Vichy water? With ice and lemon?'

'Of course you can.' He ordered it, wrenching his eyes away from her bosom with transparent difficulty. 'Now tell me what you've been doing today.'

They sat for hours over dinner and afterwards; just talking. There were two brief Annunciata-type interruptions, one from a very flashy-looking, rather middle-aged-looking blonde who came and hugged Piers rapturously as if she was meeting him after a five-year separation, and who bestowed a look of breathtaking suspicion on Chloe, and another from an intensely beautiful young man with black curly hair who hugged Piers almost as rapturously as the woman had, and called him 'love'. Piers introduced them both to Chloe as colleagues, talked to them fairly briefly, told her that the woman was an agent, the man the lyricist who was working on *The Lady of Shalott*.

The relentless intensity of his interest in her flattered her into confidence. She talked little; sat and listened to him, and tried to eat. Much of the time he talked, told her of his own life. She heard about a jolly father, an adoring mother – now in a nursing home in Sussex – a happy childhood, a 'slightly dashing war in the RAF'.

'When it was all over, feeling a bit of a fraud, I tried for RADA and got a place.'

'And?'

'And oh, I did OK.'

'Which means?'

'Well,' he said, smiling at her slightly ruefully, 'which means I won a few prizes, and a part in repertory. God, that was fun. That was when I met and married Guinevere. My first wife: Guinevere Davies. An actress, and a girl from the valleys. With all the music of Wales in her. And we were happy. For a bit. Then – oh, well, she got her break before I did. Played Ophelia at the Bristol Old Vic. And got a little grand.'

'Was that why you broke up?' asked Chloe, gently careful.

'Well, you know, one really should be able to live with these things. It's what you expect in the theatre. I think we might have been all right even then. But she – she –' He looked at her, and there was pain, fierce raw pain in his grey eyes.

'She what?' said Chloe.

'Oh, it doesn't matter. You don't want to hear this. The ramblings of a middle-aged man.'

'Yes, I do. I do want to. Please tell me.'

'Well.' He hesitated, then said, 'All right. She was pregnant. The day she found out she was offered Jennifer Dubedat in *The Doctor's Dilemma*. Bristol Old Vic. It was no contest really. She – she had an abortion. I couldn't handle it. We parted.'

There was a long silence. Chloe was deeply, painfully shocked, shocked at his patently still-alive grief, and at a breed of woman who could discard a baby simply in order to be in a play.

He smiled at her rather shakily. 'I vowed, that day, the day she told me, I would never marry again, until I found someone whom I could – well, trust.'

'And you never have found the someone?'

'I never have.'

'Oh, I see,' said Chloe, and loathed herself for the fatuousness of the response.

She heard of a burgeoning career: a series of small parts, then second leads, Horatio, Mercutio, Victor in *Private Lives*. 'After that I became that dreadful thing, a male lead, and then I hit the screen and – well, maybe you know the rest. If you don't, it doesn't matter.'

Chloe didn't like to say she didn't really know the rest, but she smiled, and said, 'So did you go to Hollywood?'

'I did. Not until I was quite an old man though. At the end of the fifties. That was to make *Town Cousins*. Did you see *Town Cousins*?'

She shook her head. 'Sorry. But Joe told me about it,' she added hastily.

'Darling, don't be sorry. It was a very silly film. But it made me a household name. And a lot of money. And then the next one, *Kiss and Don't Tell*, that great genre, the comedy thriller, made it possible for me to get into directing. Dear me, this is turning into a crash course in theatrical history. I'm sorry.'

'That's all right,' said Chloe, trying to work out why she felt so heady suddenly, and realizing it was because he had called her darling. 'I love it. I just feel so silly not knowing about it. So you didn't think of going to Hollywood earlier? When you were young?'

'Oh, no,' he said, taking out his cigarette case, fishing in his pocket for his gold lighter, 'I never got into that. The cattle call culture. Professional suicide. Now, Miss Hunterton, it's late, nearly twelve, I must take you home. I do hope this hasn't been too boring. I expect you spend most evenings at the Saddle Room and the Ad Lib, with groovy young men.'

Chloe shuddered. 'No, I don't. Honestly. And I've loved this evening, every minute of it.'

'Good. Let me drive you home and you can talk for a little bit for a change. I want to hear about your horrible brothers and your unhappy childhood. I presume it was unhappy, most people of any note seem to have unhappy childhoods these days.' As the car pulled up outside Joe's flat, he leant over and kissed her gently on the mouth. 'You impress me you know,' he said. 'You impress me very much. I think you're lovely.'

Chloe was quite unable to think of anything to say.

When she got in, Joe was waiting, sitting at the table, struggling with an article. He hadn't been there when she went out; he looked her over in her black crepe dress, her piled-up hair, her double lashes and smiled. 'Wow,' he said, 'you look amazing. Who's the poor unfortunate sucker?'

'I don't know what you mean,' said Chloe loftily and some instinct told her to keep the identity of the sucker to herself. Joe would not like it, she knew, in the very least. And she wanted to think about the evening, to savour it, to savour the kiss, the fact that Piers had told her she was lovely, to explore the way she felt about him, to examine the sensations that were flooding her, flooding her emotions, her body, her very self. She smiled at Joe, kissed him on the top of his head and went straight into the bathroom, and thence to bed. She lay for a long time, staring into the darkness, listening to Joe's typewriter, wondering what was happening to her and where it would end; she awoke in the night, hot, restless, and found, half ashamed, half amused, that one of her hands was cupping her own breast and the other was moving with a gentle insistence in the moist tenderness between her legs.

Joe was waiting for her when she came in the next evening, with a face like thunder. 'Chloe, did you really go out with Piers Windsor last night?'

Chloe met his eyes with a coolness that surprised her. 'Yes I did. How do you know?'

'He just rang.'

'Well, I can't see what it's got to do with you. Did he –' (now, Chloe, sound casual, don't give anything away) 'did he leave a message?'

'Yes, to ring him. Chloe, what on earth is this about? Why did you go out with him?'

'Joe, because he asked me, that's what it's about.'

'Oh, really? And you go out with everyone who asks you, do you?'

'If I want to, yes.'

'Chloe, the man is –' Joe stopped abruptly.

'Yes?' said Chloe. 'The man is what?'

'Oh – totally unsuitable. I just don't understand you. Understand any of it.'

'There's nothing to understand,' said Chloe, 'and I don't see why he's so unsuitable either. I think he's lovely.'

Well that had been a mistake, that sweet, naïve word. She should have said something sophisticated, like Piers was charming, or delightful, or amusing: not lovely.

'Whatever else Piers Windsor may be,' said Joe, 'he is not lovely. He's devious, smooth, manipulative –'

'Joe, don't be ridiculous,' said Chloe. 'He's none of those things. He's been extremely good to me. And I like him very much and I shall go out with him if I want to. I don't see what it has to do with you.'

'Chloe, please don't,' said Joe and she was quite startled by how upset he seemed. 'I do assure you there is no way it is going to bring you any happiness whatsoever. And it has a great deal to do with me. I care about you very much.'

'Then you should do me the kindness of acknowledging that I am actually an adult, Joe, and able to make simple judgements like who I go out with myself.'

'Are you going to see him again?' said Joe, pushing his hair back in a particularly wild gesture.

'Yes, I probably am. Don't look like that, Joe. I'm only going out with him, I'm not going to marry him.'

Two weeks later Piers took her to bed. He had seen her almost every night since the first dinner at the Ritz; he cancelled all but the most pressing engagements, and turned his rather intense energies on her. She was genuinely baffled by his attention, his apparent obsession with her.

Infinitely easy to please, she enjoyed everything. He took her to the theatre: *The Odd Couple* and *Half a Sixpence*; to the cinema: *The Ipcress File* and the new James Bond, *Thunderball*; he took her out to ever more beautiful restaurants, to Inigo Jones and the Arethusa, and the Caprice; he drove her out to his house in Berkshire on Sunday and showed her his horses: thoroughbreds, which he was just starting to race, and even offered to allow her to ride one of the smaller ones round the track but she refused with such vehemence that he laughed and said it was all right, it wasn't compulsory.

She was swept along on the tide of Piers's romanticism; any doubts she might have had in the beginning about her feelings for him, whether they were genuine love, or merely infatuation, gratitude, an acute sense of flattery, faded in the brilliance of his courtship: flowers, presents, poems read in his beautiful voice to her over the phone, anniversaries remembered (four weeks ago today since you did the lunch for me, a fortnight since we first went to tea, exactly a week since you told me you thought you might love me) – it was all too much for her; irresistible, irreversible, she tumbled, rushed, fell over into love.

The strange intensity that her accident had brought to their early relationship, the mingling of her pain and his concern, her suffering and his tenderness had undoubtedly accelerated their affair. They had learnt much of one another very fast, had confronted raw emotion together; weeks, months of more easy contact had been accomplished in as many hours.

But that had only been the beginning; she had travelled far since then. For the first time in her entire life, she felt valued, important, strong; she was happy, joyful, and filled with pleasure. It was heady stuff. She gave no thought to the end of the thing: clearly an ending there would be, and it would be painful and dreadful, but in the meantime every day was a new delight and nothing, not Joe's increasing and patent disapproval, not her mother's cool questioning about 'this man', not even the anxiety of any of her friends who knew of her affair, could disturb her.

She could see why they were all worried, but it amused, rather than concerned her, that they should all assume that she was so foolish, so blind, so naïve that she could see no dangers in the situation herself.

She could see them all clearly, horribly clearly: Piers's age, her own age, his sophistication, the life he led, the people he knew, spent his life with, famous, glittering, household names; all these would be terrible, insurmountable barriers to her happiness. But as she clearly had no need to climb the barriers, as this was a finite thing, she gave them little thought. She was with Piers, for a limited time; she was not part of his life, his difficult, grown-up life, she had no need to be, she was living out a fantasy that he had created, and she was enjoying every possible moment of it.

'I'm only going out with him,' she kept saying, laughing at their worried disapproval. 'I'm not going to marry him.'

He seemed to her to be quite rich; indeed he acknowledged that he was. 'I did what everyone tells you not to do, and put some of my own money into various productions. Everyone, happily, has turned out to be wrong.'

He had what he called a small flat in London, in Sloane Street; it seemed quite large to Chloe, and was furnished in a rather bland, although clearly expensive style, with a great deal of antique furniture, pale beige carpets, which Chloe was so frightened of spilling things on she refused to take so much as a cup of tea out of the glittering white kitchen, and a great many extremely modern-looking paintings all over the white walls. There were also, on every surface, photographs of famous people, either with Piers (including the Queen, shaking his hand at a première) or on their own and signed in a variety of theatrical excessiveness, ranging from 'Darling Piers with best love Vivien and Larry' to 'Piers, me old mate', from Michael Caine. Chloe would walk round and round studying these with ever-increasing awe; how anyone who had clearly been on (at the very least) friendly terms with Julie Christie, Vanessa Redgrave, Jane Asher (currently going out with Paul McCartney) and Hayley and Juliet Mills could possibly want to spend so much time with her was completely beyond her comprehension.

Then there was the country house, in Berkshire, Stebbings Hall, more personal, and a great deal more beautiful, a perfect example of the classic Georgian country house, furnished and decorated with sympathetic and flawless taste; there were fewer of the photographs there, and the walls were hung with eighteenth- and nineteenth-century paintings. There was a small cinema at Stebbings; Chloe begged to be allowed to see at least one of Piers's films and, protesting and laughing, he put *Kiss and Don't Tell* on for her and she sat watching it in total awe. 'You're so good,' she kept saying. 'You're so good. I can't believe it's you and I know you.'

Piers kissed her at the end, and told her she was obviously just saying it, that he was hammy as hell in it, but she insisted that she thought he was wonderful, and even wanted to see it again.

He had been, ever since the first night, reticent about his personal life. He assured her that there was very little more about him to know, that he had told her everything, and when she asked about other women, other relationships, he said vaguely that there had been several, a few of them quite long term, but none of them remotely important. 'I told you, I haven't risked myself again.'

She believed it because she wanted to; but she was aware there was some effort involved. The light easy charm that lay on the surface of him concealed, as she had swiftly discovered, an intensity, a capacity for darker, more brooding passions that did not seem entirely compatible with a harmonious emotional life. But it seemed something she could ignore, discard almost; her concern with Piers Windsor being so ephemeral, so almost unreal. All that mattered was what he wished her to see, what he presented to her; and that was all she wished to see also.

And then, after the two weeks, and one particularly joyful evening, after dinner at the Ritz again ('Because it is our anniversary,' he said, smiling at her), he looked at her over his brandy and said, 'Chloe, would you like to come back to the flat now? It isn't very late.'

'Yes,' she said, her brown eyes meeting his in an odd mixture of pleasure and bravado. 'Yes, I'd like that very much.'

She had thought a great deal about this: had alternately longed for and dreaded it. She was a virgin and he clearly knew she was a virgin, but that didn't stop her being apprehensive, embarrassed. He had been kissing her a great deal; and he had been caressing her, her breasts, her thighs, her buttocks. Chloe liked that; and she was relieved to find she liked it. Knowing she was not overtly sexy, she had been worried that she might be actually frigid; but if the shafts of delight that went through her body when Piers's hands were on her meant anything at all, they had to mean she was at least not that. She was silent going along in the car; it was a pale grey Rolls-Royce (which Joe Payton had remarked, with a stinging accuracy, exactly matched Piers's eyes), driven by a uniformed chauffeur, and she found it inhibiting whenever she was in it, but now she was nervous, not merely of what was to happen to her, but of how she would feel, and how she was going to conduct herself. Just what was she meant to do, she wondered; how much should she move, respond? And would it hurt? She had heard so many times that it did, and she wasn't exactly afraid of it being painful, but she couldn't see how she was going to be a very rewarding partner. She looked at him, as he sat beside her, his profile rather serious, and felt so apprehensive that she almost thought of ducking out even now. She could always say she had suddenly got the curse; or she felt sick; or simply that she had changed her mind. He was so indulgent towards her, so apparently pleased by everything she did that she was sure he would forgive her, take her home and deliver her on her doorstep as usual.

But no. She wanted to go to bed with him because she loved him, she loved him absolutely, she would quite literally have died for him. In the two weeks they had been together he had not once done anything, anything at all, that she had not liked. And she wanted him to be her lover, so that their affair was complete. It couldn't be going to last much longer, he would tire of her soon, go off with one or other of the infinitely beautiful and sophisticated women he knew, and she had to see it as gloriously to its end as she could. And lose her virginity in what would at the very least be style. She just had to be a bit brave, that was all. A bit brave and very relaxed. She sat back, taking deep breaths. She would be all right. Of course she would.

The first thing that happened was that she broke something. A glass by his bed, a cut-glass tumbler, set there with a bottle of Glenfiddich malt whisky and a carafe of water. She had been fiddling about, looking at the books on the table, trying to appear nonchalant, and it had gone, knocking against the table as it went and cracking right through. Just like that. Piers came in from taking a phone call in his dressing room to find her on her hands and knees in tears, looking at it.

'Hey,' he said, 'now what have you broken?'

'Your glass,' she said, great tears forming in her eyes, 'I'm so terribly terribly sorry.'

'I'm not. It doesn't matter. How many more times do I have to tell you, I like your clumsiness. You're like a puppy, and I like puppies.'

'I don't want to be like a puppy,' said Chloe, slightly indignant. 'I want to be like a – a sleek, exotic cat. That never knocked things over.'

'Well, you're not and I'm glad you're not. Now dry your eyes, and wait there, I'm going to get some champagne for you and another glass for me, so we are both as relaxed as we can be. All right?'

Chloe nodded forlornly. 'All right.'

While he was gone, she looked round the room; she had not properly taken it in before. It was rather less spartan than the rest of the flat; in fact had she not known (or hoped she knew) that there was no Mrs Windsor, she might have assumed there was. The walls were covered in beigey-pink silk, the carpet was white, the curtains and the cover on the bed a purple and pink William Morris pattern. There was also, just off the room, his dressing room; she looked in it and had to make a huge effort to keep silent. It was like a clothes shop: all open, instantly visible, the cupboards with sliding doors, most of them open, showing rails of suits, jackets, trousers, dinner jackets, shirts stacked high on shelves one side of the room, sweaters on the other. There were four racks of shoes, three trouser presses, rows and rows of ties and belts. There was also a dressing-table with a great many bottles of cologne on it. Chloe, who had a classic country girl's antipathy towards men who wore what Toby would have called pongs, told herself they were probably only for wearing on the stage – although she had noticed some strongish, though not disagreeable, scents emanating from Piers at times – withdrew from the dressing room quickly and returned to exploring the rest of the room.

There was an antique desk in one window bay and a chair, and there was a chaise-longue in the other; the walls were covered not with the inevitable modern paintings but with nineteenth-century watercolours. It was a soft room, a gentle one; the pile of books on the bed intriguing too: *Far from the Madding Crowd*, *Jane Eyre*, and *Rosemary's Baby*. Women's books, as Joe would have said, all of them. She saw Piers's own face staring at her from the cover of the *Sunday Times* magazine: that must contain Joe's article, the one that had brought them together. Thinking of Joe (again), knowing what he would do and say if he knew she was here, she turned away, and walked over to the window. She felt chilled and very lonely, all at once.

'Now then,' said Piers, coming through the door, smiling at her, oddly nervous himself, 'now then, come and sit on the bed, and we will have a drink, and talk a little more. And if you like you can go straight home again. I promise I won't keep you here against your will.'

'All right,' said Chloe.

She sat on the bed, looking at him, sipping the champagne. He bent forward and kissed her, gently at first, then, as she responded, harder, his tongue seeking hers. He took the glass from her and laid her back on the quilt.

'I don't want you to be frightened,' he said, 'and I want you to know how I feel about you. I want you terribly. I think you are very beautiful, and I want to give you pleasure and make you happy. Because you've made me very happy, these last few weeks. Very happy. I cannot believe quite how happy I feel.'

Chloe was silent, her eyes exploring his. He moved his hands and began to caress her breasts through her silk dress; she pushed them away, sat up, pulled it easily, quickly over her head. Underneath she had on a black slip; he slid it off her shoulders, kissing them, moving down, kissing the top of her breasts, and then licking them, working his tongue down, in the salty warmth of her cleavage, and then tenderly, teasingly, round her small rosy nipples, first one, then the other.

Chloe closed her eyes; delicious sensations filled her, flooded her, she felt hot, liquid, alive. She flung out her arms, thrusting her breasts, her body at him; he pulled away from her briefly, looked at her expression and smiled.

'Don't be frightened,' he said, 'please don't be frightened. I'll look after you.'

It was all over terribly quickly. One minute he was stroking her, kissing her, telling her he loved her; and almost the next, it seemed, she was lying there, feeling a little bleak (and rather sore) and oddly lonely again, all the warm and wonderful sensations gone, all their bright promise unfulfilled somehow, hearing his voice telling her how beautiful she was, kissing her, kissing her hair, her neck, her shoulders, thanking her, and promising her that next time, next time it would be as wonderful for her.

'Well,' he said in the morning, as she woke to see him sitting on the bed, dressed in a rather wildly printed silk nightshirt, watching her as the sunlight streamed across the bed, 'well, here you are then, an old woman of the world. How do you feel?'

'Fine,' said Chloe slightly untruthfully (for she was still sore, and the second time had been just the same, wonderful in the beginning, then quick and almost frightening).

'I am going to organize some breakfast,' he said, looking at her rather oddly, 'and then we have to talk.'

'All right,' said Chloe. So this was it. She had been hopeless, absolutely hopeless and he was going to tell her that it was all over. Well at least she wasn't a virgin any more. She hoped she wasn't pregnant. Or perhaps she hoped she was. She lay back exploring the prospect, and drifted slightly uneasily back to sleep; he woke her with a kiss on her forehead.

'Come along, sit up. We have work to do. Orange juice? Croissant?'

She nodded, although she knew she wouldn't be able to swallow a thing. She took the glass of orange juice and sat very still, bracing herself for the awful, dismissing words.

'Chloe, look at me.'

She turned her head, met his grey eyes; they were gentle, smiling.

'What do you think is to become of us?' he said.

'Well – I don't know,' said Chloe. 'Nothing, I suppose.'

'Well that would be a waste,' he said almost cheerfully. 'Tell me, how do you see the rest of your life?'

'Well, I told you,' she said. 'I want to get married to someone and have lots of children.'

'So do I,' he said.

There was a long silence. Chloe sat chilled, frightened by it.

'Chloe,' he said, 'Chloe, I think you are a very special person. Very special. You're terribly young and yet you seem to me to be very mature. Far more mature than a lot of people twice your age. I also think you're very beautiful, very sexy, and very very nice.'

Gentle let-down, thought Chloe; giving her something nice to remember.

'I – I feel I've been looking for someone like you all my life. Well, I have been. And I don't want to let you go again. But then I've only known you a few weeks. It's an absurdly short time. To base a serious decision on. For either of us. Drink your orange juice.'

Chloe drank it obediently; he refilled the glass.

'But I'm afraid, terribly afraid of losing you. And I've always been good at making swift decisions. Of course you may not be. Anyway, I asked you once two weeks ago, in Fortnum's, and now I'm asking you again. Chloe, I'd like you to marry me. Please.'

Chloe said nothing. She sat staring at him, for what felt like a long time. Then she smiled, gave out a great whoop of pleasure and threw her arms round his neck, covering his face with kisses. The orange juice spread slowly and stickily over the white sheets and the purple-patterned silk bedspread.

First interview with Richard Davies, brother to Guinevere, for Love and Marriage chapter of *The Tinsel Underneath*. Might agree to be quoted.

I just hated him. Right away. Couldn't see what Guinevere saw in him. He was a clever, conceited bastard, and he was no good for her. They met at RADA and from the first moment she was obsessed with him. She said she'd never met anyone like him. Well, I wish it had stayed that way. Of course I didn't understand all that theatre stuff, or theatre people, and their ways are not ours, but even so a person is a person, and they don't come any more genuine and through and through good than Guinevere.

She made a breakaway for our family, going into acting. My dad is a farmer, and my grandad and great-grandad before him. I'm a farmer too. My mother is a teacher though, so maybe Guinevere gets it from her. The talent and the brainpower. You should hear Guinevere talk. It's like reading a book. Every other word a quotation, from Shakespeare or something. Only you don't feel she can help it, it's not that she is trying to show you how clever she is. Oh, but she is clever. Can remember a part, or a poem or a speech and only read it once or twice. And under your eyes she becomes an old woman or a young man, and no costume or make-up or anything, just her own skills. I shall never forget the first time we saw her on the stage, apart from little school plays; it was at the theatre that RADA have for their students, the Vanbrugh I think, something like that anyway. They did *St Joan*, and she was St Joan, and she stood on that stage and she said that speech, you probably know it, about, what is it now? Yes, perpetual imprisonment, 'Am I never to be free?' And I sat there, and I cried. I could hardly believe it but I cried. And my mother cried and even my father cried. And she was there, on that stage, our Guinevere, making everyone, all the audience cry. Oh it was wonderful.

Anyway, that was the night we met him. 'Oh,' he said, 'how terribly proud you must be,' and I felt like saying, you know, up yours. And I'm not like that at all, not really. And we *were* proud, all of us. My mother liked him, but my dad felt like I did. Fancy creature, he kept saying, fancy creature, what's she see in him then?

We couldn't understand it, any of us, not even my mother really. Guinevere knew, I think, and she only brought him home to Wales once, apart from the wedding, she knew it wouldn't work. She was very defensive though, wouldn't hear a word against him, she really loved him. The wedding was terrible, so awkward and strained, apart from Guinevere, and she was so happy, she seemed to float down the aisle in the chapel. She organized it all herself, made her dress, chose the music and the readings and everything. One of his friends read a poem; David Montague his name was, he was a conductor, but he had a beautiful voice, I'll give him that. Guinevere read a poem too; it was very beautiful – 'The birthday of my life is come', was one of the lines. I stood there, listening to her, looking at her lovely face, and all her hair falling like a veil down her back, and I thought, why him? And of course it was terrible, not at first, not the first year or so, but after a while I think he got jealous of her, to tell you the truth, and they quarrelled a lot, it was hopeless really, and awful to see her happiness dying. And then she was pregnant, and after that everything went really wrong. I never knew quite why, only that she wanted that baby so very much, and he left her and she lost it.

Chapter 15

1966

'I'm going to see the other great love of my life,' said Joe. 'The one in America.'

Caroline looked at him sharply; it was one of Joe's tricks to present her with unpleasant truths dressed up as jokes. 'Who?' she said.

He grinned at her, picked up her hand and kissed the fingers. 'I love it when you're jealous. It really turns me on.'

'I'm not jealous,' said Caroline irritably.

'Yes, you are. Anyway, she's another redhead with the longest eye-lashes you ever saw.'

'Joe, stop it, who are you talking about?'

'Yolande. Yolande duGrath. My old friend in Los Angeles.'

'Oh,' said Caroline, her voice flat suddenly. 'The one who knew Brendan.'

'That one.' It hurt him oddly, how deeply affected she was by the memory of Brendan. He tried to tell himself it was just that the guy had been the first love of her life, but of course it was more than that. Brendan was not someone she had grown out of and simply cherished foolish fantasies about; he lived on, not just in her heart, but in reality, in his daughter. The daughter Caroline longed to get close to, the daughter she was obsessed with, the daughter who haunted not only her, he knew, but Chloe too.

And, Joe would admit (but only to himself and only when he had had too much to drink), of course she haunted him as well; he found Fleur oddly disturbing. It wasn't just her beauty, her Irish beauty, the fair skin, the small fine features, the dark blue eyes, the almost black hair, nor was it the tall, slender body, the surprisingly full, luscious breasts, the long beautiful legs; nor even her sensuality, the undoubted presence of strong hungers in her; it was the odd blend of vulnerability and intense courage, of toughness and tenderness, the longing to be loved and the insistence that she needed no one. He thought of her more than he cared to admit even to himself.

'I wish you wouldn't go away at the moment,' said Caroline irritably, 'I'm worried about this thing with Chloe and Piers Windsor.'

'Oh I'm sure there's nothing to worry about,' said Joe easily, who was sure of nothing of the kind. 'It's just a schoolgirl crush. She'll get over it. And he'll get bored.'

'Well, I wish I had your confidence,' said Caroline. 'We've hardly seen Chloe for weeks.'

'I have.'

'Yes, I know, but you say yourself she's out with him every night. It's ridiculous. I cannot imagine what you were doing introducing her to him.'

'I didn't,' said Joe. 'She introduced herself. I've told you. Spilt wine over one of his thousand and one suits.'

'You know perfectly well what I mean. She'd never have met him if it hadn't been for you.'

'Well, I'm sorry,' said Joe. 'Pardon me for living, as Mr George Harrison said only the other day. But I have to go to LA, I have a series to write, and I have people to visit in New York as well.'

'Will you be able to see – to see Fleur?' said Caroline.

'I'll try,' said Joe. He hoped he sounded as casual as he intended.

'This is such fun,' said Fleur. 'I'm so glad you came.'

He had called her at her office, invited her to lunch; she had suggested a picnic in Central Park, and had brought chicken, bagels, cheese, fruit and Joe had brought a bottle of wine and half a dozen cans of the Diet Pepsi he knew she preferred.

She was wearing cut-offs and a white T-shirt; her dark hair, grown a little longer, caught up in a pony-tail. It was high summer, and very hot; she was tanned and her eyes looked especially dark blue. The sun had brought out some freckles on her nose; she was grinning at him, her teeth white and perfect. She had great teeth: American teeth. What did they do, this side of the Atlantic, he wondered, that made teeth grow porcelain-white and die-straight? Even Chloe had slightly crooked teeth.

'You look great,' he said.

'Thank you. It was really nice of you to come and see me.'

'Well,' he said, 'I feel I have to keep an eye on you.'

'Why? I'm a big girl now.'

It was true, and he had been right; she was no longer in the least childlike. She had grown up even since his last visit, there was a coolness about her, a greater self-assurance, a slight distancing from him. Well she was – what? twenty-one now, officially an adult. Joe tried to keep his mind from what else might have been happening to her, to effect the change. He found it absurdly disturbing.

'I know you are,' he said. 'But Caroline worries about you.'

'I can't think why,' said Fleur and suddenly the old truculence was there.

He grinned at her relievedly. 'Then you're very stupid. Anyway, I'm off to California in the morning.'

'Oh, God,' she said and her blue eyes were dark with longing. 'Oh, God, I wish I could come with you. I really feel I'm beginning to get somewhere now, you know, only I can't progress it because I can't get there, and it's terrible, it's worse than before I began.'

'Well, come with me,' he said, feeling his heart thud with pure fear and excitement at the prospect, shocked at the irresponsibility of what he was saying.

There was a very long moment's pause, and then, 'I can't, Joe,' she said, 'I just can't. I'm in the middle of about six campaigns, I should be working right now, Saturday though it is. And besides, I don't have the money. I practically don't have the money for my fares to work every day. Later in the year, that's what I've promised myself.'

'Fleur, I know we always have this conversation, but do you need any money? Because your mother –'

'No,' she said, her face closing stubbornly inwards, her eyes flashing dangerously. 'No, I don't. I can manage perfectly well. Thank you,' she added slightly reluctantly.

'OK. But I don't like to think you're having real problems.'

'I'm not. Really. Now, will you be seeing Yolande while you're there?'

'Of course.'

'Could you please ask her if she knows who and/or where Kevin Clint or Hilton Berelman might be. They're not in New York. I've tried everything, even went to the addresses the old witch gave me. Nothing, nobody there even heard of them. And I wrote to Yolande, oh, weeks ago and she didn't answer.'

'Fleur, do you really think . . .' His voice tailed away as hers lashed at him.

'Yes, Joe, I really do think. And I really do have to. It's so incredibly important to me. It's beyond me why you can't understand.' She looked at him, and sighed. 'However many more times do I have to tell you? Somehow, Joe, I've got to find out what happened. Everyone else may have forgotten my father, but I haven't.'

'Your mother hasn't,' said Joe carefully.

'Well she has a strange way of showing it.'

'She's not like you,' he said. 'She doesn't wear her heart on her sleeve.'

'I'm glad to hear you think she has one,' said Fleur briefly.

There was a silence; then he said, 'You could get hurt with all this, Fleur.'

'That's what Yolande said. I'm hurting already. It can't get worse.'

'I hope not,' he said and his voice was very gentle.

'It won't. What are you going to LA for anyway?'

'Oh – *Sunday Times* series on the Californian myth.'

'What myth?'

'That what happens there today happens in Britain tomorrow.'

'Oh,' she said, 'that old thing.'

'Yup. That old thing. And of course I'll ask Yolande. I haven't heard from her either. Not even a birthday card. It's unlike her.'

Yolande was not in her dusty, cluttered apartment in Venice. She was in the state hospital, waxy yellow, her eyelashes still on but askew, her red hair sparse and grey.

'So silly,' she said, 'they insist I'm ill and I'm perfectly well. I'm going home next week, I've told them.'

Joe patted her hand. 'Sure. Don't let them push you around.'

'What are you doing here, Joe?'

'Writing a series of articles. I've become a bit of an authority on the place.'

She patted his hand. 'Good for you. How is that darling Fleur?'

'She's fine, I think. I don't often hear from her, of course. But she loves her job and if the watch she was wearing is anything to go by, she's doing well. Although she says she's terribly hard up.'

'I'm glad she's happy. Poor little thing.'

'She said she wrote to you,' said Joe carefully.

'Yes, she did. About Clint and Berelman. She's combed New York for them without success and wants to know if I can help. I didn't know what to do, and while I was thinking I got sick. Please tell her I'm sorry. I just wish we could dissuade her from this trail, Joe. I really do.'

'Just try stopping Fleur doing what she wants to do,' said Joe. 'Yolande, who exactly were those guys?'

'Clint was an agent, and Berelman, he was a talent scout. They were equally horrible.'

'But – did they have anything to do with – with Brendan?'

'Well, yes, they did,' said Yolande. 'In the beginning. They brought him here. But –' Her face distorted with pain suddenly. 'Joe, my darling, ring for the nurse, will you? I think I may need a little shot.'

The nurse came, gave her a little shot. Yolande sank back on the pillows, her face gradually softening, easing out of pain.

'That's better. I think I may – may need to sleep for a while. Come back tomorrow, darling, will you? See me then.'

Joe bent and kissed her. 'Yes, of course I will.'

She had cancer, the doctor told Joe, breast cancer with secondaries just about everywhere. 'It's in the lymph glands. There's nothing we can do, but help her along. She's a very lovely person,' he added, 'you should hear some of the stories she has to tell.'

'I have,' said Joe.

He went back in the morning; her bed was empty. She had died in the dawn. Joe stood staring at it, stricken, feeling totally bereft.

'She was lucky,' said a passing nurse gently. 'She had a heart attack. It saved her a lot of pain.'

'Sure,' said Joe. He sat outside in the hospital car park, rested his head on the steering wheel and wept.

He was not the only one at her funeral. Dozens of them came, the actors and actresses she had taught and coaxed and bullied and teased; some of them big names, some of them nobodies. The funeral alone was going to make great copy. Hating himself for doing it, Joe made copious notes in his head. Afterwards, he went back to the hotel and turned them into an article. Then he sat down and wondered what he could say to Fleur.

Fleur would be so upset: on two counts. She had been genuinely fond of Yolande, and she had been frantic to get a lead to Clint and Berelman. Joe was not entirely uninterested in them himself; and he was torn between irritation and amusement that Fleur's investigations into Brendan FitzPatrick's past had been marginally more fruitful than his own. Well, Yolande was no longer there to help them, and the trail had once again petered out; maybe they would never pick it up again, and may be that was as well. Nothing else that Fleur could learn about her father could possibly make her feel any better, or do her any good.

Joe lay on the bed and thought about Brendan FitzPatrick: of what Caroline had told him and what he had learnt for himself. The two portraits did not add up too well. To Caroline he had been a hero, a gentle, dashing hero who had arrived in Suffolk in the middle of the war and swept her off her feet. He had come riding into town, like a fucking prince in a fairytale, only in a Jeep rather than on a white charger, and they had fallen in love. And to everyone else he had spoken to he had been a no-hoper, weak, untalented, albeit charming, and hopelessly indiscreet. What was he to make of this enigma, he wondered that night after the funeral, for the hundredth, the thousandth time, of this man Caroline had loved so much, who Fleur had loved so much and who so clearly deserved neither of them?

Or did he? Who was the real Brendan FitzPatrick, and what had he truly been like, what had actually happened to him? It was the apparent paradox of the man that kept Joe working away as tenaciously as Fleur herself at finding out precisely what had led him to his death. The story that he had told in his book, that had served almost as an introduction to the other famously great Hollywood scandals, of Lana Turner and Johnny Stompanato, of Errol Flynn and the rape charge, of Charles Chaplin and his predilection for young girls, of Robert Mitchum and the drugs case, the story of Byron Patrick, its details obscured in the tangle of time, intrigued and haunted him. And even as he had come to resent and even dislike, if not Brendan, then certainly Byron, the person that he had become, Byron Patrick, God damn him, with his dazzling smile and his rippling muscles, he felt a compulsion, like Fleur, to get to the bottom of the story, to find out who had betrayed him, hated him enough to talk to the scandal sheets about him, and how he had actually come to sink so low. For after all, Byron had led him to Caroline. And to Fleur.

Joe lay on his bed, drinking bourbon and thinking about Fleur. Now what did he do about her? The best thing he could do was obfuscate the trail, not help her to follow it. Only – only she would never give up. She would give him that terrible, scornful, angry look and go right on past him, and carry on alone. And she would get to the end of it, she would find Clint and Berelman, and anyone else she needed to find, and he had to be there, to help her through. It was the least that he owed her, the least he could do.

* * *

He woke at three in the morning, sweating. He was still dressed and the air-conditioning was off. And he had had a horrible dream, that he had been driving a car on the Pacific Coast Highway, and a drunk had come weaving towards him, shouting and waving his hands and begging him for something. But what? Joe pulled his clothes off and lay naked on the bed, the sweat drying on him, making him cold. To distract himself from the nightmare of Brendan, he began to read his piece again, raking over the details of the funeral in his mind, trying to make sure he hadn't missed any particularly delicious little tableau. And then he remembered that he had. A nauseating guy in a toupee and an over-firm handshake, who had come up to him for no reason and said, 'Hi. Perry Browne. Publicity director. What a very lovely lady Yolande was. How terribly sad. You wrote the *Scandals* book, didn't you? Such a wonderful piece of research. I enjoyed it so very much. Maybe we could work together some time.' And he had pressed his card into Joe's hand. He had not been the only person to do so that day; there was a crumpled grubby handful in Joe's pocket, a testimony to Hollywood tastelessness.

Perry Browne hadn't seemed to be a publicity director for anything in particular, just eager to impress anyone impressionable. Fired long since no doubt, and one of the teeming hundreds of freelance writers who scratched out a living on the overworked soil of Hollywood gossip. Well, if he had known Yolande, and he had read *Scandals*, he might very well have known Byron. He would call him in the morning. It was a long shot, but worth trying.

Perry Browne lived out at Westwood; he was touchingly pleased to get Joe's call. 'Joe! It is really lovely of you to remember me. Can I buy you a drink? The Polo Lounge at twelve? Wonderful! I'll book a table.'

In the event, they weren't allowed into the Polo Lounge of the Beverly Hills Hotel, because Joe wasn't wearing a tie, but after some argument by Perry and the rather more persuasive sight of Joe's press card they were allowed to sit by the pool. Perry ordered a margarita and Joe a beer.

'I'm so pleased you called,' said Perry. 'So very pleased. What a touching ceremony that was, Joe. I have to tell you I saw much of it through a blur of tears. This town will never forget Yolande, never.'

Joe opened his mouth to say it seemed to have done a pretty good job while she lay in the hospital and then shut it again.

'Now, Joe, what can I do for you? I have to tell you I would just love to work with you. I have many many contacts here, and I admire your writing so much. What exactly are you working on at the moment, Joe, and for which paper?'

'A series for the *Sunday Times*,' said Joe.

'The *Sunday Times*! How wonderful!' said Perry. 'Oh, that is just such a coincidence. I dined with Michael Boxman last time he was over and he said I had only to come up with an idea, and he would commission it just like that.'

Joe presumed that by Michael Boxman he meant Mark Boxer and smiled at him weakly. 'So what happened?' he asked with a touch of malice.

'Oh, well, you know, I've been so busy, I just haven't had the time. But I will, Joe, I certainly will – although of course I don't want to crowd your space.'

He smiled his gleaming smile, and patted his toupee a little uncertainly. It was windy by the pool. The wind wafted the strong smell of his aftershave in Joe's direction. Joe felt glad they weren't in the Polo Lounge.

'Uh, Mr Browne –'

'Oh, please call me Perry. Please!'

'Perry. OK. I'm researching a new book. On the old studio system. I thought maybe you could help me with that.'

'Well, surely I will. I'd be glad to. Of course I'm not actually tied to a studio any more, but that makes me lighter on my feet. Er – what kind of a fee did you have in mind, Joe?'

'Oh – I don't know,' said Joe helplessly. 'It would depend.'

'On what?' said Perry. He looked sharper, suddenly, like an ageing ferret. 'I mean my time is precious, Joe, I don't have to tell you that. *Time* magazine are paying huge sums, and we're talking really huge here, for their show pages.'

'Oh, really?' said Joe. 'You must tell me who you're working for there. I did a piece for them last week and got fifty dollars for it.'

'Oh, you did?' Perry looked uncertain. 'Well, I suppose we all have our little areas of expertise. Joe, suppose we do it on the basis of fifty dollars a day. That way we'll all be happy.'

'Sure,' said Joe easily. He had no intention of using Perry for five dollars' worth of day. 'You can invoice me. Now, Perry, which studio were you with?'

'Oh, well, Joe, I was with all of them in my day. Universal. MGM. Paramount. ACI . . .'

Joe felt a stab of violent excitement. Byron had been at ACI. This was better than he had hoped.

'When were you at ACI, Perry?'

'Well, I was there at the time Naomi MacNeice was there. We worked very closely together. Poor Naomi, she is so ill you know. I take tea with her every week or so.'

'So you were there when Byron Patrick was there?'

'Well, in his early days there, Joe, yes, I was.'

'Really?' said Joe, concentrating as hard as he could on the drink in his glass.

'Yes, and I would have talked to you very gladly about him for your book, had I known, but of course I had left by then, fallen out with Naomi. A very difficult woman, Naomi.'

Joe nodded agreeably at Perry. 'So I gather. Did you know Byron well?'

'Well enough,' said Perry, and there was a pained look on his face. 'He was difficult, you know, Joe. Very difficult. And he could be quite rude. I sometimes felt he didn't like me.'

'Surely not,' said Joe carefully.

'Well, I have to tell you I did. But – well, it's all blood on the tracks now. He was foolish. And I was truly sad when he died. Very very sad.'

'Indeed?' said Joe. 'In what way would you say he was foolish, Perry?'

'Oh, the friends he made. The company he kept.'

'Yes,' said Joe. 'Not very savoury, I imagine. Did you see much of that company?'

'As little as possible,' said Perry with dignity.

'Perry,' said Joe, fighting to keep his voice calm, 'Perry, do you remember an English actor in his crowd? At that time?'

Perry sounded mildly impatient. 'Joe, I told you, I kept away from them. There were a lot of English actors here. Fighting to get breaks. I dare say he knew several of them. He put himself about a great deal, I have to say. He really had only himself to blame, you know, in the end.'

'Oh really?' said Joe. 'All he needed maybe was a friend.'

'Well, I think a little more than that, Joe. This town is very unforgiving.'

'Yes,' said Joe. 'Yes, I suppose it is. Tell me, Perry, did you know a pair of guys called Clint and Berelman?'

Perry's eyes were watchful again. 'Hilton I knew. Kevin not so well. They were very big at one time.'

'Uh-huh. And did Byron know them?'

'Well, he certainly did!' said Perry. 'He and Hilton were really very close when Byron first came to Hollywood. Kevin discovered him, of course, in New York. But you know, and it may shock you to hear this, Joe, because I'm sure you would have imagined Byron to be a nice person, he fell out with them, and then once he had made the big time, he would have nothing to do with them. Nothing! I think that kind of behaviour is so unnecessary.'

'Yes, but if they were big –'

'Joe, we all need one another,' said Perry, looking pained. 'And Hilton was having a difficult time. It would have meant so much to him if Byron had put just a little business his way. But he didn't. I think Hilton was very hurt by that. Very hurt.'

'So you were quite close to Hilton, were you?'

'Oh, well now, Joe, it depends how you mean! Professionally yes, but personally no. I didn't admire his style. Not at all.'

Joe reflected that whatever Hilton Berelman's style had been, he would undoubtedly have preferred it to Perry's. 'And – er, what has happened to them now? Do you know?'

'Kevin is still in New York, to the best of my knowledge. Hilton has gone to live in San Francisco. He has friends there, and he felt he could start all over.'

'In the same business?'

'Of course. He was very talented.'

'So tell me, Perry, in what way did you not admire his style? Here, let me get you another drink. Same again?'

'That'd be wonderful. Thank you.'

Joe waved his arm at one of the starched retinue of barmen standing round the pool, ordered more drinks. He leaned back, enjoying the warmth in the air, the sun on his face, the ice-cold beer. Every time he opened his eyes he saw yet more beautiful women, wearing the minimum of clothing. He could get to like this life.

'What were you asking me?' said Perry, sipping daintily at his margarita through the pink straw. 'Oh yes, about Hilton. Well, he was a little flamboyant. And he could be rather tasteless.'

'In what way?' said Joe, amused. He was completely unable to imagine any behaviour which would seem tasteless to Perry Browne.

'Well, he used bad language. In mixed company, which I have never liked. Have you, Joe? No, I thought not. And he used to tell very questionable stories. I once did confront him. I said, Hilton, that is not the kind of story we want to hear at a dinner table.'

'And what did he say?' asked Joe, intrigued.

'Oh, he was very rude to me. In fact I wouldn't like to repeat his exact words. But I think one has to take a stand sometimes, don't you, Joe? Over what one believes in.'

'Oh, I do,' said Joe.

Perry suddenly looked at him more sharply.

'Anyway, Joe, I really don't think you want to hear any more about Hilton Berelman. We're here to talk business. Now you tell me which studios you're interested in and I'll see what I come up with for you in the way of ideas. I have a contact book second to none, believe me.'

When Joe got back to his hotel, there was a message to call Fleur. He ordered himself a large bourbon and settled down at the phone.

'Hi, Fleur.'

'Joe! Why have you been so long? It's five days since our picnic.'

'Darling, I have some bad news. I'm sorry.'

'What kind of bad news? Doesn't Yolande remember anything about Clint and Berelman?'

'Fleur – sweetheart – she doesn't remember anything about anyone any more.'

There was a long silence. Then Fleur's voice came down the lines and across the thousands of miles, careful, frightened. 'What do you mean, Joe? Is she – is she –'

'She died, Fleur. Three days ago. I'm so sorry.'

'Shit. Shit, Joe, why didn't you tell me? Did they have the funeral yet?'

'Yes, they did. Yesterday.'

'Shit, Joe, I really hate you.' He could hear the pain cracking her voice. 'I would have come. You know I would. She's been so kind to me. God, I hate you.'

The phone went dead. Joe sat staring at it, feeling slightly shaky and very sick. God, he was an insensitive, thoughtless lout. Why hadn't he called Fleur at least to tell her, to give her the chance to come if she could? Once again, Fleur had needed them, and once again they had failed her. No wonder she was so hurt, so hostile to them all.

He decided to go for a walk; drove down to Santa Monica and wandered for a couple of hours along the shore, hating himself. He didn't eat dinner when he got back, but sat in his room, trying to work, getting drunk. Then the phone rang. It was Perry Browne.

'Joe? I have some people for you to talk to down at Venice. Just mention my name and I know you'll find them very co-operative.'

'Thanks,' said Joe, and sat there while Perry reeled off a list of names, not even bothering to write them down. 'Thanks,' he said when Perry had finished; he was half asleep.

'Oh and Joe? I have a number for Hilton Berelman for you.'

Joe woke up with a start. 'Yes?'

He scribbled the number down, feeling suddenly alert and rather heady.

'Oh, do please call me Hilton,' said the light, amused voice down the phone. For some reason, Joe felt he would greatly prefer him to Perry.

'Well – Hilton. I'm actually researching a book into the Hollywood star system. I'd be really grateful if you could give me some case histories.'

'This your first book?'

'No,' said Joe carefully. He had thought about this one. 'I wrote one earlier. About Hollywood scandals.'

'Oh yeah. Didn't read it.'

'You didn't miss much. Now tell me, Hilton –'

'How'd you get my name?'

'Oh – from a lady I think you may remember. Yolande duGrath.'

'Sure. She was a one-off. How is she?'

'I'm afraid she died.'

'You're kidding me! Now that is really sad. Recently?'

'Quite. I was very upset. She was a good friend to me. Anyway, these things happen.'

'Yeah. Poor old Yolande. What a great shame.' He was silent for a moment.

Joe decided it was time to cut the sentiment. 'Now, Hilton, if you could give me a few case histories, I'd be really grateful.' He got his notebook out and made some notes out of sheer force of habit. He was so tired the page was blurring. As much to wake himself up as anything, he said, 'Hilton, does the name Byron Patrick mean anything to you?'

'Sure it does. He was one of mine. Originally. How d'you know about him?'

'Oh – Yolande had mentioned him.'

'He was no good really. No talent. He deserved all he got.'

'What did he get?'

'Well, in the end, nothing, nothing at all. He was killed. Run down. He was drunk at the time, weaving up the Pacific Coast Highway. He'd been living on the beach at Santa Monica. Destitute.'

'But why did he deserve that?'

'He didn't treat people very well,' said Berelman briefly. 'His agent, Kevin Clint and I, we did a lot for him. Kevin was a real ace. Could spot a face anywhere. Not so hot on whether there was any talent there though. He's dead now; I really miss him. Anyway, we got Byron to Hollywood, got him signed, bought him nice clothes, you know the whole thing. Then when he got taken up by that MacNeice woman at ACI he didn't want to know. Wouldn't even speak to us at parties.'

'I – see.' Joe hesitated, not knowing quite what line to take. He didn't want to sound over-sympathetic, but something was clearly called for, if he wasn't to cut Hilton off mid story. 'Well, that certainly doesn't sound too nice. But –' He had obviously said the right thing. Hilton went on chatting easily.

'Anyway, his past found him out. And Kevin too, of course.'

'His past?'

'Yeah. He was declared guilty of the one crime Hollywood won't forgive. Still. Not officially anyway. Not in its heroes.'

'You mean Byron was a – a homosexual?' said Joe sounding carefully innocent.

'He certainly was. Quite a wild little boy, as I recall. AC-DC of course. I mean Rose Sharon always swore he was straight. But I can show you plenty of people who could personally testify to the opposite.'

'Rose Sharon?' said Joe. 'Did she know Byron? I didn't realize.' He felt confused, irritated at having missed this titbit: Rose Sharon, one of the great Hollywood stars of her generation, three Oscar nominations, every picture an enormous box-office success. Why hadn't he heard about this connection before? And why hadn't Yolande mentioned it?

'Joe, it was a real love story. When they were young. Romeo and Juliet. Type-casting. Naomi broke that one up, of course, along with the rest. Anyway, like I say, Byron hit the scandal sheets. Usually when that happened, when the studio got wind of it, they'd do a deal. I mean they say there was a huge trade done over Rock Hudson, huge. When *Confidential* offered Jack Navaar ten thousand dollars to talk. But Byron just wasn't worth that kind of cover-up. They just let him go down the pan.'

'I see,' said Joe. 'So who was it talked to this magazine? Do you know?'

'Joe, I don't know.' Hilton sounded bored suddenly, irritable. 'Some stringer. Hollywood swarms with them. Hookers most of them. Now look, this is really old news. We should talk about something more interesting. Joe, can you use anything on Floy Jacoby? I tell you that chick is going to be big. And we could both get big with her . . .'

Joe sat down in the morning and wrote a long, careful letter to Fleur. He asked her to forgive him for not telling her about Yolande, he told her that he had discovered that Kevin Clint was dead, and that Berelman had long since left Hollywood. After a great deal of thought he told her that he had also discovered that her father and Rose Sharon had had a love affair in the early days in Hollywood. 'That was long before she was a big star. Or even a small one. Apparently Naomi MacNeice broke it up with great efficiency. I really don't think she'd talk to you, but I suppose it's worth a try.' He hoped it wasn't irresponsible of him but he felt he had to offer Fleur something to try to redeem himself.

She would almost certainly try to see Rose; Rose would almost certainly refuse her request; and after that, maybe, dear God, how he hoped so, Fleur would finally give in and let things rest.

Only letting things rest was not really Fleur's style.

Transcript of telehone conversation with Hilda Foster, sister to Kirstie Fairfax, for Lost Years chapter of: *The Tinsel Underneath*.

I'm sorry, but I don't want to get involved. I never have, and I never will. She died, she's gone, she can't be brought back; what's the point of stitching up some bastard over twenty years later? Well, that's what you're doing, isn't it? And like I say, it won't help Kirstie. Poor kid. Starstruck, that's what did it for her. They all were, all those kids. Whoever the guy was she got mixed up with out there, I'll bet he was too. I didn't know his name, I tell you I don't want to get involved. We had all this at the time with the Los Angeles police, and we couldn't help then. She never wrote, hardly ever called. All we knew was she met him at some casting session and he tried to help her. And he was very taken with her. Obviously it went wrong and he knocked her up in the process. Well, that's life. It's tough. Sure it was sad at the time, but it's a long time ago. Life goes on.

Transcript of telephone conversation with Lou Burns, cameraman at ACI during 1950s.

Sure, I remember Byron. He was a real nice guy. Couldn't act his way out of a paper bag, but he had the looks and he had Miss MacNeice, and who needed more? He was doing OK when all that shit hit the fan. I never could make out the truth of any of it. You never knew who was doing what to who in this town. Still don't. It's all an act. I tell you, even going to the toilet's an act here. He was his own worst enemy, Byron was. Too trusting. He just never saw trouble coming. Yeah, I remember Kirstie Fairfax. Only because she died and she was here the day before, so the cops came round. He'd tried to help her. I mean there's a for instance for you. Got her tested for some film with him, then when she doesn't get it, she blames Byron. She was a tramp. Slept with half the town. Girls as well as men. On just about everything. Knocked up, wasn't she? She comes in with some funny little dancer guy. Queer as a nine-dollar bill. 'Where's Byron?' she says. 'I wanna tell him something.'

I say he's gone and she says tell him Kirstie called. Tell him we've passed the message on. Then she's gone, and I never see her again.

Chapter 16

1966

'The thing is, I'm pregnant,' said Chloe, looking rather fierce, 'so there's no point trying to stop me. It's either an illegitimate grandchild, or you agreeing to the wedding. I'm twenty now, so I shall be able to do what I want next year anyway. Sorry, Mummy.'

Joe looked at her, pale and tired, standing there so bravely in her mother's drawing room, making her announcement, and thought that if Piers had walked in now he would find it quite difficult to refrain from some kind of physical assault on him.

'I told Piers not to come,' she said, fiercely defensive, anticipating what he might say. 'I knew you'd be horrible, and it would be worse if he was here.'

'Well, let us not waste time and energy debating that,' said Caroline. 'This is nonsense, Chloe, of course you can't marry Piers Windsor.'

'Caroline,' said Joe, warningly gentle, 'let Chloe at least tell us whatever she wants to.'

'I've told you,' said Chloe. 'I'm going to marry him. Very soon.'

'But poppet, why? What's the rush?'

'I'd have thought that was obvious. I'm pregnant.'

'Chloe,' said Caroline, clearly struggling to be calm, to digest the situation, 'you don't have to get married. Just because you're pregnant.'

'Oh really? I suppose you want me to have an abortion.'

'Chloe, don't be silly. Of course we don't. But you don't actually have to get married. Until – until, well, you're sure.'

'I am sure. And why shouldn't I get married? You don't seem to understand. We love each other.'

'Chloe, you've known – Piers –' Caroline plainly had trouble getting the name out, without spitting – 'known him for about four or five months. That isn't very long.'

'It's long enough.'

'Chloe,' said Joe, and he could hear himself saying the words, very slowly, very cautiously, as he struggled not to alienate her, not to drive her faster into the disastrous course she had set herself on, 'Chloe darling, I know you do feel quite sure about this. But first of all please try to understand this is something of a shock to us. We're trying to be calm, but it isn't easy.'

'No,' said Chloe and for the first time she looked slightly less hostile. 'No, I can see that. I'm sorry.'

'It's all right. And then please, please think. Piers is at least, at the very least, twenty years older than you are. He leads a life of which you know nothing. You will find yourself, if you do marry him, having to contend with situations which you will find extremely difficult, and people with whom you have nothing in common. It may not seem very important to you now, but later, when the first excitement has worn off, it will. Your life will be terribly difficult; you're shy, you're – well, you're very young. I just don't see how you can be happy with him. Or rather,' he added, still desperate to be tactful, 'with his life.'

'Well, I can,' said Chloe, and he could see she was near to tears. 'I know I'm shy, that's half the point. All my life people have put me down, thought I was stupid. Boys don't really like me. I hate the kind of men you'd want me to marry. Of course I'm shy. But Piers loves me and thinks I'm wonderful and wants me to be his wife. That makes me a lot less shy, I can tell you.'

'But, Chloe –'

'Don't keep saying but. I'm going to marry him. And just in case you think he shouldn't have got me pregnant, it was absolutely my fault. He thought I was on the pill and I wasn't. So don't blame him for that.'

'Chloe, that is absurd.' Caroline's face was very white and there were two brilliant red spots on her cheeks. 'There is a way of not becoming pregnant that neither of you seem to have considered. You don't have to go to bed with someone just because you are in love with them, you know.'

'Oh really?' said Chloe, turning on her like a small, cold fury. 'Well there's certainly no way I could have learnt that from you.'

'Chloe!' said Caroline. 'Please don't.'

'Don't what?' said Chloe. 'Talk about you? About it? Why not?'

'Because it's totally irrelevant to all this,' said Caroline, 'that's why not.'

'Oh really?' said Chloe. 'Not totally, I wouldn't have said. If we had been closer, if you'd had a bit more time for me, if –'

'Chloe, don't,' said Joe, suddenly very sad. 'This is getting us nowhere. We want your happiness, poppet, that's all.'

'Yes, well, my happiness is with Piers,' said Chloe. 'I'm an adult now, and I know what's best for me. I thought you'd be like this, not even try to understand. I'm going back to London now. I just wanted to let you know.'

'Chloe, wait,' said Caroline.

But she was gone.

'I just can't understand it,' said Joe. He and Caroline were sitting by the fire in the drawing room an hour later; it was a cold August day, and the scene with Chloe had made it seem colder. 'I can see why she's infatuated with him, but I don't understand why he wants to marry her.'

'Well, maybe he's infatuated too,' said Caroline, rather bleakly. 'She's young and very pretty. She is – or rather was – a virgin. No doubt it all rather panders to his monstrous ego.'

'But he knows dozens of very pretty young girls,' said Joe. 'All dying to take off their knickers for him. Much more his style as well. Chloe simply isn't.'

'Maybe that's the point.'

'Maybe. I don't know. I actually would have said pretty boys were more his thing.'

'I presume you're joking,' said Caroline.

But he could see the unease in her eyes.

Later she said he must talk to Piers.

'It's all your fault anyway.'

'Thanks. Why is it my fault?'

'You introduced them. Didn't you?'

'Not really, no,' said Joe wearily, wondering for the hundredth, the thousandth time what Caroline would say or do if she knew the original reason that he had been investigating Piers Windsor's past. Thank God, thank God the investigations had drawn a blank, that the drift of information had proved nothing, an entirely fragmented straw in the wind.

'Piers? Joe Payton. I think we should talk.'

'Of course.' Piers's voice was as always silken smooth. 'Yes. I've been expecting you to call. Can I buy you lunch?'

'If you like,' said Joe. He might as well get what he could out of the bugger.

'Look,' he said, as they settled to Steak Diane at the Savoy Grill, 'I want to know why you're marrying her. Why not just an affair? Why not make her your mistress? It's very destructive, what you're doing.'

'Joe, please!' Piers's grey eyes were very wide, his face very candid. 'I love her. I really do.'

'If you loved her,' said Joe flatly, 'you wouldn't marry her. You'd leave her alone.'

'How very unfair of you. Why should I leave her alone?'

'Because she's not going to be able to cope with you. With your life. With any of it,' said Joe desperately. 'She's young, she's only twenty, Piers, for Christ's sake, and a young twenty, totally unsophisticated, terribly shy. She'll suffer agonies. Once the first flush is over. And she won't be a very satisfactory wife to you either. She's not what you want, Piers.'

'You're quite wrong there,' said Piers easily, draining his glass. 'You underestimate her, Joe, totally. She is a person of sterling character. And she is what I want.'

Joe looked at him, suddenly intent. 'How much do you know about her, Piers? About her background?'

'Oh – as much as I need to know,' said Piers. 'I know she's a typical product of her class, her education. I know she's shy and lacks self-confidence. For which I have to say I blame her mother.'

'Oh really?' said Joe sharply. 'Why do you say that?'

'Isn't it obvious?' said Piers. 'Caroline is very unaffectionate, very detached. She hardly has a relationship with Chloe. She clearly adores those boys, favours them quite appallingly over Chloe. I think it's hardly surprising she's shy and insecure.'

So he didn't know. Well, that was interesting. And probably a good thing.

'Anyway,' Piers went on, 'I think she will cope splendidly. And I will help her.'

'Do you call this pregnancy helping? It's absurd, it's making things twice, three times as difficult. She's not well, she's exhausted, she's –'

'I'm not entirely happy about that,' said Piers quietly. 'I have to tell you. For her sake, not mine. I had no idea she was – well, she told me she was on the pill. I'm very sorry about it. I can see how you must feel. She's quite wilful, you see,' he added with a slightly wry smile. 'She's not the helpless malleable creature you seem to imagine. But – well, I'm sorry, Joe. I asked her to marry me long before I knew she was pregnant. I love her. I want to have her with me. I need her.'

'Yes, but why? Why do you need her, Piers?' said Joe. He looked across at him, hating him, at the famously beautiful, chiselled face, the wide grey eyes, the girlishly long eyelashes and the awful sprayed-on hairstyle.

'I told you,' said Piers, gently firm, an expression somewhere near reproof in his eyes, 'I love her. And you really mustn't worry about her, Joe. I'll take the greatest care of her. She's doing beautifully.'

Chloe would have been surprised to hear this conversation. She did not feel she was doing beautifully at all. Despite her adoration of Piers, his constant affirmation that he adored her, it was hard: she would not have believed how hard. There were times when she would have run away, had it not been for the baby, but she knew it was too late to change her mind. She would have run away, not from Piers, but from the life she found herself thrust into. The theatrical tribe is arguably the hardest of all in which to gain acceptance. Its language, its customs, its initiation ceremonies are all absolutely exclusive; no experience of any other people can prepare for it. While Chloe was only trying to gain acceptance as a member, she was seen, by the women within the circle, as an interloper of the highest order, a plunderer, stealing a glittering and unearned prize.

Most people in Piers's circle treated her with an initially overt and gushing politeness, and then proceeded to ignore her, occasionally tossing her a courtesy smile. She had many times sat for over an hour at a lunch or dinner table, completely silent, neither speaking nor spoken to, while Piers's friends exchanged jokes and gossip, discussed their present and future work and frequently invited him to join them for all manner of social and professional happenings without so much as glancing in Chloe's direction. She sometimes thought if she had to listen to one more conversation about how John Osborne had changed the English theatre beyond recognition, or how breathtakingly brilliant Tom Stoppard was, how magically talented Vanessa Redgrave, how Bernard Levin's review of *Rosencrantz and Guildenstern* had just slightly missed the point, she would scream very loudly indeed. But of course she never did, she went on sitting, smiling politely, trying to look intelligent, praying no one would speak to her, ask her opinion. Not everyone was like that; some people were kind and courteous, particularly men, and those of Piers's generation, but both older women and young girls regarded her at best tolerantly and at worst with contempt.

She struggled not to mind, she struggled to join in the conversations, to ignore the hostility, the coolness, to tell herself it was only a phase, something that had to be gone through, that it would surely get better and that anyway it didn't matter, and that Piers loved her and that was all that mattered – and still it was hard.

There had been one particularly appalling day, just before the wedding, which weeks later she could hardly bear to think about: they had been invited to a lunch party, given by Maria Woolf at her house in Oxfordshire. Maria Woolf was the leading member of the circle concentric to Piers's own: not theatrical, but café society, rich, smart, high profile ('They love to boast about being in each other's worlds,' Joe had explained to Chloe: he was a great source of information on such matters, she had discovered); Maria Woolf was an over-dressed, over-jewelled blonde, with wide blue eyes and a rosebud mouth which totally belied a ruthless ambition and almost complete self-absorption; she was married to millionaire industrialist Jack Woolf and nobody knew quite why he put up with her. 'You know what they used to say about Fred and Ginger,' Piers said to Chloe once in an unusually humorous comment, 'she gave him sex and he gave her class: same with Maria and Jack, except he gives her money.' Maria was a heavy investor in many of Piers's productions, including the *Lady*, and was important to him. Piers had assured Chloe that she would love the party, that she would have the greatest fun, that there would be all sorts of amusing people there, that he would be with her, and that most people would kill to be going. Chloe would have killed not to be going.

The party was huge: Piers's pale grey Rolls pulled through the iron gates of the Woolfs' house – a beautiful Queen Anne mansion near Oxford – and she saw, with a thud of terror, innumerable groups of people, all immensely glamorously dressed, scattered everywhere. Most of them seemed to know Piers and waved at the car; countless women blew him kisses. Chloe shrank into her seat, forcing herself to keep calm, and debated saying she felt ill and wanted to go home, but she knew that would be a mistake. She had to go through with this. She had to. It was part of the deal, as she had told herself so many times during the past two months, part of becoming Mrs Windsor. She forced herself to smile, to ask Piers who people were, and became instantly confused against a background of, 'Oh, that's Lila Beauchamp, wonderful girl, she and I were at RADA together, and that's her husband, very big banker, darling, do be nice to him, and there's old Foggy Fanshawe, we were at school together, and that's his new lady, Dulcima, isn't she lovely, now that's Caroline Outhwaite, she's so sweet you'll love her, her husband will adore you, he's a wicked old rogue, always causing trouble in the House of Lords, he's probably in the bushes even now with some dolly bird and that's . . .'

It didn't really get too bad until lunch-time: Maria Woolf greeted her with a chilling courtesy before kissing Piers effusively on the lips and telling him she had missed him and she wanted to hear every tiny detail of what he had been up to; but then she was mercifully distracted by yet another guest, and Piers led Chloe off, his arm through hers, introducing her to endless people. Chloe stood, smiling prettily, trying not to notice how bored everyone seemed by everything she had to say, got caught up in a conversation with someone and then suddenly realized Piers was gone from her side and, panic-stricken, excused herself and went off through the crowds trying to find him.

Then: 'Lunch' came a cry from the terrace of the house, and Maria Woolf stood there, ringing a bell loudly, and laughing, with Piers beside her; whereupon they disappeared into the house, a great snake of people following them. Chloe hurried forwards: at least now she knew where Piers was. She found it hard to get into the house; she kept pushing gently, and saying 'excuse me', hurried straight past the vast buffet table, heaped with silver dishes of whole salmon, rose-pink beef, chicken baked in golden pastry (noting even in her misery that that was a nice idea and one to copy), of piles of new potatoes and asparagus and mangetouts and great bowls of salad, thinking that Piers would surely have her food ready for her, would not have completely neglected her, and arrived, slightly breathless, in the dining room, with its seemingly endless tables, and there at last was Piers. Only he was not looking for her, and had no extra plate in front of him, but was sitting between Maria Woolf and another woman, and was engaged in filling their glasses with wine, and listening with rapt attention to what Maria was saying while slightly absent-mindedly patting the hand of the other. Every other chair at the table was taken by people all of whom knew one another and were chattering and laughing; he had clearly forgotten all about her. Chloe felt sick; she backed out, her eyes fixed on his face, like a rabbit in front of a fox, praying he would not see her, and bumped into one of the waiters, his arms full of bottles of wine.

'Oh,' she said, 'oh, I'm so sorry, could you possibly tell me where the lavatory is?'

The waiter looked at her with a chilly courtesy and said, 'Yes, madam, through the lobby just over there.'

She fled to it, bolted herself in and sat there, numb with misery, not knowing what to do, but somehow insanely praying that Piers would notice that she was missing and come in search of her; he would send someone in perhaps, she would hear her name. But no one came; and after ten or fifteen minutes she came out and brushed her hair and put some perfume on, and went cautiously into the hall.

Everyone had disappeared: there was a huge heady hum from the dining room. Chloe went forwards and looked cautiously through the door; the room was full, there were no empty spaces at any table. Piers was still engrossed in conversation with Maria Woolf, careless of her absence. A couple of people looked up amusedly at her and half smiled, then returned to their food; she stood there, as if turned to stone, a great lump in her throat, feeling conspicuous, ridiculous, humiliated. She was just about to run again, when she felt a hand on her shoulder.

'Hallo, Mrs Windsor-to-be. Got delayed? Me too. You're much too pretty to eat lunch by yourself. Shall we go in together, and you can sit and tell me all about yourself. Come along, pick up a plate and we'll find a quiet corner and can get to know one another.'

Chloe looked up and found herself staring at one of the most outrageously good-looking men she had ever seen. He was tall, and very heavily built; he had thick fair hair, and intensely blue eyes in a tanned face, and he had very shaggy eyebrows which gave him a slightly rakish air, made his looks less too-good-to-be-true. He was rather over-dressed for the occasion, she noticed, even in her confusion, in a dark grey suit, although he had removed his tie and his striped blue and cream shirt was open at the neck. He was about thirty-five, she thought, maybe a little older, and when he smiled at her, his face crinkled up in a way that somehow made him look like a small boy.

He settled her in a corner, and said, 'I'm Ludovic. Ludovic Ingram. Lawyer by trade although not by nature. Friend of our hostess, friend of your fiancé. Funny to think of old Piers being a fiancé. He looks much too old for you. Why don't you ditch him and marry me instead? I'm a free man, just divorced, it'd be much more fun for you.'

And she had sat there, listening to him, not required to say anything at all, picking her way through her food, and feeling slowly better suddenly, and thinking that she had never felt more fond of anyone in her life. By the time Piers finally saw her, came over and said, 'Chloe, there you are, wherever have you been?' she was able to say quite coolly, 'Talking to this extremely attractive gentleman, Piers,' and even when they were going home in the car she didn't make a fuss, didn't make an issue of it. But ever since then she had remembered that day, and its total misery and, more than that, a sense of rage with Piers that he had allowed it to happen to her; it became a yardstick by which she measured other unpleasant things, and very few of them came near to it.

A few days later she was able to talk to Piers about it, to try and explain how terrible it had been, how hurtful she had found his behaviour; but he had laughed and taken her in his arms and told her she was imagining things, that he would have been delighted had she come over to the table, and he knew she was going to love such occasions in no time at all. 'You mustn't be so sensitive, darling, everyone loves you, really they do.'

She doubted that; what she did not doubt was that Piers loved her. Or that she loved him. Whatever she had to endure, whoever she had to deal with, it was worth it. She just wished everyone else could see how wrong they were, and how happy she was.

They were married on a golden late September day, in a small, rather bleak ceremony at the register office in Ipswich, followed by a small and really very charming reception at the Moat House. Joe and Caroline had been surprised by Piers's insistence that he wanted no fuss, and that he wanted it kept out of the papers; for a man who liked the maximum of fuss about everything, whose life indeed was dedicated to fuss, it seemed a strange remark.

His mother was too old and frail to come: she had a bad heart and could not leave the nursing home in Sussex, but Chloe told Joe that she had met her several times, that she was a sweet, rather beautiful old lady called Flavia, had told Chloe she was so thrilled that Piers was finally going to settle down again and with such a lovely girl that she really felt she could dance at the wedding. Piers's best man was Damian Lutyens, who was writing the lyrics for the *Lady*; he was a very nice young man, with wild dark hair and burning dark eyes, whom Chloe liked very much, but he still seemed a puzzling choice to Joe, who didn't like him, and in his darkest hours, and in the privacy of his own thoughts, wondered about his exact relationship with Piers; why, after all, could there not have been some long-standing friend produced, more his own age, rather than this somewhat exotic young man? It all contributed to his sense of panic and foreboding.

The Woolfs had been invited, because Piers said Maria would be so outraged if they weren't that she would withdraw her backing from the *Lady* immediately; Chloe was appalled, but hadn't argued. Also David and Liza Montague were coming: Liza was an opera singer, a diva, and David a conductor, and they were rather different from the Woolfs, and very kind to Chloe. Liza had known Piers from RADA days, and had been a close friend of Guinevere's, but it didn't seem to prejudice her against Chloe in any way. She was dark and imposing, rather large and very beautiful and much given to taking Chloe to her large bosom and telling her if ever she needed a friend, she would be there. The only other guests from Piers's side were Tabitha Levine, which delighted Joe, a young playwright called Giles Forrest, who was being hailed as the new Osborne and had written a play called *The Kingdom* which Piers was reading, 'with a capital R, you understand,' he said to Chloe, and Giles Fawcett, one of the new wave of theatre critics, some said the new Tynan, a very close friend of both Piers and the Montagues.

Apart from the Woolfs, and just possibly Tabitha Levine, Chloe was happy with the guest list and her only problem was finding guests of her own to match up to it. There were her friends, none of whom were at all impressive, indeed she wondered what on earth the Woolfs would make of them, and more importantly how they would behave towards them; there was dear Mrs Brownlowe who was in any case doing the catering so would be there in a rather below-the-salt capacity anyway; and, with the exception of Joe, there was nobody other than her family, and of course the Bamforths, whom she wanted. The thought made her feel miserable and more of a failure than ever; the unbidden thought that Fleur would no doubt have had dozens of clever, smart people to invite to a wedding entered her head and she had some trouble dismissing it. In the end, she decided to ask three of her closest friends and their escorts, her brothers and the Bamforths and leave it at that. Piers was faintly amused at the invitation to the Bamforths and even questioned its wisdom, but Chloe was uncharacteristically firm. 'There have been times when I couldn't have got through without Jack and they're coming,' she said, and walked out of the door.

She asked her mother if there was anyone she would like to ask, and Caroline had said she really thought it would be better not, that the mix was daunting enough already without hurling Suffolk middle-aged society into it, and Chloe had said fine, that was absolutely all right by her, and was about to leave the room when Caroline called her back.

Chloe,' she said, just slightly carefully, 'I don't suppose you've thought about telling Piers about – well, about your –'

Chloe, flushing with something approaching outrage, said of course she hadn't, that it was nothing, absolutely nothing to do with him, with them, with anybody, and she hoped, indeed prayed, that Piers would never hear anything of it. 'I hope you agree,' she added.

'In that case,' said Caroline crisply, 'we certainly shouldn't ask anyone from old Suffolk. You never know what someone might say, what might slip out. And yes, Chloe, I do agree with you.'

Two days before the wedding, Piers rang Caroline: 'Caroline, I wonder if it would be too awful to inflict one more guest on you?'

'Not too awful, but quite,' said Caroline coldly. 'Who is it?'

'A journalist friend of mine. He's been away in the States. I wasn't expecting him to be in the country, but we go back a long way and he'd be very hurt if he was excluded.'

'Oh, all right,' said Caroline with a sigh, 'but you know it's sit-down, I'll have to rejig everything. I hope he's not married?'

'He's not. Thank you, Caroline. His name's Magnus Phillips. I expect Joe will know him.'

Joe was at once intrigued and amused. 'Magnus Phillips is the original yellow journalist. The worst sort. He's just been writing a gloves-off book about the ballet. Very nasty. I'm extremely surprised Piers should claim him as a friend. Must have misread him. You'll probably like him,' he added.

'Why should I like him?' said Caroline.

'Because you like rough trade,' said Joe, kissing her briefly, 'and they don't come much rougher than Magnus.'

Caroline turned her face away from him.

Chloe wore a dress by Ossie Clark for her wedding, in cream crepe, long and slightly high-waisted which dealt with any suspicion of a burgeoning bump in her stomach. She had her hair dressed in a tumble of tendrilly ringlets with fresh white roses set in it, and she looked so lovely that even Caroline had a lump in her throat as she looked at her coming into the register office on Joe's arm. Piers was wearing a very light grey suit for the wedding, with a cream silk shirt – 'specially made for my wedding,' he said to Joe – and a dark red tie; he looked ridiculously handsome. Damian was more flamboyant in cream linen; but he also looked wonderful.

Joe was in the suit he had bought for lunch at the Caprice with Tabitha (a fact he did not feel it necessary to acquaint Caroline or Chloe with), but he arrived very late the night before the wedding having managed to leave his only respectable shoes behind in London. He had enormous feet and none of even Toby's shoes fitted him; it was a question therefore of wearing either the white plimsolls he had arrived in or a very heavy pair of brogues which had been William's, and which Caroline had for some reason kept, or alternatively dashing round Ipswich in a panic just before the wedding.

Chloe said she thought the plimsolls would be better, and more in keeping with the rather eccentric occasion, but Caroline said she thought the brogues; they both agreed that if they let him loose on Ipswich they would never see him again. In the end Joe wore the brogues which were a size too small and made a very loud noise as he walked in them, and then changed into the plimsolls when they got back to the Moat House: none of which escaped the beady attentions of Maria Woolf, and which distracted Chloe very efficiently from her nerves.

Maria was wearing a white suit, and a very ostentatious white fox stole which she flung about her dramatically whenever she felt attention being withdrawn; she also insisted on making a short speech before they all sat down to lunch, saying she knew she was something of an interloper on a wonderfully charming family occasion, but she was absolutely too thrilled to be there. They had all forgotten about the mysterious Magnus Phillips, who had not in any case been coming to the register office, when there was an immensely loud throbbing noise coming up the drive and they all watched through the drawing-room windows as a leather-clad figure dismounted from a very large BMW motorbike.

'Good Lord,' said Piers, 'it's Magnus. Old devil.' He was obviously very impressed.

Magnus walked in through the front door, pulling off his helmet. 'Good afternoon,' he said to Caroline, 'Magnus Phillips. I'm so sorry I'm so late. Bike failure. I did my best. Can I change?'

'Of course,' said Caroline, icy with composure, 'we're just going into lunch. Janey, do show Mr Phillips one of the guest rooms.'

She was unduly ruffled and upset by Magnus Phillips's behaviour; his reappearance ten minutes later, looking rather different, in a dark suit and very sober tie, only slightly soothed her.

He bent over her hand and bowed, elaborately formal. 'Lady Hunterton,' he said, 'again, let me apologize. I broke down in the middle of the A12. It hasn't ever happened to me before. I hope I haven't disrupted the nuptials.'

'No, of course not,' said Caroline, slightly irritably, struggling to sound polite, 'I'm sorry you've had such trouble.'

Magnus Phillips straightened up and half smiled at her and she found herself unwillingly and helplessly disturbed by what she saw. He was dark-haired, almost swarthy, average height, very heavily built, with powerfully broad shoulders and very large, strong-looking hands. He was expensively dressed in a dark grey three-piece suit, which had appeared from a bag on the back of his bike and was only slightly creased, light blue shirt and grey and red striped tie and he wore rather too much jewellery: gold watch, large gold signet ring, ostentatious gold cufflinks. He looked, she thought, like a successful gangster. His brilliant dark eyes were fixed on her with immense interest, as if she was worthy of close and careful study, and, at the same time, with great appreciation.

'Are you really the mother of the bride? Not a sister of some kind?' His voice was deliberately working class, deep and rough, and very sexy.

'No,' said Caroline, briskly detaching herself from his gaze. 'Very much her mother. Now do come along in. Piers, your errant guest is ready, shall we go in?'

Lunch went well: Caroline sat next to Damian and found him charming and engaging, and watched Joe patently finding Tabitha charming and engaging at the other end of the table. Maria was busy impressing Giles Forrest and Sir Jack was patently hugely charmed by Chloe's best friend, Lucinda Bryant Smith, from Wycombe Abbey. The Montagues chatted to everyone, and kept distracting Jack Bamforth from his role as wine waiter to ask him about a racehorse they were in the process of buying, and Chloe sat in a daze of happiness and wondered when she might wake up.

After lunch Joe made a short and very sweet speech about how he wasn't exactly losing a daughter, because he didn't have one, and hoped he wasn't gaining a son because he was much younger than the bridegroom. Then Piers stood up and said he did know that his good fortune was truly quite incredible, and that he knew he had a wife whose gifts and attributes were simply too long to list, but he would make a start by saying she was beautiful, clever, sweet-natured and quite incredibly brave in taking him on, and that he would do everything in his power to take care of her, and then he bent over her and took both her hands in his and kissed them and said, 'Thank you for marrying me, Chloe.'

The muffled but unmistakable sound of Toby and Jolyon making sick noises quite cheered Joe and got him through the day.

After that everyone got very relaxed, and drank a great deal more. Damian tried to explain to Caroline what a lyricist was, and Giles Forrest said he hoped Damian's work on the *Lady* was better than his work on *Angels*, and Damian said so did he. Caroline asked what was *Angels*, and Magnus Phillips, his dark eyes bright with malice, said it was a show that Damian and Piers had collaborated on a couple of years earlier that had flopped.

'Unfair,' said Piers. 'It got wonderful notices, the public simply didn't like it.'

His eyes were uneasy suddenly, even as he smiled: Magnus asked him what he thought they hadn't liked about it.

'Oh – chemistry,' Piers said. 'There are some things that just don't work. That don't seize the public imagination. This didn't. I still don't understand why; although I have to say that if the director had agreed to set it in the thirties, as I had originally envisaged, I think it would have worked better. But he held those particular purse-strings. Anyway, it's all history now. Doesn't matter.'

'Sure,' said Magnus. His face was very respectful; Joe suddenly decided he liked him better.

'Well, I adored *Angels*,' said Maria, 'I thought it was desperately unfair. Never mind, Piers darling, we shall have our revenge.'

'Yes indeed,' said Piers and then Magnus said enough theatre chitchat and asked Joe how his *Scandals* book had done.

'OK,' said Joe briefly.

'Did you enjoy it, Lady Hunterton?' said Magnus. Caroline said yes, she had, very much, and felt uneasy suddenly, she wasn't sure why.

The conversation became more general and then Chloe and Piers went upstairs to change; Jack Woolf moved over to talk to Caroline, and Maria moved into an incredibly explicit conversation with Jack about mares standing for stallions, and a mare of hers who would never stand for the stallion, only the teaser, and Tabitha started chatting up the boys who, apart from the sick noises at the end of Piers's speech, had behaved very well. Toby was growing into a distinctly plain young man. He was very tall and heavily built, and threatened to be fat ('My father's build,' said Caroline), and he had thick slightly wavy dark hair and very dark brown eyes. He had loved Eton (unlike his brother) and Chloe was quite sure it was simply because no one dared bully him, on account of his size and his quite extraordinary self-confidence. Jolyon was smaller, slighter, and far better looking; he had his mother's dark red hair, and his father's rather diffident manner, and although his behaviour was appalling when he was with his brother, when he was on his own he was comparatively civilized. He even went so far as to say to Chloe on the morning of the wedding that he hoped she'd be very happy, and if Piers Windsor wasn't nice to her he'd see that Toby knocked his block off, which enormously touched Jack who had been listening in the doorway, and for the first time in his entire life he felt a wave of affection for Caroline's boys. Joe, who was chatting up Liza Montague with a view to doing a profile of her, was so benignly and magnificently drunk that he actually found himself managing to feel a wave of affection for Piers. And then very shortly after that Chloe and Piers were gone, lurching up the lane in the Rolls bound for Paris, waving and laughing and leaving everyone in that condition of flat euphoria that always follows a wedding.

'Well,' said Caroline, 'more drink everyone? Coffee?'

'Coffee would be wonderful,' cooed Maria, 'and then, Jack dear, we must go.'

'Fine,' said Caroline, disappearing into the kitchen.

The kitchen was empty; released suddenly from the strain of smiling, of being gracious, of pretending to be pleased, she sat down suddenly at the table, and felt – most unusually, for Caroline hardly ever cried, always said Joe shed enough for both of them – tears filling her eyes.

She thought of Chloe, offered up like a sacrificial virgin on the altar of Piers's vanity, and thought how ill equipped she was to deal with it, and with a fervour that made it almost a prayer, hoped she would manage to be happy, somehow. And then, unbidden, came the thought of her other daughter, of how swiftly and effectively she would have dealt with Piers Windsor had he come her way; and she thought, too, that she had lost both of them now, and she felt a great ache in her heart, She rested her head briefly on her hands, and struggled to regain control of herself.

'Caroline. You all right?' It was Jack Bamforth; he had come into the kitchen in search of soda water.

Caroline looked up and said, 'Not really, Jack, no. I don't know how she's going to manage.'

'She'll be all right,' he said, putting his arm lightly round her shoulders. 'Tougher than she looks is Chloe. Always was.'

'Oh Jack, I don't know. She seems such a baby to me.'

'Well, she would,' said Jack, smiling down at her. 'Always babies to their mothers, people are. But she isn't, Caroline, and she'll be all right, she'll manage.'

'Do you think so? I hope you're right. God, it doesn't seem a moment since she was born, does it, Jack? Or the boys. Longer since – since I had – well, since Fleur.'

'Yes, well, that is a while,' said Jack, patting her gently, rather as if she was a horse. 'I was only thinking about that the other day.'

'Were you, Jack?' Caroline lifted a tear-stained face. 'Were you really?'

'Well, it was a bit of a time, wasn't it? One thing and another. The baby being born, and then you marrying Sir William and then – well, as I say, it was a bit of a time.'

'Yes, it was,' said Caroline. 'And now it's all over. Jack, could you make some coffee? I'm just going upstairs to redo my face, I must look frightful and –' She stood up and turned towards the doorway; standing there, an expression of considerable interest in his dark eyes, was Magnus Phillips.

'That is one gorgeous woman,' said Magnus to Joe. 'All yours, I take it?'

'Absolutely all mine,' said Joe, draining half a tumblerful of brandy. He was very drunk; he needed to be, it was his only defence against his loss of Chloe, his fear and sorrow for her. 'And absolutely all gorgeous too.' He struggled to focus on Magnus. 'Magnus, what are you doing coming and being here?'

'Very old friend of Piers's,' said Magnus, enunciating with as much difficulty but rather more skill.

'Old friend, my arse,' said Joe. 'Writing something beastly about him, are you?'

'Absolutely not,' said Magnus, with an attempt at dignity. 'Just a short piece for the *New Yorker*. Idea tickled his vanity. Good brandy, Joe. Lovely girl, the blushing bride.'

'Lovely girl. I love her like my own. Wish she was. Wish she was. Have some more brandy, Magnus. All yours. All yours.'

Caroline came in with the coffee and smiled composedly at everyone.

'She is gorgeous,' said Magnus again. 'You must be no end of a fine fellow, Joe Payton. Having a woman like that.'

'I am, I am,' said Joe, beaming at him modestly. 'No end of a fine fellow.'

'Can't believe she's the mother of three grown-up children.'

'Well, she is,' said Joe, hiccuping gently, 'their mother. All of their mother.'

'And when –' said Magnus, but Caroline, who had been watching them with a degree of intentness, came over and said, 'Joe, the Woolfs are leaving, come and see them off,' and Joe rose, extremely unsteadily, and went out to the drive to wave off the Woolfs' pale blue Rolls which was marginally larger and certainly flashier than Piers's.

There was a great deal of going and goodbye-ing after that, and finally Magnus himself went upstairs again to change back into his leathers.

He bowed again over Caroline's hand in the drive, smiling at her, and she thought that he looked much more at home and interestingly less gangster-like in them than in the suit. He was also interestingly more sober.

'I have so enjoyed meeting you, and being here today,' he said and his eyes as he studied her were watchful. 'And I'm sorry again I was late.'

'That's all right,' said Caroline. 'Are you sure you're OK to drive or whatever you do on a bike?'

'I'm fine. The air will sober me very quickly, I assure you. You are,' he added, 'the most beautiful mother of the bride I have ever been privileged enough to meet. I really mean it. And thank you for your hospitality.'

'My pleasure,' she said, in tones that implied it had been nothing of the sort, and then added, looking at Joe who was walking rather unsteadily towards the house, in his plimsolls, his jacket on inside out, his arms round the two boys, 'I must get Joe inside and into a horizontal position. Will you excuse me?'

'Lucky old Joe,' said Magnus. 'I wish you'd get me into a horizontal position. Some time. Goodbye, Lady Hunterton,' and he was gone in a roar and a belch of exhaust.

Caroline went in to find Joe who was already asleep on the drawing-room sofa, and was not to be woken.

She called the dogs and took them for a long walk. She felt uneasy about Magnus Phillips. She went over and over the conversation with Jack Bamforth in her mind, and told herself, tried to persuade herself, that the conversation had meant nothing, nothing at all really, to someone who hadn't known about Fleur, about her history, and indeed managed quite effectively to calm herself. But then, unbidden, she would see again and again Magnus Phillips's brilliant, fiercely interested face, his thoughtful, probing eyes, and even after she had come home, picked at the leftovers, got Joe up to bed, had a bath and read three chapters of Pierre Salinger's brilliant book *With Kennedy*, she still felt chilled and troubled by what Magnus had overheard and what he might do with it, should he so choose.

Background to Love and Marriage chapter of *The Tinsel Underneath*. First taped interview Liza Montague, long-term friend of Piers Windsor, wife of David Montague, conductor, since 1959. Agreed to be quoted.

I first met him in – what? – 1953. He'd just met Guinevere, and they were still in the very first flush. My God, he was in love. Of course Piers is like that. Obsessive. He falls in love with someone – man, woman, child, idea, and that's it. Nothing else matters. They met at RADA. I was at the Royal College of Music, and I'd met Guinevere at a Christmas carol concert. She had a lovely voice herself. Filled with music, very very Welsh. She should have trained as a singer, I often told her. One evening in the next term, I bumped into her at a concert. Oh, she said, oh, Liza, I'm in love. The birthday of my life is come. She does that, Guinevere, talks in quotations all the time. We all had supper together one night, at Jimmy's. You know Jimmy's? Underground restaurant, near Leicester Square, all tiled, like a men's lavatory. Well, you like that kind of thing when you're young, I'm afraid. Great food, really cheap. Anyway, I just wasn't sure, you know? He was divine to look at, stayed so until he died, poor darling; and very charming. He had this way of asking very intense detailed questions, so you really thought he seemed absolutely fascinated by whatever you had to say. I swear he could seem entranced by your bowel movements, if he thought it was necessary. But it was all a fake, a trick; he'd really only be half listening. Women always fell for it. And the men if he put his mind to it. Anyway, he and Guinevere were completely gaga. Couldn't keep their hands off each other. Darlings, I said in the end, why don't you just go home to bed and have a good fuck? Guinevere said OK, they would, but Piers seemed slightly embarrassed. He hated women using bad language or even speaking very frankly. He was a bit of an old woman himself really, you know.

They got married at the end of that year; Guinevere seemed blissfully happy with him still. It was such a strange wedding. Her family seemed slightly bemused by it all. Her mother obviously thought he was wonderful, but her father and her brother were more doubtful. And all the Welsh relations, well, it was a bit sad really. The wedding was at their home, but all us London lot trailed down and we're rather noisy and flamboyant, you know, terrible show-offs, and I think the family just couldn't really cope. Piers made this frightful speech, I wanted to die. He got up all filled with burning sincerity and said how wonderfully happy he was, and what a gift the Davieses had given him, and then he went over to Guinevere and said, 'Thank you for marrying me, Guinevere.' I wanted to be sick. And he was terribly over-dressed. I know it was his wedding, but it had been agreed no morning suits, and he had a grey suit on with a very long jacket, and a black velvet collar. He looked like a rather smart, posh Teddy Boy. It was very insensitive, that was the thing. And his mother, dear Flavia, she was completely overdressed too, in a cream lace suit. She sobbed into her hanky right through the service and then was terrifically ladylike and radiant right through the reception, even made a little speech, since Dad Windsor of course had long since disappeared. Straight out of Noël Coward. I did love Flavia, but she did spoil him so. It was where the whole trouble started really.

I met my husband at their wedding; he'd come down with a party of other Londoners. He was standing next to me, while Piers made his speech, and he hissed in my ear, 'Ridiculous creature, isn't he?' I had to agree.

I didn't see them for a year after that, I was touring with some awful company; then I bumped into Guinevere in London. She was a bit subdued, I thought; she said everything was fine, although things were tough. She said she was doing OK, getting the odd thing, but Piers was having more trouble. 'He won't go for the tiny parts, Liza,' she said, 'so half the time he doesn't get any.'

I asked her how the marriage was and she said, oh, wonderful, but that was it; she changed the subject and asked me about what I was doing instead. A few weeks later, they asked us to supper: it wasn't very happy really. Piers was touchy and difficult; Guinevere had warned me not to talk about work, and I did try not to, but there really wasn't much else. The main thing was that Piers seemed to have got rather – hostile is too strong a word – distanced from her. Distanced and critical. She couldn't do anything right. The lamb was overcooked, the flowers were overdone, even the light bulb was too bright. And she was trying just a bit too hard. Darling this, darling that, sorry, Piers, didn't mean to, Piers, when what he needed was a kick in the balls.

After supper, Piers suddenly suggested to David they should go to the pub, which seemed extraordinary, in the middle of a reunion dinner, and I said to Guinevere when they'd gone, what on earth is going on, and she said, and I shall never forget it, oh, Liza, love cools, love cools. She wouldn't talk about it any more; she said she was fine, just being silly, and we talked work after that. It seemed safer; what I couldn't make out was whose love had cooled. Then.

The men came back, looking more cheerful, and we all got very drunk, and then I didn't think about either of them for another year, or not much because I was in Milan, doing rather well, and David was in New York. When I came home, I heard they'd split up. I phoned Guinevere's mother, because I couldn't find her in London, and she was really upset, said she would never have believed it of Piers, and I said what, and she said walking out on a pregnant wife. Well, of course, it wasn't that simple – is it ever? – and it took me years to get to the truth of it, because Guinevere had lost the baby by the time I saw her, and was on a kind of fake high, playing Jennifer Dubedat at the Bristol Old Vic, and said she didn't want to talk about Piers or anything to do with him. It had all been an awful mistake, and she couldn't believe she had been so stupid. Later, years later, when I was having trouble with my own dear husband, and I was vulnerable too, she told me all about it, really told me, and I understood. But at the time he just seemed like a spoilt, selfish, arrogant child. Which of course he was; but it was a little bit more complex than that.

And then I didn't see him for years, because he avoided me very thoroughly; ashamed, and guilty I suppose. I didn't want to see him anyway, I felt so angry, and so loyal to Guinevere. He only came back into my life when he was a film star; and then he felt he could get close, and talk to me, explain how he saw what had happened, against the background of his own success, rather than the failure. Which tells you everything about him, of course.

He really was a very dangerously complex personality.

Chapter 17

1967

Chloe stood in the foyer of the Princess Theatre, holding Piers's arm, smiling into the flashbulbs, turning her head to greet this person and that, and wondered what they would all have to say if they knew she had no knickers on.

In every other way she was most carefully and elaborately dressed for the occasion: in a long white lace dress, hung with hundreds of crystalline droplets, high-waisted and stunningly low-cut to set off her newly magnificent cleavage, her dark red hair piled high and set with pearl droplets also, a glorious baroque pearl choker round her throat, her make-up, darkly dramatic, with double fake lashes on her brown eyes, professionally done by a girl sent from *Harpers & Queen* for a photographic session with Piers that very afternoon, all designed to distract from her hugely burgeoning eight-and-a-half-month-pregnant stomach. There was a white fox cape hung carelessly on her shoulders, white satin slippers just visible beneath the billowing hem of the dress; but knickers she wore none, had not indeed for some weeks now, as the task of putting them on had become increasingly difficult. She had intended to put some on tonight, and tights too, but after several minutes of struggling, first sitting, then standing, had given up; she would have asked Piers, but he was too ill with nerves, too engrossed with his own wardrobe – dinner jacket, genuine Victorian ruffled evening shirt, black velvet cape lined with crimson silk – to give her more than the briefest attention, to say 'Yes, of course you do,' in response to her shaky 'Do I look all right?' and certainly to get involved in the intimate indignities of pulling up her pants for her.

Well, it was his night, the brightest yet in a brilliant history, the world première of *The Lady of Shalott*, the culmination of two years of work, of inspiration, the drawing together of the finest talents in the land, of writers, lyricists, composers, designers; of actors, musicians, dancers; he was offering it to the world, his creation, brought to birth from his own dazzling imagination, courage, vision – and steely, unflinching determination. Chloe looked at him, smiling the tight, taut smile that she had come to know so well and, sick with nerves and misery as she was herself, felt a great pang of compassion for what it concealed, a desperate, all-consuming terror that the *Lady* would fail, and he with it, and that all these people here, the glitterati of the theatre, the press, the innest of the in crowd, ostensibly come to share his triumph, would turn Judas and bear witness and even rejoice in his downfall.

Unlikely, she knew, really extremely unlikely, almost an impossibility: but in his perfectionist self-obsession already almost a reality. 'There is no paranoia like the actor's,' he had told her, when she was just beginning to get to know him. 'We all await failure, court it almost, even in the midst of some wild success, it's a kind of superstition. And of course there is no one more superstitious than an actor either.'

She had learnt about most of those superstitions, since then, as she had learnt so many other things in her crash course in Being a Famous Actor's Wife: never say the word Macbeth, merely the Scottish Play, never have fresh flowers on the stage, never say good luck, always wear the same shoes to arrive at and leave the theatre; she could have written a book or at least a chapter in a book on the subject.

Chloe looked surreptitiously at her watch: still only ten past seven. She seemed to have been standing here for hours, the ache in her back developing nicely. The Princess Theatre was already surely packed to capacity, and there would be at least twenty more minutes before they would go to their seats, thirty before the curtain finally rose; waves of people were pouring through the door, smiling, waving, kissing, cooing at one another and at them, growing ever larger, more engulfing. She was beginning to think if she heard one more voice saying, 'Piers darling,' in rapturous tones and then, 'Chloe!' in rather more subdued ones, she would raise her own in a piercing scream, when a heavy arm went round her shoulders, a real kiss reached her cheek, and a wonderfully welcome, slightly husky voice said in her ear, 'Hallo, honeybunch, you look much too grand to be any relation of mine.'

'Joe!' said Chloe. 'Oh Joe, I'm so glad to see you. Stand right here and hold my hand, and make me feel I do matter just a tiny bit.'

'Right,' said Joe, positioning himself carefully, elbowing gently but extremely firmly a large billowing blonde, who was struggling to reach across Chloe to kiss Piers, and taking her hand in his. 'Good turn-out, poppet. Piers must be happy.'

'Of course he's not happy,' said Chloe. 'He wants to die. He's been telling me all day. The *Lady* will flop, the critics will slaughter him, the investors will lose all their money, and the workhouse awaits us.'

'Oh, right,' said Joe, 'of course. Talking of investors, is the terrible Maria here yet?'

'Of course. She's over there, look, just dying to get into the theatre and her place next to Piers in the front row. Now you're sitting next to me, and don't let Mummy change things, will you? Where is she anyway?'

'Coming on separately,' said Joe. 'She's been to have her hair done or something like that.'

'Goodness, I'm honoured. You look as if you've been doing something to yours as well, Joe. It's very tidy. Although a tiny bit lopsided maybe.'

'Well, I went and got it cut for you,' said Joe, 'and I would have had one of those fancy blow jobs on it even, but a call came through from the *Observer* that could I have a few words with Tabitha about life as the Lady, and I really thought that was more important. They actually didn't quite finish cutting it, which is why it's a bit long on the left.'

'Well, it looks wonderful,' said Chloe, smiling at him tenderly, before leaning forward to receive a fulsome embrace from yet another over-perfumed fan of Piers. He made her feel so much better, just by being there, smiling at her tenderly, his green eyes watchful for her in his angular face, his shabby dinner jacket, clearly hastily pressed for the occasion, with a double crease in one of the trouser legs, and she thought that whatever passion, whatever adoration she might feel for Piers, it came nowhere near what she felt for Joe in warmth, comfort, reassurance.

'Chloe, darling!' Piers's voice was tetchy, taut, beneath the words. 'Look, here is Damian, and Liza too.'

What he meant, she knew, was 'Stop talking and smiling at Joe, concentrate on me and my people.' She shifted slightly in an attempt to ease her backache, forced a smile at Liza Montague, received her kiss and gently embraced Damian, and kissed him back.

'You look beautiful, Chloe,' he said now, 'simply beautiful. How is the great man?'

'Very unhappy,' said Chloe, smiling at him. 'Knows it's going to be a complete disaster, probably best to call the whole thing to a halt now, before the curtain ever goes up.'

'Of course,' said Damian and squeezed her hand. 'Oh God, there's Maria, I'd better go and kiss her feet.'

Maria Woolf came bearing through the crowd towards them, tall and stately, her ledge-like bosom encased in black satin, her legs (still slender beneath her considerable frame) revealed through a long skirt slashed to the thigh.

'Damian, my darling boy. How wonderful you look. Isn't this exciting? How proud I am of you all. Piers, shouldn't we be going in soon? The theatre is filling up.'

'Not just yet, Maria, dear,' said Piers, and Chloe, who heard it so often, recognized the edge in his voice as Maria did not. 'Why don't you go on in? Is Jack here yet?'

'Oh yes, somewhere about over there,' said Maria Woolf carelessly. 'He's so useless at these things, never can remember names or anything. No, I wouldn't dream of going in without you. Chloe, dear, you look a little warm, why don't you ask Mr Payton to get rid of that stole?'

What she means, thought Chloe, is that my face is red, that my fur looks silly, and that she wants to get Joe out of this line-up. Maria didn't like Joe, he didn't treat her with the deference she thought she deserved, and had once written some rather harsh words about her in a piece about patronage of the arts; she certainly wouldn't like to see him standing there, unmistakably family, on what she saw as her night as much as Piers's.

'Hallo, Chloe.' It was her mother, coolly elegant in black, her dark red hair swept up on top of her head, a slightly distant smile on her face. 'Joe, whatever time did you leave the flat? I've been ringing you for hours.'

'Hours ago obviously then,' said Joe easily. 'You look very nice, Caroline. Can I get you a drink?'

'No, no thank you. Chloe, how are you feeling?'

'OK,' said Chloe. 'Fine. Considering.'

Caroline nodded. 'Good,' was all she said,

No words of comfort, thought Chloe, no compliments, no reassurance, not even a kiss. She often wondered if her mother was warmer, kinder to Joe; she presumed she must be although she had never seen it. She smiled at her rather weakly, and then saw Magnus Phillips, looking more like a boxing promoter than a first-nighter, in his dinner jacket, coming towards them, a blonde of incredible fluffiness on his arm, her hair piled on the top of her head like a bouffant soufflé, dressed in a black lace dress of awe-inspiring shortness.

'Hardly worth putting that dress on,' whispered Joe in Chloe's ear, 'there's so little of it between the neckline and the hem.'

Chloe managed a rather weak smile.

'How very beautiful you look, Mrs Windsor! Even more so than on your wedding day.'

'Thank you, Mr Phillips. A little larger, I fear.'

'Well, only in the one extremely well-contained place. Otherwise, exquisitely the same. And Lady Hunterton, how nice.'

Caroline nodded coolly; Magnus kissed her hand, Chloe's cheek and moved on to Piers.

'Good evening, Piers. Congratulations.'

'Save them for later,' said Piers, slightly irritable.

'OK. And I mustn't say good luck, must I? Break a leg, old chap. We must get together soon, discuss this book idea. This is Sally-Ann, Piers. Sally-Ann has theatrical pretensions as well. Come along, my dear,' he said to Sally-Ann. 'Let us go and find our seats.'

'Round to Mr Phillips,' said Joe, grinning appreciatively at the back of Magnus's head.

'Well,' said Piers finally, just as she thought her back would snap with pain and strain, 'well, perhaps we should move in now. Good evening, Caroline, how wonderful you look. And Joe, how nice.' He turned, proffered his other arm to Maria; she took it, somehow managed to draw him forward, away from Chloe, who was left trailing after them, slightly uncertain.

She looked round wildly; she had lost Joe, who was talking to Caroline, had indeed lost everyone; Damian had gone with Liza, and here she was, looking huge, hideous, flushed, abandoned; as she tried to pull herself together, to smile, to look confident as she walked alone into the stalls, she felt it: deep within her body, buried almost, but unmistakable, a taut, hard tug that was half pain, half pressure, and she knew exactly, even though she had never felt it before, what it was. She was going into labour, two weeks early, in the front row of the stalls, at the most publicized first night of a decade, in the presence of dozens of photographers and journalists, and on the most important night of her husband's life.

Chloe stood quite still, trying to be calm. The pain, if indeed it could be dignified with such a word, was already receding; on the other hand, there was absolutely no doubt, no doubt at all that it would return. What should she do? Piers was already gone, lost to her; Joe and Caroline had disappeared into the throng of people; she could hardly ask Damian or even Liza Montague to help her.

For want of anything else to do, she decided to go to the Ladies. In any case she already needed to pee, quite badly, in spite of having carefully drunk nothing all afternoon, and having spent most of the half hour before leaving the house sitting on the loo. Piers had been very emphatic that she was not to spend the whole night rushing into the lavatory: 'I know it's a problem of your condition, darling, but I also think it's partly nerves. And it really isn't very – well, very attractive.'

'I'll give you attractive,' said Chloe to herself as she hauled her dress, with immense difficulty in the space of the tiny theatre loo, up over her vast stomach and eased herself down on to the seat. Sitting there, feeling her heart thumping painfully, she took deep breaths, and tried to remember everything her natural childbirth teacher had said. For a start, of course, first babies took for ever to arrive. At the very least twelve hours, and probably longer. So the baby was actually extremely unlikely to make its entry into the world in the stalls of the Princess Theatre. The clue to how things were progressing, how serious they were, she also had been told endlessly, was the regularity of the contractions and the intervals between them. If she watched that carefully, she would have a very good idea exactly what was happening to her. Chloe shivered slightly as she stood up, eased her way out of the cubicle; she was more than a little frightened of what lay ahead of her: although less frightened of that than of how Piers was going to react when she told him what was happening. Well, that was too bad. This was one thing she really couldn't help.

As she looked at herself in the mirror, smoothing her hair, stroking her own forehead without quite realizing why, she heard the final bell go. God, he would be going completely insane. She picked up her skirts and fled, through the now deserted foyer, into the darkening auditorium, down the central aisle. She sank, gratefully, breathlessly, into her seat in the front row, just as David Montague came in, took his place on the podium, to tumultuous applause; Piers's face, tense and white in the darkness, looked at her with a rage so violent she felt sick. 'Sorry,' she mouthed, and he looked away. Next to her Joe put out a hand, took hers.

'You OK?'

She nodded; as she did so, the tug came again. Just slightly stronger, longer, just slightly nearer pain. She looked at her watch: exactly 7.40, exactly ten minutes after the last one. Fear gripped her, alongside the pain;

what was she to do? She took a deep breath, consciously trying to relax: she sensed Piers's hostility, even at that slight sound.

And then the curtain went up, and the haunting overture died away, and she momentarily forgot everything except what was before her eyes.

She had seen sketches of the set, models even, had heard it discussed endlessly, of course: as she had seen drawings of the costumes, had read the words, heard the music played on the piano at home, had heard Tabitha and Julius Hovatch, who played the Knight, singing with Piers and David as they rehearsed, also at home, in the early days, but none of it had prepared her for the finished reality. Piers had never allowed her near any rehearsals, and so it was for her almost as fresh, as enchanting as it was for the rest of the audience. The set was ravishing: 'four grey walls and four grey towers' at the left of the stage, and against it great urns of lilies and rose trees; two vast trees, real willows, trailed into the orchestra pit, which was itself transformed into a river, painted as closely after Millais as was possible; to the rear of the stage, hazily set behind gauze, fields of barley and of rye met a blue sky; in a window high in the tower was the figure, the strange enchanted figure of the Lady of Shalott, weaving her web, and as the music swelled again echoing the crescendo of the overture, the tower turned slowly and the Lady was there, on a great platform within it, sitting in her enchanted prison, weaving her web with the great mirror before her, reflecting the scene she was forbidden ever to directly see. Then the music changed, became sweeter, softer, and Tabitha Levine, moving with a deathly, enchanted slowness, sat there, her lovely gaze fixed on her mirror, and sang the first song, 'Sick of Shadows'.

It was an enchantment: and as the song ended and Tabitha took the first of her many tumultuous ovations, Chloe looked at Piers and saw that he had tears standing in his eyes, and she was, in spite of everything, moved by the fact.

Lydia Wintour, who had designed the set and the costumes, had done a magical job: the dazzling colours of the troupe of damsels, the crimson-clad page, the funeral with its plumes and lights, flickered against the greyness of the mirror and were gone; and as the moon rose and the two young lovers, lately wed, appeared, the audience again caught its throat audibly and sighed with pleasure and a ripple of applause ran through the theatre, very quietly, as if not to disturb the enchantment.

It was as well it did: for it was then that Chloe felt again, and more fiercely, another wrenching pain, and despite herself caught her breath and thrust her fist into her mouth, lest some sound of distress might escape her. The time on her gold Cartier watch, a wedding present from Piers, was precisely eight o'clock; and she was beginning to realize that she was going to have to act.

She glanced at Piers, sitting there in total concentration, his face looking as if it was carved from stone; she knew she could not possibly disturb him with what would seem to him the most gross intrusion. She turned to her other side, and thanked God for him, for Joe, as she put out her hand, touched his and whispered, shakily, fiercely into his ear, 'Joe, I think I'm having the baby.'

Joe turned to look at her; she saw in his face, alongside concern and love and a degree of panic of his own, a sense of acute amusement that such a thing should be happening to her.

'Can you hang on till the interval?' he whispered in Chloe's ear. 'I'll get you out then,' and she turned to him and smiled briefly, rather wanly, and nodded and he took her hand in his and held it very tightly.

She forced her attention back to the stage, concentrating, almost meditating on the ebb and flow of the music, forcing calm within herself. Suddenly, almost immediately it seemed, timed perfectly to coincide with the shock of the Knight's bow-shot, brilliantly executed by a sliver of white light and an echoing scream of the strings, the pain came yet again, fierce, forcing, and despite herself a slight but audible whimper escaped her. Joe turned away from the stage, away from the Lady, away from Sir Lancelot as he rode through the yellow field in her mirror, and as Sir Lancelot began to sing 'Riding down to Camelot' and the orchestra was huge and loud he said, 'Now?' and she nodded, biting her lip, and then she saw again, watched Piers's face flashing at her, at both of them, a look of pure hatred as he said, 'Be quiet. Please be quiet.'

And then, mercifully, it was the interval and she stood up, smiling bravely, released again from pain, and made her excuses, pushing through the crowds as they fought to get near Piers, and Joe followed her, ignoring Caroline's puzzled face, and he put his arm round Chloe as they reached the foyer, and she said, 'Go and get a taxi, Joe, I have to write a note to Piers.'

She handed it to one of the ushers and then made her way towards the door. Joe was waiting for her, standing by a cab; he helped her in, took her hand, held it tenderly.

'The London Clinic,' he said to the driver, 'and hurry.'

'Blimey,' said the driver, 'my chance of being famous. I think I'd rather not.'

The cab leapt forward as he put his foot down.

Another pain came, gripped Chloe, fierce, hard, longer; she clung to Joe's hand, fearful, seeking comfort.

'All right?'

'Not really,' she said and tried to smile.

'You'll be all right when you get to the hospital,' he said. 'I've already rung them. They thought I must be Piers of course.'

'Yes,' she said, 'of course. They would.'

And even in the midst of her fear and pain, she could hear the bleakness in her own voice.

Joe helped Chloe into the clinic (bent double now, white-faced, gasping), called out for help and finally, released from responsibility but not from pity, from fear, from love, watched her being wheeled away, her eyes large with pain and apprehension, the absurd necklace pulled off, held in her hand, the elaborate hairdo crumpled and tousled into nothingness, a nurse now holding her hands, talking to her calmly, and he thought that if Piers Windsor was to appear now he would surely kill him.

'Mr Payton? I heard you were here. How very loyal. It's a girl, a beautiful little girl, and she and Mrs Windsor are both fine. Tired, but fine.'

Mr Simmonds, the gynaecologist who had seen Chloe through her unbelievably short, fierce labour, impressed by her courage, her stoicism, moved by her lonely triumph, had come into the waiting room to find Joe to tell him the news.

It was as well they had left the theatre; Pandora Windsor had made her entrance into the world just as the audience at the Princess Theatre was giving a standing ovation to the stars of the show, and the curtain had fallen and risen again for the seventeenth time. Many of the women were weeping, and had been ever since the final song of Lancelot's: 'She Has a Lovely Face', and the whole house was shouting 'Bravo' and cheering. Piers Windsor, the man with the vision to mount the show, the catalyst who had brought together the actors, designers, musicians and enabled them to work their magic, who had drafted the original adaptation, whose idea the whole wonderful magical thing had been, stood between the Lady and the Knight, holding their hands in his. It was the only place he could have been, of course: certainly he could not have left, on that night of all nights, just to be at his wife's side, just while she had his baby. Of course not. Out of the question. Absolutely out of the question.

'Joe! Oh, it's so lovely to see you.' Chloe lay on her pillows, reached out for his hand. 'Thank you for everything. At one point, when it was getting really bad, I wondered if I shouldn't after all try and get Piers here, but of course I couldn't. This is his night. I can't spoil it for him. Can I?'

'No, of course not,' said Joe, lying staunchly, betraying everything he believed in out of love for her, looking at her face, blanched with pain and exhaustion, her baby, Piers's daughter, cradled in her arms.

'I'm sure he'll be here soon; well, certainly after the party. Mr Simmonds did phone the theatre. What a night to choose, Joe, how tactless of me!' Her eyes were fever-bright, her voice slightly shaky.

Joe sat down, picked up one of her hands and kissed it. 'You did so well, Chloe. So well. I'm so proud of you.'

Mr Simmonds put his head round the door. 'Mrs Windsor, you have another visitor.'

'Oh,' said Chloe, struggling rather feebly to sit up, 'oh, Piers,' and her eyes shone and her face was paler still; but it was not Piers who came in, it was Caroline, holding a huge bouquet of lilies, and Chloe sank back on her pillows, her eyes suddenly dark and dead.

'Darling, how are you?' said Caroline. Joe could never remember her calling Chloe darling before.

'I'm fine,' said Chloe, smiling with clearly enormous effort. 'Thank you. It's a girl, Mummy, look, isn't she lovely?'

'She's beautiful,' said Caroline, and she appeared to be genuinely moved by the sight of her granddaughter. 'These flowers are from Piers, who says' – her voice froze briefly, then she managed to smile – 'says I am to tell you he loves you, and he will be here as soon as the party is under way. He felt he couldn't leave his guests quite unreceived.'

'Of course not,' said Chloe, as she looked down at Pandora's small head, and bit her lip. 'I understand.'

'He was so thrilled,' said Caroline, talking rather faster than usual, 'so thrilled. And Chloe, the show was wonderful. Seventeen curtain calls.'

'Goodness,' said Chloe. 'Seventeen. How clever he is. Mummy, Joe, I'm so sorry, but I feel terribly tired. Would you mind if I went to sleep for a bit? I don't mean to be unwelcoming but –'

'Of course,' said Joe, 'we'll leave you. Goodnight, darling. Well done.' He bent and kissed her cheek; as he stood up again he tasted the salt of her tears.

He went back to the clinic next morning. Chloe was looking less pale, and rather determinedly happy.

'It's lovely to see you,' she said. 'Is Mummy coming again?'

'Tomorrow possibly. She had to rush down to Suffolk this morning, it's Jolyon's half term. She sent lots of love.'

'Thank you. She sent me some sweet flowers. Look. Much nicer than those ridiculous lilies.' She smiled at him rather fiercely.

'And what time did Piers finally manage to get here last night?' asked Joe, forcing his voice into lightness, otherwise he knew he would have shouted.

Oh, she said, oh, he was there well before three, probably earlier, she had been too sleepy to notice the time, but it had been so hard to leave that party, and his guests, on such a night, and he had been so thrilled and so proud, and how wonderful that Pandora should have arrived on such a night for him, to crown his triumph, and he would be back quite soon this morning. He had a press conference at eleven and then he would be over. All the time she was talking flowers were arriving, and cards and telegrams; at one point the nurse came in entirely hidden by an immense basket of white lilies, roses and freesias, and Chloe took the card out, read it, then flushed and laughed and said, 'Oh, how ridiculous.'

'Who are they from?' said Joe, intrigued by her reaction.

'Oh,' she said, 'someone called Ludovic Ingram. A friend of Piers's.'

'You look rather as if he were a friend of yours,' said Joe, picking up the card, trying to find somewhere to set the basket down. 'To the loveliest mother in England,' it said. 'If only she were mine. Ludovic.'

'Who on earth is he?' said Joe.

Oh, she said, a famous lawyer, a barrister, divorced, terribly sophisticated and clever, who was conducting a silly flirtation with her.

'Is he good-looking?' asked Joe.

'Yes, he is, ridiculously good-looking. If he was in movies, as they say, he'd always play romantic leads.'

'Well, darling, I'm happy for you,' said Joe, smiling. Then there was a delivery from Harrods of a huge bouquet of red roses, with a small box at its heart, which she opened; it contained a diamond eternity ring, and Chloe looked at the card, said 'Aah' though her voice was not quite right somehow, and while she put the ring on, and sat looking at it on her finger, Joe read the card. It said, 'To my darling Pandora's darling mother with all my love,' and he thought how easy it must have been to call Harrods and have it sent and how difficult, almost impossible, to have left the theatre to see Chloe through her labour last night and how just the same that was what Piers should have done, what he, Joe, would have done, what any man properly in love would have done.

Joe sat down, took her hand. 'How's my sort-of grand-daughter?'

'She's wonderful. What a thought, you don't look a bit like a grandfather, step or otherwise. In fact, you actually look much younger than Piers. Only don't tell him I said so.'

'I won't,' said Joe, 'but I don't see why it should matter, I am much younger than Piers.'

'Yes, of course you are.'

The phone rang. Chloe picked it up.

'Hallo? Oh, Piers darling, hallo. It's lovely to hear you. We're both absolutely fine. Yes. She's wonderful. Longing to see you. What? Oh, well that's a shame. No, of course it doesn't matter, as long as you're here tonight.' Her voice was determinedly bright, shakily cheerful. 'I'm fine. Joe's here anyway, keeping me amused. And Mummy's probably coming in later. Yes, of course. And it's wonderful about the film. What? Yes, I have, every single one. They're all marvellous, aren't they? Even the *Guardian*. Bye, darling. I'll see you in a little while. Don't – don't be late.' She sank back on her pillows and looked out of the window.

'All right?' said Joe.

'Oh – oh, yes. Fine. It's so exciting, some Hollywood mogul is flying in to talk to Piers about film rights for the *Lady*.' She sighed. 'So he won't be able to come in after all this morning. He's so excited though, the reviews have all been amazing, you know, every single one has raved about the *Lady*. I was reading them last night. I seem to have married something of a genius, Joe.'

'Really?' said Joe.

She was quiet, and then she said, 'Joe, I know you don't like Piers very much, but I really am very happy, you know. He is so good to me, and he loves me very much.'

'Of course,' said Joe, hoping his voice would not betray him too thoroughly. 'And if you're happy, poppet, that's all that matters.'

'Well, we're both happy. I suppose you think it's odd, him not being here now, but you must admit it's a difficult time for him. He'll make it up to me, I know he will.'

'Of course,' said Joe again.

'I can't wait to get home and be a proper family,' said Chloe, reaching out to Pandora's cot and touching her head. 'And I'm going to find it quite easy, I think. I have a wonderful maternity nurse, and then a dear sweet nanny coming after that, so between the three of us we should be able to keep Pandora happy. I didn't really want a proper nanny, actually, but Piers says he doesn't want me to be tied down at home, and I suppose he's right.'

'I don't know,' said Joe carefully, 'isn't that the place for a new mother, at home with her baby?'

'Well, normally, yes of course,' said Chloe, 'but most new mothers aren't married to the leading man of the English theatre, as the *Daily Express* called him last week.' She smiled at Joe, but she looked wistfully at Pandora in her crib, and bent over and stroked her face. 'Isn't she lovely, Joe? Don't you think she's beautiful?'

'Not as lovely as her mother,' said Joe, giving her a kiss.

'Oh, I'm afriad you're wrong there. I look a bit washed out and I'm so terribly fat,' said Chloe with a sigh. 'Piers wants me to go to a health farm in a few weeks, to get back into shape, but I actually hate the idea.'

'I hate it too,' said Joe. 'You're a mother, not one of his starlets. Tell him no.'

'Oh, I have,' said Chloe hastily, 'but Joe, you're not to think badly of him, it was only because I was moaning about being fat and having a horrible stomach, honestly. He's so sweet to me, and he tries so hard to take care of me.'

'Well, that's what he's there for,' said Joe.

'Yes, I know,' said Chloe. 'And I take care of him. He's not at all how you imagine, Joe. Not really very confident at all. Terribly highly strung and sensitive.'

'I'm sure,' said Joe. 'Chloe, have you ever told him – I mean does he know about –'

'No,' said Chloe quickly. 'No, I haven't. Not because he'd mind, of course, but because I would. It's not really anything to do with me, anyway, it's Mummy's life, Mummy's past. I might tell him some time, but not yet, Joe. And I don't want anyone else telling him either.' Her eyes were brilliant suddenly, her cheeks flushed; she looked upset.

'No one's going to tell him if you don't want them to,' said Joe.

Chloe lay back on her pillows again, smiling at him; she put out her hand and touched his. 'You're lovely, Joe. Mummy's so lucky. I hope she knows it.'

'I hope so too,' said Joe, smiling at her as convincingly as he could.

Interview with Damian Lutyens, for central section of *The Tinsel Underneath*. Happy to be quoted.

He was a wonderful friend. I know everyone thought we were more than friends, but they were all wrong. I was his best man when he married Chloe. You don't ask your lover to be your best man. He was terrified the night before. He took me out to dinner at the Ritz; he got very drunk. 'I can't believe I'm doing this again, Damian,' he said, 'I really can't. Why should it be all right this time? I'm no different.'

I tried to calm him, to reassure him, but it was difficult, because I couldn't see why it should be all right either. He shouldn't have been marrying anyone, and certainly not Chloe. It was a very strange relationship. I mean she's sweet and lovely and we all adore her, but there was just no way she was a wife for him. She got better at it, over the years, but it was awful at first. I don't think either of them had the faintest idea how awful it was going to be.

She was one of his obsessions; it was no more than that really. There was always someone. And every time he thought it was the answer. To all the problems.

'She's pregnant you know, Damian,' he said, staring into his food. He didn't eat any of it, all night; the waiters got very upset.

I didn't know; I was shocked. I wondered if maybe she'd done it on purpose, to trap him. I said so, as delicately as I could.

'Oh no,' he said, 'no, she's not up to that. I've been caught like that before, Damian. As you know.'

I didn't know; so he told me.

'Guinevere did that to me,' he said. 'I was leaving her, and she knew it, and she got pregnant, thinking I'd stay. I couldn't. Not under the circumstances. I just couldn't. I thought she was better without me. I really did. I believed that, Damian. Do you think I was right?'

I said I didn't know. He was almost in tears by then.

'I'm a bit of a case, Damian,' he said. 'Bit of a case. You wouldn't believe the mess my life is in.'

I said most people's were; he said his was worse than most, that he had seen a life wrecked, someone incredibly dear to him. I asked him how and he said he couldn't tell me.

'But I'm trying to put it right now,' he said. 'I really am, Damian.'

I didn't think too much about it, to be honest; he did get very carried away at times, especially when he started thinking about Guinevere.

He was getting rather agitated by then; I thought it was time to get him home. He's always being recognized, you know; I thought the last thing we wanted was a picture in the gossip columns of him crying into his beer, or rather burgundy, the night before his wedding. I paid the bill, and got a taxi; I went with him, back to Sloane Street. He was being driven out to Suffolk very early next day.

'Terrible place, East Anglia,' he said to me. 'I hate it. Couldn't spend a night there.'

When we got back to Sloane Street he asked me in for a drink. I said it was very late, but he said he'd go to pieces if he was on his own. Said he was frightened. Just a quick one, Damian, he said, just a quick one. So I went in, very reluctantly.

He had a picture of Chloe, a big one, on the piano in the drawing room. I thought that was a good sign. I said how pretty she was; yes, he said, she is, lovely, a lovely child. What am I doing to her, Damian? He kept on saying that. What was he doing? It was very sad, really awful. I thought of telling him it wasn't too late, but I was too scared. He might have agreed. I should have done really. I still regret it.

Chapter 18

1967

'Oh, look, Pandora. Joe's book!'

Chloe was pushing her small daughter down the King's Road in her pram, gazing enraptured at her, watching people smiling at her; and smile they might, for she had climbed halfway out of her pram despite the constraints of her harness, and was kneeling the wrong way round, smiling toothlessly – or almost toothlessly – at anyone who came into her orbit. She looked terrible, really; Chloe had given her a ginger biscuit to chew on, and it was drifting down her chin in a slobbery stream. Other remnants of it adhered to her cheeks, her hands and her forehead. But oh, she was so pretty, Chloe thought, so perfectly beautiful, with her wide grey black-lashed eyes, her dark red curls (in which there were yet more ginger crumbs, mercifully camouflaged), her creamy, perfect baby skin. Everyone said she was exceptionally pretty, even her grandmother Caroline, even her uncles Toby and Jolyon; and as for those rather more likely to voice such an opinion, her other grandmother, her father, her father's friends, they never stopped exclaiming upon it.

Piers had become a doting and adoring father, insisting on doing the most unlikely things like bathing Pandora, reading her (somewhat prematurely) fairy stories at bedtime and even very occasionally changing her nappy. Chloe, still helplessly in love with him, learning painfully slowly to be more at ease with his life, felt absurdly grateful to her small daughter for her contribution to the situation.

The public part of her life was comparatively easy; she was naturally efficient; she had no great trouble running Stebbings and the new London house they had bought, tall and stylish, in Montpelier Square. But she was still finding the private part of it difficult. Piers, she was inevitably discovering, was a complete mystery to her. Intensely loving as he was, he seemed increasingly – what? – out of reach was the nearest she could get to defining it. He would never talk about his feelings (except how much he loved her), his hopes and fears (except in regard to the next production and the next and the next); he seemed indeed to have a near-neurotic need to keep a part of his life to himself. He would disappear up to town sometimes at the weekends, for a few hours, saying vaguely that he had to meet someone, would come home very late, long after dinner, without warning, would become suddenly rather withdrawn and distant from her, and she would catch him looking at her oddly, coldly almost. And then there were the endless trips to the States, either to New York or Los Angeles, usually with some vague explanation about meetings with producers, actors, agents; never for long, just a few days, but as frequently as once a month. She had suggested that she might sometimes accompany him, but he had discouraged her, sweetly dismissive at first: 'Honestly, darling, you'd be so bored, just sitting around all day waiting for me,' and then tersely firm: 'Chloe, I've told you, this is all part of my life, and you have to learn to accept it; there is absolutely no point your trailing across the Atlantic with me all the time.'

'It's not all the time,' Chloe had said, stung into courage. 'I'd just like to come sometimes. I've never been to America.' But then she had given up entirely, seeing that she would never manage to persuade him, that the request only irritated him.

He, on the other hand, was almost hysterical in his need to know where she was, every moment of her day; there had been occasions when she had been at friends' houses, often with Pandora, chatting, careless of the time, had stayed perhaps for lunch unexpectedly, and would get home an hour or so later than she had said, and he would be waiting for her, deeply distressed, even angry sometimes, wanting to know exactly where she had been, what she had been doing. At first she had tried to tease him out of it, but she had learnt it was hopeless, he genuinely minded, so she always phoned home with endless messages and got appallingly tense if she was held up in traffic, or some other situation where she couldn't contact him. He was jealous of her friendships, too, with her girlfriends; she learnt to play them down, to say she had lunched or shopped or taken Pandora to the park alone when in fact she had been with someone, several other people, and then worried that he might have seen her, and known she was lying. It was as well, she thought, she was so helplessly in love with him, and there would never be the slightest reason for her even to look at anyone else; he would undoubtedly have killed him. He was also fiercely jealous of Joe and any time she spent with him, so she would lie about that as well, imploring Joe to back her up in her deception if the need arose. Piers, on the other hand, however, had any amount of intense friendships, with Damian, with David Montague, with David's wife Liza, with Giles Forrest, and had endless long conversations with them, far into the night, while she sat feeling chilled and alone, and ended up either falling asleep on the sofa, or going quietly up to bed. But then he would make it up to her, swear desperate undying love, take her to bed and make love to her almost frantically, as if he was aware he might have hurt her.

And then there was the making love itself, the sex; she really still found that the hardest thing to deal with. It was as unsatisfactory, as much of a letdown still as it had been the first time: the wonderful build-up, the longing for him, the confidence (waning now, she had to admit) that this time, this time, it would be all right, that the darts of pleasure would be allowed to grow, the soft tenderness would turn to triumph, but somehow it never was and she would be lying there, yet again, near to tears, fearful that he must be finding her as disappointing, wondering what she could, should do. She tried once or twice to talk to him about it, but her courage failed her; he thought she was simply asking for him, so feeble were her approaches to the subject, and so for now she had given up, a little sad, disappointed even, feeling oddly helpless. The only comfort – and it was a big one – was that he seemed perfectly content with her in bed, always told her afterwards how wonderful she was, how glorious it had been. Well, it wasn't everything: it wasn't even nearly everything. When she was feeling really bad, really afraid, she would remind herself that he had had no need to marry her, he could have had anyone, any beautiful, talented, self-assured creature he chose. There could be no doubt, no possible doubt really that he must love her, and that she pleased him. She was doing well, she told herself. It was all going to be all right. And in time, she was sure, her sense of aloneness, of anxiety both with herself and him would ease.

And then she saw Joe's book. *Scandals*, it was called, published years ago, just before he had met her mother in fact, and she had been wanting to read it for ages, but it was out of print. She had grown weary of his assurances that he had no copies left, that he had lost his own, lent the very last copy to a drunken colleague, that he would try to get her a copy from his publishers. She had even asked Piers if he had it, knowing there was some stuff in it about the theatre, but he had said no, absolutely not, he'd never even heard of it, and it wouldn't interest him anyway. Anyway, there it was, in a second-hand bookshop, marked down to a pound; she tucked it beneath Pandora's pram cover and continued on her walk home. When they got home, Pandora was tired and fretful; she hurried in to bath her, calling for Rosemary, the nanny, and forgot the book until the next morning, when she was looking in the pram for a glove.

So it was that when Piers came down for a very late breakfast she was sitting with it, flicking idly through the pages, not interested enough to read the whole thing, a lot about political scandals and financial ones; she dipped with rather more enthusiasm into the chapter on Hollywood, where the name Byron Patrick caught her eye. Ten minutes later she had not moved, apart from turning the pages, absent-mindedly feeding Pandora with bits of eggy toast; she looked up at Piers, smiled at him quickly and nervously and hurried out of the room, the book in her hand, thanking God that Piers (who considered newspapers purely as vehicles for reviews and theatrical gossip and had, like many of his colleagues, a slightly hazy view of world events) had been so engrossed in an article about the Royal Court Theatre and its financial future that he had not noticed it.

'Joe,' she said, her voice shaking, 'Joe, I've just bought your book. The one about the scandals. Joe, why didn't you tell me?'

'Tell you what, poppet?' said Joe and she knew at once he knew what she meant.

'You know what, about Byron Patrick, or Brendan, or whatever his name really was,' she said. 'The man, Fleur's father, I didn't realize he'd died like that, that it was all so horrible. I wish I'd known.'

'And why do you wish you'd known?' said Joe, gently. 'What difference would it have made?'

'I don't know. It just would. I might – well, it's so sordid and sad. I think I ought to have known. I think it makes me feel – well, differently. About her. About his daughter. Sorrier for her. Less hostile.'

'Well, it's all a long time ago now. She – Fleur – she's fine now. She's got over it perfectly well.'

'Oh Joe, how could she? If she has any feelings at all. You should have told me, you really should.'

It seemed unbearably sad somehow that Fleur's father, Brendan, or Byron as Hollywood had rechristened him, the handsome actor playing on the beach with the starlets, the brave hero who her mother had loved, had died, in squalor and obscurity, after some terrible scandal; Fleur seemed less strong, less dangerous somehow, and more important in her life, and she wanted, if a little half-heartedly, to know the rest. She wondered if she should not perhaps be brave and ask her mother about it, and maybe tell Piers about Fleur, about all of it, that it was too important to have lying between them, a sad sorry secret. She was about to go down and ask him if he had the time to talk to her when the phone rang and Piers picked it up and then came flying up the stairs into her room, to say that David Montague had just called to say that the *Lady* was up for Best Musical with the Variety Club, and was almost certain to get it. It didn't seem right to bother him with something so complex and difficult at that point, and then he was out for days, and had to go to New York for three weeks, and then she discovered (wonderfully) that she was pregnant again. After that Fleur and her father seemed part of such a distant and different past that they were best left there. After all, they had nothing to do with her own life now; absolutely nothing at all.

Joe sat staring at the phone after she rang off, uncertain as to why he felt so uneasy. Then he realized and felt slightly sick. There had been a copy of *Scandals* in the library at Stebbings; he had seen it himself. Surely Chloe would have found it, if it had still been there. And if it hadn't – why on earth not?

Fleur was thumbing through an edition of *Harper's Bazaar* one chill and dark November day, checking out one of the Juliana ads, when she came across a feature entitled 'Good Wives'. 'Chloe Windsor,' the caption said, beneath the picture of one of the good wives, 'ravishing young redhaired wife of English actor and impresario Piers Windsor, seen here with her new baby daughter Pandora. Mrs Windsor, who holds refreshingly old-fashioned views on motherhood and says she sees no more satisfying career than caring for what she hopes will be a large family, is pictured here in her London home wearing a white satin ballgown from Belville Sassoon. Pandora's lace robe is from the White House.'

Fleur felt as if she had been hit very hard, first in the stomach and then over the head. Was it? Could it be? No. No, it was impossible. It would have been the most absurd, the most horrible coincidence. It was a ridiculous idea. It was just the name. That was all. Chloe – well, there were hundreds, thousands of Chloes. She had never actually seen a picture of Chloe, had never wanted to, had strenuously discouraged Joe even from talking about her. Sweet, Joe had always described her as. An old-fashioned girl. Well, this was no old-fashioned girl. This was a gorgeous, very contemporary woman. But – when had that been? When he had said that? Years ago. Well, even so. No, she was just being silly. But what about the red hair? The dark red hair: like Caroline's. Well, so what? Dozens of girls with red hair. Called Chloe? Yes, of course. She must know several herself. She actually couldn't think of any.

'Poppy,' she said, and her voice sounded odd, 'Poppy, do you know any girls called Chloe?'

'Don't think so,' said Poppy. 'Why? You all right? You look terrible.'

'Yeah, I'm fine,' said Fleur. She didn't feel fine. She felt sick. She had to find out. She had to. Ridiculous, absurd as it was, she still had to find out, for sure. She sat as if in a trance for the next three hours, ostensibly trying to think of something original to say about mascara and actually doing absolutely nothing.

When everyone had gone, she picked up her phone and called Joe collect in London.

She heard his voice, giving the number; heard him asked if he would pay for the call, heard him hesitate. Finally, 'Yes, OK,' he said, and she was put through.

'Joe? This is Fleur.'

'I guessed it was,' he said, and her heart turned over at the drawly, gravelly voice. 'How are you?'

'I'm fine. Joe, I'm sorry to bother you, but I – you have to tell me something. Did – is – Chloe married to Piers Windsor? The old actor guy?'

There was a brief silence. Then he said, 'Yes. Yes, she is. Although,' he added with a sudden lightening of his voice, 'I wouldn't call him exactly old.'

'He looks pretty damn old to me,' said Fleur. 'When – that is, how long ago were they married?'

'Oh,' he said carefully, 'well over a year ago.'

'How nice for her,' said Fleur. 'Er – I suppose this is a silly question, but didn't anyone think to tell me? She is my sister.'

'Well, Caroline felt – that is . . .' Joe's voice tailed off weakly.

'Oh, I expect Caroline felt I didn't need to know. Well, I am a bit of an embarrassment, I can see that, when it comes to family. Not that I *am* family of course. What on earth does he make of us all? Whatever did Caroline tell him about me?'

'Well she didn't,' said Joe. 'Obviously.'

'I see,' said Fleur. She felt very sick suddenly, and extraordinarily fragile, as if she might faint. She picked up her cup of cold coffee and took a huge swig; the room swam about her oddly.

'Fleur, are you all right? I'm sorry if this has upset you.'

'Oh, yes,' she said, fighting down the hurt, the raw misery of this latest rejection, that Joe of all people could be so crass, so insensitive, 'I'm absolutely fine. Don't worry about me, Joe. I'm not in the least upset. Why should I be?'

'Fleur,' he said, 'Fleur, it isn't –'

'I don't want to discuss it,' she said, and put the phone down.

Later she sat, staring at the picture, looking with a sense that was almost wonder into Chloe's serene brown eyes, knowing at last what she looked like. All these years she had been thinking about her, had built her up into – what? Not a person at all, just a faceless, anonymous being, but an enemy none the less in possession of everything she didn't have. Now, she had not just a face, but a personality, a facile personality; she wore clothes (beautiful expensive clothes), she lived in a house (a flashy, expensive house), she spoke foolish sentimental words, she held an absurdly dressed baby. But oh, how did she do it, how did she go on having it all, love, luxury, security, everyone caring for her, protecting her, the petted pampered wife of a rich and famous man? How had she won such a prize, for heaven's sake, this vapid creature, even if she was pretty; how could it have happened? Well, she could certainly see why they couldn't have mentioned her: why, of course, obviously, they couldn't have. That would have cast a shadow over things, an illegitimate sister, sent off by her mother to the other side of the world. That all would have sounded very shoddy; might even have put him off.

Suppose she had even suggested coming to the wedding, to what had been no doubt an immensely grand and fashionable occasion, probably in Caroline's fucking great country house, with everyone there, smiling, being happy, being proud of Chloe: suppose she had turned up, like the wicked fairy at the feast. No, obviously they couldn't have told her about the wedding; couldn't have told the wedding about her. Obviously.

'One day,' she said to the picture, 'one day I'll get even with you. One day we'll be quits, you and I.'

Just before Christmas Piers suddenly had to go away again. 'Sorry, darling, only for a few days, I just have to see a producer in LA about a new idea I have, such a wonderful idea, just a tiny gleam in my eye at the moment, I'd better not tell you about it at least till I get back, it might be unlucky.'

Chloe was cross, miserable, feeling unwell with her pregnancy; she hated the thought of him being away; nevertheless she put a brave face on it, packed his bag for him, drove him to the airport, and then, faced with a long day ahead with nothing to do, decided to go and visit Piers's mother in her nursing home. She phoned Rosemary at the house to make sure Pandora was all right, and said she'd be back at tea-time, phoned the nursing home to say she was coming if Mrs Windsor was up to it, and then made her way down to Sussex.

She adored Flavia; she wished she could see more of her. But Piers was not over-attentive; there was always some excuse not to visit – although when he did, they were clearly so besotted with one another, had so much to say, that Chloe had initially felt slightly awkward, playing her usual role of outsider; but then Flavia had been so sweet to her, so affectionate, told her she was so absolutely delighted to have a daughter again, that she had longed to see more of her.

She had offered several times to go and visit Flavia on her own, but Piers had frowned on the notion, had indeed been quite hostile to it: 'She's very fragile,' he had said, 'not nearly as strong as she seems. She needs delicate handling.'

'You make her sound like a nervy horse,' said Chloe irritably. 'Anyone can see she just can't have enough chat. Please let me go, Piers, I'd love it and so would she.'

'I really think it best that you don't,' said Piers. 'Her doctor has stressed that she must be kept quiet.'

Chloe thought that the kind of conversations Piers conducted with Flavia, endlessly frenetic anecdotes, requiring intense admiration and boundless laughter, hardly qualified as keeping her quiet, but she didn't say so. She was becoming so irritated by his endless absences, and his refusal to take her with him, that the thought of disobeying him was soothing, positively pleasurable. Besides, it would give Flavia pleasure too: she couldn't get many visitors.

Flavia was sitting in a chair by the bed when Chloe arrived, not doing anything, just looking out of the window: she was still a pretty woman, with thick, wavy white hair and large grey eyes exactly like Piers's. She was wearing a pink robe over a frilled white nightdress; there was a gold locket round her neck, and several very beautiful rings on her thin fingers; she had told Chloe on their first meeting that she still spent quite a lot of time trying to look as nice as she possibly could. 'I may be a bedridden old woman, but I don't intend to look like one.'

'Flavia!' said Chloe. 'Hallo.'

Flavia's face looked at Chloe, taking a few moments to come back from the distant country her thoughts were fixed in; then she smiled, her enchanting sparkly smile. 'Chloe, my darling, how lovely, how lovely to see you. And what beautiful flowers, freesias, my favourite, they make the room smell so wonderful. Have you brought that naughty husband of yours with you?'

'No,' said Chloe, 'he's on an aeroplane on one of his endless trips to Los Angeles.'

'Good. Then we can have a really lovely talk. Men are all very well, but they do go in for such heavy conversation.'

Chloe would not quite have called the kind of conversation Piers and Flavia had heavy, but she didn't like to say so.

'I've brought you some pictures of Pandora,' she said, bending to kiss Flavia, 'I would have brought her in person, but she's very exhausting at the moment. And I've also brought you some really nice news.'

'Darling, what?'

'I'm pregnant again,' said Chloe, blushing slightly.

'Oh, darling, how lovely. Oh, I'm so thrilled for you, and so happy for Piers that he found you. He always so longed for a family, it's just wonderful, and so good for him too. It will make him grow up a bit,' she added slightly sternly.

Chloe was surprised at such frankness from so adoring a mother. 'He seems quite grown up to me.'

'My darling, he is still a baby. Never had any responsibility, always been the centre of attention. It's my fault, of course, I spoilt him when he was little. And since then the whole world has spoilt him. The only person who refused to do so was my darling Guinevere. And then look what happened,' she added, a look of great sadness in her large eyes.

'But I thought –'

'Oh, let's not waste time talking about anyone else,' said Flavia quickly. 'I don't suppose you have very long, do you? I'm going to ring for some tea for us both and to get a vase for those lovely flowers and then you can show me the pictures. Now when is this next little darling due?'

'In May,' said Chloe.

'A summer baby, so much easier than the winter. And hopefully this one won't be born on a first night. Bad timing there, my darling. But how marvellous Piers was able to dash over and see you before the party.'

'Er – yes,' said Chloe. Obviously Flavia had got the details muddled. It was hardly surprising.

'And how are you finding it all? Those difficult people, and so on?'

'Oh – better now,' said Chloe. She looked at Flavia and said, 'I didn't think you'd understand so well.'

'Well, of course I understand. It must have been a nightmare for you. They haven't always been terribly kind to me, you know. Many's the first-night party I've stood and found myself ignored.' She leant forward and patted Chloe's hand. 'I think you're doing wonderfully. And you're so young. What are you, still only twenty-one? Of course it's better in a way. You learn faster. I was only twenty when Piers was born. Nineteen when I was married. To a considerably older man also.'

'Yes,' said Chloe, 'yes, I know. Piers told me about him.'

'Not very much, I imagine,' said Flavia briskly. 'Piers is very adept at ignoring difficult facts. I was married to a bit of a brute, darling. Oh, he didn't knock me about or anything, and he kept us very well provided for. But he was always away, Piers seldom saw him, and he was a miserable old creature. That's why we were so close, Piers and I. All the world to one another when he was little.'

'I see,' said Chloe.

The nurse came in with a tray of tea, and the flowers.

'Now, darling, you be mother, and pour. Tell me more about Pandora. Is she saying anything yet?'

'Well, actually . . .' said Chloe and was off, on the litany so beloved, so familiar to mothers, of noises that might be words, of movements that were clearly about to be crawling (or walking), of skills mastered (holding, waving, hiding eyes), of anxieties (how will she take the arrival of the new baby?), of pleasure (she is such good company already, you can't imagine), of delicious laughter, of touching tears, of naughtiness, of goodness, of sweetness, of cleverness, and Flavia sat enchanted, responding occasionally (although not too much) with stories of Piers's own childhood, and it was quite dark when Chloe suddenly realized she was looking tired and was leaning back in her chair, and speaking less and less.

'Oh Flavia, I'm so sorry, I've worn you out. I must go at once. Shall I ring for a nurse?'

'My darling, I'm fine, really. And I would far rather be tired in your company than well rested in my own. Now I think you should have another cup of tea before you go and perhaps a biscuit, it's a long drive, and you're looking tired yourself. Oh, and you can give me a little advice before you go. Hand me my bag, darling, will you? I had a letter the other day, from a journalist, called – let me see, yes, Magnus Phillips. He wants to come and see me.'

'What on earth for?' said Chloe. She didn't really trust Magnus Phillips, and she was surprised Piers did; it was a relationship that baffled her.

'He says he's researching a book on Piers. And he wants to talk to me about him. Here, look.'

Chloe looked: a polite letter, on *Daily Sketch* paper, full of apologies for intruding, of promising not to take too much of Mrs Windsor's time, of immense gratitude should she be able to see her way to helping. It looked harmless: but if Piers was going to have a book written about him, why let Magnus Phillips do it? His last book had been outrageous, a terrible series of revelations about a politician and his sexual and professional misdemeanours; Phillips had interviewed half England getting the truth – and who was to say it was the truth? – about the man. She wondered if Piers realized that Magnus was already working on the book, which had been mentioned in the vaguest terms, and who else he might have written to; probably he did, she thought with a sigh, and it was yet another example of his devious behaviour, his compulsion to conceal things from her.

'If I were you,' she said carefully, 'I should check it with Piers first when he gets back. Make sure he's happy about it. He's a perfectly nice man, he came to our wedding as a matter of fact, but I had no idea he was actually working on anything, b— well, you never know.'

'Yes, darling, I will. How clever of you, I knew you'd know what to do. Tell me, darling, do you mind Piers being away so much?' she asked, casually, as Chloe started gathering her belongings.

'Oh – well, you know, of course I do miss him. But it's nice when he comes back.'

'Where is he this time? Hollywood? Of course it doesn't seem quite so far away these days. When he first went, I could hardly bear it, it seemed like the other side of the world.'

'What, when he went off to make *Town Cousins*?'

'Oh, no, darling, long before that. He made an earlier foray – hasn't he told you about it?'

'No,' said Chloe slowly. 'No, he hasn't.'

She could hear Piers's voice now, very clearly, at the Ritz, that first night; she knew she was right, every word of that evening was etched on her mind: she'd asked him if he'd gone to Hollywood in his early days and he had said, very firmly, 'No, I never got into that. The cattle call culture. Professional suicide.' Why should he lie about such a thing?

'He's a bit sensitive about it,' said Flavia, smiling, seeing her confusion. 'It was a disaster, and it was when he was still upset about Guinevere. He doesn't like people to know. You'd better not let on I've told you. Silly boy. I told you I spoilt him. Now, darling, off you go, give that baby a huge kiss from me, and take care of yourself. And thank you for coming. It's been such a lovely day.'

Chloe drove home slowly; she was very tired and for some reason the information about Piers being in Hollywood had upset her. Not because it mattered, but because it was yet another example of his near compulsion to keep so much of his life to himself.

Chapter 19

1968

Fleur was stark naked when she saw Piers Windsor for the first time. She had been getting ready for bed, and had switched on the news (one of the perks of her job was a colour TV paid for by the agency, so that she could see their own and the opposition's commercials), and there he was; she stood and stared at him, transfixed, at the absurdly handsome chiselled face, the fine, wide eyes, the patrician nose; at his beautiful clothes, the perfectly cut suit, the hand-made shoes (a quirky side benefit of her affair with Nigel had been an ability to recognize hand-made shoes), the overcoat slung over his shoulders, the slim leather briefcase in his hand. Well, he was certainly a looker. She'd give him that much. If you liked that sort of thing, which she absolutely didn't. Chloe was welcome to him.

He was being interviewed arriving at Kennedy; she listened to the famously beautiful voice, so perfectly modulated, so English, so musical, talking about how delighted he was to be in New York, how proud to be putting on the *Lady* there. 'How long are you going to be here, Mr Windsor, and will you be doing any auditioning during that time?' 'Oh, about three weeks,' he said, maybe four, and yes, of course, a great deal of auditioning. If there were any marvellous actresses and dancers out there, longing for a part in the *Lady*, would they contact him immediately. (This to camera, with the slow, perfect smile.) Where would that be, Mr Windsor, where could they find you? Oh, the theatre, naturally, where the *Lady* was to be put on, the Warwick. And was there no chance now that Tabitha Levine who had made the part her own in England would be bringing it to New York? Very little, said Piers Windsor (and Fleur, watching him intently, saw the muscles of his jaw tighten just a little, noticed the slightly less easy smile), New York Equity had made it very difficult for her to get her card, but he was still hoping, because although of course it would be marvellous to find a new actress and watch her create the role, there was not a great deal of time left and it was not a part that could be just knocked into shape overnight, it needed care and understanding and love of a sort and . . .

Fleur switched off the TV; she could take no more. What a creep! What a pure-bred, A1, record-breaking creep. The thought that he was some kind of a relation of hers, her brother-in-law in some convoluted, warped way, made her want to throw up. Well, she was very unlikely to meet him, she supposed. Thank God.

'Fleur, can I come in?'

Mary Steinberg was at the door, baby at her breast; she looked exhausted.

'Of course. Coffee?'

'Might as well. I'm not going to get any sleep tonight anyway. This one is a nightmare. Anyway, there's a letter for you. It got mixed up with ours this morning. Sorry.'

'That's OK,' said Fleur, slitting it open. 'I –' and then she was silent, stunned, her eyes racing over the words, her heart thudding furiously.

Coldwater Canyon Road, Los Angeles. April 1968

My dear Fleur,

Good news! I am coming to New York for a couple of days next week and I thought we could maybe meet at last: have a meal or something. I'll be staying at the Pierre, arriving Monday. Call me. I can't wait to see you!

Yours,

Rose

'Holy shit!' said Fleur. 'Fuck me! Oh, Mary! Oh, my God.'

She had written to Rose Sharon at MGM which was where all the movie magazines said she belonged, after quizzing Joe ferociously on the phone about any possible consequences of the trip to L.A. after Yolande's death. He had been carefully vague, but had finally told her about Rose and that she and Brendan had been 'like Romeo and Juliet'. 'I really don't think she'll see you, Fleur.'

'She won't if I don't ask her to,' said Fleur. 'You're a seriously negative person, Joe,' and rang off.

There had been no reply. She had been upset, but not surprised. Stupid spoilt, stuck-up bitch, of course she wouldn't reply to a letter from a girl she had never heard of, who came at her out of the blue, telling her she wanted to talk to her about a man far into her past she had once had a love affair with. It was six months later that she read that Rose Sharon was in India, filming, and realized that in any case she had written to the wrong studio, that she was no longer with MGM but with Universal. She tried again, putting Please Forward on the letter and enclosing a self-addressed envelope. Universal wrote back and gave her the address of Rose Sharon's fan club; she tried that, and got a signed photograph and a membership card.

Tearful with frustration she wrote again to Universal putting Personal and Urgent all over the letter: finally almost a year after her first attempt she got a note from Rose Sharon's secretary saying that Miss Sharon was away filming in Europe, but that when she got back, she would certainly pass on Miss FitzPatrick's letter.

Just after Christmas that year, finally a slightly guarded note came from Rose, saying how lovely to hear from her, that of course she remembered Fleur's father, and that she'd always be very welcome if ever she was in Los Angeles.

Fleur wrote back and said she didn't get over to LA too often, but thanked her for writing, and said she really wanted to talk to her about her father. A warmer note came back, saying Rose would be in New York in the spring and that she would certainly be in touch then. Yeah yeah, said Fleur crossly to the letter, throwing it in her trash can as a gesture – not many people could throw away a personal letter from a world-famous film star, it made her feel good for at least an hour; and now, only a few weeks later, this wonderful letter had arrived. Maybe Rose Sharon wasn't such a stupid, spoilt, stuck-up bitch after all . . .

She wasn't. She was lovely. She still looked wonderful, despite being quite old, at the very least (Fleur calculated) thirty something; she had golden-brown hair and blue eyes, and a real peaches and cream skin, and an oddly gentle, very sweet smile, and Fleur thought that if she could have coped with her father being in love with anyone it would have been Rose Sharon.

She was staying in a suite at the Pierre: a woman with iron-grey hair, a rather severe electric-blue suit and a very fierce face came down to meet Fleur and she thought for a dreadful moment that she was Rose. But of course she was not, she was Rose's secretary, Martha Johns. Fleur was taken upstairs and led into the suite, where Rose stood up, smiling, and said, 'Fleur! If you only knew how often I've thought about you. You know you look just like your father.'

'Do I?' said Fleur. 'That's really nice. I think,' she added and burst into tears.

Rose Sharon signalled to Martha Johns to disappear, and passed Fleur a handful of Kleenex. Then she said, 'I feel so terrible, never getting in touch with you. But – well, I didn't know how much good it would do. And you were such a little girl. And Yolande said not to. It was stupid of me. But anyway –'

'I wish Yolande was still alive,' said Fleur, sniffing hard, wiping her eyes.

'Me too. I miss her so. It just broke my heart. I was away when she died, you know, all that time, filming in India.'

'Yes, I know,' said Fleur.

'You do? You're obviously a very good detective.'

'Not really,' said Fleur. 'But I try.'

'Coffee?' said Rose.

Fleur nodded.

'Come and sit down. Tell me, how old are you?'

'Twenty-three,' said Fleur.

'Oh, my God! Well, I suppose you would be. I know your dad told me you were only ten or something when he left you. Oh, my goodness, he had such remorse over that. And he missed you so.'

'Did he?' said Fleur. 'He had a very strange way of showing it.'

'Really? No letters?'

'Almost no letters,' said Fleur. 'And he never sent for me either. He promised he would, and he never even mentioned it ever again.'

Rose's face was thoughtful, careful. 'Fleur, he couldn't. Believe me. In the beginning he didn't have any money, none of us did. And later on – well, he just couldn't have. It would have been impossible.'

'Why?' said Fleur.

'Naomi wouldn't have allowed it. You know about Naomi?'

'I met her,' said Fleur.

'You met her?' Rose's voice was amused. 'You really are a good detective. When?'

'Oh – a couple of years ago. She was completely gaga.'

'Still is, darling. Well she would be. I can see it's terribly hard for you to understand even now, but there was no way anyone in Naomi's pocket would have been allowed to have any kind of life of their own. She swept me away from Brendan's door very effectively; she certainly wouldn't have stood for you.'

Fleur liked it that she called her father Brendan, rather than the terrible Byron.

'Why did you let her? Sweep you away?'

'Fleur, you have to live in Hollywood to understand that. It's just the toughest place on earth. Hundreds, thousands of people all fighting to get noticed, for just a moment. And about as much chance of making it as an icicle in hell. If you got that chance, you jumped. You did what you were told. That's all your dad was doing: what he was told.'

'But – didn't you mind?'

'Of course I minded. Like hell. But I understood.'

'Oh,' said Fleur. She was beginning to feel very miserable, not better.

Rose looked at her. 'Fleur, what can I actually do for you? I mean, presumably you have a reason for getting in touch, or are you a journalist elaborately disguised?' She laughed. 'I warn you, I don't like journalists.'

Fleur managed a smile. 'I'm trying to find some answers,' she said, 'to some very tricky questions. I had never ever thought you might be able to help. But – will you?'

'I'll try,' said Rose, cautiously. 'Who put you on to me?'

'Oh, it's such a long story. But it was through someone called Joe Payton. He's a journalist. He said he'd been told you and my dad were – well, as he put it, were like Romeo and Juliet. Is that right?'

Rose smiled, and her clear blue eyes took on the sweetly thoughtful look familiar to a million, ten million film fans all over the Western world. 'That certainly is,' she said. 'I loved him, the son of a bitch. Really loved him. He was a kind, funny, gentle creature, almost totally untalented – sorry, Fleur, but it's true – and we had a really good time together. We lived in a tiny apartment on La Brea, and we were very hard up, I worked as a waitress and he worked pumping gas and I never was so happy in my life.' She smiled at Fleur slightly sadly. 'They were such good days.'

'But he – he did tell you about me?'

'Of course he did. I told you. And your mother and that whole romantic war story, it would make a great movie.'

Fleur shuddered. 'God forbid.'

'Yes, God forbid. But yes, he did, he talked about you a lot. He was so proud of you. He used to say so often he was going to get you over here to live, when he hit the big time. Which of course I never thought he would. Hit it, I mean.'

'But he did.'

'Yes, he did. God knows how. Well, he was very good looking. And extremely photogenic.' She refilled Fleur's cup. 'And acting is a kind of bonus, at a certain level.'

'And of course there was Miss MacNeice.'

'There was indeed.'

'I like it that you call him Brendan,' said Fleur suddenly. 'I feel you really did know him.'

'It was such a lovely name. Brendan FitzPatrick. Only Hollywood could want to change that. Me too: I was called Rose Kildare. So they called me first Rose de Sharon, gave me a biblical ring as I was dancing in a terrible film about Moses, and then we dropped the de. Dear God.' She laughed. 'Now then, tell me what exactly it is you want to know.'

'Well . . .' Fleur hesitated. 'Well, you see – oh, it's so difficult to explain, I just don't –'

Rose put out her hand, a slender beautiful hand, and covered Fleur's with it. 'Let me say it for you. You want to know how it all happened. How that story ever got into *Inside Story*. Whether it was true.'

'Yes,' said Fleur simply. 'And who was to blame, I suppose.'

'Now that is a difficult one. You could say all manner of people were to blame, from Naomi to the publisher of *Inside Story*, to everyone else in Hollywood. And maybe to an extent your father.'

'But that's what I don't understand. How it was him. What did he do?'

'Two things, Fleur. He made some enemies. And at one time, I think, he . . .' She hesitated, as if debating whether she should really go on, and then said, 'Yes, Fleur, I do think he might have had one or two homosexual relationships. Albeit fleetingly.'

'Oh,' said Fleur. She made a small, sad, shocked sound. 'Oh, my God.'

'You hadn't heard?' said Rose. She looked shocked herself. 'Oh, Fleur. Fleur, I'm so sorry. I thought you must have seen the article, heard the gossip.'

There was a long silence. Then Fleur said, her voice very strained and odd, 'I think I always feared it. From what – well, from what Miss MacNeice said. But she was so mad. I just buried it.'

'And you didn't see the article?'

'No,' said Fleur flatly. 'No, they kept it from me.' She looked at Rose, and saw her face was very white, very concerned. 'Do you have it?'

Rose hesitated. Then she said, 'Yes, I do. Do you want – do you really want to see it?'

Fleur lifted her chin. 'Yes,' she said, 'yes, I do.'

Rose looked at her for a long moment. Then she said gently, 'It isn't terribly nice reading, Fleur. And it isn't that informative. Just some very strong innuendo.'

'Could I see it?'

'Yes. I'll get it. Have another coffee.'

Fleur shook her head. She noticed that the knuckles of her hands were quite white from gripping the arms of her chair.

'Byron and the Boys Brigade,' said the headline.

> What does Byron Patrick, determined bachelor and second-division lead at ACI, have to say to allegations that he was very close indeed to certain Hollywood gentlemen in the days when he was hanging around the casting couches? Predictably, 'No comment,' echoed by Perry Browne, his press agent. These guys really should think of another line. Byron, who was signed by Naomi MacNeice fifteen months ago, and is often to be seen three paces behind her at premières and parties, is said to be close to Lindsay Lancaster, new hot property at ACI. Does this boy know exactly what he's supposed to be doing?

'Who was Lindsay Lancaster?' said Fleur. Her voice seemed to come from a long way away, not to belong to her.

'Oh, darling, no one. Just some little starlet at the time. I seem to remember she's married now to some poor sucker who runs a canning factory or something like that.'

'Oh. Oh, I see.' Fleur read it two more times. Then she dropped her face into her hands and started to cry.

Rose got up and sat beside her and put her arms round her. 'Don't,' she said, and her voice was odd and strained itself. 'Don't cry, Fleur. I'm so sorry, so terribly sorry.'

'You don't understand,' said Fleur. 'You couldn't. I loved him so much. He was perfect, he was so kind and strong and brave and such fun. Even when things were really really bad, he was fun, he could make us all laugh. He was never cross, never too tired to play, to invent games, to do whatever I wanted. And now – now –'

'Now look,' said Rose, 'let's take a good look at all this. Just because he was – was homosexual, that doesn't mean he wasn't all those other things. Wasn't fun and brave and strong. He hasn't changed. Not in himself. He's still your dad, he still loved you. You can still love him, love what he was. I did.'

Fleur stared at her. 'Did you? Could you?'

'Somehow, yes, I did. Fleur, listen to me. Hollywood is a terrible place. Morality takes a nose-dive as you move into it. Nobody knows who or what they are any more. It's – well, a place where you become very pragmatic.

Especially if you're hungry. And even more especially –' she paused and smiled at Fleur – 'if you have a little girl who's hungry.'

Fleur stared at her. Then she said, 'So who do you think put the story about, Rose? Someone like Perry Browne or Hilton Berelman? My father certainly upset both of them.'

'Yes, he did. But they wouldn't have talked to *Inside Story* direct. Too much against their own interest. Deliberately to get your name linked with a homosexual scandal would be seriously unwise. Besides, those stories were almost always supplied by stringers. People paid an enormous amount for information.'

'How do they get it?' said Fleur in a small voice.

'Oh, darling, it's not difficult. Sometimes from private detectives, sent out by the magazines – they have this dreadful cover organization called Hollywood Research – sometimes from . . . well, from call girls. Call girls with tape recorders in their purses. Left on the bedside table, you know?'

'Yes, but if the gossip was that my dad was homosexual, why should he tell a call girl that?'

'Oh, I'm not saying in his case it was a call girl. Just letting you know what a filthy business this is. Are you really sure you want to go on with this?'

'Yes.' Fleur felt more and more as if she had strayed into a strange country, where night was day, black white, and all the signposts had been turned round, so that there was no hope whatsoever of finding her way out again. 'But you really think this would have been enough to finish my father off?'

'Well – yes. Yes, it was. As we saw. And then he dropped very fast: they took everything, the apartment, the clothes, the car; he tried to get work as an extra. That's hard when you've been a star, sitting at the long table, with all the other extras, hanging around the set. But he couldn't even get that. He was bad news by then, you see. Poor baby. And then – well –'

'What then?' said Fleur.

'Oh, he – well, things got very bad.'

'What sort of very bad?' said Fleur. The pain was so terrible, she couldn't think it could be worse. 'You have to tell me.'

'He got into the blue movie culture. Fleur, I tried to help. Really. But there was very little I could do. I mean I still didn't have much money. Or any clout. And he was terribly proud. And he felt bad about me. Obviously.'

'Yes, of course.'

'Then he started drinking, I mean really drinking. And – well, you know the rest.'

'Yes,' said Fleur. 'Yes, I suppose I do.' She managed to smile at Rose. 'Some of it. Rose, who do you think sold that story to the magazine? Did he ever – did he talk to you about it?'

'To me? No, not really. Only after it was much too late. Even then only in passing, only by inference.'

'And what did he say? Please tell me.'

'He said – do you want his exact words?'

'I want his exact words.'

'He said, "I talk too much, Rose. Always did. I've been an even bigger fool than I thought." '

'Oh,' said Fleur again.

'And then he wouldn't say any more about it. I said did he want to, was there anything I could do, and he said no, it would only make matters worse and the less I knew the better. Probably true. Then he just said, "Mud certainly sticks, Rose. Remember that." And we never talked about it again. But, Fleur, I really don't want you to think he was some kind of a raving gay. I can tell you we lived together for almost a year and he absolutely was not.'

'And – and not – well, not promiscuous?'

'I don't think so. Fleur, he just did what he had to do. I'm sorry, there isn't a pretty way to say it. It was silly, crazy if you like, but there's an awful lot of people doing awfully well in Hollywood out of exactly that kind of behaviour. You have to be very strong to resist success, if it comes looking for you, even if you don't like the terms. And especially if you need it. Sillier than sleeping with some casting director or whatever, I have to say, was alienating people like Berelman and Clint when he got to the top. That was very unwise. And he was – well, he *was* silly. He trusted people, talked too much. You can't do that there.'

Fleur was silent. She felt, against all the odds, strangely comforted. Then she said, 'Rose, I just have to find out who did that. Who talked. Can you understand that?'

'Of course. I loved my dad too. I'd feel the same. But you have a tough job ahead of you. It's so long ago.'

Fleur smiled at her rather weakly. 'I'd be so grateful if you could help in any way at all. You don't think that starlet, Lindsay Lancaster or whatever her name was, might have known, do you?'

Rose looked at her and smiled. 'I doubt it. But of course everything's worth a try. And I'll see what I can come up with, although I really have told you everything. I think you're very brave, Fleur. The important thing to remember is that in spite of all this, all the squalor and mess, your dad stayed basically a nice, kind, good guy. I was really very fond of him. And he was so afraid you'd find out.'

'Was he?' said Fleur. 'Well I did, I'm afraid.' She felt horribly near to tears again.

Rose stood up and said, 'Time for a drink. Do you like champagne? Good. And now shall we talk about something else for a bit, like you, and what you do with your life?'

Outside again, wandering in something close to despair in Central Park, Fleur wondered if Joe had known all along. She decided he probably had and had been too much of a coward to tell her. She hated him more than ever, and thought how if she had had to discover such a thing, Rose Sharon had been the perfect person to see her through it. She felt she had truly discovered a life-long friend. She didn't have many of those.

* * *

She felt terrible. Part of her was in shock, another part acknowledged that she had always known or, certainly, instinctively suspected, and fought the knowledge off. Every part of her hurt, ached physically. She couldn't eat; her habitual sleeping problem was exacerbated; she lay awake night after night, restless, feverish, hanging on to Rose's words: 'He was still your dad, he still loved you.' But it was hard. Very hard. She became, as always in misery, fierce, hostile; only Reuben dared to ask her what the matter was. Fleur told him she didn't want to talk about it. 'That's fine,' said Reuben. He gave her a hug. Fleur thought for the thousandth time that he was the most emotionally restful person she had ever met. She was also slightly uneasily aware that she very seldom repaid him for all the support and love he gave her. Soon, very soon, she told herself, when she was feeling better, she would make a huge effort to make it all up to him. And then something happened that did make her feel better: and drove Reuben even lower on her list of concerns.

Ten days after watching Piers Windsor's arrival at Kennedy Airport, she was invited to a boardroom lunch with Julian Morell and Camilla North. It was to present the final campaign, the layouts, the photography, the copy for the fake tan campaign; she was pleased by her inclusion.

'Thank you,' she said to Mick when he stopped by her desk to tell her he wanted her at the meeting. 'It's a nice surprise.'

'Well, darling, you've made a considerable input. And in the other spring campaign. In fact you could say the whole Flatter Yourself concept sprang from your talented little typewriter. We're not entirely stupid, you know.'

'Of course not,' said Fleur, smiling at him sweetly.

The meeting went well; so high on excitement indeed was Fleur that she almost missed what Nigel said to Camilla at lunch. Almost, but not quite.

'I expect you've met Piers Windsor?' were the actual words and for the rest of her life she would hear them, and the ones that followed, over and over again, played until they were worn thin, worn out in her brain.

'Yes, once or twice. He's over here now, isn't he, setting up his new show?'

'Yes, he is, and for my sins, I have to have dinner with him tonight. Serena is desperately trying to co-opt him on to one of her charities and she's on the board of the Warwick Theatre, where this show, what's it called? oh yes, *The Lady of Shalott*, is to be put on.'

'Oh, really?' said Camilla. She was making it very clear that if Nigel was trying to impress her, he was not succeeding. 'I'm afraid I really don't like those kinds of musicals. I'm one of the very few people who hated *West Side Story*. A fault in me, I'm sure, but there it is. I'm sure Mr Windsor is extremely clever, and I would travel hundreds of miles to see him do Shakespeare. I wonder if you ever saw his Hamlet?'

'I did,' said Nigel, 'and I thought –'

But Camilla was not to know what he thought, for Julian had called her over to discuss some finer point of copy, and with a gracious smile at Nigel she went across to him. Fleur stood there, quite still, staring at Nigel, enjoying on one extremely superficial level the discomfiture he was enduring at Camilla's defection mid-sentence from their conversation, even while her conscious mind was occupied with something quite different, something extraordinary and disturbing and exciting. Piers Windsor had come within her reach, within her, Fleur's, grasp; Fleur, the unsuitable, unmentionable sister, the person who of course couldn't be mentioned. Supposing she met him, supposing she actually talked to him: supposing she told him who she was. What a dreadful thing that would be for Chloe and for Caroline; having to explain her away, and not only her, but the fact that they had not explained her before. What an irresistible prospect. Here was revenge, delicious, sweet, wonderful revenge, dangled before her, there for the plucking. How could she resist it? How could she possibly resist it?

She excused herself from the boardroom briefly at around half past one, and went straight up to the fourth floor, and Nigel's office. There was just a chance, just a faint chance, it would not be locked. It was locked. Damn. Mavis Delmont would never in a million years let her near Nigel's diary if she was there.

Who else might know? Well, Serena would know. She could ring her. 'Oh, hi, Serena, this is Fleur, I just wondered if you could let me know where you're dining with Piers Windsor tonight, I wanted to pop by and take a look at him, say hi.'

Serena's secretary would know. Serena's housekeeper just might know. Who else, who else? Perkins! Perkins would know. Dear Perkins, Nigel's driver, who had always been so kind to her. He would know. But would he tell her? Probably not. Well, nobody else would, it was worth a try.

She knew where he'd be. In one of two places. He never left the building while Nigel was there, just in case he was needed. Nigel was capricious, changeable, it could not be assumed that just because he was hosting a boardroom lunch he would not suddenly decide to transport his guests to a restaurant, a club, even his home. There had been a dreadful occasion, early in Perkins's career, when he had gone out to buy a Christmas present for his grandson, secure (as he thought) in the knowledge that a very heavy client meeting was in progress in Nigel's office, and Nigel and Mick had decided to take the client to see a location in Chinatown in the hope of persuading him to a campaign; Perkins was not to be found, and they had had to take Mick's car, which was a rather dirty if valuable 1950s Oldsmobile. Perkins had been lucky to keep his job that day, he was given very clearly to understand; since then, if Nigel was in the office, he was too, usually in the small car park under the building. Fleur looked at her watch; she had already been gone ten minutes, she really couldn't stay any longer. She would just have to hope to catch Perkins later.

The lunch wound up soon after two; Camilla, who drank nothing and ate very little either, did not greatly enjoy any function that encompassed either activity and encouraged its speedy conclusion. It was hard to imagine, Fleur thought, watching her pushing a piece of celery round her plate, that she could take a great interest in any other carnal pleasures either.

'Could I go?' she said to Mick, as soon as the lift doors had closed. 'I have so much to do.'

'Sure, darling. Thanks for coming.'

'My pleasure,' said Fleur, smiling sweetly round the room, focusing particularly on Bella, and left.

Perkins was down in his small kingdom; he was actually reading the situations vacant column in the *New York Times*, ringing various entries in red, and didn't hear her come in. Fleur, deciding there was a God after all, and moreover near at hand, crept up behind him and put her hands over his eyes.

'Who's that?' said Perkins. 'Karen, if that's you I'll –'

'It isn't Karen, whoever she is, you wicked old thing, it's Fleur FitzPatrick.'

'Miss FitzPatrick. Well I never did. What are you doing down here? Frightening an old man to death.'

She took her hands away, moved round to the front of him. 'Looking for a job, Mr Perkins, I see.'

'No,' he said, uneasily, uncertainly. 'Course not. Not for me. For my boy.'

'Oh,' said Fleur. 'Oh, I see. I thought he was a welder, Mr Perkins, not a –' she bent forward and looked at the paper – 'not a driver, with experience, English preferred.'

'Miss FitzPatrick, you really are a bad girl. You all right, my love?'

'What? Oh, yes, I'm fine. But, Perkins, I need a spot of information.'

'What sort of information?'

'Oh – let's say, geographical.'

'Oh, really?'

'Really. Mr Perkins, where is Mr Silk having dinner tonight?'

'Now why on earth should I tell you that?'

'Mr Perkins, I need to know.'

'What for? You're not – he's not –'

'No, of course not. I just need to know. Badly.'

'I can't tell you that, Miss FitzPatrick. More than my job's worth.'

'It looks to me as if your job might be on the line anyway, Mr Perkins. If Mr Silk knew you were looking for a new one. No reference, either. Oh dear, oh dear . . .'

'Miss FitzPatrick, what did I ever do to you?'

'Nothing except be very kind to me. Of course I wouldn't tell him.' She paused. 'Unless I had to. Go on, Mr Perkins, please tell me.'

He looked at her. She put on her tragic face, willing misery into her eyes.

'Mr Perkins, let me say this. The reason I want to know has nothing actually to do with Mr Silk. Or Mrs Silk. It's the gentleman they're having dinner with. I just need to see him. I swear I am not going to make a scene, or embarrass the Silks, they won't even know I'm there, probably. They certainly won't know why. But I need to know. It's so important to me, Mr Perkins, desperately important.'

'Well . . .' He hesitated. 'No. No, I can't.'

She reached forward, tweaked the paper off his knee. 'Mr Perkins. Come on. You don't even like Nigel Silk.'

'Well – you're trouble, you are, Miss FitzPatrick. All right. Four Seasons. Eight o'clock.'

'Mr Perkins, I love you. Here's your paper back.'

'Reuben, don't argue. You don't have to pay even for a glass of water. Just be there, OK? In a suit. I know you have one. See you there. Eight thirty. All right? Table in your name.'

She spent two hours getting ready. She showered, she washed her hair, she shaved her legs; she drenched herself in Joy, she got out every single dress she possessed (all three) and tried each on, finally settling on a black crepe shift, slit up the side, a Norell copy she had blued over half a week's salary on, telling herself it would be worth it. 'And it was,' she said aloud, through teeth that were chattering slightly with nerves. She did her hair, scooping it up in a pony-tail, with her new fake fall tumbling down her back and great dark kiss curls on either cheek. She made up her face, palely dramatic, her eyes elaborately shadowed, with false lashes top and bottom; she clipped great shimmering dangling Paco Rabanne-style earrings on, with twin bracelets to match; and then she put on her coat, a rainbow-dyed fun fur, gave herself a last spray of Joy, put her money (all she had had left in her bank account) in a small beaded bag she had bought in the flea market and went out to catch a cab and capture her prey.

She arrived at the restaurant at eight twenty; perfect time, they would be settled, at the table, Reuben would not be there. She paid off the cab, took six deep breaths and walked into the restaurant, the rainbow fur over her arm. She stood there in the entrance, looking round the room: and at first it was all a blur, a fast-beating, heart-thudding blur, she would have recognized nobody there, nobody at all: and then through the noise, the hum, the careful, ordered dance of the waiters, moving around from table to table, the maître d' gliding round the room, through the chatter, the interested glances of the women at her, the admiring, intrigued looks of the men, she saw them, saw the Silks, Nigel leaning back in his chair, gracefully attentive to the woman next to him, and next to her, a man she did not know, and next to him, Serena Silk, exquisite blonde hair dressed high, set with pearl drops, shimmering bead-encrusted dress, small perfect chin resting on small elegant hand, pale blue eyes fixed on – fixed on, yes, dear God, on him. On Piers Windsor, who was looking at her, smiling at her, saying something.

As if propelled by a force entirely out of her control, Fleur walked forward, smiling, towards them all, towards the table and said, and was amazed at the calm, the levelness of her voice, 'Nigel! How nice to see you. And Mrs Silk, what a lovely dress. No, no, don't get up,' as Nigel and the other men moved as if to stand for her, and one of them did, he did, Piers Windsor stood up for her, a tall, slender figure.

He looked down at her, smiling at her and said, without moving his eyes from her face, 'Nigel, can we be introduced to this lovely friend of yours?'

Her first thought, her first instinct, was that he was homosexual; it was not so much the looks, not even the slightly intense charm, it was something else, very subtle, a sense of delicacy, of perception, impossible to determine, to define; and then, seeing the expression in his eyes, moving over her face, she was less sure, and Nigel, his face tense with nerves and embarrassment and probably, Fleur thought, rage, said, 'Yes, of course, this is Fleur FitzPatrick, she works for us, and Fleur, this is Piers Windsor, who of course you will have heard of, and this is Henry and Sybil Fletcher, friends of ours, and you've met my wife, have you not, Fleur?'

Fleur said yes, indeed, she had and held out her hand to Serena who touched it unbearably briefly, as if it might burn her, and then to the Fletchers and then turned again to Piers Windsor and said, 'I can't tell you how excited I am to meet you, I've dreamed of it ever since I was quite a little girl.' Then Reuben arrived, looking remarkably civilized and neat in a suit, but didn't see her and was shown to their table which was mercifully quite far from the Silks so she said, 'Oh, there is my boyfriend now, I have to go. So nice to meet you, Mr Windsor, and Mr and Mrs Fletcher, Nigel, Mrs Silk. Good evening, enjoy your dinner.' She backed away gracefully from the table with a final all-encompassing smile and turned and walked towards Reuben, her arms held out, and bent and kissed him on the cheek, aware that the eyes of every man in the restaurant were fixed upon her, but most especially the grey ones of Piers Windsor which had been, ever since he heard her name, dark with shock.

As she sat down, smiling at Reuben, taking the menu, staring at the menu, while quite unable to see it, her mind raced, whirled round the memory of those eyes staring at her, shocked, almost scared eyes, in a face that had turned white, the lips taut and drawn, and she tried and tried to make sense of it and she couldn't even begin. She only knew that she must clearly pursue Piers Windsor, to find out more about him and his reaction to her; and that given only the merest breath of a following wind, it was perfectly within her power to do so.

Nigel Silk was very cold with her in the morning. She had known he would be and she had also known that there would be absolutely nothing he could say to her. She had been in the restaurant with her boyfriend, and it had been the purest chance that he had been there too. She had every right to eat in the Four Seasons, and it would have been discourteous of her not to have spoken to him. And Serena and his guests.

What she wanted to do now was talk to Piers Windsor. Face to face, one to one, woman to man. That would be fun. As well as investigating him, his reaction to her name – and it had been her name, not her, he had reacted to, it meant something to him, that name, it had more than surprised him, it had frightened him. So – was it possible – could he have known her father? Surely, surely not. It was too unlikely, too almost laughably unlikely. And yet – well, there was something there. Something very strange. She had to get to know him, find out for herself. It was too important to leave. As well as that, his sexual proclivities intrigued her. The more she had thought about him as she lay awake through the long night, the more she had felt there was something at the very least ambivalent there. Well, that would be causing Chloe a few little problems. Oh, this was fun. She was enjoying this. She was not hurt, not even angry any more; just high on excitement and triumph and intrigue. She could see the danger of what she was doing and it filled her with pleasure; it was almost sexual in its intensity.

She went down to see Mr Perkins, a bottle of Scotch whisky in her hand – this was expensive this revenge business – and said, 'Tiny present. Thank you for your help. You see I didn't cause any trouble, did I?'

'Not as far as I know,' said Perkins darkly.

'Mr Perkins, after you took Mr Windsor back to the Pierre the other night –'

'Plaza,' said Perkins automatically as she had known he would, and then looked at her sharply. 'What's it to you?'

'Nothing, nothing at all,' said Fleur, smiling at him with particular sweetness.

'May I speak to Mr Windsor please? Mr Piers Windsor? Thank you.'

There was a long silence Then: 'May I ask who's calling, please?'

'This is Fleur FitzPatrick. Mr Silk's friend.'

Another long silence. 'Mr Windsor is out at the moment, Miss FitzPatrick. Can I take a message?'

'Sure. Tell him I called, and say could he call me. At my office, that's 212–765–7657. Oh, and could you just say I just wanted to tell him something, and it won't take a minute.'

Fleur settled back in her chair and waited for her phone to ring. There was no way he wouldn't call. It would look too bad.

Twenty minutes later her phone went. 'Miss FitzPatrick? Piers Windsor here. I got a message to call you.'

'Oh, Mr Windsor, that is so kind of you. Thank you. I just wanted to tell you that – oh, dear, it's a little embarrassing. You don't want to hear it.'

A very long silence. Then: 'Well it's a little hard for me to make a judgement. I might.' The voice was amused, light; he didn't sound awkward or worried. Well, don't forget, Fleur, this is one of the finest actors of his generation.

'It's just that – oh dear. Well, all right. The thing is, Mr Windsor, and this is really naughty of me, but having met you, I kind of thought you'd understand; my aunt has a most terrific crush on you. I mean seriously terrific. She's seen every single one of your films, and she saw you in *Hamlet*, when you did it here, queued for hours and hours. And she isn't very well, and I mean long term not very well, you know? It would mean so much to her if you could sign a photograph for her, with a message. Would that be the most terrible thing to ask?'

She could actually hear the relief, hear it spilling, oozing down the phone. 'Well, of course not, Miss FitzPatrick, it would be a great pleasure. I'll have my secretary put it in the post.'

'Oh – well, that is really kind, but you see she's off tomorrow, into hospital for – well, for some tests. And I'd really like to give it to her, to take in with her. It would make all the difference. So I wondered if I could possibly call by your hotel, and pick it up?'

'Of course. I'll leave it in reception.'

'That is so kind of you. I can't thank you enough. You are very understanding and – and sweet. Er – could it be in the next hour or so?'

'Well . . .' He hesitated, the sweetness and patience easing off slightly, removed, she thought, like greasepaint at the end of a performance. Then, 'Yes, I don't see why not.'

'Thank you. Thank you so much. It'll mean such a lot to her. Will you be there? So I can thank you personally?'

There was a silence. Go on, go on, you bastard, say yes. Give in. What harm would it do? You could get another look at me. See if you think I really might be who you think I might be. Fleur. Brendan's daughter. That's what you're afraid of, isn't it? Isn't it? And anyway, you liked me. Admired me. I know you did. Go on, Piers Windsor, say yes. Say yes, say yes.

'Well – yes. All right. I'll be in the lobby at five. All right? But I'll be very much on the wing.'

'Oh, that's wonderful. Thank you again.'

She was sitting in the lobby when he came down. He looked very slightly – what? Not nervous. Tense, perhaps. But he smiled as he came towards her, holding an envelope. She stood up, and held out her hand.

'This is so kind of you.'

'Miss FitzPatrick. How nice to see you again. Now I could only find this picture, and it's a little old, or perhaps I should say a little young, but I don't travel with a huge store of them, I'm afraid.' He smiled a rueful, slightly bashful smile. 'Anyway, it occurred to me that I don't know your aunt's name, and it would make it nicer for her if I could put that in.'

'Oh, how thoughtful,' said Fleur. 'It's Edna.'

'Right.'

He sat down, and she sat down again beside him; she had worn her shortest skirt, and she could feel his eyes on her legs. He certainly liked them. But then homos often liked her. She got on with them, she had the kind of body, of psyche they appreciated, felt at ease with. And she was at ease with them. Oh well, what the hell. It really didn't matter. Except that Chloe must be even more of a fool than she had thought. She intercepted his gaze, smiled at him; slightly confused, responding to the signal, he smiled back.

'Right then. To Edna. With very best wishes for a speedy recovery, Piers Windsor. How's that?'

'It's wonderful. You must have to sign so many hundreds, it must be so boring.'

'Well,' he said, 'not so much these days. But in any case it certainly isn't boring. It's so delightful that people are interested, like one that much. And that one can give them pleasure.'

Shall I throw up here, wondered Fleur, or should I try and hold it? 'Well, even still. It's very kind. May I buy you a drink or something, to say thank you?'

'Oh dear,' he said, 'you are obviously one of these liberated women. The kind I can't really handle.' He was obviously relaxing; feeling that whatever it was that had frightened him she knew nothing about.

She felt his eyes on her again, moved her legs, so that there was just slightly more thigh, looked at him very levelly and smiled. 'I'm sure you can. We're really nothing to be afraid of, you know. We're no different from the other sort, except that we say and do what seems right at the time. Anyway, this is nonsense, you must meet hundreds of extremely liberated women in your business. And what about your wife, she's young, isn't she? I'm sure she's not an old-fashioned girl.' God, this was unreal: talking to Piers about his wife. Her sister. She felt scared suddenly; she mustn't let this get out of hand.

'Oh, but she is. A really old-fashioned girl. That's why I married her.'

'Well – that must be very nice for you.' She bit her lip. 'You won't tell Nigel, will you? That I've done this? He'd probably fire me.'

'Surely not. He seems charming. What do you do for him? Are you his Girl Friday or something?'

Shit, he was a nightmare. What on God's earth was Chloe doing with him? She must be a thousand times worse than she had even imagined. And a thousand times more stupid.

'I am not,' she said and she couldn't keep the indignation out of her voice. 'I'm a copywriter.'

'Oh, I'm sorry. Now I've really put my foot in it. Look – maybe I'd better buy you a drink. Just to make amends.' His confidence was growing; she could feel it. The fear had almost gone. He thought he was safe, and now he just wanted to have a flirtation with her. Creep. What a creep. With a wife and two tiny children.

'Oh, but –'

'Come on.' He stood up, smiling down at her. 'And I promise to try not to say anything more unfortunate.'

'Well – all right. Thank you. Thank you very much.'

She had done it. She was on her way.

Chapter 20

1968

Chloe was driving up from Stebbings early in the morning when she heard the news: the terrible, almost unbelievable news, causing her to slam on the brakes and pull into the side of the road and sit there, shaking, tearful, almost frightened. She had been engaged upon the weighty problem of whether she should ask Ludovic Ingram to be godfather to her new son, Edmund (named after the actor): Piers was very set upon that course, but Chloe felt Ludovic would see the invitation as an incitement to pursue still more ardently what could only be described as his courtship of her, when the music she was enjoying suddenly ceased. '. . . bring you a news bulletin,' said the male voice, shaken itself. 'Senator Robert Kennedy, brother of the late President, remains in a condition described by doctors as extremely critical as to life. Senator Kennedy, who was gunned down in the corridor of the Ambassador Hotel in Los Angeles last night, has undergone three hours of neural surgery at the Good Samaritan Hospital, Los Angeles. He had just arrived to make his victory speech after defeating Senator McCarthy in the Californian Democratic primary elections. Mrs Ethel Kennedy is at the hospital and –'

Chloe switched off the radio: Piers was in Los Angeles. Somehow it made the news more sickening, more shocking. Not because she felt he was in any danger, but because it personalized the news, brought it nearer to home. What a violent, frightening country America was: only two months since Martin Luther King had been shot, five years since Jack Kennedy. It was horrible, obscene: the world was going mad.

She sat there for a while, pulling herself together, and then drove slowly on to London and sat staring at the television, watching the scene run and rerun, watching Bobby, the white hope of the Kennedys, cut down, lost to the world he had seemed genuinely to want to change, lying in a pool of blood, a rosary pushed into his hands, on the floor of the Ambassador Hotel. When at lunch-time the announcement came that the Senator had died, she wept as bitterly as if it had been her own family; wept for Ethel and all the Kennedy children; for Jackie, forced to relive the nightmare of Jack Kennedy's death; for Rose, called upon to bear the murder of two sons, wondering even as she did so why she felt it so keenly.

She decided she must speak to Piers; somehow she thought he might make her feel better about it. Very unlikely really, of course: he didn't make her feel better about much. Increasingly, it seemed to Chloe that she was the source of strength in their relationship, she who must provide stability, normality in an increasingly quixotic life. Piers could bring her his distress, anxiety, self-doubt; she must not trouble him with hers. But she was worried, worried that he was there, in the centre of this awful storm; she needed to speak to him: there might be rioting or something, there had been so much lately. She dialled the operator and gave her the number of the Beverly Hills Hotel.

'Mr Windsor, please,' she said when she was put through, 'Mr Piers Windsor.'

'I'm sorry, ma'am, Mr Windsor is no longer here. He checked out twenty-four hours ago.'

'Checked out?' said Chloe stupidly. 'He can't have done. Are you sure?'

'I'll just double-check that for you,' said the girl. She returned to the phone after a minute or two, sounding irritatingly cheerful, almost smug. 'I'm sorry, ma'am. He's gone.'

'Well, do you have an address? Or a number, where he's gone?'

'No, ma'am, I'm sorry. May I have a name should he return, ma'am?'

'No. No, it's all right – I'll leave it.' She wasn't going to afford her the pleasure of thinking she was a duped wife. 'Thank you.'

'Very well, ma'am. Have a nice day.'

Now what? Now where was he, where had the bastard gone? How could he do this to her, tell her he was somewhere and then just go, move out? Suppose there was some kind of an emergency, then what would she do? Then she started to wonder why he might have done such a thing, who he was with. 'Shit, Piers,' she said, staring at the phone, tears of frustration and misery welling in her eyes, 'where are you, what are you doing?'

The phone rang suddenly; she snatched it up. It must be him: the hotel had obviously made a mistake. She must tell him to give them a ticking off.

'Piers? Piers, I . . .'

'Sorry, Chloe, not Piers.' It was Magnus Phillips's voice. 'What's the matter, you sound upset?'

'Oh,' she said, dashing the tears out of her eyes, trying to make her voice level, 'oh, not, not at all. Not really. Hallo, Magnus.'

'Yes, you are. What's the matter?'

'Oh – well –' She knew this was foolish, began to regret it the minute she started to speak, but she had to tell someone. 'It's just that Piers has – well he's not where I thought he was.'

'Which was?' The deep, slightly rough voice sounded kind, even if mildly amused.

'At – at the Beverly Hills Hotel.'

'Well, I expect he's out at some important meeting with some Hollywood moguls,' said Magnus soothingly.

God, thought Chloe, he must think I'm totally witless. 'No, he isn't. Well he might be but that's not the point. He's checked out and he didn't tell me. Didn't leave a message or anything. Of course I wouldn't worry normally,' she said quickly. 'I mean he's always dashing around all over the place, it's just that with this Kennedy business I wanted to speak to him. Make sure he was all right, you know?'

'Chloe, I'm sure he's fine,' said Magnus. 'I don't suppose he was anywhere near the Ambassador Hotel at the time, and if he was –'

'No, of course not,' said Chloe, 'I just thought there might be riots or something, you know?' She was horribly aware that she sounded increasingly silly: exactly the sort of person all Piers's friends thought she was. She would have given anything not to have started this conversation.

'There aren't any riots,' said Magnus firmly, 'but if you like I'll confirm that with the news desk and ring you back. Would you like me to try and track the old bugger down? We hacks have ways and means of doing these things.'

'Oh, no,' said Chloe, horrified at the thought of Piers's reaction should Magnus be successful in his tracking down. 'Of course not. You've been very kind, Magnus. Really. Thank you. I'm sorry to have been such a nuisance.'

'You're not,' he said, his voice unusually gentle, and rang off; two minutes later he rang back. 'No riots,' he said. 'LA reported totally calm and peaceful. A lovely day. I expect he's taken off to the beach.'

'I expect so,' said Chloe miserably. 'You won't mention this to him, will you, Magnus? That I told you I was worried and everything? He tends to be a bit mysterious, it's just one of his little ways.'

'Of course not,' said Magnus. 'Your secret is safe with me.'

She often thought of that remark in the years that followed.

Next morning Piers rang.

'Hallo, darling. Everything all right?'

'No,' said Chloe, 'not really. I've been frantic with worry, Piers. Where have you been?'

'What do you mean? You know where I've been.'

'I don't actually. I rang you yesterday, at the Beverly Hills, and they said you'd checked out. Where were you, for heaven's sake? And why couldn't you have told me? I get so sick of you doing this sort of thing, Piers. Suppose there'd been a crisis. I was worried to death about you being there, when Kennedy had been shot; it's so unfair, you know how much I –'

'Oh, for God's sake,' he said, 'how many more times do we have to go through all this? I've told you a dozen times, Chloe, I am not some suburban husband, on call every hour of the day. I went over to Herb Leverson's place, we were working on this deal, putting this production finally together, it got late, I stayed over, I'm still here. Now are you satisfied? I really have to have freedom to move, Chloe. I can't tell people like him that I have to get back to my hotel in case you're looking for me.'

'You could have rung me. Or left a message.'

'I tried to. All the lines out of town were jammed. I don't suppose you thought of that. Anyway, I'm going to stay in LA a couple more days. We're thrashing this thing out slowly and it's a painful process. I don't want you ringing me here, things are at a delicate stage, but I'll call you again tonight, if you want me to. Otherwise I'll be back at the Beverly Hills tomorrow.'

'Fine,' she said. 'Don't bother ringing, Piers. I really don't want to talk to you.'

She put the phone down. Bastard. Bastard. She was too angry even to feel hurt. Later she felt remorseful: it was all true, he did need to have time and space to work, he couldn't be expected to check home all the time, it was terribly unreasonable of her to behave as she did. Now they'd be off on the wrong foot when he did get home. And she'd made a fool of herself with Magnus Phillips. Oh, God.

Early that evening Joe turned up on her doorstep, a bunch of rather wilting flowers in his hand. 'I wondered if you'd like to come out and have supper with me. As you're all alone.'

'Oh – Joe, you're so kind. I don't think I want to go out, though. I'm awfully tired. Ned's got a cold and never stops crying. Stay and we'll eat something here.'

'Fine. Anything'll do.'

She made him an omelette and a tomato salad; they consumed nearly a bottle of white wine, and she began to feel better, told Joe how silly she had been about Piers.

'It doesn't sound too silly to me. He ought to tell you where he is.'

'I know. But I'm sure it's difficult sometimes. And I was upset anyway. About Kennedy. It's so terribly sad. That family seems to be doomed. I feel so sorry for Ethel, all those children. Just as well Piers isn't here, really, I've been crying about it, it always makes him cross when I cry.'

'Oh really?' said Joe, in the cool voice he always adopted when she said anything about Piers he didn't quite approve of. 'Why should he be cross because you cry?'

'Oh, I expect it's awfully irritating. You know how emotional I am.'

'Not really,' said Joe, 'you always seem very steady to me.'

'Well, maybe you don't see as much of me as he does.'

'Unfortunately. Well, never mind. When's he back?'

'Oh, in a couple of days, I think.'

'He likes it over there, doesn't he? Always going there.'

'Yes. Well, he has lots of friends there. He and it go back a long way, I suppose. I expect it seems like a second home to him.'

'Maybe. Is it really such a long way? Back I mean?' His voice was very casual, almost disinterested.

'Much further than we're all supposed to know,' said Chloe and her voice was amused, almost indulgent suddenly. 'He really is such a baby, Joe. You've no idea.'

'In what way?'

'Oh, you know, he's so – well, so over-sensitive. Can't bear criticism. Oh, it's naughty of me to be running him down when he's not here.'

'Darling, you're not running him down. Seems to me you pander rather to his little vanities. I call that sweet.'

'Well, I don't know. Not really.'

'So what's all this about us not knowing about him being in LA.'

'Now you are not to mention this, Joe, his mother told me, and I promised her I never would, but I know I can trust you. Well, he went to Hollywood for a bit, years before he was such a hit. And he's always kept quiet about it, denies it even, because he was a total failure, never even got a screen test. Isn't that sad? And sweet really, that he should be so insecure.'

'Very sweet,' said Joe. 'Darling, let's finish that bottle, and then have you got any red? I suddenly feel like a full-blooded drink.'

Now that was – interesting. Joe fought to keep it as only interesting. Nothing more. Interesting that a man so successful, so gifted, should be ashamed of an early unsuccessful foray to Hollywood. Interesting that he should be so ashamed he denied being there. Interesting that Naomi MacNeice, who had been so intricately involved with Byron Patrick's downfall, should have mentioned an Englishman and a film of Piers's in her ramblings about that downfall. Only interesting.

Piers returned from Hollywood high on the triumph of having actually interested a Hollywood producer in a film of *A Midsummer Night's Dream* he had long wanted to do. He seemed totally uninterested in Bobby Kennedy's death, in Chloe's sorrow over it, but at least he had forgiven her for making a fuss about disappearing: in fact he seemed particularly delighted to see her, and brought her a huge bunch of red roses and a bag from the Beverly Hills Chanel shop. 'You must come next time I go to LA, darling, you'd love it.'

'I expect I would,' said Chloe, too relieved that he had forgiven her to point out that he had always discouraged her from doing anything of the sort.

Ned was to be christened in the small church near Stebbings. Piers, high on his successful deal with Herb Leverson and the fulfilment of his ambition to film *A Midsummer Night's Dream*, was using it as an excuse for a party.

'You will come, won't you, Joe? You and Mummy?' Chloe's voice on the phone was anxious. 'I'm going to need you. Badly.'

'Of course we'll come. Try and keep us away,' said Joe, his heart sinking at the thought of yet another of Piers's theatrical bashes.

Chloe had asked Jolyon to be Ned's godfather. 'I know it's funny, when I hated him so much all the time I was growing up, but he's really sweet now, and he loves both the little ones.'

'And who are the others?'

Chloe's voice darkened slightly. 'Well – the godmother is Maria Woolf. She's backing Piers's new venture.'

'What, the film? I thought he had Somebody B. de Somebody from Hollywood doing that?' said Joe.

'Yes, he does. This is different, a modern play, by someone frightfully grand, the new John Osborne, everyone keeps calling him.'

'Oh,' said Joe, 'not Nick Grimond?'

'Yes, that's right. Is he good?'

'He's not bad,' said Joe. 'His first play won all kinds of awards last year.'

'Yes, and so will this one, Piers says. It's about politics.'

'Sounds thrilling.'

'Joe, don't be naughty. Anyway, Maria is backing that. And Piers wants to thank her. Quite rightly.'

'Quite rightly.'

'Any other godfathers?'

'Well, you see, I thought Damian would be good. But Piers seems to have gone off him, I don't know why. We haven't seen him for months. It's so odd, when he used practically to live here. So it's someone else quite surprising really, Magnus Phillips. Not really very godfatherly, I wouldn't have thought, would you, but Piers is very keen. He thinks Magnus is wonderful. Well, he is of course, he was very kind to me when – well anyway, I do like him.'

'Is he still doing this book about Piers?' said Joe.

'No. Piers has taken fright now at the idea. He read that one about the politician and backed off.'

'Quite right,' said Joe.

'He even wrote to Flavia, Magnus I mean, wanted to talk to her. I think that was what put Piers off. I was very relieved, to tell you the truth. But like I said, I do like Magnus. And I think he's very sexy.'

'So does your mother,' said Joe. He was quite sorry Magnus Phillips would no longer be writing a book about Piers. It would have been a lot of fun to read. He might even have offered the odd anecdote himself.

The day of the christening was beautiful: warm and cloudless. Joe and Caroline arrived with Jolyon at midday; there was a marquee on the lawn of Stebbings, tables set with champagne and glasses under the great chestnut tree, and a man dressed in white tie and white tails sat at a white piano playing music from popular classics, *West Side Story*, *Hair* and (inevitably) *The Lady of Shalott*. Piers was standing on the steps of the house, greeting his guests; he was smiling, at ease, smoothly happy. He was wearing white trousers with a pink shirt and white loafers; he was very tanned, and his hair was indisputably lighter, streaked with gold highlights. He held out his hand to Joe, put his arm round his shoulders at the same time. 'Hallo, Father-in-Law,' he said. 'Great to see you.'

Joe particularly hated this joke. 'Morning, Piers,' he said briefly.

'And Grandmother! You look so wonderful, Caroline, impossibly glamorous and young. What a lovely dress. Jolyon, good to see you. Remind me to have a chat with you later about that job. Maria, my darling, how glorious you look, and Jack, dear boy, welcome. Do all go through and help yourself to a drink, find Chloe. Have to stay here, doing my hostly duty.'

'What job?' said Joe suspiciously to Jolyon.

'Oh – he might be able to get me a job in some theatrical agency,' said Jolyon. 'Just for a couple of weeks, at the end of the summer. Before I go to college,' he added hastily.

'How too kind,' said Caroline sweetly. 'He might have talked to me about it, I think.'

'Oh, Mum, don't get heavy,' said Jolyon. 'It's really kind of him.'

'Yeah, sure,' said Joe. He felt a dreadful unease suddenly and he couldn't think why: it was kind of Piers, very kind, to get a callow eighteen-year-old boy a job for the summer, in a place where he might very well be a nuisance. He would just have preferred Piers to talk to Caroline first.

'Oh, there's Chloe,' said Jolyon, patently eager to distract them. 'Chloe! Over here!'

Chloe, stunningly pretty in a floating pink lawn dress, and a huge-brimmed straw hat with pink streamers tangled with real pink roses in it, was patently nervous, and immensely relieved to see them. 'Mummy, you look lovely. Hallo, Joe.'

'Don't I look lovely?' said Joe plaintively.

'No, you don't,' said Caroline. 'I'm sorry about the shirt, Chloe, he spilt coffee down it when we stopped on the way, and of course had nothing to change into. I'm so embarrassed.'

'It doesn't matter,' said Chloe, 'and anyway, they're all so style-conscious here, they'll probably think it's a new thing, having a brown stain right across a white shirt.'

'Hey,' said Jolyon, 'hey, Chloe, you're getting quite witty in your old age.'

'Thank you,' said Chloe, smiling a sweetly barbed smile. 'Love you too. That really is a great dress, Mummy.'

'Thank you,' said Caroline graciously. 'It's Ossie Clark.'

Joe looked at her in surprise. He never really noticed what she looked like any more.

The dress was nice: very floaty, in a kind of blue and green, with flowers printed into it. He resolved to look at her more carefully in future.

'Magnus!' said Chloe. 'How nice! Come and talk to us.'

Magnus smiled at them all, kissed Chloe's hand and then fixed his attention on Caroline.

'Mother of the bride,' he said. 'You look more like her sister than ever.'

'Shall I kick him or will you?' said Chloe, laughing.

'Neither of us,' said Caroline. 'I always like that one.' Her lips smiled, but her eyes, held by Magnus Phillips's dark ones, were solemn.

Joe felt a sudden rush of fear, then stifled it. The guy was a shyster. And vulgar with it. Not Caroline's type at all.

'Oh boy,' said Jolyon, breaking into a slightly awkward silence. 'Now who is that? Boy, what a pair of legs.' The legs belonged to a girl of extraordinary height and slenderness, with a great tangling cloud of dark hair and huge dark eyes.

'Oh,' said Chloe quickly, lowering her voice, 'that's Annunciata. Annunciata Fallon. Actress. Or rather would-be actress. Desperately wanted to be the Lady. Beware, Jolyon, she eats big boys for breakfast.'

'I'm game,' said Jolyon. 'Can you introduce me?' He stood, his eyes huge with awe, gazing at Annunciata who was wearing a white satin shirt, slashed almost to the waist, and white satin shorts.

'All right. But you've been warned.'

'Such suitable attire for a christening,' murmured Caroline.

Chloe called Annunciata over. 'Annunciata, can I introduce my mother, Caroline Hunterton, and my almost-stepfather, Joe Payton. And this is my brother, Jolyon. And of course you know Magnus Phillips, don't you?'

Annunciata looked at them all very coolly, and nodded almost imperceptibly. 'How do you do?' she said, an expression of acute boredom on her delicate disdainful features. There was a long silence.

'Er – have you known Piers long?' said Jolyon rather helplessly.

'Oh yes. Ages. Well. You know.'

'Annunciata is an actress,' said Chloe quickly. 'She may be in the new play.'

'How exciting,' said Caroline, almost as cool.

'Well, you know,' said Annunciata again, more distant still.

'This is a great house, isn't it?' said Jolyon. 'Lovely part of the world. Do you live near here, Miss Fallon?'

'No, of course not,' she said, as if he had suggested something entirely ludicrous. 'I live in London.'

'I wish I did,' said Jolyon. 'Whereabouts?'

'South-West Three,' said Annunciata. 'Do excuse me. Magnus, darling, do tell me all about your book. It sounds so exciting. Politics are so sexy.' She tucked her arm into his and drew him away.

'I did warn you,' said Chloe, smiling gently at Jolyon's scarlet face.

'Oh, no, she's gorgeous,' he said. 'Gorgeous.'

'Hmm,' said Joe.

'Chloe, my darling, at last! I've been looking for you everywhere. My God, you look beautiful. Couldn't we run away together straight away, forget this tedious christening?'

'Maybe later,' said Chloe, laughing. 'Joe, Mummy, this is Ludovic Ingram. He's – well he's – what are you, Ludo?'

'Well, I'm in love with your daughter,' said Ludovic to Caroline, 'I keep trying to persuade her to leave Piers and run away with me, but she won't. I work on it as a project tirelessly. And in my spare time I'm a barrister.'

Joe looked at him, at this wonderfully good-looking, charming, and yet patently nice man, and thought how much better for Chloe it would be if she did run away with him. Then he set the thought determinedly, if regretfully, aside as impracticable. It was nice at least that Chloe had a friend in this circle.

A little later he saw Magnus standing alone, glass in hand, studying a group of people with an expression of intense amusement; Piers was at its centre.

'Working?' asked Joe with a slightly grim smile.

'Of course,' said Magnus, returning it. 'Fascinating, this lot, aren't they?'

'Yup.' Joe looked at him, his green eyes very thoughtful. 'I understand from Chloe,' he said, 'that you're dropping the biography of Piers.'

'I think so, yes,' said Magnus, his face suddenly blank. 'He seems a little too bland for my attentions. Unfortunately. I do like a degree of dirt to work with. As you know. So unless I happen upon some fascinating scandal in Mr Windsor's past, or present of course, which seems so unlikely as to be laughable, I am turning my attentions elsewhere. I have a fancy for Miss Taylor at the moment. Or Mrs Onassis.'

'Don't we all,' said Joe. 'And besides, you could hardly expose a scandal in the life of a man whose son you were godfather to.'

'Hardly,' said Magnus, grinning at him broadly.

For the first time in his life, Joe felt a flash of something approaching sympathy for Piers.

He and Caroline found themselves sitting at a table at lunch-time with Jolyon and seven people they didn't know. Chloe was rushing about looking distracted, trying to settle people who had loaded their plates and couldn't find anywhere to sit, and Piers was lounging at a particularly noisy table near the door, laughing and refilling everyone's glasses with champagne.

'No sign of the guest of honour,' murmured Caroline.

'Who's that?' said Joe.

'Ned. You know? The one whose party this is.'

Joe smiled at her, leant forward and kissed her suddenly on the nose. 'Sometimes,' he said, 'I realize exactly why I love you.'

But she wasn't looking at him; following her gaze, he saw she was staring at Marcus Phillips.

He turned slightly to his left: a rather intense middle-aged man was shovelling food into his mouth, and talking at the same time. It was a very unattractive sight. Beyond him sat a woman in her thirties, very beautiful, heavily made up; she caught his eye, and smiled at him slightly. 'Felicia Strang,' she said.

'Joe Payton,' said Joe. 'This is Caroline Hunterton.'

'And how do you know Piers?' she said, immensely gracious.

'I'm his wife's mother,' said Caroline, more gracious still.

'Oh,' she said, a little vaguely, 'oh yes. Such a pretty girl. You must be very proud.'

'Of what?' said Joe.

'Well, of her marrying Piers. How marvellous for her.'

'We think it's quite marvellous for him actually,' said Joe. 'Could you pass the butter?'

The man with the food had finished eating, and was shouting across Joe and Caroline at a younger man who was wearing a white suit and a panama hat.

'I hear you're going to Edinburgh,' he said. 'Marvellous.'

'I hope so,' said the Panama Hat. 'It's always a bit of a lottery.'

'Oh, I don't know,' said Joe, determinedly. 'Pretty reliable, Edinburgh. The castle and everything. Nice hotels.'

They ignored him. 'What are you going to do?' said the Food.

'Oh, a marvellous one-act play, by this girl everyone's talking about, Sacha Simons,' said the Panama Hat. 'It's – well, I don't know how to describe it really. It's a comi-tragedy. As opposed to a tragi-comedy. Do you know what I mean? The balance is just slightly different.'

'Fascinating,' said the Food.

'Are you going?'

'No. I'm desperately disappointed, but we go into rehearsal at Chichester on September first. Anouilh season. I bumped into Harold Hobson the other night at a party, and he's promised to come.'

'Wonderful. I adore Anouilh. Such a voice still. I don't know if you saw the production I was in of *The Man Who Came to Dinner* – oh, two years ago. The scope of that play is truly amazing. I could never get tired of it. I was talking to Johnny Mills about it the other night, he'd seen it and he said he thought it would make the most marvellous film.'

'Oh really? I wonder if . . .'

Joe ceased to find the conversation even amusing; he tuned in to two girls opposite him who were talking across Jolyon about where they were getting their Ascot clothes: 'Two of my chums have dared each other to wear dresses from Biba,' said one of them. 'With really super hats of course.'

'Oh what fun,' said the other. 'Do you really think they will?'

Jolyon looked frantic with embarrassment and boredom. Joe winked at him, saw Annunciata heading in their direction and hissed at him, 'Do you want to see some action?'

Jolyon looked puzzled; Joe leant right back in his chair, reached out his arm, touched Annunciata on the hand. She looked at him very coolly, half smiled and said, 'Hi,' with such acute disinterest it took even Joe's breath away.

'I just wondered if you could spare me half a minute,' said Joe.

'Well, I'd love to,' she said, 'but I really have to tell Piers something. I could try and come back.'

'It won't take a moment,' said Joe. 'Honestly. It's just that I'm a journalist, work for the *Sunday Times*, and I'm doing a series on young English actresses. If you were at all interested, you could give me a ring. Here's my card.'

Annunciata looked at him, and her face softened, sweetened. 'Why, how frightfully nice of you,' she said. 'I'd love that. Really love it. Goodness, I can't think why you should want to include me. Although I can tell you I'm almost certainly going to play Portia at Stratford next season. I don't know if that's the sort of thing that would interest you? Um – Fergie, budge up, you old bore, let me share your chair.' She sat down, one buttock on the Food's knee, pushed back her mane of hair, fixed her large dark eyes on

Joe's face. 'How interesting your job must be, I'd adore to do something like that.'

'Well, it has its moments,' said Joe. 'You must excuse me, I have to see someone over there.'

He turned to Caroline, but she was gone; looking, slightly irritably, for her, annoyed that she had missed his performance with Annunciata, he saw her on the other side of the marquee, talking just a little too intently to Magnus Phillips.

Ned was very good at the christening; he submitted to the vicar's ministrations in the small church, didn't cry, and even managed a toothless smile at his mother when she took him back from his godmother.

'What a treasure,' said Maria Woolf, smiling at him slightly nervously. 'Doesn't he look exactly like Piers? I hope I shall fulfil my duties well. I'm afraid I'm rather hedonistic to be a godmother.'

'All the better!' said Piers, raising her hand to his lips and kissing it. 'You can initiate the boy into all kinds of pleasures in the fullness of time. And how lucky he will be.'

'Oh, Piers, really! Now look, can we have a tiny chat about this new play? And then Jack and I must take our leave, we have guests for Sunday sups. Oh dear, that baby's dribbled on my sleeve. Chloe, dear, could you go and find a cloth or something?'

When finally all the guests had gone, Joe and Caroline, with Jolyon, sat down in the kitchen with Chloe. The nanny had whisked away the baby and Pandora, who was overtired and fractious, had just been extremely sick all down her white frilled dress. Piers was nowhere to be seen. 'He's talking business to someone, I expect,' said Chloe vaguely. 'It was lovely to see you all. Jolyon, you did wonderfully well. And Annunciata specially told me how good looking she thought you were.'

'Gosh,' said Jolyon, blushing scarlet again.

'Well, well, well,' said Joe. 'I liked your admirer, Chloe. Mr Ingram. Very nice. We talked some more over christening cake.'

'I like him too,' said Chloe.

Piers appeared, flushed, excited. 'What a marvellous day, and how wonderful you were here to share it.'

'Well, Piers, they are family,' said Chloe. 'Of course they'd share it.'

She spoke sweetly, but there was a slight edge to her voice. Good, thought Joe, she's learning, learning at last.

'Marvellous,' said Piers again, 'and darling, Maria is definitely going to put money into *The Kingdom*. What a girl she is. And what a hat that was. I was terrified it would fall into the font.'

'It was bigger than the font,' said Caroline, with a frosty smile.

'Yes, it was, wasn't it? Now then, have you enjoyed yourselves? I do hope so. I saw you talking to Fergie, he's the most marvellous amusing man, and the most brilliant character actor of his generation. Not my words, I hasten to add: George Devine's. He was here, did you meet him? He founded the Royal Court, you know. Now Joe, he would make a marvellous subject for you. I could fix it any time.'

'Thanks, but I could probably manage on my own,' said Joe. 'Er – Piers, I wonder if we could have a word?'

'Of course,' said Piers. 'As a matter of fact, I wondered if you might write a piece about this film project I'm planning. The musical version of the *Dream*, you know, with Tabitha as Titania; wouldn't that make a terrific story?'

'Probably, yes,' said Joe. 'Let's talk about that too.'

'Fine. We can stroll down to the yard. I can show you my other new baby. A colt.'

'I'm not very fond of horses,' said Joe. 'As long as he's tied up.'

'Oh, good Lord, yes, he's in a stall,' said Piers. 'Will you be all right, Chloe darling, for a few minutes?'

'Oh, I think so,' said Chloe.

Piers led him out of the house and down a long, hedged path towards the stables.

'No anxieties, I hope?' he said. 'Chloe is marvellous, such a wonderful little mother.'

'No, no, not at all,' said Joe. 'She looks very well.'

'Now, this piece about the *Dream*,' said Piers.

'Love to do it,' said Joe, truthfully, 'when it's in production. I'm sure the *Sunday Times* would be very interested. No, it was Jolyon I wanted to talk to you about.'

'Jolyon? Oh, yes, very stage-struck he is. Well, I would be delighted to help, in any way. He's a sweet boy. Wonderful manners.'

'Yes. And of course he'd probably love to work in your agent's office. If you can really fix that. That was a nice surprise. To Caroline as well.'

'Well, of course. He'll be nothing much, just a messenger really. But it'll give him a feel for the business.'

'The only thing is, it's a long commute for him,' said Joe, 'and I don't really think I want the responsibility of him living with me, in my place in Primrose Hill. I'm out such a lot, and he's very young.'

'Oh, that's absolutely no problem!' said Piers. 'He can stay with me in the London house. I'm there all the time at the moment. Of course Chloe's down here, but I'm in every night practically, learning lines and working on the *Dream*. I'll take very good care of him, I promise.'

'How kind,' said Joe. 'Well, look, I hadn't quite expected that. I'll have to talk to Caroline.'

'Yes, of course. Well, was that it?'

'Oh yes, it was really. Is that the horse?'

'It is. Isn't he beautiful? Such a wonderful rich, dark bay. His name is Dream Street. Damon Runyon, you know?'

'Yes, I know,' said Joe.

'Fantastic breeding. He's going to be superb. I plan to race him for a few years, on the flat, and then retire him to stud.'

'He looks very excitable,' said Joe, looking with alarm at the animal's rolling eyes and flaring nostrils. 'Will he quieten down?'

'I hope so. I certainly don't want to have to geld him. I see him as a very long-term investment. I've put a lot of money into him.'

'Well, as long as Chloe doesn't try and ride him,' said Joe.

'Chloe! My dear chap, I wouldn't get near this fellow myself. Strictly for the professionals. Shall we get back to the house?'

'Sure,' said Joe easily. He looked at Piers, smiling at him in his silky, just-off-patronizing way, and thought how much he disliked him; and catching himself almost unawares, he said, 'I understand you were in Hollywood, Piers, in your youth. I wish I'd known before, you might even have been able to help me with the research for my book.' He half expected still to do no more than embarrass him; he was totally and deliciously unprepared for the effect it had on Piers. He turned not just pale, but a ghostly greenish colour, and then a dark flush spread up from his neck to his face; his pale grey eyes leapt with – what? Joe wondered. Fear? Rage? Shock? It was certainly a great deal more than embarrassment.

He stood there, staring at Joe, and Joe stared back and recognized his terror; then he leant quite casually against the wall, and looked down at the linen suit he had changed into for the christening, picking an imaginary piece of fluff off it, and when he looked at Joe again, his face was normal, his eyes amused, his voice light and confident.

'Good Lord,' he said, 'who on earth told you that?'

'Oh,' said Joe, relieved for the first time that Yolande was safely with the angels (as she surely must be, he thought), 'a wonderful lady, who did help me with my book, called Yolande duGrath. A drama coach at Theatrical. You don't remember her?'

'Sadly not. I wish I did. What a name though, Yolande duGrath. She should have been an actress, herself.'

'She was, in her youth.'

Piers looked at him, and Joe could read behind the bland open gaze, the rueful smile, knew what he had decided: that this one was too dodgy to deny, better gone along with, defused that way.

'Well, Joe, I'm afraid you've found out my guilty secret. Not even Chloe knows. I like to play that one down. Stupid, but I really am not proud of my time there. It was only very short. Less than a year. I did some dreadful things, dreadful. A couple of frightful costume dramas, even played a dancing pirate in a musical about a mutiny ship.'

'I'd certainly like to see that one,' said Joe. 'So – when exactly were you there?'

'Oh – mid fifties.'

'Really? Then that was exactly the time I was researching. Did you read my book?'

'What book was that, Joe?'

'Oh, it was called *Scandals*,' said Joe. He was watching him very intently.

'No,' said Piers, and his gaze meeting Joe's was open, almost amused. 'No, I've never even heard of it. Did it do terribly well?'

'Not terribly,' said Joe.

'Well, that must have been so disappointing for you. But I'd certainly love to see it. Do you have a copy, Joe? That you could lend me?'

'No,' said Joe, 'I don't. Only one left I gave to my dear old mum. Chloe was asking for it too, she said she wanted to read it, now she's in the business so to speak.'

A flicker of alarm was in the grey eyes and then gone again. 'Hardly in the business, poor darling. She still finds it all rather hard to cope with, I'm afraid. But she'll get used to it I'm sure.'

'Yes,' said Joe, 'I'm sure she will. With you to help her. Anyway, one of the scandals I was researching at that particular time was concerned with a young man called Byron Patrick, who was quite a rising star, but got mixed up in something very unsavoury. You never met him?'

'No,' said Piers, after the briefest pause, and it seemed to Joe he spoke with particular and enormous care. 'No, I never met him. Never heard of him, I'm afraid. What a wonderfully typical Hollywood name. Byron Patrick. Good God. What a place that is.' They were back at the house now, and he was completely relaxed, utterly at ease. 'Ah, Jolyon, I was just saying to Joe here that when you come to work at my agent's, you can stay with me in Montpelier Square, if you like. We can keep each other company. Would that appeal?'

'That'd be great,' said Jolyon. 'Thank you very much, sir.'

'I think perhaps we should check that with your mother,' said Joe. 'Come on, we must get back, I've a piece to write tonight.'

As they drove away, down the winding drive of Stebbings, Joe knew with absolute certainty that Piers had been lying. It was quite impossible, unthinkable even, that anybody living at that time in the extremely small and incestuous town that was Hollywood would not have known about Byron Patrick. Byron Patrick, Hollywood's First Grand Master of Wine, juvenile lead at ACI, the subject of countless column inches in the gossip columns; Byron Patrick, high-profile plaything of the high-profile Naomi MacNeice; Byron Patrick, centre of what had emerged as one of Hollywood's many unsavoury small scandals. It was absolutely beyond all reasonable doubt that Piers Windsor would not have known about him; and since he had chosen to lie about it, then it was equally beyond all reasonable doubt that he had something to hide. To hide from any one of a great number of people; but from Joe Payton in particular who had written a few pages in his book about Byron Patrick, and who was pursuing the real reasons behind his death with an ever-increasing interest.

Chapter 21

1968

One of Joe's favourite games was What If, in both matters large and small: What if Lincoln had been unwell on 14 April 1865 and not gone to the theatre? What if, he would say, it been raining in Dallas on 22 November 1963 and Jack Kennedy's car had had to be covered? What if Adolf Hitler had been just a little more talented and had been accepted rather than rejected by the Vienna Academy as an art student? What if (laughing) Michelangelo had suffered from vertigo, or Mozart had been just a little more robust, lived just a little more wisely, and not succumbed to typhus at the age of thirty-four? And what if (more soberly now) Caroline had been out that day, when he had been on *Woman's Hour*? How differently everything both large and small would probably have turned out. And what if, as he thought over and over again, in the years to come (keeping this particular version of his game entirely to himself), what if an exceptionally vile woman in ice-blue satin had not come up behind him as he left the Carmel Hotel on Santa Monica Broadway, one of his favourites, being charming and modestly priced without being shabby, and stolen his cab? What if he had not had to wait for another three minutes and he had not therefore arrived at LAX three minutes later as he did? Then so much of his personal history and that of those dearest to him would have been changed, rewritten, redirected. And greatly for the better, perhaps, almost certainly indeed.

But the vile woman was there, she did take his cab; and he arrived at LAX tired but pleased with the work he had done, the people he had managed to see: a story on Brits making a rather unexpected conquest of the town, most currently and notably Jacqueline Bisset, fresh from her triumph in *Bullitt*; charming she had been to him, charming and beautiful and unbelievably sexy (although rather regrettably skilful at fielding questions), and now he wanted sharply to get home. As he reached the airport, sitting in his cab in the slow-moving line, the rush-hour traffic edging slowly forward, he saw a man and a girl leaving the airport.

The man, who was dressed in a beige linen suit, pushing a trolley piled high with what looked like extremely expensive luggage, was very familiar to him: it was Piers Windsor. And the girl, who was laughing up at him, her hand joined with one of his on the trolley, and wearing a pink shift dress that left very little to the imagination, was more familiar still. It was Fleur.

He just didn't know what to do. What to think, how to act, how to react. He would have given everything he owned (not a great deal these days, but still) not to have seen her, not to have known; but he had and clearly something had to be done. He thought of Chloe, trustingly at home in London, with her small family, and had it been anyone with Piers, anyone at all, he would have wished to kill them both. The fact that it was Fleur, Chloe's own sister, wittingly, horribly cheating on her, made it a hundred, a thousand times worse. And what exactly was Fleur doing? Was she simply playing around, amusing herself; or was she having some kind of revenge on the sister she had hated all her life?

Either way it was intolerable: she had to be stopped. She was mad and bad and sad, he thought to himself, remembering the sorry epitaph on all women coined by – who was it, some psychologist guy? Stopped so that Chloe might be saved, so that Fleur herself might be saved from the worst excesses of herself. As for Piers – Joe closed his mind to Piers. He couldn't begin to think about Piers. Not yet.

He sat on the plane, drinking bourbon as if it was going out of style, staring into the growing darkness, feeling progressively more unhappy, more ill, more afraid. And another emotion too. One he did not dare to acknowledge, not even to himself.

When he got home, back to the blessed sanity of his own flat – thank God, thank dear God he had kept it – he put in a call to Fleur at the agency. She was away, for a week, they told him: on vacation.

'Would you ask her to call me the minute she gets back?' he said. 'It's Joe Payton. I'm in London. Tell her it's important.'

He sat and waited for her call, in a mixture of rage and dread.

'Joe? Hi, this is Fleur. Is something wrong?'

'Yes,' he said, and he knew his voice, even across the Atlantic, was heavy, filled with rage. 'There's something wrong.'

'What?'

'Oh,' he said, 'oh, you know what's wrong, Fleur, as a matter of fact. You know very well.'

'No, I don't,' she said and her voice was puzzled, wary. 'Of course I don't.'

'It's you, Fleur, that's what's wrong, and what you're doing to Chloe, her children and her marriage, her happiness. What are you doing, Fleur, what the hell do you think you're doing?'

'I – Joe, what are you talking about?'

'For both our sakes, don't come over innocent with me. I've just been in LA, Fleur. I saw you.'

'Oh.'

'Fleur, how could you? How could you do such a thing? You are worse than I ever suspected. I knew you were a liar, I feared you were a cheat, I didn't know you were totally heartless into the bargain. Stop it, Fleur, stop it at once, or I swear to God I shall see that you do.'

'Joe,' she said, 'Joe, it isn't –'

But he put the phone down. He couldn't bear to hear any more.

The whole incident had upset him horribly. He felt physically toxic; sick and aching, day after day. He didn't know what to do: whether to confront Piers, to write to Fleur; there was no one to talk to, to discuss it with. Caroline sensed there was something wrong, started questioning him about it, and then when he refused to discuss it, as so often happened these days, withdrew from him. They were increasingly distanced: that too upset him, made him feel worse. He tried to concentrate on his work but that seemed impossible; he was sitting at his desk one day, three weeks after he got back from Los Angeles, when the phone rang. It was Magnus Phillips.

'Joe. Hi. How's things?'

'OK,' said Joe guardedly. He didn't trust Phillips: somehow felt (absurdly) that he knew too much about them all.

'Could I buy you a beer?'

'You can buy me a beer,' said Joe, 'but I may not be willing or able to give you what you want in return.'

'I don't want much,' said Magnus Phillips.

'Well, I'll drink your beer anyway,' said Joe.

'El Vino's? Lunch-time tomorrow?'

'Fine.'

El Vino's was the journalists' pub almost opposite the law courts. There, and in Poppins, the pub next door, enough beer went down throats worn dry by a morning's work to float a small craft down Fleet Street. By the end of a long lunchtime or a longer evening a considerably larger craft could follow it, as the dry throats, freshly lubricated, became dry once more with the exchange of gossip, news, conjecture and the recounting of usually long and frequently filthy jokes and needed further lubrication still. Like all quasi clubs El Vino's had its mores, its unwritten rules, its standards of dress (not generally high); there was a requirement for a strong head, an iron nerve, an ability to watch your back, and a genuine esprit de corps. Women were not allowed to stand at the bar and order drinks, but had to sit in a special section designated to them at the back. Joe, like most jobbing journalists, had spent many of his happiest hours in El Vino's and, like most of them, was able to remember very few of them with great clarity. He wondered, as he always did as he walked through the door, to be hit by the noise, the heat, the cigarette haze, why he did not go there more often.

Magnus Phillips was standing at the bar talking to David Farr from the *Chronicle*.

'Congratulations,' said Joe to Farr, who had just won an award as News Reporter of the Year. 'Well deserved.'

'Thanks,' said Farr. 'I'd rather have your job, though, Payton. Chatting up all those starlets all day long.'

'Yeah, well, it has its moments,' said Joe modestly.

'What'll you have, Joe?' said Magnus.

'Pint,' said Joe, resolving firmly not to have any more. His head at lunchtime was not strong.

Three pints later, he was sitting in a corner with Magnus and another journalist from the *Sketch* trying to persuade himself he wasn't as drunk as he thought.

'Got to go,' said the *Sketch* man. 'Got a briefing on this anti-Vietnam demo in Grosvenor Square tomorrow. Could be nasty.'

'Bloody Yanks,' said Magnus, slightly surprisingly. 'What do we care about their bloody war? Using expensive police time, carving up our horses.'

'Oh, it's got nothing to do with Vietnam,' said the *Sketch* man cheerfully. 'Excuse for some violence, beat up a few coppers. Good copy though. Cheers, Magnus, cheers, Joe.'

'Cheers,' said Joe.

'Right,' said Magnus. 'What next?'

Joe looked at him, slightly surprised. 'I thought you wanted something.'

'Oh – not really. Have another drink.'

'No thanks. Well – maybe I'll have a very large tonic. Clear my head.'

'You can't drink neat tonic water in here,' said Magnus, 'it'd be like allowing women at the bar. There's talk of that. These feminists getting ideas above themselves. Silly cows. Whisky? That'll clear your head.'

'Yeah, that'd be good,' said Joe. 'Then I must go.'

The whisky looked suspiciously large. He drank it very quickly. He thought it might have less effect that way.

'I met Germaine Greer once,' he said. 'She's very sexy. Very beautiful.'

'Don't believe it,' said Magnus.

'You should believe it. You wouldn't refuse her.'

'I would,' said Magnus. 'I can't stand the thought of any of those dykes.'

'Magnus, she is no dyke. I told you. She's very sexy.'

'Someone ought to lock 'em up,' said Magnus firmly. 'And throw away the key.'

'Yeah, well,' said Joe equably, 'that's a view. Another drink, Magnus? That went down rather well. Shall we sit down for a bit?'

'Sure. I'll grab that corner.' He shot an amused look at Joe, who was too drunk to notice. Sitting down was not an activity that went on a lot in El Vino's: the hollow leg of the journalist tends to work better standing up.

'Just read your book,' said Magnus, picking up his whisky.

'Which one?'

'*Scandals*. Great read. You must have had fun with that.'

'I did.'

'The Hollywood stuff was great. I really liked it.'

'Yeah?'

'Did you ever actually meet that Patrick guy?'

The name pierced Joe's confused brain; he suddenly felt alert, wary, almost excited. 'No.'

'How'd you hear about it? About that story?'

'I met this lady called Yolande duGrath.'

'Yeah? What does she do?'

'She taught.'

'Uh-huh. What?'

'Drama. She was a drama coach.'

'And full of stories, I bet.'

'Oh full,' said Joe. He was enjoying this.

'I need someone to talk to over there.'

'Why?'

'Oh – doing a series on the place. Not unlike your own. Not as good of course.'

'Of course not,' said Joe and grinned.

'Only I'm going deeper into the gutter. Going into the police files.'

'Yeah?'

'Yeah.'

'Expensive,' said Joe.

'A bit. But the *Sketch* is still quite a rich paper.'

'Sure.'

'So – do you think your friend Yolande would talk to me?'

'I'm afraid not,' said Joe, a deep sadness in his voice.

'Why not?'

'She's dead.'

'Bastard,' said Magnus Phillips equably. There was a silence. Then he said, 'Did you ever come across a starlet called Kirstie Fairfax? Or any stories about her?'

'Nope,' said Joe truthfully. 'Why?'

'Oh – she was mixed up with your Patrick guy.'

'She was?' said Joe, interest rising in him like a physical force. 'How?'

'Don't know. He'd been trying to help her get a screen test. Or so the papers said.'

'Can't help,' said Joe, speaking very carefully. He felt he was walking on glass. 'Sorry. Why was it in the papers? What's happened to her now?'

'Oh, she's dead. Long dead. Killed herself. Or so the papers said.'

'Ah,' said Joe.

'Got any other ideas? People I could talk to?'

'Not really,' said Joe, raking his mind frantically for some harmless, innocent name he could give Phillips. It looked seriously obstructive, suspicious almost, to say no one. Then he said, slightly – but only slightly – reckless, 'You could try Naomi MacNeice. Casting director at ACI. Byron Patrick was her plaything. She knew everyone and everything. She's out at Malibu now, I think. I could check for you.'

'She's not,' said Phillips briefly. 'She's in what they call a Twilight Home. And she's totally gaga and she's dying. I tried.'

'Well, in that case,' said Joe, 'I really can't help. Sorry, Magnus. I must get back now. It's been great.'

Later that evening, nursing a hideous hangover, he wondered with immense foreboding what on earth Kirstie Fairfax had had to do with Byron Patrick, what Magnus Phillips was actually up to, and what if anything he could or should do about it.

Fleur was walking out of the office when she saw Joe. He was standing by the swing doors, watching her intently. It was over a month since she had got back from her trip to LA with Piers; Joe had written to say he was coming to New York, that he had to see her: he had obviously come to find her. She sighed, and went towards him. There was no point doing anything else. This was going to be grim.

'Hallo, Joe.'

He looked at her, and his eyes were dark with hostility, and a kind of savage rage she would never have believed him capable of. His face was very drawn and white. He was looking particularly shabby, in a crumpled, rather dirty raincoat, a navy sweater and faded jeans and shoes which had seen no polish for a very long time. His hair was particularly untidy, and she felt weak with her old half-forgotten longing for him.

'I think,' he said and his voice was so cold, so bleak she shivered physically. 'I think we should go back to my hotel and talk. On the other hand, I might be tempted to kill you. So perhaps it had better be somewhere more public.'

'Well,' she said, looking him up and down rather pointedly, 'you're hardly dressed for the Plaza.'

'Shut up,' he said and his gentle face and lazy voice were both distorted, made harsh with anger. 'Shut up. We'll go to a bar.'

'No,' she said, and her own voice was sad, full of pain. 'We'll go to your hotel. If you hate me that much and you want to kill me, then I'd rather you did.'

Joe looked at her and she could see that just for a moment, a brief moment, she had pierced his rage, touched a more tender nerve; then he hardened again.

He was at the St Regis as usual. He had a cheap room on the mezzanine where he had stayed for years. They went in, sat down in the bar; Joe ordered a beer. 'What'll you have?'

'I'll have a beer too. No, I won't, I'll have a bourbon.'

'No drink for a lady.'

'I'm no lady. As you know.'

'I do know.'

They sat in silence for a minute or more, drinking, not looking at one another.

'You are becoming a regular little jet-setter, aren't you?' she said. 'You and that guy David Frost.'

'He gets his fare paid,' he said.

'Don't you?'

'Not this time, no. But I decided I had to come. Had to talk to you.' Then he said, 'Fleur, I cannot tell you how shocked I am.'

'Joe, why? Why are you shocked? What did I do that is so dreadfully shocking?'

'If you really don't know,' he said, 'then I am more shocked still. Fleur, that is your sister's husband you are sleeping with. I imagine you're sleeping with him?'

'Oh, yes,' she said, 'I'm sleeping with him.'

'Fleur, why? In God's name why? What good will it do you?'

'A lot. I hope.'

'But what?'

'Joe,' she said, and in spite of her resolve to keep calm, she felt rage and pain rising up in her in a great hot physical shaft. 'Joe, I think you owe me at least to listen to me. It isn't quite what you think.'

'Oh, really?' he said.

'Yes. Really. Joe, that man had something to do with my father. I know he did.'

'Oh, Fleur, for the love of God –' Something in his voice was different, changed; she stared at him, he looked away.

'Joe, what is it?'

'Nothing.'

'Yes there is. Joe, I know there is. You know something, don't you?'

'Fleur,' said Joe, 'leave me out of this, please.'

'How can I, Joe? When I can see you're involved. Don't lie to me, Joe. I know you too well.'

'Fleur, this is getting us nowhere. Let's return to your charming little fantasy, shall we? How did you meet Piers anyway? How did you engineer that?'

'He was having dinner with my boss. I went to the restaurant.'

'Deliberately to meet him?'

'Deliberately to meet him.'

'Fleur, why?'

'I'll tell you why,' she said and she could hear the pain in her own voice, 'I'll tell you, Joe Payton. It was because of something you said as a matter of fact.'

'Oh, really. So it's my fault, is it? That you're having an affair with your sister's husband?'

'Yes and that's exactly it, she's my sister, we have the same mother and I am still, still, after all this time, kept hidden away, a nasty, dirty, inconvenient little secret. "Oh, we didn't tell Piers about you," you said. "Obviously we didn't tell Piers about you." Obviously not. I mustn't exist, as far as he's concerned, must I, Joe? In case he doesn't like it all, doesn't approve. Chloe, dear Chloe can't have her brilliant marriage put at risk, can she? That would be too terrible. So obviously we won't mention her illegitimate sister.'

'Fleur,' said Joe. 'Fleur, it wasn't –'

'How do you think that made me feel, Joe? Do you think it made me feel valued, worthwhile, good?'

'No,' he said quietly, 'no, I don't suppose it did.'

'Too right it didn't. It hurt so much, Joe, I can't begin to tell you how much it hurt. But I took it on board, along with all the other things. I have so much on board, Joe, I'm going to sink one of these days. Well, I guess that'll be pretty convenient for you all.'

'Fleur, don't be –'

'So that's how it began. I thought I'd hurt you all. Tell him who I was. And then – then I met him.'

'And? I suppose you're going to tell me you fell passionately in love with him.'

'Oh, go fuck yourself,' said Fleur. 'The guy's a – well never mind what he is. The point is, he heard my name and, Joe, he was shitting bricks. It was incredible.'

'What did he say?' Joe's voice was interestingly sharp. She felt her senses quicken, tauten.

'He didn't say anything. Of course.'

'Fleur,' said Joe, and she could feel him relaxing, easing again, 'Fleur, this is insanity. You clearly have absolutely nothing to go on. It's a kind of terrible paranoia, this thing about your father. You've got to stop, got to let it go.'

'Joe, I can't. Please, please try to understand. It was there. In his eyes. Those famously beautiful eyes of his. Terror. Sheer, spooked terror. It was like he'd seen a ghost. Which I guess he had. In a way.'

'And then what?'

'Then I excused myself politely and went and ate my dinner. And the next day I called him at his hotel and said would he sign a photograph of himself for someone. And he realized, or thought he realized, I didn't know anything about him, and he asked me to have a drink with him. And now he thinks he's safe, and I'm getting close to him. He likes me. A lot. He wants to be with me. That gives me quite a bit of pleasure, Joe, you know. In various ways.'

He looked at her and she thought she had never seen such coldness, such distaste on a face. She shivered.

'So you're getting close to him. Has he confirmed all these suspicions of yours? Has he said, hey, Fleur, I knew your dad, we were in Hollywood together, or words to that effect?'

'No. No, in fact he denies having been in Hollywood. At the time.'

'Oh, really? Well that certainly proves everything, doesn't it?'

'Oh, Joe, for God's sake. That's the whole point. Of course he's not going to tell me he knew my dad. If he did do something – well, something wrong.'

'Fleur, I despair of you. On the strength of a moment of fevered imagination, you move in on your sister's husband, have an affair with him –'

'Joe, it was not imagination. Believe me. That man knows something about my father, and he won't say what and that makes me think it was something bad.'

'And I suppose it couldn't have been something bad your father did? There's a lot of evidence stacking up against him you know.' He was sounding more reasonable now, calmer, he was listening to her. She felt just slightly better.

'I don't know, Joe. To be honest, that had crossed my mind, but I don't think so. He looked scared, Joe, that's the only word for it. And I have to find out. I have to.'

'And how long are you going to pursue this?'

'As long as it takes. Joe, if Piers Windsor did do something that hurt my father, if, just supposing, if it had been him who talked to that magazine, I want revenge. I've been very lonely and very unhappy for a great deal of my life because of him. I want him to be lonely and unhappy. At the very least.'

'Fleur, you just don't know what you're talking about. It is simply a rather – what shall I say – neurotic notion.'

'I do know, and it is not neurotic.'

'I see. And this revenge – is this to be on Chloe too?'

'Oh, I don't care about Chloe,' said Fleur, meeting his eyes. 'She may get hurt along the way, I'm afraid. Quite honestly, it doesn't seem very important.'

'That is a very sad and ugly attitude.'

'I am sad, Joe. I'm sorry, but I am. I don't know about ugly.'

He was silent for a while, looking at her. 'I still don't know what you hope to achieve.'

'Well,' she said, 'first I have to establish for certain that he did do something. Make him tell me himself. It's the only way I could think of. And then I want him to know the pain, the awful misery it caused me. I want to frighten him. I want to make him realize.'

'I don't know when I felt more angry,' he said, 'or more sickened.'

Fleur stared at him. 'That really hurts,' she said. 'I thought you were my friend.'

'I was once,' he said, 'I loved being your friend. Loved helping you. You blew that one, Fleur. Your fault.'

'I know.' She spoke quietly.

'But now – now you are really wreaking havoc. Destruction. It's insane. Terrible. For nothing really. Hurting everyone. Yourself included. What about that nice boyfriend of yours? How do you think he would feel? Or does he know?'

'No,' said Fleur quietly. 'No, he doesn't know.'

What Reuben would make of her pursuit of Piers was something she kept buried, pushed to the bottom of her heart.

'I hope he doesn't find out. Have you thought of that?'

'Yes, I have,' said Fleur, tears of guilt and exasperation springing to her eyes. 'Of course I have. But –'

'He has to go along with it, I suppose. Take it on board. Poor bastard.'

'Joe,' said Fleur, 'Joe, don't. I have to do this. I know there's something. I know.'

Joe stared at her. She could feel him withdrawing from her, feel his dislike. It hurt, but she had to live with that.

'Oh, Fleur!' Joe lay back in his chair and she could see something at the back of his eyes that she recognized but couldn't quite define. 'Fleur, this is total insanity. You detect or think you detect some reaction in the man to your name and base an entire case for the prosecution on it. And behave with the most appalling callousness into the bargain. You have absolutely no morals, no sense of decency. Now please, Fleur, I beg of you, drop this. Stop seeing Piers Windsor. Stay out of his life. I suppose you're not going to tell me you're falling in love with him?'

'No,' said Fleur, 'of course not. I can't stand him, most of the time. He's a creep. I'm sorry for him, I suppose. I don't want to be, but I am.'

'Why are you sorry for him?' said Joe and there was genuine interest in his eyes, replacing the hostility briefly.

'Because he's pathetic,' she said. 'He's a pathetic mess. I don't know what your beloved Chloe has told you about him, but –'

'Nothing, obviously,' said Joe. 'She seems very happy with him.'

'Well, she's a fool,' said Fleur.

'Why? Why is she a fool?'

'Oh, no,' said Fleur. 'I'm not going to be pulled into this one, Joe. I'm not doing any of your work for you. If you can't see what's wrong with Piers, with their marriage, with everything, I'm certainly not spelling it out for you. But I'm sure you do. I'm sure even you are not that stupid.'

Joe looked at her, and she could see in his eyes that he did know, of course he must, and that at the same time it must not be spoken of between them, not named, not defined, for fear it would become an active, swift, deadly danger, rather than something still contained, locked away, for as long as possible. And as she caught him unawares, vulnerable, acknowledging that truth, she knew this was the moment to tear into him, ripping open his guard, pursuing the other.

'Joe,' she said, 'Joe, you know something, don't you? You know something about Piers. About all this?'

'Of course I don't,' he said quickly, too quickly, and didn't look at her directly.

'I don't believe you.'

'Fleur, leave this. Leave it, please.'

'Joe, tell me. Look at me, and tell me.'

And he looked at her, and his eyes told her.

'So he was there? At that time?'

'Oh, Christ. Fleur, don't. Don't do this.'

'Was he there? Was he?'

'Yes,' he said. 'Yes, he was there.'

'When?'

'At – at that time. That's all I know, Fleur, I swear.'

'You bastard,' she said. 'You bastard. When I needed the truth, needed your help so much, you kept it from me. How could you, Joe, how could you? How did you find out, Joe, and when?'

'Oh – by accident. It was mentioned. By his mother to Chloe. I didn't tell you for exactly the reasons you should leave this thing alone. None of it means a thing, it's the merest shred of information; he says he likes to keep it quiet because he failed so totally, didn't even get tested. Oh, Fleur, what would have been the point of telling you?'

'I would have known,' she said quietly. 'It would have been something to go on.'

'It's nothing. Nothing at all. Now I don't give a toss about Piers, Fleur, you can do what you will with him; but there are innocent lives here, terribly at risk. Think of Chloe, Fleur, she has no part in all this, she is innocent of any guilt, any blame, she is struggling to make that marriage work. Please, Fleur, I beg of you, leave it alone.'

Fleur looked at him, and a searing white light seemed to dance in front of her eyes. She felt hot, blazing, ragingly hot, and physically shaky. She stood up and looked down at Joe, and started to speak and all the hurt, all the betrayal she had ever felt were in those words. 'Don't talk to me about Chloe, Joe, about hurting Chloe. I can be hurt, that's fine, I can be abandoned, sent off to America, away from my mother, so that I wouldn't litter up her life. I can be hurt, left alone while my father went off to Hollywood, and I can be hurt, left alone when he died. I can be hurt, learning all those terrible things about him, and I can be hurt trying to unravel what really happened, what was behind it. And now I can be hurt again, by you betraying me, lying to me, keeping from me the one thing I really need to know, and then you think you can just ask me to leave it all alone. Just to save Chloe, to leave her safe with her famous husband and her perfect children and her undamaged little life. How could you, Joe, how could you? You of all people, you who are supposed to be my friend. OK, OK, so I've blown that, and if you weren't so stupid, so dumb, you'd be able to understand. Well, I can't leave it all alone, and I won't, do you understand, because – because –' She stopped suddenly, unable to go on, her voice dying, smothered by pain and tears.

Joe was standing up and his face had quite changed: it was tender, and shocked, and there were tears in his own eyes; he put out his hand and touched her face, traced her tears and, for a moment, just a moment, she thought he was going to go on, go forward, and she stood there, staring at him, hardly daring to hope, to think.

But then he said, and his voice was changed, hesitant, very quiet, 'I'm sorry, Fleur, but I can't accept that. I know what you've been through, and I know how hard it's been for you, and I can see what a rather – unhappy view of your family you have. But it does not give you the right to behave as you have. As you are doing. I'm terribly fond of you, Fleur, as I hope you know, but I can't condone this thing. I'm sorry. It's callous and amoral and it shocks me. Please, please stop it. For me if for no one else.'

'I can't,' said Fleur, and she felt a deadly misery creeping into her, a disappointment and a profound sense of betrayal. She stood looking at Joe, who had been her friend for so long, her ally, Joe who had taken the time and trouble to explain things to her, to try to help her, Joe who she had adored for years, who she had fancied rotten, for God's sake, and in that moment love died, totally, and with it trust, and she felt more lonely than she could ever remember being in her life.

'You can't? You mean you won't,' he said, and his voice was very cold.

'I mean I can't. If you understood anything, you'd understand that,' she said and turned and walked out of the hotel, and stood in the street looking for a cab, crying hard, desperately, like a small abandoned child.

It hit her hard, very hard: what she saw as Joe's betrayal. She longed to talk about it, to tell Reuben, or maybe Poppy, to receive comfort, support, understanding, but she couldn't. This was too private, too painful, something she was locked into alone, quite alone now. She felt shocked, almost bereaved; she ached, physically; she felt she had been kicked, bruised, dragged through an assault course. She had more trouble sleeping even than usual; her appetite, usually so healthy, so hearty, failed her; if she ate she developed stomach pains. Tears overcame her: suddenly, shockingly, in meetings, at lunch, over her typewriter. Mick and even Nigel noticed, asked her if she was all right. Fine, she said, fine, glaring at them, hating them too, men, the common enemy.

And then, as she began to recover, to feel better, a hard, hot anger slowly replaced the pain. And something else. An even stronger, fiercer clarity of vision. She no longer just wanted to hurt Piers Windsor, and whoever else had damaged, ruined her father: she wanted to hurt all of them, Chloe, Caroline, and most of all now she wanted to hurt Joe, let him learn what it was like to feel misery, rejection, loneliness.

She was haunted, too, by Joe's words, his concern for Reuben; his heavy 'poor bastard' invaded her head at the most unlikely moments. What kind of person was she, that she could deceive, so remorselessly, someone who loved her so much? She kept pushing the thought aside, but it pursued her.

'Want to talk about it?' he had said the very next day when she suddenly started to cry over dinner, hot, helpless tears. She shook her head, and forced a smile, and he smiled back, shrugged and said OK; he saw her home and hugged her very close to him on the doorstep, didn't even suggest he came in.

'Oh, Reuben,' said Fleur, looking up at him, at his gentle, ugly face, soft with concern for her. 'Oh, Reuben, you are just the best.'

She didn't deserve him, as Joe had said; but he was there and he wanted to be there. She often felt she would have lost all faith in everything without him.

Background to early Hollywood section of *The Tinsel Underneath*.

Extract from *Scandals*, by Joe Payton. Permission to quote from publishers.

There can be little doubt that what actually killed Byron Patrick was the Hollywood system. It requires that all the players both on and off screen are absolutely one hundred and one per cent acceptable. They must be agreeable, good-looking, glamorous and well-behaved beyond a certain line. Anything unacceptable, sexually or socially, has to be kept completely off-limits. Hollywood may be filled with cocaine addicts, adulterers, and homosexuals; the wildest indulgences, designed to satisfy the most salacious appetites, may take place within its tinsel walls: all absolutely fine so long as the public does not get to hear about it. A great deal of money and effort goes into buying that silence. The trade-off has to be that the subjects are worth the price. In Byron's case he was not: not a big enough star to be worth protecting. It was cheaper to junk the investment made in him thus far, and let the scandal sheets do their worst, than to buy them off. Hollywood built him up, and then without a second thought, knocked him down again. He was a victim, in that late summer of 1957, not just of the journalist who wrote the story, or the person who tipped the journalist off, but of the whole tawdry town. He hadn't a hope; they were all too clever for him.

Note: insert here: 'But who was it in particular who was too clever for him?' Pithy and powerful.

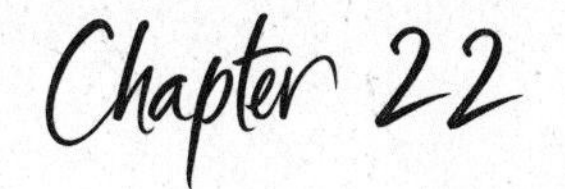

Chapter 22

1969

'Lady Hunterton? This is Magnus Phillips. I wondered if we could meet.'

Such straightforward, innocent, harmless words: belying so totally what they were to unleash. For ever afterwards, for the rest of her life, they haunted her, those words, echoing through her head, down the years.

And well, she had said, well, I don't know: sensibly cautious, afraid for many reasons, suspicious of his motives, wary of anything that might worsen her already deteriorating relationship with Joe, wary of Magnus and his professional reputation, the way he wrought havoc with people's lives, wary of herself and how she might react to temptation, sexual temptation, and if ever a man embodied for her sexual temptation it was Magnus Phillips.

'What don't you know?' he said, and she could hear him smiling into the phone, arrogantly amused.

'Whether we should meet,' she said, and promptly felt cross with herself, knowing what the next question would be, and it came, promptly, on cue.

'Why not? Why on earth should we not meet?'

'Well,' she said, hauling herself together, feeling her way cautiously into a position of more control. 'For one thing, I'm in Suffolk, for another I'm very busy, I have no intention of coming to London and I cannot imagine –' She paused, not sure what it was she was going to be unable to imagine, but mercifully he interrupted her.

'That's fine, in fact it's the whole point. I'm also very busy, but I have every intention of coming to Suffolk. If you'll have me.'

'Yes, but –'

'Let me make things a little clearer. I'm writing an article about the racing game for my paper. I thought you were the person to talk to about it.'

'Why isn't your racing correspondent doing it?' said Caroline tartly.

'I forgot you were involved with another hack. Very good. It isn't that sort of piece. It's about the people involved, and all that sexy stuff about stallions and stud farms and covering mares. And I thought that charming friend of yours, Mr Bamforth, might be able to help me too.'

'Oh, well, that would be fine,' said Caroline, relief and disappointment flooding her in equal quantities. 'Jack's forgotten more about breeding and bloodlines than –'

'I know, than most people know,' said Magnus. 'That'd be great. When could I come down?'

'Well, any time,' she said, 'any time at all. Jack's always here.'

'Oh, but I wouldn't want to come all that way and not see you as well. That would be seriously stupid. Don't you think?'

And Caroline, aware that it was she who was being seriously stupid, arranged to give him lunch at the Moat House the following Thursday.

He arrived at eight in the morning, on his motorbike; it was only just getting light, and she was still not dressed.

'I'm a little early for lunch,' he said, grinning at her over his crash helmet, his dark eyes roving over her as she stood there in the doorway, pulling her silk dressing-gown closely round her like a virginal schoolgirl, cursing herself for not getting up early, for being here, bleary-eyed, un-made-up, miserably aware of looking every moment of her forty-seven years, 'but I thought there was probably a lot of ground to cover, and the roads were clear, I had a great run.'

'You must have left London at about five,' she said.

No, he said, four actually. 'I don't go in for a lot of sleeping. Waste of good time. Death's brother.'

'What?' said Caroline, looking at him blankly.

'Sleep and his brother death. Shelley. I don't suppose you thought I'd know about Shelley, did you?' he said, grinning at her. 'Working-class boy like me. You'd be surprised what we get up to, in between picking our noses and dusting off our flat caps.'

'Oh, don't be silly,' said Caroline crossly. 'I never thought about whether you might know about Shelley or what class you came from for that matter. Do you want some coffee?'

'Love some. Dry work, biking.' He followed her into the house, sat down in the kitchen, watching her with frank pleasure as she put the kettle on the Aga; the dressing-gown swung open revealing a rather shabby elongated T-shirt; she hauled it back round her. 'This is a great house. Did your late husband own it?'

'No,' said Caroline. 'My father owned it. And my grandfather and my great-grandfather if you really want to know.'

'I don't especially. But I suppose now you've told me it is slightly interesting. Do you mind if I smoke?'

'No, of course not,' said Caroline, who minded very much, but was afraid of looking even more like a virginal schoolmistress than she did already if she said so. Magnus Phillips got out a rather squashed packet of Disque Bleu and an incongruously expensive-looking gold Dunhill and lit up, his eyes through the smoke fixed on her breasts beneath the silk robe. For the rest of her life, Caroline was unable to smell French cigarettes without feeling sexual discomfort.

She ground the beans, poured the water into a jug; the smell of coffee joined that of the cigarette, and of motorbike oil. It all seemed strangely erotic.

'You make a good cup of coffee,' said Magnus Phillips. 'It's a rare talent in a woman.'

'Really?'

'Really. Chloe was a cook, wasn't she? Must get it from you.'

'Yes, she was. But I'm no cook. Do you know,' she said, without being able to imagine why she should be telling him such a thing, 'I have never made a cake in my whole life.'

'Good Lord,' he said, 'and you the mother of – three.'

'Yes,' she said, and a stab of fear, a sense of danger went through her, as she wrenched her gaze away from him. 'Do you want anything to eat?'

'Well,' he said, 'I don't suppose you've got any Cooper's Oxford marmalade, have you?'

'Of course I have,' said Caroline, slightly indignantly.

'Then I'd like some with some toast please. I'm addicted to the stuff. Eat it at all hours of the day and night. Thanks a lot.'

She made him some toast, passed him the jar of Cooper's. He spread it extremely thickly, and wolfed it down.

'Well,' he said, finally, with evident regret, 'that was good. Lead me to the man, Lady Hunterton. Or tell me where to find him. I imagine he's an early starter.'

'If you wait five minutes,' she said, 'I'll get dressed, and take you down there.'

'Five minutes!' he said, grinning at her. 'That's very quick for a female. Do you undress quickly as well?'

Caroline, enraged, felt herself blushing. 'I've never timed it,' she said and walked quickly out of the kitchen.

She carefully didn't make him lunch: too much danger of intimacy, she felt, after the morning, and it showed too much desire to please. 'I thought we'd go to the pub,' she said, walking into the stable yard at lunch-time. 'Jack, you'll join us, won't you?'

'Mustn't be long,' said Jack. 'Got a pony to look at this afternoon, for Pandora. Mr Windsor asked me to keep an eye out for one.'

'Really?' said Caroline. 'I didn't know. What did Chloe have to say about it?'

'You don't know everything, Caroline,' said Jack, grinning at her as she climbed up into the Range Rover. 'And Chloe wasn't keen, you're quite right. I'll bring my own car, then you don't have to rush off when I do.'

They sat in the smoky warmth of the Hare and Hounds, eating large plates of shepherd's pie; Magnus and Jack drank beer while Caroline, still uneasy, afraid of relaxing, drank tonic water. Jack continued to talk about bloodstock, about National Hunt racing, about the flat, about yearling sales, and Caroline sat silent, watching Magnus make notes, and wondered why she felt so sure he was not remotely interested in anything Jack was saying.

Finally Jack rose. 'Got to go, Caroline. See you later.'

'Bye, Jack. Thank you. Don't get anything for Pandora unless you're absolutely sure, will you?'

'Of course not. Bye, Mr Phillips.'

'Cheers, Jack,' said Magnus. 'Very much appreciated. Nice bloke,' he added, as Jack left the bar. 'Very unfeudal, isn't he? Calling you Caroline and all that.'

'Jack is a friend,' said Caroline simply, forgetting to be watchful of what she said. 'He may be my groom, but he's been here all my life, and he knows more about me than anyone in the world. He's eased me through all kinds of crises, the death of both my parents, and of my husband –'

'The births of all your children?'

'Yes,' she said smoothly, 'and he is the most marvellous man. Very special. I love him.'

'Strong words.'

'Strong feelings.'

'And what does he make of your son-in-law?'

The question threw her slightly. 'I don't know. We haven't discussed the matter.'

'I'm surprised. Since you're so close. Perhaps you don't need to discuss it.'

'I don't know what you mean,' said Caroline.

'Oh, I think you do. He's hardly – well, hardly what you would have chosen, is he? Any of you?'

'Magnus,' said Caroline, and her eyes were very steady as she looked at him, 'be careful. Please.'

'Sorry. I don't like him either. Don't know how I got mixed up with him really.'

'I didn't say I didn't like him,' said Caroline with dignity.

'No, you didn't say it.'

There was a silence.

'You're not writing this book about him, then? So I understand.'

'No. Well, I don't think so. I haven't quite given up the idea.'

'Really? Chloe says Piers told you he didn't want to go ahead.'

'Yes,' he said, 'Piers did say that. But – well, you know, there's no law against biography writing.'

'But surely –'

'You can do what's known as an unauthorized biography. Written without the cooperation of the subject. Usually scurrilous, and often, although not always, inaccurate. Mine are accurate and scurrilous.'

'But you wouldn't do that to Piers, would you?'

'What, write something scurrilous?' He was grinning at her, looking particularly saturnine, with his dancing, almost black eyes, his uneven, very white teeth. 'Not unless there was something scurrilous to say. Which I'm sure there isn't.'

'So why haven't you given up the idea?'

'Oh – I have really. Just keeping a tiny option open. That's all. Don't look so worried.'

'I'm not,' said Caroline.

'Although, as you must be aware, there is – gossip about him,' he said, taking out a cigarette from the crumpled packet, offering it to her.

She shook her head. 'What sort of gossip?'

'Oh – you know. The usual sort. That surrounds so many of our actors.'

'No. No, I don't.'

'Caroline!' He shook his head solemnly, his eyes brilliant, boring into hers. 'I cannot believe you are quite so naïve. Gossip about homosexuality of course. There always has been. Utterly meaningless, fairly harmless, very malicious. Ask your friend Joe. I cannot believe he's never come across it.'

'Well, if he has he's certainly never mentioned it,' said Caroline, hoping she sounded as positive as she meant to. 'When you say gossip, do you mean people just – just talking about it? Fairly harmlessly? Or deliberately spreading it, with intent to – well, to do damage?'

'Oh, very much the former,' said Magnus. 'Dinner party tattle. Green room gossip. For the most part. Which can, I have to say, be extremely damaging in its own way.'

'But nothing in the press?'

'Oh, no. Not yet at any rate.'

'You sound as if that was something inevitable,' said Caroline. She was beginning to feel alarmed.

'Not inevitable,' he said, his eyes thoughtful as he looked at her. 'But it's always a possibility. Although of course the libel laws are very clear in this country.'

'So what are you saying?' said Caroline.

'Oh, that I think there is little for Piers to worry about. Whatever the facts.'

'Magnus,' said Caroline, angry suddenly, with herself for being drawn into such a discussion, as much as with him, 'I have to tell you I find this conversation fairly offensive. You're talking about the man who's married to my daughter. And I do very much hope you're not implying –'

'I'm not actually very given to implication, Caroline. Blunt sort of chap. I'm sorry if I've offended you. I did preface my remarks by saying it was very prevalent, this sort of thing. The gossip, as well as the behaviour,' he added with a grin. 'Tell me, did you ever meet that guy Byron Patrick?'

The suddenness of the question, on top of the disquieting conversation about Piers, completely disarmed Caroline. She sat staring at Magnus Phillips, feeling her face drain of colour, her heart falling away into the depths of her body. 'What did you say?'

'I said did you ever meet that guy Byron Patrick? The one in Joe's book?'

'No,' she said, closing her eyes briefly, trying to steady herself. 'No, of course not. Why should I have?'

'Oh, I wasn't sure how far back you and Joe went. It's possible. You've read the book, I presume?'

'Well – sort of. Not really my sort of thing.' She was fighting for time, to recover herself.

'Oh. Oh, well. Just a thought. You don't know anything about all that then? His death and everything? And the article in that scandal sheet?'

'Absolutely not, no. Is this something to do with your article on bloodstock?' asked Caroline tartly. She felt better now, and suddenly furious with Magnus Phillips for trying to trick her.

'No. This is to do with a book I'm thinking of writing. About Hollywood. And various goings-on.'

'But not Piers?'

'No, not unless some strange new facts emerge.'

'Surely you're not going to write about the same people as Joe?'

'No. Not really. But they all interwine and overlap, that lot. You'd be surprised. It's been said before, I know, but Hollywood is a very small town.'

'Oh really?' she said. 'I wouldn't know. But anyway, I certainly can't help you. Look, I have to be getting back. I have work to do.'

'Me too.'

'Really?'

'Yes. I have to write my article about horses.'

'Do you know, I slightly doubt that,' said Caroline.

Magnus laughed. 'You're a cynic, Lady Hunterton.'

'I'm a realist, Mr Phillips.'

She worried and fretted through the rest of the week. What was the bastard up to: all those veiled hints about Piers: what should she do? Who should she tell? Was he trying to warn her, or to tell her something? It was worrying, scary almost. She almost phoned Joe, dialled his number even, but then put the phone down. It would sound very odd, casually mentioning she had had Magnus Phillips down for the day. Chloe? No, definitely not Chloe, it would worry and frighten her. Especially as they were all living in LA for a year while Piers made his film. Piers himself? Obviously not. No, there was nothing she could do, nothing at all. Just hope it was going to stay in the green rooms and round the dinner tables. She might ask Joe casually if he had heard anything more: although she rather thought he would have told her if he had.

The question about Brendan, clearly designed to catch her completely unawares, had been more frightening, more disturbing: had Magnus been even remotely deceived by her response? Probably not. What was he up to? Why ask her about Brendan, and not any of the other people Joe had written about? Did he have any real grounds for thinking she might have known him? He was like that detective on television, the one in the crumpled raincoat, always turning up unexpectedly with apparently innocent questions. Not that it would be so very terrible, she supposed, if it did all come out now. None of them had committed a crime, done anything wrong. She just didn't want it all hauled into the open, and certainly not by a journalist from the gutter press. It had been so sneaky, so rotten, the way he had introduced the subject. He was a devious, clever bastard, and a dangerous one, and she had been right to mistrust him. She cursed herself for letting him come down. Gullible, naïve, pathetic behaviour. In future, she would steer very clear of him. If there was an article in the *Daily Sketch* on bloodstock by Magnus Phillips on Saturday she'd go and personally kiss his arse.

* * *

On Saturday, Jack Bamforth came up to the house grinning from ear to ear; he was carrying a copy of the *Daily Sketch*.

'Here it is,' he said.

'Secrets of the Stud' ran the line across the top of the paper. 'Magnus Phillips opens some very smart stable doors.'

Caroline sat down and began to giggle rather weakly.

'What's so funny?' asked Jack.

'Oh – nothing. I was just thinking how glad I was I kept at least some of my thoughts to myself.'

Later that morning Magnus phoned.

'Did you and your nice Mr Bamforth see my piece?'

'Yes, we did,' said Caroline. 'It was full of inaccuracies. And what my friend Jane Pinchbeck is doing right this minute I dread to think. On the phone to her solicitors, I imagine. I hope you didn't get any of that from Jack.'

'Of course not. Well, thank you anyway.'

'That's all right. Er – Magnus.'

'Yes?'

'That stuff you were telling me about Piers, about the gossip.'

'Yes?'

'You see quite a lot of them. You don't think it – well, upsets Chloe, do you?'

'I don't imagine so. In any case, Chloe's innocence and adoration of your son-in-law is such that if she found Piers personally beating up an old lady in a dark alley, she'd think he was merely indulging in a little method acting.'

'I hope you're right,' said Caroline. 'And I wish you wouldn't refer to him as my son-in-law. It makes me feel old. Goodbye, Magnus.'

'No,' said Chloe. 'No, no, no. I'm sorry, Piers, but it's an appalling, horrible idea, and it makes me feel physically sick. Please don't ever mention anything like it again.'

'Oh, for fuck's sake,' said Piers, and the grey eyes were granite-hard as he looked at her, 'don't be so melodramatic, Chloe. I'm only asking.'

'I know what you're asking,' said Chloe, 'and the answer is no. And don't use that horrible language, I hate it. If you so much as mention it again, we are going home, the three of us, and you can stay here and do whatever you like.'

'Dear God, you are ridiculous,' said Piers. 'I cannot believe we are having this conversation.'

'Well, unfortunately I can,' said Chloe. 'Now please go away. Go and finish making that horrible film as fast as you can. I want to get out of this house and this town as you call it, and this whole miserable business.'

'Chloe, for God's sake,' said Piers and his face was oddly desperate as he looked at her, 'I need Pandora for this. It's just a few small scenes. She would be perfect, and I could wrap this whole sequence up.'

'Piers, Hollywood is full of children dying to get into movies. With mothers who are dying for them to get into movies. Go and find one of them.'

'Chloe, you don't seem to understand. That could take days, weeks. I want a very small and beautiful child with red hair. We happen to have one in the next room. Now we are horribly over-budget and overtime as it is, it would be one small thing you could do to help. You're not over-strong in that direction. Why not make an effort just for once?'

'You bastard,' said Chloe, surprising herself by the violence of her own reaction, 'you bastard. I do everything I can for you, against considerable odds, and –'

'Oh, spare me,' said Piers, 'I cannot stand this self-abasement. The point is, you could do this one thing for me, and make my life immeasurably simpler, and you're deliberately making it much harder.'

'I'm sorry if I am making your life hard, Piers. I happen to be more concerned with Pandora's. I can't and I won't agree to this. If necessary I shall take Pandora home to England. I'm desperately homesick anyway.'

He stared at her in silence for a moment, and then said, 'You really are unbelievably unsupportive, you know. I have grown extremely weary of your whining.' The phone rang. He picked it up and not only his voice but his face changed, became warm, smiling. 'Oh,' he said, 'oh, Robin, hi. No, it's fine of course. Sure. Yes, I'll be there in five minutes.' He put the phone down, looked at Chloe. 'I'm going now,' he said, 'I'll see you later. When you feel a little calmer, perhaps you would consider this again.'

'I'm perfectly calm,' said Chloe, 'and there is nothing to consider. Pandora is not going to become a Hollywood brat. Goodbye, Piers.' She picked up a magazine and began reading it very intently.

Piers glared at her, and then walked out, closing the door very quietly behind him. He never shouted or slammed doors; he lost his temper in an icily controlled way. She found it disturbing; she would have preferred slams and shouts.

When he had gone, she got up very slowly and wearily, and walked into the shower. She stood there for ages, in the pounding hot water – even showers in California were excessive – trying to decide what to do. If Piers really wanted Pandora in his wretched film, he would have her. There was nothing she could really do to override him. All her threats were empty and he knew it. Unless – unless she did take her home, home to England. She decided she would actually be prepared to do that. It seemed to her the most terrible prospect: to have the child, already precocious and spoilt beyond belief, acutely aware of her beauty, her charms, her talents, dragged into the claustrophobic spotlight of appearing in her father's film; being on the set every day, pampered and praised, watched, admired, cosseted, exclaimed over. It would be appalling. Chloe, who loathed the film business more every day, shrank from the prospect. And if Pandora herself got an idea that it might happen, a very noisy, multicoloured balloon really would go up. Pandora was enchantment herself if she got her own way; if she didn't, then demons paled beside what she became.

Chloe walked out of the shower and into her room; she could hear Pandora now, outside, laughing, playing near the pool, and looked down; she was wearing the sky-blue bikini Piers had bought for her (and Chloe didn't approve of that either, she hated seeing little girls dressed up like starlets, she had told him, and Piers had laughed and said Pandora was a star to him, not a starlet, a very special little star), her small body golden brown, her dark red curls tied in a bobbing topknot. Tiny, little more than a baby really, not yet three, she was beautiful; she would make an enchanting attendant for Titania (with her own dark red hair), a companion to Peaseblossom (who had a dazzling, brilliant red mop); she could see why Piers wanted her. But he wasn't going to have her. Somehow she would stop it.

She spent a miserable day; she was sick of the sunshine, sick of the pool, sick of the whole damn thing. It was spring now, and they had been there since just before Christmas. Christmas was Los Angeles at its most ridiculous with fake snow piled up and set with Christmas trees at strategic points along Hollywood Boulevard, fairy lights strung between the palm trees in Beverly Hills and carols like 'In the Deep Midwinter' playing in all the elevators. Chloe had been initially amused by it, and then became ferociously homesick. Spring seemed very little different, apart from the lack of the fake snow: one of the things she hated most was the lack of seasons. They were living in a rented house in Bel Air, and she hated it, lush and lavish as it was, hated being there; she was lonely and bored, and missed everyone, her friends, Joe, even her mother, terribly. Joe had been out a couple of months earlier and, slightly to her surprise, so had Magnus Phillips, researching, he said, some article on the casting couch culture. Piers had been cool towards him, and had not encouraged Chloe to invite him to stay, but she was so delighted to see a friendly face, hear an English voice (and a humorous one at that, standing in a corner with her at one party and whispering scandalous comments on almost everyone in the room) that she had insisted. Magnus only actually stayed in Los Angeles for four days, then disappeared, saying rather vaguely that he was off down the coast for a day or two; when he came back, he stayed less than twenty-four hours and flew out, much to Chloe's disappointment and Piers's patent relief.

'I thought you liked Magnus,' she said to him, as they ate dinner that night, at the appallingly Californian hour of six o'clock, and he said he had liked him, very much, but he had heard just one too many stories about his untrustworthiness and he would prefer to have less to do with him in future.

'Then you shouldn't have asked him to be Ned's godfather,' said Chloe light-heartedly, but Piers seemed genuinely troubled by the whole thing, so she abandoned the discussion, and diverted his attention by asking him about the problems he had been having with his lighting director which led to a hour-long exposition on the difference in lighting fantasy and reality, something which the director clearly didn't understand. Chloe didn't point out that Piers had hired the lighting director personally and at immense expense.

She had made a few friends at the dance class she had enrolled in, but they were not soul-mates, to put it mildly; although charmingly easy to get along with, they seemed to her to lack a sense of either humour or proportion, and would discuss with equal intensity and at equal length, as they sat around their identically shaped and landscaped swimming pools, their weight, their skin, their exercise routines, their sexual responses and the progress of the Vietnam War. Sometimes as she sat in the sunshine, Chloe would grow a little sleepy and confused, and would drift off over one set of LA-speak encompassing personal therapists, inadequate responses (both intellectual and sexual), hormonal imbalances and multi-orgasmic tendencies, and come to over another, taking in abuse of power, a moral edge, radicalization and imperialistic tendencies. It seemed to her that most of the phrases were interchangeable.

Piers, on the other hand, with his perfect ear for accent, for dialogue, for phrasing, loved it all; he could switch from his own perfect classic English to a kind of mellifluous west coast mid Atlantic without it sounding in the least phoney or patronizing; and he could use the words too, the Hollywood talk, the self-indulgent egocentric conversations that were not really so different from London theatre talk, but with psycho-babble thrown in. The first time she had heard it, had heard him debating in all seriousness whether the fear of his physical self or the fear of what the camera might find was the prime force in creating a character on screen, she had almost laughed, thinking he was sending himself up; but she had learnt quickly that while he was saying those things, with those people, he meant them, believed them, believed in what he was saying. And then of course, she knew, he would get back to the dining rooms of London and repeat them, word for word, only laughing, indulgently to be sure, but still laughing at the people he had left behind, who were so intellectually unsophisticated, so intense, so creatively shallow, compared with the company he now found himself in.

She had learnt to cope with it all, had learnt to perform quite skilfully at the life there, the screenings, the self-indulgent, narcissistic, egocentric gatherings, to sit and smile at least at the parties, even the wild, hedonistic affairs, where the cocaine was laid out in one room, and the sexual activities in another, but she still didn't like it. She felt lonely, small, of no importance, even more so than she did in London, there on sufferance, although everyone tried so hard to be nice to her (which made her feel guilty in itself); and to protect her, latterly at least, from the humiliation of the latest gossip, the scandal, which of course she was aware of. How could she not be, after – what? – two, three years now of it, of finally recognizing there was some basis to it, facing it, accepting it? Never spoken of, of course, never acknowledged between them, between her and Piers, just a darkness, a haunting wretchedness. Each time, every time, she thought she could stand it no longer; every time she swallowed it, swallowed her pride, her humiliation, told herself it was nothing, of no importance, that it was her Piers truly loved, wanted, needed – above all needed, that awful stifling claustrophobic need that had once seemed so precious, so wonderful and was now such a terrible, heavy burden.

Chloe went shopping after lunch and bought herself three extremely expensive dresses; she always spent money when they had had a row, it was the only way she could think of to get at Piers. He had told her to ease up on their spending briefly: that they had a slight – 'only slight' – cash-flow crisis, that the year in Los Angeles was proving expensive. Well, that was the least of her worries. She felt sore with misery, and also with self-doubt; was she really unsupportive, did she really whine all the time? Well if she did, she thought, with a flash of sudden violent rage, he had only himself to blame. He had hardly worked at shoring up her self-confidence. Nevertheless, she had to live with it. Make the absolute most of it, concentrate – no, not concentrate; what were the words of that song? one of Joe's favourites – accentuate the positive. Certainly at this particular moment in time she had no choice. She had got herself into this hot, lumpy, acutely uncomfortable bed, and she had to lie on it.

She prepared dinner herself, put some wine on ice, changed into one of the new dresses. She waited for Piers by the poolhouse; at ten o'clock she put the wine back in the fridge, the dinner in the freezer. She knew, or supposed she knew, where he was; she shut it determinedly from her thoughts. She had grown very skilful at doing that. It was the only way she could handle it. He didn't come home until after midnight; he didn't call, didn't even send a message. She heard him come in; she lay awake for hours, half dreading, half hoping he would come to their room. He didn't.

In the morning he looked white and drawn and was totally cold towards her. He kissed the children goodbye and left after a breakfast eaten in stark silence. Chloe spent another wretched morning by the pool, and then, on a whim, and in a desperate burst of courage, decided to go down to the studio and share the lunch break with Piers. She hated doing it, hated exposing herself in all her Englishness, her unsuitableness, to the cast, the crew, the intensely staid little world they all inhabited (although they were always friendly, always made her welcome when she did appear on the set); but the fierceness of her quarrel with Piers had made her uneasy and she felt as always it was she who should try to set it right. It would probably please him that she had made the effort, gone to the studio, and he would certainly not be publicly hostile to her; it was one of his virtues anyway that he forgave swiftly and easily, never bore her grudges.

She put on another of the new dresses, a white silk from Valentino, and drove across town towards West Hollywood and the studio in the pale blue Mercedes convertible that Piers had hired for her, feeling sick with nerves. She knew it was silly: that everyone would greet her rapturously, that Piers would, whatever his feelings, kiss her fondly, make a space for her at the table (he always ate with the crew, never stayed alone in the caravan; it was all part of his rather studied conviviality). And, sure enough, the man at the gate smiled at her and saluted and said, 'Hi, Mrs Windsor,' and as she walked across the parking lot she met a couple of actors she knew who kissed her ecstatically and said what a treat it was to see her, and told her she looked wonderful. 'They're just shooting the last scene, on Stage Two,' said one of them, so she made her way over to Stage Two, slipped quietly in through one of the side doors and edged her way very slowly towards the set, marvelling as always at the huge number of people who seemed to have to be present at even the smallest scene: not just the director, the cameramen, the lighting cameramen, the sound engineers, the make-up people, the hairdressers and the dressers, but dozens more, carpenters, gofers, grips, and a whole crowd more who seemed to be there only to watch. She thought (as she always thought, every time) how extraordinary it was that this great shuffling, hustling, apparently disorderly and disparate group of people standing there behind the cameras were all actually as much a physical part of the film as the actors themselves, crucial, essential to what was going on before it, with equal parts to play, talents to contribute, and yet in the final result, up there on the screen, they became invisible, except in a small line in the credits. She joined them, slightly nervous that she would be noticed, would spoil things in some way, would cause problems.

It was indeed the last scene and: 'Give me your hands if we be friends,' Puck had called out, reaching out to Piers, to Tabitha, and they, laughing, gave their hands. Chloe, enchanted, forgetting her distress, stood and stared at the breathtaking beauty of the drifting fairy forest, seemingly sprung up in the middle of the set, wonderfully real and strangely believable despite the steel girders above it, hung with wires and lights, the cameras mounted high on trolleys, the concrete floor, the constant ebb and flow of people wearing dirty jeans and dirtier T-shirts: that was what mattered, that was real, the banks of flowers, the trailing ropes of foliage, the swirling blue-white mists, peopled with drifting fairy folk with pale ethereal faces. She looked at Robin's wild faun-like face, turning from Piers to Tabitha and back again, calling out, his sweet light voice singing into music, 'And Robin shall restore amends,' and she believed in it totally, just for a moment or two; then someone behind her swore under his breath, lit a cigarette, and sharply the whole scene epitomized for her the confusion and lack of reality in this strange world, the nightmare of the whole situation; she looked at Robin Goodfellow, or was it Robin Leveret, damn him, God, she hated him, standing there, holding Piers's hand, and was it her fevered imagination, or was he really massaging his palm insidiously gently, and were the loving, tender eyes turned to him really Oberon's, or were they Piers's own? She felt she had no idea where the midsummer night ended and the harsh, hot day began, where Athens ceased to exist and Los Angeles took over, where Titania ceased to be and Tabitha became herself again; the whole thing was a long, ceaseless, confusing nightmare. If only, she thought, her heart aching, if only it were true, that their time here was truly over, if only they, as well as Puck, were speaking the very last words on the Hollywood stage, if only they could go home to England, to London, to Stebbings, if only she were back in a soft, cool climate with flat English voices and calm English ways instead of the heat and the sunshine and the California drawl and the Beverly Hills excesses, the gilded, open prison that was Hollywood.

Well it was nearly over, here at least; only another few months or so. And then they would be home, home in England.

She realized the scene was over, that everyone was breaking up; she took a deep breath and went further forward towards the stage, where Piers was talking intently to the assistant director, and to Robin Leveret, and she waited again, too nervous to interrupt. She studied Robin interestedly, as if he were a strange biological specimen (as indeed he could be called, she thought, smiling to herself, briefly, harshly cynical). He had a very strong, large presence, although physically he was small, and slight; he was older than he seemed too, not the beautiful boy he appeared to be on stage (and even on screen) but a man well into his twenties, possibly older. She had got a great pleasure from observing this, from noting the fine lines around his great blue eyes, the petulant droop of the cupid's-bow mouth, the drifts of white in the golden curls. The whole company adored him: Tabitha called him her darling boy, David Montague called him his muse, Liza her beloved. It had been a great coup, getting him, Piers had told her initially when he was casting the film, he was actually a dancer with the International Ballet, but with a rare talent for speaking (and singing) verse. He also, Piers had said, had an extraordinary grasp not just of his own part but of the whole production. 'One day I would like to direct a ballet, with him,' Piers had said, 'that would be a great experience,' and she had nodded, unsuspicious in those early halcyon days, merely awed as always by the range of Piers's talents and the breadth of his ambition.

'Hi, Mrs Windsor, how are you doing?'

It was Cathy, one of the make-up girls; pleased to have found a friend, Chloe chatted to her for a minute or two, and then realized Piers had disappeared. Glancing at the huge table where the lunch was laid, at the queue of people waiting for food, she couldn't see him at all; maybe he was in his caravan. It was a couple of hundred yards away. She made her way to it slowly, nervous now of the actual moment of encounter. She tried the door; it was locked. She knocked. No reply.

The windows were impregnable, heavily curtained: no point looking in there. She turned away, and looked back at the table; still no Piers. Maybe he was in someone else's caravan. Maybe – God, this was a nightmare. She should not have come, it had been a bad idea, she was trespassing in Piers's country, she had no business to be there, and she was about to leave quietly, make her way back to the parking lot, when she saw Tabitha suddenly, wandering along, smoking, her floating blue-green robe tied up round her waist, her red flower-bedecked hair tucked under a baseball cap, her feet clad in sneakers. Chloe didn't really want to speak to her, but Tabitha had seen her and there was no escape.

'Hallo, Chloe!' she said. 'How nice. What are you doing here?'

'I came to see Piers,' said Chloe. 'Hallo.'

'Does he know you're here?' said Tabitha, and no, said Chloe, no, he has no idea, it was a surprise. Tabitha said he should be at the lunch table, and slipped her arm through Chloe's and led her over.

Piers still wasn't there, but everyone was really nice to her and sat her down and fetched her food and Tabitha asked her if she'd seen any of the rushes and Chloe said yes, she had, and she thought it all looked wonderful, and Mark Warren, the assistant director, came and sat on her other side and told her they would really value her reaction; they gave her quite a lot of wine, and people kept wandering up, half of them dressed in fairy gear and the other half in jeans and T-shirts, some of them even with fairy gear to their waists and then jeans below it. Chloe began to feel very strange and not sure where she was or what she was doing. And still there was no sign of Piers: or of Robin Leveret.

'I expect he's rehearsing somewhere,' said Tabitha, noticing her discomfort. 'He often disappears at lunch-time. Or maybe he's having a sleep. He gets very tired lately. I expect you've noticed.'

'Yes, I have,' said Chloe, smiling bravely, although she hadn't, feeling horribly hopeless suddenly. 'Look, I must get back anyway; give him my love when he turns up.' She stood up and as she did so Robin Leveret appeared, looking rather flushed and bright-eyed.

He didn't notice her, sat down heavily on one of the chairs, poured himself a tumblerful of wine and said, 'Oh, my God, I need this.'

Tabitha was looking uneasy now, Chloe noticed. 'Robin, darling, look, Chloe's here. You haven't seen Piers, have you?' she said, and there was something in her voice that Chloe had come to recognize, something coded, something cautious.

'Chloe darling, how lovely! How wonderful that he isn't here, that terrible husband of yours, we can all enjoy you. Have you had lunch?'

'Yes, thank you,' said Chloe. 'I'm just going actually, but do you know where Piers is?'

'In his caravan,' said Robin just a little too casually. 'I saw him going in straight off the set hours ago.'

'You can't have done,' said Tabitha, still oddly tense. 'We've all been banging on the door for hours.'

'Well, darling, go and bang some more. I know he's there.'

'Oh, honestly,' said Chloe, 'it doesn't matter, he's obviously resting. I'll go home, leave him be, poor man.' She thought Tabitha and Robin too were oddly relieved by her reticence but Mark Warren said no, no, that was nonsense and anyway it was nearly time to get back to work and Chloe hadn't after all come all this way for nothing.

'Come along,' he said to her, holding out his hand, 'we will go and waken him together.' Chloe took the hand and followed him obediently towards the caravan, and she felt absolutely terrified suddenly, her heart thumping so heavily it hurt; when they reached the caravan Mark banged and banged on the door and called Piers's name but still he didn't come, and then Mark looked through a small window at the back where the curtains were only half shut and said, 'He's in there, the bugger, fast asleep,' and still they couldn't wake him: finally they found his dresser who had the key to the caravan, and he unlocked the door, Chloe still protesting that it was really not necessary, and they stood back courteously, so that she might go in first, and as the hot sun broke into the still more stifling heat of the van, and the light fell into the dimness, she saw how very necessary it had been that they came, for Piers was lying on the floor, unconscious, curled in the foetus position, his arms clutching his chest, his face a ghastly grey-white, a trickle of vomit coming from his mouth.

It was all hushed up very cleverly. He was rushed to hospital, and his stomach pumped, and was found to have swallowed an entire bottle of sleeping pills; his stomach also contained a fair amount of alcohol. As soon as he was stable, he was brought home; a press release was issued saying he had collapsed due to pressure of work, and was taking a short break; the strain of directing and starring in the *Dream*, and of preparing for his next venture, a Chekhov season in London, had proved too much for him. His wife was taking him to Palm Springs for a few days to convalesce.

Chloe, sick with fear, with remorse, had scarcely left his side since she had found him.

'Don't question him,' the doctor, the awful actor-style doctor, had said, 'just let him come round to it himself. He'll tell you when he's ready. Spoil him, make him feel good about himself, just give him everything he wants for a while. He's obviously feeling deeply unhappy and insecure. He's horribly exhausted, you know, and very thin.' His voice, and indeed his face, were clearly reproachful.

Piers told her, in the end, that he had no real idea why he had done what he did, except that he had been feeling desperate, exhausted, ill, misunderstood, and very alone. Chloe, knowing he was telling her only half, a quarter maybe, of the truth, desperately trying to reassure him of her love and support, and mindful of the doctor's words, found herself agreeing to allow Pandora to appear in *A Midsummer Night's Dream*.

Notes for Cracks chapter of *The Tinsel Underneath*. Quotes from *Handbook of Psychiatry*. Priest and Woolfson.

'There is no doubt often a desire on the part of the patient to seek attention or to manipulate the feelings and actions of other people.' (Attempted suicide.) 'Overdoses are ways of acting out problems.'

Those who actually kill themselves are 'men, old rather than young and of high social class'. (Poor old manipulative high-class Piers.)

Attempted suicides on the other hand are often 'young, female and from the lower social classes'. (Poor little lower-class Kirstie.)

Only her attempt became successful. Or did it? Was it really an 'attempt'? Did she mean to succeed?

'It is a myth that those who talk about it never do it.' Is it?

Kirstie is the most puzzling part of this puzzle. She was a tough little cookie. Why kill herself, just because she was pregnant? Why not an abortion? Did she do it because she couldn't get a part? According to Lou Burns she was a successful little scrubber, having a wild time. Not a despairing neurotic.

Doesn't make sense.

Chapter 23

1969

'Oh no,' said Caroline, to the piece of paper lying next to the phone. 'Absolutely not. No way.'

An hour later the phone rang. 'Caroline?'

'Yes, Mr Phillips. This is Caroline Hunterton.'

'I rang and left a message. You obviously didn't get it.'

'I did,' said Caroline.

'But you haven't had time to call me?'

'I've had time,' said Caroline, 'but I decided I wouldn't.'

'Why not?' The voice was amused, still confident.

'Because I didn't like what you did last time I agreed to see you.'

'What on earth did I do?' The voice sounded genuinely surprised. 'I seem to remember behaving like a perfect gentleman.'

'Mr Phillips,' said Caroline, 'you wouldn't know a perfect gentleman if he came and spat in your eye.'

'Lady Hunterton, I thought the whole point about perfect gentlemen was that they didn't spit in people's eyes.'

'Oh, for God's sake,' said Caroline irritably, 'this is getting us nowhere.'

'Absolutely not. Now I have something to tell you. Something I thought you ought to know.'

'I'm sure I don't want to hear it.'

'You might.' There was a long silence. Then: 'I find you totally attractive. You're very sexy, and I'd like to have an affair with you.'

Caroline put the phone down.

An hour later he rang again. 'I'll rephrase that. Even I can see that was ungentlemanly. I'd like to get to know you, and then have an affair with you.'

Caroline smiled in spite of herself. 'That doesn't sound too gentlemanly either.'

'Well, like you said, I'm pretty far removed from the genuine article.'

'Yes, you are.'

'And do you only have affairs with gentlemen?'

'I don't have affairs, Mr Phillips.'

She put the phone down, and walked into the kitchen, made some tea, sat there, feeling shaken and disturbed, and wondering why it was such a pleasant sensation. As she put the tea caddy away, she saw the jar of Cooper's Oxford marmalade, and felt a pang of quite extraordinary regret.

Much later that night he rang again.

'Magnus, please . . .'

'That's an improvement. At least you're not calling me Mr Phillips.'

'I wish you'd leave me alone.'

'I'm sorry, but I can't. Well, not just yet. Are you sure you wouldn't like to get to know me better?'

'Yes, I'm quite sure.'

'I've obviously misread you,' he said with a sigh so heavy she smiled in spite of herself.'

'Yes, you have. What did you read as a matter of interest?'

'Oh – boredom. Frustration. A certain – willingness to be approached.'

'Very wrong,' said Caroline, hoping she sounded firm.

'Well, I'm sorry. Is Joe there?'

'No. No, he's not.'

'Doesn't he live with you?'

'Well – yes, yes of course he does.'

'But he's not there in the house?'

'Well – not usually in the week,' she said and then cursed herself. What an incredibly stupid, crass thing to say.

'Well,' he said, 'well, it does sound like a passionate relationship.'

'Mr Phillips, I have no intention of discussing my relationships with you.'

'Not even ours?'

'We don't have one.'

'Ah. Could you just tell me one thing?'

'Probably not.'

'What did I do that was so terrible last time we met?'

'I don't want to discuss it.'

'Because if I upset you, talking about Piers Windsor, I'm very sorry. I know I lack – tact.'

'I rather think,' she said, 'there was more to it than that. Actually.'

'No. No, there wasn't. But of course you must think what you like.'

'And I get the feeling that all you really want is to get information out of me. For all these horrible things you're writing.'

'They're not all horrible. And you misjudge me.'

'I don't think I do. Goodbye, Mr Phillips.'

Three days later she was unsaddling her horse after a particularly good day's hunting when she heard a loud throbbing from the front of the house.

'Dear God,' she said.

Magnus Phillips was standing at the front door being told she wasn't yet back by Mrs Conway, the cleaner, when she walked into the hall. She was very aware that she was filthy, her face spattered with mud, her white breeches stained, her hair plastered to her head where her hat had been jammed on to it.

'You look wonderful,' said Magnus, grinning.

'Thank you. I'm going to have a bath. Mrs Conway will give you some tea. Mrs Conway, I think Mr Phillips would also like some toast and marmalade.' She found herself, entirely against her will, smiling at him. She had always admired persistence.

She lay in the bath soaping herself tenderly, feeling the pain of the day easing out of her; she had no intention of hurrying. She washed her hair, soothed body lotion all over herself, and then dressed in a big mohair jumper and a soft, easy woollen skirt. She brushed her still damp hair, applied just a dash of bright lipstick, sprayed herself with Joy and went downstairs, absolutely determined to refuse to enter into any kind of arrangement with Magnus Phillips.

'Have some more wine.'

'No, thank you. I really should be getting home.'

'I've enjoyed this evening.'

'Me too. Thank you.'

'Can I see you again?'

'No.'

'Why not?'

'Oh – because you know why not. Because of Joe, mostly. And – well, you know the other reasons.'

'Caroline, I swear I will never again try to get information out of you. OK, yes, I did wonder if you knew that guy Patrick or whatever. It really wasn't my main reason for coming. I genuinely needed your help with that piece. I could not give a monkey's fuck about Pier Windsor's sexual preferences, or what anyone may be saying about them. I just fancy you rotten. I think you're gorgeous. I'd like to – know you.'

'In the biblical sense I suppose,' said Caroline tartly.

'Well – yeah. Ultimately. But any sense would do right now.' He reached out suddenly and touched her cheek. A sliver of fire shot through Caroline: she tensed against it. He felt it and smiled.

'And you?'

'I told you. There's Joe.'

'There's nothing left there,' he said, 'so far as I can see. Except habit. And life's too short to waste on habit. Especially good ones.'

Caroline told him he was wrong.

He was clearly unimpressed.

'You just don't understand,' she said, 'And now I really must go home. It's been lovely, but. You're not going back to London tonight? On that thing?'

'That thing is the love of my life. Don't knock it. Yes, I am. Unless you have something more comfortable in mind.'

'Yes,' said Caroline. 'The village pub.'

'I'll stay with the love of my life.'

'OK. Now I really mean it, Magnus. This is it. Beginning and end.'

'Alpha and Omega. Don't you want to know more about me? Don't I intrigue you?'

'No,' she said, and she knew he knew she was lying.

Sleepless that night, she thought about Joe, and what Magnus had said. That there was nothing left but habit.

There was a lot more than that. Tenderness, affection, gratitude. And a relationship that worked. They didn't trouble one another, didn't demand much. Didn't give much either, maybe, any more. Neither of them. But they were comfortable, easy. She could live in Suffolk, enjoy her life there, he could be in London; they could meet when it suited them. It was peaceful, ideal really.

She was still very fond of Joe. And she knew he was fond of her. And there were times still, when she looked at him, at that shambolic grace of his, his long untidy body, his lazy smile, and her heart could turn over, and she wanted him all over again. But it wasn't very often and she actually couldn't remember now when they had last been to bed together. Months. That was sad. She would remember how good it had been, quite suddenly and sharply, and wonder at its passing. But he had withdrawn from her as much as she from him. They neither of them seemed to mind. There was no hostility between them. They had other concerns, other claims on their attention.

Just the same, it was all too good to throw away. She wouldn't see Magnus again.

He came down and took her out to dinner twice more, invited himself to the Moat House one Sunday when Joe was away, and then over dinner the following week told her life was too short to waste on any more courtship, and he needed her in bed with him. Otherwise, it was finished.

'There's nothing to finish,' said Caroline coolly, and walked out of the restaurant. She was very upset for a few days; then he phoned.

'I don't know what it is about you, but I'm prepared to invest a bit more time. How about dinner tomorrow?'

'I can't. I'm not coming to London.'

'I'll come to Suffolk. On my bike.'

He arrived, dirty, sweaty, grinning, and produced a bunch of rather squashed red roses from his leather jacket. Caroline felt faint.

'I need a shower before we eat.'

She took him upstairs to the guest bathroom. 'This was once the nursery bathroom,' she said. 'I lost my virginity in it.'

'Lose it again.'

'You can't lose it twice.'

'Yes, you can. It's a rather neat little concept of mine. Marital virginity. First time you do it after you're married. Or as good as married.'

'No, thank you,' said Caroline. 'Not in here anyway. I like my comfort these days.'

'Caroline, sex shouldn't be comfortable. No wonder you look like you do.'

'How do I look?'

'Frustrated,' he said.

Caroline walked out of the room.

He didn't pester her that night; he bought her dinner, told her she was the sexiest thing he'd met for years, talked about the new book he was writing about an American ballerina – 'not Piers, you see, not even Hollywood, you really should trust me – a bit.' The dancer, he said, looked divine, like a piece of thistledown on the stage, and then she went home and indulged in troilism, one girl, one boy. And snorted cocaine. And had a long-standing affair with her father. And had the world at her feet, presidents, prime ministers, all inviting her to their parties and things.

'It sounds like a horrible book.'

'It'll sell. I'm going now, I have to get back to London and write a story. I'll call you in the morning. I really do wish you'd see sense over all this.'

He roared off up the street, breaking the sweet silence of the Suffolk night, leaving her feeling fretful and unused.

She struggled to remain loyal to Joe. He had been depressed, recently, more distant from her than ever. He had refused to talk about it, indeed about anything, even on the short holiday she suggested they took (as much to get away from Magnus and his importunings as a desire to help Joe). He hadn't even been down to Suffolk at a weekend for over a month. Toby was working in Citibank's New York office; Jolyon was living in London, at art school, studying theatrical design; Chloe, increasingly uncommunicative anyway, was in Los Angeles; Fleur had refused even to have lunch with her, when she went to New York.

It was that as much as anything that made her give in to Magnus. What was she doing, trying to be good, to remain loyal to a family that didn't want her?

She rang him as he had told her to if she changed her mind.

'I'd like to see you,' she said.

'Supposing I didn't want to see you any more?' he said.

'I'd live,' said Caroline.

'I'll meet you at my place tonight.'

'No, I'm not coming to London. You can come to Suffolk again.'

'All right. On condition we can use the nursery bathroom.'

'We can use the nursery bathroom,' said Caroline, weak, limp, liquid at the very thought of him.

'It isn't just sex,' she said to him afterwards, when she was lying weak, almost tearful with pleasure, with fulfilment, 'that makes me want to be with you.'

'Oh really? What else is it?'

'I don't know. You make me feel – clever.'

'You are clever.'

'I know. I think I'd forgotten.'

'Tell me about your family,' he said the next morning, bolting huge mountains of toast and marmalade.

'It's very complex,' she said, 'it would take me weeks.'

'We should have weeks,' he said, kissing her. 'I have to go now. I'll see you soon.'

They did have weeks. They tipped into one another: fervent, vivid, joyful weeks. Caroline felt young once more, raw with sex and desire.

'I can't think why me,' she said one night, as she lay quiet at last after hours of shouting, crying, exultant love-making. 'Why not some beautiful young creature?'

'You're beautiful, and I don't specially like them young. Self-absorbed. You are a great woman, in and out of bed. You please me. I please you. As far as I'm concerned that's a pretty good formula. Stop looking for trouble.'

He was seven years younger than her, just forty. He was formidably clever; he could persuade her of anything. He came from a working-class family, his dad had been a lorry driver. 'But he was a very well-read lorry driver, he was self-taught, a marvellous man. Hence the fancy name. I was named after a Norwegian medieval king who was known as Magnus the Lawmaker. I bet you never heard of him.'

Caroline shook her head humbly.

'My father always dreamed of me being a lawyer. That's what he wanted for me. A judge really. Nothing second-rate. It was the best day of his life when I got the eleven plus, the second best when I got a place at Bristol.'

'How about when you published your first scurrilous article?' said Caroline tartly.

'He'd died by then,' said Marcus briefly. 'Killed in a pile-up on the Ml in a fog.'

'I'm sorry.'

'Yes. So was I.'

Caroline sat silent, angry with herself at her crassness, wondering how she could put it right.

'But actually,' he added suddenly, 'you're right. He would have been very disappointed.'

'And your mother?'

'She died when I was fifteen. Cancer.'

'So it was just you and your father.'

'Yes. And he wasn't there much. He was always out on the road. Working.'

'Difficult for you,' said Caroline carefully.

'Very difficult. But it taught me self-sufficiency.'

'I suppose it would have done.'

He had got a First in English and then moved up to London and got a job on the *Daily Sketch*.

'I'm ideal for you,' he had said to the editor at his interview, 'I'm a socialist-voting Tory, an educated working-class man. Just what you need.'

The editor, irritated at his arrogance, nevertheless agreed and took him on.

He was a brilliant reporter; he could get a story out of anyone. He was ruthless; nothing, no shreds of conscience held him back. He could make the great seem mediocre, and the truly good appear hypocritical. No one could twist a quote like Magnus Phillips; no one could place a comment after an innocent remark and turn it to a death knell.

He was tireless; he could sit half the night outside a house, waiting for his victim to return home, turn in a story, go to the all-night pub, and then be at his desk again at ten thirty. His heavy frame, his rather lumbering walk concealed a fierce, a restless energy; he could never sleep for more than four hours, could not sit at his desk for more than twenty minutes. He paced the office, while he wrote even a long story, often with a large whisky in his hand, smoking, scowling at people, returning to his desk and his typewriter every so often to beat out a few more sentences. For recreation he played squash with a ferocity that terrified his opponents, and rode his bike up and down the M1 at over a hundred miles an hour. He said it released his inhibitions.

Women either found him dislikeable or irresistible, and occasionally both. He did not waste time on honeyed words, tender gestures; his approach to Caroline had been typical.

He told her he had timed his approach to her very carefully. 'Straight away, I wanted you. At the wedding. I kept getting a fucking great erection, sitting at your dining table. Listening to Piers's wanky speech. But I knew it wouldn't do me any good. Not even after the christening. You were still looking just a bit too settled. So I waited. I'm good at waiting,' he added with a grin.

She liked him more as time went by. He had an odd set of morals, harsh and dispassionate, but they were at least consistent, and he had a fierce honesty. He was ruthless, unconcerned about the havoc he caused in people's lives. He saw – or said he saw – no harm in any of it. He doorstepped, eavesdropped, inveigled himself into the confidence of neighbours, teachers, friends of his victims, and felt no compunction about any of it.

'No compassion either?' she had said once, shocked, in the early days.

'Not really,' he had said, grinning at her. 'People set themselves up, they deserve to be shot down. If they have something to hide, I think they have a reason. Usually a bad one.'

'But, Magnus, what about the children, the parents . . .' She was thinking about Brendan.

'Caroline, before people do something immoral or unfortunate, they should think of their children and their parents. I can't be held responsible for other people's irresponsible behaviour.'

She learnt about him slowly; he had been married (once) to a girl from university, and divorced her a couple of years later. 'She disapproved of me which I could forgive and I found her boring, which I couldn't.' He had lived with another girl for a long time and the reason for the termination of that relationship was more obscure. 'It just didn't work any more.' She learnt in time that the girl had been having another relationship concurrently for months. Caroline suspected that being cuckolded had hurt Magnus more than simply losing out to someone else. And then a long series of semi-permanent relationships.

'And now you. Very nice.'

They were having dinner in London; Joe was away in the States.

'I'm not even semi-permanent, Magnus. I'm a pseudo-married woman. In love' – she felt, rather than heard herself stumble over the words – 'in love with the man I live with.'

'Bollocks. And.'

'What about children?' said Caroline after a pause.

'Yes, well, what about them?'

'Wouldn't you have liked them?'

'Not really, no. I don't like children. I don't have any egotistical need to reproduce myself. And I like to come first in relationships, which children certainly preclude. Tell me about your children. And why didn't you have any with Joe?'

'It was never that kind of relationship.'

'Very wise. So tell me about the others.'

'Other what?'

'Relationships. And children. Caroline, you're being very obscure.'

She told him about William; and about Chloe and Toby and Jolyon.

'So why did you marry this boring old fart of a bart?'

Caroline was angry suddenly; she stood up. 'Don't use your tabloid language on me. I loved William very much. Goodnight.'

He shrugged, watched her leave the restaurant.

She drove home shaking with rage.

At six the next morning the phone rang. It was Magnus.

'I'm sorry. Sorry I offended you.'

She was silent.

'Can I come in?'

'Where are you?'

'Just down the street.'

She sighed. It was exactly the kind of behaviour she couldn't resist. 'All right.'

He came in looking almost shamefaced. He was unshaven, filthy dirty.

'I've been on the bike for the last three hours. I went down to Brighton.'

'You're mad,' said Caroline.

'I know it. Can I have a shower?'

'Yes, all right.'

'Want to share it?'

'No. Absolutely not.'

They stood in the shower together, the water thudding down; he held her, kissed her, differently, gently.

He pushed her down; she was kneeling, kneeling in the warm waterfall; he knelt before her.

'Sweet, sweet Caroline,' he said, pushing her legs gently apart.

She felt him moving into her; the water confused her, she felt strange, odd, removed from herself, aware only of his penis entering her, her vagina welcoming it, sweetly wantonly welcoming. She pushed herself on to it, on to him; began to rise and fall. Her climax came swiftly, sharply; his took longer, he knelt there, pushing into her, harder and harder, impossibly far, and when he came, she came again with him, following him, calling out with pleasure.

The water ran cold; they wrapped themselves in towels, sat in the kitchen drinking coffee. She wondered how she could do this, in Joe's home. She was shocked at herself.

'Caroline, I'm tempted to say all kinds of things to you,' said Magnus, reaching out a hand, pushing back her wet hair.

'Don't,' said Caroline. 'Please don't. It's too dangerous.'

But she still didn't tell him about Brendan, about Fleur.

It was too precious, too secret, too much her own. And besides she still didn't quite trust him. In any way.

Chapter 24

1969–70

Fleur wondered what Piers's fans would think if they could see him now: lying on his back, his mouth open, a whining snore coming from his throat, a slight dribble of saliva leaching from the side of his mouth. His hair, his wonderful gold-streaked hair, was ruffled sideways; the roots, she noticed with interest, were a shade or two darker than the rest, and studded with grey. Hardly Romeo: more like Romeo's dad.

She turned away, unable to contemplate him and what she was doing there with him, in the vast double bed in his suite at the Algonquin, and tried to decide whether she should strike now, today, this morning, when he woke up, surprise him, lash out, ask him, or whether she should continue to take a more subtle approach. Subtlety was palling; she had been working on him for almost a year, and despite all her efforts, he was still sticking to his story, that he had not been in Hollywood until 1959. Of course it wasn't really a year: they had only met four times. And apart from the long weekend in California, all very short, overnight stops. Even the long weekend had been short, not even a weekend at all; he had been interestingly anxious not to stay in LA itself, but had whisked her off to Catalina Island and the wonderfully Victorian Glenmore Plaza as fast as was decently possible, and then had proceeded to leave her there for thirty hours, without explanation, saying only that he had to go, it was business, but he would be back. She hadn't exactly minded, but it had been irritating and a big bite out of the weekend.

If it had all been a bit more fun, she might have minded less; Nigel had at least had the virtues of generosity, and a sense of humour. Piers had neither. He wasn't exactly mean: he always booked into expensive hotels and ordered the best champagne, that sort of thing, and he obviously spent a fortune on his clothes – his vanity was inordinate, womanish, he required admiration, appreciation – but he never gave her proper presents, just flowers, maybe a scarf. And there was certainly no humour: Piers's idea of a joke was a long theatrical story about someone else going wrong.

He was absolutely ghastly in bed; she had never thought to feel sympathy for Chloe, but the occasional pang did enter her, along with Piers's very small, incompetent penis. He either came almost immediately, or went on seemingly for ever, with about as much imagination and variation as a truck on the highway; afterwards, in either case, he would lie looking pleasedly at her, telling her how wonderful it had been for him, and he hoped for her. He was better at the early bits, especially at kissing; she supposed he must have learnt a few tricks from his co-stars, and he made a great thing of talking in bed, both before and afterwards, which she imagined would be all right if you really liked him; it was all very poetic and supposedly flattering. Fleur just thought it was irritating.

She had, with exquisite skill, got him talking about Chloe quite a lot; he obviously found her a bore and an entirely unsatisfactory wife. 'Of course I adore her, but she is so very young, and unsophisticated, and she finds it terribly difficult, poor darling, to cope with all the social side of my life. And of course, she doesn't really understand my work, how could she, and as if it mattered really. But I feel with you, Fleur, even though we've known each other such a little while, you actually can see what I'm trying to do, with this film for instance. I find that very exciting.'

He plainly adored his children; or rather he adored Pandora: 'I can't expect you to appreciate such a thing, and it's dreadful of me even to talk about her to you, but she is so exquisite, and so intelligent, has incredible sensitivity, for such a tiny little thing. I'm so proud of her.'

Fleur found that really boring; but stories about Chloe were fascinating, even what she looked like. 'She's really very pretty, in that English rose way, a young English girl, that was why I fell in love with her, totally unspoilt. Not terribly clever with clothes, but I suppose that will come, poor darling. She's wonderful with the houses though; we have such a pretty house in London, and of course my house in the country, I've had for many years, and that's very much more mine, but even that I feel I can trust to her . . .'

She was fascinated by his sexual inclinations. Her initial instinct that he had been homosexual had been not entirely correct: she was quite convinced that he had strong tendencies in that direction, but there was no doubt that he genuinely enjoyed having sex with her. Indeed he was, although not skilful, very highly sexed; he could produce an erection several times a night – not bad for an old guy, Fleur thought – and he was tremendously tactile, he liked stroking, kissing, cuddling even. She found that about the only engaging thing about him; she was sure a psychiatrist would have traced it all back to his childhood and the mother he so patently adored, but in the lack of anything more satisfactory, she read a lot of quasi-medical articles, mostly in magazines like *Forum*, about homosexuals and bisexuals and decided he was probably the latter.

She disliked him increasingly; his vanity, his conceit, his self-absorption. He had virtues: he was easy-tempered, genuinely kind, and could be thoughtful. But they were greatly outweighed by the faults. Well, not that she was immune from faults. As always on these occasions, these nights, and however hard she tried not to, she thought suddenly, sharply of Reuben, his sweetness, his gentleness, his trust; how hideously he would be hurt if he knew what she was doing (no matter what the end might be), how unlikely and how unsatisfactory her explanation. She found it quite unsatisfactory herself, at times; she was supposed to love someone, really love them – well, she wasn't supposed to, she did, she did – she had a wonderful sexual relationship with him, and then when it suited her, for some rather dubious end of her own, she just went to bed with someone else. She must stop it, Fleur decided, stop it very soon, before any real harm was done, before she broke Reuben's heart and lost her self-respect. She wasn't gaining anything, getting anywhere; it was a pointless exercise. Interesting, initially, but pointless. And disappointing. Very disappointing. No need to say anything, make a big deal out of it; she would just say she couldn't see him next time he called. Easy. She felt more cheerful suddenly, less remorseful about herself; she might even manage to go to sleep.

God, it had been a long night. She looked at her watch: Nigel's watch. Only three. She had a really big day ahead: she was going for an interview; she'd been headhunted by Browne Phillips Ivy, one of the most prestigious, medium-size, blue-chip agencies in Manhattan. It was only a would-you-be-interested-in-a-chat call, but she knew what it meant: we want you. Every time she thought about that, ever since the phone had rung, she had been high, high on exhilaration and a huge shot of self-esteem. Fleur was low on self-esteem; her last encounter with Joe had brought it even lower.

Sometimes she realized, thinking idly about leaving Silk diMaggio, what it would mean, and she felt quite a sense of regret over Nigel. Especially when she was with Piers. At least he had been honest with her. Well, almost. She would miss him, if she left. And Mick. She would really miss Mick. Apart from adoring him, he was her Svengali, he'd taught her everything. She couldn't actually imagine how she was going to get along without him, without his funny, brilliant, tough guidance, his originality, his ferocious perfectionism. Maybe she could take him with her. That'd be fun. Maybe – she realized her mind was finally hazing over, drifting into irrelevancies, that she was going to sleep. She turned over, pulled the pillow over her ears against Piers's snores, and fell into a complicated dream about Mick and Nigel and Poppy all making a film of *Romeo and Juliet*.

When she woke up, it was still dark: thank God, she was always afraid they'd forget the Wake Up call. She looked at the clock: five thirty. What had woken her? She turned cautiously: Piers was no longer in the bed. She heard him moving in the bathroom, then heard the phone gently picked up; Fleur half sat up, listening, totally awake.

She couldn't hear all the conversation, and she didn't dare pick up the extension; but what she did hear was so extremely interesting, she felt all her patience, all her endeavours had been worthwhile. She said goodbye to him at eight thirty, and went off to her interview at Browne Phillips Ivy with her heart flying. This was clearly going to be altogether a good day.

'This is a very nice portfolio, Miss FitzPatrick. Very nice indeed. Impressive for someone of your age and – what – five years' work.' Chuck Laurence sat back in his chair and smiled at her. He was one of the creative group heads at Browne Phillips Ivy and he did not look too much like Mick diMaggio. More from the Nigel Silk mould, very WASP, very old money, but less sleek, less smooth, tall and slightly gangly, with neat brown hair and piercing blue eyes. 'Very nice indeed. I specially like the work on T. & J. Stores. We have a relevant account here, as you know. And the cosmetic work is interesting too. Now, then, tell me why you're thinking of leaving Silk diMaggio. You obviously have a very successful relationship with them.'

'Well, one has to move around,' said Fleur. 'I think six years is quite a long time really in this business. I love it there, but I've got itchy feet. And I want some new challenges. I got your call, or rather the call from Macphersons, and it was a kind of a nudge. In absolutely the right direction. So – here I am.'

'Well, I'm pleased you are. Look, I have to talk to some other people here, and then I'll get back to you. I'm very glad you came in.'

'Fine. Thank you for seeing me.'

He called her later that day, asked her to go back to meet Baz Browne. She had to tell Poppy, it was so exciting.

'My,' said Poppy, 'Baz Browne, eh? You really are on your way, Fleur.'

'I really think I am,' said Fleur.

'I have some news too,' said Poppy. 'I'm getting married.'

Poppy's man did not seem nearly good enough for her; his name was Gill Hillman, and he was very good looking, tall, Jewish, he could be extremely funny, and was an excellent dancer, but that was where his virtues ended, as far as Fleur could see. He was moody, often morose and occasionally extremely bad tempered; he was a lawyer, with a medium-size firm in Manhattan, and was not doing terribly well. Fleur could see why. If she was paying someone a fortune to sort out her problems, she'd want encounters with him to be pleasant, not an assault course. Maybe he made more effort with his clients than he did with her, but whenever she had a conversation with Gill Hillman she came away feeling intellectually incompetent. The phrase most often on his lips was, 'I'm afraid you've missed the point.' He clearly didn't like Fleur, seeing her, no doubt, she thought, as a rival in his affections for Poppy, and he made no attempt to disguise the fact that he thought Reuben was little better than a buffoon. When Fleur discussed this with Reuben, he shrugged and said in his even-tempered way that Gill was a bit of a superior bastard, but Poppy liked him, so he must be OK.

'He's not marrying me,' he said with his sweetest smile.

Mrs Blake was also clearly not entirely happy about the relationship; Gill made an effort to be nice to her, but she confided in Fleur that she found him a little hard to talk to. For someone who was Reuben's mother, Fleur felt this was quite an observation. 'But Poppy adores him, so I'm sure things will be fine. She's very sensible.'

Poppy did adore Gill; she came right out and confronted Fleur's anxieties one evening over a great many glasses of wine. 'I know you all think he's a little difficult, and he is. That's exactly what I love about him. He needs me. He's awkward because he's shy and unconfident, and he knows he isn't charming, and when he's relaxed and we're alone together he is just the sweetest guy in the world.'

Fleur thought of Gill telling her she had entirely missed the point about *Midnight Cowboy* which they had all seen together the previous night, and the progress of the Vietnam War, and tried to believe her.

'That's great,' she said, slightly uncertainly.

'And he adores me. I'll tell you something else, Fleur, when it comes to bed, he is just fantastic. I never had such sex. Ever.'

'Now that I can relate to,' said Fleur.

She didn't quite know what to do with the information she had acquired that day, listening to Piers on the telephone, but she felt it was important and valuable. Only little threads, really, half of them obscured, muffled, through the wall; a person-to-person call to a somebody Zwirn (there couldn't be that many) on some exchange she hadn't been able to identify (but within the United States). A tender enquiry about someone else, a hope expressed to be 'over soon' (over? over where?) and, most important, a promise to 'increase the allowance'. She stored it away in her brain, and returned to it two or three times a day, checking it over, feeling pleased with herself for acquiring it.

Browne Phillips Ivy made her an offer of senior copywriter on a group of three accounts, at a salary of thirty-five thousand dollars a year. Fleur took a deep breath and said she couldn't think of moving for less than forty thousand dollars and felt sick for a whole morning until they came back and said OK, but she'd certainly be earning it. Fleur said she certainly hoped she would, and went to tell Mick. She knew it was slightly rash before BPI confirmed in writing, but she trusted them, and she wanted to get the nasty part over. It was very nasty, because Mick was so nice; he was clearly upset, and told her they'd miss her terribly, and he really didn't know what Julian Morell would have to say about it. He also said he thought the whole idea was for her to be FitzPatrick Advertising, not part of some other lousy set-up, and she had said it was, but she needed a little wider experience first. Nigel was less upset, and more put out, but he and Mick took her out to a wonderful lunch at the Four Seasons on her last day, and they all returned extremely drunk and got a lot drunker on the champagne Fleur had blued her entire first month's raise on. She was planning to spend most of the other month's raises on a new apartment: 'I adore it here,' she said sadly to Mary, 'but it is a little uncomfortable a lot of the time, like when it's very hot and very cold. And I've seen these lofts on Central Park West and they just blew me away.'

Mary hugged her as closely as her latest pregnancy allowed and said she hoped Fleur wouldn't be too grand to visit sometimes.

'Mary,' said Fleur, and there was a touch of pain in her voice, 'you're the nearest to family I've got. Just try and keep me away.'

She put in a call to Rose Sharon in Los Angeles. The maid told her she was away filming for another three months, but she would certainly have her call her when she got back.

'Thanks,' said Fleur and put the phone down, feeling rather bleak. Rose had been a bit of a disappointment. Nothing more from her about the starlet, Lindsay Lancaster, nothing about anything. Well, she obviously had a great many claims on her time. And it must all seem very unimportant to her.

Sometimes Fleur felt faintly, just faintly tempted to give the whole thing up. She was busy, she was happy, she was successful; and it was all such an old, cold trail. It was all so slow, so painfully slow; hardly surprising, when it was just her, pitted against the whole world. What did she think she was going to achieve, except a lot of newly awakened grief for herself? Then she would remember, as sharply as ever, the feeling of outrage when she had heard about her father's death and the way it had come about; she would get out the cutting from *Inside Story*, and read it, and look at her father's handsome, smiling face, and remember how he was, and how different from the way *Inside Story* had presented him, and how much she had loved him; and she knew she couldn't betray him by simply leaving things, leaving him the sad sordid subject of a sad sordid story. He deserved better than that. And no one else was going to give it to him.

Browne Phillips Ivy was a very different place from Silk diMaggio: larger, older, more formal, less fun. Senior management was very senior, distanced from the other departments: the thought of any of them wandering into an office and peering over a shoulder, as Nigel did, was laughable. They were known by their second names only, and when Fleur was introduced to Baz Browne, and Col Ivy, they both called her Miss FitzPatrick, and she knew they would continue to do so for some time. It was not one of the giants, not a JWT or an Ogilvy's, but it was a large and seriously rated agency, and both Browne and, even more, Matthew Phillips, were both originally creative men who had been brought in in the late fifties by Col Ivy: Browne from JWT, Phillips from Bates. The triumvirate had quadrupled its growth in five years; all three were considered gurus in the business. The agency was based on Madison, a couple of blocks down from Silk diMaggio, in rather more sober offices; the accounts people presented an extremely conservative front, wore dark suits, didn't lark around in office hours and had individual offices, rather than open plan, and the creative people were certainly not encouraged to think they had carte blanche to behave in any way irresponsibly. Indeed, it was one of the tenets of the agency that the creative departments were forced to give very serious consideration to such sober and grown-up matters as budgets, spend, research, and media. Fleur liked that; she had always considered the rift between account management and creative far too wide; it was one of her personal credos.

Browne Phillips Ivy were not currently considered so creatively brilliant as Silk diMaggio, but they had a solid history of famous campaigns, two of which – for Mayer's Whisky and Holden's Airlines – were part of advertising history. Life there was less like a party and more like hard work, and although Fleur had some misgivings about the culture shock, she welcomed the insistence that was placed on what she thought of as account experience, and knew that working in a large, blue-chip agency was not only crucial to her career pattern, but would introduce her to entirely new aspects of the advertising business.

Her accounts were Morton's, a cheap clothes chain, Stobbs, a small publishing house specializing in glossy heavily illustrated books, and Pettit's, who fought a fierce ongoing battle with Petfoods for the number one slot in the pet food war.

She worked with two art directors, neither of whom she considered especially talented, Ricky Pentry on Morton's and Pettit's, and Julia Miller on Stobbs, but both of whom liked her and seemed enormously grateful to have her in their team. They took her out to lunch on her first day, and told her that Sol Morton was a nightmare 'in and out of the office' said Julia darkly, that Dick Rankin, marketing director of Pettit's, used the agency in general and the group in particular as his own personal New York office, and Bernard Stobbs was the sweetest man in Manhattan, but 'as much use as a client as a steeplejack with vertigo'.

'The group head won't hear a word against any of them,' said Julia. 'So be warned.'

'I'm warned,' said Fleur.

Her first tough meeting was with Sol Morton. He was Jewish, short, thickset (although not fat), dark-haired, wore an enormous amount of gold jewellery, and smoked huge cigars whatever the time of day. He was aggressive, rude, defensive about his shops – and could be extremely funny. Fleur liked him.

'Well,' he said, looking her up and down after their initial introduction. 'I can see you've never been into Morton's in your life.'

'I certainly have,' said Fleur with dignity. 'I go in all the time.'

'Since you were put on to this account.'

'No, long before I knew about this account.'

'Really? What did you buy there?' His darting little black eyes were sharp, cynical.

'Bags.'

'What sort of bags?'

'Those gorgeous little leather shoulder bags. The quilted ones, that look a bit like Chanel. And about ten silk shirts.'

'How did you hear about it? Through the ads?'

'No,' said Fleur, taking a deep breath, and looking nervously at Chuck Laurence as she spoke. 'I heard about it through a friend.'

'Mmm. Says a lot for your ads, Chuck. I want to tell you I think this new lot stinks. Stinks. Pictures of women in plastic bags: puhl–lease! I want a reason for going into Morton's, not some fucking arty-farty rubbish. Let's see what Fleur here thinks of them.'

Fleur met his gaze steadily. 'I couldn't possibly begin to comment.'

'Don't give me that shit. You're new to this account. You're still a consumer, near as dammit. Tell me how you react to plastic bags. Come on. I'm waiting.'

'You'll have to wait,' said Fleur. 'You can't expect me to comment, you know you can't. This is my first week, Mr Morton, it's totally unfair. You're out of line.'

'Sol, darling, Sol.' He laughed suddenly, blew a cloud of cigar smoke out. 'OK, I'll ask you in your second week. Let's talk media, Chuck. No sense discussing creative. That campaign has to go straight down the toilet, I'm telling you. Let's see what Fleur here can come up with.'

It was a long morning; he rejected everything, every newspaper, every magazine, except *Cosmopolitan*, every TV slot. He told them they were fart-arses, that they knew less about advertising the retail trade than his great-grandmother, that they shouldn't feel remotely comfortable about retaining the account.

'I'm looking around, Chuck, I warn you. I want advertising, not Thoughts for the Day.'

They took him out to lunch inevitably; to the Roosevelt Hotel, which was just around the corner from the agency. It was a great haunt for advertising people at the time: not a smart hotel, but a good restaurant and in the heart of adland. Sol Morton ate his way through the card, drank two large martinis, more than a bottle of claret, and finished with two double brandies. He appeared marginally more sober at the end than when they began. He sat next to Fleur and spent most of the meal rubbing his leg against hers. She endured it good-naturedly, reckoning that she could find a way to handle it when she knew him a little better.

When they got back to the office, Ricky collapsed into his chair, threw his arms above his head. 'Jesus wept,' he said.

'We all will if we lose that account,' said Chuck. 'Fleur, what do you make of friend Sol? You handled that rubbish about what you thought of the roughs very well. I felt for you.'

'So did Mr Morton,' said Fleur tartly. 'Right through lunch.'

'Oh, God,' said Chuck. 'I'm sorry. Maybe –'

'Don't worry about it,' said Fleur. 'It's my problem. For now. Can I take a look at the research tonight and talk tomorrow?'

'Sure. That'd be good. You'll see there's something about the English market in there, Fleur; he has some fantasy about opening there.'

Her new apartment was gorgeous; it was exactly what she had promised herself, a loft conversion on the Upper West Side: a huge studio room, a small bedroom, and a kitchen and bathroom. She even had someone to clean it and do her laundry once a week. 'I work such terrible hours now, worse than ever,' she said to Poppy, slightly embarrassed, 'and I can afford it, it's my present to myself.'

'Look who's complaining,' said Poppy with a grin. 'You can hire a fleet of servants if you like, Fleur, it's entirely up to you.'

'I know, but I feel bad about it,' said Fleur. 'They didn't have maids in Sheepshead Bay.'

'Well, that didn't do either the maids or the people in Sheepshead Bay any good,' said Poppy, who was a staunch democrat. 'You do your bit for the economy, Fleur, and get your laundry done at the same time.'

The maid was called Tina, and she was black, extremely fat and extremely cheerful. She came to Fleur either early in the mornings, often arriving before Fleur had left, or late at night; she liked to work the same time as her man, who worked on the subway. 'We get up together and we go to bed together,' she said, grinning, her mountain of flesh shaking. 'My man likes me with him. All the time.' And she dug her large elbow into Fleur's ribs, giggling loudly. She took a maternal interest in Fleur and worried about the hours she worked, and how little there always was in her fridge, and the fact that she seemed to be alone in the world, without a man.

'You put on some weight, Miss Fitz, you'll find some man to cuddle up to you for always,' she said.

Fleur tried to tell her she didn't want a man to cuddle up to her for always, but Tina clearly didn't believe her.

Tina was there when she got home the night after her lunch with Morton, putting away the laundry.

'They changed us to nights,' she said by way of explanation. 'I made you some soup. You don't eat enough, Miss Fitz.'

'I eat plenty,' said Fleur, sitting down wearily to the soup which looked and smelt wonderful, 'but I certainly like this. You mustn't spoil me, Tina.'

'Ain't nobody else here to spoil you,' said Tina pointedly. 'And you look tired.'

'I am tired,' said Fleur. 'Hard day. Heavy lunch. Dirty old man.'

'Honey, lead me to him. My Rob, he hasn't laid a finger on me now for four nights. I think he got another woman.' The bulk heaved; Fleur smiled at her.

'You wouldn't like him, Tina. Not your type.'

'I'm telling you, Miss Fitz, after four nights anyone's my type. He going to be any good to you, now?'

'I don't think so. Not in the way you mean, anyway. Tina, did you ever go to Morton's for clothes?'

'Morton's? The chain? No, I never did. Too small for me.'

'I guess so. But if they weren't, would you?'

'I don't think so, Miss FitzPatrick. They're too pricey for me.'

'You're wrong, Tina, they are seriously cheap.'

'You're kidding me. They don't look it.'

'That's interesting,' said Fleur. 'Thanks, Tina. See you in the morning.'

Her last waking thought was that Morton's was reckoned tacky by the rich, and pricey by the poor.

'Everyone's got it wrong,' she said to Chuck Laurence three days later, after two dozen more conversations on the subject.

'Got what wrong?'

'Morton's. Or rather, nobody's got it right. I mean, it says in the research that it has no image, that it's just there; that's nothing new. But no two people I talked to had remotely an idea what it was really like. Comments varied from sleazy to flash, cheap to expensive.'

'Anecdotal evidence, Fleur. Beware of it. We're very suspicious of it here.'

'I know, I know. But, like I say, the research bears it out. The thing about Morton's is that it's so unexpected. I mean what are they, those shops? Boutiques? No. Department stores? No. Madam shops? No. They're unique. They just – just . . .' Her voice tailed away. She stared at Chuck and she could feel the colour draining away from her face. 'I might go away and think for a while,' she said. 'I have a kind of an idea.'

'I like it,' said Sol Morton. 'I like it very much. It's clever. Needs more work, of course. But it certainly says a lot more than those shitty plastic bags. "Just Morton's." It has style. Real style.'

'You must put that on the shitty bags,' said Fleur. 'In the corner, above the logo. The word "Just" I mean. And on the bills, everywhere. So that everyone will start thinking of it as Just Morton's. Unique, not like anywhere else, not like any other shop in town.'

'No,' said Sol Morton. 'Couldn't do that. Too expensive. We have a million of those bags. Anyway, it seems to be overworking the point to me.'

'Not at all,' said Fleur, 'and when this campaign gets going, those million bags will all be gone. You can put it on the next lot, although we're talking corporate here; it ought to start right away, or when the campaign breaks.'

'It'll be great on the radio and on TV,' said Sol. 'I like that jingle. It's cute.'

'Everyone'll be singing it,' said Chuck.

He looked like he was about to start singing himself, thought Fleur.

With Bernard Stobbs she had a different problem altogether. They all did. He was white-haired, sweet-faced, charming, cultured and deeply appreciative, and he had absolutely no idea what he wanted to say; and if he did he changed his mind again the very next day.

'Let's go visual,' he would say, and they would do a series of beautiful ads, showing his book jackets, or the houses featured in one of his latest books, and he would shake his head and say, no, no, they're lovely, but I think copy is the way to sell books, just words, telling 'em what they're going to get.

She finally cracked that one by just letting Bernard Stobbs talk, lovingly, charmingly about his books (as he would do all night, if allowed) and printing what he said. The type was quite large and interspersed with pictures from the books, and of their jackets. The campaign made wonderful posters, and people would stand stock still on the subway, and in the street, and even fail to move off at green lights because they were reading his charming amusing words. It won Fleur a raise and, just as importantly, it won her Bernard Stobbs's intense gratitude: not because the sales of his books increased considerably (which they did) but because visits to the agency had become pleasurable occasions, rather than stressful ordeals.

She was too busy to think about anything else but her job: everything else was put on hold. She worked late, she worked early; she socialized almost entirely within the profession. There was a lot of that. It was a time of high visibility, when everyone was extremely busy being seen: eating the right things in the right places, wearing the right clothes. 'It's almost as if you couldn't star in a Broadway play so you do this instead,' said Fleur, collapsing in a chair in Mary Steinberg's kitchen one Saturday afternoon near Christmas, after recounting a week of almost frenetic busyness. 'It's wearing me out, I tell you.'

'It sounds wonderful to me,' said Mary, reaching out and wiping noses on a couple of small faces with one hand, while spooning apple sauce into the mouth of a third with another. 'You don't have any vacancies for a once bright girl with an attention span of up to five seconds, do you?'

'No, but all our ads are for people with attention spans of up to five seconds,' said Fleur. She looked at Mary consideringly. 'If you ever found yourself with more than five seconds to spare, we're always looking for market researchers, you know, to ask people how they feel about some ad or some product. You could do that from this kitchen, Mary, wiping those very noses. How about it?'

'Sounds wonderful,' said Mary. 'Just lead me to it.'

Then early in December Rose called.

'Fleur. I'm so sorry. I've been in Mexico. Forgive me.'

'Of course,' said Fleur, trying not to sound cool. 'It doesn't matter at all. How was Mexico?'

'Beautiful. You'd love it. Maybe we could go together one day.'

'Maybe,' said Fleur. 'Er – Rose, nothing about Lindsay Lancaster, I don't suppose?'

'Nothing. She is, as I thought, married. Moved away. Not in movies. Not a lot I can do really, Fleur. I did try. I'm so sorry.'

She sounded genuinely regretful; Fleur was touched for a minute, then she hardened her heart, remembered this was one of the greatest actresses of her generation. She could turn on regret, remorse, love, desire as the first millimetre of film began to move through the camera.

'Oh well,' she said, 'never mind.' And then, rashly, foolishly perhaps, she heard her voice saying, because she simply had to say it to someone, 'Rose, does the name Zwirn mean anything to you? Michelle Zwirn? Or Gerard?'

There was a long silence. Then Rose said, 'No, darling, I really don't think so. I'll rake my memory for you. And if it turns over any bright little embers, I'll let you know. Why?'

'Oh – nothing really,' said Fleur, 'just something somebody said.'

Piers sent her a very extravagant Christmas card of his country house which she studied with great interest; it looked to her like a real English stately home. God, he must be rich. A very large bouquet of roses also arrived from him, with a card that said, 'I've missed you since May. Next year must be better.' Fleur threw the card in the trash can and took the roses round to Mary.

She read in the *New York Times* that Piers Windsor's *Midsummer Night's Dream* was up for an Oscar, and that his wife was expecting her third baby.

Against every odd, she had hoped to hear from Joe Payton over Christmas, and did not; Caroline as always wrote and sent her a cheque (a very large one this year, five hundred dollars, which would mean she could carpet her apartment, great). She wrote a letter of thanks to Caroline rather earlier than usual, and told her she was welcome to visit any time. She knew Caroline never would. She saw an article Joe had written syndicated from the *Sunday Telegraph* about theatrical wives, and found the copy about Chloe offensively flattering.

Sol Morton took her out alone for a Christmas lunch at the Seafare of the Aegean, and told her he thought she wasn't just gorgeous, but extremely talented, and that if she ever wanted to go into business on her own, he would be interested in backing her, and would certainly give her the Morton's account. He also made it very plain that he would like to put their relationship on a more personal level.

Fleur told him she was flattered by both offers, that she thought the latter would upset the very good working arrangement they had, and that if ever she did go solo, she would certainly be looking to him for his custom.

Reuben asked her to spend Christmas at his mother's home in Sagaponack; Poppy was to go to Gill's parents in New Jersey, and Mrs Blake was feeling bereft. Fleur said she would adore it. The three of them had a wonderful time, eating and drinking a great deal, walking on the South Shore, playing backgammon and discussing Gill and what Poppy might see in him at great length.

Julia Miller announced at the beginning of January that she was moving to Greys. One of the applicants for the job as her replacement was Bella Buchanan. Fleur was forced to tell Chuck Laurence with great regret that she had worked with Bella before and she really didn't consider her talent worth a row of beans.

Sol Morton had decided he wanted to do a new corporate design on his shops. Seven design shops pitched for the account, and it was won, with the help of some charmingly diffident recommendations from Fleur FitzPatrick, by a rather eccentric young man called Reuben Blake.

* * *

Poppy and Gill were married in March, at the Brotherhood Synagogue in Gramercy Park, and had a rather subdued lunch party afterwards at the Carlyle, just the families and a few friends. Fleur, who was Poppy's attendant, and honorary family, sat between Reuben and Mrs Blake, who was alternately excited and weepy. Poppy looked charmingly original in a white lace mid-calf dress and a little lace bonnet; Gill looked a cliché in a dark grey suit and a brocade waistcoat. He made a long and pompous speech, which made Fleur doubt more than ever Poppy's claim that he was shy and insecure. His parents were a surprise, rather modest, nervous people, and plainly not very well off; she had been expecting rather arrogant carbon copies of Gill. Gill and Poppy left around five for a honeymoon in the Bahamas, and Reuben and Fleur offered to take Mrs Blake out to dinner to cheer her up. She said she couldn't eat a thing, and what she'd really like to do was go to the movies; they saw *Bob and Carol and Ted and Alice* and after it Reuben took Mrs Blake home after kissing Fleur tenderly and saying that Natalie Wood was beautiful, just like her.

Fleur lay awake half the night, wondering if what she felt for Reuben was indeed really love.

Then, later that month, just when she had begun to forget all about the mysterious Zwirns herself, a letter arrived from Rose.

'My darling Fleur,
Forgive me (again) for being such an age. But I'm afraid that once again there is nothing to tell you. I have asked around, talked to old friends, gone through my old contact books, raked through my memory, really worked at it for you: but no records anywhere, of anyone called Zwirn. None even in the phone book. I'm so sorry, Fleur. I'm not much help to you, am I?

Come over and see me soon.

Best love,

Rose.

Fleur sighed and put the letter away in her desk. Rose was very sweet, very kind, but as a help in her quest, she was absolutely no use at all.

Chapter 25

1970

'Oh, Joe, really! I'm surprised at you, a journalist and all. *Private Eye* are very behind with their gossip.'

'But, Chloe –'

'Honestly, Joe, I can't remember when people weren't going on about all this,' said Chloe. She sat back on the huge sofa in the drawing room at Montpelier Square, holding her new baby daughter tenderly in her arms, and smiled serenely at Joe. 'It comes up every year with the daisies. Piers is homosexual, Piers is going to leave me, Piers has a boyfriend in Los Angeles. Damian Lutyens, Robin Leveret, old Uncle Tom Cobley. I didn't know they had him and David Montague in bed together, I must say. Whoever told you that one?'

'Oh – I got it at a *Private Eye* lunch,' said Joe.

'Don't they realize he and Liza have been married for more than ten years?'

'I don't know,' said Joe. He looked confused, more miserable than she could ever remember.

'Oh, well, no doubt it will keep on surfacing for a bit. There are always nasty rumours circulating about Piers, about most actors; he warned me himself, they don't mean anything, they keep people amused, and the public from getting bored. The only thing to do is ignore them, not even bother denying them.'

'But, Chloe –'

'Yes, Joe?' She could hear her own voice growing sharper, feel her smile less sickly sweet. Christ, she thought, I should be in movies myself.

'Oh – nothing.'

'Look, Joe,' said Chloe, leaning forward. 'If Piers was a homosexual, I'd know. And I can tell you, I'd have left him. Taken the children and left. Now he has his faults, and he can be very difficult, but I' – she heard herself hesitate almost imperceptibly, then went on – 'I love him and we have a good marriage. You were all wrong, you see, and I was right. Now could you please just forget all about this, don't repeat it to anyone and tell your friend Mr Ingrams that if a word of this reaches the pages of his horrible paper, Piers will sue. He's always said so, and he would.'

'Right,' said Joe. 'Well, I'm sorry, darling, and I wouldn't have upset you for the world. I – we – just felt we should warn you. That there might be some mud flying about.'

'Well – thank you. That was most kind,' said Chloe politely, as if he had just asked her to go for a drive with him, or to have another helping of pudding, 'but I – we – can look after ourselves.'

'Yes, of course you can,' said Joe.

Later, telling Caroline about the conversation, he was still very upset. 'Either she's been taking acting lessons herself, or she really believes what she says. I think possibly the latter. Maybe even it's true.'

'Let's hope it is,' said Caroline. She sounded uncertain.

Joe looked at her sharply. 'You don't sound very confident.'

'Oh – I don't know.' She avoided his eyes. 'You always said you thought he was queer, Joe. You know you did.'

'Yes, I did. And I've heard the odd innuendo over the years. But Chloe's quite right, there always are these rumours about actors. They can hardly be surprised. The way they carry on. I mean look at Piers, all those clothes of his, having his hair streaked, the way he hugs people. Men, I mean. I don't give a toss what he does or is, except if it hurts Chloe, but he can hardly be surprised if people talk about him.'

'Well, he obviously isn't. Surprised, I mean. Anyway, let's hope your friend Mr Ingrams is wrong. He often is.'

'He often isn't actually,' said Joe. 'He has this great gift for seeking out, boring out the truth. Nigel Dempster once said to me that he was completely unafraid of pursuing a story. "Just keep on going," he says, "don't let anyone stop you; if you think it's true, keep after it." It's what makes him a great journalist.'

'Great journalist,' said Caroline with a shudder. 'Putting all those terrible stories about.'

'Well, Chloe seems to have it under control. Not too upset by it. Thank God. Mind you, if she found Piers putting arsenic in her tea, she'd say he thought it was sugar.'

'That's exactly what Magnus said,' said Caroline and then met Joe's eyes slightly confusedly. She was blushing.

'Magnus? When were you talking to Magnus?'

'Oh – the other day. Well, not the other day. The last time Chloe and Piers had a party. You must remember.'

'No, I don't really.' His eyes were thoughtful as he looked at her. 'But then I never remember anything much.'

'No,' said Caroline, 'that's true.'

Later that day, Chloe pushed little Kitty through the park, wondering how much longer she could stand it. The hurt, the humiliation, the rejection, the necessity to dissemble, and to people like Joe, people she loved and cared about. She thought of his concerned, troubled face when he had warned her about *Private Eye*, clearly having had to brace himself with several stiff drinks, and almost laughed. They evidently all thought she was a sweet, wide-eyed innocent still. If they only knew. How she really felt, what she really had to endure. Would they be shocked? Understanding? Supportive? Well, however much she could do with some support and understanding, she couldn't run the risk of going looking for it. But it was very hard. The whole awful cycle was hard, from the beginning, the increased absences, the vague explanations, the elaborate excuses, to the end, the grief, the confrontation, the self-abasement, the promises. Half the time, she knew nothing happened more than a passionate flirtation, an emotional game very much like the one Piers had played with her in the early days; he had a near craving for flattery, admiration, appreciation. At other times the relationships proceeded, became more serious, more intense – and more often than not, then, were consummated. She found it less distressing these days, and more wearying. She had grown more tolerant towards the cause while increasingly intolerant of the effect. Most of all she was weary of the promises at the end, that it would never happen again, that he had changed, that he was truly contrite, that he would be faithful to her, that it was over. They left her unmoved, those promises, except in so far as she could hardly bear to listen to them. The early shock, humiliation at her discovery, had given way to a sense of resignation; there was nothing to be done, absolutely nothing at all, except leave him, and she was not prepared to do that. She still cared about him, she supposed – certainly cared about her children, about the family she had so longed for and was determined to preserve. They were still together: still a unit, still a family, still arguably even a happy family. She was going to keep it that way, was not going to have her children exposed to a broken marriage and all its attendant miseries.

But it wasn't easy. In fact it was horribly difficult. Because her personal life and her family were everything to her, because she had no work, nowhere to hide, nowhere to bury herself and her hurt, she was forced to confront it, to live with it, all the time. There was no one she could talk to about it, no one even she could tell; it was too dangerous and so it went on like some awful wound, refusing to heal, that she had to conceal from everyone.

She astonished herself constantly by her ability to do so. She had at one stage become so helplessly unhappy that she had gone to a psychotherapist for help, a kind gentle woman who had waited patiently as Chloe had struggled against her own loyalty to tell her about Piers, about his sexual ambivalence, had finally eased it out of her, and had encouraged her to talk for many hours, for what amounted to days; who had urged her to try first to understand what Piers endured himself: an endless sense of frustration and longing, an uncertainty of what he really wanted, a lack of sexual fulfilment in everything he did.

'He's not a homosexual, from everything you tell me, especially his considerable sexual demands on you, he's bisexual – as I might say we all are, to some extent – but with the constant dissatisfaction that implies: always looking, always searching; and there's always something missing,' she had said, and urged patience, kindness, tolerance, and tried to help her to reach an understanding of Piers and also to come to terms with her own unhappiness. She also suggested Piers might like to seek support and help himself; Chloe suggested it to him, freshly concerned for, sympathetic with him, in her new perception of his behaviour; and there had been rages, scenes, and finally tears for days. He had been down that road once, he said, with all its attendant miseries and humiliations, and it had yielded nothing. 'Stop treating me like a bloody pariah,' he had finally shouted. 'I love you, I want you, a bloody sight more than you want me, I might add, what more do you want?'

Nothing, she had said, frightened, alarmed at his rage; nothing, of course, it's all right, Piers, I'm sorry, I shouldn't have suggested it, and had lain in bed that night, as he made love to her furiously, frantically, hating it, shrinking from him, hearing her therapist's gentle voice: 'He needs to trust you, Chloe; above all, he is afraid you will fail him.'

She found a most unlikely ally in Liza Montague who met the issue head-on one day when she found Chloe in tears in the loo at a party. Piers was standing with his arm around Damian Lutyens, very drunk, a bottle of champagne dangling from the other hand; they were singing in high falsettos the old music-hall duet, 'Tell me Pretty Maiden'. It was very funny; except that Chloe didn't find it so.

'Bit near the bone, wasn't it?' said Liza, cheerfully kind, after giving her a hug and handing her a handkerchief. 'You poor little soul. I did tell David at the time we should have warned you, but he wouldn't have it.'

'I wouldn't have listened,' said Chloe, blowing her nose, smiling a rather wobbly smile at Liza. 'I'd have thought you were yet another grown-up trying to spoil my happiness.'

'Oh, how ageing!' said Liza. 'But that's what David said. Listen, sweetie, it doesn't mean a lot you know. He loves you very much. Very very much. He's told me so. Many times.'

'Has he?' said Chloe, staring at her.

'Yes, he has. You have to hang on to that. Either that or leave him.'

'Oh, I'd never do that,' said Chloe, 'I don't think. I believe so much in marriage, you know? And the family. I've got three children, I have to think of them. It's just – well, so painful. I love him so much, still, and it seems such a dreadful rejection.'

'Yes, of course it is,' said Liza briskly. 'But what you have to remember, darling, is that Piers is an actor.'

'I do remember,' said Chloe tartly.

'What I mean is that you can't judge him by conventional, traditional standards. You just can't. Actors are gamblers. They gamble with life.'

'I don't know what you mean,' said Chloe.

'I mean that they're risk-takers. If you're successful in the theatre you're extremely tough, extremely shrewd, extremely ruthless. You have a huge capacity to stay the course. The going is very difficult and you escape in various ways. Sometimes it's drink, sometimes drugs, sometimes religion. And quite often sex.'

'Yes,' said Chloe. Her voice sounded very dull, very tired. 'Yes, I can see that.'

Liza smiled at her. 'David Niven once said this to me and it's so true. With very great difficulty you climb to the top of the tree and you see a bough and you think I can stay there for a bit, just gently mop my brow, there isn't much higher I can go, I've arrived. And then just as you settle down it breaks, snaps. Think of Piers on that bough, Chloe, waiting for it to snap. He's living on the edge of everything. He can't be a homebody. Even for you.'

Chloe didn't like to say, when Liza was being so kind, that she thought there might be some middle course between being a homebody and having a large number of homosexual affairs, but she was oddly comforted by the conversation.

She was permanently and seriously tempted herself by Ludovic Ingram. He had continued, in his quasi-serious way, to declare an undying passion for her; whenever they met he implored her to run away from Piers, and marry him. She found him extremely attractive and his behaviour beguiling; trapped in a situation where her self-esteem was sent constantly plummeting, she needed a source of reassurance. He was not only excessively charming and amusing, he was very sexy; hungry herself, aware at least now that the sexual problems she had were at least partly due to Piers, and not some underlying frigidity, the thought of going to bed with Ludovic was at times irresistible. He had affairs, from time to time, and he always talked to her about them, as if he needed her approval, and assured her they meant nothing, that he was merely waiting for her. At times she believed him, certainly wanted to; he kept her physically at a distance, saying if he once so much as kissed her he would not be able to resist her any longer. But when sometimes they were dancing together, and she would be in his arms, acutely aware of the strength, the sheer physical power of him, she longed more than anything in the world to give in, to have an affair with him at least. Once, on such an occasion, he had looked down into her eyes and said, very quietly, 'I mean it all, you know, Chloe. I am madly in love with you,' and she had smiled up at him, slightly uncertainly, and had seen that a word from her and they would both be lost, and had fled there and then from the dance floor, and indeed from the party as soon as it was decently possible, afraid of herself and what she might do.

He had rung her in the morning, as light-heartedly flirtatious as ever, clearly to defuse the situation, had said he would continue his campaign, that he would live in hope, but in the meantime they would have to remain friends. And friends they were; but she trembled at the thought of what might happen if he knew exactly how unhappy and how unsatisfied with her marriage she was.

And then things threatened to get really out of hand.

It began when Flavia died: suddenly, quietly and sweetly as she had lived, she slipped out of life. Piers was away; it was an appalling shock to him. He cried for hours, like a small child: 'I loved her so much,' he said, 'so very

very much. She was always there for me. We were everything to one another for so long.'

Chloe didn't know how to comfort him; she had never seen him so upset. For days he hardly came out of his room; he spoke a eulogy at her funeral and broke down before he had finished. Not even Pandora could distract him from his grief. Then he embarked on a wild round of socializing, in what she could only describe as excitement; not an evening, not a lunch-time even, could he bear to be with fewer than a dozen people. He insisted on her giving endless dinner parties, house parties at Stebbings at the weekends, accompanying him to gatherings all over the country, becoming ever more manic in his enthusiasm; drinking an enormous amount, and then falling into bed in a near stupor at the end of each day. Chloe was bewildered, sought help and advice from her therapist; she was soothing, comforting.

'It's his way of escaping from the grief. It's not the best way, it means he hasn't faced it. You must try and help him do that. Because one day, when he does have to do that, whether over her or someone else, he may not be able to handle it at all.'

Chloe often thought of her words in the years to come.

And then Piers's escape took a different route altogether.

'Chloe? Hi. This is Jolyon.'

'Hallo, Jolyon. How are you?'

'I'm fine. Is Piers there?'

'No, he's having lunch with some moguls. Talking about some Chekhov revival.'

'Well, that's exactly what I want to talk to him about.'

'Really? Why?'

'Well – well, he said I might be able to work on it.'

'Jolyon, how marvellous. I'll tell him you called. Maybe you could come for a drink this evening.'

'OK. Fine.'

How sweet, she thought, Piers going out of his way to help her little brother. Really, in spite of everything, he was a truly nice man. She was lucky. In spite of everything.

Jolyon came for a drink that evening; Piers seemed delighted to see him, told him that yes, he had spoken to the designer and he could start working as soon as Lydia Wintour was free of a rather tedious opera set she was doing.

'You'll like Lydia,' he said to Jolyon. 'She's wonderfully talented. She did the set for the *Lady*.'

'I know,' said Jolyon. He was scarlet with pleasure.

Chloe looked at him, smiling gently to herself. He was such a sweet boy these days, so gentle and self-effacing, and so phenomenally good looking, with his dark red hair and his brown eyes. So different from the ghastly Toby, who was every bit as dreadful as he had seemed set to be in his childhood: he had somehow managed to pick up every rogue gene going. He was large and clumsy and heavily built, with a florid face, small dark eyes and a rather loose, full mouth; and he was possessed of the extraordinary and rather oafish self-confidence peculiar to the more unintelligent ex-public schoolboy. He wore either very formal suits for his City job, or what he perceived to be the latest fashion in the worst possible taste, extra-wide flares, loud floral shirts and high stacked boots; his dark hair, which was just too wavy, was cut unfashionably short, with enormous wedge-shaped sideburns which looked as if they had been stuck on. He had a tendency to sweat and as he believed (and indeed had been heard frequently to proclaim) that any kind of cosmetic was strictly for woofters, he very often smelt strongly. Piers couldn't stand Toby and had told Chloe he really would rather he came to the house as little as possible; she was happy to concede.

But Jolyon was a delight, a frequent visitor, much loved by his little nieces and nephew. He still nurtured a hopeless passion for Annunciata Fallon who, once Joe's piece about her had failed to materialize, had ignored his existence, even if she was sitting next to him at supper, which she often was. Annunciata was one of Piers's favourites, and a frequent guest; Chloe was baffled but no longer troubled by it. She found Annunciata tedious, complacent and self-centred, but she served a purpose in a tireless bolstering of Piers's ever-hungry ego, and relieved Chloe of at least a little of that task. The theatrical ego never failed to amaze Chloe: the extra-ordinary combination of towering self-confidence and almost pathological self-doubt. Piers had often told her, and indeed so had many of his friends, Annunciata included, that all actors were desperately shy, that they were actors for that very reason, it gave them another persona to hide behind. Watching them at parties or round the dinner table, talking (almost always about themselves), pontificating, play-acting, she found the shyness claim laughable and indeed enraging. Shy to Chloe meant feeling sick for hours before a party, shrinking from making an entrance, dreading conversation with new people, and an almost physical condition that slowed the traffic of ideas from brain to tongue, so that you stood there, helplessly mute, pathetically dull, apologetic for your very presence, relieved when someone finally excused themselves from your side and moved on.

'You are not *shy*,' she had shouted at Piers one day, when she had been particularly anxious about a dinner they were getting ready for and he had told her not to complain and that he was as shy as she was. 'You don't know what it means.'

He had looked at her irritably, almost angry and said, 'Chloe, I assure you before I go anywhere, anywhere at all, I am terrified. I shrink from a roomful of people.'

'Oh, Piers,' she said, 'how can you say such ridiculous things, when the minute you're anywhere you're laughing, joking, telling stories, moving from person to person.'

'You just don't understand,' he said. 'All that time I am acting. Acting at not being dull. At being amusing. At being good value. It's just as difficult for me, darling, believe me.'

'I don't,' said Chloe, 'I'm afraid. But never mind.'

Much of the time she felt her life with Piers was conducted from within the confines of a soundproof room, from which she struggled to communicate with him.

Jolyon left his scarf behind that evening. It was a very nice scarf, cashmere, brand-new by the look of it, from S. Fisher in the Burlington Arcade, not cheap, she thought, almost surprised: obviously a present from someone. He would be missing it. She put it in an envelope and addressed it to his flat in the Fulham Road.

'Rosemary,' she said at breakfast, 'could you possibly pop this scarf into the post for me on the way to taking Pandora to nursery school? It's my brother's, he'll be missing it.'

'I'll take it, darling,' said Piers, looking up from the paper, 'I'll be leaving first. Darling, you must read this piece about Peter Brook's *Dream*. It sounds quite extraordinary, so different from ours. Terribly modern; the fairies are all to be dressed in sackcloth, apparently, and the set just a stark white box. Very clever I'm sure, but I wonder how dear old Joe Public will take it. I have a sneaky feeling they still prefer something like ours.'

'Of course I'll read it,' said Chloe, knowing that she wouldn't. 'Are you doing anything special today, Piers?'

'Oh – not really. Busy with Chekhov. I just long for Vanessa, but I don't know if I can get her.'

'Are you lunching with anyone?'

'No, definitely not. Shackled up with a lot of very boring agents. Why?'

'Oh – nothing. Just wondered. I might go and have lunch with a friend. That's all.'

'All right, darling. Good Lord, *Jesus Christ Superstar* looks set to break a few records. Clever young chap, that Lloyd Webber. We might ask him to dinner one evening.'

'Yes, all right,' said Chloe.

As she spooned egg custard into little Kitty at tea-time, there was a ring at the door. It was Jolyon. He was wearing the scarf.

'Hallo, Chloe. I left my book behind last night. Steinbeck. *Mice and Men*. Have you found it?'

'No,' said Chloe, 'but I'll have a look. You seem to have left everything behind last night, Jolyon. How on earth did you get your scarf so quickly?'

'Oh – Piers brought it to lunch,' said Jolyon carelessly. 'He was a bit cross with me actually, leaving it around.'

'You had lunch with Piers? What, at his agent's office?'

'No,' said Jolyon, 'at the Ivy actually. Celebration. Of my involvement with the Chekhov, you know?'

'Yes,' said Chloe slowly. 'I do know. This was just a sudden thing was it, Jolyon?'

'Well – fairly sudden. He called me very early to arrange it and to tick me off about the scarf and suggested it.'

'What's very early? Before breakfast?'

'Oh yes. Around seven thirty. He woke me up.'

'I see.' Keep calm, Chloe, it probably means nothing; just Piers playing Mystery Man as usual. 'And why was he cross about the scarf?'

'Well, because he gave it to me. The other day.'

'Piers gave you that scarf? Jolyon, it must have cost a fortune. What on earth for?'

'Oh – I did him a small favour. Suggested someone who could paint a mural for a friend of his.'

'That's a pretty big thank-you present,' said Chloe. She felt very sick, and was too frightened even to think why.

'Do you mind, darling, if I stay in London this weekend?' said Piers. 'I have so much to do.'

'Of course not. I'd quite like a London weekend myself.'

'Oh, no, sweetheart, you mustn't do that. You know how the children love to go to Stebbings.'

'Piers, they don't care where they are. As long as they're with us. And Pandora is with you.'

'But darling, Pandora wants to ride. She told me so.'

'She can ride in London. In the park, she likes that too.'

'Well – oh, all right. But it's going to be fearfully boring, lots of chat about Chekhov.'

'I'll stay out of your way,' said Chloe briskly.

Two hours later the phone rang.

'Mrs Windsor, this is Peter.'

Peter Walton was the new groom Piers had hired. He was very nice; she liked him.

'Oh, hallo, Peter. There's not a problem is there?'

'No problem at all, Mrs Windsor. But I just had a call from a yard in Oxford, and they've got a pony for Pandora for you to look at. He sounds perfect, little grey, thirteen hands, very good temperament. The thing is they say they can only hold him for a few days. Could you come over on Saturday with me?'

'Well – oh, yes, all right, Peter. I was going to stay in London this weekend, but Pandora would never forgive me if we lost the perfect pony.'

'She certainly wouldn't.'

The pony was very nice: dish-faced, with a very long forelock hanging almost into his calm eyes. His name was Misty. Pandora fell in love with him.

'Please, Mummy, please. I want him so much.'

'Well, I'll have to ask Daddy. I'll phone him now.'

'She likes him,' she said to Piers, laughing. 'What shall I do? Buy him?'

'Well – you're not the greatest judge of horseflesh. I'd like to have a look at him myself, I think.'

'But, Piers, they can't keep him after tomorrow. Peter thinks he's very nice.'

'OK, I'll have a look at him tomorrow. I'll come down. Around lunch-time, can't make it before.'

'But I was going to come back to London.'

'Well don't. Stay down there, and I'll see you tomorrow.'

'Oh – all right,' said Chloe. She was very tired. She didn't really fancy driving all the way back to London with three fractious children. Rosemary had the weekend off.

She made them all high tea, sat and watched *The Muppets* with them, and put them to bed. Then she poured herself a large glass of wine, and settled down in front of the television again with the *Radio Times* to plan her evening.

The offerings on TV were predictably fatuous; but late on BBC2 she noticed there was a documentary on theatre designers, one of whom was Lydia Wintour. Jolyon ought to see that; he'd never notice it for himself. She picked up the phone and dialled his number. There was no reply.

Well, there wouldn't be, on a Saturday night, she told herself, and then wondered if Piers would like to see the programme. She phoned the house: there were several rings and then the answering machine clicked on. Funny. Obviously Piers didn't want to be disturbed. She waited for the message to begin, and then stiffened, her hands gripping the receiver so tightly her knuckles were white. It was a new message, in Piers's most actory voice, even a little pompous: 'This is Piers Windsor. And no, I'm not actually here. Sorry. But leave a message and I'll ring you before the evening is out. And thank you so much for calling.' It wasn't the message that upset Chloe; before it cut to the bleep there was a lot of scuffling and then a sudden fit of giggling in the background. She knew that giggle. It was Jolyon.

OK, Chloe, keep calm. So Jolyon's there. Why shouldn't he be? He's part of that production. Of course he would be. And of course Piers wouldn't have mentioned it, he never does tell me more than he absolutely has to. It was just coincidence about the pony, making me stay in the country. All weekend. Of course it was. Piers wouldn't. He just wouldn't do such a thing. Not even Piers. Just have another glass of wine and stop being hysterical.

He phoned at nine thirty, sounding contrite. 'Darling! I'm so sorry. We were engrossed in casting and I just couldn't bear the thought of being interrupted. What can I do for you?'

'Oh – nothing. There's a programme on later. Lydia's in it. I thought you might want to see it.'

'Bless you, darling, how sweet of you. I will watch it, if I possibly can. We're pretty engrossed here.'

'Who's we, Piers?'

'Oh – Geoffrey. Of course. Jim.'

'Jim Prendergast? Why is he there?'

'Because we're talking money, darling. You don't seem to believe me. Do you want to speak to him?'

'Of course not. Who else?'

'What's this, the tenth degree? Tabitha, actually. I want her for Masha and by a miracle she may be free.'

'Oh. Is – is Jolyon there?'

'Jolyon? Of course not. Why on earth should he be?'

'Oh – I don't know. I thought if you were really talking Chekhov –'

'Darling, I adore your brother, but I don't think he has that much to offer just yet. Now we'll watch the programme if we can, and bless you for thinking of me. Goodnight, darling. Meet you at the yard tomorrow. Get Peter to come along, won't you?'

'What? Oh, yes, of course, Goodnight, Piers.'

She waited until nearly eleven and rang Jolyon again: and at twelve. No reply. Obviously he was out clubbing somewhere.

Misty was pronounced everything Piers would have wished and duly purchased; Peter drove him back in the box to Stebbings and Piers and Chloe went back to London in convoy, Pandora weeping copiously all the way because having finally got her pony she was now not to see him until the following Friday. In the end Chloe flashed Piers down in the Rolls and transferred Pandora into it. 'She's your daughter,' she said slightly grimly. 'You deal with her,' and went again before he could argue. He shot off at a great speed towards London, and when she got back Pandora was asleep on the sofa.

'She'll be fine now,' he said, looking down at her adoringly. 'She's so terribly excited, bless her little heart. I've promised we won't make her get off Mr Misty next Saturday even to have her lunch.'

'Oh, Piers,' said Chloe wearily, 'she'll hold you to that.'

'That's fine. You won't have to do a thing.'

Next morning was lyrically beautiful: spring had arrived. Chloe shook off her morbid suspicions, drove Pandora and Ned to school and then, taking herself by surprise, rang her mother. She made a huge effort to keep in touch with her for the children's sake; she knew if she didn't she would probably only see her once a year at the most.

'Mummy? It's me. I wondered if you'd like a visit some time this week or next, just for a couple of days. Piers is so busy, and I'd love to come and see you. I could leave Pandora in London with Rosemary and just bring the little ones.'

Caroline sounded unusually flustered. 'Oh, Chloe. How nice. Well, of course it would be lovely, but – well which day were you thinking of?'

'I don't know. Whichever would suit you.'

'Well, I'm not sure, Chloe. Not next week. I'm rather busy. The new horses, you know, and everything. Perhaps the next one. Ring me again. Nearer the time.'

'Oh. Oh, all right,' said Chloe. She felt surprisingly hurt. 'I – I don't have to be looked after all the time, Mummy. I am family.'

'Yes, of course. But – well, if you do come I'd like to have time for you. I'm sorry, but we have two of the new mares being covered next week and – well, it just isn't a good time. How are you?' she added, clearly feeling she was not being maternally correct.

'Oh, I'm fine,' said Chloe coolly. 'Well, Mummy, just ring me when you have time. Goodbye.'

'Goodbye, Chloe. See you soon. Oh, and Chloe –'

'Yes, Mummy?'

'Thank Piers for taking such an interest in Jolyon, would you? He had such a marvellous time on Saturday.'

'On when?' said Chloe. The day had darkened around her; she tried to fight down her panic.

'On Saturday. Was it? Yes, because it went on into Sunday. When Piers had that great meeting at your house. Jolyon was so flattered to be asked.'

'Yes,' said Chloe, 'yes, of course I will.'

Chloe went into the small room she called her sitting room and wrote a letter to Piers telling him she was leaving him and why. Then she told Rosemary to pack some of the children's clothes together, they were going to stay with her mother for a few days.

'I know Pandora shouldn't miss school, but I need the break. I'm sorry. You don't have to come: take the rest of the week off.'

She packed some things for herself, and spent the rest of the morning pacing the house. At lunch-time she sent Rosemary to get Ned from nursery school and collect Pandora from school. She told her teacher that her mother wasn't well and that she had to go and stay with her for a few days. Pandora was delighted.

'Goody. Will Jack take me riding? Could we have Misty brought over?'

'Darling, it's much too far. But I'm sure Jack will ride with you.'

'Is Daddy coming?'

'No,' said Chloe. 'Daddy isn't.'

She arrived at the Moat House soon after seven. She hadn't rung her mother; she couldn't face the excuses. If she arrived, Caroline would have to keep them all. She had to go somewhere and she didn't want to go to Stebbings or a hotel. And she had a somewhat surprising yearning, in the midst of all this misery, for Suffolk. Suffolk and home.

As she pulled into the drive, she saw a huge motorbike parked by the front door.

'Motorbike,' said Ned excitedly. 'Want to ride it.'

'Edmund, you can't. I wonder whose it is. Some workman, I suppose.' The front door was locked; she went round to the back of the house, carrying Kitty. The kitchen, the downstairs of the house was deserted. Pandora and Ned were running round the garden, released from the boredom of the journey; she called her mother's name. No reply. Kitty was soaking wet; she would have to change her. She carried her up the stairs, to the old nursery; there were still some threadbare old nappies there. Nanny used to say with great pride that both Caroline and Chloe had worn them.

As she went along the corridor, she heard a noise. A loud, strange noise: a wild desperate cry. It came from the nursery bathroom. What on earth was going on? It sounded as if some wounded animal or something might be there.

'Mummy?' she called, anxious, fearful. The cry halted; she half ran down the long corridor, hanging on to Kitty, fumbled with the handle, pushed the door quietly open.

Lying on the bathmat stark naked, with Magnus Phillips astride her, was her mother, her arms flung back, her eyes meeting Chloe in a mixture of shock, embarrassment and – without doubt – more than a flash of humour.

'Chloe, have a drink!' Magnus, dressed now in a towelling bathrobe, a delighted Ned hanging round his knees, waiting for his promised ride on the bike, was clearly enjoying the situation.

'No, thank you,' said Chloe. 'I don't want a drink.'

'You need a drink.'

'I don't need one either.'

'Chloe, have a drink. And try to be a little more sensible.'

'Sensible! I find you and my mother making love on the nursery floor, and you tell me to be sensible.'

'She is over twenty-one,' said Magnus calmly.

'Yes and she's supposed to be – well, as good as married. To Joe.'

'Well. I don't think I should get into this. I'm going to get dressed and then take Ned for a ride.'

'You are not taking Ned on that dreadful thing.'

'He'll be fine. Won't you, Ned?'

'No,' said Chloe.

'Yes!' said Ned and burst into noisy tears. Kitty joined in, startled. Pandora meanwhile was ringing at the front door bell, which was a jangling pull, endlessly. The dogs started to bark very loudly.

Caroline appeared, fully dressed, white-faced and slightly wild-eyed, in the doorway. 'Chloe, for God's sake. What is going on here? Would you please keep those children quiet.'

'How could you?' said Chloe, and her voice was vibrant with anger and rage. 'How could you? Cheat on Joe like that. You're disgusting.'

'Chloe, please –'

'Don't Chloe me. I just can't understand you. Joe, who's so good and kind and loyal. All these years. Even – well, you obviously haven't changed one bit.'

'Chloe, how dare you? How dare you speak to me like that!'

'I dare because it's true. You know it is. All your life you've cheated on people. Me, Daddy, even – well, even Fleur. Yes, even her. You failed her very nicely, didn't you? Being a perfect mother to us and just leaving her –'

Caroline walked forward and slapped her hard on the face. There was a stark silence; then Magnus Phillips stepped forward.

'Caroline. That was uncalled for.'

Caroline stared at him, her face distorted, ugly. Then she turned and walked out of the room.

Ned started crying again; Magnus picked him up, and he cried harder. He handed him to Chloe, and produced a bar of chocolate from his dressing-gown pocket. 'Unless boys have changed greatly since I was one, this'll shut him up.'

'He's not allowed chocolate,' said Chloe, aware even in her misery that she sounded very prissy.

'Dear me!' said Magnus. 'Your mother's not allowed sex, Ned's not allowed chocolate. Is there anything at all that you approve of, Chloe?'

'Nothing that you would understand,' said Chloe coldly.

'OK, I'm the villain of the piece. I'm old enough and ugly enough to cope with that. Come on, have a drink.'

'No! I keep telling you, I don't want a drink,' said Chloe and burst into tears.

Magnus Phillips was very good. 'I just might join in this crying jag myself,' he said, taking Ned, handing him the chocolate, placing Kitty, who had gone back to sleep, tenderly on the sofa next to her mother.

Then he sat down on the other side of Chloe and put his arm round her.

'Now come on. I can see you're very upset, that it is very upsetting, but it's not as terrible as you seem to think. Your mother and Joe have been drifting apart for some time. You must have noticed. He hardly ever comes here. Here' – he passed her his handkerchief – 'dry your eyes. That's better.'

Chloe blew her nose; then she said, 'I'm sorry, Magnus. But I think it is terrible. I'm so fond of Joe, he's been like a father to me. He's such a nice, good person. It seems so – cruel.'

'Well, life's cruel, Chloe. It just is.'

'Oh and that's supposed to make it all right, I suppose. We all do exactly what we like, just because life's cruel.'

'No, of course not. But we all do wrong and stupid things – sometimes. Mostly we get away with them.'

'Do we?' said Chloe. 'Well some of us try not to do them in the first place.'

'And the rest of us are human,' said Magnus, looking at her rather interestedly.

Then right on cue, Caroline came back into the room and the phone rang. She picked it up.

'Hallo? Oh – Joe. Yes, yes, I'm fine. No, that's right, she's here.' She handed it to Chloe, her eyes confused, startled even.

Chloe shook her head. She couldn't face him, knowing about this betrayal. 'I can't talk to him now.'

'Chloe, he says it's very urgent.'

'Oh.' She took the phone, held it for a moment against her, pulling herself together.

'Joe? Yes?'

'Chloe, darling. I'm sorry to do this to you. But you have to get back to London. It's Piers. Rosemary rang me. He's – he's taken an overdose.'

Later, much later, when Chloe had left again, had been driven by Magnus to the station, put on to the train, with Joe meeting her at Liverpool Street, and Magnus had agreed to meet the nanny at Ipswich off the first train in the morning, and Ned had been given the promised ride on Magnus's bike, to stop him crying, and Pandora had been allowed to ride in the floodlit ring to stop her crying, and they had all been put to bed by a besotted Janey, and read to by Caroline, and peace had settled, albeit it briefly, on the house, Magnus sat down in the drawing room and passed Caroline a very large brandy, and said to her, 'And now, my darling, I'm afraid you simply have to tell me. Who the hell is Fleur?'

Introduction to True Love chapter of *The Tinsel Underneath*.

If Guinevere Davies was not the love of Piers Windsor's life, he was certainly hers. She adored him; from the moment she met him until the day he died. She did not only love him, she admired him and his talent intensely; she was fiercely loyal, totally selfless, gave him everything she had, and she staked everything on a desperate gamble when she feared she was losing him and she didn't know what else she could do.

Her family are divided on him: her mother, Megan, speaks with an odd fondness for him; her brother, Richard, absolutely loathes him. This is not surprising: Megan is a sensitive, educated woman, clear-sighted, with a piercing sense of humour. Richard's view is more uncompromising; he saw only a man he didn't trust who then went on to vindicate that view by, as he saw it, abandoning his sister when she was pregnant.

Megan recognized Piers's complexities, and the difficulties he had with relationships, even with her own daughter; she liked him, she enjoyed his company, while fearing for the future of the marriage. It was not, as she saw it, entirely Piers's fault: what ever is? It grieved her to see her daughter suffer, but she could acknowledge that at least some of the fault could be laid at Guinevere's door.

There is a view, propounded by some psychologists, that to become pregnant deliberately, without the knowledge and against the wishes of a partner, is the female equivalent of rape. This was what Guinevere did; she feared she was losing Piers, she couldn't stand it, and a child, their child, seemed to her a powerful weapon in her battle. A battle she lost: twice. First Piers, who felt the strictures of family life closing in on him like a vice; and then, even more tragically, the baby. And then perhaps a third time, in Piers's lie: that she had had an abortion, in order to keep the part in *The Doctor's Dilemma*. A wicked lie, a selfish, slanderous lie; that she could love him after that bears testimony to her passion for him.

Chapter 26

1970

Magnus Phillips sat back and took a first, appreciative sip at the glass of claret his publisher had poured for him.

'Very nice,' he said, 'very nice indeed.'

'Good. Well, it's nice to see you, Magnus.'

'Nice to see you, Richard. Literally.'

Richard Beauman looked exactly like the popular conception of a successful publisher. He was very tall and slim and elegant; he had white hair and a rather long face with a hawkish nose and very brilliant brown eyes. He always wore what his enemies called five-piece suits, tailored exquisitely for him at Gieves and Hawkes, hand-made shoes, and a gold pocket watch with a chain. He had been to Winchester and then to Balliol, where he had got a First in English literature. It was virtually impossible to name a book he had not read, he could converse in fluent Latin, played championship chess, and had a ruthless commercial instinct that was renowned not only in England but in America as well. His publishing company, Beaumans, had three imprints: Peerage which published classic literature; Gabriel which published hugely expensive art books; and Impression which published highly commercial fiction and non-fiction and which made the modestly respectable balance sheets of Peerage and Gabriel look like petty cash.

In the past year, he had published *Heaven's Gates*, a steamy saga set in the banking business, *Fortunes* (another, similar, about a prostitute who came to own a chain of brothels masquerading as hotels) and *The House* by Magnus Phillips, an explosive study of one or two of the more colourful members of the cabinet. One or other of them had been in the bestseller lists throughout the entire twelve months. *Dancers*, Magnus Phillips's new book, was due out in November.

'So to what do I owe the honour of this visit?' said Richard Beauman. 'You're right, this is a very good wine.'

'I have got one hell of a book for you, Richard. It makes my balls creep, just thinking about it. I even have a title for it.'

'Oh yes? What is it?'

'*The Tinsel Underneath*. Quote from Sam Goldwyn. Good one-liner,

Goldwyn was. He said, "I'd like to tear down all this false tinsel and show the real tinsel underneath." Talking about Hollywood.'

'Sounds all right. So what is it, this book? Biographical, I presume. Not about Mr Windsor surely? I thought you'd gone off the idea. I hear he's in the running for a knighthood in the next birthday honours.'

'No, it was he who went off the idea,' said Magnus. 'I stayed with it. Fortunately. Interesting about the knighthood. That might add a few pounds to the bidding for the serial rights.'

'So it is a biography? On Windsor?'

'Yes and no.'

'Magnus, I do hate riddles.'

'Biographical, yes. Mr Windsor, yes. And a great deal more besides.'

'Indeed? Try and make my balls creep a little, there's a good chap. Steak all right?'

'OK. I'll try,' said Magnus. 'Steak's fine, thanks.'

At the end of the lunch, they walked back in the early spring sunshine to St James's, where Richard Beauman had his office.

'I'll talk to your agent, Magnus. I imagine he has a figure in mind.'

'He does indeed. Of course, other publishers would be salivating at this one too.'

'Bastard,' said Richard Beauman good-naturedly. 'We don't have much money in the kitty at the moment, Magnus, I have to tell you.'

'Oh, really?' said Magnus. 'Tell Henry that, Richard, I'm sure he'd be interested. Thanks for the lunch.'

Richard Beauman put his phone down rather wearily an hour later, having heard himself, to his own considerable regret, if not surprise, giving a verbal agreement to an advance of one hundred thousand pounds to Henry Chancellor, Magnus Phillips's agent – 'Providing he can really deliver something solid rather than what is after all only a few rather wild and unconnected anecdotes at the moment' – for the world rights of a book which, as Henry pointed out, would incorporate just about everything that would make the public rush out in their thousands and put their money down on the bookshop counters: fallen idols, famous names, scandal and betrayal, sex and heartbreak, Hollywood glitz, theatrical glamour.

'And it's all true,' said Henry in rapturous tones, smiling down at the pad on which he had been doodling throughout the hour. 'And he's hardly begun. Now, then, as I understand it, Richard, twenty thousand pounds on signature, and then a further –'

'Hold it, Henry, hold it. No signature even, until I have rather more to go on than what Magnus was talking about over lunch. I want names, interviews, possibly tapes, a fully worked outline with corroborating evidence.'

'You'll get it,' said Henry calmly. 'He's never failed yet. I really don't know how the man does it, Richard, do you?'

'By being a ruthless conscienceless bastard,' said Richard. 'Good afternoon, Henry.'

'You're a ruthless, conscienceless bastard,' said Caroline, 'and I wouldn't trust you further than I could spit. Which isn't very far.'

'Quite right,' said Magnus, kissing her naked shoulder tenderly. 'So you shouldn't. Now look, my darling, I'm going to be away for a few weeks. I don't want you fretting and thinking I've forgotten about you. Because I couldn't.'

'Where are you going?'

'Oh – here, there and everywhere,' he said, and his dark eyes were very blank as he looked at her. 'Researching a new book.'

'What's it about?' said Caroline, trying to crush a tiny shoot of fear that was thrusting up into her chest.

'Ambition,' he said.

Chloe couldn't ever remember feeling so tired. Not even after having the babies, not even after having the third baby, and Rosemary being ill the day she came home, and Piers insisting she gave dinner – 'nothing elaborate, darling, just an omelette, anything' – to a visiting mogul from America.

Joe had met her at Liverpool Street that terrible evening, and that added to her distress, knowing what she did about her mother and Magnus; she had found it almost impossible to look at him even, to talk to him, had prayed he would just think it was her own shock. He had taken her straight to the Ethica Clinic in Harley Street and left her with Piers, who was lying looking oddly small, absolutely white, a drip in one arm. 'He's going to be all right,' Roger Bannerman, their GP, had said to her soothingly. 'We got it just in time, thank God; lucky your nanny hadn't gone away.' Yes, said Chloe, yes it was lucky, unbelievably lucky, horrified at herself at what she had done, her cruelty, her insensitivity in attacking Piers for what she had been shown, told, knew was not his fault, putting him and her whole family at risk. She sat by his bed all night, watching him, dry-eyed, terrified that he might suddenly become worse, that his heart might fail; it did happen, it could happen, hating herself; her mind returning from time to time to the dreadful scene at the Moat House, reliving that as well.

'Of course,' Roger Bannerman said, just a little too firmly, 'of course it's so easy to do, taking sleeping pills instead of pain-killers, Poor old Piers was obviously terribly tired, and on top of all that vodka and the red wine for dinner.' Yes, she had said, yes, it must be terribly easy, she must be more careful in future about leaving him on his own when he was so tired and of course he had been worried about the new play, and his new project for the next year, it was hardly surprising he'd done that, got them muddled.

Rosemary had met her at the house. 'I found this,' she said carefully, giving a note to Chloe. 'It was on the kitchen table. I thought I'd keep it for you.'

'Rosemary,' said Chloe, 'you are quite wonderful, so sensible. You've done all the right things, I can never thank you enough.'

She sat in the taxi, reading the note over and over again, until it bore a groove in her brain: 'My darling, Please forgive me. I can't go on any longer. I love you. Piers.' It had been lying on the kitchen table, Rosemary said, propped against the big salt mill, just a piece of the stiff, deckle-edged paper Piers always used, folded over. No envelope.

Not too incriminating: not even entirely clear. Only Rosemary, who had been through the attempt in Los Angeles, would have grasped instantly what it meant, gone flying upstairs into Piers's room (conveniently not locked) and then phoned for the doctor. And only Rosemary would have had the calm, the common sense to have kept the note quietly, for Chloe alone to see, once she had known Piers was safe, was not actually going to die.

'Of course,' said Roger Bannerman cheerfully the next morning, when he popped into the Ethica to see Piers, and then talked to Chloe outside the room, 'of course, he hadn't taken nearly enough to – well, to do anything – drastic. Not that that was the idea, of course.'

'No,' said Chloe, 'no, of course not.'

'Look,' he said, gently, 'you look all in. Why don't you go home? He'll be staying here another day. You'll need your strength for when he gets home, I'm afraid. Oh and Chloe –'

'Yes?'

'I think he should perhaps see a psychiatrist. You know. Just to talk. I know an awfully good man. Nervous exhaustion they call this sort of thing. Professional help can make all the difference.'

'Yes,' said Chloe. 'Yes, thank you. I might go home. A bit later. I'll go and see him for a bit now. He seems more himself.'

'Yes. But don't push him. Don't question him. All right?'

'All right,' said Chloe.

Piers was fretful, almost tearful, contrite.

'I'm so sorry, darling, so terribly terribly sorry. About everything. You must forgive me, you must.' He grasped her arm; his hand felt bony and hot.

'Piers, it's all right. I do forgive you. For everything. Don't talk, darling. Just rest.'

'My throat's so sore,' he said. 'It's ghastly what they do, you know, push a tube down it, then flood your stomach with water, until you – well it was horrific, I came to vomiting, vomiting everywhere, couldn't breathe –'

'Piers, don't, please, please,' said Chloe. She knew exactly what he was doing, making sure she knew what he had been through, had had to endure, making it plain that in spite of his apologies, his self-abasement, he held her at least partly responsible.

'So wonderfully lucky,' he said, reaching out with his other hand for the glass of water. 'I'm only allowed tiny sips, you know – so wonderfully lucky Rosemary hadn't gone out. Goodness knows what might have happened.'

'Goodness knows,' said Chloe. 'But she hadn't. Piers, you must rest now.' She stroked his forehead gently. 'Everything's all right. It's going to be all right. We must put this behind us. All of it.'

It was weeks before she discovered that Rosemary had actually told Piers she was not going out but having a TV supper in her room.

And then, as if that wasn't enough to cope with, there was this awful, hideous knowledge about her mother and Magnus. That was truly horrible. Any respect Chloe had ever felt for Caroline had gone in that moment, looking down at her on the bathroom floor; all the revulsion and shock she had felt when she had first found the letters, the letters about Fleur, came back, as if it was the first time.

She just didn't know what to do about it. She wanted to tell Joe, to warn him, but she knew she couldn't. Probably shouldn't. It wasn't her story to tell and she was incapable anyway of inflicting that kind of pain. So she avoided him, embarrassed, awkward, shunning his offers of lunch, of drinks, his invitations for himself to come over to the house, pretending that it was because of Piers. She knew he was hurt, puzzled, but she didn't see what else she could do. She was also worried, afraid, about her mother associating with Magnus. He was danger, she felt instinctively: a charming friend if he was on your side, interesting, colourful, amusing, but he was a tabloid journalist of immense influence; there was no telling what he might do with any succulent little story that came across his path. Like Piers Windsor's wife having an illegitimate sister, who nobody knew about, who the family pretended didn't exist. She shivered whenever she thought about it; and because she could do nothing else, tried not to think about it very often.

'This is wonderful, Joe. I really like it.' Caroline looked up from the *Sunday Times* colour supplement and smiled at him: the first time, it seemed, for weeks.

'Good,' said Joe. It was a great relief: he had slaved over the bloody thing, a profile of Elton John, for weeks, far longer than the fee justified. Increasingly he felt work was the only thing he was remotely good at: Caroline (despite her sudden warmth) seemed increasingly withdrawn from him; he seemed to have lost Chloe's affection as well, she was avoiding him, was awkward, tense with him; middle age was stalking him with relentless tenacity; he still trembled when he opened his bank statements.

They were sitting in the kitchen at the Moat House: it was a perfect summer's day. Peaceful, golden, undisturbed. The dogs slumbered by the Aga; sunlight drifted in in dusty shafts through the open door; the bees in the honeysuckle that grew around the window were working, noisily, relentlessly. Later Chloe was arriving with the children (but not Piers); a good day, a happy day.

The phone rang, breaking into the peace: it was Joe's agent, Will Niven.

'Joe, this is a fantastic piece. Sorry to disturb you on a Sunday, but I had to congratulate you.'

'Thanks.'

'We should do a book of these profiles.'

'Think we could?' said Joe, pleased and surprised.

'Yes, I do. Have to find a peg for them. But they're too good to waste. I even have a title. It's *Love at First Sight.*'

Joe laughed. One of three questions he always asked his interviewees was 'Do you believe in love at first sight?' He said the answers were always intensely revealing. 'It's certainly a seller.'

'Yeah. Well, I'll look into it. Talking of books, this one your friend Magnus Phillips is working on sounds like dynamite. How does Piers feel about it?'

'Sorry?' said Joe.

'Don't tell me you haven't heard. It's a gloves-off job. Apparently Magnus started researching Piers and his past, and came up with some very interesting stuff. All kinds of excitement. Hollywood and all.'

'Oh, not all those old chestnuts,' said Joe quickly. He felt rather sick.

'What old chestnuts, Joe?'

'Oh, the slave system, and all that. I can't believe Piers would give a toss about it.'

'From what I've heard,' said Niven, 'there's a lot more to it than the slave system. Of course it's totally under wraps. His agent is walking around looking like the cat that got the cream, and the bidding's gone sky high.'

'Isn't Beauman publishing it?'

'Oh, yes. We're talking American rights here. And serialization. Joe, you must have heard about all this.'

'I've been down here a lot lately,' said Joe.

He put the phone down and looked at Caroline.

'What on earth is it?' she said. 'You look terrible.'

'I feel terrible,' he said and told her what Niven had said.

Later they went for a walk; Caroline was distraught and he couldn't quite understand why; it added to his unease. She wasn't that fond of Piers, and she certainly had no idea of any possible connection between him and Brendan.

'You've got to stop it,' she kept saying. 'You've got to.'

'I'll try,' said Joe. 'But I don't think it's very feasible.'

He wondered if he ought to warn Chloe, warn Piers. It sounded seriously worrying. What on earth had the stupid fucker thought he was doing, ever suggesting Magnus might write his biography? Vanity, he supposed, the all-consuming, overweening Windsor vanity. He decided he should tell them, picked up the phone on three separate occasions and dialled the number only to put it down again, completely unable to face not only the conversation but the implications of it, the questions they might ask, the answers he might have to give. Every time he thought of Magnus's questions about Byron Patrick, about the girl, Kirstie Fairfax, of what he would make of the whole story if he ever got hold of it, he felt violently ill. He told himself that Piers had enough people looking out for him to warn him anyway, and that Chloe had enough to worry about for the time being without this. In any case, she was odd, distant with him at the moment; she seemed to want to avoid him. It was sad; he missed her. She was without doubt one of his favourite people: probably his very favourite. Poor little thing. She'd taken on more than any of them had ever suspected when she married Piers.

'Magnus? Joe Payton. I'd like to talk.'

'Sure.' The voice was blank, easy. Bastard, thought Joe, bastard.

'American Bar at the Savoy? Tomorrow evening? Six thirty?'

'I'll be there,' said Magnus.

Joe got there at six, so determined was he to be in control of the conversation. He was still furious, shakingly furious – and scared too. Of a great many things, and one dark, stalking menace in particular. One he hardly dared even look at.

Magnus arrived at exactly six thirty, smiling, relaxed; he looked suntanned, sleek. He held out his hand to Joe; Joe shook it briefly.

'Drink?'

'Yes. I'll have a bourbon. I've been in the States a bit lately. Developed a taste for it.'

'Oh really?' said Joe. 'Researching your book?'

'Researching my book. Fascinating stuff, Joe. Of course you may be familiar with just a little of it.'

'Magnus,' said Joe, 'what exactly are you going to do?'

'Write a book, Joe. About Piers, and his great successes. I hear he's talking about doing *Othello*, playing Iago and the Moor on alternate nights; is that right? Yes, I thought so, and he's up for the knighthood and then there's the Oscars, three for the *Dream*, the man is clearly a genius. And the gorgeous young wife and the perfect family: truly the gods have smiled upon him. All good stuff.'

'Magnus,' said Joe, 'I am not a complete fool.'

'No, Joe, I know you're not. Oh, excellent, drinks. I've had a tough day, talking to American publishers.'

'Magnus,' said Joe, 'do you realize the damage you're going to do? If you write what I think you may be going to write?'

'I'm going to write the truth,' said Magnus. 'I have a great regard for the truth, Joe. Always have had.'

'Oh, really?' said Joe. 'That seems a fairly spurious justification for wrecking lives, to me.'

'Joe, if people behave well, the truth can't harm them. If they behave badly – correction, if they behave badly and then try to cover that behaviour up, then in my opinion they deserve everything they get. Piers Windsor is an arrogant, self-aggrandizing, vain creature; what's more, he originally came to me, Joe, suggested I might write his biography. Now what he had in mind was clearly rather different from what he's going to get: but the fact remains he was seeking, overtly seeking, a great slug of sycophancy between hard covers. I find that rather distasteful. He can hardly blame me if in the course of my investigating his unarguably golden past, I find a little dross. Can he?'

'That's shit and you know it,' said Joe. 'Think of Chloe, think of the children; you're a family friend, or supposed to be, Ned's godfather; think of – well, all the others involved. Christ, I don't like the guy, but I really don't feel he deserves this.'

'It's not shit, Joe. It's hard fact. I'm sorry for Chloe, sure, but I'm more sorry for her because she's married to the bastard, being manipulated by him. These suicide attempts, what kind of creep does that? To someone like Chloe? Jesus, Joe, it turns me up.'

'You turn me up,' said Joe, 'trying to justify what you're doing.'

'And what precisely do you think I'm doing?' said Magnus. There was a dangerous look now in his almost black eyes.

'Making an obscene amount of money. Increasing your own reputation, feeding your own ego. Setting yourself up as the arch-exponent of the publish-and-be-damned revelations.'

'Oh, Joe,' said Magnus, 'I already have an obscene amount of money, as you put it. In my bank account at this very moment is probably ten times more than my father earned in his entire life. Without any input from this little number. My ego is in no danger of starvation. It was actually born slightly overweight. As for my reputation it probably stands to be damaged rather than enhanced by all this.'

'Well, why the fuck are you doing it?' said Joe, wishing his voice sounded slightly less desperate.

'Above all, because it is the most riveting, fascinating project I've ever happened upon,' said Magnus simply. He drained his glass, signalled at the waiter. 'Same again, please. Where was I? Oh, yes. It's got everything, Joe. Sex, scandal, household names, nostalgia. Wonderful stuff.'

'Nostalgia, eh?' said Joe.

'Nostalgia. And coincidence. Extraordinary how stories, lives cross, tangle, and then weave into a pattern. Haven't you found that yourself? Again and again. When you were researching something? So yes, indeed, plenty of nostalgia. It's a most crucial part of the story.'

He put his hand in his pocket, pulled out a packet of Disques Bleus, offered one to Joe. Joe shook his head. Magnus lit the cigarette, and the pungent smell of strong French tobacco filled the air. It increased Joe's sense of panic.

'Look,' said Magnus and his dark eyes were amused, watchful. 'Look, Joe, I know what you really want, you want to know exactly what I'm going to write, and of course I'm not going to tell you. Nobody knows that, not my publisher, not my agent, no one. To be absolutely honest, I don't know myself yet. I'm still digging. This is one hell of a story, Joe. I can't let it go.'

Joe felt very sick. He was afraid to say any more, any more at all, for fear of giving something away, something that Magnus had not discovered; but he thought back to the conversation he and Magnus had had in El Vino's, all those months earlier, the apparently disconnected questions about

Byron Patrick and Kirstie Fairfax and he knew without doubt that it was all going to go in, Brendan, Caroline, Fleur. He decided to risk one last, dangerous, double-edged question.

'Have you thought about what this will do to me and – and to Caroline?'

'Joe, really! I know you're very fond of Chloe, but if you were honest, you'd surely admit you'd quite like to see Piers squirming a bit. And Caroline is a very beautiful, very self-contained, successful woman of – what? Well, forty-something. She has wealth, position, an adoring family. Do you really think the revelation of some youthful indiscretion, twenty-five years ago, will hurt her so much? Of course not. Her shoulders are broader than that. If they're not, they should be.'

'You're a bastard,' said Joe. Shock waves were going through him, increasing in violence with every one. Somehow, somehow Magnus Phillips knew about Fleur. And Caroline knew he knew. No wonder she had been so distressed. Christ almighty. This got worse every minute. How the fuck had he known? How could he have found out? And then he thought of other things, all slotting neatly into one another, Caroline's distancing from him, Caroline's voice saying 'that's what Magnus said', when he had made some comment or other on Piers, Chloe's awkwardness, embarrassment with him recently. She obviously knew. No doubt half London knew. God, they must all think he was a fool. Which he was. A blind, bloody fool. He picked up his glass and noticed his hand was shaking violently.

'You're a bastard,' he said again.

'Yes, well, you're entitled to your opinion,' said Magnus Phillips easily. 'I'm sorry I haven't manged to change it in any way.'

Joe stood up. His glass of Scotch was still full, and the ice in it had not yet melted. He picked it up and threw it into Magnus's face, very hard. One of the cubes hit him in the eye, clearly hurt.

Magnus didn't flinch, merely picked up a napkin and wiped his face with it, picked the ice-cubes off the front of his suit where they had settled and set them down on the table. The waiter had rushed forward, was signalling at the barman for help.

Magnus waved him away. 'Don't worry. It really doesn't matter. Just get me another bourbon, will you. Joe, you must read the book. It may not be exactly what you expect. In fact I'm sure it won't be.'

Joe grabbed Magnus by the front of his shirt and hauled him to his feet. He was very strong and heavy, but he was taken by surprise. Joe pulled back his fist and punched him very hard in the face, then sent him staggering into his chair.

Magnus stood up again immediately; a trickle of bood was emerging from his nose, his mouth looked slightly odd, but his eyes were still almost amused. He took hold of Joe by his lapels and said, 'This is no way to play this, Joe. No way at all.'

Then he pushed him aside and stalked out of the bar.

'Oh, for God's sake,' said Caroline. She had the *Daily Mail*; there was a picture of Magnus, leaving the Savoy through the swing door, holding a handkerchief to his nose, and another rather old and unflattering one of Joe. 'Dogfight in the Savoy,' said the headline. 'Rival hacks in punch-up.'

'How on earth did they get this? How did a photographer just happen to be there? Joe, you are a fool.'

'There are always journalists in that bar,' said Joe. 'One of them must have phoned his paper. Oh, I don't know, Caroline, I was only trying to help.'

'Well all you've done,' said Caroline, 'is make things worse. Have you read this?'

'No, but I can imagine what it says.'

'Well, stop imagining and listen. "Magnus Phillips, author of the hot seller *The House*, a real-life study of politics, and currently working on a biography of actor Piers Windsor, was in a brawl yesterday at the Savoy Hotel, with a member of Windsor's family, journalist Joe Payton. The waiter who served them said they had been engaged in a heated discussion when Payton threw his drink at Phillips and then pulled him to his feet and punched him in the face. Both Payton and Phillips refused to comment on whether the disagreement concerned the book which is rumoured to be fairly sensational in content. Piers Windsor, whose film of *A Midsummer Night's Dream* has just won three Oscars, and who is working on a new production of *Othello*, is confidently expected to get a knighthood in the forthcoming birthday honours. Both Piers Windsor and his young wife, Chloe, were unavailable for comment yesterday."

'God,' said Caroline, 'this gets worse and worse. I can't believe you did this, Joe. What on earth did you think you'd achieve?'

'Personal satisfaction, I suppose,' said Joe, 'and I can assure you I did.'

'Well, I'm delighted. Chloe just rang. She says Piers is distraught.'

'What a shame,' said Joe. 'Not grateful, I suppose, that I was trying to help?'

'Joe, I don't think he quite saw it as help.'

Joe looked at her. She was very pale, and her eyes were very hard as she met his. 'Well, thanks for your support,' he said. 'Much appreciated.'

'What do you expect?' she said. 'It was such a dangerous, stupid thing to do.'

'Oh, really?' he said and anger, sick, fierce anger shot through him, giving him courage. 'Well now, talking of dangerous, stupid things, Caroline, would you mind telling me how Magnus Phillips came to hear of what he describes as your youthful indiscretion?'

An hour later, he drove away from the Moat House, his battered old leather suitcase on the back seat filled with the very few things he had moved down there.

He had always thought he never liked the place; but when he looked back at it, just before he drove away, its image was blurred with his tears.

Chapter 27

1970

Fleur could never remember feeling so sick-scared. She just hoped it didn't show; thank God for the darkness. She knew her face was parchment white, that her mouth, for all the determined firmness of its smile, was quivering; she could feel the prickle of sweat breaking out in her armpits, the clamminess of her hands; her stomach was heaving, her bowels churning. One more minute, one more moment even and she would have to make a rush for the toilet.

As if from very far away now, she could hear the voice, the voice on which she was rather oddly trying to fix her concentration, and yet at the same time to escape; she felt a hand in the darkness reach out for hers and resisted the temptation to grip it. She was not going to give herself away, show how much she cared; that would be a weakness she knew she would regret for ever.

'And the winner is' – another stifling pause – 'Browne Phillips Ivy for "Just Morton's" .' A roar of triumph from their table, of applause all around the room; there were hands pushing her to her feet, clapping her back, and Baz Browne was standing up, ushering her and Ricky Pentry forward, and she was walking up through the long tangle of tables to the podium, and running, running up the steps, pushing back her hair, laughing at Ricky, and they stood there, holding it between them, the treasure, the holy grail, the advertising industry's top creative award, the Golden Pen, and she looked out into the huge room, a blur of smiling faces and fluttering hands and felt, for the first time in her whole life, not just triumph, not just delight, but absolute self-assurance.

'To Fleur and Ricky! The stars!' Baz Browne raised his glass to the two of them, sitting there, the centre of attention, as people ebbed and flowed around them, congratulating them. Mick diMaggio had been one of the first at the table, hugging her, telling her she was wonderful; Poppy had rushed to her side, her eyes streaming with tears; Nigel Silk had walked over, more slowly, but smiling in genuine pleasure none the less and raised her hand to his lips. Reuben, who had been invited as part of the Morton team, and who was sitting across the table from her, had said nothing, but had pushed a note across to her on which he had written 'Good.' Sol Morton, who had been massaging her thigh with great enthusiasm most of the evening, or at least at every moment of the evening when Sylvia Morton was not watching him, now had his arm fixed extremely tightly around her waist and refused to take it away; Matthew Phillips had kissed her, discreetly, and told her he was very proud of her, in his drawling Boston accent; and Col Ivy, sitting on her other side, had told her she was a great girl and he would like to see her first thing in the morning in his office.

Much much later, they left: for the Four Seasons, where there was more champagne, more laughter, more congratulations; and then finally, at half past two, when she was so drunk she could hardly stand, Reuben said he thought it was time to go, and led her out to the limo waiting to take them home, courtesy of Browne Phillips Ivy, and they drove off almost as if they had just been married, with the entire party waving to them from the kerbside.

'Oh, my God,' said Fleur, settling against him with a sigh of pure pleasure, 'that was just the best. Wasn't it? Didn't you think so? Can you even believe that all happened?'

'It was OK,' said Reuben. But his smile as he looked down at her was brilliant.

Fleur was always turned on sexually by her work; tonight she was frantic with hunger for Reuben. She half ran up the stairs, dragging him after her, fell on him on the bed, biting, kissing, stroking, wanting him. They made love for a long time, slowly, exquisitely, and as she rose to her final climax, soaring flying into it, it seemed to her to echo the soaring, flying joy of the whole evening, of knowing she had made it, she was someone, she had arrived. And as she opened her eyes, looked into Reuben's, saw the love there, she was ashamed, ashamed of the absolute selfishness of herself and the way she behaved. She got up, fetched them some water, lay in the crook of his arm, wondering why he loved her so much, wishing she could love him in the same way.

'I'd like to marry you,' he said suddenly, and she laughed, laughed aloud, said, 'Oh Reuben, really,' and then she turned and looked at him, smiling, so sure he was joking, and saw the hurt, the pain that she should think such a thing; suddenly desperate to make amends, to stay on her high, to take him back up with her, and because she was so fond of him, loved him so dearly, she said, and her panic rose higher with each word, 'Yes, Reuben, I'd like that too.'

Fleur got into the office early the next morning nursing a formidable hangover: award or no award, she had a meeting with Bernard Stobbs at eleven and she'd promised him an ad for his latest baby, a series of art books for children; and she had to see Col Ivy at ten.

Col was smiling, almost effusive, plied her with coffee and said he would like to give her a raise of ten thousand dollars a year. 'We're very pleased with you. Very pleased. Well done. Miss FitzPatrick –'

'Yes, Mr Browne?'

'There could be a vacancy for a creative group head in the pipeline. I'd like you to think about it. Of course it would mean you moving to different accounts, but – well, put it into your back tooth, as my old grandmother used to say, and let me know if you want to talk some more.'

'I will,' said Fleur. 'Thank you.'

She left the office, and walked rather slowly down the corridor, her heart thumping. She really was doing it, making it; she was becoming all the things she wanted to be, getting all the things she knew she wanted to have. Except one. Except still one.

'Fleur? Sol Morton.'

'Oh, hi, Sol. How's your head?'

'My head's fine,' said Sol, who contended that hangovers were all in the mind, their only victims hapless no-hopers who shouldn't drink at all if they couldn't carry it. 'Fleur, I'd like to have lunch with you soon. You and Reuben. No one else.'

'Why, Sol?' said Fleur innocently.

'Got an idea. That's all. How about next Wednesday?'

'Next Wednesday'd be good. You'd better ask Reuben yourself though.'

'I already did.'

'Great,' said Fleur.

She rang Reuben.

'What do you think Sol wants?'

'Us,' said Reuben.

'Yes, but what for?'

'Himself.'

'Uh-huh. What do you feel about that?'

'Depends.'

'On what?'

'Terms. Got to go.'

'Bye, Reuben.'

'These are lovely, Fleur,' said Bernard Stobbs, smiling at her over her roughs and her copy, which talked of quite complex things like cubism and impressionism in a way that even a six year old would not only understand but be intrigued by. 'Charming. I couldn't be more pleased.'

'Good,' said Fleur, smiling at him. If she were to move, either to a different group, or to whatever Sol Morton had in mind, she would miss Bernard Stobbs more than anyone.

'Can I buy you lunch?'

'That would be lovely. But I mustn't be long.'

'We won't be long. I don't like long lunches. They send me to sleep over my books. How does pasta and Pellegrino sound to you?'

'Like a lovely cookery book. You should do one.'

'What a nice idea.'

Over their lunch, he chatted, charmingly, about his new range, his latest bestseller (a biography of Callas), his pleasure in sponsoring a children's art exhibition to tie in with his new range of books. Then he said, 'I don't really like the way the publishing industry is going these days. Very cut-throat, very scurrilous.'

'Oh, really?' said Fleur. She was winding a long strand of fettucine round her fork; it was giving her trouble.

'Yes. There is some new book coming out, sounds little better than tabloid journalism, doesn't deserve the name of a book. Half the houses in New York are scrabbling over it. English, which makes it worse: I like to think there are some gentlemen left in the business over there.'

'Doubtful, I would think,' said Fleur briefly.

Bernard Stobbs looked at her amusedly. 'You sound very cynical, my dear.'

'I feel it,' said Fleur, 'about the English. Hypocrites to a man, in my experience.'

'Dear me.'

'Anyway, what is this book about?'

'It's about an actor. Well, that's only the half of it, obviously. All kinds of – what shall we say – subplots.'

'Have you read it?'

'Oh – only the outline. Sent me by the author's agent. Which was very uninformative, as these things always are. Designed to get us all salivating.'

'And you remained dry-mouthed, I hope,' said Fleur, smiling at him.

'I certainly did.'

'Who's the actor?'

'Oh, he's very famous, a great classical actor. It's very depressing really, if half the innuendoes in this thing are true. You might have seen him, he's done some Shakespeare on Broadway and he did that film, that was so very beautiful, of *A Midsummer Night's Dream*. Piers Windsor, you must have heard of him. Good gracious me, my dear, you'd better have some water. I didn't think people could choke on pasta.'

Magnus Phillips was sitting in his study transcribing some tapes, and smiling pleasedly as he did so, when Richard Beauman's secretary phoned him to say she had received a call from a girl in New York called Fleur FitzPatrick and was it all right to give her Magnus's address and telephone number?

Magnus said it was perfectly all right, and experienced such a rush of adrenaline he felt physically light-headed.

He waited, frantically impatient, for her to call: she didn't. He decided she must be writing and shadowed the postman down the street every morning for a week. But there were no letters from New York. He called Beaumans every day, asking if she'd phoned, even though he'd been assured they'd let him know the minute she did. He pestered his agent, asking him if he was sure, quite quite sure there hadn't been any messages for him, that no one had let this precious call through. They were sure. Quite sure. Christ, he'd been trying to find the bloody girl for six months; how could God, fate, whatever, do this to him, dangle her in front of him and then snatch her away again? He even thought of phoning Caroline, but decided it was too dangerous. Caroline had cut him out of her life with a ruthless thoroughness that had impressed him.

'You are disgusting,' she had said simply, standing in the doorway of his house, refusing so much as to cross the threshold. 'I've never known anyone truly rotten before. It's been an interesting experience. Goodbye, Magnus. Don't ever try to contact me. If you do I shall call the police.'

He felt he should have found it amusing, and was surprised and upset to find it hurt. Quite a lot.

He was actually finding the book quite hard to take. The truths he had unearthed in his research for it, even thus far, had shaken him. More than once he had been tempted to jack the whole project in, to say it simply wasn't worth the angst. But then he would go back and read what he had actually written – about half the length now – and look at what he was yet to write, and it was so exciting, on so many levels, that he couldn't quite bring himself to jettison it. It was like writing a thriller. Or rather living a thriller. And he still wasn't finished. There were huge holes in its fabric, unresolved mysteries, unexplained actions. God, he needed to find the daughter. To get her theories, to test them against his own: to have her views of her father, simply to know how much she knew, what lies she might have been told as well as what truths. It was all important, all frighteningly relevant.

He was lying in the bath, nursing a hangover, one morning in early October when he heard a taxi pull up outside. Good: that would be the roughs for the cover of *Tinsel*, as everyone called it. The publishers had promised them first thing this morning. There had been endless arguments about it. More schemes had been put up for it than there were chapters, ranging from straightforward photographs of Piers, to montages of Hollywood, with every possible variation in between. There had even been a montage of Hollywood interspersed with a montage of Piers's life. The latest idea was the Hollywood sign, bedecked with tinsel; Magnus felt they were at least getting warm. The bell rang once; he sighed, settled more deeply in the bath. It was too good to leave. They would leave the package on the doorstep: the taxi company knew to do that when there was no answer.

The bell rang again, strongly, imperious. Bloody man, must be new. He climbed out of the bath, cursing, dragged on the towelling robe he had stolen from the Bel Air Hotel – well not exactly stolen, they'd written the usual 'we know it must be a mistake' letter and he'd sent them a cheque for an absurd number of dollars, far more even than if he'd bought it in Harrods – and ran down the stairs, shouting, 'All right, all right,' at the front door.

As he opened it, and drew breath to complain, to curse, to threaten to shoot the messenger, he stopped, halfway through the first obscenity, shaken, shocked, stunned into silence, and stood there, absolutely still, finding it hard momentarily even to breathe. For on the doorstep stood a girl, a girl of considerable beauty, young, young enough to be his daughter, tall and very slender, with almost black hair tumbling in tendrilly layers on to her shoulders, and very dark blue eyes, fringed with immensely long black lashes, Irish eyes; her face was unmistakably Irish too, pale and delicately boned, with high cheekbones and pointed chin, and the expression on the face was interesting, wary, challenging, confident, all at the same time. It was familiar to him, that face, and he could not for a moment think why and then it came to him, hit him with a force that was even stronger than the sense of her immense sexuality and his attraction to her. For it was a face that unarguably and greatly resembled one that he had been poring over for months, in old Hollywood photographs, old film magazines.

'Magnus Phillips?' she said, and he nodded, his eyes still fixed on hers, and she said, holding out her hand, 'My name is Fleur FitzPatrick. I've come to talk to you about your book.'

'I've come to talk to you about your book,' said Fleur again, settled in the Charles Eames chair in Magnus's black and white study, a large mug of coffee in her hand.

'Yes,' he said, 'so you said. How did you hear about it?'

'From one of my clients.'

'What do you do, Miss FitzPatrick, that you have clients?'

'I work for an advertising agency. In New York.'

'That sounds very smart.'

'It is,' she said briefly.

'And what does this client do?'

'He's a publisher.'

'Ah. Well, I'm glad my book is the talk of literary New York.'

'I didn't say that.'

'No. But it seems that it possibly is.'

'I want you to tell me about it.'

'Oh, I can't do that.'

'Mr Phillips, you have to.'

'Why?'

'Because – because it concerns me.'

'In what way?'

'I can't tell you that.'

'Neither of us are going to get very far,' he said with a smile, 'if we continue in this rather negative vein.'

Fleur looked at him. He reminded her of Sol Morton. Sol Morton gone first class. Not the sort of class Julian Morell and Nigel Silk had, but hard-edged, fine-tuned, thousand-watt, hundred-per-cent brainpower class. He was also one hundred per cent sexy. He bothered her; bothered her senses. She tried to put that thought aside.

'Well, I could tell you a little,' she said. 'I suppose.'

'OK. And then I could tell you a little. At least we'd be making progress.'

'I – know Piers Windsor,' she said.

Magnus Phillips's face showed nothing; no shock, no surprise even. He merely nodded. 'Right. Well?'

'Pardon me?'

'Do you know him well?'

'Pretty well.'

'Uh-huh. Am I to understand you mean know in the biblical sense?'

'I – know him pretty well,' said Fleur briefly. 'We don't need to get any further than that.'

'OK. Right then. Now I'll swap that for a bit of information. I know who you are.'

'I'm sorry?'

'I said I know who you are. I mean really who you are.'

Fleur felt rather breathless suddenly, odd, almost frightened. 'I don't know what you mean.'

'Your mother is an English lady called Caroline Hunterton. Your father was an American actor called – well, really he was called Brendan FitzPatrick. Known as Byron Patrick to his fans. More was the pity.'

'Fuck,' said Fleur. 'Fuck me.' And then, greatly to her own distress, she burst into tears.

'I'm sorry,' she said a little later, when Magnus had supplied her with a large box of tissues, and a fresh cup of coffee, a part explanation. 'I'm really sorry.'

'For what?'

'For crying. And for swearing. I always swear when I'm excited.'

'I don't mind either of those things,' he said.

'What I cannot understand,' she said, blowing her nose loudly, 'is how my mother came to tell you about me. I'm the skeleton in the family cupboard. Nobody, just nobody, gets to be told about me.'

'Well, let's say it slipped out.'

'How well do you know my mother?'

'Probably as well as you know Piers Windsor,' he said and grinned at her, conspiratorially. 'Or rather I did. She's a little – cross with me at the moment. I suspect that may get you swearing again.'

'No,' she said, 'not quite.' There was a silence. Then, 'Shit,' she said and grinned. 'Does – does Joe know? About you guys, I mean.'

'I'm afraid he does. They're not – together any more. You didn't know that?'

'I don't know anything about them,' said Fleur. 'Any of them. I told you. They like to pretend I don't exist.' She got up and walked over to the window, and stared out. When she turned again, her face was white and strained. She looked less in control. 'So can we talk about the book now?' she said and her voice was a little shaky.

'Well – maybe. What exactly do you want to know about it?'

'What exactly it's about.'

'Ah. Well, now we seem to have come full circle. Because I can't tell you. Honestly I can't, because I'm still finding things out.'

'About?'

'About Piers Windsor. About his life and his wives and his past.'

Fleur looked at him very directly. She waited for a moment, gathering her courage and then she said, 'I think there's a chance that my father figured somewhere in his past. That their paths crossed.'

There was a long silence. She sat there, listening to it, watching him, trying to decipher at least something that was going on behind his dark eyes. Magnus looked back at her, his face absolutely blank; then he reached out, picked up a pack of cigarettes from the desk. He held them out to her.

'Want one?'

'No, thank you,' said Fleur.

He lit one, looking at her through the smoke; she managed somehow, still, not to move, not to speak. Finally he said, 'I think there's a chance of that too.'

'Ah,' she said. She felt very sick suddenly, rather scared.

Then he said, 'We could talk about your father. Who I happened upon in Joe Payton's book. I imagine he must occupy a great deal of your thoughts.'

'Well,' said Fleur, 'he certainly does. But why should you say that?'

'I would imagine you must be – what? Twenty-five years old?'

'Yes.'

'And for at least ten of that twenty-five, I would imagine you've been feeling pretty upset about your father. Nice guy like that. And how he died. In such a – well, a horrible way. Wanting to know exactly why it happened. Why he got into that mess. And then maybe be able to put the record straight.'

Fleur sat and looked at him, and wondered how it was that this total stranger, who she most certainly didn't trust, who she felt could not possibly be up to a great deal of good, whose existence she had not known of until a few days ago, should understand, should know how she must hurt, how much she must hurt, how long she had been hurting; and it was as if she had been locked up in some dark, airless room for a very long time and now someone had come along, opened the door, and she had stepped outside into the sunlight and the sweet fresh air. She sat there staring at him, with a sense of such gratitude, such astonishment that it clearly showed in her face, for he said, half laughing at her, 'What did I say?'

'Oh,' she said, 'oh, nothing really. Everything. Not many people kind of grasp it.'

'I'm surprised,' he said, 'I'd have thought it was fairly – well, obvious.'

'Not so,' said Fleur briefly.

'Doesn't your mother understand? Or the nice Mr Payton?'

'No. They don't.

'How extraordinary of them,' he said. 'Look, I'm going to have some breakfast. Well, some toast and marmalade. Do you want some?'

Fleur realized suddenly that she was ravenous. 'That'd be good,' she said.

Sitting in the kitchen of his house (which was, like his study, very modernistic, all stainless steel and marble: marble floor, marble surfaces), watching him eat slice after slice of thick toast spread with thicker marmalade, she felt oddly relaxed, warmed, easy. She tried to tell herself it was dangerous, that she should be feeling nothing of the sort, that a man like Magnus Phillips who wrote the sort of books he did, who was clearly at war with her family (if you could call them her family which she actually didn't), who had had an affair with her mother, who was writing a scurrilous book about her sister's husband, a man like Magnus Phillips, clever, ruthless, albeit charming, was not to be trusted for one thousandth of one second. But she found she was not listening to herself too carefully. Maybe it was because she was tired, maybe it was the emotion of the past hour, the series of shocks she had received; whatever it was she felt soothed, softened, she just wanted to stay here, talking to this man, telling him things, telling him about herself, telling him everything he might wish to know, and more besides. And she also felt there was a great deal she would not need to tell him, that he would understand, would not need to have explained.

He looked up finally from his fourth slice of toast and licked his fingers, one by one, and said, 'I really should go and get dressed. I don't usually entertain strange women in my kitchen wearing virtually no clothes.'

'Oh really?' said Fleur, smiling at him.

'No, really,' he said. 'Make some more coffee if you like,' and he disappeared up the stairs.

She wandered around the kitchen, taking in the clues it offered: a row of cookery books (mostly virginally unused), a notebook and pen set neatly near the phone, a pile of newspapers (*The Times*, the *Daily Mirror*, the *Daily Mail*, the *Daily Worker*) and of magazines (*New Statesman, Private Eye, Nova, Campaign*) on the table, a heap of unopened letters, many of them plainly circulars, a large wine rack filled with bottles, including a great deal of champagne, a set of framed black and white photographs, signed by David Bailey, not of glamorous model girls, but of men she mostly didn't recognize, apart from Mick Jagger and David Hockney. There was a bulging address book by the phone, and she was just idly starting to flick through it when Magnus Phillips appeared again, and picked it up rather firmly.

'Private property,' he said, and although he smiled at her, there was a very hard expression in his dark eyes. 'You've obviously been badly brought up.'

'I was very well brought up actually,' she said, 'by my grandmother.'

'Would that be Brendan's mother?'

'Yes, it would.'

'I cannot tell you,' he said, 'how pleased I am to see you. I've been looking for you for months.'

Fleur looked at him coolly over her coffee mug. 'You can't have tried very hard,' she said.

'I tried extremely hard. But you have to understand some very brightly painted red herrings were placed in my path. Your mother told me first that she had no idea where you lived, then – now what was it? – "somewhere near Chicago".'

'Oh, for God's sake. Why on earth should she say that?' said Fleur, her face reluctantly amused.

'I imagine she didn't want me to find you.'

'Oh,' said Fleur, and sat and processed this piece of information. Of course they wouldn't want Magnus to find her. Not if he was writing a book about Piers. They'd be shitting themselves at the thought he might find her. Well, Joe would. She wondered if Joe had ever told her mother, or Chloe, about her and Piers. Probably not. God, they were a filthy lot. She could actually imagine the conversations. Discussing whether they should tell her not to have anything to do with Magnus, not to tell him anything, if he approached her: deciding that would be a mistake, that she was likely to do the opposite of anything they might say; at that she laughed aloud, at that and at the realization that she actually, finally, had the whip hand over them, all of them.

'What's so funny?' said Magnus.

'Oh – nothing.' She looked at him and then said, 'There might be things I could tell you. People I could tell you about. That would help you with your research. Do you think that might be an idea?'

'It might,' said Magnus Phillips.

Interview Tabitha Levine. Wishes to be anonymous.

Now look, I do mean anonymous. I was very fond of Piers, and I'm very fond of Chloe, and I don't want to make her feel worse. But I guess if you're doing the book anyway, I might as well tell you what I know.

OK. Two things. I mean without doubt he was sexually ambivalent. Fighting it: sometimes harder than others. But more than that, he was just generally promiscuous. He tried to have an affair with me, but (a) I didn't fancy him and (b) I just didn't think it was a very good idea. I mean I was his leading lady, he was directing me, and it gets in the way, that sort of thing, and then it goes wrong and your professional life gets fucked up along with your emotional. But he found it very hard to resist any attractive person. I don't mean he had to get into bed with all of them, but he liked to make them like him, want him, admire him, enjoy him. He was certainly a pushover for anyone who might be after him.

The other thing was that he had a really strong moral sense. I know that sounds odd, coming after the promiscuous number, but after all, what's sex? What does it matter? But I can tell you this, Piers would never ever let anyone down: never gossip; never rat on a friend. He had awful faults, he was vain and phenomenally self-centred, and conceited, and not very honest, and very manipulative. But he was so loyal. You can ask anyone, anyone at all, even his enemies, they'll all say the same thing. Nobody ever got dropped in the shit by Piers Windsor. That's why all those stories about Guinevere and the baby were so awful. Piers would just not have left her if or because she was pregnant. He wouldn't. There had to be another explanation. I do hope you've got that one sorted for your book. That would be really cruel, to perpetrate that old myth. In a funny way, he was actually a bit of a victim.

Chapter 28

1970

'Ludovic,' said Chloe, 'I'm desperately worried. I don't know what to do.'

'Marry me?' said Ludovic.

'Oh, Ludo, please don't joke. It isn't funny.'

'I'm not joking.'

'Ludovic, *please*!'

Ludovic composed his features. His blue eyes settled on Chloe in sober contemplation. 'I'm sorry, darling. Tell me what's bothering you.'

'Well obviously,' said Chloe, 'this book.'

'Ah,' said Ludovic, 'yes, the book.'

'You've – heard about it?'

'Hard not to, my darling. The press are rather taken with it, are they not?'

Chloe sighed. 'Yes, I'm afraid so.'

'What does Piers think about it?'

'Piers won't talk about it,' said Chloe and her voice had a desperate, slightly wobbly edge to it.

'Ah.'

'He says that there's no point even discussing it, that all we can do is carry on with our lives. The point is, Ludovic, this book could stop him carrying on with his life.'

'Not literally, I hope,' said Ludovic. He smiled at her, but his voice was gentle; Chloe felt herself growing hot. She lived in terror of Piers's suicide attempts becoming public knowledge: not least because she felt convinced that on both occasions she had been in large part to blame.

'No. No, of course not. But – oh, Ludovic, I'm so frightened. There are terrible, awful things that book could say about him and –'

'True? Or not?'

Chloe looked down at her hands; they were, she noticed with some surprise, twisted in the most extraordinary way in her lap. 'I – don't know.'

'Chloe,' said Ludovic, 'Chloe, look at me. That's better. Now listen. I might be able to help you and I might not, and certainly, at the very least, I can recommend a very good libel lawyer. But what you have to understand is that he does need to know the truth. If what the book says is libellous, then we can do a great deal about it. Stop its publication altogether – possibly. Threaten the publishers with legal action if they go ahead. If, on the other hand, there is some truth in it, then it becomes very much more difficult.'

'In what way?'

'Well, there is a great deal of difference between knowing something bad is going to be published about you, and fearing something is going to be published about you which is simply not true. Now which of those two things are we talking about here?'

'Well I – oh God, Ludovic, it's so difficult. I just don't know what to think, what to do . . .' Chloe's voice rose in a near wail.

Ludovic smiled at her tenderly. 'Well, you certainly don't have to talk to me, my darling. Save it all for the lawyer. But in any case, it won't be for you to talk. You can't do anything. The defamation, if such it is, is a defamation of Piers. The action has to go through him. Not you.'

'Yes, but – I mean if he won't do anything.'

'Then we must try and persuade him. Unless it simply isn't worth worrying about. I mean is there not the slightest possibility that this book is simply a rather racy biography?'

'Absolutely none,' said Chloe, trying to smile. 'Dynamite is the word that's most bandied about.'

'Yes, I have seen that one. It's Magnus Phillips, isn't it? Writing it? I never did like the fellow.'

'I did,' said Chloe, with a feeble smile. 'He's Ned's godfather, you know. I always thought he was – well, interesting. Kind, in a rather rough way. Joe always said he was a baddy.'

'Did he indeed? Poor Joe, getting beaten up in the Savoy over it.'

'He wasn't beaten up,' said Chloe indignantly, 'he did the beating.'

'He must have taken Phillips very much by surprise. He's about half his size.'

'He is not,' said Chloe, 'he's much taller than Magnus. He's thinner, that's all.'

'I can see I shall have to watch Mr Payton. He seems to have a considerable slice of your heart.'

'He does,' said Chloe. 'I love him very much. He's been a second father to me.'

'But he's no longer with your mother.'

'No,' said Chloe shortly.

'Am I allowed to ask why?'

'She – was having an affair with Magnus Phillips.'

'Fuck me!' said Ludovic. 'I beg your pardon, Chloe. I had no idea. This is more complex than I realized.'

'Oh, Ludovic, it's a lot worse than that. I can't tell you how much worse.'

'Look,' said Ludovic, 'it's nearly lunch-time. Why don't we pop round the corner to the Savoy, and you can tell me all about it?'

'Ludovic, I wouldn't dream of telling you all about it in the Savoy. Of all places. I think the entire family should steer very clear of the Savoy for quite a time to come. Just think of who might be listening. I really don't even know if I ought to tell you all about it anyway.'

'You should, my darling, otherwise you are going to do something desperate. I can see it in your exquisite little face. And then I'll find a very good, very kind, and very ugly libel lawyer to take it over. Now I suggest we have lunch in a locked room, with all the light fittings checked for bugs. How about that? In here?'

'Yes, that'd be lovely,' said Chloe, trying to smile.

When she'd gone, after picking her way half-heartedly through a smoked salmon sandwich and describing rather slowly and haltingly precisely what she thought the book might say, Ludovic picked up his telephone.

'Nicholas? Ludovic Ingram. Got a very knotty little problem here. Can I come and see you? What? Well, because I have a tasty little morsel for you and besides you owe me a lunch. Friday'd be fine. Cheers.'

* * *

'I've written to Rose and asked if we can go and see her,' said Fleur. 'She is really nice, a kind, sweet person. She and my father had a – well, a relationship when they were young.'

'Really? Were they close?'

'Very close. I mean they lived together. Until he got taken up by Naomi MacNeice. Then he had to drop her.'

'Had to?' said Magnus.

'Yeah, Naomi just told him Rose had to go.'

'And how did Rose feel about that?'

'Oh, she was just amazing about it. I mean she was when she talked to me about it. I don't suppose she felt quite that good at the time. She said Hollywood was like that, that kind of thing just happened all the time, that you got used to it, that she hadn't liked it but she'd understood.'

'What a remarkable person she must be,' said Magnus. He sounded slightly unconvinced.

'Yes, well she is,' said Fleur defensively. 'It's hard to believe she's so world-famous and successful. She's so – real somehow. I'm sure she'll talk to you.'

'She doesn't have a husband, does she? At the moment?'

'No, she doesn't. Why, are you thinking of applying for the job?' asked Fleur drily.

'I don't think Miss Sharon would suit me too well,' said Magnus.

'But you'd suit her, I suppose?'

'In some ways, yes, I dare say I would.'

Sitting on the plane going back to New York, Fleur thought over this remark and wondered why it had made her so cross. She finally decided it typified Magnus Phillips's arrogance. He was the most arrogant man she had ever met. He made Nigel Silk and even Julian Morell look quite self-deprecating.

She wished she knew what she really thought about Magnus. Whether she was mad to trust him; whether she liked him; whether she ought to be helping him at all. He was infuriatingly vague about what he might be writing about her father: said he would let her read it when he had everything in place. Which would be a while yet, he said. He had a lot of – what was the phrase – oh yes, digging to do yet. She had told him so much, told him to go and see her aunts, to get a fuller, more perfect picture of her father, talked about him for hours herself, about how perfect he had been, loving, caring, fun. Magnus had told her just to go on talking, made tapes of it, asking her the occasional question; she was amazed how skilful he was at getting her to talk, prompting half-forgotten memories, half-lost emotions. She had been very brave and told him about Rose and the things she had said. She had shown him the article in *Inside Story*; and she had even told him about Piers and how he had denied being in Hollywood at the same time with her father – and how he had looked when he had heard her name. She had even told him about the mysterious Zwirns. He'd better be on the level, she thought, picking rather half-heartedly at the approximation to food that Pan American called lunch, he'd just better be. She'd made an awful fool of herself if he wasn't.

But he was. She was sure he was. She was slightly worried that she'd rushed her judgement, tempted into recklessness by the empathy she had with him, his swift, almost astonishing grasp of how she felt, by what she could recognize, even as she responded to it, as skilful, clearly well-practised questioning – not even questioning, a sort of easing out of answers. But after a week of fairly intense exposure to him, she still felt oddly easy about him. He was one of the good guys. OK, he'd had an affair with her mother, when she'd still been with Joe, and he'd written a couple of fairly ruthless books, and a whole lot of very revelatory articles, but she found his justification for doing it – for telling everyone the truth – totally acceptable. It was her own morality exactly: an end you cared about justified any means. Never mind hurting, getting hurt, along the way: if something mattered enough, it was worth anything.

Joe sat in his flat, feeling very bleak. He missed Caroline more than he had even expected. The fierce pain, the hurt pride that had assaulted him when he had first discovered she was having an affair with Magnus Phillips had become a dull, throbbing nausea that invaded everything he did. Worse even than the discovery itself had been the discovery of how long it had been going on: a quick fling he could have forgiven, but not nearly a year, a year of subterfuge, of duplicity. A year while she had greeted him smiling, warmly even, on Friday evenings, when he arrived at the Moat House, talked to him, listened to him, fed him, laughed with him, slept with him occasionally, led him to believe she was still fond of him, still needed him, and all the time she had been doing all those things, not just fucking – no doubt a great deal more and more enthusiastically – but talking to, listening to, eating with, laughing with Magnus Phillips.

'Who else knew?' he had said, sitting in the chair, the battered old chair that she had designated his, because it suited him, she said, by the fire in the drawing room at the Moat House.

'No one,' she said, 'no one at all, except Chloe, only Chloe and then only for a very short time.'

'How could you?' he said. 'How could you, with that creep, who is working to destroy your daughter's life, her happiness, both your daughters' probably?'

She had looked at him in silence, her hands spread helplessly, and said she did not know, she could see how terrible it looked, indeed it was terrible, but she had seemed not to be able to help it, had decided, every time, to finish with Magnus, not to go on, had felt it as shocking as he did, but somehow – well, somehow it had not been possible. Not just for another few days. Or weeks. She had not attempted to excuse herself, had not asked him to try to understand, to forgive her, like most unfaithful wives: had simply said she understood how he felt, and she would feel the same. He wasn't sure if that made him feel better or worse at the time: looking back he admired her honesty. Her honesty had been one of the most important things about her: its betrayal had been what hurt most.

Well, it was over. It had to be over. He couldn't go back to her now. Too much had been destroyed. Even if they both wanted it, he couldn't imagine anything being sufficiently powerful even to begin to bring them together. The rift was too shockingly wide. He would have to set her and life with her aside and somehow, some way, begin again. With someone very different and new. He wasn't at all sure he had the stomach for it; maybe he should accept the fact that it was all over, that he was to spend the rest of his life leading a life of celibate solitude. It didn't look like a very happy prospect. He was only thirty-nine, and he seemed to be all washed up. No wives, no children, no one even to talk to. Even Chloe was avoiding him: he wondered what on earth he had done to her. Maybe she was simply embarrassed by her mother's behaviour. He had just decided, whatever the reason, she was too big an absence in his life, to confront her and ask her what the matter was, was sitting indeed with his hand on the phone, when it rang.

'Is that Joe Payton?'

'It is.'

'Joe, this is Fenella Maxwell.'

Joe felt a strong urge to stand up. Of all the women editors in London at the moment, Fenella Maxwell of *Life Style* was the most powerful and successful. She was also extremely attractive.

'Good morning, Fenella,' he said.

'Joe, are you busy at the moment?'

'Depends,' said Joe.

'Well, how busy would you be if I asked you to interview Rose Sharon?'

'Not at all busy.'

'Good, because she's coming to London. To promote her new film. I put in a request, and she said she'd do it if you could write it. She said she liked the way you wrote. Have you ever met her?'

'Yes, once,' said Joe slowly, 'only briefly. In LA. I was doing a story on the Brits there, and she was at a party at Jackie Bisset's studio. I didn't think I'd made that much impression.'

'Well, obviously you did. Anyway, you'd better make another one. Call her agent and fix a time; she hits town the week after next according to the Celebrity Bulletin. Staying at the Savoy.'

'Right. Well, thank you very much, Fenella.'

'My pleasure. Goodbye, Joe.'

Joe put the phone down and sat gazing at it thoughtfully for quite a long time. It was very nice that Rose Sharon had said she liked his work so much she wanted him and him alone to interview her for *Life Style*, but he didn't really quite believe it. Well, it might be true, but it seemed likely there might be something else behind it. He couldn't imagine what though. Maybe when he met her, he could find out. He picked up the phone again and dialled her agent's number.

'I'm going to need some more time on this one,' said Magnus to Richard Beauman. 'Sorry.'

'Magnus, you can't have more time. It'll go off the boil. You gave me early spring as a delivery date, and as far as I'm concerned that's when I want it. The sales force are all geed up, the trade are wetting themselves, we'll look like idiots if we don't deliver, we'll lose credibility and, I might say, a fair bit of money. We've already invested quite a lot in this one, and –'

'Oh, come off it, Richard, what money? The promotion hasn't begun, you haven't even had to spend any of your extremely expensive time reading anything. The only possible cost has been those roughs of the cover. Which are all terrible.'

'Thanks,' said Beauman. 'Magnus, I've put in an enormous amount of groundwork with the trade: dinners, lunches, there's a preliminary promotional package doing the rounds, we've briefed the advertising people, they've been working on it –'

'Balls,' said Magnus. 'Absolute balls. Anyway, even if you'd spent millions on it I wouldn't let you have it. I can't. I've got a whole lot more stuff to follow up and you don't want to publish some half-arsed load of rubbish, do you? I'm investing quite a lot in it myself, Richard, turned down countless thousands in journalistic projects to write it. Including an interview with our illustrious Prime Minister the other day. Which I've been trying to get for ages, I might say. Every time I see a poster that says "Ted Heath talks to the *Mail*. Exclusive", I feel quite sick.'

'My heart bleeds for you,' said Beauman.

'So it should. Sorry, Richard, the book's got to be right, and that's all there is to it. Apart from anything else, with all this talk of injunctions going on, we need to be one hundred and one per cent certain of every single detail.'

'So how much longer are we talking?'

'Let's say six months,' said Magnus.

'Six months! For fuck's sake, Magnus, I can't wait six months. I'm going to have to talk to Henry.'

'OK,' said Magnus cheerfully.

'Magnus, this is not entirely professional,' said Henry Chancellor.

'It's very professional,' said Magnus. 'The story is getting better by the day. I have more leads to follow up. What would be unprofessional would be to leave any of them unfollowed. I'm sure you'd agree with that, Henry.'

'I'm not sure that I would. You could go on for ever with a story like this, Magnus. I have every sympathy with Richard. It's going to leave a huge hole in his summer schedule.'

'In his cash flow more like it,' said Magnus. 'Look, Henry, he's lucky to be getting this book. I've had endless offers for it. Remind him of that, why don't you? You make enough song and dance about not having an ongoing contract or whatever with anyone. Why not use the fact?'

'But, Magnus, you did say originally say this autumn for delivery, then the spring. Now you're saying – what, next autumn? I think Richard Beauman has every right to be worried. I'm worried myself.'

'Oh, go and play with yourself, Henry,' said Magnus good-naturedly. 'What you're worried about is getting your rake-off from the next tranche of the advance. You'll get it and much bigger royalties at the end of it if you leave me be. Now get off my back, there's a good chap. I've got work to do.'

'Chloe, where is Piers?' said Ludovic. He sounded faintly exasperated. 'It's very important.'

'He's not here. He's gone to the States for a few days. Why? What's happened?'

'Nothing's happened, darling, don't sound so frightened. But Nicholas Marshall needs to get together with Piers as soon as possible, and he says his secretary is being unhelpful to put it mildly. Well, of course that's what secretaries are paid for: but in this case she's not really helping him at all. He rang me and asked me if I could get on to him.'

'Oh. Well, I'm sorry, but he really isn't here. Can't it wait?'

'Not for long. It's like asking him to work with his hands tied behind his back, or whatever the equivalent of that is for lawyers. Having all his books locked up. But of course if Piers is really away, that's different. Do you have an address for him, a phone number?'

'Well, sort of. He's staying with Herb Leverson in Hollywood. The man who produced the *Dream*, you know? But he doesn't like me ringing him there unless it's terribly important.'

'This could be called terribly important.'

'Oh – well, all right. I'll try to get hold of him.'

She dialled Herb Leverson's number straight away, before she could lose her courage. A man answered the phone, one of those asexual, transatlantic

Hollywood butler voices: No, Mr Leverson was away for a couple of days, and no, Mr Windsor was out of town as well. He was expected back very shortly, maybe next day. Should he have Mr Windsor call her? What name should he say?

'Say Mrs Windsor,' said Chloe and slammed the phone down. She was near tears.

She called Ludovic back. 'He's not there. Sorry.'

'What's the matter?'

'Nothing,' said Chloe.

'Want me to come over?'

'No. Yes. Oh, Ludovic, I'm so sick and tired of all this.'

'Put the kettle on,' said Ludovic, sounding genuinely concerned as well as amused. 'I'm on my way.'

'Now then,' he said, after listening to her for half an hour, and his voice was at the same time gentle and insistent, 'I think enough is enough. The time has arrived.'

'For what?'

'For you and me.'

'Oh, Ludo, don't,' she said. 'Not now.'

'Why not now? This is exactly now. Chloe, darling, look at me.' They were sitting on the sofa in the upstairs drawing room at Montpelier Square; Ludovic was holding one of her hands. 'What are you hanging on to?'

'Don't be silly. My marriage.'

'Chloe, you don't have a marriage. You really don't. Look at you. Distraught, lonely, betrayed.'

'Don't be so dramatic, Ludovic,' said Chloe with an attempt at a smile. 'I'm perfectly fine.' And she burst into tears.

Ludovic held out his arms. 'Come here.'

Chloe moved forward, and crawled into them, lay there for a long time, her tears drenching his shirt.

'I'm sorry,' she said finally, looking at the large dark patch she had made, 'I'm really sorry. I just needed to cry.'

'You need more than to cry,' said Ludovic tenderly.

'Oh really?' said Choe, smiling at him, aware that she must look appalling, she always did when she cried, her eyes puffy, her nose red, even her mouth distorted in some way.

'Yes. You need to be loved and cared for and' – he said kissing her – 'kissed, and comforted and, well, all kinds of other good things which it would be unseemly to go into now. When you're so upset. Now dry your eyes, I'm going to go down and get you a nice strong brandy –'

'I hate brandy,' said Chloe,

'All right, strong coffee then. You're going to have a bath, and do yourself up a bit. Then I'm going to take you out to dinner.'

'Oh, Ludovic, don't be silly. I can't come out to dinner with you.'

'Why not?'

'Someone might see us.'

'I hope they do.'

'And anyway, Piers might ring.'

'I hope he does. I shall tell Rosemary to tell him you're with me, what's more. Now, darling Chloe, dry your eyes, and I'll be back in a minute.'

'Oh – all right,' said Chloe, sniffing. It was easier to give in.

'Now then,' he said later, much later, as they sat over dinner at the Caprice, and she was smiling into his eyes, happy briefly – and knowing it was briefly made it the sweeter, the more intense, 'now then, Chloe, we have to make some kind of a commitment.'

'Ludovic, what are you talking about? What kind of commitment?'

'To me,' he said, suddenly serious. 'I haven't been joking all these years, Chloe. I saw you that day at that terrible woman's awful lunch, and I fell in love you, there and then, with your dear little frightened face, and your despairing brown eyes. I looked at you and I thought there she is, just exactly what I want –'

'Yes, well,' said Chloe, slightly irritably, 'I've changed a lot since then, I'm not frightened any more although I am still despairing, and besides, I'm tired of being someone sweet and pathetic, I'm a grown-up now, Ludovic, and –'

'I know, I know,' he said, reaching out, touching her face gently, 'you are immensely grown up and sensible and strong, and I just love you all the more for it.'

'Don't patronize me,' she said. 'I can't bear it.'

'I'm not patronizing you. Oh dear, I seem to be making a hash of this. Let me start again. I love you, Chloe, and I want you more than I know how to tell you. And I might point out I'm pretty good at telling people things, I make an impressive living of it. Now, will you please turn if not your back then your side on that miserable non-marriage of yours and do something that you won't regret for a change?'

'Which is?' she said, laughing in spite of herself.

'Have an affair with me.'

'Ludovic, I can't. You must know I can't.'

'I know nothing of the kind. What's your problem, lady? I can show you a good time. Or do you find me totally unattractive?'

'Ludovic,' said Chloe, 'I find you terribly attractive. As you very well know. But I don't approve of people who have affairs.'

'Well, I can handle that. I don't mind being not approved of.'

'Ludovic, I'm not talking about you. I'm talking about me.'

'Well, stop talking about you. Stop talking about it altogether. Just do it. Come to bed with me. I promise you you won't regret it.'

'But Ludo –'

'Listen,' he said, and there was such passion in his voice, such solemnity it startled her; she had only ever known him laughing, light-hearted, teasing. 'Listen, Chloe, I love you. I love you very much. I've watched you, over the years, being brave and loyal and good. I think it's time you were a bit less good. You deserve it. And anyway,' he added with a grin, 'so do I. I've been incredibly faithful to you.'

'Ludovic Ingram, don't be ridiculous. You've had at least three love affairs with perfectly gorgeous creatures since I first met you.'

'They didn't mean anything,' he said, smiling. 'I was just marking time. Waiting.'

On and on it went, as he cajoled, flattered, reasoned with her, telling her that Piers had no kind of claim on her any more, that he did not deserve her, that he was a monstrously unsatisfactory husband; and she sat smiling, increasingly confused, no longer arguing, wishing, wishing above all things that she could say yes, yes, she would have an affair with him, knowing that almost any other woman in the world in her situation would have done so, and quite unable to admit to him the one overpowering reason that was holding her back: not the children, not Piers, not her marriage, but the bleak, sad fact about herself.

Finally, growing just a little impatient, a trifle weary of the excuses, he said, 'Now come along, Chloe, what is it really, why won't you come to bed with me?'

She replied, weary herself, irritated even by his refusal to accept what she said, 'Ludovic, does there have to be a reason? Beyond the fact that I'm married and I have three children?'

'Married?' he said and suddenly there was real rage in the easy voice, dark anger in the smiling eyes. 'That is not a marriage, Chloe, that is simply another performance Piers is putting on. And moreover, you don't even have the starring role.'

Chloe, startled by the anger at first, felt a stinging rage of her own: not just that he had verbalized her misery, but that he was right, that it was not a marriage, not such as she had dreamed of, hoped for, worked for, and knew as well that he had finally pierced her, weakened her, and precisely why he had done it.

'Ludovic,' she said, standing up suddenly, 'I want to go home.'

He drove her home in silence, clearly put out, his pride wounded, his ego (which was, his most devout fan would have admitted, monstrous) dented, and didn't even kiss her goodnight and she went in and lay down on her bed, on the bed where she had been so unhappy with Piers, and cried for a very long time and wondered what on earth was the matter with her, that she was rejecting happiness from a man who was in every way perfect for her: charming, amusing, tender, sensitive, and proclaiming loyalty to another who deserved none of it.

'You're mad,' she said aloud, 'completely mad,' and she finally fell asleep fully clothed and woke just before six to hear a banging at the front door.

She went down, feeling terrible, looking terrible she knew; and there on the doorstep, looking wonderful, freshly shaved and smiling, as if he had had at least eight hours' sleep, was Ludovic, holding an enormous bunch of red roses.

'I got them from the market,' he said, bending to kiss her tenderly, 'and I love you, and I have come to say that I know what the matter is, and I won't say another word about it, as long as you let me in and give me some coffee.'

She let him in and led him to the kitchen, still confused, made a jug of coffee and set it down at the table, and poured out two mugfuls. He leant over and pushed her heavy hair back and said, 'You're so pretty, even when you've just got out of bed. Could we go up to the drawing room? I don't like kitchens.'

'All right,' she said, smiling rather feebly, and led him upstairs to the drawing room, and put her mug down and turned to open the curtains and the shutters.

As she reached up she heard him move over behind her, and she tensed, and he said, 'Leave the curtains, Chloe, we need them closed' and 'no' she said, 'no, really, Ludovic, I –' and then she was silent, for his hand slithered down the front of her dress and was fondling, very gently but with extraordinary firmness, at her breast.

'Beautiful,' he said, 'so beautiful. I've dreamed of these breasts,' and she stood there, savouring him, the warmth of his hand, and the pressure of him behind her; then he pushed his hand further down, towards her stomach, and smoothed and stroked her; still she didn't move; and then his fingers were in her pubic hair, reaching, probing; she tensed, and he said, 'Don't. Chloe, don't be afraid of me.'

She pulled away then, turned and faced him, and the tears began, gently at first, then stronger. 'You don't understand,' she said, 'you don't.'

'I do,' he said, 'I do, Chloe, really. Kiss me.'

And she started to kiss him, felt herself become fluid, melting under his mouth; then tense, wary again as his hands moved down over her hips, cupping her buttocks.

'Darling Chloe,' he said, 'I love you.'

He pulled at her dress, pulled it up over her head and she stood there, in her drawing room, feeling faintly absurd, wearing only her pants and he knelt and started kissing her there, and she stood, totally still and taut, afraid, afraid of him and afraid that at last he would discover her awful sad secret.

'Come along,' said Ludovic, and he went over and locked the door; then he removed his clothes, all of them, and she looked at him, a great golden body, his penis jutting out of his red-gold pubic hair, tanned, every inch of him – 'The boat,' he said, smiling, interpreting her amused surprise, 'I always sunbathe naked on the boat' – and he lay down on the floor, on the white bearskin rug, and said, 'Come along, I'm going to get cold.'

'No,' she said.

'Yes,' he said, 'otherwise I shall shout and pretend to be a burglar and then what will you do?'

Laughing, she sat down on the rug beside him and said finally, confused and afraid, 'Ludovic, you don't understand. I – I don't like it.'

'Oh, but you will,' he said, 'I promise you will. Now take those very elegant pants off and I will tell you exactly what to do.'

Laughing again, she took them off, still half afraid; and he said, 'Now, understand, exactly what I say, all right?'

'Yes all right,' said Chloe, 'but you have to know, Ludovic, before we go any further, I won't – I can't – I'm numb, I –'

And he sat up, and said, 'Please stop talking,' and started to kiss her, and his hand was feeling for her, gently, so gently in her bush, and in further, and she sighed and he said, 'Don't sigh, it's going to be wonderful,' and then he lay down again and said, 'Come and lie on top of me.'

And she did; just lay there, unthreatened, untroubled somehow; and gradually, without realizing why she was doing it, she spread her legs until she was lying astride him, and very slowly, very slowly, she felt him pushing up against her; and she was afraid again. 'Easy,' he said, 'easy, Chloe, be easy,' and then he was in her, right in her and she still felt nothing except fear and a dead loneliness.

Then he pushed her very gently upwards, pushed her body up, so that she was sitting there, astride him, his penis sinking deeper and deeper into her, and she felt – what? A softening, a lightening; nothing more. But it gave her courage, and she moved, cautiously, gazing down into his eyes, his careful, watchful eyes; his hands were on her buttocks, moulding them, but otherwise he was quite, quite still. She moved again; she felt, within her, his penis follow. Nothing then: again, and this time, yes, there was a dart, just a faint flickering dart of pleasure.

'Ah,' he said, 'ah,' and he moved too, and the dart sharpened.

Chloe gasped, tensed, bit her lip; moved again.

'There,' she said, 'there. Now.'

Ludovic pushed suddenly; she felt herself ease, round, tauten all at once, within.

'Good?' he said gently.

'Good,' she said, her voice very faint.

And she was sitting there, on him, her eyes closed, waiting, willing the pleasure back, when he said, quite briskly, 'That will do then,' and very gently eased her off him, and kissed her rather as if he had indeed just dropped in for a cup of coffee.

Chloe opened her eyes and stared at him. 'What?'

'I said that will do. Enough for today. We will continue. How about another coffee, before I go?' He was laughing, his eyes all over her, her naked body, her tousled hair, her face which she knew must be shocked and raw.

'You bastard,' she said, genuine anger sweeping her. 'You bastard. How dare you come in here and – and patronize me? How dare you?'

'I dare because I love you,' said Ludovic, more cheerful still. 'And I'm not patronizing you, I'm taking care of you. I'll be back tonight.'

'I shan't let you in,' said Chloe.

But she knew she would.

* * *

Rose Sharon was a very skilful interviewee. She was also extremely attractive. Joe, who had become suspicious of and bored by famously beautiful and sexy actresses – 'I tell you, they'd be asking you what you thought of their latest movie right up to the moment of orgasm' – found Rose genuinely charming, slightly diffident, and most engagingly interested in him, and what he had been doing since she had last seen him.

'Not a lot,' he said. 'Well, not a lot that's worth talking about. Wrote a lot of articles I wasn't really pleased with. Interviewed a lot of people I wasn't really interested in. Got even more overdrawn . . .'

'And didn't go shopping often enough,' said Rose, laughing. 'Last time I saw you, Joe Payton, you had a rip in your shirt, this time you don't have any buttons on it. I've heard of casual chic, but this is ridiculous.'

'I'm sorry,' said Joe, surprised and oddly charmed she should even remember what he had been wearing at all, let alone that his shirt had had a rip in it.

'Don't be. I rather like it. Do you just hate shopping or what?'

'I just hate shopping,' said Joe.

'Doesn't your wife do it for you?'

'I don't have a wife.'

'Or anything?'

'Or anything,' he said and knew from his voice and the expression in her large blue eyes that she understood beyond the actual words.

'I've been having a horrible time too,' she said. 'Did a film I hated. The one I'm supposed to be talking about this minute . . .'

'Really?' said Joe. 'What do you hate about it?'

'It's a me-too. *Son and Daughter of Bob and Carol and Ted and Alice*. I should never have agreed to it. Then we took the last film, the thriller, you know, *Buckle My Shoe*, to Cannes, and it did really badly. Have you ever been to Cannes?'

'Only once,' said Joe.

'Well enough to know, I expect. Talk about vultures. Rows of them, sitting in the sun. Waiting for you to fail. Oh, that awful thing of going to a party the day after your film didn't win. People smiling, sweetly, saying how wrong the jury had been, talking to you just long enough and then rushing over to chat up the winners. Horrible. And looking at all those babies of seventeen, all over everywhere, and telling yourself how ridiculous they are and then catching sight of yourself in the lobby mirror. Oh, it was awful.' She sighed, then smiled at him. 'Well, at least this is nice. Now then, what can I tell you about? My miserable childhood, that's always a good one –'

'It's amazing,' said Joe, interrupting her, 'how many people have had miserable childhoods. Mine was really happy, I loved almost every day of my first eighteen years.'

'Well, you're very lucky. How about the next eighteen?'

'They were mostly OK too. The last one's definitely been the worst so far.'

'Well, let's hope a pattern isn't setting in. Now look, Joe, we don't have to do all that early stuff do we? You know it, all the getting discovered in the Garden of Allah, and everything. You can get that out of the cuttings.'

'Sure. Can I mention Byron Patrick? All that stuff?' he said.

'If you want to. I mean I'd rather you didn't go into it all too deeply, because it's not actually too relevant, and anyway it's rather well-worked soil. But of course, yes, if you think it matters.'

'Well, I'd like to mention it,' said Joe. 'If only because I covered his story in my book. Which I'm sure you never heard of . . .'

'You sound like a movie star, Joe. Of course I heard of it. Of course I read it. I thought it was excellent, really well researched. I think that was truly one of the saddest episodes in my entire life. Darling Yolande helped you with it, didn't she? Oh, I miss her. I still miss her.'

'Me too. She became a real friend.' Joe looked at Rose carefully, while ostensibly pulling his notebook, pen, notes out of his shabby briefcase. He wondered if Rose had really been fond of Yolande, or if it was an expedient fondness, designed to make him like her more. He decided that, unlikely as it might be, it had probably been genuine. She was gazing out of the window of the Savoy, down the river, an expression of rather distant sadness on her face. Then he shook himself mentally. She was an actress, for God's sake. She had a fine line in sadness, distant or otherwise. Watch it, Payton, you're getting soft.

'Look, I tell you what,' he said, 'I'll read you that bit over. Take out whatever you're not happy with. You're right, it isn't very relevant. It's just rather sweet, boy and girl stuff. Is that OK?'

'Of course.'

'I'm much more interested,' he said, 'in why you've never married again. After David Ezzard. Only one husband. All this time.'

'Don't say all this time,' said Rose, laughing. 'It takes me straight back to Cannes. Oh, Joe, if I knew the answer to that question I'd probably be married again now. If you see what I mean. I think I'm just afraid. So many Hollywood marriages mean no more than lunch. If you see what I mean. Well-publicized lunches. David was different, and I loved him to pieces and it really broke me up when we split. But I've never met anyone since who was worth risking it again.'

'But you've had – relationships?'

'Oh, dozens,' said Rose, laughing. 'I hope you're not implying there's anything suspect in my single state, Joe. I'm as red-blooded as the next girl. Yes, of course. But I don't name names on that one. Sorry.'

'You must regret not having children?'

'Well – I do. Of course. Everyone wants children don't they? It's a stake in immortality. But I don't want children without a fully present husband. I don't believe in it. I'm an old-fashioned girl, I think there has to be a mummy and a daddy, all the time, every day, for ever and ever, Amen. You see, I believe having children is about love and tenderness and security, not just sex . . .'

Joe realized she had settled into interview mode, was trotting out her usual line, carefully dressed in just slightly different colours for him, because she liked him, and he let her talk. *Life Style* would want lots of stuff on sex and relationships, she knew that and he knew that, and she was delivering the goods, in return for being on the cover to coincide with her new picture. It was a very fair deal, really. He just got a bit tired of tying it up sometimes.

After they had finished, and Rose had given him a very good two hours' worth, a very nicely accomplished blend of philosophy, anecdote and self-publicity, she got up and stretched and said, 'These things always make me feel atrophied. Do you have anything much to do for the next hour or so? Because I'd really like a walk, and I could use some company. This can be a lonely city. Or would you feel propositioned?'

'I'd like to feel propositioned,' said Joe, laughing. 'And yes, sure I'd like a walk. Only won't you be mobbed?'

'Of course not. People actually don't see you if you don't want them to. Laurence Olivier once told me that. If you go out, looking to be noticed, you will be, but if you walk quietly along, where nobody's expecting you, just doing ordinary things, you usually get away with it.'

'But surely everyone knows you're here.'

'Yes, they do. But if you went out the front door and brought a cab round to the River Entrance and I was there, especially if you'd let me wear that revolting raincoat of yours, and we took the cab to somewhere like Hyde Park, I bet we wouldn't be noticed. In fact I bet you a hundred dollars we wouldn't be noticed.'

'I can't afford to bet a hundred dollars,' said Joe.

He was glad he hadn't because she was right. She came out of the River Entrance dressed in a pair of jeans, a sweater, and his raincoat, and not even a pair of dark glasses, just make-up-less, with her long hair scraped back, and nobody glanced at her. They told the cab to go to St James's Park – 'Much nicer,' said Joe, 'less moth-eaten' – and walked around it, chatting easily, and then out into the Mall and down towards the palace. It was a perfect gold and blue autumn day; Queen Victoria glittered gold in the sun, Buckingham Palace looked carved stolidly white out of the blue sky.

'This is a very regal area,' said Rose. She took Joe's arm. 'I love London. Some of my happiest times have been here.'

Joe smiled at her slightly foolishly. He was beginning to feel a little light-headed.

'I must get back,' said Rose with a sigh. 'Awful publicist coming to see me in half an hour. This has been such fun, Joe. It's been so kind of you to spare me the time.'

Joe looked at her. He found it very hard to believe he was the only person she could genuinely wish to be spending time with this morning; on the other hand he couldn't think of a single reason she should be bothering with him if she didn't want to.

They were nearly back at the Savoy when she provided it.

'Joe, could I ask your advice about something?'

'Of course.'

'I've been approached by someone called Magnus Phillips, to be interviewed for some book he's writing about Hollywood. What do you think I should say?'

'I think you should say no,' said Joe, trying to sound light-hearted, to ignore a cold dread striking at his heart. 'He's a fairly terrible man. A real gutter journalist. Works for the tabloids. You wouldn't like him at all.'

'Well, that settles it,' said Rose. 'I just didn't know what to think, and I was sure you'd have a view. The thing is I don't know many of the press here, and it's so hard to know where to go for advice. He's very successful though, isn't he?'

'Yes, very,' said Joe. 'The last two books have been bestsellers. But honestly, Rose, he'd sell his own grandmother if it was going to make a good story. As we say over here. Did he give you any idea the sort of area he wanted to interview you about?'

'No,' said Rose. 'No, it was all rather vague. Of course if I was going to do it, I'd have gone into it all very carefully. But I shan't even bother with it. Thank you so much for the advice, Joe. I'm really grateful.'

'That's OK,' said Joe. He felt rather hurt and foolish suddenly.

Rose looked at him; her blue eyes were very gently watchful. 'You think I only wanted to spend the morning with you so I could get your advice, don't you?' she said.

'No. No, of course not.'

'Yes, you do and you're very silly,' she said, smiling at him. 'I could have asked you that hours ago. I wanted to spend the morning with you so I could spend the morning with you. I'm having the tiniest party tonight.'

'Yes?'

'If you come a little bit early I'll mend your shirt for you.'

'I'll buy a new one,' said Joe and walked off into the autumn afternoon feeling as if he had plunged down Alice's rabbit hole.

Much, much later that night as he lay in her arms in her suite at the Savoy, wiping the tears away that she had shed, sweetly sad after he had made love to her, she said, 'You've no idea how lonely it is to be me, Joe. No idea at all.'

Interview with Perry Browne, for Lost Years chapter of *The Tinsel Underneath*. Happy to be quoted.

Well, I certainly had no idea Piers Windsor was here then. If only I had! I could have helped him so much. How very sad that no one introduced him to me. Such a wonderful man, and such a very great actor. We could have flown to the moon together, Mr Phillips, made the most marvellous team. It makes me quite wretched, just thinking about him, and what I could have done for him. I had such contacts in those days. Well, I still do of course, but it's not quite the same.

He can't have been here for very long, or I would have met him. There was no one, but no one, that I didn't know. I was at all the parties, of course, every single one. It was so much more glamorous in those days. So much more fun.

Kirstie Fairfax, no, rings no bells at all. There were so many of them, you see, so many girls, and boys for that matter, all desperately trying to make names for themselves. Missing out all for the want of a little expertise. They're so arrogant, the young: they need help and they won't ask for it. She died you say: how sad. I'm sorry to have to say this, Mr Phillips, but it happens terribly frequently. Drugs, alcoholism, body abuse generally. She was pregnant: well of course that was hardly unusual. The doctors made a lot of money. Of course if she had no money – well, they usually found some way or another.

Now you want to know about Gerard Zwirn. I do remember him. A charming, charming boy, terribly handsome, with the most wonderful very dark hair and eyes, and a beautiful dancer. And such lovely manners; I met him at a private function, he and two girls did a delightful little cabaret. I sought him out afterwards, gave him my card, told him I would be happy to represent him if he wished. He said he had no money, and I was so impressed by him that I said I'd work on a no-fee basis, on the understanding he would repay me when and if he became successful. Even then he refused, said he couldn't take charity from anyone; I thought it was rather sweet of him, if misguided. I said well, anyway, he must let me advise him on a purely friendly basis, on things like contacts, and how he should approach people. I asked him to have dinner with me one night, and he accepted; it was all arranged, then at the last minute he had to cry off. He wasn't well: or did he have an audition? I can't remember. He lived with his sister, out at Santa Monica. She was a rather coarse girl, not in the least like Gerard. I tried to get along with her, made a great effort, but she was always rather abrupt.

I was able to do him a good turn at one point: one of my clients, Patrice Dubarry, I'm sure you'll know of her, was giving a big party and wanted a cabaret. I told her about Gerard and she hired him. He did a marvellous turn, a Fred Astaire impersonation. Everyone thought he was quite wonderful, and then I was able to introduce him to all sorts of people afterwards, quite influential people in the business. He was so grateful to me.

He got very little work, I'm afraid. As I say, I know I could have helped, but he was very proud. He taught dance at a little school in Santa Monica, and that kept the wolf from his rather shabby door. I sent him the occasional pupil, and when they had a performance, which they did each term, I always went and took a few friends with me. I don't know if it's still there. It was called Tip Top Tap which I always told him was misleading, 'people will think you only teach tap, Gerard,' I said, and I suggested several names which I thought would be better. I remember particularly Stage Door. Don't you think that's rather clever? Anyway, he was very stubborn, wouldn't hear of changing it.

He left town rather suddenly; I hadn't seen him for a while and I called a few times; he was always busy, said he'd call me back. And then never did. Well, I didn't mind too much, in fact I was rather pleased for him, obviously he was making some headway. Then he just disappeared. I called and called, spoke to Michelle, that was the sister, and she said he was away, and then finally they both just moved away, leaving no address. That was hurtful; I'd done my best for him, after all, and I felt he could have at least thanked me. Now you wanted to know if he had any connection with Byron Patrick? I really couldn't tell you that. I'm afraid I lost touch with Byron. He was very unfriendly towards me, once he'd made his name. I find that sort of thing very hard to forgive. He owed me a lot, you know. I wouldn't say I was glad when he fell from grace, that would be very unpleasant of me, but I did find it hard to be especially sorry.

There is one possible connection between them, and I really don't know if this is helpful, but I do know Gerard knew Kevin Clint. You've heard of Kevin of course? One of the most important talent scouts in the fifties. He discovered Byron, in New York, and to be frank with you, I did wonder if he'd made a mistake. I mean Byron was wonderful-looking, but quite honestly he couldn't act his way out of a paper bag. Well, of course, dear Miss MacNeice handled Byron so brilliantly, he owed everything to her. She – with some small input from me, I have to say – made him the star he was. I think he thought it was because he was talented, but that was very far from the case. Anyway, Kevin did know Gerard; he'd had him on his books briefly. But I don't think, you know, that he quite understood Gerard's personality; he wasn't just another dancer, he had very real acting talent as well. It needed bringing out, developing; I mean, when I think what Miss MacNeice could have done with him! I did try to persuade her to see Gerard, but she wouldn't. She said she didn't need any dancers. It saddens me to think of all that care and attention being lavished on someone like Byron, it really does.

1971

'She says she won't see you,' said Fleur. Her voice was very flat, carefully casual. 'I'm sorry.'

'That's all right. It isn't your fault. Does she give a reason?'

'She says she's paranoid about the press. Well, I suppose that's reasonable.'

'Not entirely,' said Magnus. 'It's done quite a bit for her, over the years, the press has. Arguably more than it's harmed her. Fleur, do you have any marmalade in this terribly smart kitchen of yours?'

'What? Oh, yeah, sure, over there, look, that whitish jar.'

'Fleur, I'm sorry, but this is not marmalade. It's syrup playing hard to get with some citrus flavouring. I'll have to go and find some.'

'Couldn't you have jelly or something?'

'For breakfast? Oh, sorry, I forgot you call jam jelly over here. No, I couldn't. I'll go down to the deli, see what I can find. Need anything else?'

'Yes, some milk, I need some more coffee. Intravenously. Then I have to go to work. You got plenty of change?'

'Sure.'

He went out, and bumped into Tina in the doorway; her bulk, arguably greater than his own, quivered against him. Magnus put his hands on her shoulders to steady her, smiled into her slightly protuberant eyes.

'I'm terribly sorry. Forgive me.'

'Miss Fitz!' said Tina, in a voice of awe, looking at him as he disappeared down the stairs. 'Who is that?'

'Oh,' said Fleur casually, 'just a friend.'

'A friend? You can have a man like that in your apartment and say he's your friend?'

'Yes, I can,' said Fleur, slightly irritably. 'Tina, he's twice my age, I should think. Not my type. Very nice, but a friend.'

'Then, honey, let me loose on him. That man is sex on legs. I'll give him a little more than friendship, just about right away. He married?'

'No, Tina, he isn't married.'

'He spend the night here?'

'Yes, Tina, he spent part of the night here. On the couch.'

'Lordy, Lordy,' said Tina, and went over to the sink, shaking her head.

Magnus reappeared, his arms full of milk, bagels, orange juice – but no marmalade.

'They didn't have any,' he said mournfully, smiling at Tina. 'I'm sorry I knocked you over like that.'

As he had scarcely even disturbed Tina's mass, this was an acutely flattering remark. Tina bridled at him, fluttering her eyelashes. 'You can knock me over any time,' she said. 'And what did the deli not have?'

'Cooper's Oxford marmalade,' said Magnus. 'I can't live without it.'

'Is that some special kind?' said Tina. 'Do something for you?'

'It certainly does,' said Magnus. 'It does a great deal for me anyway.'

'I'll get it for you,' said Tina. 'Zabars they'd have it. Or Bloomies. Want me to go out now, Miss Fitz, and find some for the gentleman?'

'I most certainly do not,' said Fleur. 'I want you to get on with waxing the kitchen floor, Tina. Thank you. Magnus, I have to go when I've had my coffee. Will you be able to –'

'Miss Fitz, don't you worry about the gentleman,' said Tina, 'I'll take great care of him. Anything he wants, I'll provide.'

'That sounds wonderful,' said Magnus solemnly, 'but I have to check into my hotel. Right away. My secretary fouled up my hotel bookings and Fleur here took pity on me, took me in.'

'I'm telling you I'm sure she didn't mind one tiny little bit,' said Tina.

'Well not till now,' said Fleur shortly.

She sat in the cab going downtown with Magnus and his luggage, feeling irritable and generally upset. She had been so sure Rose would see them, had predicted it so confidently, had wanted so much to impress him, and here she was forced to say sorry, got it wrong, silly me: he would probably doubt all the other things she had told him as well. She had even put in a preliminary request to get the following week off, so she could go to LA with him, deliver Rose into his lap like some glittering prize: now there didn't seem much point.

'Oh well,' she said, 'my aunts aren't too much like Rose Sharon, but at least they'll be interesting.'

'I think I'll probably have a much nicer time with your aunts,' said Magnus. 'I like the sound of Miss Sharon less and less.'

'Oh God!' cried Chloe. 'Oh God, God, don't, don't, no, no, shit, oh. God, please, please, God it's – it's –' and then she cried out, loudly, wordlessly, and then the sound died away, and she lay back, gasping, fighting for breath, slowly restored to calm, her fists unclenching, her body limp, still.

'For a girl who assured me she was frigid,' said Ludovic Ingram, 'you're learning very fast.'

Chloe opened her eyes, looked into his; put out her finger, traced the shape of his face.

'You're a great teacher,' she said simply and shifted slightly beneath him; deep within her it started, stirred again, the wonderful, insistent, pulling brightness; she moved, it moved with her, stronger, more insistent. 'God, Ludo,' she said, and reached around him again, pulling him into her, searching, longing for his force, his strength.

'Chloe!' he said, laughing, 'Chloe, my darling, I can't.'

'No you must,' she said, 'it's there, it's there, please, Ludovic, please.'

He smiled into her eyes and said, 'OK, just for you,' and he was moving in her again, a little fragile at first, then growing, wonderfully growing, and she could feel it, the strong sweet pushing of him in her, at her, working on the sensation, caressing it, tending it, and he was kissing her, his mouth gently, wonderfully erotic on hers, his tongue exploring her, as it had explored other parts of her, and the memory inspired her, prompted her, and she moved, suddenly frantically, and the sensation in her sharpened, peaked, grew, peaked again, and there were endless rivulets of pleasure now, feeding off one another, and she felt it would go on for ever, for eternity, and then as she rose, rose again, to meet him, crying out, calling his name, he suddenly collapsed on her with a great groan and said, 'Chloe, you are wearing me out. Now this is quite enough for now.'

She lay beside him on the pillow, smiling, released at last, happy, sweetly weary, gently used, and could not believe how happy she was.

Sex was wonderful; she could hardly believe she could have lived for so long with all this potential for pleasure within her and not known about it. She could not have enough; she was frantic for it. Starved of it right through her marriage, she now ran appalling risks to assuage her appetite. She would go to Ludovic's flat in the Albany at lunch-time, early in the evening, first thing in the morning even, any time when she knew Piers would be occupied, and within minutes of arriving she would be naked, in bed with him, exploring, discovering, abandoning herself to pleasure. She shocked herself, at the departure from the nicely brought-up girl, the beautifully behaved young matron she had always been; and at the same time she was proud, exultant at herself and the things she could achieve.

She became swiftly familiar with her own body; what it liked, where it responded most swiftly. She loved what it could do, what she could do for Ludovic as well as he for her. Modesty, inhibition did not exist, after the first few times: he led, and she followed willingly, laughing, crying, shouting with pleasure. She did not always come swiftly; sometimes it took her a long time, and she would lie, clinging to him, sweating, whimpering with frustration. They were the best times in the end; the orgasm when she finally reached it, found it, tumbling over her in great drenching sheets of pleasure.

She was so happy, so alive, she had no room, no time for guilt. Piers came back, full as usual of excuses, of protestations of love, and she listened, smiling politely, feeling detached as if he were simply a rather distant acquaintance; thinking, remembering only how she had felt the day before when on the third time Ludovic had made love to her he had brought her to her own personal edge of pleasure and tipped her over into it. And she had lain there afterwards, weeping sweet, tender tears of relief and of triumph, staring up into his face, soft with delight of his own, his eyes smiling down into hers, his fingers tracing gently, tenderly the shape of her face, his voice telling her over and over that he loved her, and she had thought she had never even dreamed of such happiness. 'How did you know?' she said, gazing at him almost in awe after the first time. 'How did you know I could do this?'

'Not you,' he said, laughing. 'Me. Don't flatter yourself. I did it.'

'Oh,' she said, laughing back, 'oh, all right, how did you know you could do it?'

'Well,' he said, 'I watched you, and I loved you and I knew, I knew you weren't – what were the words you used? – oh yes, "numb". I knew no one like you could be numb.'

'And I don't even feel bad,' she said.

'Why should you feel bad?' he said.

And she said why, because of Piers, and he said she was not to feel bad, that Piers had made her feel bad enough for long enough, and she owed herself a little, no, a great deal of pleasure. She gave herself up to pleasure: she ceased to worry about anything. She turned her back on the book, on Magnus Phillips, on her mother, even on Joe, who she felt being so close to her must surely guess her sweet, terrible secret. She went through the days automatically, caring for her children, seeing to her household, accompanying Piers to functions, attending to his needs, nurturing his ego, soothing his anxieties.

He had come back from Los Angeles anxious, distracted: he told her it was because of a new project he was working on and she did not entirely believe him, but she was too caught up in her own concerns to properly care. He was at once withdrawn from her, yet increasingly dependent; demanding her attention, her time, while (mercifully, God how mercifully) leaving her with a tender kiss each night to sleep alone in his dressing room. She had no idea why, and she had no desire to ask, she was simply grateful that in a rare act of generosity, fate had freed her to celebrate her new discoveries about herself.

And she was, as well as glowing, sleekly warm, with sexual pleasure, in love with Ludovic. The emotions he evoked in her were the ones she had first known with Piers, but deeper, stronger, more confident. She felt within her a great well of happiness, of belonging, of being absolutely at peace with herself and with him. That too eased her guilt, made her feel more joyful, less afraid. And he loved her too, he told her tenderly over and over again, had always loved her, always would, and helpless, dizzy with happiness, she allowed herself to know it was true.

It was hard to believe entirely in the niceness, the sheer uncomplicatedness of Ludovic. She kept thinking she must find a flaw in him, some hidden awful darkness that no one had expected. But weeks went by and she saw more and more of him, and still she found none. He did not even pressure her in any way to proceed with their relationship, to take decisions on it: he told her that they had enough for now, and time would take care of the rest. And for now, she found that quite easy, quite acceptable; clearly they must move on, she could not go on for ever living with one man and loving another, but just for a while she was satisfied, they both were, with what they had discovered and what they could enjoy.

He was forty years old, most amicably divorced from his wife, the daughter of an earl, who had left him for an American folk singer ('You know how these guys love English class'). He was, as well as dazzlingly good-looking and very rich, brilliantly clever, and had left Eton for Balliol on a scholarship and proceeded to get a First in law. After a comparatively short pupillage, he had gone into chambers with another Balliol man; within five years they were up and running, star names in a starry profession. Ludovic had a talent for self-publicity; he attracted attention. His first notorious case had been defending a high-profile banker in a libel case against a Sunday newspaper; he had won him damages of forty thousand pounds, and a grovelling apology in print. From then on, he was made. He belonged to that rare (and fortunate) breed of people who are popular with both sexes; women fell determinedly in love with him, but men liked him enormously also, respecting his brilliant mind, his capacity to amuse and his awe-inspiring prowess on the squash court and at the sails of his yacht. He led a charmed life; his only sorrow (on the departure of his wife) being that he had as yet no children. He owned a beautiful house in Hampshire where he kept his boat, and a charming flat in the Albany; he dressed well, rode adequately, and was greatly sought after at the dinner tables of London.

And he was, unbelievably, in love with her.

Things had gone very quiet on the book. Spies put out by Ludovic and Joe in the trade reported a six-month, possibly a year's delay in publication. 'I wouldn't like to bank on it,' said Ludovic to Joe, 'but it seems just possible they've been scared off. A libel action is an extremely expensive thing, and publishers are not newspapers, they don't have that kind of telephone-number money.'

'I certainly wouldn't bank on it either,' said Joe. 'Magnus Phillips doesn't scare easy.'

'Well, that's true, but it's not just Magnus we're dealing with, after all. It's the publishers and the publishers' lawyers. And quite possibly the lawyers of some of his witnesses.'

'I hope you're right,' said Joe, 'but I don't feel very confident about it myself. What does Piers say?'

'Very little. Extremely reluctant to talk about it. Says he leaves it in our hands. Extraordinary when the story could be so damaging.'

'Maybe it's a kind of death wish,' said Joe.

Fleur was beginning to feel uneasy about Magnus Phillips. She wasn't sure what about, what had prompted it; but she just knew all was not well, was beginning to regret being quite so reckless with her information.

He was so secretive for a start: disappearing off to places for days on end (Chicago last week, upstate New York this and with no apparent interest in going to LA or San Francisco) without telling her who he was seeing or why.

He told her he always worked like that, and she told him he wouldn't be working at all on this particular tack without her help. He laughed and told her not to flatter herself, that he was a great detective; and then more seriously that she would get to hear all about it, all in good time.

'Would you show your clients the first line of your ads without working out the rest of it?'

'That's different,' said Fleur. He had met her from work on his return from Chicago, told her he owed her a drink while refusing to tell her why.

'It's exactly the same. Did they like my fridge idea?'

'I'm not sure,' said Fleur untruthfully.

She had been struggling over a copyline for a new fridge which had absolutely nothing to commend it but the fact that it was more expensive than any other fridge on the market; Magnus had found her desperate one evening, beating her brains out, read the research and said, 'Just say exactly that. That it's the most expensive fridge on the market.'

'So?'

'So anyone who's got it can afford it. Is rich. Has money to burn. Or freeze. It's the pure silk of fridges. How about that?'

'It's fucking brilliant,' said Fleur, staring at him.

He smiled at her suddenly. 'It's sweet the way you do that.'

'Do what?'

'Swear when you're excited. Does any other kind of excitement have that sort of effect on you, or is it just verbal?'

'I haven't really thought about it,' said Fleur briefly. There was no way she was going to get into that kind of territory with the devious bastard.

Her aunts had been charmed by him, especially Kate.

'He seems so keen to put the record straight,' she said ecstatically to Fleur, 'so anxious to present Brendan in the best possible light. I told him to go and see Father Cash, and he was most enthusiastic about the idea.'

'Oh, really?' said Fleur.

'Yes, and he sent me the most beautiful bouquet of flowers next day, and a note saying he hoped I might have time to see him again if necessary. He is one of nature's gentleman, Fleur, no doubt about it.'

'I'd say there was quite a bit of doubt,' said Fleur.

She worried about his ability to make people talk: even Reuben, to whom she had been forced to introduce Magnus one evening in the lobby of the agency, saying Magnus was an old friend of her mother's.

Magnus had promised to buy her a drink, dinner even, and had promptly invited Reuben too, to Fleur's intense irritation; it became even more intense as she discovered a passion in Reuben (entirely unsuspected) for motorbikes and she finally went home alone in a cab, leaving them in the midst of an animated discussion about throttles.

'Nice guy,' said Reuben next day.

'I'm not so sure,' said Fleur.

* * *

'I like your boyfriend,' said Magnus. 'He's one of the good guys.'

'I'm glad you liked him so much,' said Fleur. 'The feeling was mutual. He rather seems to prefer you to me.'

'Oh, not entirely. I'm sure you can give him things I could only dream of.'

'Why didn't you tell me you were interested in motorbikes?' said Fleur irritably to Reuben.

'You never asked,' said Reuben.

'Sometimes, Reuben, you drive me way up the wall.'

'Sorry,' said Reuben.

Her irritability and sense of unease spilt over into her work: she found it hard to concentrate, and harder to care. For the first time in her life she found the obsession with who was buying what and why faintly ridiculous, and even her enthusiasm for Bernard Stobbs's latest list was lukewarm. It was only when Sol Morton told her that if she didn't get her elegant arse into gear and come up with a new line for his Summer Fantasy he'd look around at other agencies that she was galvanized into any kind of painstaking thought and even then she knew that what she presented him with was not truly first rate. More significant, however, was that she had managed to persuade herself it was good enough.

She didn't want to go out; and she got bored and fractious staying in. Reuben irritated her, and she kept making excuses not to see him; she only wanted to see Magnus, and find out what was going on, and then when she did see him, she felt worse, because it was so unsatisfactory and she didn't find anything out at all. He had become very friendly with Reuben and they went off out on to Long Island on hired motorbikes every Sunday afternoon that Magnus was in New York.

She had even more trouble than usual sleeping, and she had what seemed to her an almost constant headache.

Finally Baz Browne took her out to lunch and said he thought she had been overworking and suggested she took a vacation.

Fleur stared at him in alarm. 'You don't mean the old joke about two vacations a year of six months each?'

'No, of course not. Two weeks, just once. Enough to put some life back into you. We need you firing on all cylinders for the autumn campaigns.'

'Don't talk to me about cylinders,' said Fleur wearily.

When she got back to the apartment that night there was a letter from Rose.

Dearest Fleur,

Would you be terribly sweet and ask your Mr Phillips to stop pestering me. I'm sure it's not your fault, but I must have had half a dozen letters now and as many phone calls to my secretary. He doesn't seem able to take no for an answer. I wouldn't trouble you, but I know initially it was your idea I should talk to him, and you might have more influence over him than I do.

Best love,

Rose

Fleur swore and picked up the phone, dialled the number of the slightly seedy hotel where Magnus was staying on the edge of the Village.

'Just what the fuck do you think you're doing?' she said when she finally got through to him.

'I'm sorry?'

'Pestering Rose Sharon. She's actually been driven to write to me, to ask me to call you off.'

'Dear me. What a sensitive little flower she is,' said Magnus.

'Magnus, what is this?' said Fleur. She found to her horror she was near tears. 'Rose Sharon is a friend of mine, she's been sweet and good to me –'

'In what way exactly?'

'I'm sorry?'

'I said in what way exactly?'

'Well – she's been kind and friendly. Generally.'

'Oh,' he said, 'oh, I see. Yes, of course. I wonder, did she get in touch with you after your dad died, write to you, that sort of thing?'

'She couldn't. She didn't know where I was. Magnus, do you have any reason for your hostility to Rose?'

'No, of course not,' he said and his voice was amused. 'I just find your loyalty to her rather touching, that's all. And her sensitivity slightly amusing.'

'What?'

'World-class film stars generally have hides that would put oxen to shame. Except of course when their own egos are ever so slightly bruised.'

'This is getting us nowhere,' said Fleur, exasperated.

'I didn't start it.'

'Oh, for fuck's sake, Magnus, of course you did. Hounding Rose like that. Until she had to write to me.'

'Oh, yes, of course. Sorry. Well, I won't do it again. I'm going back to London tomorrow.'

'For how long?' said Fleur, hoping her bleakness didn't sound in her voice.

'I don't know. Quite a long time probably. It is my home.'

'Yes, but you haven't finished here, surely.'

'Yes, I have.'

'You haven't been to LA or San Francisco.'

'I don't know that I need to.'

'Oh, for God's sake,' said Fleur and heard her voice growing heavy, wretched, 'of course you do.'

There was a long silence. Then Magnus said, 'Fleur, are you all right?'

'Yes, of course I'm all right.'

'You don't sound it.'

'I'm all right,' she said. 'Why don't you just fuck off back to London, leave me alone.'

She put the phone down, got rather wearily out of her clothes, ran a bath. She ached all over, and her skin felt sore. So did her heart.

She was just settled in the water, her head resting on the bathpillow, when the intercom bell rang. She decided to ignore it, settled herself deeper. It went again, playing a dum-de-de-dumdum rhythm. Cursing it, she heaved herself out, went to the phone.

'Yes?'

'Fleur, it's Magnus. I want to see you.'

'I don't want to see you,' she said and slammed it down again.

She had only just got back into the bath when the bell went again. She ignored it. It went on. After twenty minutes she broke.

'Just fuck off, will you?' she shouted into it.

'After I've seen you.'

'Oh, for God's sake,' she said, 'all right. Come on up,' and pressed the buzzer.

'I'm in the bath,' she shouted through the door when she heard him come in. 'You'll have to wait.'

'OK.'

She realized none of her clothes were in the bathroom, which opened on to the studio, and that she had even shed her bathrobe by the entryphone in her rage. The only towel in the bathroom was small – hardly big enough to cover her. Fuck it. Fuck it, fuck it, fuck it. She put it carefully round her, checking her back view – yes, it covered her arse, just; and then the front. It dangled perilously on her nipples, but it was decent. She opened the door: Magnus was sitting facing it, smiling expectantly.

'Nice towel.'

'Oh, shut up,' said Fleur.

'I don't seem to be able to say anything right tonight.'

'No, you don't. Look, I didn't ask you to come. Don't expect sweetness and light.'

'I certainly wouldn't,' he said, grinning cheerfully. 'Not from you. Not sweetness anyway.'

Tears, treacherously hot, stung at Fleur's eyes. Magnus saw them.

'Hey,' he said, 'what's this? Don't tell me you have a heart after all. Tears from the iron maiden.'

'I am not crying,' said Fleur and put up her hand without thinking to dash the tears away. The towel promptly dropped off. 'Oh shit!' she said and stooped to pick it up. 'Fuck, Magnus, why don't you just go away?'

'Bad language!' he said. 'Excitement. Good sign. This could be my lucky day.'

'Oh please!' she said, and suddenly she couldn't stand any of it any longer and burst into tears.

Magnus moved very slowly towards her. He picked up the towel and wrapped it round her, carefully, tenderly, as if she was a baby, tucking in the end just above her left breast, put his arm round her gently, held a handkerchief to her nose.

'Blow,' he said. 'That's right. That's better. You smell lovely,' he added, almost casually. 'Quite lovely. Now go and get something slightly more respectable on, although I have no objection to the present outfit, and then come back in here, and I'll have a hot drink ready for you. And you can tell me what the matter is.'

When she came out from the bedroom, wearing a large sweater of Reuben's and a pair of jeans, he was waiting for her with a mug of coffee.

'I shouldn't drink that,' she said, 'I have enough trouble sleeping as it is.'

'You do?' he said. 'Me too. Imagine neither of us knowing that about the other. I go for rides on my bike. What do you do?'

'Get up and work,' said Fleur. She felt cross with him again, as if her insomnia was his fault as well as everything else.

'That's really bad for you,' he said, 'your brain never gets a chance. You should dance or listen to music or something like that. Rest your eyes.'

'Maybe that's why I have to wear glasses,' said Fleur.

'Probably is. How about sex?'

'I'm sorry?'

'I said how about sex? I mean as a way of getting to sleep.'

She laughed, slightly unwillingly. 'Yeah. That works.'

'Works for me too. But I'm told it's not so good for your half.'

'My half of what?'

'The human race.'

'Oh,' she said and was silent, suddenly uncomfortable at the thought of her mother's presence in Magnus's past, in his bed.

'Now then, what exactly is the matter?'

'You should know,' said Fleur, her anger surfacing again, that he should ask, 'and I'm sure you do. Actually.'

'I'm sure I don't. Actually.'

'OK,' she said, 'take a look at it my way. I hear you're writing a book about – well, about things that concern me. Deeply, desperately concern me. I trust you enough, God knows why, to tell you lots of things, personal, private, precious things, some of them. And what do you do? Say, hey, that's great, I'll use that, thanks, see you around.'

'Fleur, I –'

'It may be just another book to you, about just another set of unsavoury people, like your politicians and your dancers. To me it's my one chance to set the record straight about the one person I really truly cared about, loved more than I ever loved anyone. Don't you understand that, Magnus? Don't you see? And can't you see how frightened I am, how concerned that it won't work for me and for him, won't put things right? You just go off, seeing people, God knows who, God knows where, making them talk, making them tell you things, and then you say fine, that's it, time to finish, and never mind about anything else. Well, I wish, I wish to God I hadn't ever met you, seen you, talked to you. I'm so scared, so scared of what you're going to do. Don't you understand?'

She was really crying now, tears pouring down her face, her voice jerky, rich with pain. She got up and went over to the window, looked down over at the park, wondering when, if, how this was ever going to end, this hurt, this awful hurt of hers; and then she suddenly heard behind her Magnus Phillips's voice, gentle, quiet as she had never imagined it could be.

'I'm sorry,' he said. 'I'm so sorry. Please forgive me.' She turned and he was looking at her, his eyes genuinely full of remorse, of distress. 'I'm so sorry, Fleur. I just – well, I suppose I just didn't think.'

'No,' she said, 'no, I don't suppose you did.'

There was a long silence.

Then she said, 'What have you learnt, Magnus? What are you going to write about him?'

'I don't know,' he said, 'honestly, I don't know. Yet. You have to believe that. When I know, I'll tell you. I'm learning, all the time; things are changing. Don't make me tell you too soon. There isn't any point.'

Fleur sighed. Then she said, 'All right. All right, Magnus. I guess I have to trust you. But is it going to be all right?'

Magnus Phillips looked at her and there was something near to tenderness in his almost black eyes.

'I hope so, Fleur,' he said, and sighed. 'I do so very much hope so. Now I think I should go. Before I upset you any further. And can I just say one thing. You said you wished you'd never met me, seen me. I cannot tell you how infinitely glad I am that you did. Goodnight, Fleur.'

And he bent and kissed her, very gently, on the mouth.

Interview with Lindsay Lancaster, re Lost Years chapter of *The Tinsel Underneath*.

I don't remember Piers Windsor at all. I don't think I ever met him. He was certainly around at the time, but he never got anywhere. Yeah, sure, I always thought it was him talked to those scandal sheets about Byron; that was just because of something Byron said. It seemed to add up. I told Rose about that. Years ago.

I really liked Byron. He had manners, you know. More than I can say for Naomi MacNeice. She was a real, numero uno, ace bitch. You know the kind of thing? Jewish princess from Manhattan, Seven Sisters school, always fucking someone up. She was ruder than anyone I ever met. She made rudeness an art form. She was also very clever and very powerful. Byron was no match for her. Just no match at all. I don't really know why she liked him. I suppose he could deliver the goods. And he looked good, on her arm. Or rather walking three steps behind her, which is what she made him do. Everywhere, into parties, at premières, award ceremonies. Funny thing is, he never really bad-mouthed her. He said she was honest. Byron liked honesty. It was honesty that did it for him. In every way.

I really don't remember all that stuff about Kirstie Fairfax. There are a lot of tragedies in this town. B-movies tragedies. Byron never mentioned her, but then why should he? He must have known dozens and dozens of those girls. All trying to make it; trying to make him too, I guess. I certainly don't think he had anything to do with her. Certainly wouldn't have knocked her up. Listen, he never got near enough any girl to hold her hand without Naomi getting up his arse. And he knew not to risk it. But he would have tried to get her a test, sure, get her a part, if he'd known her. He was like that. He was kind. Really kind. A gentleman, like I said.

Chapter 30

Autumn 1971

'Think of me as a priest,' said Nicholas Marshall encouragingly. 'In the confessional.'

He often used this analogy, to soothe nervous clients, and generally it worked beautifully. It didn't now.

'I'm sorry,' said Piers Windsor. 'I really would rather not go into any kind of detail.'

'Look, Mr Windsor,' said Marshall patiently, 'this is a potentially very – difficult business. As I understand it, this book is being written, you feel it could be seriously defamatory of you, and you want it stopped. Now it would help me greatly if you were to tell me in what way you feel it could be defamatory, and how sound you think the author's sources might be. If it contains a libel or a series of libels then there are several courses of action we can consider; but we do need to be fairly sure of our ground. We need to know, in other words, what the book contains. Otherwise, we shall all be wasting a great deal of time, and you of course' – he paused, smiled carefully – 'you will be wasting a great deal of money.'

'It's – extremely difficult to say,' said Piers.

'What is difficult, Mr Windsor?' Christ, this guy was trouble. He must remember to do Ludovic Ingram a disfavour in return.

'There are several things which the book might be saying which would be libellous or defamatory. It is very hard for me to assess what and how many of them there might be.' He smiled suddenly: a rather haunted smile.

He didn't look well, Marshall thought: he was very thin, very pale. Well, it was hardly surprising. 'And you don't feel you can tell me about them?' he said.

'Let me say I would rather not. At this stage. Would you like to tell me what the various courses of action might be?'

'Very well. You are fortunate, Mr Windsor, I might say, in living in the libel capital of the world. You might not fare so well in America. Over there you have to prove malice before you are able to sue for libel. Not impossible, obviously, but more difficult.'

'Well, at least I have something in my favour,' said Piers. He smiled with obvious difficulty.

'Indeed. Well now, the first thing would be for you to talk to the author direct. As I understand it, he is – or rather was – a friend of yours. It might be possible to appeal to his better nature. Persuade him not to write the book. Or at least to tell you what he intends to write in it. That would be a start.' He paused. 'I need hardly tell you that unless you can exert some very powerful pressure on him, that is a little unlikely. As I understand it, he has been paid a huge advance by his publishers. And no doubt is very keen to write the book.'

'No doubt,' said Piers. 'Er – would you accompany me on such a mission? Or would I go and see him alone?'

'Oh, I would have thought you should go alone. If I were to come with you, then no doubt Mr Phillips would bring his solicitor. It would be more formal, harder to get any sense of personal appeal into the occasion.'

'I see. And then what might or might not happen?'

'Well, the next step, presuming you are unsuccessful, would be for us to ask to see copies of the book. They will almost certainly refuse. The point is, you see, Mr Windsor, that if the publishers are confident that what the book contains is the truth, and they will have had the author's sources most painstakingly checked out, then they are not going to be too worried by any threat of ours.'

'Can we not take out an injunction, to prevent it being published altogether? That is what I was hoping for,' said Piers. He fiddled with his tie: the Garrick Club pink and green stripes. He was paler than ever; there was a light sweat on his forehead.

This is a seriously worried man, thought Marshall. He felt a pang of sympathy, wished he was getting more cooperation. 'An injunction does indeed prevent publication. But, Mr Windsor, I would advise you most strongly against such an action. The point about an injunction is that it is extremely difficult to get if the defendant – that is to say the author – insists that what the book contains is true. It is also a requisite basis for such an action that what the book contains cannot be compensated for by damages – however great.'

Piers looked at him. 'If my reputation, indeed my life are ruined by this book, if everything I have worked for, both on a personal and professional level has been destroyed, then no damages can compensate me. If – what shall we say – allegations have been made, and people believe them, no amount of money paid to me is going to change their minds.'

'Well, you see, Mr Windsor, the law doesn't quite see it like that. If the damages are large enough, then what the court has done is state categorically that it has found the book to contain serious libel: the information in it is without foundation, and the perpetrators of the libel must be forced to admit that they have been in error.'

'I'm afraid I don't find that very satisfactory, Mr Marshall,' said Piers Windsor. 'To use a vulgar phrase, mud sticks. I cannot imagine any sum of money which would compensate me for what I fear this book might contain. No, we have to stop the publication beforehand. Somehow.'

'Well, if we are to stop it, we have to be sure that the book is not only defamatory, but untrue. If a man who is a pillar of the community is beating his wife and nobody knows, and then a book is published stating that he does so, he has not been libelled: merely defamed. I cannot stress this too strongly, Mr Windsor. It is why I would urge you to take me into your confidence.'

Piers looked at him for a long time: then he said, 'I think perhaps I should begin by going to visit Mr Phillips. I shall go alone, and then I shall report back to you.'

'Very well. I wish you every good fortune.'

'How kind,' said Piers and gave him one of his sweetest smiles and left the office.

Nicholas Marshall sat looking after him in silence for a while; then he remarked, to the floor-to-ceiling bookcase that was his normal confidant on such occasions, 'There goes a guilty man.'

Caroline was in the stables when Piers phoned: she had been for a long ride with Jack, it had rained most of the way, her back ached, and she was tired and irritable. She felt tired and irritable a great deal of the time at the moment, wet rides or not; she could see she had only herself to blame for the disagreeable form of her life, but it didn't make her feel any better. She missed Magnus horribly; but she also missed Joe and she was missing Chloe and the children with a fierceness that surprised her. Chloe had cut her from her life with a ruthlessness that had startled her. She had never really apologized for her outburst at the time; and had not made a single overture to her mother since. If Caroline phoned her, she was coldly polite. She made an excuse not to see her at Christmas, she wrote polite notes to say thank you for presents, and she sent flowers on her mother's birthday. When Caroline phoned her, made her confront the issue, she said simply, 'I love Joe very much. I just can't bear the way you've hurt him,' and put the phone down.

Caroline couldn't quite bear the way she'd hurt Joe either. It was completely impossible to justify, to make excuses for. She had hurt him beyond all endurance, and he had done nothing, nothing at all, to deserve it. He had not married her, but he had most certainly loved, cherished and, in the truest sense of the word, kept her, had been loyal to her, been there always when she needed him, taken on her children, cared for Chloe, helped her with Fleur, and for the sake of a little sexual excitement, a desire for adventure, she had rejected him totally, deceived him, damaged him almost beyond endurance. She felt shocked at herself, shocked and sickened; and alone in her distress. She talked to Jack about it, he being the only person with whom she could have such a conversation, and not even he was able to help, to reassure her about herself and the way she had behaved.

'We all make mistakes, Caroline,' he said simply. 'Life's about trying to put them right again.'

The problem was, she couldn't see how she could put this one right. She wrote to Joe, a short letter, telling him how sorry she was, how ashamed; anything more seemed nauseatingly hypocritical. Joe had not replied. She had finished swiftly, angrily with Magnus, as much appalled by his behaviour as her own; but once the rage was over, she found herself sadly bereft. He had been such a strong, powerful force in her life and for quite a long time; she found herself not merely alone, but alone in a flat, bleak landscape with no light or shade in it, and no hope as far as she could see of finding any ever again.

And seeing pictures of Joe in the papers with Rose Sharon, with whom, they both insisted, he was just good friends, didn't help in the least.

Jack took the call: 'It's Mr Windsor,' he said to her, his face and voice equally blank.

'Thank you, Jack. Tell him I'll take it at the house.'

'Piers? Is anything wrong?'

'No, no, everything's fine,' he said. 'Chloe and the children are all well. I just wondered if I could ask you a possible favour, Caroline.'

'You can certainly ask, Piers. I don't know if I'll be able to deliver.'

'I don't either. But I think it's worth trying. It's about this book. That your – friend' – he made the word sound particularly obscene – 'Magnus Phillips is writing.'

'Ah, yes,' said Caroline, 'the book.' Against all logic she felt a sudden loyalty to Magnus.

'I . . .' He paused, clearly searching for exactly the right word. 'I very much need to know what he's likely to write in it. About me.'

'Yes? I hope you're not going to ask me to find out, Piers. Because he certainly won't tell me. And I certainly don't know.'

'Well, I just – wondered. If you could give me any clues. I'm taking legal action and any information I can glean will be invaluable.'

'Yes, Piers, no doubt it will. But I'm afraid I can't help. Can't help at all. Magnus and I are not on speaking terms.'

'I just wondered if you might have any clues . . .' His voice sounded strained, slightly odd.

'No, Piers, I'm sorry,' said Caroline and put the phone down.

Then she sat looking at it and felt remorse creeping over her slowly. This book, this wretched book, that was threatening to tear their lives apart, pulling in so many strands from so many directions: it was not just going to damage Piers, but almost everyone she loved or had loved, everyone who had been important in her life. Chloe, her sweetly conventional life and status disrupted, made ugly, not only by present scandals, but by past ones, an illegitimate and, more importantly, an unacknowledged sister exposed, a past indiscretion that was in no way her fault reaching out and spreading into every corner of her life; and Chloe's children, of course: Pandora at least was old enough to be hurt by it. That indiscretion, her indiscretion, its sweetness turned sour, a sacrifice made with such honour, such courage, made to seem ugly, furtive. And then Fleur, already so hurt, so confused, so starved of love, what would it, could it, do to her, to have her history misrepresented in the pages of a book, written with the express and sole purpose of sensationalism? She realized with a sense of acute shock that since her affair with Magnus had begun, she had scarcely thought of Fleur; had relegated her to her past, her distant past, when she had been another person, with other concerns. Maybe, just maybe, that was where Fleur did now belong; they were clearly never to be close, never friends. But this book, this awful horrible book, would that not revive all those emotions, rip the skin off them, make them raw again? And what might it, would it say about Brendan, this book? Would his sad history, retold, refurbished, with the same purpose, become yet more disgraceful, move further from its truth?

Caroline sat there, suddenly careless about all the others, thinking only about Brendan, as she so rarely dared to do, and as she sat, he became alive again. Alive and young, and brave: a hero, her hero, her love, with her, walking, talking, loving. She saw him, with total clarity, the dark blue eyes flicking over her, the tall, almost gangly body, young, oh so young that body had been, so hungry, so potent; the cropped dark hair, the slow, lazy smile. She heard his voice again, his light, American voice, with its distant touch of Irish, calling her name, talking to her, tenderly, sweetly, telling her how much he loved her, how he was going to take her home with him, marry her, make her his for ever. And she felt him, felt his hands on her, felt his mouth on hers, felt him in her again; and felt her love for him, certainly, determinedly happy.

Then he was gone again, lost from her, and with him, her small, beloved daughter, gone both of them, far away, to the other side of the world, lost for ever, taking with them all of her happiness, all of her youth, leaving her a shell, a painful shell, living out a marriage with someone she did not love, and motherhood to another daughter who had meant then almost nothing.

And it was remembering Brendan, seeing him, hearing him, feeling him with such force, such clarity that gave her the courage to fight for him and for Fleur, to justify what she had done, however wrongly, just one more time. Not for Piers, not for Chloe, not for Fleur even, but for Brendan, that he might finally be shown to be the person she had known, the person he had truly been.

Magnus returned her slightly nervous, tentative call within half an hour.

'Caroline! How charming to hear from you.'

Shit, he had the sexiest voice she had ever heard: deep, roughed up, slept in. She felt, despite her hostility, a pang of longing so fierce she had to close her eyes, grip the edge of the hall table. 'Magnus. Yes. Well, I expect you know why I've called.'

'One of two reasons. You want me back. Or you want to know about the book. Possibly even both.'

'I absolutely do not want you back,' said Caroline. 'What I said at our last meeting still holds.'

'What was that? Oh, yes, that I was disgusting. Strong words, Lady Hunterton. To describe a humble seeker after truth.'

'Don't give me that, Magnus. Seeker after truth just possibly, providing it's going to pay its way one way or another, humble absolutely not.'

'My darling, you do have a way with words. I don't know why you don't try your hand at my business.'

'Thank you, Magnus, but I wouldn't care to. I'd be too worried about my immortal soul.'

'Oh, Caroline, I'm sure your immortal soul has a place very safely reserved for it up there, whatever you did from henceforward.'

'How kind of you.'

There was a silence. Then he said, 'So you want to know about the book? What I'm going to write and about who?'

'Yes,' said Caroline briskly. 'That's what I want.'

'Well, it's quite a lot to ask.'

'I don't know. Since we've provided you with most of the material.'

'Now there,' he said, 'you are quite wrong. Hopelessly wrong. This book, my darling, extends a very long way further than any boundaries set by you and your charming family.'

'What do you mean?'

'I mean it has a cast of thousands. In the best Hollywood tradition. I can never remember finding a project so enthralling, so all-encompassing. All human life is in this book. You'd be amazed.'

'Would I?' said Caroline.

'Yes, you would. Do you really want to know about it?'

'Yes, of course I do.'

There was a very long silence. Then he said, 'Which particular aspect of it, Caroline? Which aspect concerns you the most?'

She was silent, trying to form the words, to lead him; he cut into her thoughts.

'You know I can't tell you, don't you? You know I can't even think about telling you.'

'You could,' she said, her voice heavy with pain. 'Really you could.'

'No, Caroline, I couldn't. It would be wrong, and besides, it would serve no purpose. I am writing this book, because above all it has become immensely important to me. The story in it is an extraordinary example of distorted truth. The more I discover, the more astonished I become. And the more I feel the real, the true truth should be straightened out. Held up to the light. Offered for consideration.'

'Magnus, please! Please don't.'

'Don't what, my darling?'

'Destroy us all.' She could hear the words sounding ridiculously dramatic even as she spoke them.

'Caroline,' said Magnus, 'this story is not going to destroy you all. I promise you that at least. And a great many people that I have talked to feel it should be told. That it brings credit where credit might not be expected.

That is my defence. I can't stop it now. It's too late. In every possible way.'

Caroline put the phone down.

Magnus sat looking at his own phone and shook his head at it reprovingly. Then he put on the thick horn-rimmed spectacles he wore at his typewriter and returned to the chapter he was writing on Piers Windsor's schooldays. It was very sad, and rather touching reading: it brought a lump to his throat.

'Magnus Phillips,' he said aloud, 'you are one hell of a writer.'

Two hours later, he had a crashing headache; he decided to go for a long walk. He smiled with sheer pleasure as he set out along the Brompton Road towards Knightsbridge, looking at the taxis, the people, the firework-bright shop windows, and thought of the walks he had occasionally been persuaded to go on with Caroline, endless cold disagreeable things, with nothing to look at but hedges and fields, and usually to the accompaniment of a great deal of driving rain. The countryside and her love of it had been one of the worst aspects of the relationship he had had with her.

He missed her though: he hadn't realized how much until he had heard her voice that day. It hadn't been love – at least he didn't think it had been love, he was a little unfamiliar of the emotion, wary of it – but it had certainly been true affection. And great sex. Really great sex. She was an extraordinarily joyful and imaginative creature in bed. And fun. Lots of fun. He was sorry it was over. And sorry she was so upset as well. Was he really such a shit? Should he really pack this whole thing in? Was it really going to destroy so many lives?

He stood quite still for a full minute, considering this, and then moved off again, deciding that this was, as always, not a consideration for him. Lives were there, held by their owners, to do as they wished with, and they must accept the consequences. It was a tough philosophy, but he genuinely perceived it as the truth. Magnus held immense store by the truth: it was the one thing he felt worth fighting for. This book told the truth, and a strange and fascinating truth it was: and, like a piece of good surgery, it would first hurt and then heal. They would all get over it. They were all strong enough. Even Chloe. Certainly Chloe. He smiled for a while, thinking of Chloe. He was extremely fond of her; it was that fondness, the sympathy for what she had to endure in the form of Piers Windsor and the hoops she was dragged so persistently through, that had made him want to explore the background to the whole thing in the first place. She would find that very hard to believe, of course: that and the fact that he was so fond of her. But he was: Chloe was – Magnus struggled to find the right word to describe Chloe and could only manage good. She was good, through and through, transparently and sweetly good: loyal, brave, loving. Too good for her own cause. Piers didn't deserve her. Christ, he didn't deserve her.

He had walked a long way now: right up Piccadilly, almost at the Ritz. He was feeling much better: a drink might complete the cure. He went into the Ritz, had a whisky, and left again almost at once. He wanted to get back to work now. He hated having to break; it was almost like having to stop making love, the disentangling of concentration, but work was easier to get back to: a permanently eager mistress. He would walk on down to Piccadilly Underground station and get the tube back. Back to Piers and his schooldays and his loneliness and his terror: he started thinking of Chloe again, of how she might have responded to that unhappiness, of how much she would have heard about it, and thinking about her with such intensity that he seemed suddenly to see her with extraordinary vividness, her long red hair slightly wild, her sweetly serious pale face a little drawn, with its great brown eyes anxious, her body taut and tense. Then he realized that it was not in his imagination or his memory at all that he saw this Chloe, but in actual fact; for she was there, in front of him, perhaps ten yards away, standing alone, hailing a taxi. No time for her to be out, a respectable young matron and mother like her, it was bedtime, bathtime, story time. And then he realized, his mind moving into its highest level of professional perceptiveness, assimilating that fact and her patent agitation, as taxi after occupied taxi went past her down Piccadilly in the six o'clock rush, that she had emerged from the Albany, alone. Confused, anxious, and physically less self-contained than usual.

Who lived in the Albany? Magnus wondered, watching her finally capturing a taxi, throwing herself into it, leaning back in patently huge relief as it waited to swing round in a U-turn and take her off in the direction of Knightsbridge and her home: why, a most interesting person lived there, in bachelor splendour, Magnus had been there for drinks parties, even once or twice for dinner, before he had become so totally Chloe's long-term admirer. Ludovic Ingram lived there.

Then he saw, dreadfully, Chloe's face change as she saw him too, saw him watching, realized what he had seen and what the significance of it had been, her eyes grown wider still with terror, with horror, and then she really was gone, dragged away from him, her tormentor, into the anonymity of London.

Only the anonymity had come a little late.

'I'd like to come and see you.' Piers's voice was clear, firm, oddly confident. Magnus was surprised.

'But of course. When would you like to come?'

'As soon as possible. Tomorrow morning perhaps.'

'Well, you'll be very welcome. Of course. Do you want to make it a breakfast meeting?'

'Thank you, no. I'd like it to be as brief as possible.'

'Fine. My house, ten o'clock?'

'Ten o'clock.'

Now why was the bastard sounding so confident? Magnus poured himself the third whisky of the evening and settled down to the evening papers. His attention was caught by an article in the *Evening News* entitled 'Star and Stripes Billing'; it was a highly reasoned piece, on the distinct, if distant, possibility of the instalment at the White House of Mr Ronald

Reagan, star of *Bedtime with Bonzo* amongst other distinguished movies, and now appearing with arguably greater success in his latest role as Governor of California and President Nixon's stand-in on foreign tours, most recently the Far East in the company of his glamorous co-star, Mrs Nancy Reagan.

'It'll never happen,' said Magnus, shaking his head over it, and thinking that none the less if you were going to typecast the movie, Reagan would probably get the part.

Piers arrived promptly at ten o'clock. He was, Magnus thought, looking very thin, but he was, as always, impeccably dressed in a three-piece suit and a herringbone tweed overcoat with a velvet collar; he could have been ready for a day in the City were it not for his hat which was large and black, with a very wide brim. The guy was obsessed with clothes, thought Magnus; he must try to talk to his tailor. If it was one of the old guys, they might not talk, but the promise of a plug and, failing that, a few fivers might produce a good quote or two from one of the new, high-profile tailors all the rock stars had made famous.

'Piers,' he said, 'do come in.'

'Thank you.'

'Let me take your coat. Coffee?'

'No, thank you.'

He sat down and looked at Magnus in silence for a long time. Magnus was interested to discover he felt mildly uncomfortable, and wondered for the second time if Piers knew something he didn't.

'Right,' said Piers, finally, his eyes very brilliant and hard, 'let me come to the point. I have been advised by my solicitors to endeavour to divert you from writing or publishing this book.'

'Indeed?' said Magnus.

'Yes. Or at least to ascertain exactly what you intend to write in it.'

'Yes?'

'I fancy both courses are ones you are unlikely to follow.'

'You fancy correctly.'

'I thought so. It seemed worth making the approach.'

'Sorry, Piers. Can't do it. Too late not to publish, and I really have no intention of telling you what I'm going to write.'

'As I thought. Would I be right, however, in thinking that your material and your research have been quite painstaking?'

'You would indeed. I have – oh, God knows how many hours of taped interviews, all painstakingly checked. I take great pride in my powers of detection.'

'How admirable. Your publishers are very fortunate.'

'Yes, well,' said Magnus lightly, 'that is what they pay me for.'

'I suppose so.'

There was another silence. Then Piers said, 'Well now, Magnus, I have just come to give you a warning.'

'Indeed? How interesting.' Magnus smiled at him, easily, casually. But he was still not quite as calm as he would like.

'Are you familiar with *The Merchant of Venice*, Magnus?'

Magnus looked at him thoughtfully. 'Not as familiar as you are, I suspect.'

'I suspect so too. I would like to remind you therefore of Portia's speech. To Shylock. After she has conceded that he is indeed entitled to his pound of flesh. But –' Piers turned, walked over to the window, looked out for perhaps half a minute, in a long, potent silence, then turned back, his grey eyes thoughtful, very distant. 'But Magnus

if thou cutt'st more
Or less than a just pound, be it but so much
As makes it light or heavy in the substance,
Or the division of the twentieth part
Of one poor scruple – nay, if the scale do turn
But in the estimation of a hair,
Thou diest, and all thy goods are confiscate.'

His voice faded; a voice that had become, eerily, magically not that of a middle-aged actor, but of a beautiful and brilliant young woman, totally in command of the situation and the others in her presence. He looked very intensely at Magnus. 'I hope you see what I am trying to say. This book, Magnus, this book is your pound of flesh. You are entitled to it, to write it, to publish it. But if the truth within it, which I do know to be cruelly complex, and much of it buried in quite a distant past, if that truth turns the scales towards untruth, but in the estimation of a hair, then, Magnus, please know that, indeed, all thy goods are confiscate. And now I must go. I have work to do. Good morning, Magnus.'

Half an hour later Magnus was still sitting at his desk, his mind shocked into impotence, totally and terrifyingly unable to work.

Chapter 31

1971–2

Rose Sharon had had many gifts bestowed upon her by the fairies at her christening: beauty, brains, talent, charm, but above all, an extension of her charm perhaps, an ability to create a feeling of self-worth in the people she was with. A conversation with Rose was not simply an exchange of views, of ideas, or even a confirmation of arrangements: it was (for the other person) a sense of pleasure, a feeling that he (or she) was perhaps, definitely indeed, more interesting, more amusing, more desirable, even than they had considered themselves to be. And she did not simply work her magic on the important people in her circle, directors, producers, fellow actors, Hollywood hostesses, or even the arguably and equally important outer ring of it, head waiters, dress designers, her housekeeper; but on everyone she came into contact with, car park attendants, bank clerks, messenger boys. Such was the power of this quality of hers that even her critics, or someone who had slipped her net in some way, someone who felt hostile to her, could be won round, persuaded in no time at all that any slight coolness they might feel towards her for whatever reason was a fault on their part, not hers, and to be pleased, delighted even, that she was caring about them now.

Fleur FitzPatrick had been feeling a certain coolness about Rose in the last few weeks: well, not coolness, but certainly disappointment with her. It did not seem to her to be asking so very much that Rose should talk to Magnus Phillips about her early days in Hollywood and her memories of her father. Of course, she didn't like the press, she was very wary of journalists, but even so, this wasn't some probing article about her present private life and her failure to make a lasting relationship with anyone, as so many of them were. Fleur tried to tell herself that she was being silly, that it was perfectly understandable, and that probably half the trouble with her was Christmas and that the other half was finally agreeing that she and Reuben should work for Morton's full time. The offer had been in the end irresistible, but she knew they should have resisted, it felt wrong without knowing why. She was going to Poppy and Gill for Christmas to their new, smart apartment not far from her own, with its red walls and black furniture and already-impressive collection of modern paintings. Reuben would be there of course, and Reuben's and Poppy's gorgeous mother, and they would eat themselves into a stupor, exchange all sorts of expensive and stylish things, play endless stupid games and it would all be great fun, and Mrs Blake would ask about every five minutes when she and Reuben were going to get married. For God's sake, thought Fleur miserably, why didn't they know, why hadn't she agreed to anything yet? – and then her phone rang.

'Fleur? Darling, this is Rose.'

And there it was, the charm, Rose's charm, and instead of continuing to feel cool about her, she felt as if she had been given a present, or a glass of absolutely perfectly chilled champagne, and instead of sounding cool, she flushed, and said with considerable warmth, 'Oh, Rose, how lovely to hear from you.'

'How are you? What have you been doing?'

'Not a lot,' said Fleur with perfect truth.

'Lots of Christmas parties, no doubt. How's the high-powered job?'

'It's – OK,' said Fleur. It wasn't; it was part of her dissatisfaction with everything, with her unspoken, unacknowledged unease about Reuben, with the disappearance of Magnus Phillips and the book from her orbit – God knows how many weeks it had been since she had heard from that bastard – that her work had become so tedious. And second-rate.

'You don't sound too sure.'

'I'm not.'

'It sounds as if you need a change of scene.'

'Maybe I do.'

'Why don't you come to Los Angeles for a few days?'

'I'm sorry?'

'I said come to LA. And bring your friend Mr Phillips with you. I've decided I should see him after all.'

'I'm sorry?' said Fleur again, too stupefied to believe what she was hearing.

'Darling, you seem to be only half awake this morning. I'm inviting you over here. Don't you like the idea?'

'Like it? I love it,' said Fleur, her heart suddenly beginning to fly. 'But – what made you change your mind, Rose? I don't understand.'

'Well, let's say I've been doing some remembering. And some thinking. About your dad, mostly. I loved him so much, Fleur, he meant so much to me. If someone can put the record straight, finally, I'd be so happy. It seems very foolish and wrong to try and block that.'

'Well I – well, I'm just so pleased,' said Fleur. Her voice sounded suddenly exultant even to her; she felt she could fly.

'Good. Well, speak with your friend, and then get back to me. I'm here all over Christmas and New Year and right through January. After that, I go away for a while. All right?'

'All right,' said Fleur, 'and thank you. Thank you so much, Rose.'

'That's all right, darling. Bye now. Oh and Fleur –'

'Yes?'

'New Year'd be good. Then we could see it in, start the new one together.'

'I'd like that too,' said Fleur.

Magnus was enragingly unimpressed.

'It seems like pretty short notice to me. And what's made her change her mind?'

'She said she'd thought about it and she wanted to help,' said Fleur irritably. 'You don't seem to understand, Magnus, she is just hugely famous. She doesn't have to do this. She hates the press. She's doing it for – well, for me. And my dad. She loved him.'

'Well, I'll see what I can do,' said Magnus. 'It'll certainly have to be after Christmas,'

'Magnus, what is the matter with you? I thought you really wanted to see Rose.'

'I do. But it's Christmas. I'm busy. Things to do, places to go –'

'If you don't fucking well make some kind of an effort to do things here, it'll be too late,' said Fleur. She found, enraged, that she was close to tears. 'Magnus, please! It's so important –'

'All right, all right,' he said, sounding more impatient than amused. 'I'll move some things around if I can. I'll call you back.'

'Sweet of you,' said Fleur and put the phone down.

He had sounded odd. Less sure of himself, less obsessively keen. She hoped he wasn't cooling on this thing altogether. She just about couldn't stand it if he did. She'd call Bernard Stobbs in the morning, ask him if he'd heard any more about the book. There'd certainly been nothing in the spring catalogues about it. The stupid bastard was going to miss the boat altogether if he didn't get his act together. Arrogant, ignorant creature. He just didn't deserve the kind of input he was getting from her. If it mattered even the slightest bit less she'd just dump him.

By the time she'd calmed down, she was feeling much better about not being in love.

After lunch Reuben called.

'Walk? In the park?'

'Oh – no, Reuben, I don't think so. I don't feel like walking. I have a headache.'

'Cure it.'

'No, honestly.'

'Movies then?'

'Oh, Reuben, I don't know. What's on?'

'*Love Story*.'

'Ugh. No thanks.'

'OK. *Sunday, Bloody Sunday.*'

'All right,' said Fleur and laughed.

She hated the film. It was so terribly English, and it reminded her of Magnus Phillips.

'Supper?' said Reuben.

'No, thank you, Reuben. I'm not hungry. Sorry.'

'That's OK,' said Reuben, and sighed. It was a very light, very faint sigh; but she heard it and was moved to a strong sense of remorse. She did not deserve this man, this lovely, unselfish, undemanding man; she really didn't. She slipped her hand into his.

'Let's just go back to my apartment.'

'Fine,' said Reuben.

She was riding on a rich wave of pleasure when Magnus Phillips called, her back arched beneath Reuben, her arms flung wide, her cries loud and wild, and as rhythmic as the great ripples taking her to her climax.

The sound of the phone pierced her pleasure; she reached blindly for it, picked it up, slammed it down again, only it missed the receiver and went on to the bed just as a huge groan escaped Reuben and she cried out, 'Shit! Yes, yes, yes, Reuben, shit, yes . . .' and then as the world steadied, she surfaced into it again, her body easing, relaxing, falling into release; she looked at the phone and realized it was silent, not giving out the dialling tone, and that someone was clearly listening on the other end.

'Hallo?' she said cautiously, trying to breathe more evenly.

'Hallo,' said Magnus Phillips's voice, amused, laughter surfacing into it. 'Fleur? I would judge from your bad language that you must be experiencing some excitement. Do you want to call me back?'

'No,' said Fleur, fiercely angry at herself, at him, at everyone suddenly, even perversely Reuben, 'no, of course not.'

'I admire your control. Now then. Miss Sharon.'

'Who? Oh, oh yes, of course.'

'I could come over there the second week of January. Any good?'

'I'll have to check with her,' said Fleur, 'and get back to you. It should be fine.'

'Good. Well I'm sorry to have disturbed you.'

'That's perfectly all right,' said Fleur and put the phone back carefully this time, wondering why she felt so bleak and upset.

Chloe felt so terribly frightened all the time, she didn't know what to do with herself. She couldn't quite believe she had been so stupid. Leaving the Albany like that, in the middle of the rush hour, when everyone knew Ludovic lived there, when half London could have seen her; and then who did exactly that, who had to witness her flight, of all the people in the world, but Magnus Phillips. The man who was out to destroy not only her, but her entire family. It was like some terrible nightmare.

'Why didn't we go to some hotel?' she wailed to Ludovic from a phone box next day, after a long fearsome night lying awake, fretting, tearing at her nails.

'Because my flat is so much nicer,' he said soothingly, 'and we were just as likely to bump into someone in the corridors of the Ritz or the Savoy as in the middle of Piccadilly and it would have been twice as compromising. Did it not occur to you that it might seem just remotely possible to anyone who saw you that at six in the evening you might not have been committing adultery, but doing something innocent like shopping or having tea with your mother?'

His voice was relaxed and amused; it was all right for him, Chloe thought, he had nothing to lose. Well, almost nothing.

'Of course I couldn't, the shops were all shut and my mother is in Suffolk.'

'And of course all London knows that,' said Ludovic. 'Darling, don't fret. Please. You're being hysterical. Anyway, you have to tell Piers some time. Maybe this will be the catalyst you need.'

'I can't,' said Chloe, 'not now, you know I can't, with this bloody book hanging over him and the disappointment over the honours list again, and –'

'All right, sweetheart, all right,' said Ludovic soothingly. 'Look, don't panic. Just keep calm. You don't know if the wretched man actually saw you, he was probably looking the other way; it's your guilty conscience –'

'It is not!' said Chloe. 'He was looking at me, in that awful amused way, you know. He knew, he knew exactly what I'd been doing and –'

'Exactly?' said Ludovic. 'I do hope not. Not exactly. It was particularly imaginative, as I recall, what you were doing.'

'Oh Ludo, please!' said Chloe in an agony. 'Please don't tease me. And anyway –'

'Anyway what?'

'Oh – oh, nothing,' she said. 'Now please, please, don't ring me for a few days. All right?'

'All right. Now calm down, darling. And remember I love you.'

'Yes,' she said, 'yes, I'll try,' and put the phone down, feeling suddenly desperately sick.

She knew why she was feeling sick and it wasn't just terror.

And she hadn't slept with Piers for weeks.

'Mrs Windsor, this is the Charing Cross Hospital. I wonder if you could come over straight away. We have your husband here, in Casualty.'

Oh God, thought Chloe, oh God, he's done it again, and this time she knew why: he had found out, Magnus Phillips had told him, had told him she was having an affair with Ludovic. This time it was really her fault, and what was she to do? It could not be cured this time by long periods in therapy and analysis, this time there was no blame attached to him, it was not that he was accusing her of not helping him by forbidding him to use their daughter in his film, nor that she was accusing him of conducting a flirtation with her brother, this time it was her fault for betraying him, hurting him when he could least stand it, having an affair with one of his friends. Publicly, dreadfully, the blame lay not only squarely but absolutely fairly at her bedroom door. And what could she do about it? How could she possibly endure the guilt, the terrible, awful disgrace, what could she do even to begin to put things right again? Nothing, it was beyond remedy, beyond hope –

'Anyway, nothing to worry about,' the voice was going on cheerfully, 'it's a nasty break, but clean, it will soon mend, as long as he understands he has to rest.'

'I'm sorry?' said Chloe, trying not to sound stupid. 'Did you say break?'

'Yes, my dear, he's broken his ankle. Slipped on this miserable ice— Are you all right, Mrs Windsor, you're not crying are you? He really is fine.'

'No,' said Chloe, 'no, I'm not crying. I'm afraid I'm laughing.'

'It really isn't funny, you know,' said the voice reprovingly. 'He's in quite a lot of pain.'

'No,' said Chloe, 'no, of course it's not funny. I'm sorry.'

She got out her car and drove to the hospital; it took ages, in the near-Christmas traffic. When she got there Piers was sitting in Casualty looking very white and very angry.

'What on earth have you been doing? Hours ago they said you were on your way. I could have got a cab home long before this.'

'Oh darling, I'm terribly sorry. The traffic was awful. And your poor leg. Is it very painful?'

'Very. So stupid. And here I am about to go into rehearsal for *Othello*. All the times I could have done it, staging ridiculous fights, and I have to slip on the pavement of the Strand. God.'

'That's what I thought,' said Chloe, stifling the uncharitable thought that he would have minded a great deal less if it had been broken in rehearsal and he could have made a wonderful publicity story out of it. 'Never mind, darling, I'm sure it will soon heal. Can you walk?'

'No, I can't. But they said they'd lend us a wheelchair. Good thing I hadn't got one before, I'd have felt even sillier sitting in that for an hour.'

'Piers, I'm really sorry. Look, I'll get a chair, and we'll go home. You'll feel better then.'

'I don't suppose I will,' he said, glaring at her. He clearly felt the whole thing was at least partly her fault.

Chloe, released from a greater guilt, was happy to be castigated. 'Please forgive me, darling,' she said, 'I'm so terribly sorry.'

She finally got him home, and up to bed. Pandora went into paroxysms of sympathy and sat by him, stroking his hand and putting cold compresses on his forehead; Ned and little Kitty were kept carefully out of the way.

Chloe called Roger Bannerman, the GP; he prescribed some strong pain-killers, told Piers he had to stay in bed for at least two days, and that he'd be back in the morning and then walked down the stairs with Chloe.

'Nothing to worry about,' he said, 'well, not with the ankle. Worst he'll endure from that is a little inconvenience, and some enforced rest which will do him no harm.'

There was something in his voice that disturbed Chloe; she looked at him sharply. 'Is there something else I should worry about?'

'Well, he seems rather frail to me. It's what – a month since I've seen him, and he does seem to have lost more weight. And I don't like that cough. Oh, I know we've done X-rays and everything, but it hasn't really cleared. I wish you could stop him smoking.'

'I wish it too,' said Chloe. 'But he says he needs it. He says if he didn't smoke he'd drink still more.'

'Well, that might be better. I'm surprised it doesn't affect his precious actor's voice, the smoking. I know he only gets through twenty a day, but even so, it can't do it good.'

'He says it does. He says it gives it timbre.' She raised her eyes to the ceiling and then smiled at Bannerman.

'He's not worried about anything, is he?'

'Well – you know. Only the usual things,' said Chloe hastily, praying that it were true. '*Othello*. He was very upset not to have got his knighthood this time. Took that terribly hard. But otherwise: no, I really don't think so. He's seemed much more – well, steady lately, actually.'

'He's not worried about money, is he?' said Bannerman suddenly.

'No. Not as far as I know.' Chloe was genuinely surprised. Of all the things that troubled Piers, money had never even been on the agenda. There had always seemed plenty; he spent it with something she could only describe as determination. 'In fact he's just bought three more horses. One absolute dead cert Derby winner, I'm told, a gorgeous grey he's potty about.' She laughed. 'No, honestly, I don't think so. Why?'

'Oh – just something he said. About my bill. It was meant to be a joke, but I thought it was a bit heavy. I wondered if he was – well, trying to open up a discussion.'

'I'll see if I can sound him out,' said Chloe.

'Well, take it steady. And I'll be back in the morning. Don't fuss over him too much. It isn't necessary or good for him. It's only an ankle.'

'Try telling Pandora Siddons Nightingale that,' said Chloe darkly.

'Come on, darling, time for bed,' said Chloe. 'He's all right without you now for a bit.'

Pandora looked at her, her grey eyes, so exactly like her father's, slightly hostile. 'I could stay,' she said, 'I could sleep on the floor. In case he needed anything in the night.'

'Darling, I'll be here if he does,' said Chloe firmly. 'And besides it's very late and you have school tomorrow.'

'I could stay at home.'

'No, Pandora, you couldn't. Now, come along, let's get you into your bath.'

Pandora slithered off her chair, blew Piers a kiss and walked slowly to the door, where she stood gazing back at the bed, her small face a mask of tragedy. Chloe tried not to feel irritated with her and failed.

'Pandora! Come along.'

She sat down rather wearily when she had finally got Pandora settled, and flicked through the television channels, more to distract herself than anything else: she longed to phone Ludovic, but didn't dare. But the ten o'clock news, a rerun of the *Forsyte Saga* and a documentary about the new phenomenon, world chess champion Bobby Fischer, did nothing for her and she started worrying about Piers instead. And then moved inevitably on to herself. He was very thin; every so often she would notice it herself, but he seemed perfectly well, and fit; he went to the gym twice a week and played squash at the RAC Club as if possessed. His lungs surely couldn't be too bad if they could support him through that sort of thing. And he'd seemed much steadier and more stable lately and, surprisingly, almost coolly untroubled about the Phillips book; that baffled her, but he refused to discuss it, said it was in good hands, and that he had more important things to worry about. He had been very upset about once again not getting his knighthood, but he'd been more or less promised he'd get it next time around. He'd been showered with honours throughout his career, three Oscars for the *Dream*, a BAFTA award, and the *Evening Standard* Best Actor for *Uncle Vanya*: he could scarcely claim disappointment and failure.

Their private life was something rather different, of course: Chloe realized somewhat to her shame that evening that she no longer knew how Piers viewed their marriage. It seemed years since they had had a serious, constructive conversation about it. There was too much to be afraid of behind that conversation, too much darkness, too much mistrust. At times she would remember how fiercely, how passionately she had loved him once, and believed him to have loved her, and the change, the sad sorry change, made her literally weep. She imagined, although she did not know, that he viewed her dispassionately, as the mother of his children, the keeper of his houses. Someone he was fond of, someone fairly if not entirely suitable, someone certainly necessary. That she did know: how necessary she was to him. Not just to care for the children and the houses, but to provide substance to the fantasy of their happy, stable marriage, his image as a redblooded, entirely heterosexual male. Without her, he would be frail, suspect, vulnerable; it would be a heavy blow to deal.

But it had to be dealt. She knew that: she could not stay with him for ever, could not live out the rest of her life with someone she did not love, who did not love her. She had to go, she had to be with Ludovic, and she had to tell Piers she was going; she could tell, if only by a dusting of occasional darkness, like wispy clouds drifting slowly up on a perfect summer morning, that Ludovic was growing just a little impatient. If he knew that she was pregnant, he would be considerably more so, she thought distractedly, looking down at her entirely flat stomach, thinking almost fearfully of what lay there, growing steadily, determinedly, of the havoc it would cause. Every time she had seen him, in the three or so weeks since she had discovered the fact, she had determined to tell him, and then her courage had failed her. Not on her own account, but on his, and on Piers's and the truly terrible storms the news would unleash. Well, she had a little time: it was less than three weeks since she had missed her period, Ludovic was not familiar with pregnancy, did not know of minor things like gently swollen, tender breasts, an increased need to pee, a tendency to be over-emotional. But she knew them: experiencing them for the fourth time, there had been no doubt, no doubt at all for her, not from the very first day. Well, it was her own fault: she was notoriously bad at remembering to take her pills; no doubt, she thought, deeply Freudian. She hoped Ludovic would be understanding, would not be angry, or accuse her of trying to trap him. She didn't think he would; he would probably be delighted, and a wonderful father. Which was more than she could say for Piers, with his outrageous favouritism of Pandora, his virtual lack of interest in the other two.

And Pandora was a worry, so precocious and difficult, and Piers was no help with her, no help at all, he just laughed at her tantrums, her ridiculous behaviour, and gave in to her, refused to allow Chloe to discipline her at all much of the time. On the other hand, in spite of everything, Pandora was a nice little girl at heart, and very loving; she was clever and very talented; after the *Dream* came out, there had been lots of offers for her, but part of the bargain Chloe had made with Piers had been that she wouldn't appear in anything again until she was at least a teenager, and he had for the most part kept to it. There had been a small part in Chekhov, and a tiny TV appearance in *Black Beauty*, but that had been all.

'I don't like theatrical brats either,' he had reassured Chloe, smiling rather weakly at her as he convalesced in the house lent them by a friend in Palm Springs, 'but Pandora won't be one, she's too sweet and bright and intelligent, and anyway I won't allow it. We'll keep her ordinary, darling, don't worry.'

So Pandora went to Kensington High School with a lot of other ordinary little girls, and led a perfectly ordinary little life; but the fact remained that she was not ordinary, she was exceptionally lovely to look at, and exceptionally bright: she could read at three, was writing little stories already and had a photographic memory that could commit any number of facts to heart in no time – and she also led a very high-profile life. Nothing Chloe could do would persuade Piers not to have Pandora at the dinner table from time to time, at rehearsals, interviewed, photographed, quoted even: and at nearly five, she was self-confident, socially accomplished, and had a rare penchant for telling jokes – not the usual five-year-old lavatorial variety, but stories she had heard her father tell, word for adult word; her delivery was brilliant, she knew exactly how to time a punch line, how to get everyone's attention. Her adoration of her father was almost, Chloe feared, unhealthy; not serious at the moment, but there would surely be trouble when she was an adolescent. Chloe looked ahead to clashes of will, female rivalry, side-taking, and, horrifically, possible separation from her father, by way of divorce, and shuddered.

Ned and Kitty were easy children: less remarkable, less gifted. Ned at three was a sweet little boy, with dark floppy hair and his mother's steady brown eyes and gentle disposition, while Kitty was too young to be anything much at all, apart from a roly-poly carrot-top, with immense blue eyes with which she surveyed the world from within a permanently dirty face. However hard Chloe and Rosemary, the nanny, tried, Kitty's face was permanently coated with dust, with honey, with egg, with mud, and washing it was apparently a complete waste of time.

But oh, God, it was not just herself she would be tearing from her marriage, but those children: and how would they, and especially Pandora, be able to bear it?

Now, because of this new baby, the break would clearly have to be hastened. Piers would know the baby was not his: Ludovic would want to claim it, and all that it implied. She could not hide very much longer. But if Piers was ill, as Roger Bannerman seemed to be implying, if his ever-fragile emotional health was at risk, then how was she to do it to him? Not for the first time in the last few months, Chloe longed for Joe, to talk to, to confide in, to consult; she missed him terribly; but Joe was avoiding her, avoiding all of them, partly because of the break-up with her mother, partly, she feared, because of the book. Joe without doubt knew more about the book than he would reveal, and he chose to deal with the problem by not confronting it, refusing to discuss it. It was horrible. Oh God, thought Chloe, throwing her head back in the chair, closing her eyes, that book: it was like some awful bird of prey hovering over them, casting a huge dark shadow over everything they did.

Chloe suddenly realized she was getting sleepy; she would go to bed, forget everything. Even her new baby. She tried not to think about the baby too much. Ludovic's baby. Tried to keep it as something detached from herself; otherwise it would overwhelm her. When she did allow herself to think about it, to envisage it, to imagine it, bearing it, suckling it, caring for it, loving it, seeing it smile, hearing it cry, watching it sit, crawl, stagger, laugh, her eyes filled with tears of almost unimaginable love.

So don't, Chloe; don't. Don't think about it. All it is at the moment is a missed period, a nausea, a problem. Not a baby. She stood up to go to the kitchen, to make herself a hot drink, and on the way passed Piers's study. She heard Dr Bannerman's words again: 'Does he have money troubles?' and felt a disproportionate stab of anxiety; it would do no harm to assuage it, she thought, just for her own peace of mind. She didn't usually interfere in Piers's private things, but if he was unwell and worrying, if this might, God forbid, be going to trigger some new crisis, she should know about it.

She went to his desk, looked through the papers on the top of it. Nothing there, no bank statements, nothing. She tried the middle drawer: rather a lot of bills, unpaid, but that was typical of Piers, didn't mean anything, he was hopeless at administration and his accountant was in permanent despair about him. Bank statements? She opened the next drawer: a mass of letters, unfiled, cuttings, reviews, destined one day for his scrap books, but no statements, nothing of any kind.

The bottom drawer was locked. Well, that was frustrating, but not surprising. It was all part of his near compulsion to preserve much of himself for himself. In the early days, she had been deeply suspicious of it, thinking it to relate to his sexual behaviour, but in fact it seemed a perfectly harmless quirk of his personality. He hardly ever told her where he was staying, when he was out of town, and she had to find out, if she needed to (always embarrassed), by phoning theatres, his agent, or his part-time secretary, nice Jean Potts; usually there was no reason, no reason at all for such nonsense, and he would be doing nothing more sinister than simply sitting alone in some perfectly respectable provincial hotel, reading, learning his lines, watching television. It was something she had learnt to live with, if not accept.

She went out now to the kitchen, where his keys hung on a hook; a large number and it took five minutes to try them all in the desk. None of them fitted. Chloe sighed. Oh well. She was probably worrying about nothing. He had never indicated for a moment that she should spend less money: rather the reverse. She heard him calling her, fretful, irritable, and ran up the stairs: he wanted whisky in hot milk, more painkillers, ice for his ankle. It all seemed a lot more pressing than where his bank statements might be.

At Bannerman's insistence, Piers took a month off the *Othello* rehearsals. His plans for *Othello* were ambitious; he planned to play Othello and Iago on alternate nights, with Ivor Branwen, the sensational Welsh actor, risen to fame and acclaim with petrifying speed, playing opposite him. There were among the critics some more acerbic spirits proposing the view that Piers Windsor felt threatened by Branwen and was doing this audacious thing in order to lay the ghost.

They spent Christmas at Stebbings, and Piers gave Pandora a new pony, a beautiful little grey which he had christened Oberon, Ned an electrically powered miniature Range Rover and Kitty a doll's house as big as her small self. He gave Chloe an antique gold bracelet, a painting he had commissioned of Stebbings, and a very beautiful and ornate eighteenth-century French clock. He didn't seem to be overworried about money.

But he still didn't make love to her, or even join her in their bedroom.

Chloe spent quite a lot of the holiday making excuses to go down to the village where she could phone Ludovic from the public phone box; he was away for two weeks after Christmas, sailing in the Caribbean. Chloe spent the entire time sick with terror and jealousy, absolutely convinced he would fall in love with someone else. When he finally got back and phoned her to tell her he loved her and had missed her almost beyond endurance she burst into tears and put the phone down on him.

She got back to London a nervous wreck, quite convinced that her pregnancy was clearly visible to anyone who so much as glanced in her direction, and wrote a total of fourteen letters to Ludovic telling him about it, all of which she tore up.

Fleur always thought about Chloe at Christmas time. She tried not to but she couldn't help it. Sitting there, in her perfect house, with her perfect family, trimming some perfect tree, going to church, having all the work done by some family retainer, everyone smiling, smirking round the table, no doubt with Caroline there as well, sharing in it all: no real problems, nothing to worry about. Fleur didn't like Christmas. She had hated it ever since her father had gone away. Before that it had been wonderful, they had had such fun with her grandmother and all her aunts, always lots of games, and midnight mass of course, and after that, her father carried her home on his shoulders singing carols all the way; but ever since he had gone, it had been the lowest spot of the year, apart from her birthday which anyway followed so hard on its heels, a dark, hollow occasion, with all the joy knocked out of it.

The years since she had left home had been better of course: she spent it either with the Steinbergs who celebrated Christmas determinedly and joyfully, the tree in one corner of the kitchen, the Hanukah candles in another, or at Mrs Blake's house at Sagaponack, where they ate their way through the holiday; but it was still something she always dreaded, wished over. This year had been strange: the Blakes, especially Mrs Blake, were beside themselves with pleasure at the engagement, which Reuben had announced with a certain informality at Christmas Eve supper with the words, 'Like the ring?' and Fleur had sat there, being kissed and exclaimed over and smiled at and welcomed into the family, smiling, laughing, holding Reuben's hand, her own eyes filled with tears of what was clearly, had to be, happiness; and finally lying in her own small room (for Mrs Blake held strong views about pre-marital sex) telling herself the reason she was unable to sleep was because she was so excited and happy.

Now she was on a plane to Los Angeles, and so, she supposed, was Magnus Phillips, only coming from a slightly different direction; she had told Reuben she was going on family business and told him she'd explain when it was all settled, and he'd gone to Kennedy with her and kissed her goodbye tenderly and said he would miss her.

'I'll miss you too,' said Fleur, hugging him hard at passport control.

'March'd be good,' he said, and then he turned away and she watched his tall, awkward body making its way through the crowd and felt very unhappy as she went slowly through the departure lounge and joined the queue for her flight.

Rose had sent her driver to meet her at LAX: a grizzled Hispanic with mournful black eyes in a strangely incongruous grey uniform. 'Miss Sharon sends her apologies, she's at the studio till dinner time. I'm to take you back to the house, and see you settled.'

'Thank you,' said Fleur, 'that sounds good.'

* * *

Rose lived in a house off Coldwater Canyon, set up high from the road by a winding drive, and barred from view by a pair of high wrought-iron gates. Inside there were lush gardens, bank upon bank of flowering shrubs, bougainvillaeas, azaleas, camellias, and a sloping lawn leading at the side of the house down to the pool and a white poolhouse. The house itself was low and square, built of the glorious rose-golden stone so beloved of the best of Beverly Hills architects; a huge wisteria grew over the heavy, double grey door, and sprawled around the upstairs windows.

A young woman opened the door, smiling, held out her hand to Fleur: 'Hi. I'm Sue. Rose's housekeeper. May I show you to your room? Ricardo, bring Miss FitzPatrick's cases.'

Sue did not look too much like any housekeeper Fleur had ever known; she was pretty, tanned, with curly brown hair, dressed in a linen shirt-dress. She talked entirely in questions, most of which needed no reply.

'How was your flight? Aren't you terribly tired? Would you like a swim when you're unpacked? And some ice tea? Or maybe something stronger? Did Ricardo explain that Miss Sharon is at the studio? Now, will you be all right until she gets home, or will I call her there for you? She said to do that if you needed anything special.'

Fleur said she'd like a swim, and some ice tea, that she didn't need anything else in the world, and was lying by the pool, sipping ice tea and feeling rather as if she should be in movies herself when Ricardo brought out a telephone.

'Call for you, Miss FitzPatrick.'

'For me? Oh, thank you.' She took the phone. 'Fleur FitzPatrick here.'

'You sound very at home,' said Magnus Phillips's voice. 'I bet you're playing at movie stars. They said you were by the pool.' He sounded amused.

Fleur scowled into the phone. 'I am most certainly not playing anything. I'm waiting for Rose to get back.'

'Ah. Where is she?'

'At the studios. Where are you?'

'At the Beverly Hills Hotel. You'd love it.'

'I have been there,' said Fleur with dignity. 'And I quite like it. I prefer the Bel Air myself.'

Her sole experience of both had been on a whistle-stop tour with Joe: the Bel Air they had only peered at from the car park on the wrong side of the bridge. But she was not going to let Magnus Phillips think she was some hick who thought LA began and ended with the Hilton and the Star Homes tour.

'Well, I wondered if you and Miss Sharon would like to dine here with me tonight? Or maybe it would be beneath you?'

'Of course it wouldn't be beneath me,' said Fleur irritably, 'but I'll have to ask Rose. She may have other plans.'

'Of course. Well, just ring me. I'm in Bungalow 12.'

'Fine. I will.'

'You OK?' he said suddenly.

'Yes, of course I'm OK. Thank you.'

'Good. I'll wait to hear from you.'

Rose got back from the studio at five thirty. She looked tired, and thinner than Fleur remembered. She hugged Fleur, told her it was good to see her, then sighed, and said, 'I'd like a swim and then a quiet dinner. It's been a tough day.'

'In what way?'

'Oh – contract problems. Nothing that my agent can't fix, but the wretched studio people will try to twist your arm when you're not looking.' She laughed. 'If that isn't a mixed metaphor.'

'It isn't,' said Fleur. 'Er, Rose, Magnus Phillips is here, he's invited us to dinner at the Beverly Hills tonight. I said I'd have to ask you.'

'I can't think of anything worse,' said Rose. 'Please thank him though. I'll meet him tomorrow. Here would be much nicer. Sue darling, would you fix us some dinner for – would seven be all right, Fleur?'

'Of course.'

'Good. We'll just have some chicken, something like that, OK? Is the pool warm enough, Fleur? It can get a little brisk this time of year.'

'It's gorgeous,' said Fleur. 'It's all gorgeous. I love your house. It's so – gentle somehow. Like you,' she added, and promptly felt silly.

Rose smiled, put out her hand and touched Fleur's cheek. 'How sweet,' she said. 'Thank you.'

They sat by the pool until the swift dusk came down at six thirty, bringing a cool to the air, then moved inside. The house was infinitely charming, its background all shades of gold: golden wooden floors in the living rooms, natural slub silk wallpapers, chintz curtains and covers; the kitchen had large golden-rose tiles on the floor, pale oak tables and chairs, the bedrooms pale golden beige carpets, print papers, silk drapes. Every wall was covered with pictures, photographs, book-shelves, every room was filled with flowers, plants, baskets of dried flowers.

'I've lived here for ten years,' said Rose, 'and every year I've added to it, without changing it. I love it, it's my family this house.'

They were sitting, drinking Californian Chardonnay, chilled to the exact temperature that only Californians seem able to attain; Sue's meal had been deliciously perfect, Parma ham and asparagus, cold chicken mayonnaise, with wild rice, and a great basket of fruit. Fleur had already eaten her way through a pound of strawberries, a pineapple, half an ogen melon, a great bunch of grapes and was now idly peeling a pear.

'I wouldn't like to keep you in fruit,' said Rose laughing, pressing the tiny buzzer on the table: Sue appeared. 'Coffee, Sue, please, and some more grapes. My guest has polished off the lot.'

'I'm sorry,' said Fleur apologetically. 'I just can't ever seem to stop eating the things. Once I start.'

'Darling, you don't have to. I was only teasing you. I'm happy for you to eat California clean of grapes. Tell me about this boyfriend of yours.'

'Oh – well, he's very nice,' said Fleur.

'Handsome? Rich?'

'No, not at all handsome. Or rich. But very sexy. And sweet and funny. He manages to be funny without saying more than five words max at a time.'

'That's clever,' said Rose. 'And are you getting married soon?'

'Oh, yes, very soon,' said Fleur quickly. 'This spring, I guess. There doesn't seem much point waiting.'

'I guess not. He sounds perfect.'

'He is,' said Fleur. She suddenly recognized the sensations she experienced when she was talking about Reuben, or even when she was with him and thinking about their future: it was like trying on a dress that was absolutely what she had been looking for, the right fabric, style, length, colour – but for some reason not as perfectly flattering as it should be. She stifled the thought and smiled quickly at Rose.

'What about you? Do you have a boyfriend?'

'Oh – dozens,' said Rose, laughing. 'All beating a path to the door. No, not really. I haven't been very lucky in love, Fleur. I don't know why. Too wrapped up in my career, myself, maybe. I seem to pick the wrong one every time. Except your dad of course. He was – well, he was perfect.'

'Oh, Rose, you can't think that!' said Fleur protesting. 'He treated you like – well, not very well.'

'I know he did, and that wasn't so nice. But while we were together, it was really so good. We were so happy. Just the two of us, no thought for anyone else, no worries, except where the rent was coming from. All we wanted was each other. It was – good,' she finished simply. The wide blue eyes that had gazed so raptly, so tremulously into the camera and out of the screen for more than a decade, enslaving a generation of romantic young men, looked thoughtfully out into the soft darkness of her lush garden. She sighed, then looked quickly at Fleur. 'Sorry, you must think I'm ridiculous. The ramblings of a middle-aged woman.'

'Oh, Rose, don't be silly,' said Fleur, 'you're not middle-aged. You can't be much older than me.'

'I'm thirty-five, darling. Getting on a little bit. Too old probably to have babies. Or anyway lots of babies. That's sad. I dreamed of a big family, you know. But still. I've been very lucky in lots and lots of ways. More wine, darling?'

Fleur nodded. She could have sat here for ever, in this exquisite room, listening to Rose talking in her beautiful musical voice about her father, how perfect he had been. She looked at Rose, sitting in a rocking chair, moving gently backwards and forwards, thinking it was almost incredible she was thirty-five, she looked like a young girl, with her sheet of light brown hair, her perfect skin, her slender body. She was wearing a white dress, a silk shift; her feet – and even they were perfect, narrow, elegant feet – were bare, her legs, stretched out in front of her, occasionally pushing against the floor to keep the rocker going, long, beautiful, golden-brown legs.

'Do you . . .' She hesitated. 'Do you have any pictures of my dad?'

'Of course. I thought you might want to see them. Stay there, I'll go get them.'

She was back in a minute, smiling, a big album under her arm. 'Look,' she said, 'look, here he is outside Schwab's. With me. They're mostly with me, I'm afraid. And here we both are, pretending to be film stars, at the Garden of Allah. On the beach, look: oh, that was a wonderful day. We went to Malibu, tried to surf. He was just terrible, I wasn't so bad. He got so cross, I can't tell you.'

Fleur looked at the young man, the young man she had loved so much, laughing into the camera; exactly as she had remembered him, fun, confident, making life good. It was a talent, that: she was afraid she didn't have it. Rose had it; she could see why they had been so good together.

'They're lovely,' she said, oddly shy, 'thank you.'

'Did you see any of his movies?'

'Of course,' said Fleur. It seemed an odd question. She saw them all: over and over.

'He was no actor really,' said Rose, 'but boy, was he a looker. The camera adored him.' She looked at Fleur and smiled. 'You look so like him. I can't tell you.'

'So – how long were you together?' said Fleur.

'Oh – about a year. Properly. We were friends before that, shared this terrible room. And then – love arrived.' She smiled at Fleur, bit her lip. 'It still makes me sad, you know. To remember. How happy we were, and how wrong it went.'

'Yes. It must do,' said Fleur. 'But it wasn't your fault. Yours least of all. Maybe my dad's – a bit. Mostly Naomi MacNeice. And the system, I guess. Yolande always said it was the system.'

'Dear Yolande,' said Rose. 'Fleur my darling, you must forgive me, but I have to go to bed. I'm so tired. Now when is your friend Mr Phillips coming tomorrow?'

'Just whenever you want him,' said Fleur, 'I said he wasn't to come until we called him.'

'Good. I can't say I'm looking forward to it.'

'It's so sweet of you, Rose. I'm so grateful. He really isn't so bad. Honestly.'

Magnus was finally permitted to arrive at the house next evening, at six.

'You're to come for drinks and then you can stay for dinner,' said Fleur rather fiercely. 'And you're not to upset her, Magnus, because she's really nervous about it.'

'What a sensitive little soul she is,' said Magnus.

He arrived just a little early; they were still by the pool. Fleur was in her bikini, having a last swim: Rose was swathed in a huge white towelling robe.

Fleur had done a length underwater; she surfaced, and saw him standing there, slightly blurred through the sparkling water in her eyes, on her lashes. He came into focus, large, dark, brooding; he was wearing navy linen trousers, and a beige linen jacket, and looked more Mafioso than ever. He was smiling; she smiled just a little cautiously back, walked up the steps at the shallow end of the pool. His eyes went over her; she remembered the last time she had seen him, and felt herself, to her huge irritation, blush.

'Good evening,' he said.

'Hi,' said Fleur, and held out her hand, feeling faintly silly. 'Rose, this is Magnus Phillips. Magnus, this is Rose Sharon.'

Magnus looked at Rose for a long moment, taking in her famous beauty, the candid, almost challenging expression in her wide blue eyes, and then took her small white hand in his huge brown one and raised it to his lips.

'This is the greatest honour,' he said.

And Rose Sharon looked up at him, into his almost black eyes, held them in hers for a while and then smiled, sweetly, relievedly.

'You're not at all what I expected,' she said.

Fleur wrapped herself in her own robe, feeling awkward and suddenly oddly superfluous.

'So,' said Magnus, as they sat back after dinner, a more formal, impressive affair that night: artichokes, dressed lobster, strawberry pavlova, served formally, with lace cloths, candles on the table, Sue dressed in a severe navy dress, with Marcie, Ricardo's daughter, a ripe peach of a sixteen year old, helping to serve. 'So, Rose, tell me how you met Brendan.'

He had been listening to her patiently, prompting her for hours about her own career, recalling movies, scenes, plots with formidable skill. She was clearly enchanted by him, relaxed; she even acceded with perfect grace to his request to record the conversation.

'On one condition. You let me have a copy of the recording.'

'Of course,' he said, plugging in his machine, setting the tape rolling. 'I hate this thing, it's so big and awkward. I was listening to a guy in the hotel last night, and he said there was something on its way called a personal stereo. Size of a packet of cigarettes, you'll be able to listen to or record on it, carry it around with you.'

'Sounds purest fantasy to me,' said Fleur. They both looked at her, almost surprised to hear from her, so silent had she been.

'I think I would also like to hear a little more about your book,' said Rose. 'Before I start baring my soul to you.' She was smiling, but her eyes were very distant, almost hard.

'Hardly your soul,' said Magnus lightly, 'but yes, of course. Entirely reasonable. What would you like to know?'

'Well – you have a publisher?'

'Of course,' he said, looking amused.

'Magnus is a bestseller, Rose,' said Fleur. 'I told you.'

Magnus looked at her quickly, frowned imperceptibly, and turned back to Rose. 'My publisher is Beauman. Very blue-chip, English house. We're planning to publish this one just before Christmas.'

Rose raised her eyebrows. 'That sounds like cutting it a little fine. If you're still doing research.'

'It is. But the research has gone on rather, we're running very late and Mr Beauman wants to get his money back.'

'And over here?'

'Oh, several people interested. Crown. Doubleday.'

'My goodness, Mr Phillips, I hadn't realized it was such a big deal number,' said Rose. 'And it's a biography?'

'Well, not exactly. My books are more portraits of the world certain people inhabit, rather than biographies as such. How those people function in it. *Dancers*, for instance, surveyed the entire ballet scene, as well as one or two particular dancers; *The House* was a look at British politics and all its shenanigans, as well as a handful of politicians. Big scandals, like Profumo. And this one is actually subtitled *A Story of Hollywood*. Which is where Brendan comes in.'

'What's the title?'

'*The Tinsel Underneath*.'

'Oh, the old Goldwyn quote. Yes, I see. And who is your main subject?'

'Well, as far as there is one, Piers Windsor.'

'Piers Windsor! You're kidding me! What in God's name does Brendan have to do with Piers Windsor?'

She looked so genuinely astonished that Fleur was taken aback. She felt a thud of intense, painful disappointment.

'Well, it's pretty remote,' said Magnus easily. 'Let's call it ideological. It's the Hollywood connection, really. Have you ever met Piers Windsor?'

'I certainly have. He was here a year or so ago, filming the *Dream*, you know? I met him at some parties then. And his pretty little wife.'

'Did you like the pretty little wife?' asked Magnus mildly. Fleur shot him a look of pure venom.

'I thought she was adorable,' said Rose. 'And that little tiny daughter – she was just delicious.'

'Uh-huh. But you hadn't met him before?'

'No. Not really.'

'Not really?'

'Well, I mean, I think we once met at an Oscar. Something like that.'

'So you didn't know him – earlier?' said Fleur.

Magnus looked at her; his eyes were very hard. She flushed, looked down. It had been the condition of her sitting in on the interview that she didn't say anything.

'Earlier – what do you mean, earlier?' said Rose.

'Oh – nothing,' said Fleur. 'Sorry, Magnus.'

'It doesn't matter,' said Magnus. He turned back to Rose. 'The thing is, my books are rather like spiders' webs. I start in the centre and work out. Extraordinary links emerge. That's why they're so fascinating. And so – if I may sound immodest – unique. Piers is very far from being the only subject. Merely a hook to hang the book and its concept on. Other actors. Film directors, theatre managers, agents. Money men. Backers. English society. New York society. And lots and lots of Hollywood. Every conceivable area a career of that kind of calibre might be expected to extend into.'

'Well – of course I'll tell you what I can. But I still don't see any possible connection with Brendan,' said Rose.

'At this stage, there seems to be none whatsoever,' said Magnus, 'but it's those early Hollywood days, the struggles, what people did to one another, that fascinate me. And Brendan typifies that.'

'But Piers wasn't here in the early days,' said Rose patiently.

'I'm pretty sure he was. For a brief time.'

'Piers Windsor? Here? And nobody knew?' Rose stared at him. Then she began to laugh, her joyful, throaty, infectious laugh. 'That is the most ridiculous thing I ever heard. Do you really think we would have let him get away, that someone somewhere wouldn't have seen him, snapped him up?'

'Stranger things have happened,' said Magnus equably.

'But, Magnus, he is the most brilliant actor, and probably one of the most photogenic men in the world. Of course he would have been discovered.'

'Well, maybe he wasn't so hot then. I believe Laurence Olivier did none too well at first. Isn't the film business full of people telling how they missed Gable and Monroe and Hepburn first time around?'

'Oh, puh-lease! I'm telling you, it couldn't have happened. OK, maybe he might not have made it, but there's no way someone wouldn't have known him, noticed him. Or at the very least remembered him later on.'

'Well, maybe my informant was mistaken,' said Magnus easily. 'That's one of the reasons I'm here, to go over and over the same ground, from every possible angle. I'm very pleased, in a way, that you're so positive. It makes me that much more careful. Anyway, as I keep saying, it's the ambience of those days I want to get over. The dreams. All that sort of thing. What it was like to be a struggling young actor. I want to know how you, for example, moved from being a Young Hopeful to a Major Star. I hope you can hear the capitals. And by contrast, how Brendan moved from being a Major Star to a Casualty, a no-hoper.'

'Well – I don't know,' said Rose. 'I didn't realize it was going to be quite this sort of book. I thought it was just another book about – well, like you just said, about – Hollywood.'

'It is,' said Magnus. 'Hollywood. And also Broadway. Shaftesbury Avenue. Stratford. Big names, big stars. And I want you to be in it. I want you to grace its pages.' He smiled at her, and his eyes moved over her face, lingering on her lips. Then he sat back, picked up his glass. 'But of course I shall understand if you feel you can't. Absolutely. I have no wish to worry you, make you feel uncomfortable.'

Rose hesitated. 'Can I read it? Before publication?'

'Of course. I shall have proof copies sent to you.'

There was a long silence. Then she suddenly said, 'All right. Start the interview.'

'Thank you. How did you meet Brendan?'

'Oh, in the best possible way,' said Rose, smiling down at the hand holding her glass, at the memory, 'at a cattle call. A cattle call at Theatrical. Which was then in West Hollywood. You know about cattle calls, Mr Phillips?'

'I do think,' he said, 'you should call me Magnus. After all, you said I should call you Rose. And yes, I do know about cattle calls.'

'Fine. Well, there he was, Magnus, standing in line, and I just looked at him, and – oh, this is going to sound like one of my movies –'

'And why not?' said Magnus. 'What better way to sound?'

Shit, thought Fleur, he is ladling it on with a shovel. Slimy bastard. She wouldn't have expected it of him. She was sure Rose could see straight through him. Although she didn't appear to; she was sitting with her pretty little pointed chin resting on her hand, her large eyes fixed on Magnus, her face just slightly flushed. She was wearing a black dress, cut very low, her brown breasts pushed very high and full; he was clearly captivated by her. Fleur was finding it amusing, in the light of his early hostility.

'Well, maybe,' said Rose. 'Anyway, he looked at me and smiled, and I looked back at him and smiled, and hours later, when neither of us got anything, we caught the bus and went back down to Schwab's, because he had buddies there, and he bought me a beer and I guess that was that.'

'Tell me about Schwab's. Wasn't that where everyone got discovered?'

'Supposedly. Of course they weren't really. But it was such a fun place to be, almost like a family, and they took messages for you and . . .'

The light, musical voice drifted back into the past, telling charming, amusing stories, sad stories, anecdotes, about the people who had been around Schwab's in those days, hopeful, struggling people, all of them talented, all of them waiting for the big chance, the big break; Fleur listened, half interested, half bored. Rose's certainty that Piers had not been in Hollywood had upset her. She would surely know. All this time, and she had been making a fool of herself, wasting time. She sighed, forced her mind back on to Rose and her stories. 'And like I said,' she was saying, 'that was it really. For Brendan and me.'

'But I thought – forgive me –' Magnus hesitated.

'Yes?'

'I thought that at first you were just friends.'

'Oh, you have done a lot of homework.' She spoke lightly, but was clearly irritated at her story being, however slightly, queried. 'Who told you that? Fleur here?'

'Indeed.'

'Well, Fleur my darling, I shall clearly not have to employ you as my ghost writer when I do my autobiography,' said Rose. 'You'll take all the magic out. Yes, that's right. We were friends for a while. Friends and housemates. Then one night, oh, I don't know, the moon was full, I guess, and the air was warm, and – things changed. Friends become lovers rather naturally, I always think, don't you, Magnus?'

'Sometimes,' he said. 'I prefer the compartments kept very separate myself. Love, for me, is a singular creature, with one thing and one thing only in mind.'

'Indeed,' she said, smiling at him, reaching out for the wine, refilling his glass. 'Well, perhaps we had better not get on to that for now.'

'Perhaps. And so . . .?' His voice tailed away.

'And so – we fell in love. We were inseparable. Everything to one another. I loved him. Very much.'

'And that lasted for?'

'Oh, around a year. He had a tough time. Well, we both did. He'd arrived on a three-month contract, didn't make it; well, you'll know all this from Joe Payton's book.'

'You've read it, then?'

'Oh yes,' she said quickly. 'Of course. Are you surprised?'

'No. No, of course not. Besides, it's a good book.'

'I thought so too. Anyway, we had that year, Brendan and I. Hard up but happy. Living in a little cold-water apartment off La Brea. We had fun.'

'How would you describe him?'

'Oh –' Her blue eyes took on a hazy, tender look. 'Kind. Generous. Gentle. Funny. All the good things.'

'No bad ones?'

She met his eyes very steadily. 'Not then, no. Unless you could count trusting people too much.'

'Hardly a fault.'

'In Hollywood, that's a fault.'

'I can see it might be. How was he as an actor?'

'Pretty bad. Sorry, Fleur. He really wasn't good. But he did something to the camera, it liked him, he looked good, moved well. There was one film, a comedy, he played a young lawyer, when I really thought maybe he was getting somewhere. But – well . . .'

'Did he think he was a good actor?'

'He certainly did.' She laughed, easily, tolerantly. 'And I certainly didn't disabuse him of the idea.'

'I would hope not. Fragile egos we have, us men. Did he talk about Fleur?'

'Of course. A great deal. He loved her very much.'

'And he wanted her over here?'

'Yes, he did. But he couldn't bring her. It wouldn't have been suitable. Nowhere to live, no money.'

'Of course. Did he talk about Caroline?'

'Who?'

'Fleur's mother?'

'Oh – oh sometimes. He had obviously loved her very much. But then I might have been jealous, don't you think?' She smiled at him, sweetly provocative.

'I suppose so. How old were you then?'

'You should never ask a lady her age.'

'How old were you, Rose?'

She laughed. 'How offensive. I was – eighteen.'

'Ambitious?'

'Very.'

'I see. Well now, what went wrong? With this idyllic state of affairs.'

The eyelids lowered: the long black lashes swept down, concealing emotion.

'He met Naomi MacNeice.'

'What was she like? She fascinates me.'

'Casting director ACI. Powerful, dangerous, very clever.'

'Beautiful?'

'Not at all.' Rose sounded almost amused. 'Icy cold eyes, hard face, much too thin, rude, God, she was rude. She had more enemies than anyone you could possibly think of.'

'So Brendan wasn't personally taken with her?'

'Of course not. He found her very unattractive. But – she was success. At last. And she signed him up, and took him off.' Her voice was brittle, determinedly amused.

'And he wasn't allowed to see you any more?'

'No, he wasn't.'

'And' – Magnus's dark eyes were careful, watchful – 'and how did you feel about that?'

'Oh – terrible. Of course. Very upset.'

'Angry? Surely you must have been angry?'

'No. Not angry. Not exactly. I suppose I found it hard to believe. After – well, after what we'd had. And of course there were scenes. But it was very – Hollywood. You just have to accept that kind of thing.'

'Really? I find that terribly hard to believe.'

'Listen,' said Rose. She leant forward earnestly, pushing back her golden-brown hair. 'You come to Hollywood to make it. To get famous. Successful. It's a tough club to get membership, and the rules are very simple. You do what you have to do. Otherwise you just go home. Brendan had to become Naomi's lapdog.' Her eyes were calm, but gently, amusedly contemptuous. 'I didn't like it, I was very hurt, but I accepted it. And I didn't want to go home. Magnus, would you like a brandy? Some Armagnac maybe? What about you, Fleur?'

'Armagnac would be very nice,' said Magnus. He was awe-inspiringly sober, despite the bottle and a half of Chardonnay he had consumed. Fleur supposed it was years of training. She refused anything more to drink, sipped slightly compulsively on mineral water.

'Now,' he said, 'when did you hear Brendan had fallen from grace?'

'Oh, very quickly. This is a small town. And he had been quite high-profile. The story hit the scandal sheets and he was out. Just like that.'

'Did you go and see him?'

'Yes, I did. Of course.'

'That was nice of you.'

'Well, I figured he needed a friend. I suppose I'd loved him enough to be able to be that to him.'

'It was still nice of you.'

She shrugged, gave him her sweet smile. 'I'm a nice girl, Magnus.'

'I can see that.'

God, thought Fleur, I shall throw up in a minute.

'And what did you make of the allegations in the magazine? Were you shocked?'

'Not shocked exactly. Surprised.'

'But you believed them?'

'I still don't know. I think probably I thought, and I still think, that there was maybe a minor indiscretion or two, and they were – well, oversold, shall we say? I honestly didn't take a great deal of notice at the time. Those publications were always raking along the bottom of the muck heap, destroying reputations, people, lives. That Dan Dailey was a drag queen, that Lana Turner and Ava Gardner shared a lover. Half the time they were bought off, the scandal sheets. They made as much money out of blackmail money as sales. But within that framework, I guess I thought it might have been – feasible. Anything's feasible here. I can't stress that enough.'

'But you'd certainly had no idea? That he might have been – capable of such behaviour?'

'Of course not. None.'

'Not even though he'd been brought to Hollywood by two raving queens?'

'Magnus, half of the actors in Hollywood are there by courtesy of raving queens.'

'Yes, I suppose so. And he'd never talked to you about past indiscretions?'

'No. Never. It's not the kind of thing you tell your girlfriend, is it? Magnus, I'm awfully tired. Do you think we could carry on tomorrow?'

'Of course we can. I'm so sorry. I thought you were busy tomorrow.'

'Oh, not really. Costume fittings, that sort of thing.'

'Well maybe I'd better be getting back to the hotel. Could your driver take me?'

'He could, but you're welcome to stay. It's very late. The poolhouse is free. There's everything you need in there. Including pyjamas.'

'I don't wear pyjamas,' he said. 'But thank you. I'll take you up on the offer.'

'And we can talk some more in the morning.'

'Indeed we can.'

Fleur could see the poolhouse from her room. The lights were on for almost two hours after they all went to bed.

In the morning Rose was sparkling, awesomely bright. She had done thirty lengths, she told them, before either of them had even been up. She sat by the pool in a pale peach robe, her face totally bare, her wet hair slicked back, and looked as perfect as if she had spent three hours in make-up.

She offered Magnus fruit salad, eggs, croissants. He spurned them all.

'I only like toast. And do you have any marmalade?'

'I certainly do.' She picked up the house telephone on the poolhouse wall.

'Sue! Bring some marmalade out, would you?'

'Er – I'm afraid it isn't just some marmalade,' said Magnus. 'I only eat Cooper's Oxford. Otherwise honey'll do.'

'It'll have to,' said Rose Sharon. 'What in God's name is Cooper's Oxford?'

'The only real marmalade there is,' said Magnus. 'All the rest is counterfeit.'

'We only have the counterfeit. Sue, can we have some honey? Fleur darling, you look tired.'

'I am tired,' said Fleur. 'I couldn't sleep.'

'Oh, darling, I'm sorry.'

'It doesn't matter,' said Fleur, 'I hardly ever can.'

'Did you try herbal tea?'

'I tried everything.'

'Acupuncture?'

'Everything,' said Fleur firmly. She had no intention of letting some Hollywood crank stick needles into her.

That morning Magnus sat and recorded at least sixty minutes more of conversation with Rose about her early career, her struggles, how she got her first big break. 'I was working at the Garden of Allah, and this guy came in, said I should be in pictures and he could help. I said sure, what was his name, Harry Cohn? He said no, but he was one of Harry Cohn's scouts. I didn't believe him, of course, but it was true.'

'A real Hollywood fairytale,' said Magnus.

'Yes, I suppose it was. Anyway, that was that. I signed, made my first picture, and then I was on my way. I mean really on my way. The comedy with Cary Grant, and then . . .' More film titles, more co-stars. Fleur crushed the disloyal thought that Rose could become a little boring on the subject of herself and tried to concentrate.

'And this was – after Brendan had died?' said Magnus after another twenty minutes.

'Well, not getting my break, signing my first contract,' said Rose quickly. 'He was still with Naomi, still with ACI then.'

'That must have given you some satisfaction?'

'Pardon me?'

'Well, to think you were catching up on him. Cinderella was getting to the ball.'

'I suppose so. Yes. To be honest I didn't think about him much any more.'

'But you still went to see him after the scandal?'

'Yes, I did. I told you, I thought he'd need a friend. He was living in some terrible place –'

'Where was that?'

'Oh, I don't really remember. Downtown somewhere.'

'I still think it was very sweet of you. Very forgiving.'

'Yes, well –' She shrugged, looked at him. 'God, it's bright, would you just excuse me while I get my sunglasses?'

'Of course.'

She disappeared; Fleur looked at Magnus. He grinned at her; he seemed mildly embarrassed.

'Nice lady.'

'I can see you think so.'

'This must be – painful for you,' he said suddenly.

'Not really. Rose agrees with me, you see. That there was some minor indiscretion, and then someone hated him enough to frame him, sell his story. And I like it that she loved him so much.'

'Well, she certainly seems to have done.'

'Magnus, why did you tell her so much about the book, and Piers and everything? Was it necessary?'

'Absolutely. She'll hear about it quite soon, all the hype that's going on, and then she could get me for talking to her under false pretences. Very dangerous. And don't forget it's all been recorded. You have to be very careful.'

'She seems pretty sure he wasn't here,' said Fleur heavily.

'Yes, well, I think –'

Rose came back, smiling. Her sunglasses were huge and very dark. 'That's better. I get the most terrible migraine without these things. I've asked Ricardo to bring out some wine. Where was I?'

Magnus switched on the recorder again. 'You'd been to see him, in some terrible place.'

'Oh yes. Yes, and he looked so awful, haggard, thin, exhausted. He'd been having the most terrible time. And he said, "I talk too much, Rose. Always have done." That was his problem. Like I said, he trusted people too much.'

'Well,' said Magnus with a heavy sigh, 'it's clearly a dangerous thing to do here. He didn't give you any indication who he'd talked to?'

'No. I asked him, of course, but he said it could have been one of so many people.' She was silent, staring into the pool. Ricardo arrived with an ice bucket, a bottle of Chardonnay, another of mineral water. She smiled at him rather vaguely; she looked upset, disturbed.

'Do you have any ideas of your own?' said Magnus.

'No. I've worn a groove in my brain, ever since, thinking about it. I would guess probably some kid he'd rejected. Something like that. Wouldn't that make sense to you?'

'It would seem to, yes. So did you see him again, before he was killed?'

'Once or twice. I tried to get him a job. You know, bit parts, walk-ons, anything to keep him going. But I had no real power at that time. And he was bad news. If you're bad news here, you're very bad news. People don't want to be associated with you.'

'It was brave of you then. To try,' said Magnus.

'Magnus, I'd loved the bastard. I had to try. But I – failed. Then he just disappeared. I didn't know where to. Of course afterwards we all knew it was the beach. But –' She smiled, a shaky smile. 'I'm sorry. It still hurts, thinking about it.'

'I'm sure. Rose, does the name Kirstie Fairfax mean anything to you?'

Fleur stared at him. She had never heard of Kirstie Fairfax.

'Not much,' said Rose, after a moment or two. 'She was on the edge of Brendan's crowd for a while. I never really met her. She was trouble, that's all I know.'

'What kind of trouble?'

'Oh, the usual. You name it, she was into it. Sex, drugs, alcohol. I think she did a little blackmailing on the side.' She spoke carelessly, started undoing her robe.

'Blackmailing?' said Magnus, sharply. 'What kind of blackmailing?'

'Is there more than one kind? She got her hooks into people, discovered the soft underbelly and then wouldn't let go. Until they gave her money. Or something.'

Fleur felt excited suddenly: her flesh crawled. Blackmail. That was what those scandal sheets were really all about. Everyone said so. In which case . . .

'Where is she now?' she said, feeling herself flush. 'Do you know?'

'I'm afraid we do,' said Magnus, laughing. 'And it isn't heaven.'

'You mean she's dead?' said Fleur.

'Very dead. She was killed. Or rather she killed herself. Or that's how the verdict came in.'

'I see,' said Fleur. 'You seem to know a lot about her.'

'I do. All part of the research.'

'How does she come into all this anyway?' said Rose.

'Well, you said yourself she knew Brendan. And he gave evidence at the inquest. He was supposed to have been trying to help her get a part.'

'He did? I didn't realize that.' She sighed. 'Well, I guess there was a lot I didn't realize. You have to remember I just never saw him at that time.'

'And you can't tell me any more about her? Friends, family, anything? You never talked to her?'

'I never did.'

'Did Brendan ever talk about her? Afterwards? When you were – helping him?'

'No, he didn't.' Rose stood up suddenly, slipped off her robe; she was wearing a sliver of a bikini in brilliant stinging pink. Fleur took in the perfect body, the full breasts, the flat stomach, the endless legs before she dived in, a scissor-flash of colour against the blue. She turned and looked at Magnus; he was staring at Rose, and she thought she had never seen sexual desire written more clearly on a man's face. God, they were a pathetic lot. All the same. All the fucking same.

'Come in and join me,' said Rose. 'Both of you. It's wonderful.'

'I don't have anything to wear,' said Magnus.

'You don't need a lot to wear in the water.'

'I'm terribly shy,' he said, grinning down at her.

'There are plenty of shorts in the poolhouse. Have a look.'

'OK.'

He came out again wearing a pair of navy and red shorts. His body was very heavy, very muscular, but totally without any spare flesh. He was tanned, very hairy; it was without doubt a powerfully sexy body. Fleur looked away, feeling unsettled, upset.

Magnus stood on the edge of the pool, grinning down at Rose; she reached out a slender arm, took his hand, pulled him in.

'Come on, Fleur,' she said, 'it's gorgeous.'

Fleur shook her head. She felt sixteen again, in the presence of adults, awkward, out of it. 'I'm fine,' she said.

They fooled around for a while; Rose kept pulling Magnus underwater, he kept swimming very fast away from her. They were both laughing, having a patently wonderful time. Fleur watched them and wondered what she should do to make herself feel better. The only thing she could manage was drinking two glasses of the wine, very quickly, which made her feel dizzy and slightly sick, but otherwise just the same.

She closed her eyes, wishing she was anywhere else in the world, when Magnus climbed out, shook himself dry and sat down in the chair next to her. He grinned at her, his teeth awesomely white in his wet brown face; he looked particularly saturnine. The wet shorts clung to his penis; the bulge was very large. She looked away with difficulty.

'You OK?'

'Yes, of course I'm OK.'

'I've never known you so quiet.'

'Well, you haven't known me very long,' said Fleur irritably, and closed her eyes again.

'I guess not. Can I try you on another name?' he called to Rose.

'Sure.'

'How about Zwirn?'

Rose looked thoughtfully up at him from the water. 'Fleur asked me about that. It really doesn't mean a thing. And it's not a name you'd forget.'

'No indeed,' said Magnus.

'Am I allowed to ask what he or she might have done or not done?'

'We don't have an idea. It's just another name that's cropped up. In old cuttings.'

'Is Mr – or Mrs – Zwirn resident in LA?'

'No. Well if he is, he's not listed.'

'Oh dear. I really don't know how much help I've been. Not a lot. I'm sorry. But I did warn you.'

'Yes, you did. Now you're absolutely certain, are you, about Piers Windsor? That he wasn't here, didn't know Brendan?'

'Of course. If he had done, I'd have known.'

'But –'

'Look,' said Rose, 'what is this, an inquisition or an interview? I said I'd help, tell you everything I could. Here I am doing that and you're arguing with me.' She smiled, sweetly, but there was a tension, a tautness behind it.

Fleur looked at her, looked at Magnus. She felt lost, confused, suddenly bitterly disappointed and sad. Magnus was smiling easily at Rose.

'I'm terribly sorry,' he said, 'you're right. Of course you'd know anything, everything that went on here. You have to forgive me. I'm just a hick reporter from England. It's well known we don't have any manners. Interview over.'

'I enjoyed it – most of it,' said Rose. She was towelling her long golden-brown hair, smiling down at him, quite relaxed again.

'You have wonderful hair,' said Magnus suddenly. 'It's so nice you never went blonde.'

'Thank you.'

'I suppose you have one of those power hairdressers who goes round the world with you on every film? Appears on the credits, that sort of thing?'

'Yes, I do.'

'Would I recognize her name?'

'I doubt it.'

'Try me.'

God, thought Fleur, what is this piece for, an interview in *Hair & Beauty*?

'She's called Dorian Roth.'

'You're right. Doesn't mean a thing. Can I buy you dinner tonight, Miss Sharon, just to say thank you?'

'I'm sorry,' said Rose, sounding as if her heart was breaking, 'I'm busy tonight.'

'That's a shame. Maybe tomorrow. You've been marvellous. Hasn't she, Fleur?'

'Marvellous,' said Fleur, wishing she didn't feel quite so wretched.

'Well, let's all swim, and then have lunch, and just enjoy being friends,' said Rose, reaching for her robe. 'I still haven't got over the pleasure of finding Fleur.'

'Neither have I,' said Magnus.

After lunch Fleur developed a splitting headache. It was the combination of the sun, the wine they had drunk, her sleepless night. 'I might go and lie down,' she said, 'if you don't mind. I don't feel too good.'

'Of course I don't mind,' said Rose. 'Magnus, what do you want to do? Have some more wine? Swim? Play tennis? Go back to your hotel?'

'Don't you have to go to the studio this afternoon?' said Magnus, looking at her thoughtfully.

'I should. But I don't really have to.'

At that precise moment, Marcie appeared, put-putting up the drive on a small motorbike.

'Hey, that's fun,' said Magnus. 'Could I have a ride on that?'

'Of course you can. Is that OK with you, Marcie?'

'Sure,' said Marcie. She smiled up at Magnus.

'Do you like bikes?' said Rose.

'I love 'em. Perfect form of transport. I have a Harley Davidson at home.'

'You do?'

'I do. Love of my life.'

'Come with me,' said Rose.

She stood up and walked him over to the huge garage that stood on the other side of the house, half submerged in trees and shrubs. She pushed the door up: inside, next to the pale blue Cadillac, was a massive BMW bike, gleaming black and silver in the sun.

'Be my guest,' she said. 'It'll make up for the marmalade.'

'You going to ride behind me?'

'No,' she said, 'you're going to ride behind me. We'll run down to the coast.'

She sat on the bike, and he settled behind her; his muscular legs pressed up under hers, his arms around her waist, the wet shorts still outlining his cock. Fleur could see he had an erection, and from the way Rose thrust her small, perfect bottom back against him, she could see she felt it. The image she was left with as the bike roared down the drive was of intense and blatant sexuality. She went to her room, pulled the curtains and lay on her bed, crying quietly from a mixture of rage and misery.

Chapter 32

1972

'Chloe, my darling, you have to tell me what the matter is. I can't stand this hostility any longer.'

'I'm not hostile, Ludo. Just – well, just upset.'

'I can tell you're upset. It's written in every line of your pale, funny little face. And it's obviously making you ill. You looked terrible last night, at that party. I suddenly understood what ashen meant.'

'Ludovic, I –'

'Chloe, listen to me.' His voice, normally so gentle, so relaxed, was urgent, almost harsh. 'I've been very patient for a very long time. It hasn't been easy. And I think the time has come for things to be clarified. It isn't going to get any better as time goes on. Rather the reverse.'

That's true, thought Chloe, resting her aching head on the wall behind the bed (she had taken to coming back to bed when she had driven Pandora to school in the morning, so sick and weary did she feel).

'Chloe? Chloe, are you there?'

'Yes, of course I'm here.'

'Not in the full sense of the word, I fancy.'

'Ludo, don't treat me like one of your witnesses, please.'

'My witnesses pay rather more attention to what I say. Now then, I'm going to deliver an ultimatum. Otherwise I can see this situation going on until we are both old and grey, and that would be rather a waste. Unless you talk to Piers by the end of next week, I shall come and see him myself.'

'Oh Ludovic, please –'

'Don't "Oh Ludovic" me. I'm sorry, darling, but this is not just a piece of glorious adultery. Although it is exactly that. I love you, and I need you, and I want this thing settled. All right?'

'Yes, Ludovic. All right. But you're not to talk to him. I will.'

'Well, darling, do it. Or it will make me ill as well as you.'

'All right, Ludo. Thank you for ringing.'

'Any chance of a meeting?'

'No. No, I think we shouldn't,' said Chloe, feeling panic rise, join her nausea, 'not until I've talked to Piers.'

'Well perhaps that will spur you on. Or maybe you've just gone off the whole idea.'

'Oh Ludovic,' said Chloe and the passion in her voice made it a near groan, 'oh Ludovic, if only, if only you knew.'

'I think I do,' he said, sounding infinitely more cheerful, 'but I don't want to be complacent. I love you. Now why don't you go and have lunch with one of your girlfriends and cheer yourself up a bit.'

'It wouldn't do any good at all,' said Chloe, thinking with foreboding of the fate that befell most of her food at the moment. Thank God, thank God, Piers was so engrossed in *Othello*. He would hardly notice if she gave birth to a large blonde freckled baby in the middle of Piccadilly Circus.

As January dragged on (and somehow she won a reprieve of another two weeks from an exasperated but resigned Ludovic) and the opening of *Othello* approached, Piers started smoking heavily again, and his cough became more troublesome. Bannerman insisted on an X-ray and phoned the results to Chloe, saying that bronchitis and quite possibly pleurisy were 'minutes away'.

'He has to have a break. Take him to the sunshine for a few days, make him rest completely. Otherwise there'll be no *Othello*, no anything.'

'I'll try,' said Chloe, panicking at the very thought of being alone with Piers, and not only because of her almost constant nausea, 'but I don't think –'

'Chloe, you have to succeed. This is serious.'

Chloe decided she had to act; maybe this was the catalyst she needed. Maybe she could break the news to Piers while they were away; maybe he would take it better. Maybe. Maybe not. Anyway, she clearly had to do what Bannerman said. She picked up the phone immediately after she had put it down, phoned their travel agency, and booked two flights to Antigua, and a bungalow at the Jumby Bay for a week. Then she called the theatre, to say she was coming to collect Piers personally. It was a bold move; it was a measure of her desperation that she was making it.

When she got there, Wally, the doorman, said they were running very late, and why didn't she slip round and watch. She said Piers would be furious and Wally said what Piers didn't know wouldn't hurt him, and to go up to the dress circle and watch from there. So she went round to the front of the theatre and up to the circle and sat down, very quietly, behind a pillar and looked down at the stage. And saw the Piers she had fallen in love with all over again.

She had never been to anything but a dress rehearsal: had never sat in a half-lit empty theatre, with all its attendant flatness and drabness. Piers wouldn't allow it. He liked her to see what the public saw, the brilliance, the polish, the magic. There were several people sitting in the stalls, about five rows back, but the house lights were out and she couldn't see who they were: the producer, she supposed, and the director, maybe the set designer, the costume designer. The stage was empty: empty and dusty. There were a great many cigarette ends on it. No scenery, no props, except one extremely ugly chair. Piers sat on the edge of the stage, calling out to the row of people in the stalls.

'I know, I know,' he was saying, 'but I just think it would work. Let me try it. Please.'

'OK. But it won't work. And we don't have Desdemona. She'll be at least another ten minutes. She's gone to get her fucking cleaning. And we're running out of time,' said one of them. A woman. Chloe wasn't sure who she was.

Piers walked off into the wings, and there was a long silence. Then he came on again, and he wasn't really Piers any more. He was dressed the same, in the baggy flannels and checked shirt he always wore for rehearsals, and he carried no props, but he was someone else altogether, someone tortured, someone wretched, someone in horror. He stood, his back turned to the audience, bowed his head, raised his hands, and pushed them, with a kind of gentle, frantic desperation, through his hair. And then dropped them, heavily, to his sides. And then, without moving again, he spoke, wonderfully, resonantly, every note, every syllable clear, and the voice she knew so well, the marvellous, musical, confident voice was changed, charged with pain, with uncertainty, with terror, and as he spoke, suddenly Desdemona was there, despite her absence, despite the empty stage, dead, murdered, smothered by this tortured creature who spoke, slowly as in sleep, nightmared sleep: 'No more moving? Still as the grave. Shall she come in? Were't good? I think she stirs again. No . . .' And then, as the great voice roared and shook into the climax of the speech, 'my wife! my wife! I have no wife,' she found tears pouring down her cheeks, and she knew that whatever he had done, whatever he might do, she had married and loved an extraordinary and most gifted man, and she wept as much for the death of that love as for the emotion he had evoked in her with his speech.

She slipped down as the speech ended, as the long debate began about whether his back should be turned entirely or just three-quarters to the audience, the position of the bed, of Desdemona on it (Desdemona having now returned), of the lighting, of the timing of Emilia's entrance, and made her way back to the stage door, where she stood, waiting patiently, still entranced, still shocked by the beauty and the sheer power of what she had witnessed.

'I should go in, my love,' said Wally, 'they'll be talking till daybreak, unless you do.'

'All right,' said Chloe, and went down towards the dressing room, but Wally had been wrong: Piers was alone in his dressing room, and he was very pale, shaking slightly, and was lighting a cigarette.

'Piers, don't,' said Chloe, too anxious, too altogether disturbed by what she had witnessed to be tactful, careful, 'don't do that, you've got to stop smoking at once.'

'Oh, for God's sake,' he said, 'not you as well. Don't nanny me, Chloe, please.'

'I'm not nannying you, it's Roger Bannerman. He's just phoned through your test results, and you're what he calls minutes away from bronchitis, possibly pleurisy. He says you need immediate antibiotic treatment, some sunshine and a complete break, and I've booked us a week in Antigua. Don't look at me like that, Piers, if you don't go, Dr Bannerman says there'll be no *Othello* anyway.'

Piers agreed to go.

Two nights before they were due to leave, Ned started to run a temperature and to cry with pain; later he was very sick.

'Appendicitis,' said Bannerman briefly, and had him admitted to St Thomas's.

The appendix had almost ruptured; Ned was quite ill. Not dangerously, but wretchedly, feverishly, painfully ill. There was no way Chloe could leave him.

'We'll forget this trip then,' said Piers and she could hear the relief, the triumph in his voice; but Bannerman said he was not to forget it, that he needed the break and the sunshine, that Piers really must not underestimate the danger of ignoring the infection in his chest, that he would be joining Ned in hospital if he did.

'Go out alone,' he said, 'Chloe can join you in a day or two.'

Piers hesitated; then he said, 'I hate travelling alone.'

'Well, take the other woman in your life,' said Bannerman. 'Take Pandora. She'll love it.'

Piers thought for a moment and then said he would love it too.

On the third day after he had gone, Chloe returned from the hospital at midday; she was sleeping there and indeed spending most of her time there, but Ned was better and she needed a break. She could see a considerable miracle had been worked on her behalf, that she was not going to have to go to Antigua; and almost as the plane had taken off, she had stopped being sick and in fact had begun to feel much better. Piers had phoned once to say he and Pandora were having a wonderful time and that she had been snorkelling on the reef and they had both been waterskiing and they had been dancing together after dinner. Chloe had tried to keep the disapproval out of her voice, and said she was very glad it was such a success. Kitty had been missing her badly; Chloe was sitting on the nursery floor, playing with her, and wondering if she might phone Ludovic and suggest dinner, when the nanny came in and said there was a call for her.

'I'll take it in my room,' said Chloe.

It was Mr Lewis from the bank.

'Mrs Windsor?' He sounded apologetic. 'I'm sorry to trouble you, I really wanted to speak to Mr Windsor.'

'I'm afraid he's away, Mr Lewis. He's in Antigua, with our small daughter. He hasn't been at all well.'

'Oh. Oh, I see. Well, in that case . . .' His voice tailed off.

'Mr Lewis,' said Chloe, 'my husband and I have no secrets from one another.' (God, if only that were true.) 'If there's a problem, you can tell me.'

'Yes, well – it could wait, I suppose,' said Mr Lewis. 'It's simply that I've just been presented with a cheque, made out to a racing stable.'

'Yes,' said Chloe, 'yes, of course. Piers has just bought a new horse. So?'

Mr Lewis sounded more embarrassed still. 'Well, to be blunt, Mrs Windsor, I really don't think I can pay it. Unless I receive some monies or certainly unless I am reassured that there are some in the pipeline.'

'What?' said Chloe. 'Mr Lewis, I don't understand.'

'Well, you see, Mrs Windsor, the account is considerably overdrawn. Very considerably. Now I have always allowed Mr Windsor a great deal of latitude, naturally, he is a very important and valued customer of this bank, and it is an honour to have him with us. But the overdraft is at a very high level at the moment, and frankly, I don't have the authority to sanction any further borrowing. I'm so sorry, Mrs Windsor. You obviously had no idea.'

'No,' said Chloe, 'no, I didn't. Er – what is this high level, Mr Lewis?'

There was a pause; then Mr Lewis said with enormous reluctance, 'Ten thousand pounds. On current account. Plus – well, plus some more on a loan account.'

'How much more, Mr Lewis?'

A long painful silence. Then: 'Another ten thousand pounds.'

Chloe felt as if she was falling from a huge height; she actually put out a hand to the wall, requiring physical steadying. Then she said, 'Well, clearly there is some mistake. I mean, some transfer or whatever has not been made. I will speak to my husband as soon as possible, and ring you. Thank you so much, Mr Lewis.'

When she put the receiver down, she noticed it was wet, where her hand had been sweating.

Piers was mildly indignant but mostly amused about the state of the account.

'I'm sorry, darling. There's a series of payments coming through from the States; in fact the first one should have arrived by now, and it can go straight into the account. If it hasn't, ring Jim Prendergast and get him to chase it up; he'll make you an advance in any case if it hasn't come.'

Jim Prendergast was Piers's accountant; yes, he said, that was quite correct, there was a cheque for twenty thousand dollars arrived that morning, and he would send it round to the bank by messenger immediately.

It all seemed slightly hand to mouth, but Chloe felt for the most part reassured. She phoned Mr Lewis and told him a payment would be with him by the end of the next day, and that he should clear the cheque to the stables.

'Well, Mrs Windsor, I'm so sorry to have worried you. But I'm sure you will understand my predicament.'

'Yes, of course, Mr Lewis.'

'Er – there is just one other thing.'

'Yes, Mr Lewis?'

'The cheque he writes each month in dollars: to the company in Santa Barbara, California. I presume you are familiar with this one?'

'What? Oh – yes, of course,' said Chloe hastily. Probably some theatrical workshop Piers was on the board of and contributed to. There were dozens of them, all of them sent money to succour the ventures and his vanity. 'Well now, this has also just been presented to me for clearance. It is, as of course you will know, quite a large sum. Presumably you would like me to go ahead and pay this one at the same time?'

'Well, I suppose so. Is it really such a large amount?'

This was getting out of hand; Piers must clearly be stopped from making donations he couldn't afford.

'Well – quite large. You didn't know?'

'Not the precise amount,' said Chloe carefully.

'Ah. Well perhaps I shouldn't –'

'Mr Lewis. My husband is away. He hasn't been well. He expects me to take care of things. Is this the – let me see, the hundred-dollar payment?' She had pulled the figure out of the air. It seemed to come into the category of quite large.

Mr Lewis sounded once again guarded and exasperated. 'No, Mrs Windsor. Not a hundred dollars.'

'Then –'

'Mrs Windsor, I really don't think –'

'Mr Lewis, please. Look, I have access to all my husband's bank accounts. As you know.' This was absolutely true; Piers's generosity did not end with extravagant gifts.

'Indeed. Well, the amount is, as I said, quite considerable. One thousand dollars per calendar month.'

'Oh yes,' said Chloe, and she was astounded at her calm, her icy control, 'yes, of course. That one. Well, Mr Lewis, I think provided funds are available, you should pay the cheque. What was the name of the company?'

'Zwirn, Mrs Windsor. Gerard Zwirn.'

'Oh, Zwirn, yes of course. No, that's absolutely right, Mr Lewis. Zwirn of Santa Barbara, fine, put it through.'

'Thank you, Mrs Windsor.'

Fleur was finding it increasingly hard to think clearly. She had felt like this for two weeks now, ever since she had left Los Angeles. Well, no, before she had left Los Angeles; ever since that horrible day when Magnus and Rose had driven off on the motorbike, and come back hours later, laughing, excited, had found her by the pool, and begged her to join them for dinner.

'No, really,' she had said, 'I feel lousy, I must have some bug, please forgive me,' and had watched wretchedly as they disappeared into the house for quite a long time before Magnus emerged and said he was going back to the hotel to change and just to call him if she changed her mind.

'I won't,' she said, trying to sound normal, not like some spoilt, thwarted child, 'I really do feel terrible, I keep throwing up. And somehow I have to get back to New York tomorrow; my boss called, there's a huge meeting with a difficult client, who's just trying to trash a whole campaign. So –'

'OK, OK,' he said, putting his hands up, grinning down at her; but his eyes were kind, concerned almost. 'You do what you have to do. I hope you feel better.'

He bent to kiss her on the cheek; she smiled up at him with a huge effort.

'Have a good dinner. She's so nice, isn't she?'

'She is indeed. A remarkable lady. Disappointing in some ways, but most certainly not in others.'

'Magnus –'

'Yes, Fleur?'

'I – oh, it doesn't matter.'

'Look,' he said, 'I'm coming to New York before I go home to England. I'll see you there. We can talk then.'

'How long will you be?'

'I don't know. A few days.'

'Oh.' She was silent, feeling the pain as she contemplated the few days and how he might be filling them, and then, angry with herself for caring so much, she said, 'Do you always get so close to your interviewees?'

'No,' he said, 'very seldom. It's very seldom worth it.'

She had booked a flight into New York early next day, and sat staring out of the window for much of the five hours, fretful with disappointment and frustration, and at the sense that she had lost Rose as a friend, thinking about her father and how they seemed as far as ever from knowing what had really happened.

She had half expected a message from Morton's on her answering machine, but there was nothing. Well, they were still in the post-Christmas calm, the eye of the storm Mick diMaggio used to call it. God, she missed Mick, she could do with some of his inspiration right now. She was enjoying Morton's, she supposed, but it was tough, and she found – as she had feared right from the beginning – that having one account, one client, was creatively stultifying. Shit, she should have resisted the whole idea. Apart from anything else, it meant – Fleur closed her mind to what it meant apart from anything else, and went for a long walk in Central Park, cooked herself a chilli, and wondered how she was going to fill in the rest of the week she had taken off. She finally decided to go in the next day anyway, and catch up on some admin. They wouldn't be expecting her, she would get some peace. She certainly couldn't face staying in the apartment any longer. And besides it was one of Tina's days and Tina was in a state of intense excitement about Fleur's engagement to Reuben, and talked of little else, when the wedding would be, where it would be, what she was going to wear, how many guests they would have, and whether (Tina's voice would rise in anticipation at this point) Reuben would then be moving in permanently with her.

'It'd be real nice to be running around after a man, Miss Fitz, doing his laundry and clearing up his mess. I like a man's mess. Seems more worthwhile somehow.'

'Well, I certainly don't like it,' said Fleur briskly. 'Any mess around here, and I can tell you, he goes right out the door again.'

'Miss Fitz, you're talking through your face. By the way, what happened to the other one, the English one? Man, was that a sexy man.'

'Tina, I told you a hundred times, he is just a work associate.'

'Yeah, yeah, and I only weigh a hundred pound,' said Tina equably.

She hardly slept, in spite of taking a sleeping pill, and got into Morton's at seven, before anyone else was in. She sorted through the mail and memos on her desk – mostly trash – and reread some copy she'd written on the prospective cosmetic range just before the holiday. Shit, it wasn't good enough. There was no magic to it. The range was coming on nicely, and she was really happy with the packaging Reuben was working on, plain white cartons for the skin care, with splashes of colour to indicate skin type: stinging pink for oily skin, brilliant aquamarine for combination, and what she described as bluebell pink for dry. The cosmetic colours were great too, good strong assertive colours, nothing pastel, even the creams and beiges were sludgy; they had tested them on some volunteer customers and got rave results. But her copy just didn't work. It was meant to be saying 'Here it is, what you always wanted and never could find before', and it was simply saying 'And now here's some Morton's make-up'. She really must pull herself together. What was the matter with her? Six months earlier she'd have sat up all night, rather than turn in crap like this. Mediocre crap. Of all the things Fleur despised, mediocrity came top of the list. Better a good checkout girl than a mediocre copywriter, dancer, actress.

That reminded her of her father: he had been a mediocre actor. Or so everyone said. So Rose had said. No doubt that would be reported in Magnus Phillips's fucking book. Fucking Magnus Phillips and his fucking book. That was largely to blame. She should never have allowed herself to get so involved with him and his book. Well, it was too late now. She had better things to worry about. Like her copy. At least she could see how terrible it was. She decided to rewrite it at once, while the sense of distaste was so strong. She'd just get some coffee – she never could write so much as her own name without a mug of coffee set right by her typewriter – and do it.

She went down the corridor towards the coffee machine – filthy stuff, but at least hot and wet – and found it was empty. She decided to go up to the boardroom kitchen and make herself a proper cup. She was just walking past the studio when she heard Reuben's voice. He was on the phone. She was just going to push the door open and tell him she was back when she heard her name. Fleur was nothing if not pragmatic; she stood listening, holding her breath. There was no way it was going to be a long conversation.

Reuben regarded a telephone call the way most people regarded a visit to the dentist.

'Fleur isn't here, Poppy. She's in LA. What? I don't know. I'm worried about it. She seems so – distant. I have asked her. No. OK. Well maybe. She won't say a date. Won't even discuss it. I don't know why, she just won't. What? Well, I am scared. I can't help it. Look, I have to go. Bye, Poppy. See you tonight.'

He sounded heavy-hearted. Fleur's own heart ached, went out to him. What was the matter with her, that she had this lovely, loving, sexy man who adored her, and she was just pushing him around? It was a terrible thing to do. If she wasn't careful she'd lose him altogether. Fleur carefully and determinedly crushed the thought that she would never lose Reuben, whatever she did to him, and walked very quietly back down the corridor, down the stairs and into her own office. She sat at the desk for a minute, looking out at the still-dim morning. Far below her New York was roaring on its way, cold, noisy, dirty; up here, in the silence of her double-glazed, air-conditioned room, removed from reality, she felt no part of it. It seemed to her to echo her feelings for Reuben. They were there, she knew they were, but they were distant, remote, muffled. Well, she had to work on them. She had to. She loved him and she was going to marry him, and she would be very happy. She was lucky, very lucky. Swiftly, decisively, before she could think about it for another moment, she picked up the phone, dialled his internal number.

'Reuben? It's Fleur. I'm here. What? Here in the office. Can I come up and say hallo? LA was OK. Nothing special. I'll tell you about it later. Now listen, Reuben, just before I got on the plane you said something about March. Would you be good enough to be just a little more explicit, Reuben? I mean did you mean dinner, or the cosmetic launch, or what?'

An hour later, a beaming Sol Morton was opening a magnum of champagne to celebrate the announcement that Fleur FitzPatrick and Reuben Blake were to be married on 24 June, midsummer day, that it could be no sooner than that if the occasion was to receive the attention it deserved, and that he was going to stand in as father of the bride and throw a party they'd never forget at his new duplex on Park Avenue as a wedding present.

Reuben said he was really sorry, but he had to go out that night. He had a meeting with some designers on the cosmetic range, and then he was going to see *Godspell* with Poppy and her husband. 'I thought you'd be away,' he said mournfully. 'I could cancel if you like.'

'Don't be ridiculous,' said Fleur. 'Of course you must go. Those tickets probably cost several arms and legs. Anyway, I have to rewrite some truly terrible copy.'

'Who wrote it?'

'I did.'

'OK,' said Reuben.

* * *

She got home feeling terrible. Her head throbbed, she felt sick, and she was experiencing a sense of rising panic that nothing seemed able to crush. What had she done? What in God's name had she done? Don't think about it, Fleur, just don't think about it. You're a lucky girl, concentrate on that.

She went into her apartment, drank almost a whole bottle of mineral water, and sat down on the couch staring out of the window at Central Park, trying not to think about it. The trouble was the only other thing she could think about was Magnus Phillips, roaring down the Pacific Coast Highway with Rose Sharon.

She was in bed and half asleep when the phone went. She picked it up, sounding groggy.

'Fleur FitzPatrick.'

'Fleur, this is Magnus. I'm in New York. I promised I'd call.'

'You did? I don't remember,' said Fleur, struggling to sound disinterested.

'Yes, I did. You OK?' he said, and his voice was genuinely concerned. 'You sound terrible.'

'I'm fine. Never better.'

'It's early. I'd quite like to see you,' said Magnus Phillips. 'Are you busy?'

'Yes, I'm very busy.'

'Fleur, are you sure you're OK?'

Fleur burst into hysterical tears, told him to fuck off and put the phone down.

Half an hour later her buzzer went. She shouted into the phone and told him to fuck off, and he said he was very good at not fucking off and he wanted to see her. 'I promise I won't stay long. And I have a present for you.'

'I don't want a present.'

'You'll want this one.'

Fleur, with extreme reluctance, pressed the buzzer and, anxious to avoid a repetition of his last visit, dragged on a pair of jeans over her nightshirt.

She felt as she always felt when she was first confronted by Magnus: slightly weakened, as if the huge force of his energy somehow attracted some of hers, drew it off. She forced a smile; there was after all no reason to be hostile to him.

'Hi.'

'Hi.'

'Do you want a drink?'

'What I'd really like,' he said, 'is some –'

'Toast and marmalade. Sure, I'll fix you some. Coffee?'

'Please. So your sexy lady cleaner got me some Cooper's, did she?'

'Yes, she did,' said Fleur, putting it on the kitchen table. 'I tried it, it's horrible. So strong.'

'I like strong-tasting things. I like curry and chilli and pickled onions and very strong lemonade,' he said.

'Me too,' said Fleur. 'Very strong lemonade, anyway.'

'You look tired,' he said.

'No, I'm fine. Well, maybe a bit tired. I got up very early this morning.'

'Couldn't sleep?'

'No,' said Fleur. She was aware he was genuinely concerned for her and smiled at him apologetically. 'Sorry. I do feel really shitty.' She made a huge effort to be more friendly. 'What have you been doing?'

'Oh – talking to your friend Miss Sharon some more.'

'My friend! I would have thought she had become yours,' she said, She had meant to sound light-hearted, amused, and she knew it sounded harsh and hostile.

'And if she had?' Magnus's dark eyes were gently amused.

'Well, fine,' said Fleur. 'I'm delighted for you both.'

'You don't sound delighted.'

'Oh, for God's sake. What am I supposed to do?' she said. 'Congratulate you? Send flowers?' and promptly burst into tears. 'Oh shit,' she said, 'shit, Magnus, you'd better go. I'm sorry, I do feel perfectly awful.'

Magnus stood up and walked out of the kitchen, into the living room, and sat down on the big couch by the window. He patted the seat beside him.

'Here,' he said, 'come and sit down. Tell me what the matter is.'

'Nothing,' said Fleur, sitting down slightly warily beside him.

'I think there is. Come on, tell me. I'm a very good listener.'

'Yes,' she said, her voice tart again, 'so I observed.'

'Oh, Fleur. That was work. That was professional.'

'Oh, really? Like sitting behind her on that fucking bike and telling her every other minute how gorgeous she was?'

'Yes,' he said, quietly. 'Yes it was.'

'Well, good,' said Fleur, and sat feeling very silly.

'Look,' he said, putting his hand into his pocket, 'look what I have for you. Rose sent it.'

'Rose did?'

'Yes she did. She was concerned for you. She said it came with her best love.'

Fleur took the package he handed her. She had been expecting some fancy. Beverly Hills wrapping, and was surprised to see some plain white tissue wrapped round what felt like a frame. She opened it cautiously: it *was* a frame, and the picture in it was of herself, aged about eight or nine, sitting on the beach at Sheepshead Bay with her father beside her, his arm round her. He was smiling, and his head was very close to hers. She was dressed in shorts and a T-shirt, and her hair was very long and blowing in the wind, and she wasn't just smiling as her father was, she was laughing, laughing so wholeheartedly and happily she could almost hear herself.

'Oh,' she said, 'oh, I remember that day, it was my dad's birthday; we had such a good time, we took Grandma and she made us a wonderful picnic, I can even remember what it was, fried chicken and coleslaw, and she brought a birthday cake; we couldn't get the candles to stay alight for even a minute, but he blew them out anyway, and we sang Happy Birthday and he built a sandcastle and he said, "One day, Fleur, we'll have a real castle, you and I." In the evening we went to Coney Island, and we only had enough money for two rides, and I just didn't care.'

'Did you have a friend with you?'

'No, of course not,' said Fleur, surprised he should ask. 'I never wanted a friend, if my dad was there. He was my best best friend.'

'I see.' Magnus looked at her thoughtfully. Then he leant over and took the frame. 'You have to see what's inside.' He took the back off; tucked between the picture and the cardboard that held it in place was a note. In Brendan's writing.

'Fleur, aged nine,' it said. 'The real love of my life. Just so you don't get too complacent. Brendan.'

'Oh, shit,' said Fleur. The words blurred as she looked at them. She wiped her eyes with the back of her hand, and sat staring at herself, at the little girl she had been, the happy little girl, with the father she adored, unthreatened, unhurt, safe, infinitely loved, and she thought of the woman that little girl had become, hurt, angry, toughened, difficult, and she felt a sense of such loss she could hardly bear it. Not just for her father, but for the child that she had been.

'Shit,' she said again, and she turned and looked at Magnus, saw him watching her, tenderly, concerned, and she tried to smile, tried to be brave and she couldn't, just sat there, staring at him, struggling to hold back the great flood of her grief.

'I'm sorry,' he said gently, 'I'm so sorry,' and he took her in his arms, and held her, and suddenly, inexplicably, her pain was gone, her tears magically dried and she lay there, surprised by the fact, soothed, restored to herself, for a long time.

'That was nice of Rose,' she said suddenly, 'really nice.'

'I thought so too,' said Magnus. 'She was most insistent you should have it. She was very upset you left so suddenly.'

'Oh dear,' said Fleur, and then she looked up at him, and grinned and said, sounding and feeling much more herself, 'but I'm sure you were able to console her.'

'I tried,' he said, 'although not quite in the way that perhaps you think.'

'Oh yeah?'

'Oh yeah. She really is not my type.'

'And what is your type?' asked Fleur tartly, sitting up away from him, pushing back her hair. 'You must be very hard to please.'

'I am,' he said lightly, and smiled at her and then suddenly he stopped smiling, and the whole room, and indeed time itself, seemed to freeze: Fleur stared at him, feeling she had never seen him before, or rather as if he had always been out of focus before and now had come clear, sharp, easily read. She felt she was not just discovering him with her eyes, but with all her senses; she was drawn, pulled towards him, she could hear no sounds except his breathing, was aware of no movement except his own eyes, exploring hers. And then very slowly, very carefully, as if afraid of breaking the spell, he reached out and took her hand, picked it up, without looking away, and turned it over and kissed the palm. Gently, tenderly at first, and then slightly harder, his tongue began to move on her hand, feathering over it, then pushing into it, exploring it, first the centre of her palm, and then the fleshy part by her thumb, his tongue becoming harder, more insistent, and it was the most extraordinarily and powerfully sexual thing she had ever known. She put out her other hand and touched his face, very gently, stroking it as he kissed and tongued her hand, and all the violent emotion of the past few days, the frustration, the jealousy, the pain, the remorse over her relationship with Reuben, all centred somewhere deep within her, and then became less emotional, more physical, a great shifting, violent force, and she moved, still without taking her eyes from Magnus, nearer him, nearer, nearer; he lifted his head and stared at her, his expression almost shocked, and without dropping her hand, he leant forward and began to kiss her. His mouth was slow, careful at first: then as it had been on her hand, harder, more erotic; Fleur closed her eyes, moaned gently. They sat there for a long time, kissing, then suddenly he set her back, sat staring at her, looking shocked, almost frightened.

'Dear God,' he said, 'I think I'd better go.'

And Fleur, as shocked as he by her desire for him, by what had so nearly happened, nodded, said, 'Yes, I think so too.'

He stood up and walked over to the door and she followed him, her legs weak, aching, her entire body feeling strange, light, shaken, as if she had just had some terrible shock, and she stood at the door, and said, 'Goodbye, Magnus,' and he said, 'Goodbye, Fleur,' and she shut the door behind him, swiftly, desperately, and leant against it as if he had been some intruder she had managed to evict. As, indeed, she supposed he was.

Chapter 33

January – February 1972

Chloe's first thought was that she must have died. Her second was of thankfulness that she had done so. Then she realized that she was in considerable pain, that she had a drip in her arm, and that standing at the foot of her high hospital bed was Joe, looking at her with an expression of great tenderness and concern. Her mouth was very dry; she licked her lips, tried to smile.

Joe went forward, handed her a glass of water. She took a sip with an enormous effort and then lay back on her pillows, exhausted.

'Sorry to sound corny, but where am I?'

'In the London Clinic. They said I could visit you for a minute. Piers is on his way. He should be here in a few hours. How do you feel?'

'Terrible,' said Chloe, and then she remembered everything suddenly, and turned her head away from him, and started to cry.

'Chloe, darling, don't cry. Please. It won't help. Try not to. It may be all right still.'

'What?' said Chloe stupidly.

'The baby. They may still be able to save it.'

'Oh, God,' said Chloe and cried weakly on.

Joe sat on the bed, carefully, took her hand. 'Honeybunch, don't. Hang on.' He managed a smile. 'The nurse will send me away if you cry.'

'Oh, Joe,' said Chloe, 'oh, Joe, if only you knew. There is so much to cry about. So much. Oh, God, this hurts.' She managed a feeble smile of her own. 'Poor Joe. You're always with me in some awful gynae situation, aren't you? Childbirth, miscarriage . . .'

'Shall I get someone?'

'No. No, it's all right. I think – yes, Joe, please do. Please.'

He rang the bell; she hung on to his hand. Waves of pain going through her, sharper, harder, more raw than anything she could remember of childbirth: awful, dead, hopeless pain. Joe was banished; a doctor came, examined her, injected her with something, asked her if the pains had any kind of pattern. Chloe shook her head through clenched teeth. The drug took effect, the pain receded, became at least duller.

'I'll get someone to sit with you,' he said.

'Am I going to lose the baby?'

'I – don't know. Of course we hope not. But it seems – possible. I'm so sorry. So very sorry.'

'Is Mr Simmonds coming? He might . . .' Her voice tailed away. What was the point anyway? Of anything Mr Simmonds might do.

'Mrs Windsor, he's away. But your husband will be here. In a few hours.'

'Oh God,' said Chloe, her voice rising in panic, realizing the implications of this, 'you mustn't tell him. You must not tell him.'

'All right,' he said soothingly, and she could tell he thought she was simply a foolish, hysterical woman. 'All right, Mrs Windsor, we won't tell him anything you don't want us to.'

'No, really, you mustn't. He mustn't know. He didn't – oh, God –' The pain seemed to be winning its battle against the drug; it was rising again. It was very bad.

'Try to rest. It's all you can do. For the baby's sake.'

She lay back, trying to be calm, to distract herself, remembering, remembering, like some terrible horror movie, the events of the day – or was it the day before – playing and replaying in front of her eyes.

The endless wait while International Directory looked for a number in Santa Barbara for Zwirn. 'Would that be B. Zwirm, ma'am?'

'I don't think so, no – G. For Gerard.'

'Nothing under that name, ma'am. Just B. Zwirm, with an "m", that's a store, in Salinas Street, and then a Stanley Zwirne, with an "e". I could give you those, ma'am, if that would be helpful.'

'No,' said Chloe. 'No, it's all right. They aren't what I'm looking for.'

She slammed the phone down, sat looking at it, impotent tears stinging at the back of her eyes.

God, who were these people, sent like demons to haunt her? Where were they that they were not listed in the phone directory? And who, what were they to Piers that he sent them a thousand dollars every month, and she had never ever heard of them? What had they got on him, what had he done? Should she ring him, confront him? Would that be better? But no, he wouldn't tell her, and besides, she wanted the truth, not some carefully contorted lie.

She remembered suddenly the bottom drawer, the locked bottom drawer that she had so blithely assumed to contain such innocent things as bank statements and birth certificates. That must, surely, contain a clue. That was what she needed. She ran down to Piers's study, pulling, tugging, kicking the drawer; it remained stubbornly, defiantly locked.

Well, it was going to be opened. It had to be opened. Who could open a lock? A locksmith. Yes, that was what she needed, a locksmith. But how did you find a locksmith?

'Rosemary,' she called to the nanny, 'Rosemary, I need a locksmith. Can you think how we can find one?'

'Yellow Pages?' said Rosemary.

'Yellow Pages. Of course. Wonderful Yellow Pages. Thank you, Rosemary.'

She could tell from Rosemary's face that she thought she must have been drinking.

'Should I go to the hospital, Mrs Windsor? To be with Ned?'

'What? Oh, no, Rosemary, it's fine. I need you here for Kitty. I'll be going back myself later.'

Locksmiths, locksmiths. God, there were dozens. Better get a local one, otherwise it would take days. Like – yes, like James and James, Locksmiths, New Kings Road. They would do.

James and James were unable to help. They only did business locks. Could they suggest Faulkners, Lower Sloane Street? Faulkners said they could come in the morning. Around eleven. They were extremely sorry, but they had a long list of calls to make.

Fuck, said Chloe most uncharacteristically and went back to Yellow Pages. Dysart in the Fulham Road. They sounded nice and hardworking. Dysart were all out. Finally, three calls later, a nice-sounding lady called Mrs Adams said she would tell Mr Adams the minute he came in that it was an emergency and she was sure he'd do what he could.

Mr Adams rang about twenty minutes later. He said he'd have his tea and then come right over.

'Tea?' said Chloe stupidly. 'Tea? What time is it?'

'Nearly five thirty, madam.'

'Good Lord,' she said, genuinely amazed. 'I thought it was lunchtime.'

'Time flies,' said Mr Adams conversationally, 'when you're having fun.'

He arrived just before seven, full of apologies. Chloe had in the intervening period drunk half a bottle of Piers's finest claret. It was the only way she felt she could take revenge on him at that particular time. Later she would think of something else.

'Mr Adams,' she said, 'how kind. It's this drawer, you see. One of the children has thrown the key away and I've locked something absolutely crucial in it, my birth certificate actually, and my passport has expired, and I have to renew it immediately, because my husband wants me to join him in Jamaica and –' She stopped talking; Mr Adams was clearly not interested in her story. 'Would you like a drink, Mr Adams? It is after opening time.'

'Well, now,' he said, fiddling with his tools, 'I don't mind if I do. As it's after opening time. Port and lemon is my drink, madam. If that would be at all possible. Otherwise a small sherry.'

There was no port, so Chloe poured a large glass of the claret; she couldn't find any lemons, so she added a tablespoonful of Jif Instant Lemon. The thought of what Piers would say if he knew made her feel more hysterical still.

'Thank you, madam. Now this is difficult. A double lock. Not easy. But never fear. Adams is here. That is our company motto, madam. Now then, I think a little easing here – and here – and – yes, there we go. Open. Good. My word, this is nice port, madam.'

'I'm so pleased you like it. Er – how much do I owe you for that?'

'Oh, shall we say five pounds? And could I take just a little more lemon?'

'Of course,' said Chloe.

* * *

The drink had been a mistake; Mr Adams became garrulous and started telling her about Locks I Have Opened. The owners of the locks included a famous actress, a racehorse owner and a member of the nobility, none of whom were clearly safe on the streets, in Mr Adam's opinion. 'I did think, madam, a man who could lock his own gun away was not to be trusted.'

Chloe rather rashly said she thought a man who locked his gun away was more to be trusted than one who didn't, and Mr Adams said he'd never thought of that, but she certainly had a point; after a while Chloe opened a second bottle of the St Emilion Grand Cru, 1961, and poured them each a glass of that and added the Jif to Mr Adams's glass. Mr Adams said it was very nice, although not quite Beaujolais standard, and finally at eight thirty the phone rang and it was Mrs Adams, wondering what had happened to him.

'Just having a quick one with the lady,' said Mr Adams, firmly, 'and then I'll be on my way. Women never understand the importance of business entertaining,' he said confidingly to Chloe, who, suddenly afraid of him leaving, of being forced to open the drawer, the terrible crawling, obscene can of worms, eager to detain Mr Adams, to postpone the moment, said that was quite true, she never really understood it herself, and Mr Adams explained the importance of business entertaining at some length, so that by the time he finally wove rather unsteadily down the steps it was after nine. Chloe, suddenly and horribly alone, took hold of all the courage she possessed and sat down and started working her way through the drawer.

It was the usual mess, inside the drawer. Letters to Piers from his mother, from the Montagues, his army papers, old photographs from the RADA days, some pictures of her, a great many of Pandora, old programmes, yellowing cuttings and reviews. Chloe tore through them all carelessly, ripping some of them, unfolding them, pushing them back again, breathing hard, so hard that every now and again she had to sit back and consciously try to relax. Nothing, nothing, it seemed. No reason to lock the drawer. Just another example of Piers's extraordinary secretiveness, it seemed; unnecessary, tantalizing secretiveness. She rummaged harder, half sobbing now under her breath, her eyes blurred with tears; no, nothing. Nothing at all. And then she saw it: a brown envelope, newer than the rest, stuffed inside another one filled with old school photographs. It reminded her of another occasion her life had been shattered by a search through old photographs and she stopped briefly, remembering that hurt, that pain, wondering if she should put it all back again, walk away, wipe it from her mind, tell herself that yes, Gerard Zwirn must be a drama studio, a theatre workshop, forget the whole thing. But she couldn't; it wasn't possible, and, watching her hands trembling, she opened the envelope.

Bank statements: the only ones she had ever seen Piers file, bank statements from the year 1957, a dollar account with his own bank, a standing order made out in favour of G. Zwirn, in a bank first at Playa del Rey, and then at Santa Barbara; a regular amount, only two hundred and fifty dollars initially, then slowly mounting over the years to the current sum of one thousand dollars. Payments into the account erratic, sometimes quite small, inadequate, but just about levelling up, every time: every so often a very large one, three or four thousand dollars, one huge one in 1964, for twenty thousand dollars, and then back to the regular amounts. Chloe sat staring at them, trying to make some kind of sense: blackmail, she thought, it had to be, this Gerard Zwirn was blackmailing Piers; he must have something on him, had done for years, before she had even known him. She could imagine with horrible clarity what it might be. As she sat there, reading them over and over again, and then rather half-heartedly tidying the drawer, refolding the papers, replacing the photographs, she suddenly remembered with a thud of horror that she had left Ned in the hospital many hours earlier, that he would be wanting her, calling for her, and she stood up, dazed, not only with shock but with the bottle or more of wine she had drunk. Well, it was just as well, she thought, that she felt dazed, otherwise she would be feeling a great deal worse. She ran down the stairs, scribbled a note to Rosemary, grabbed her keys and went out to the car.

Halfway down Knightsbridge, she suddenly felt sober, horribly, hideously sober. Tears rose from somewhere deep within her, and started coursing down her face; something seemed to be stifling her, it was hard to breathe. She tried not to panic, dashed the tears impatiently from her eyes, took deep breaths. She knew really she should stop, but the thought of little Ned, crying for her, wanting her, made it impossible. She had neglected him all day and the very least she could do was go to him now. She would calm down, sober up, and then she would be able to think what to do. But she needed help, advice. And suddenly she thought of Ludovic. He would know what to do, he would help her, comfort her. She suddenly, more than anything in the world, longed to hear his voice; she saw a phone box by the road, halfway along Piccadilly, and felt a rush of relief. She would ring him, tell him to come and see her, maybe he could even come to the hospital to pick her up. Or just sit with her. She needed him so badly, so very badly. She pulled in sharply towards the phone box, and as she did so, heard a terrible noise, several terrible noises, a blaring of car horns, a screeching of brakes, a loud bang and then a deathly silence, broken only by a human scream, going on and on. It was only much later when she awoke in hospital, and was able to recall at least some of the accident, that she realized the human screaming had been herself.

By some miracle no one else had been hurt, although three cars had been damaged. She was hurt quite badly: concussed, a broken wrist, a knee cut through almost to the bone – and clearly, from the knives of pain running through her almost constantly, a threatened miscarriage. But no one else had even been scratched. The police told her that, sternly but kindly, as they sat with her waiting for the ambulance while she swam in and out of consciousness. They didn't ask her if she had been drinking. She presumed they could tell that for themselves.

Chloe supposed she had known she would lose the baby. Nevertheless when the pain grew so bad she was crying out, and she was bleeding so much they started talking about transfusions and when finally the doctor came and said they were taking her down to theatre, that there was nothing, nothing else at all that they could do, she turned her head into the pillow and wept endlessly, bitterly for the loss of her baby: Ludovic's baby: her hope for, and her stake in, the future.

'So I'm afraid she's lost the baby. I'm terribly sorry. She's lost a lot of blood and she's very shocked. But the concussion is not serious, nor the broken wrist, and she's young and strong. There should be no lasting damage.'

The young doctor looked at Piers slightly nervously. He was white under his extremely expensive-looking tan, and the muscles in his face were taut with fear and – what? Outrage? Rage?

Piers said nothing. He just sat there, staring at him. Then he said, 'Can I see her?'

'You can, but she's very heavily sedated. She's only been up from theatre for an hour or so. And she's very shocked. I would urge you not to tire her in any way.'

'Of course I'm not going to tire her,' said Piers. 'What do you think I'm going to do, drag her out of bed and start playing charades?'

'Of course not,' said the doctor, keeping his face straight with an effort (and was that right, he wondered, was the great actor trying to be funny – being funny even?). 'But very often relatives make emotional demands, even while they're being sympathetic. Above all, don't question her. She really isn't up to it.'

'I am not going to question her,' said Piers, speaking quietly with what was obviously a great effort. 'I just want to see her. That's all.'

'Fine. Come with me.'

Chloe kept surfacing to consciousness and drifting under it again. The drifting was nice, an easing of pain, of misery; the surfacing was horrible, a nightmare of fear. Any moment now Piers would arrive and if she wasn't careful the doctor would tell him she had had a miscarriage. Even Piers would know there was no way she had become pregnant by him. He would want to know how it had happened. And then he would go home and find the ransacked desk, the forced-open drawer. Every time she thought about that, and what the drawer had contained, she began to cry weakly; then a nurse would come, stroke her forehead, sponge her hot face, and she would drift off again. And Ludovic: he would hear about it, he would discover she had had a baby, would know it was his baby, a baby he had never known about, that she had been too much of a coward to tell him about. Ludovic, who wanted children more than anything in the world; Ludovic, who would be as hurt, maybe more hurt even than Piers. God, how had she got into this mess? How was she ever going to get out of it?

'Chloe, hallo, darling.' It was Piers; he looked nothing but tenderly, gently concerned. She was amazed how good it was to see him; she reached out her hand and took his.

'Piers. Hallo. I'm sorry to spoil your holiday. How was it?'

'Wonderful. Thank you. How are you?'

'Oh – you know. A bit sore. I hit my head, cut my knee. That's why they put this stupid drip in.' She closed her eyes, trying to smile, exhausted by the long speech.

Piers was silent; a long time later, from a far distant place, she heard him say, 'Chloe, it's all right. They told me. About the baby.'

Chloe opened her eyes; he was looking at her without anger, just a terrible sadness. She closed her eyes again, very tightly, to blot this awful vision out.

'Piers,' she said weakly, summoning the last of her strength, 'Piers, you have to tell me something. Who is Gerard Zwirn?'

She forced herself to look at him again, and watched his eyes darken with shock, with horror almost, saw him turn first waxy pale, and then flush, a dark flush, rising to his hairline.

Then the nurse came in and told Piers it was time he left, and he bent and kissed her and said, 'I'll leave you to sleep. Don't worry about anything.'

And then he was gone.

'Piers, this is Ludovic. Thank God you're back. I've been so worried about Chloe and you know what they're like in these places, won't tell you anything. How is she?'

'Not very well.' Piers's voice was infintely weary, dark, heavy. 'Oh, she'll be all right. But she's not very well at the moment.' There was a pause, then he said, 'She's concussed and shocked, and oh, yes, she's had a miscarriage.'

'A – a miscarriage?'

'Yes, I'm afraid so. Oh, we hadn't told anyone, it was early days. But – there it is. Always sad. Anyway, she's coming out in a day or two. Then I'm sure she'll be pleased to see you.'

'Yes, sure. I'll – phone.'

Ludovic put the phone down, and sat staring at it for a long time. Then he told his secretary not to put any calls through, laid his head on his arms and for the first time since his mother had left him at his prep school, he wept.

Magnus Phillips was feeling contented: a somewhat rare state of affairs. *The Tinsel Underneath* was in the pleasant honeymoon period, the early chapters, when it was apparently writing itself, something which he knew would swiftly change to it refusing to be written at all, but which was pleasant while it lasted; he had received in his morning mail a very large royalty cheque for *Dancers* which was still selling fast in America, and he had had a very good dinner with Richard Beauman at the Stafford Hotel, at which Richard had outlined some rather satisfying promotional plans for *The Tinsel Underneath*.

'I thought we'd use posters: countrywide, and particularly cross-track ones on the Underground, with an excerpt from a particularly tantalizing chapter. It'll get them reading it and then the train'll come and interrupt and they'll want to go and buy it. Plus the usual space in magazines and newspaper, and I thought possibly a radio campaign on a few of the commercial stations. Capital in particular. That's a very interesting news media. You can really grab the imagination.'

'Sounds good,' said Magnus.

'I suppose the book's almost finished,' said Beauman casually.

'Almost,' said Magnus.

The minute he opened his front door, he could sense something was wrong. The house felt cold for a start; and he always kept it very warm. The kitchen door which he always kept open was closed; and the radio which he always left playing quietly upstairs when he went out was off. He shut the door quietly, put down the rather large briefcase he was carrying, and pushed open the kitchen door gently. It was empty, quite quiet – and in chaos. Every drawer, every cupboard had been ransacked. The oven door was open, and so was the fridge. There was food on the floor, where it had been pulled out. He turned and went into his study: worse. Nothing had been left. His desk drawers, his files, his interview tapes, his notebooks, all thrown on the floor. His typewriter turned over; his books pulled off the shelves, even his leather chair had its seat slashed. The same scene of horror continued upstairs. Every room had been turned over. In the bedrooms, the carpets had been torn up. Magnus walked through the house, slowly, surveying the damage, occasionally pausing to right an upturned lamp, to replace an ornament. Finally he went back down to the study, lifted the phone and called the police.

'You seem very calm, sir,' said the sergeant, handing his report to Magnus to sign.

'I feel very calm,' said Magnus, smiling at him cheerfully. 'They didn't take the one thing that mattered, and the damage is minimal.'

'Really, sir? What would that have been?'

'Oh – something I've been working on for a long time.'

'Would that have been very serious, sir?'

'Very serious.'

'Very valuable to you, I suppose, sir, but maybe not to anyone else.'

'No, that's probably right, Sergeant.'

'So where was this, sir?'

'Oh,' said Magnus, 'I had it with me. All of it. It's in that briefcase over there, as a matter of fact. Never go out without it. Even to do my shopping.'

'Very wise, sir.'

He could see the sergeant thought he was completely mad. He thought by the time *The Tinsel Underneath* was published he probably would be.

'Piers,' said Chloe, trying to keep her voice calm, 'Piers, we have to talk.'

'I'm sorry, darling, I really can't. Not now. Late already. See you tonight, darling. I'll be late again, I'm afraid. Goodbye, my darling Pandora. Bye, Kitty and Ned. Have a nice day, take care.'

He bent and kissed Chloe gently and left, closing the front door quietly. Chloe stared after him, wondering how much longer she could stand it.

She had been home for a week now; a sad, lonely week. She was still frail, still subject to severe headaches, still unable to drive or indeed do more than hobble about the house. She could never remember being so unhappy.

Ludovic had written to her: a cold, hurt little note. He said he couldn't quite understand her behaviour, but he felt that if she could be so secretive about such a matter, it did not bode well for their future together. He said he hoped she would soon be feeling better and he wished her well. He signed the note simply 'Ludovic'.

Chloe phoned him the moment she had read it. His secretary was polite and said Mr Ingram was in conference with a client, and she would certainly pass the message on. Ludovic did not ring. It was inconceivable that he could not have got the message, but Chloe tried once more, just in case. His secretary assured her that she had given the message to Ludovic personally.

She tried him at home: left two messages on his answering machine which he left permanently on. The first message was calm and asked him to ring her: the second was desperate and begged him. Ludovic ignored them both.

Chloe wrote a letter, pages of explanation, about her panic, her terror of upsetting Piers, always so dangerously emotional, her obsession with getting the right moment, her fear that if Ludovic had known about the baby he would just arrive at the house and tell Piers himself, and God knew what Piers would do after that. She said she missed Ludovic, she loved him, she had things she was desperate to talk to him about: she begged him to contact her. Ludovic ignored the letter.

Chloe lost hope.

But what she did have to do, she felt, was set matters straight with Piers. She could not go on with this thing between them, this terrible, unacknowledged, desperately important thing. He must know she knew; he must have found the unlocked drawer, would probably have heard from Mr Lewis at the bank about his conversation with her. And yet he had initially refused to discuss it, went on, day after day, treating her courteously, considerately, affectionately even. He never mentioned the miscarriage either. Chloe was baffled. After the first few days, when she was beginning to feel better, he left for Stratford, where *Othello* was to be staged, and stayed down there most of the time, rehearsing from early in the morning until late at night, putting in a call to her to make sure she was all right at some time every day, but no more. When he did come home, usually on Sundays, he slept in his small dressing room. That first Sunday she had made him sit down, told him she had to talk to him, had to know about Gerard Zwirn.

'I don't want to tell you,' he had said, 'I really don't want to talk about it. It's nothing to do with you.'

'But Piers, it is. I'm your wife.'

'I know,' he said, and his eyes were very sad as he looked at her. 'I know you are.'

'Well then. It is something to do with me. You're paying him a great deal of money, you clearly have done for years. Piers, I have a right to know why.'

He was silent.

'Piers,' she said, fighting to keep calm, 'Piers, please. What is it? Is he blackmailing you or something? I have to know.'

And then he stood up and said, 'Chloe, I'm sorry, but I don't want to talk about it. No, he isn't blackmailing me, and there is nothing wrong going on. I swear to that. He's a colleague from the past, who needed my help. That's all. You don't have to worry about it. Now please accept that.'

'But Piers, it's so much money, such a huge commitment. Surely –'

'Chloe,' said Piers, sounding angry suddenly, in the terrible controlled way he sometimes did, 'Chloe, can we leave this please. I don't want to discuss it. I'm sorry.'

Chloe gave up. She told herself she was only giving up until she felt better, stronger, but she could see that unless she went out to Santa Barbara herself, she was not going to find out the truth. And she lay awake, night after night, tossing her aching head restlessly, desperately from side to side, telling herself, trying to believe, that what Piers said was true, that there was nothing wrong, nothing sinister, and failing absolutely. The other thing that haunted her, baffled her, was why he had made absolutely no attempt to discuss the miscarriage, the baby, to find out who had fathered it. But he didn't seem to want to do any such thing. And as the days turned to weeks, and February dragged on towards March, she realized that this was how it was going to be. He wasn't going to talk and he wasn't going to listen. He was safe, inside his shell, seeing no evil, hearing no evil, and he wanted to keep it that way. And there was nothing she could do about it. Absolutely nothing at all.

Henry Chancellor looked at Magnus Phillips across the room he rather affectedly called his study, and tried to keep calm.

'Now look,' he said, 'you're obviously getting cold feet about this. I can understand it. One slip and you're dead. All that. I know. It's scary. But of course you must go on. Otherwise . . .' He paused ominously.

'Yes, sure, I know, otherwise you'll lose an awful lot of money. And an awful lot of face.'

'Magnus, it's you who will be losing both those commodities. Far more than I.'

'How much?' said Magnus briefly.

'Well, for a start, you will have to return your advance.'

Magnus shrugged. 'I've only had the first tranche. Haven't touched it. Beauman could have it back tomorrow.'

'There are also the serial rights.'

'Nothing signed or sold yet. Unless you've been holding out on me.'

'No, of course not. But the Americans are snapping hard at Beauman's bait. He'd be a very angry man. He's staked a lot of his reputation on this. Especially considering not a word's been seen yet. And then there are the tabloids. Same thing there. I would say Beauman's got a good case for suing you for loss of profits. Given the figures on your last book, I'd put the figure at at least a quarter of a million. I really wouldn't do it, Magnus.'

Magnus looked at him for a long time. 'My house was broken into the other night,' he said.

Chancellor stared at him. 'Did – did they take much?' he said.

'Nothing valuable. I had what I think they were looking for with me.'

'Magnus, you're crazy. The thing isn't that hot.'

'It could be,' said Magnus.

Henry went very white. 'Are you saying –?'

'I'm saying that someone might be very anxious to know what's in it. That's all.'

'Oh, that's ridiculous,' said Henry.

'Yes, I expect it is.'

'Did you tell the police?' said Chancellor.

'Of course. They weren't much help.'

'Jesus, Magnus. This is – well, getting out of hand.'

'It does seem as if it might,' said Magnus.

'Have you any idea who did it?'

'A few, yes. Don't worry, Henry, I have it with me. All the time. You won't lose your rather warm property.'

'Magnus, I'm sorry. I didn't realize – I'd have been more sympathetic if I had. So – are you really serious about this? Do you really want to pull out?'

Magnus gave him his most intense look. He was silent for a long time. He could see Henry begin to sweat.

'No,' he said finally. 'No, I don't really. Rather the reverse, I think. It could get even more exciting. I was just – testing. Just thinking. You're right though. It is scary.'

'Magnus, I wish you'd finish the bloody thing. Then we could have the lawyers look at it, put them to work. You're scaring me now.'

'Henry, I keep telling you. I can't finish it. There's still one piece left to go. It's the piece that will let us all sleep nights. Just be patient, old chap.'

'And where is this final piece to come from, Magnus? Any ideas?'

'Yes. Little place called California. I have to get back there one more time. Then I can really start writing.'

'Start? For Christ's sake, Magnus, it's nearly the end of January. We have to deliver in July.'

'We will, old son, we will. Long before then. This thing is going to fly out of the typewriter. Have faith.'

'That's what they used to tell the early martyrs too,' said Henry Chancellor gloomily. 'Look, Magnus, if you're seriously worried –'

'I'm not seriously worried,' said Magnus. He grinned at Henry. 'I'm just shitting myself, Henry. That's all.'

Three days later Henry Chancellor's offices were broken into as well.

Chapter 34

February – March 1972

Writing and publishing a book, Magnus Phillips was fond of saying, was rather like the act of sex and procreation. There was the early, tantalizing pleasure as an idea was floated, researched, agreed upon; a growing and intense excitement, accompanied by huge effort, as the book was written; and then after the heady, sweaty climax of completion, a race to survive, to reach the safe haven of the reviewers' approval, the booksellers' welcome, the public's esteem. After that, he would say, pouring himself another brandy, beaming round the dinner table, if you were very lucky, your progeny, because of some very special quality all of its own, grew, flourished, blossomed into something special, charismatic, brilliant, something fashionable, indeed essential, took on a life all of its own, and became independent, vital, and needed you no more. This was certainly the case for *The Tinsel Underneath*: not a word of it had yet been read, apart from a brief synopsis, a few compulsive paragraphs on the jacket proof, the early press releases, and still fewer (and still more compulsive) ones in the advertising campaign: nobody knew quite what it was going to be about (save that it contained the irresistible combination of scandal and famous names) and nobody even knew quite which and how many famous names were to be in it. And yet the excitement about it, initially contained in the publishing world, moving out into the chattering classes, and then a more general public, via the media, newspaper stories, magazine articles, interviews on the late-night, highbrow chat shows, was already intense.

Richard Beauman had been heard to say, in slightly baffled tones, a pleased smile none the less on his naturally rather lugubrious face, that he had as yet made very little effort to publicize the book, and yet it had gathered reputation with incredible speed, a small glittering snowflake swiftly become a rolling avalanche. The fame had spread far beyond the boundaries of London and its theatrical and media circles: there was by that spring of 1972 a huge and hungry audience greedy for this story of the great and the good and the not so good, spanning as it did London, New York and Los Angeles, the three most charismatic cities in the world. And in one of those cities, one of the people most intimately concerned with the book, most impatient for its publication, tried to distract herself from thoughts of both it and its author with the preparations for her forthcoming wedding.

Fleur had never taken drugs, but she felt she knew now what it must be like, to be obsessed with something, to crave it so desperately you would risk anything, do anything to get it. Only her drug was not cocaine or marijuana, it was Magnus Phillips and he occupied her thoughts and indeed her feelings and evoked certain physical sensations every time she allowed the thoughts to extend beyond the most fleeting variety in a way that threatened to entirely take over her life.

Only that was ridiculous, because he did not love her, and she did not love him, and in time, without doubt, she would forget about it, and him, and be able to commit herself entirely, one hundred per cent, to dear Reuben who loved her and who of course she loved, and indeed was going to marry in considerable style in only a very few months. She watched herself in some amazement trying on dresses, choosing dresses for the small female Steinbergs who were to be her attendants, buying shoes, gloves, a hat ('I'm sorry, Reuben, but I am not going to be one of those sentimental brides.' 'Fine,' said Reuben cheerfully), talking to caterers, discussing with Sylvia Morton – who had cast herself as much mother of the bride as Sol had become father – such fine points as flowers, waitresses, speeches; she heard herself choosing hymns, readings, music with Father Donahue at the Catholic church on Columbus, where she had occasionally gone to Confession (like most Catholics, Fleur set huge store by Confession, feeling cleansed, forgiven and able to start all over again once she had left the Confessional), and where she was now to be married. And she heard herself with equal detachment telling Reuben she loved him, that she was looking forward to becoming Mrs Blake, watched herself looking over apartments with him, larger, made-for-two apartments, while all the time thinking hour on hour almost exclusively about Magnus Phillips, when she might see him again, and what might happen when she did. Only mercifully for her, her sanity and her future as a respectable matron, Magnus was in London, locked away in his house in Thurloe Square, writing eighteen hours a day, and not answering letters, the telephone, or even the door bell.

One morning in late March, as she wrestled over the copy for her cosmetic range – finally taking off, under the headline 'Just the face for Just the clothes. Just Morton's' – her phone rang. It was Bernard Stobbs.

'Fleur, my dear, I'm having a little party tomorrow night. One of my new books. I wondered if you'd like to come? I'm sorry it's such short notice, but I suddenly remembered you, and I thought it would be a nice excuse to see you again.'

'Bernard, I'd love to,' said Fleur, startling herself with the yearning in her voice, 'I really really would. Thank you.'

'Good. Just here, in the boardroom, six o'clock.'

'I might be a tiny bit late,' said Fleur, remembering she and Sylvia Morton were going to look at hats for Sylvia. God, this wedding was turning into a nightmare. Why on earth hadn't she and Reuben just run away together and got married? Because I never would have gone, she thought sadly, and then crushed the thought ruthlessly. There was no future in that. She had been worried at first that Sol would complain about her frequent absences from the office, but he seemed to be as excited about the wedding plans as his own business.

'You take as much time off as you want,' he had said to Fleur, patting her shoulder. 'It's doing Sylvia far more good than that poxy therapist she sees three times a week. She's always wanted a daughter and here you are. Ready grown, and getting married.'

'All right,' said Fleur with a sigh, removing his hand from where it was making its usual journey down towards her breast. She wasn't sure that she quite liked her wedding to be seen as an alternative to Sylvia Morton's psychotherapy, but like everything else that was happening to her at the moment, it seemed to be entirely out of her control.

After three hours of trying and rejecting hats, as being too small, too big, too fancy, too plain, she and Sylvia had a cup of tea at the Plaza, and Sylvia ate two profiteroles and a cream meringue. Sylvia was addicted to cakes and Fleur had had some problem persuading her not to have twice as many at the reception as everything else. She actually looked rather like a cream meringue herself, thought Fleur, looking at her: she was small and sweetly plump, with fluffy blonde hair, and a great fondness for lace and ribbons and glittery jewellery. Fleur had grown first to like and then to love her as she got to know her; she was permanently smiling, good-natured, generous and regarded Sol as some kind of tiresome small boy she had adopted too late to affect his behaviour in any way.

'He just can't help it,' she had said to Fleur as they discussed what she called Sol's hand problem one day. 'Show him a thigh or a bust, and he's on to it.'

'Don't you mind?' said Fleur wonderingly.

'Only if it's mine,' said Sylvia and went into peals of laughter.

She arrived at Stobbs when the party was at its peak: three glasses of champagne down every throat, the air thick with kisses, journalists assuring publishers of impossible numbers of column inches, publishers assuring authors of impossible numbers of copies already sold, booksellers assuring publishers of impossible amounts of shelf and floor space, agents assuring publishers of impossible bounty in their authors' next books; Fleur stood in the corner, surveying the scene, enjoying it, sipping a glass of Kir Royale thoughtfully, wondering who she might talk to, when a bumptious young man called Adam Coleman, reviewer for the *New York Times*, and deeply in love with his own way with words, came up to her.

'Fleur FitzPatrick! Good to see you. Haven't seen you at one of these things for months.'

'No, well, I'm not involved with Stobbs's advertising any more. Sadly,' said Fleur.

'It is sad. For all of us. What do you think of the book?'

'I think it's gorgeous,' said Fleur truthfully. It was an aerial picture-book of the States; it would undoubtedly cover enough coffee tables to reach from Park Avenue to the Midwest in a very few months.

'Me too. I'm reviewing it the week after next. I don't usually review these picture-books, as you know, but the text is charming, don't you think? Somehow musical.'

Fleur said yes, very charming, admired a couple of his more recent and florid reviews (she still read the book reviews out of habit) and asked him, her voice as casual as she could make it, her eyes widely fascinated, which books he thought would make it really big that year. She could hardly have pleased Adam Coleman more, she thought, if she had started telling him he had the biggest cock in New York.

'Well, now that's a tough one. I guess *The Breast*, that's by Philip Roth, obviously the Solzhenitsyn, there's a brilliant new satirical novel called *The Stepford Wives*, but I guess the big one, the blockbuster is that English book, *The Tinsel Underneath*. That is one book that cannot fail. Take it from me, Fleur.'

'Oh really?' said Fleur. 'Why do you say that, Adam?'

'It has just about everything. Scandal, sex – of all kinds – theatre gossip, Hollywood gossip. And of course Magnus Phillips is a very good writer. In his own rather tabloid genre. It's not for me, naturally, but, boy, will it sell.'

'You seem to know a lot about it,' said Fleur. 'Have you read it?'

'Well, not all of it, of course. Quite a considerable amount though. All fascinating stuff.'

'Really?' said Fleur, who knew perfectly well he couldn't have read any of it. 'Tell me more.'

'Oh' – Coleman tapped the side of his nose – 'can't give secrets away.'

'Of course not. When's it coming out?'

'October. On both sides of the Atlantic.'

'And what did you mean by sex of all kinds?'

'Now really, Fleur. You're a big girl. You can imagine perfectly well what kinds.'

'But I thought it was about the fearsomely respectable and conventional Piers Windsor. Mr Hamlet himself.'

'Well, we're in for some surprises about Mr Windsor, I gather. And a great many others. From all corners east and west of Hollywood. Not to mention society scandals, love children –'

'Love children?' said Fleur sharply. It was the first time she had come up against the hard fact that she would be within the pages of this book: knowing it was one thing, savouring it, even the embarrassment it would cause Caroline and Chloe, but confronting it was quite another, realizing that people like Sol, Mick diMaggio and Nigel Silk, the Steinbergs, Baz Browne, even dear Bernard Stobbs would all be reading about her. Her and her father. She suddenly felt slightly queasy. And Reuben. Dear God, why had she not thought of that before? Well, she had, of course: but not the effect it might have on him, the way he might regard her and her involvement in the whole project. She must sit him down, have a long talk with him about it very soon.

'Yes. Some long-buried scandals apparently. And then lots of wonderful stuff about Hollywood queens. Whoring their way around the studios. Brilliantly sordid, I believe.'

'I see,' said Fleur. 'Well, it's been nice talking to you, Adam. I must go and see Bernard, I've hardly spoken to him this evening.'

'Of course. Mary! How lovely to see you. I loved your book. Did you see my review in the *New Yorker*? I thought I'd touched on a couple of points the others had all missed . . .'

Fleur went out to the Ladies and sat on a toilet seat, leaning her aching head against the wall. She felt suddenly very frightened.

She couldn't sleep; at two in the morning, she put a call in to Magnus. It would be seven in England: he would be up. She got the answering machine. Where was the bastard? She knew he was there.

'Magnus, this is Fleur,' she said. 'I have to speak to you urgently. Please call me just as soon as you can.'

He rang back within five minutes. He sounded impatient.

'Yes, Fleur, what is it?'

'Magnus, I just went to a party.'

'Well, that was nice for you. Have you dragged me from my bath to tell me that?'

'Sorry,' said Fleur, hauling her imagination with great difficulty from the image of Magnus in the bath.

'That's OK. I'd been there too long anyway. Anyone interesting there?'

'Yes. Plenty. A reviewer in particular called Adam Coleman. He said you were – what was it – a very good writer, in your own rather tabloid genre.'

'How kind. I must remember to give him a kiss when I see him.'

'Talking of kissing –'

'Yes, Fleur?'

His voice had changed; become deeper, more intimate. She flushed.

'Kissing other men,' she said firmly, gripping the telephone. 'Magnus, Adam seemed to have the impression this book was very – sordid. Especially about the Hollywood scene.'

'Well, so it is. You know that.'

'I don't actually,' she said. 'I hadn't realized you were going to write so much about it.'

'Well, Fleur, I don't think you can have thought very carefully about it, in that case. You know perfectly well there is a great deal about Hollywood in it.'

'Yes, I suppose so. But he made it sound so – so tacky. I felt, you know, nervous.'

'Well, Fleur, it's a little late for that.' He sounded cheerfully impatient. 'These books are like landslides, you know. A little pebble starts them off, and then – whoosh, the whole damn lot's going.'

'Yes. Yes, of course. Um – Magnus, is there a lot about me in it?'

'As much as there needs to be.'

'Oh.' There was a silence. She suddenly felt furiously angry. Bastard. She had supplied a lot of the material for this shitty book, and now he was treating her as if it was off-limits, wouldn't even tell her how much she figured.

'You can read it when it's written,' he said, recognizing her concern.

'Yes, but before it's published.'

'Naturally. I'll send you an advance copy.'

'Magnus, you're kidding me, aren't you? I can see it before it's too late, can't I? In case I want to change anything.'

'Fleur, I have too many fucking editors round my neck already. Changing things. I'm the writer, I shall decide what's changed.'

'Magnus,' said Fleur and an icy fear was creeping through her veins, 'Magnus, I really do have to know what you're going to say about my father. That is one hundred per cent crucial. That was the deal.'

'I don't recall any deal that said that,' said Magnus lightly.

'You know perfectly well what I mean. Of course you have to let me see it.'

'I don't have to let you see anything.'

'Well, we can come back to that one. At least you can reassure me. You are clearing him, aren't you? Explaining what happened. What we know now.'

'Which is?'

'Oh, Magnus,' said Fleur, and she heard her voice crack with tension. 'You know. That he was set up. That he was a little indiscreet, but he got hammered. All that stuff Rose said. That Yolande said. That the person who talked to the magazine was someone he'd upset, someone who hated him.'

There was an infinitesimal silence. Then he said, easily, almost soothingly, 'Yes, of course. Allowing for a touch of poetic licence here and there. In the – what was it? Tabloid genre.'

'Good,' said Fleur. 'Any more information about Piers?'

'Oh – a bit.'

'And – he was there?'

'Yes,' said Magnus. 'He was there.'

'You're not going to tell me any more?'

'Not now. No.'

'Oh, go fuck yourself,' said Fleur furiously.

She put the phone down, and lay awake until daybreak, alternately sweating and chilled with fear and foreboding.

Chloe was sitting one afternoon in the drawing room, wondering wearily if her head was going to ache for evermore, and if so whether it was because of her concussion or because she was so unhappy, when the door bell rang. It was Caroline.

'Good gracious, Mummy,' said Chloe, struggling to keep her voice welcoming rather than ironic, 'what a surprise. Come in.'

'I can't stop long,' said Caroline.

'Of course not,' said Chloe, struggling rather harder. 'Would you like a cup of tea?'

'Yes, please. That'd be very nice. No, the thing is I had to come up anyway, to see my gynaecologist –'

'Is something wrong?' said Chloe, dropping teabags into mugs, looking at her thoughtfully.

'No, of course not,' said Caroline, as if seeing one's gynaecologist was an entirely sociable affair, nothing to do with one's health, 'but as I was here, I thought I'd come and see you. I've been worried about you.'

'Good gracious,' said Chloe. 'Well, I'm sorry about that, Mummy.'

'Don't be silly, Chloe. There's no need to apologize. I know you've had a horrible time. But you don't seem to be getting any better. And you look absolutely terrible. I thought you might like to talk about it.'

'Oh – no, thank you,' said Chloe, aware that she must sound as if she was refusing a cup of tea. 'But it's kind of you to think of it.'

'Well,' said Caroline, 'I am your mother.'

'Yes,' said Chloe, 'yes, I know.'

Caroline looked at her sharply. 'This miscarriage, Chloe. I can see it's very upsetting. But there can be other children. And of course you already have a very nice, healthy family.'

'Shit,' said Chloe and burst into tears.

'Oh, Chloe,' said Caroline. She looked genuinely remorseful. 'I'm sorry.'

'It's all right, Mummy. It's just that everyone says that. And it simply isn't the point.'

'No,' said Caroline, and her voice was suddenly inestimably sad, 'I know it isn't.'

Chloe looked at her. Her tears had stopped. 'Yes, I suppose you do. Know, I mean.'

'The child you lose is always the most important,' said Caroline and then looked at Chloe, biting her lip, her eyes shocked at what she had said.

'Oh, really?' said Chloe. She looked at her mother, who had so patently never loved her, never really attempted to disguise it, who had never loved her because of her sister, and moreover who had never loved her father because of her sister's father, and found her statement, no doubt meant with great kindliness, almost obscene in its insult. 'I suppose that explains how you felt about Fleur.'

'Chloe, please let us not start talking about Fleur.'

'Why not, Mummy? Why shouldn't I talk about Fleur? I think if we could have talked about her more, if you had been more understanding about my feelings on the matter, I might have found it all easier to cope with.'

'Chloe, don't be melodramatic.' Caroline took out her cigarette case, lit a cigarette, drawing on it rather hard. 'You didn't find it hard to cope with. You're exaggerating it, because it suits you. There was nothing to cope with.'

The rage grew hotter; Chloe, even while realizing it was partly because of her own tension, her own sorrow, found it hard to contain. She looked at her mother. 'Mummy, there was a great deal to cope with. Discovering her existence, that there was someone else you loved, that you had loved before Daddy, that you'd had a baby, realizing you must love her and that was why you didn't love me –'

'Chloe, you are being absurd. Of course I loved you.'

'No, you didn't,' said Chloe flatly. 'You didn't and you don't. You've tolerated me, that's the nearest you've come to love. I've had love, from Daddy and from Joe, and from – well, anyway, I can tell the difference.'

'Oh, for heaven's sake,' said Caroline. 'This is absurd. I'm going.'

'I don't think you should,' said Chloe. 'That's what you've always done, gone, walked away from it, all of it. I think for once you should stay and we should talk it through a bit.'

'Chloe, for the last time there is nothing to talk through. Your sister Fleur means nothing to me; she is far away, in America, and there has been almost no contact between us in the whole of our lives.'

'But you'd like there to have been, I think,' said Chloe. 'You'd really like that. It would bring him back as well, wouldn't it? Brendan. Brendan FitzPatrick. Or do you think of him as Byron?'

'I don't think of him at all,' said Caroline. She was flushed now, pacing up and down the kitchen.

'Don't you? I would. If I'd loved him as much as you did, I would think about him all the time. Mummy –' She put her hand out, meaning to try and comfort her mother, whose eyes were suddenly dark and brilliant with tears.

But Caroline snatched her own hand away, said, 'Don't, Chloe, this is horrible, awful. I've expended a lot of effort on putting it out of my mind. He's dead, he's been dead for a very long time now, and – and that's the end of it. As far as I'm concerned.'

'Only it isn't, is it?' said Chloe. 'Because of this dreadful book. Your boyfriend's book.'

'Chloe, don't. He is not my boyfriend. I haven't seen him since – well, for a long time now. I'm exceedingly sorry about the whole episode. For more reasons than one, as I am sure you can imagine.'

'I know,' said Chloe. 'I'm sorry. I shouldn't have said that.' She looked at her mother slightly warily and then said, 'It's a nightmare, isn't it? This book?'

'Yes,' said Caroline, 'yes, I'm afraid it is. For all of us, in different ways.'

'I try to forget it, try to pretend it isn't going to happen, and then I remember and know it is. It's like some awful bird of prey, waiting for us, and sooner or later, it's going to get us.'

'Has Piers tried to get it stopped?'

'Yes. But unsuccessfully. I don't quite understand the legalities, but there's nothing apparently he can do. At the moment at least.'

'I simply cannot believe that.'

'Nor can I. But that's what he says. And he won't talk about it. Absolutely refuses.'

'Hasn't he seen a lawyer?'

'Yes, of course. But – oh Mummy, I really can't bear to talk about it. It's so horrible. And complex. There are things – oh God, I'm sorry.' She started crying, hard, racking sobs; Caroline looked at her awkwardly for a minute or two and then sat down and put her arms round her, and held her, patting her shoulders, stroking her hair.

'Chloe, you have to tell me what the matter is. You have to.'

'I can't,' said Chloe, fighting to get her tears under control. 'I just can't. I can only cope with this by taking Piers's line, and not thinking about it, hoping it will go away.'

'But, Chloe, it won't go away.'

'No,' said Chloe, looking at her, her dark eyes blank with misery. 'I know. But maybe we can all get used to it. I'm sorry, Mummy, I can't tell you any more. It's all too – too private and personal. Not mine to tell.'

'I can imagine, I suspect,' said Caroline grimly.

'No. You can't possibly imagine.'

'Well, all right. Can't Ludovic help?' said Caroline.

'No,' said Chloe flatly, and then, because she just couldn't help it, had to tell someone, at least about the baby, she said, 'I'm afraid Ludovic isn't going to help any of us ever again.'

'Why?' said Caroline. 'Have you quarrelled or something?'

Caroline finally left two hours later. She told Chloe she had to get back, but in fact she booked into the Basil Street Hotel for the night. She had intended to ring Ludovic Ingram that night, but he was ex-directory; she had to wait until the morning, when she could get him at his chambers. She told him it was imperative he saw her that day; slightly to her surprise, he agreed to have lunch with her.

'Reuben, I'm really sorry, but I have to go to London.'

Reuben looked at Fleur. 'For long?'

'I hope not.'

'OK.'

'Oh, Reuben,' said Fleur, leaning forward, kissing him tenderly, 'you are the nicest, most extraordinary man in the world. Don't you want to know why?'

'Yes, I do.'

'It's a long story.'

'It's quite early,' he said.

When she had finished, he said simply, 'I'll come too.'

'No, Reuben, you mustn't. It's going to be terrible – I think.'

'I don't mind.'

'I know, but I think I'll be better on my own.'

'You won't.'

'And somebody has to stay and do some work.'

'This sounds more important.'

'Reuben.'

'Yes, Fleur?'

'Reuben, I really do love you.'

'Good,' said Reuben.

All the way across the Atlantic she tried to work out how she could find out exactly what Magnus Phillips was going to write. There were basically two methods: direct and indirect. She could ask him, and refuse to leave until he told her – in which case she thought she would probably be sitting in his house until eternity or beyond; or she could try to inveigle the information out of his publisher. Who was hardly likely to divulge the most intimate details of a top-secret manuscript to some girl he had never seen. She toyed with various fantasies, such as pretending to be a reporter from the *Los Angeles Times*, or a copy editor who Magnus had hired to work on the book, and finally decided her only hope – albeit a faint one – was to go and see him and demand that he came across. For some reason that made her feel better and she even managed to go to sleep for an hour or two; she dreamed that when she arrived at the house, Rose Sharon was there in bed with him, and working on the book. When she woke up, it didn't seem too totally ridiculous.

She reached Heathrow Airport at nine at night; she got on to the bus and reached the Air Terminal in the Cromwell Road at eleven. It was very convenient for Magnus's house.

'Hallo, Magnus. I thought you'd be in.'

'Fleur! For the love of God. What on earth are you doing here?'

'I'm sure you can imagine that, Magnus,' said Fleur coolly.

He looked terrible: he had several days' growth of beard, his eyes were sunk into his haggard face, he looked as if he had lost at least twenty pounds. He was wearing a track suit; his feet were bare.

'You'd better come in,' he said wearily, rubbing his eyes with his hands. 'I've no idea what the time is.'

'It's eleven thirty,' said Fleur briskly. 'Thank you, Magnus, I will.' She was very surprised by how much in control she felt: she supposed it was because she had never seen him other than powerfully alert, relaxed – albeit in his own slightly wary brand of relaxation – and patently fit.

'Coffee?' he said, leading her into the kitchen. 'I imagine you don't want to get to sleep for a while.'

'No, I don't. Yes, coffee'd be good. You look terrible, Magnus.'

'I feel terrible,' he said.

'How's it going?'

'Oh – all right. It's tough. The toughest point. I'm about two-thirds through. I always liken it to being on a raft, drifting across some vast river. I've lost sight of land, and I'm running out of provisions. It's – wearing.'

'What a shame,' said Fleur tartly.

Magnus said nothing, just looked at her and then walked into his black and white kitchen, put the kettle on, ground some beans.

'I'm going to have some toast,' he said. 'I haven't had any dinner. I don't think. How about you?'

'I don't want anything to eat,' said Fleur. 'I've been eating aeroplane food for what feels like days.'

'Uh-huh.' He started piling butter thickly on to the toast, reached into his larder for the Cooper's Oxford.

'The profits of that stuff would dip alarmingly if anything happened to you, I should think,' said Fleur.

'I suppose they would.' He handed her the coffee. 'Fleur, what do you want?'

'I want to know what you're saying in your book. About my father. About all that.'

'You know I'm not going to tell you.'

'Magnus, you have to. It's my story. Mine. You couldn't have done it without me.'

'Maybe not.'

'Well then, you have to tell me.'

'Fleur, I'm not going to. I can't. Anyway, it's not just your story. Piers Windsor could make the same claim. I certainly haven't let him read the book. Anyway, it isn't written. Yet.'

'That's balls,' said Fleur amiably. 'I don't need finished approved copy. Just a rough first draft will do.'

'I don't write rough drafts,' said Magnus cheerfully. He was clearly feeling better; he started on his third piece of toast.

Fleur looked at him, and a sensation of pure sweet rage went over her: she reached out and knocked the toast out of his hand. 'Go and get the manuscript, you bastard,' she said.

Magnus looked at her and grinned. 'You're clearly getting excited,' he said. 'I can tell by your language.'

'Oh, go to hell,' said Fleur. She looked at the doorway, wondering wildly, foolishly, if she could run through it, up to his study, lock herself in.

Magnus read her thoughts; he moved slightly to block her way.

'Magnus,' said Fleur, cursing the slight shake in her voice, 'Magnus, for fuck's sake, let me see that manuscript.'

'No.' He was smiling at her slightly, like a great complacent cat with its prey; she thought she had never hated anyone so much.

'I never thought,' she said, 'that I'd feel sorry for Piers Windsor. But I do now. I always thought he was the biggest bastard on earth. But he's an angel compared with you.'

'Compared with a lot of people,' said Magnus. 'As you'll find out when the book is published.'

'Oh, Magnus,' said Fleur and the word came out like a groan and there was suddenly no rage in her voice, only a terrible sadness, a pain. 'Magnus, when I met you, I was so comforted. That at last someone understood. About my father. About how I felt. I thought I'd found my answer. And all you've done is make things worse. I've bared my whole life, my whole fucking soul to you, and now what are you doing? Throwing it back in my face. I can't stand it, I just can't stand it. I'm going. There's no point expecting you to behave like a normal human being because you're not one. One day, Magnus Phillips, I hope someone torments you as you're tormenting all of us. I hope your life gets totally and utterly fucked up. Now get out of my way. I'm going.'

Magnus looked at her, and then he looked down at the floor; for the briefest instant she saw a flash of – what? Remorse in his dark eyes. Then he looked up again and said very quietly, 'I'm sorry, Fleur. I hope one day you'll forgive me.'

The quietness, the gentleness startled her; she stood staring at him, frightened, and at the same time oddly moved. Then he suddenly reached out and took her hand, as he had once before, looking at it, studying it; a lick of desire, entirely unexpected, shot through Fleur. She was startled by it, by its intensity; contrasting with the other emotions, her rage, her fear, her sense of loneliness, it seemed absurdly, ridiculously sweet. She knew she had to go; that she must get out of the house, quickly, and yet somehow she couldn't move, stood quite still, staring at him, hating him, furiously, fiercely angry with him – and wanting him more than she had ever wanted anyone.

And as he looked at her, still quiet, still gentle, he recognized that, saw it, and he said, 'Dear God, dear dear God, Fleur, I can't stand it, I can't stand it any longer.' He moved forward and pushed her back against the wall, and started kissing her frantically, hard, hurting her, and she felt his hand fumbling, frantic, pushing up her dress, pulling down her pants, and then with a shocking, desperate urgency he was in her; she felt him, felt his penis, pushing up hard, harder, his hands behind her pushing her buttocks inwards, and she felt she would shatter with the force of him, wanted to shatter, wanted to break, and she did, frighteningly, fearsomely soon, broke into a rain of brightness, of shock around him, sank on to him, crying out, her voice wild and strange as she had not heard it before, her arms flung wide in abandonment against the wall, her fists clenching and unclenching with pleasure; she felt him come, and then slowly, gently, he lowered her and sank on to the floor, pulling her down beside him, and started kissing her again, saying her name, over and over, and then he stopped kissing her, pushed her head back, looked into her eyes. Great breakers of the hunger grew in her, rolled, unfurled, began to travel again; she clenched herself against them, willing them to wait, wanting to stay thus, wild, quivering, lurching, knowing nothing, nothing at all but her body and its needs and its delights, its ability to give and to take, to lead and to follow. And he was thrusting, urging, resting, then thrusting again, and every time the rollers, the breakers, grew, mounted and there was a high, bright, faint spot of brilliance and she was reaching for it somehow and it grew, fiercer, hotter, larger, until she was there, reaching into it, pushing through it and there it was, a new climax, a sweet savage violence, and as it flowed and flooded and warmed and soothed her, she cried out again; then as she quietened, eased, she looked at him, saw in the depths of his dark eyes all the joy, all the remorse, all the fear, all the pleasure of what had been done.

* * *

Later, much later, they sat on either side of the fire in his small drawing room; Magnus had fetched them each a brandy; Fleur was wearing one of his large bathrobes. She felt very odd, very confused. She didn't say anything, just sat staring at him, waiting for him to clarify what had happened between them. She did not dare to let herself think of the consequences: on any level. One step, one second at a time: that was enough. Just one.

Finally Magnus spoke. 'I'm sorry,' he said. 'I'm terribly sorry. I shouldn't have done that. Forgive me.'

She shrugged, half smiled. 'It was hardly rape,' she said.

'Oh, Fleur,' he said, looking at her, and then reached out, and once again took her hand. He sat there, holding it, looking at her, his dark eyes probing into hers; finally he said, looking away, into the fire, 'I've only said this on two other occasions in my life, Fleur. But I love you.'

'Oh,' she said, and she was more afraid, more terrified by those words than she could ever remember being of anything.

'I loved you straight away. When you walked into this house before. It was like – I don't know. Being kneed in the crotch and the heart at the same time. I've tried to ignore it, tried to make it go away. But it won't. I love everything about you, from your awful temper and your dreadful language to that terrible honesty of yours, and your courage, and your fucking, fucking beautiful face. I'm sorry, Fleur. I shouldn't have told you. But I think I owe you that much.'

She was still silent, staring at him.

'I know you love your Reuben. I know you're going to marry him.'

She nodded. 'Yes,' she said and her voice was rough, cracked. 'Yes, that's right.'

He smiled, an oddly sweet smile that sat strangely on his dark brooding face. 'Good. Well perhaps the damage can be limited.'

Magnus,' she said, the truth fighting to surface, struggling to be born, 'Magnus, you don't understand. I –'

'Fleur, listen to me. Please. This is very difficult for me. Very difficult. But I really can't tell you what's in this book. It's – well, it's too dangerous. I hardly dare write it myself. If I tell you I've been burgled, and my publisher has been burgled, and I've been threatened, perhaps you'll find it easier to bear with me.'

Fleur stared at him. 'Burgled? Threatened? But – but that's preposterous.'

'I'm afraid it isn't.'

'But, Magnus, why, and by whom?'

'I don't want to tell you, Fleur. I really think it's better you don't know. At the moment.'

'But, Magnus, surely not by – by anyone to do with Piers? I mean he is a truly terrible man and a true pain in the anus, but I really can't believe he'd do anything like that.'

Magnus looked at her. 'I'd rather you didn't start questioning me, Fleur. I just want you to understand why I can't tell you any more.'

'But surely, the police –'

'Fleur, I'm raking over very old ground here. The whole story sounds purest fantasy. I want to get this book finished and then I think yes, the police may want to get involved. Incidentally' – he looked at her, half smiled – 'if you had raided my study just then, as I think you were briefly planning to do, you wouldn't have found any trace of a book called *The Tinsel Underneath*. Just a lot of files and manuscripts entitled *A History of Fleet Street*. Only that's classified information. For your ears only.'

'That's clever,' said Fleur, 'I like that. Magnus, this is all exactly like an episode of *Starsky and Hutch*.'

'Yes, I know. It feels like it sometimes. Although I don't think I'm quite as brave as those guys. Anyway' – he shrugged – 'we shall see. But no, you're right, Fleur, I don't think Piers Windsor is dangerous. In that sort of way.' He smiled at her again. 'Although, as you say, a right royal pain in the arse. I believe he's up for a knighthood this year. Sir Piers. God, what a thought. There'll be no holding him then.'

'Might your book stop him getting it?'

'Oh, I don't think so. I suppose it might.' He grinned at her again, his most Machiavellian grin. 'That would be a shame.'

'Well,' said Fleur. She felt very tired suddenly, drained of every possible emotion. 'Well, Magnus, I don't know what to think, what to do. It all sounds very frightening, very odd. And you really won't tell me what it's all about?'

'I think you're safer not knowing. And I care about you too much to put you at risk. I've been worrying about you, as it is.'

'But why? Because I'm part of the story?'

'Yes. Yes, I suppose so.'

'Can you tell me one thing?'

'I might.'

'Does any of this really terrible stuff involve my dad?'

He hesitated. Then he said, 'No. Well, not in the way you may be afraid of. No.'

'Magnus, wouldn't it be better not to publish the book? Just to go to the police, tell them what you've found out?'

'Oh, no, I don't think so,' he said, grinning at her. 'I think publishing the book is going to be very interesting. Very interesting indeed. If the lawyers let me do it, of course. What I shall certainly do is hand everything over to the police on the day of publication. That's what they taught us in crime-reporting class.'

'Shit,' said Fleur, 'shit, Magnus, suddenly I feel scared. Really scared.'

'You'll be OK,' he said, 'but just stay out of it, all right? Just be patient for a little while longer and trust me.'

'It's a little difficult,' she said, 'to put it mildly. But I'll try.'

She went to bed soon after that; alone in a small bedroom on Magnus's top floor. She lay there, wakeful, exhausted, disturbed – and afraid. Afraid of what might happen, of what was to emerge, of what dreadful things Magnus had uncovered. What scandals were to be unearthed now, what reputations to be wrecked, that people should threaten him, burgle his home, try to stop him doing – what? Publishing a book? A book? Since when had a book been that damaging, that important? As the dawn broke, as the wintry light crept round the blinds, as the traffic began to roar intermittently, she gave up on that one, wrenched her mind away, forced herself to accept what he said, that she must wait, not get involved. She trusted him. In spite of everything. She always had. It was one of the things she had recognized in him, the first moment she had seen him, that she could trust him.

She turned her mind to what he had said: that he loved her. In her wildest imaginings, she had not expected, not thought that. It was so out of character somehow – or out of the character she had perceived in him, ruthless, careless, arrogant. Every time she remembered the words, his voice as he said them, wary, reluctant almost, raw with emotion, she felt weak, shaken, literally shocked; and every time she saw herself again, standing there, against the wall, with him fucking her, invading her, pushing her, driving her into that incredible soaring pleasure, her body throbbed, tensed physically at the memory. Well, it was not a love that was going to come to anything. It couldn't. She was supposed to be – no, she *was* going to marry Reuben. Magnus sure as hell wasn't going to marry anyone. What had happened between them had been an incredible, extraordinary experience, nearer to fantasy than reality; she had to put it behind her, forget it, go home, get on with her life. That was what she had to do.

The Tinsel Underneath
Chapter Ten. Accidental Death

Every plot must have a villain and a hero. In the case of Brendan FitzPatrick, he played both.

Brendan started out one of the good guys. He was a gallant pilot; a faithful lover; a devoted son; a perfect father.

What changed him was the corruption of others: and an ability to be corrupted. Had he stayed in New York, he would have been safe. But he went to Hollywood, and was no match for it. He was vain, foolish, and not overbright; the machinations of Naomi MacNeice, Kirstie Fairfax, the PR machine and his own ambition turned him into someone dishonest, greedy, and ultimately ruthless. He could be seen as a victim; but he was actually the author of his own end.

He was playing some very dangerous games; and he wasn't clever enough to play them.

When he first arrived in Hollywood, he slept around: he was completely dazzled by what was on offer. Both men and women. Nothing new in that. Hollywood has always had a corner in sexual ambivalence. Brendan had not actually thought himself homosexual; his early inclinations were very hetero. But he slept with one man for expediency and, entirely to his surprise, developed something of a taste for the experience. He was charming, attractive, amusing; he got in with a very hedonistic crowd and, until the novelty wore off, lived life to the full.

Then he met and fell in love with Rose Sharon; became, as he put it, a reformed character, and until Naomi MacNeice began to call the shots, snapped her fingers, became again the young man he had been: nice, straightforward, loyal, loving.

But once a boundary has been crossed, it is impossible to go back entirely. Brendan was, if nothing else, ambitious; he wanted money – for his small daughter as much as himself – he wanted success and he wanted fame. Those three things lured him away from Rose, away from virtue. He literally sold out. He did what Naomi said: unquestioningly. And the rewards were considerable.

But then he got bored. Naomi was a tough mistress. The studio was tougher. He missed fun, youth, diversion. He needed relief. And he found it in Kirstie Fairfax, and her dissolute crowd.

Chapter 35

March 1972

Joe Payton was standing stark naked in his bedroom, wondering whether a clean shirt with two absent buttons would look better or worse than a slightly grubby one with its full complement, when his door bell rang. That would be the cuttings the *Sunday Express* were sending round, background to his piece on the new wonder boy, David Essex. He went to answer it; put his arm round the door to take the cuttings. 'Thanks,' he said, through the crack. 'Anything to sign? Sorry, I've got no clothes on.'

'I suppose they're all dirty,' said the voice the other side of the door. It was not a messenger; it was Caroline.

He had often wondered how he would react if – or rather as he supposed was more likely when – he saw her again: whether he would be pleased, angry, upset. He certainly could not have expected to find it funny.

'Hang on,' he said, 'just let me get something on, and I'll let you in.'

'Oh, Joe,' said Caroline, sounding impatient, 'I don't care if you haven't got any clothes on.'

'Well, I do,' he said firmly, and went to find his dressing-gown. It had a lot of toast crumbs adhering to its front, but was better than nothing. 'Come in,' he said, undoing the chain, opening the door.

She walked in, and smiled at him, her eyes moving over him in amusement. 'I think nothing would have been better,' she said. 'Hallo, Joe. Your little fling in high places doesn't seem to have affected you sartorially.'

She reached up to kiss him lightly; he bent and returned the kiss. She smelt gorgeous; she looked gorgeous, a little too thin, but leggily graceful as ever in her country clothes, her Burberry, over a skirt and sweater, her Gucci loafers, her Hermès headscarf. God, she was a class act. He'd forgotten. Worth ten of any film star.

'Coffee?' he said slightly awkwardly.

'I'll make it. You get dressed,' she said, taking off the scarf, shaking out her hair. It was still perfect, dark red: still not a streak of grey. Well, for heaven's sake, he thought, it's only eighteen months or something since we parted. He was sure he looked a lot more than eighteen months older.

'You look older,' said Caroline.

'Thanks,' said Joe.

'Still good friends with Miss Sharon?'

'No,' said Joe with difficulty, finding it hard, for some reason, to tell Caroline that the brief, briefer than brief fling with Rose was over, for she had clearly found him wanting, in every way, even as her escort when she needed one, he had so clearly not looked or acted the part; she had tired of him, and gently, sweetly, told him she had made a mistake, that it was wrong of her, that she found him very lovely, but that it was better to end it straight away, before they became any more involved. 'No, I'm not.'

Caroline didn't pursue it.

She made some coffee: strong, good coffee, handed him a mug. It was very nice; he usually made instant these days. It was all part of the slithering standards, he supposed, of living completely alone. He'd lived out of tins before, before he'd met Caroline.

'It's – very nice to see you,' he said.

'It's nice to see you.'

'Why have you come? I presume there has to be a reason.'

'I've come to talk to you,' she said, 'about all this. About Chloe. She's in terrible trouble. Poor little thing. I'm worried about her. And this wretched book.'

'Ah,' he said, 'the book.'

'Yes. I can truly say I don't care about it any more. I don't think it can hurt me. My shoulders have got very broad. But Chloe – well, it's going to be terrible for her.'

'I know. And Piers. And – Fleur.'

'Oh, Piers, yes, I suppose,' said Caroline dismissively. 'I can't get too worked up about Piers. Or Fleur for that matter. I think they both can take care of themselves.'

'Well, Caroline,' said Joe, 'this is a novel situation. You worrying about Chloe rather than Fleur.'

Caroline frowned. 'Joe, please. I'm trying to do the right thing. For once. Being at least partially responsible for the whole bloody thing.'

He shrugged. 'Well – you shouldn't be too hard on yourself.'

'Being hard on myself is my speciality,' said Caroline. 'Joe, there must be some way you can find out what's in that book. Piers refuses to discuss it, burying his head in the sand, all part of his obsession over his knighthood. Apparently the crux of the matter is knowing what's in it and that it's defamatory, and untrue. And that it contains information that is so defamatory no amount of damages could compensate. Otherwise we can't get an injunction.'

'You seem to be very well informed,' said Joe.

'Yes, well, I've been talking to Ludovic Ingram.'

'Oh really? How is Ludovic?'

'Very upset,' said Caroline briefly.

'Why?'

Caroline told him.

'So you see,' she said, pouring them both another cup of coffee, 'we have to help her. Poor little thing. She needs someone on her side. I thought it should be you.'

'I've always been on her side.'

'I know. But for once, you can actually do something useful for her.'

'Caroline, you're always so tactful,' said Joe. 'Oh God, I'm sorry. Coffee. All over your raincoat.'

Caroline left half an hour later, still wearing her coffee-stained raincoat. She said it was vital she got home, that she'd been away for twenty-four hours, that her new mare was about to foal. 'I seem to spend half my life up here at the moment. I was up a fortnight or so ago, and then I had to come up again yesterday, to see my bankers.'

'I see,' said Joe. Whatever it was Caroline was seeing her bankers about, it must be very important indeed for her to risk missing the birth of a foal.

When her cab was out of sight, he went back into his flat, feeling happier than he had done for some time, and put in calls to all the features and serialization editors he knew in Fleet Street. Then before his courage could fail him, he rang Chloe.

Chloe was touchingly pleased to hear from him. Could he come to lunch? She was feeling better, but still a bit low.

'I wanted to ring you, but I thought you'd had enough of me and my troubles.'

'I can never have enough of you, honeybunch. I'll be over at one.'

She was looking very pale, and thin, but she was full of pleasure at his visit.

'I've made us a pissaladière. One of my specialities, in the good old days. Oh, Joe, I wish I was still a cook.'

'You seem to me still to be a cook,' said Joe, carefully misunderstanding her.

The pissaladière was delicious: a golden, garlicky, tomatoey tart; eating it was like making a trip to Provence. Chloe hardly touched it.

'You ought to eat, darling. You're so thin.'

'I can't eat,' said Chloe, 'food chokes me. I'm sure I'll be better soon.'

'I hope so. How's Piers?'

'Oh – all right. I don't see him very often. *Othello* opens in three weeks. He's never here.'

'How does he feel about the book these days?'

'Oh, Joe, I don't know. I think he must be mad.' She smiled slightly weakly. 'He just won't talk about it. He won't even see the lawyers again. He says the only dignified thing to do is ignore it, then people won't think he's got anything to hide.'

'Extremely misguided thinking.'

'I'm glad you think so. I know what it is, he thinks anything he does, anything at all, may bring things to a head, endanger his chances of getting his wretched knighthood. He's so obsessed with that, Joe, it's extraordinary.'

'So your mother said.'

'You've seen Mummy? Joe, I'm pleased.'

'Yes. She – came to see me.'

'I won't ask why. She came to see me too. Do you know, Joe, for the first time in twenty-six years, I actually feel close to her. She's been really nice over all this.'

'I'm glad. I always said she loved you really.'

'I know you did. Maybe you were right.'

'I'll tell you something else. She said she was worried about the book, for your sake. Not hers, not Piers's. She even said she thought Fleur could take care of herself.'

'I'm sure Fleur can,' said Chloe briefly. 'And I really don't see it can do her much harm. It's nothing to do with her.'

'Well – I think it will cover all that early stuff about her dad,' said Joe carefully.

'Why should it? I don't even see why it should mention him at all. I know she's my half sister, and that's bound to be there – although now I come to think about it, even that doesn't seem particularly relevant – but Piers didn't know Brendan, or Byron, or whatever his name was. Did he? Although . . .' Her voice tailed away. She looked embarrassed.

'Although what?'

'Oh, nothing.'

'Well,' said Joe carefully, 'they were there, in Hollywood, at around the same time, weren't they? Piers and Brendan. Did you ever ask Piers about that, poppet?'

'No, of course not. I'm not supposed to know Piers was there at all then. Remember?'

'You mean you've never discussed that even?' said Joe.

'We never discuss anything any more,' said Chloe bitterly. 'Not even the most important things. Oh, God, who's that at the door? I really don't want to see anyone.'

'Don't worry,' said Joe, 'I'll go and get rid of whoever it is. I'll say you've gone off on a very long trip. Won't be back for ten years.'

'OK, Joe. Thanks.'

She sat back on the sofa and closed her eyes wearily. God, she felt terrible. If only, if only this wretched book was published, and everyone was actually reading it, if the stories had actually come out – and God alone knew exactly what would come out, what lies and what truths would emerge – then it would be on its way to being over. The new nightmare that haunted her was that the story of Gerard Zwirn would be there, amongst the rest. Such was the thoroughness of Magnus Phillips's research, she could only assume it might be. She didn't believe Piers's story that he was an old colleague for one moment. She was afraid to think of precisely who he might be; every so often she was tempted to try to find out for herself, to write to him, phone; but she was too frightened. Frightened and frail and sick and heartsore. And lonely. She had never felt so lonely.

She suddenly remembered what Joe had said about her mother being concerned for her and felt a stab of bitterness. A little more discretion on her mother's part, and there would have been a great deal less for Magnus

Phillips to write about. The whole thing was like sitting in the dentist's chair, and having the nerve in your tooth touched once, and waiting for it to happen again. Or having a baby, waiting for the next contraction. At the thought of babies, Chloe winced, closed her eyes, willed herself not to think about Ludovic. Although at least it distracted her from the book. She wondered if the hurt would ever ease and decided if it didn't, she wouldn't be able to stand it, would just fade away and die like a Victorian heroine.

She heard footsteps on the stairs. Oh, God, Joe must have failed to get rid of whoever it had been at the door. If it was that terrible woman from the Residents Association, she would just have to tell her to go away again.

She opened her eyes again, and saw Joe standing in the doorway; there was someone with him, and it was not the woman from the Residents Association. It was Ludovic Ingram.

'I've – got to go,' said Joe. 'Got to interview someone. Will you excuse me?'

They both ignored him; Chloe had still said nothing, nor had she moved; she was sitting, staring up at Ludovic, and he was standing, staring down at her. He looked slightly less outrageously healthy than usual, and he was holding a bunch of roses that was so large it almost completely obscured him from his neck to his waist.

'Hallo,' he said finally.

'Hallo, Ludovic,' said Chloe.

Joe went out of the room, closing the double doors of the drawing room quietly behind him, down the stairs and out of the front door.

'I'm – very very sorry,' said Ludovic. He still hadn't moved. 'I behaved extremely badly.'

'No,' said Chloe, 'no, you didn't, I did. It was a terrible thing to do. You were right to be upset. Do sit down,' she added, courteously formal.

Ludovic sat down. 'How are you? Now?'

'I'm – fine.'

'You don't look fine. You look terrible.'

'Well, thank you very much,' said Chloe irritably. 'That's exactly what I want to hear.'

'I'm sorry.'

There was a silence.

'Shit,' said Ludovic suddenly, 'I'm not very good at this. At abasing myself, saying I'm sorry. It's something to do with my profession, I'm afraid. It breeds arrogance. Chloe, don't laugh. I can't stand it.'

'I'm sorry, Ludovic,' said Chloe, 'but you do look ridiculous there. As if the judge was about to send you down, or whatever they do.'

'That's exactly what they do. How clever you are,' said Ludovic tenderly.

'Oh, Ludovic, really! I'm not clever, not in the least.'

'Yes you are, and you're beautiful and brave and lovely and I love you, and how are you ever going to forgive me for my behaviour over the past two months?'

'Oh, God,' said Chloe, 'I don't care about your behaviour over the past two months, Ludovic, not any more. It doesn't matter.'

'Chloe, it does matter. It matters terribly. I'm a self-centred, self-aggrandizing, arrogant, archetypal male. Please forgive me. It was an appalling way to behave. I feel deeply, horribly ashamed.'

'I forgive you,' said Chloe. 'Of course I do. If you'll forgive me. I was a wimp.'

'You weren't a wimp. My darling, darling Chloe. Good Christ, I've missed you so.'

'Well, I'm here now,' said Chloe, laughing. She suddenly felt strong, well again; she could have done anything . . .

'Where's your husband?'

'In Stratford.'

'Ah.'

'And my children are downstairs and so is my nanny, not to mention my Filipina housekeeper. So don't get any ideas.'

'We could go back to my place,' said Ludovic hopefully.

'I'll come later. If that's all right.'

'Oh, my darling, you will, over and over again.'

*

He had champagne waiting, in an ice bucket by the bed.

'Think of it as your wedding day,' he said tenderly, as he undressed her, kissed her lips, her eyelids, her throat, her breasts, her stomach, her thighs; entered her, gentle, loving, skilful, brought her to orgasm loudly, triumphantly, gloriously; laid her back on the pillows, gazing at her, smiling at her, telling her he loved her, adored her, that he was so sorry, so terribly sorry, that he did not deserve that she should still love him thus, that he would never, ever hurt her again.

'Ludovic, stop abasing yourself,' said Chloe, laughing, finally. 'I was wrong too. Terribly wrong. Not telling you, about the baby. Your baby.'

'Our baby,' he said, 'our baby,' and his face, infinitely and suddenly sad, made her tell him, tell him all she could, how pregnant she had been, how she had felt, how the miscarriage had happened.

'It's the nearest I've ever been to fatherhood,' he said simply, as she said no, no, he didn't want to hear, it had been just dreadfully, horribly painful and sad. 'I do want to hear,' he said, 'I really do.'

'Well,' she said, cheerfully, 'there can be other babies. Many many others. I'm nothing if not fertile.'

Joe rang Caroline.

'I thought you might like to know,' he said, 'that Ludovic called to see Chloe this afternoon. With a bouquet of red roses that almost obscured him.'

'Oh, good,' said Caroline. 'It worked then.'

'What worked?'

'What I said to him.'

'Which was?'

'That he was a self-centred, self-aggrandizing, arrogant, archetypal male.'

'Aren't we all?' said Joe.

'No,' said Caroline, sounding suddenly rather bleak. 'No, Joe, you're not.'

Chloe told Ludovic everything that night: why the car had crashed, the mysterious Gerard Zwirn, her fears about the book, that Piers would lose his knighthood. She even told him about Fleur.

'Darling, no wonder Mr Phillips has written this book. It sounds like the best kind of soap opera. I had no idea you were quite so interesting.'

'I'm not interesting,' said Chloe, 'it's just my family.'

'I find you immensely interesting. Can I meet this sister of yours?'

'I hope not,' said Chloe in alarm.

'Surely you're interested in her, in meeting her?'

'No,' said Chloe, hearing the hard finality in her voice, almost surprised by it. 'I'm really not. I don't feel any sense of – well, I suppose you'd call it kinship towards her at all. She means nothing to me. If anything I'm just scared of her. She seems so absolutely terrible. I keep expecting her to turn up on the doorstep like a wicked fairy.'

'I'm sure she won't,' said Ludovic soothingly.

He was alarmed at the lack of action Piers had taken over the book.

'He ought to get a writ out.'

'But your Mr Marshall says we can't stop it without knowing what it contains.'

'Well, you can't get an injunction. But you could take out what's often called a gagging writ. The beauty of that is the effect it has not only on the publishers and the writer, but on the printer and the distributor. It gags them.'

'What good does that do?'

'Well, publishers and writers, particularly journalists, tend to be rather hard-nosed. To put it mildly. But in threatening people like printers and distributors you are hurting the more vulnerable section.'

'I still don't see,' said Chloe.

'Well, the thing is that they are simply not going to risk it. They don't stand to make so much from the book. They don't benefit from the publicity or the hassle. It's easier for them to say well, let's not do it. So you effectively stop publication. I'm very surprised Marshall didn't suggest this to Piers. I feel rather responsible. Perhaps he's not as good as I thought.'

'Perhaps he's not,' said Chloe. 'It sounds wonderful to me.'

'There's something else he could do. Seeing as he's such an influential, high-profile old bugger,' said Ludovic.

'What's that?'

'He should tell every TV station, every radio station, every newspaper that if they so much as mention the book, he'll never appear for them or talk to it again. That might just work.'

'Goodness,' said Chloe. 'Why aren't we employing you, Ludovic?'

'I don't know. Maybe you should be.'

'Well, I'm going to talk to Piers about this gagging writ. See what he thinks. If I can distract him for long enough from *Othello*.'

Piers was not to be distracted; Chloe tried hard for ten minutes and gave up.

'We'll talk about it at the weekend,' he said. 'I admit it sounds interesting. But I can't think about it now. Still nothing from – well, from Downing Street?'

'No, Piers. Sorry.'

She put the phone down, not sure whether she felt more exasperated by his obsession with the knighthood than his ostrich-like approach to the book. Poor Piers. It mattered so much to him. More than anything, anything in the world. If he didn't get it now, because of this book, it would be – Chloe suddenly had an idea. A blindingly simple, clever idea. She picked up the phone again, dialled Nicholas Marshall.

'Yes, Mrs Windsor?'

'As I understand it, an injunction is only worth going for if it is felt that any damages cannot compensate for the – well, for the damage.'

'Correct.'

'Well, my husband is, as you probably know, in line for a knighthood. It has even been discussed at some length in very respectable newspapers. He should have got one at least a year ago. Now then, if the scandal of this book robbed him of that, wouldn't you think that would be something he could not be compensated for? By damages, however large they were?'

'Yes, Mrs Windsor. Yes, I would. But it would be a difficult thing to prove. Very difficult. And besides, if he had lost the knighthood before the book came out, then the damage would have been done, and it would not be worth taking out an injunction to limit it. It's a very dangerous game to issue proceedings when what's in the book may be true.'

'Worth a try though? Don't you think?'

'Possibly. Just possibly. But we would be talking about a great deal of money here. A great deal. You might be liable for costs. That could easily amount to a hundred thousand pounds for a three- or four-day hearing. You'd need a QC and a junior; it could drag on for weeks, witnesses being produced and so on. If they were pleading justification, that is. Which they certainly would, if they were to go ahead.'

'I'm sure we could raise it somehow,' said Chloe. 'I'm going to do some research, Mr Marshall. I'll come back to you.'

Maria Woolf was very intrigued by Chloe's phone call.

'My dear, of course I'll help if I can. I just wish I hadn't talked to Magnus for this wretched book. But he was so charming, so persuasive.'

'Yes, I'm sure,' said Chloe, thinking that if there was any justice, Maria at least would have a few skeletons unearthed from her rather tasteless cupboard by Magnus's book. 'Anyway, Maria, I just need to talk to whoever would know about recommendations to the Prime Minister for the honours list. Could you ask Jack? Please?'

'Yes, of course, Chloe. Oh dear, I do hope Piers does get his knighthood this time.'

'So do I, Maria.'

'And how is *Othello* coming along? Of course, I forgot, Piers doesn't like to talk to you about things in rehearsal, does he? Some kind of foolish superstition.'

'Foolish behaviour more like it,' said Chloe briskly. 'Thank you, Maria.'

Piers got back very late that Friday. He looked terrible. Chloe was shocked. Not just exhausted and white-faced, but very drawn and so thin. Horribly thin. For a moment her spirit quailed; she felt all she could, all she should do for him, was let him spend the weekend asleep. Certainly it was all she could do for the next twelve hours. She told him to go to bed, made him a hot toddy, and took it up to his dressing room. He was already sound asleep.

Maria Woolf rang next morning, early, while she was giving the children their breakfast.

'Chloe, my dear, some good news. I've spoken to a very close friend of ours for you. His name is Gerald Ramsey Browne. Such a charming man, a High court judge. He's on the Honours Committee. I don't know if you ever met him at any of our parties; he has a rather sweet little wife, a tiny bit shy; I've been able to help her a little here and there with parties, it's always so nice to be able to do that for people. I always enjoyed helping you in that way, as you know. Anyway, as a special favour to me, he is most happy for you to talk to him on Monday. Ring him any time in the morning, but of course do mention my name, otherwise you just won't get through.'

'Thank you so much, Maria,' said Chloe dutifully. 'I'm terribly grateful.'

Piers came in. 'Who was that on the phone?'

'Maria,' said Chloe briefly.

'Oh, God, not a party.'

'No, not a party.' That made her realize more than anything how terrible he must feel, not wanting to go to a party. 'She was just – just telling me something.'

'What?'

'Oh, Piers, nothing. Just the arrangements for all of us getting down to Stratford. Next month.'

'But, Chloe, they've all been made.'

'Well, actually they haven't,' said Chloe briskly, 'Now, Piers, do you want muesli or cornflakes?'

'Neither. I'm not hungry. Just coffee.'

'Piers, you must eat. You're so thin.'

'Chloe, I'm fine. And I don't like being lied to. What was Maria phoning about?'

Chloe hadn't intended to get into the hard stuff so early in the weekend, but she seemed to have no choice. 'It's an idea I've had, Piers. About the book.'

'Oh, Chloe.' He sounded infinitely weary. 'I wish you'd leave that wretched book alone. There's nothing we can do, as far as I can see, and this is just adding to the agony of it all.'

'Well, Piers, I think there is. Quite a lot we can do actually. I've been talking to Ludovic and –'

'Oh really?' he said, and his face was watchful 'When were you talking to him?'

'The other day.' She ignored his expression. 'Has Nicholas Marshall said anything to you about a gagging writ?'

'No. Not that I recall. He says a great deal, of course. Most of it useless. And expensive.'

'Well, I'm going to get Ludovic to talk to you. Meanwhile, listen. This is an idea I had.'

Piers sighed. Chloe felt angry suddenly, angry that he should do so little to help himself, his cause, angry that they were all working so hard on his behalf. She took a deep breath, tried to calm herself.

'You know you should have got your knighthood in the New Year. And were more or less promised it this time, in the birthday honours. Well, I thought that if all the attendant scandal of the book were to risk your loss of it again, then we really would have grounds for taking out an injunction. Because no damages, however great, could compensate for that. That's what the lawyers say, isn't it?'

'Chloe, this is nonsense.' Piers sat down wearily, reached for the coffee pot. 'Far-fetched nonsense.'

'Piers, it isn't nonsense. I talked to Nicholas Marshall and he said it wasn't. He said it would be hard to prove and might be very expensive, but we could have a case.'

'You talked to Nicholas Marshall about this? Without consulting me? And Maria Woolf?'

'Not Maria, of course,' said Chloe, 'but Nicholas Marshall, yes. Yes I did. We thought –'

'We? Who's we?'

'He and I,' said Chloe steadily.

'Well, you had no right to. No right at all.'

'Oh Piers, don't be ridiculous. This book concerns me as much as it concerns you.'

'Does it?' he said. He was looking at her very strangely.

'Well, of course it does. I'm your wife.' The tiny frail hope that she might not be forced to continue as Piers's wife drifted across Chloe's mind; she crushed it with a great effort.

'Chloe, I've told you before. I don't want to contest this book. I just want to leave it.'

'Piers, why? Why? You have to tell me.'

He was silent.

'It's this Zwirn person, isn't it? You're frightened of all that coming out. Isn't it, Piers? Look at me. Isn't it?'

He looked at her, and there was such misery, such hostility in his eyes she felt quite frightened. Then he stood up and walked heavily out of the kitchen.

She heard him upstairs, moving around, and then ten minutes after he appeared again, dressed, his overnight bag in his hand.

'I'm going to Stebbings,' he said, 'I'm not prepared to stay and be subjected to this.'

'Oh Piers,' said Chloe, and her voice rose so much she was almost shouting. 'Piers, don't. Stay, talk about it, let me help. Please, please!'

'I can't,' he said. 'I can't and I won't. Now please get out of my way. I want some peace.'

Pandora appeared in the doorway, her eyes large at the sound of the quarrelling. 'Where are you going, Daddy?'

'To Stebbings.'

'Can I come?'

'No,' said Piers and Chloe in unison.

Pandora burst into noisy tears.

Piers looked helplessly at her. 'Now look what you've done,' he said to Chloe.

Gerald Ramsey Browne was pompously, charmingly useless. He said he was quite unable to part with any information as it was of course absolutely privileged; the birthday honours were about to be privately announced and the matter was particularly delicate.

'Really? So soon?' said Chloe. 'But it's only March.'

Her head ached. It had been a horrible weekend. The children had been impossible, Rosemary had been away, Piers had left the answering machine on all weekend and refused to return any of her frantic calls, and Ludovic had been in Lincolnshire hunting. And now this old bore was telling her he couldn't help.

'I know it's March, my dear, but these wheels have to grind extremely slowly. And small.'

'Could you answer my question hypothetically at least?' said Chloe slightly desperately.

'Try me, my dear.'

'If – someone was up for a knighthood, and there was some scandal threatening him, and the powers that be –'

'Which powers would that be?'

God, she could almost see his chins quivering.

'Well, whoever it is who draws up the final list. Of honours.'

'Ye-es?'

'Well, if those people got to hear about it, would he lose the knighthood?'

'I can only tell you that is possible. I can't say more than that. It is likely, I would say, but not definite. And of course, you could never be sure that the knighthood was forthcoming anyway. It's terribly complex, you see. There are always mitigating circumstances, in everything. And it would depend on the nature of the scandal.'

'But if someone was going to be – well, let's say, named in a nasty divorce case. Would that affect their chances?'

'It could. It possibly could.'

'How could you establish that had happened? That he had lost his honour, because of that?'

'I don't think that would be remotely possible, my dear. I really don't. The lists are so highly confidential. And it wouldn't be a case – probably – of being struck off the list. This hypothetical person would probably never be considered if the scandal was truly imminent.'

'Oh. Oh, I see. Well, thank you, very much,' said Chloe and put the phone down. She felt near to tears.

Maria Woolf rang almost immediately. 'Chloe? Did you get Ramsey Browne?'

'Yes, thank you,' said Chloe listlessly.

'Oh good. Such a charmer, isn't he? So sweet of him, to give you his time. Was he able to help?'

'No. Not really,' said Chloe. 'But thank you anyway, Maria.'

There was a stony silence; Chloe promptly felt guilty, that she must have done something wrong.

'Well,' said Maria, her voice at its most shrill, 'well, I can only say you must have been asking something very difficult. He always knows the answer to everything. Oh dear, I do hope you haven't overstepped the line, Chloe, pressed him too hard. I would hate to have upset him. Perhaps I should phone, and apologize. Oh, what a pity. So unfortunate when a friendly gesture misfires.'

'I don't think I overstepped the line,' said Chloe, through clenched teeth, 'but if I did, Maria, I'm very sorry. I –'

But Maria was gone.

The phone rang again, almost at once. It was Joe.

'Hallo, darling. I've been so worried about you. I didn't dare ring over the weekend. Is everything all right?'

'Yes, it is really,' said Chloe, slightly warily. 'Joe, can you do some research for me for the next honours list?'

'Why?'

Chloe told him.

Joe said he was doubtful, but he'd do what he could. 'There's something else. Your mother asked me to find out which papers were most interested in the book. For serialization. The answer's most of them, but Beaumans are holding an auction next month. When the first draft is available for reading.'

'Oh, dear God,' said Chloe. 'Thanks, Joe.'

She sat down and buried her head in her hands. What a wasted weekend. And she hadn't even been able to talk to Piers about the gagging writ.

When the phone rang again, she shouted at the Filipina cleaner to get it, that she didn't want to talk to anyone. 'Unless it's a Mr Ingram.'

The Filipina's English was very limited; she came in beaming and said it had been a Mr Ingram. 'I told him you say you want to talk to anyone but him.'

Mr Ingram had put the phone down.

Fleur was in the middle of her orgasm when she decided she couldn't go through with her marriage to Reuben. She decided it because even at that very moment, she realized she was still trying to analyse how she felt about it, about him, about their future, and setting how she felt about him against how she felt about Magnus Phillips. She knew there was no future in her relationship with Magnus: but he occupied her absolutely, absorbed her, all her thoughts, all her senses, and she could not forget him, not in any way, not for a moment of an hour of a day, intellectually, emotionally, physically. And she knew that was what she needed, had been looking for all her life in a relationship. A one hundred per cent, consummate, unmitigated occupation of herself. What was that expression? she wondered, as she lay there, feeling her body settling, calming, easing into normalcy, wondering that she could think so lucidly at such a moment: something stern, something biblical, something absolutely demanding? I am Alpha and Omega, the beginning and the end. That was what Magnus Phillips was to her, beginning and end, and every thing and thought and sensation in between. She could not, should not marry Reuben, who she loved so much, so dearly, knowing that feeling for someone else. It just wasn't going to work. She looked at him as he rolled off her, looked at his dear, gently ugly face, his speckled hazy eyes, full of love, his huge bony hand taking her own small one in his, kissing it tenderly, and would have given everything she had to be able to spare him the pain of what she had to do to him. But she knew she couldn't. It would be dishonest and it would be cowardly, the two things she most despised. She had to stop it and she had to stop it now, at once, before another night, another day, another hour of hope and happiness on his part compounded her dreadful, cruel error.

'Reuben,' she said, 'Reuben' – and she had to stop, so huge was the pain in her heart, so strangely did his face dance through her tears.

Reuben leant up on his elbow, looking at her in tender concern, and said, 'Fleur, what is it, what's the matter, don't cry.'

And she sat up and said, 'Reuben, I'm very sorry, and I have to cry because it makes me so sad. Reuben, I can't marry you. I don't want to marry anyone else, and it has nothing to do with anything, except that I don't love you enough. I love you very much, but not enough to make my life with you.'

Reuben stared at her, as if he did not understand what she said, as if she was speaking in an entirely different language, and then after a very long time, and without a word, he stood up, got dressed, and walked heavily towards the door. He turned there, looked at her, and said, his voice cracking with misery, 'Goodbye then, Fleur,' and she heard his footsteps, his slow, heavy footsteps, moving down the stairs.

She lay, without crying, for the rest of the night, remembering him, remembering everything about him, the first time they had met, when he had sat in the Steinbergs' kitchen and said he hated Bloomingdale's because it was horrible and that had been the sum total of his conversation; remembering the way he had bought the picture for her, without telling her, simply because she liked it, how he had said Julie Christie was beautiful 'like you'; the first time he had made love to her, in all its wonderful pleasure, and told her he liked the way she didn't try to force him to talk; remembering his happiness when she finally agreed to marry him, the way he never pressed her, never probed, never pried, accepted her bad temper, her awkwardness, the way he had sent her off to London, only a month earlier, without a word of reproach or complaint; the way he had sat, listening to her carefully, as she told him her extraordinary story, and had simply at the end of it said, 'I see.' All these things she remembered, and thought how she would miss him and his goodness and how much he loved her and her heart ached with pain and remorse, but she still did not cry; but in the morning she went into the kitchen and saw, standing in the sink, their two coffee mugs and their two wine glasses from the night before, and for some reason, that made her realize finally that they were no longer two, that she had sent him away from her and broken his heart for no real reason except that she could not love him quite enough; and then finally she sat down and cried for a very long time, and realized how much, how very much she was going to miss him.

She told Sol she wanted to leave. Sol said why, and she told him; he was furious, shouted at her, ranted, raged, said she had broken his heart as well as Reuben's, that she was a fool, and a disgrace to her sex and the company and the sooner she got out of his sight the better. Fleur stood humbly, listening, knowing better than to argue, wishing that Reuben had been as hard on her. 'And what do you think this is going to do to Sylvia?' said Sol. 'You'll break her heart, she's been a new woman with your wedding to plan.'

Fleur said she was very sorry, but she really couldn't go through with a wedding to someone she didn't love, simply to make Sylvia happy, and Sol said what did she know about love, was she some kind of a moron or what? By this time Fleur was lost; she told Sol again that she wanted to leave and as soon as possible, and he told her again the sooner the better, he wished her out of his company, out of his life just as fast as she could go.

'Fine,' said Fleur, 'I'll go today,' and Sol said he would sue her if she did, sue for breach of contract, and what about the cosmetic launch? Fleur agreed to see the launch through, maybe on a freelance basis.

'What do you think you're going to do anyway?' said Sol, after a moment's consideration of this. 'Clean toilets or what?'

'Sol, I don't need to clean toilets,' said Fleur, fighting a strong desire by now to smile. 'I can get another job as a copywriter. I do have a bit of a reputation. Although, actually, I thought I might go and work in London.'

March – April 1972

Anyone who had known him intimately – a surprisingly small handful, but one which included his secretary, Marilyn Chapman, who was taking notes – could have paid testimony to the fact that Richard Beauman was nervous. He was leaning back in his office chair, beaming, a manuscript on his desk, pouring a glass of champagne for one of his bestselling authors and his agent (although rather pointedly, as always, ignoring Mrs Chapman), the very picture of a man who was confidently expecting to see profits for his company of at least a million from the manuscript, courtesy of the author; only a certain watchfulness in his eyes, a tautness in his voice, a tendency to look repeatedly, if casually, through the pages, revealing the nervousness.

'This is very strong stuff, Magnus,' he said. 'Brilliant, enthralling, compelling – I can see the reviews now – but terribly strong.'

'I know it,' said Magnus.

'This – business of the young woman's death. It is quite essential that we have an absolute one hundred per cent assurance that the events you describe took place. In precisely that way, that sequence, that there is not the tiniest area for doubt.'

'You have it,' said Magnus.

'Of course. Naturally. But I think perhaps what I am saying is I want a one hundred and one per cent assurance. The lawyers certainly do.'

'What are you saying?' said Magnus. There was a strange expression in his eyes, a mixture of wariness and irritation.

'What I'm saying is that of course I accept absolutely what you have written here. But the Windsor lawyers are out for our blood. We cannot afford to take any chances.'

'So?'

'So I have to insist, I think, that we get a sworn statement, from Mr Zwirn, that this is precisely what happened. In every small detail.'

Magnus looked at him very steadily. 'I don't think you'll get it.'

'Why not?' Beauman put down his glass, looked at him sharply.

'Well, because it took months to persuade him to see me. He's very reclusive. Not surprisingly. I just don't see him making statements to a roomful of lawyers.'

'Hardly a roomful, Magnus.'

'Even so.' He hesitated. 'I expect his sister would see you.'

Beauman swallowed rather hard, reached for his glass. 'But she wasn't there. Was she?'

'No, she wasn't. But he told her about it. Over and over again. All those months, years; he was obsessed by it. Naturally. It ended his life. In more ways than one. Robbed him of everything he loved. Believe me, she is your one hundred and one per cent reliable witness.'

'But she's not actually a witness.'

'We're splitting hairs here.'

'I don't happen to agree. I shall have to talk to the lawyers again. I think you'd better be there.'

Magnus shrugged. 'Fine.'

Beauman looked at him, amused. 'You seem very calm.'

'I feel very calm. I know it's all fine.'

'The Windsors are playing a waiting game. It's interesting. Of course, they've had their own preoccupations. All this brouhaha about *Othello*. And the knighthood. It's all excellent stuff, of course, will whip up public interest still further, improve sales.'

'Yes, it should do,' said Magnus. He looked rather bored.

'I have to say,' said Henry Chancellor, speaking for the first time, 'I feel a little sorry for Windsor.'

'Don't be,' said Magnus. 'He doesn't deserve it. Besides, in many ways, the book is very kind about him. It's a very touching story.'

'Yes, but in a rather unacceptable way. It's a very double-edged weapon, that relationship.'

'Oh, I don't know. Public opinion about homosexuality is easing all the time. It's – what, five years now since the law changed.'

'Come off it, Magnus,' said Henry Chancellor. 'I mean, yes, there's been a change in the law, but public opinion always lags behind. The theatrical crowd and all that lot may be quite happy with all their fairy friends, but the public feel rather differently. They'd bring back capital punishment tomorrow, don't forget.'

Magnus shrugged.

'And poor little Mrs Windsor has had a terrible time. Nothing to do with *Tinsel*, I hope, but not good.'

'Really? I didn't know.'

'Yes. She crashed her car, ended up in hospital, lost a baby she was carrying. Very sad. Surely you must have heard? It was in all the papers.'

'No,' said Magnus. He looked very intrigued, very thoughtful. 'I don't read the papers when I'm writing. Poor Mrs Windsor. My goodness, that is a fertile marriage. Who'd have thought it?'

'Magnus, really! Do you have no finer feelings?'

'Not many,' said Magnus cheerfully. He grinned, slightly apologetically at Marilyn Chapman. She looked coldly back at him.

'Now, there's another witness we shall need a signed statement from,' said Beauman, 'concerning the other – accident.'

'No problem there,' said Magnus. 'I'll talk to her. Now I must go.'

Marilyn Chapman, who had never liked Magnus Phillips, and had just heard nothing to change her mind, went to fetch his coat, saw him out, and went back into the meeting wishing something might happen to bring him down a peg or two. Or preferably a great many more than that.

Piers's *Othello*, which was to open the summer season at Stratford, had attracted an enormous amount of critical and press attention. Apart from the fact that he was to alternate the roles with Ivor Branwen, it was to be played in Victorian dress, in itself revolutionary, and he had had a huge row with Elizabeth Fraser, who was playing Desdemona, three nights before the opening, resulting in her withdrawing from the production and holding a very well-attended press conference at which she gave as her reason she had never tried – 'please note that word, ladies and gentleman, "tried", it's important' – to do a role with so selfish and greedy a pair of actors. 'I simply spend every moment on stage fighting to be heard, and even to be seen.'

It was only the threat of legal action, combined with a major reworking of two of the scenes which most upset her, that had persuaded her back into the production.

Chloe had only met Elizabeth Fraser twice, and had at the time found her arrogant and self-seeking; she decided, on hearing all this and even while trying to soothe Piers, to agree it was all outrageous, that she must, at some future date, go and shake her by the hand.

She drove up to Stratford quite early in the afternoon; Piers had been staying at a small hotel in the town, but had booked her into the Royal Hotel for the night. There was to be a party after the show. 'Nothing much, just drinks and so on, but I'd like you to be there,' he had said the weekend before, his white face strained and anxious, and she had remembered his glowing showy confidence at the first night of *The Lady of Shalott* and felt frightened at the change in him. He was at the hotel when she got there, and suggested they had tea. Chloe was amazed, he was normally locked into last-minute discussions, and panics with the cast at this stage; she sat and looked at him, trying not to notice the shaking hand as he lifted his cup, to crush the fear that the constant coughing must, surely, interfere with the delivery of his lines, to persuade herself that this frail, thin, pallid creature could possibly become the towering, menacing Moor of Venice.

'I've had the press on to me today,' he said suddenly, putting down his cup.

'Well, I expect you have,' said Chloe. 'I'd have thought you'd have had them on to you every day. All this business about Elizabeth Fraser and everything.'

'No,' he said, and his face was infinitely wretched. 'No, nothing to do with Elizabeth. Rumours about a knighthood, and what I thought my chances were.'

'Oh, Piers,' said Chloe, knowing the rider to this and her heart aching for him, knowing how desperate he was, 'and what did you say?'

'I said of course I knew nothing about it, nothing whatsoever, that if in the fullness of time I was to be honoured by Her Majesty, I would be thrilled and proud, but I had no reason to believe that at the moment it was more than a remote hope. A fine speech, it was. One I've made several times now.'

'And?'

'Well, and then the reporter, I think he was from the *Mirror* or the *News*, said did I feel any possible repercussions from the Magnus Phillips book might affect my chances. I said I had nothing to say about the book, that I hadn't read it, that Mr Phillips hadn't had the courtesy to talk to me about it, and I had no idea what he was going to write in it.'

'Oh,' said Chloe. 'Piers, I'm so sorry. But – don't you see? That's exactly why I thought we should try to get an injunction. If we could prove that the book contained a libel that was going to affect your chances of a knighthood, then we would have a good chance of stopping it. I think.'

Piers looked at her. 'Yes. I suppose so. And what did you say Marshall said about this?'

'Well' – she looked awkwardly at him – 'he wasn't very hopeful. But he rather reluctantly agreed it might be worth a try. If we could actually prove it. But he said it would be very expensive.'

'I don't think that's very relevant. At this point. What does expensive mean?'

'He said it could be anything up to a hundred thousand pounds. Or more,' she added with a rather weak smile.

'Well, we've got to do something.' He suddenly looked slightly better, more decisive. 'This gagging writ Ludovic mentioned. I think maybe the time has come to go for that one. I'm beginning to feel I have nothing to lose. Any more.'

Chloe didn't say anything. She just took his hand and squeezed it.

Piers looked at her and smiled his sweetest, most tender smile. 'I love you so much,' he said suddenly. 'I couldn't live without you. You do know that, don't you, Chloe?'

Piers had often talked about the actor's mythical Dr Stage, and his magical properties, the way simply going on to the stage could heal sickness, defeat pain, work miracles. There were countless stories of people going through immense four-hour performances with raging temperatures, broken limbs, in appalling grief and not merely surviving, but triumphing. But Chloe had never seen a manifestation of it until that night. The shaking, frail creature who had finally left the Royal Hotel that night stalked on to the stage at the Royal Shakespeare two hours later, a powerful brooding figure, in evening dress, a great black cloak swirling out behind him, Iago at his impatient heels; and when the marvellous, rich, emotive voice delivered its first few lines, speaking of courage, of determination, of love, no shadow of weakness, of frailty even echoing in it, she sat back in her seat and briefly closed her eyes, feeling faint herself with relief.

The performance was dazzling, from first moment to last, and when she saw again the scene she had watched that day in the empty theatre, heard not Piers, not an actor, but Othello himself say, the great voice cracked with pain, 'I have no wife,' she found herself as profoundly moved as she had been then; and when the audience rose at the end, standing, shouting, cheering, throwing flowers on to the stage, refusing to let the actors go, any of them, but especially Piers, she looked at him and felt amongst all the other conflicting emotions a sense of sheer awe at what he had accomplished.

The reviews were unanimous: the finest Othello, the finest Iago for many years, a brilliant feat, by both actors, neither drawing on the interpretation of the other. Piers Windsor, they all said, as one man, had done the impossible and surpassed himself, given his finest, most brilliant, most dazzling performance yet, and had allowed Branwen to dazzle too: this was truly great acting, great craftmanship, and, as Harold Hobson remarked in the *Sunday Times*, the great humanity of a great man.

The papers rushed to interview him: hundreds of column inches appeared, most of them referring to *The Tinsel Underneath* (although interestingly, in the briefest, most scathing terms), all of them propounding that this was his hour, that his services to the theatre were outstanding, and that he should finally be rewarded for them by the Queen in the forthcoming birthday honours list.

Fleur had decided after three weeks of indecision, lonely, sad, remorseful weeks, to call Magnus Phillips. She had left Morton's, and was working freelance from home until she had something more satisfactory sorted out; Mick diMaggio had heard of her availability with patent delight and had asked her to knock out some Juliana pack copy for him ('The new girl we have on the account feels it's beneath her, Fleur. I wish you'd come back here full time') and Baz Browne had given her all Bernard Stobbs's new books to promote ('He never stops asking for you'). They had both offered her fulltime jobs; Fleur had turned them down, without being in the least sure why.

She had heard nothing from Magnus since she had got back to New York; she told herself on alternate days, alternate hours even, and according to her mood, that there was no reason why she should, that he thought she was going to marry Reuben, that it would be very unfair of him to contact her in any way; and then her brain turned full circle and she told herself instead that if he loved her as much as he had said he did, he would want to know at the very least how she was, might, should, even, wonder if there was any chance she might not be going to marry Reuben any longer.

She found it extraordinarily difficult, even after this considerable time, to think about much else. He obsessed her: she saw his face, heard his voice, remembered him, oh God, she remembered him, everywhere, all the time. Time if anything increased her desire for him. She also thought, constantly, incessantly, about his book, about everything that he had told her, about the burglaries, the threats, about what might happen. That was upsetting her too, upsetting her horribly; if he was really so concerned about her, she thought, so anxious for her safety, then would he not have checked on her from time to time, made sure she was safe? It was outrageous: to frighten her and then to neglect her totally. He had no right to do it; no right at all. And on it went, on and on, wearing a great wound in her brain. Finally she couldn't stand it any longer, and one morning when it would have been breakfast time there, she picked up the phone and put in a call to London.

She stood there, her heart beating, thinking of, hearing, seeing even the phone, hanging on the kitchen wall, thought of him getting up from the table, putting down his toast spread with that ridiculous, foul-tasting, shitty marmalade of his, walking over to the phone; she wondered what he would be wearing, probably just his bathrobe. God, she and Magnus Phillips had seen more of one another in bathrobes than anything else and she felt a shot of pure physical hunger at the thought of him, standing there, so far away, yet within reach, and she caught her breath, waited, longing to hear his voice, to hear his reaction to hers: the phone was answered. 'Magnus?' she said quietly, too quietly to be heard. A voice said, '734–5677, Magnus Phillips's residence,' and she dropped the phone, crashed it back on the receiver, and sat down sharply in the chair, her hands clasped in her lap, rocking backwards and forwards like a demented creature, tears starting in her eyes. For the voice had not been that of Magnus Phillips, it had been another unmistakable voice, one she knew well and had once loved as well: it had been the voice of Rose Sharon.

Joe Payton was a great defender of the gutter press. He said (as indeed did his colleague Magnus Phillips) that it served a valuable function, questioning propaganda, puncturing pomposity, probing comfortable cosmetic untruth. It uncovered official lies and unofficial fraud; it mocked the sanctimonious, and laughed at the over-serious. But he was having a difficult time defending it late one Saturday night, late that April, when he had gone with Chloe to Fleet Street to get the advance copies of certain Sunday papers. The *Sunday Graphic* devoted a double-page spread to what it called 'Scandal Off-Stage', and which it had advertised extensively in its sister daily the day before; it had been Joe's idea to go and get hold of it before the rest of the world.

They stood together, he and Chloe, in the bar of a crowded, smoke-hazed Fleet Street pub, and read a long article about Piers, about his long and brilliant career, about the pleasure he had given to millions, the honour he had brought to his country by showing British talent – or, as the *Graphic* called it, Genius – to the rest of the world. It detailed his marriages, his first to Guinevere Davies, and paused briefly to say what a loss she had been to the stage, and then his second, longer one to Chloe, 'debutante daughter of beautiful society woman, Lady Caroline Hunterton'. The beautiful society woman, the *Graphic* was at pains to point out, had, after a long and happy marriage, formed a 'surprisingly swift liaison with journalist Joe Payton', which had lasted a few years, but Lady Hunterton 'now lived alone in her sixteenth-century stately home in Suffolk'.

Piers Windsor's career had been long and triumphant, the *Graphic* said, and it seemed unfortunate that it had not yet been marked by any honour; he had been passed over for a knighthood several times.

> But this oversight had been confidently expected to be corrected this summer. A source high up within the civil service revealed to the *Graphic* only last week that Mr Windsor had been almost certain to become Sir Piers in the birthday honours. How very tragic, therefore, that once again it seems possible that glory will be snatched from Mr Windsor's grasp: by the publication of a much hyped book, entitled *The Tinsel Underneath*.
>
> The book, which was initially seen as a straightforward biography of Piers Windsor, is the third in a series of 'Life Portraits' by Magnus Phillips. Essentially scandalous, the books study not only the central subject of the book, but the world he or she inhabits, his friends, acquaintances, colleagues, and ruthlessly explores relationships past and present.
>
> The book, which is attracting huge attention in other countries as well as here, promises to be a bestseller. It promises revelations concerning society figures as well as showbiz folk, and is subtitled *A Story of Hollywood*.
>
> National newspapers are vying for the serial rights of *The Tinsel Underneath*. The *Sunday Graphic* will not be amongst them. We believe everyone has a right to some privacy in their lives.

'Which means,' remarked Joe, 'the *Graphic* can't afford to bid for the rights. And have got in their two penn'orth anyway.'

'Joe,' said Chloe, her eyes wide with fear, 'we've got to stop this, simply got to.'

Nicholas Marshall read the article early that morning in the kitchen of his large mock-Tudor home in Surrey; he looked across the table at Mrs Marshall who was de-pipping grapes for a fruit salad and told her he was afraid he would have to be excused from the lunch party she had planned. 'I have to go and see Piers Windsor. This thing is getting insupportable.'

Mrs Marshall said as far as she was concerned in that case their marriage had become insupportable, and slammed out of the room. After Nicholas Marshall had phoned Stebbings and arranged to get there as soon as he could, he went to find her and told her that not only her lunch parties and her dinner and cocktail parties, but her highly expensive home, her membership of the Country Club, her children's school fees and her large wardrobe were all funded out of his day job, and he would prefer that she remembered that and gave him her support. Then he went and got into the Jaguar XK 120 that was the light of his life and set off for Berkshire.

Caroline Hunterton saw the article, which Cook had left lying on the kitchen table and took it upstairs to read in her bedroom.

'What a mess,' she remarked to her reflection in the dressing-table mirror (in the absence of anyone else to talk to), 'what a bloody awful mess.' She wondered if she was one of the 'society figures', feared she was and picked up the phone to ring Chloe. Chloe sounded very upset.

'But at least it's finally galvanized Piers into some action. He's agreed to go ahead with the writ. A bit late, but still. Nicholas Marshall is on his way over.'

Richard Beauman read the article in his large neo-Georgian house in St John's Wood in a state of mounting rage. Bloody *Graphic*, conducting what amounted to a spoiler campaign, making the book old news before it was even finished, probably reducing his chances of getting the fifty thousand pounds he had hoped for from the *Daily News*; he phoned Henry Chancellor, who was lying in the bath, waiting for the call.

Henry was dismissive of his anxieties. 'My dear Richard, it was bound to happen. It won't make the slightest difference, merely increase the public's appetite for the book.'

'I doubt that,' said Beauman. 'And how did they get all this lowdown anyway?'

'Oh, Richard, for heaven's sake. Fleet Street gossip. It was bound to happen.'

'Have you spoken to Magnus? Got his reaction? Found out who he's been talking to?'

'No, of course not. He keeps his phone off the hook to all intents and purposes, at the moment, and anyway, he'll have nothing to say,' said Henry Chancellor, who had spent most of the morning trying to raise Magnus in a state of mounting panic himself.

'Well, there's only one thing for it,' said Beauman. 'We'll have to bring forward the publication of the book. Otherwise the whole thing is going to go stale. So you'd better get hold of your client at once, and tell him to pull his fucking finger out and get the fucking thing finished.'

'I'll see what I can do,' said Henry Chancellor coolly.

Magnus Phillips read the article sitting on his motorbike on the seafront in Brighton. He had ridden down that morning, at a hundred miles an hour in a desperate bid to get away from *The Tinsel Underneath*, the telephone, and thoughts of Fleur FitzPatrick. So far he had only succeeded in avoiding the telephone.

Richard Beauman got into his office early next morning. He had a lot of work to do. He needed to talk to the lawyers about the legal aspects of *Tinsel*, he needed to write a stiff letter to the editor of the *Graphic*, he needed to get hold of Magnus Phillips. He called Marilyn Chapman at her home in Pinner and told her to get in as soon as she could. Marilyn said she had toothache and was hoping to go to the dentist, and Beauman said it could surely wait until the next day. Marilyn sighed and said all right, she would come in. She appeared an hour later, just before eight thirty, looking tired; her face was swollen. Richard felt something close to remorse, which faded as she slopped his coffee into his saucer, dropped the telephone when she answered it, and kept asking him what he had said as he gave her dictation.

Just after nine thirty, Mandy, the girl from reception, buzzed up to Richard; there was a lady who wanted to see him. She said her name was Lady Hunterton.

'I don't want to see her,' said Richard and put the phone down. The chapter about Lady Hunterton in *Tinsel* was hugely interesting; if she had heard anything about it, she could be trouble. And he was not in the mood for trouble.

Mandy rang up again; Lady Hunterton wouldn't go away, said she'd wait, 'all day if necessary. She seems a little upset.'

'Mandy,' said Richard, struggling to keep his voice controlled, 'I don't care how upset Lady Hunterton is, just get rid of her.'

Marilyn was just thinking how unpleasant a man he was, and how she really must change jobs, and wondering how much longer she could stand her tooth, when the door burst open and a woman walked in very fast, followed by a breathless, flushed Mandy.

'I'm so sorry, Mr Beauman, I couldn't stop her.'

'It's all right, Mandy, don't worry. Lady Hunterton, I'm afraid I'm very busy and can't see you now. Perhaps you should have had the courtesy to make an appointment.'

'Oh, really,' said the woman, who was tall, slim, impeccably dressed and possessed of the inbuilt, unshakeable assurance Marilyn so admired and envied (even while she did not quite approve of it) inherent in the English upper class. 'I think we should not discuss courtesy, Mr Beauman, because I don't think you'd know it if it came and settled itself on your very elegant desk. Very elegant, Mr Beauman, rosewood, eighteenth century, is it not? That must have cost a great deal of money. I wonder if it was financed by the last sordid, libellous book you published.'

'Lady Hunterton, please –'

Marilyn Chapman sat back, enthralled. She forgot her toothache, forgot Richard Beauman's rage; this was worth missing the dentist, missing breakfast for.

'Mr Beauman, please be quiet. I know you plan to publish this book about my son-in-law, Piers Windsor, and I really can't imagine that you could even begin to care how many people it hurts, how many lives are ruined. I can't imagine you'd care about anything very much except perhaps your own ego which must greatly resemble a very large heap of excrement. I have just one thing to say to you, Mr Beauman. If you do publish it, then you can be quite sure that you are going to regret it, and cease to sleep quite so soundly in what I am sure is also a very expensive bed. Because I intend to hire private detectives and see if I can't somehow, somewhere, find something in your past that you won't feel entirely happy everyone knowing about, and then I intend to make sure they do. I shall talk about it on the radio and the television – because thanks to you, Mr Beauman, I fancy I am about to become a celebrity briefly, albeit a rather dubious one, and I shall tell my son-in-law and my daughter to do the same. And I shall visit your mother and tell her about it, and your wife and your children, if you have any, if you're capable of the act of procreation which I have to say I rather doubt. Now that's all I have to say to you. Is there anything you have to say to me, Mr Beauman?'

'Marilyn,' said Richard, with, Marilyn had to admit, commendable calm, 'could you show Lady Hunterton out, please?'

'I don't need showing out of this rather vulgar office,' said Caroline. 'I can find my own way, thank you,' but Marilyn, driven by a piece of almost maniacal courage, a plan forming with almost shocking speed in her head, stood up and took Caroline by the arm, and led her very firmly and fast out of the office, into her own small one beyond.

'Let go of me, please,' said Caroline, icy cold, shaking herself free, and Marilyn said, very quietly, 'Please just let me come to the street with you, I want to say something to you.'

Caroline stared at her, and then followed her down the stairs and out on to the street; Marilyn, her heart almost stopping with terror, but still going on, on, in search of her own revenge and some sort of justice at last for the things she had seen Richard Beauman do to people, said, 'Ring me at home tonight. After eight. Here's my number. I think I can help.'

And then she ran back inside and up the stairs and settled in front of Richard Beauman's desk again, and said, a demure smile on her swollen face, 'Now where were you, when we were so rudely interrupted?'

'Piers,' said Caroline. 'Piers, I've got to talk to you.'

'Who's that? Caroline? What on earth is the matter?'

Piers's voice sounded exhausted, hoarse. He was in his hotel room, in bed; it had been his Iago night, which he found even more exhausting than Othello, for some reason he did not fully understand.

'Nothing is the matter, Piers.' Caroline's voice was coolly amused. 'But I think I have the answer. How we can stop this book. Really. Or have an extremely good try. But only you can do it.'

'All right, Caroline,' said Piers, his voice resigned, 'all right. I'm listening.'

It was mid morning in Santa Barbara. Michelle Zwirn was sitting with her brother in the garden of their small house on Voluntario Street, wondering if she really had the energy after all to get her hair done, even for something as important as the concert up at the Mission that evening, when the phone rang.

'Santa Barbara 730–4175986. Yes, sure. I'll hold. Long distance, must be Piers,' she called out into the garden, covering the phone with her hand. 'Yes, Piers, yes, it's me. I'm well, thank you. Oh, he's pretty good too. And how are you? Good, that's really good. Did *Othello* go well? Oh, Piers, I'm so pleased, and Gerard will be so terribly pleased too. Yes, and mind you send the reviews. What? Oh, Piers, I don't think I've slept since I talked to that man. I could not be more sorry, you know? But he was such a charmer, and so kind, and – well, I guess I made a bad decision. Well, I know, but – yes, of course. Anything, anything. Listen, Piers, I won't ever speak to anyone ever again, if you don't want me to. Of course. Yes. I understand completely. No, no, I'm listening. Sure. Yes, absolutely. Goodbye, Piers, and be sure you send those reviews. All right? God bless, dear, goodbye.'

She went back out into the garden, beaming.

'It was Piers. Listen, you know I've been so worried about talking to Mr Phillips about – well, about Piers. Apparently there's some legal battle going on, and they won't publish unless you or I give a signed statement to the effect that everything we said to Mr Phillips was true. Piers has asked us not to do that, not to give the statement, and of course I said we wouldn't. I can tell you, Gerard Zwirn, I shall sleep easy in my bed tonight and every night if I know that book isn't going to come out. I feel quite as if a great load has been lifted off my back. Do you want a little orange juice, dear, or are you happy with the ice tea?'

'Mummy, you really have become the heroine of the hour,' said Chloe, laughing with pleasure as Caroline related the story of her visit to Beaumans. 'That is just wonderful. You are clever.'

'Not clever, just firm,' said Caroline. 'I don't like being bullied.'

'Well, let's hope it works.'

'That nice Mrs Chapman is sure it will.' She sat back, drained the glass of the large whisky Chloe had given her, and smiled complacently. 'I greatly enjoyed it, as a matter of fact. This is very nice whisky, Chloe, I'd love another.' She picked up *The Times*, started reading it absently. 'Oh, how absurd, there's an article here that says Margaret Thatcher, you know that terrible woman who's making such a mess of education, should stand for leadership of the Tory Party. Well, that'll never happen, the sky will fall first.'

'Mummy, don't try to change the subject. I think you're wonderful, we all do. Ludovic told me to tell you you're a real star and that if you ever want a job, he'll employ you in his chambers.'

'I can't imagine as what,' said Caroline. 'I must be the most uneducated woman in England. How is Ludovic, Chloe?'

'Oh, he's fine, marvellous,' said Chloe, and stopped. A faint 'but' hung in the air; Caroline seized upon it.

'But?'

'No buts,' said Chloe firmly, 'no buts at all. It's obviously difficult for us at the moment, that's all.' She smiled brightly at her mother.

There was one though, a 'but', and she hardly dared even begin to look in its direction: she loved Ludovic, she adored him, and she knew he loved and adored her. But sometimes, just occasionally, the adoration seemed to be not a plus, but a minus in her life, so consuming, so demanding, so all-encompassing was it.

'I love you more than I can tell you,' he said, kissing her goodbye one evening, after a briefer than usual meeting in his flat, no time for more than a drink, a talk, a slightly wretched look at their situation, 'but I do wish we could put a time limit on this thing. I can see it's all very tough for Piers and hard on you, but I'm not made of iron, you know. I need you, Chloe, and I need to be with you. All the time. I want you to be Mrs Ingram, not Mrs Windsor. I can't wait for ever.'

'I know, I know,' said Chloe, 'I understand, Ludovic, I really do. But I just can't do anything about it at the moment. Please, please, understand.'

'I do understand,' he said, releasing her, 'I do. Just. But it isn't easy for me. That's all I'm saying. I want you, Chloe. I want you to myself, for myself. All of you.'

'I know,' said Chloe, 'I know you do. I must go, Ludo, I'm sorry.'

Looking back over her life, it seemed to her she had never had a time, not a week, not a day, not an hour, when she had not belonged to someone. She wondered, and scared herself by wondering it, what it would be like to belong to herself.

'Chloe, there's a call for you. It's Mr Payton.'

'Thank you, Rosemary. Joe, hallo. How are you?'

'I'm OK, honeybunch. But I've got some bad news, I'm afraid.'

'What, Joe? Not the book?'

'Not the book. Haven't heard a word, one way or another.'

'Well, what then?'

'Well – and you have to remember, this is only rumour. But it's very informed rumour, I'm afraid.'

'About?'

'About the birthday honours.'

'He's not there?'

'He's not there. I'm sorry. My mole said he'd keep digging. But he thought it wasn't hopeful. I'm afraid scandal and Honour, with a capital H, just don't go together.'

'Shit,' said Chloe, the hot tears stinging behind her eyes. 'Shit. Fucking, fucking Magnus Phillips.'

'Chloe!' said Joe. 'You sound like Fleur.'

'Good!' said Chloe.

'Look, Magnus,' said Richard Beauman, 'I don't quite know what to do here. You say the Zwirns won't talk. Won't give the affidavit.'

'That's what I said.'

'But why? For God's sake? Why?'

'I don't know. I just don't know. They talked before. Well, the sister did.'

'Well, you know what the lawyers said. They had to have this. They advise strongly against publication without it.'

'I've got you the other one.'

'I know. But that's not quite the point.'

'Well, I'm sorry,' said Magnus. 'But I can't force them.'

'Would anything force them?'

'Like money, you mean?'

'I didn't say that. But –'

'Richard, you should never do that. Ever. You pay people for information, and then when the lawyers get going, they say you paid them, and the whole thing goes down the pan. Besides, these people aren't like that. I told you. They're good.'

The editor of the *Daily News* was in a very bad temper. The purchase of the serial rights of *The Tinsel Underneath*, which he had seen as a big boost to his circulation in the summer, normally such a dud time, was not apparently so neatly in the bag as he had thought. 'I'm sorry, George,' said the features editor, Colin Firth, at the end of morning conference, 'but they've just phoned and said publication may have to be postponed.' He stood by the door, and looked uncertainly at George Jerome, who was turning the dark purplish red that only serious irritation could produce. He had not personally brought this phenomenon about before; he was fairly new to the job and very nervous, and had already incurred George Jerome's wrath in telling him that the series of exclusive interviews their star columnist had set up with what George called the Female Fuck-ups – the Germaine Greer, Gloria Steinem, Betty Friedan brigade – didn't seem to be coming together, largely because the women had got wind of the fact that their views were likely to be ridiculed rather than revered. 'I really didn't expect anything like this.'

'Well, I should hope you didn't, otherwise you'd no bloody business wasting the paper's time and money buying the sodding thing. For Christ's sake why is it being postponed? They just brought it forward. Those people don't know their arseholes from their elbows. Tell them we're not interested, whenever publication date is. I'm not paying fifty grand to be fucked about.'

'George, it's only postponed. For a month or so.'

'I don't care if it's postponed for a minute or so. I'm fed up with it. Tell them what I said.'

'Yes, OK,' said Colin Firth.

He went to phone Richard Beauman's rights editor, which resulted in a few choice exchanges, and then went to meet his old friend, Joe Payton, with whom he had worked at the *Sunday Express*, and although he knew he shouldn't, relayed in some detail the various miseries of his morning.

Chloe drove to Stratford to tell Piers; she wanted to see his face. His reaction was disappointing. 'Fine,' he said, eating the eggs Florentine that were his preferred food after a show, and which he never apparently got tired of. 'Good.'

'Piers, I thought you'd be over the moon. I don't understand.'

'Well,' he said, 'it's a little late really. Isn't it?'

'No,' said Chloe.

'Chloe, it is. There's been all this gossip. My reputation is badly damaged. I've lost the knighthood. I'm sorry, but I just can't pretend I'm over the moon. But thank you for all you've done.'

'Oh, for God's sake,' said Chloe, and walked straight out of the hotel and drove herself home again.

'Now that really is good news,' said Caroline to Joe, who had called her to tell her. 'I hadn't realized how worried I was until you told me. I'm coming up to London tomorrow, Joe, to do some shopping. Why don't I buy you lunch? For old times' sake. And to celebrate.'

'That would be very nice,' said Joe. 'Thank you.'

He was slightly puzzled that Caroline should be coming to London to shop; she always swore it was the activity she most hated. He decided to honour the occasion by buying a new shirt. She might want to go somewhere smart. You never knew with Caroline.

'This is wonderful news, my darling,' said Ludovic. 'The end must surely now be in sight. It seems to me you can now leave Piers, and marry me, very very soon, without more ado. Can't you?'

'I think I can, yes,' said Chloe.

'I love you, Chloe. Very much.'

'I love you too, Ludovic. I really really do.'

'You don't sound absolutely sure.'

'Ludovic, of course I'm sure.'

'Do you think,' said Chloe, 'that there might be a chance, even at this eleventh hour, that Piers might get the knighthood? Now the book is off, now that it's all dying down?'

'I don't know,' said Joe nervously. 'I suppose it might. But it's very late in the day.'

'Could you ask your wonderful mole?'

'I'll ask my wonderful mole. I don't want you to get your hopes up, poppet.'

'Of course not.'

'Do you realize,' said Richard Beauman, 'how much this is going to cost me? Withdrawing this book? We've already lost the deal with the *News*. Lost credibility.'

'Yes,' said Magnus. 'Yes, I think I do. Henry has spent most of the morning telling me.'

'Good.'

'Look, Richard, I'm sorry. I can't help it. What do the lawyers actually say?'

'They're thinking about it. We may decide to risk it after all. You seem pretty confident.'

'Richard, I'm completely confident. This is a totally unnecessary storm in a teacup.'

'Yes, yes, I know, but if we're sued –'

'Do you really think that you'd be sued for more than you'd lose by withdrawing, though?' said Henry Chancellor. 'It seems to me that's the big question.'

'Oh, I don't know,' said Beauman fretfully. 'I don't know what I think. I really don't.'

'I'm afraid my mole doesn't think there's a hope in hell. Not now,' said Joe.

'Oh well,' said Chloe. 'It was worth a try.'

She was in the Ritz when she saw Magnus Phillips. Her mother had invited her along to a celebration lunch she was buying Joe. The three of them had had a very nice time; Joe seemed happier than she had seen him for ages. He was also looking rather smart.

'Joe,' she said, 'a suit. My goodness.'

'Yes, it's nice, isn't it?' he said, looking down at himself in some surprise. 'I bought it a long time ago. For a lunch, as a matter of fact, with Tabitha Levine. I can still remember it.'

'Oh really?' said Caroline tartly. 'You never bought a suit to have lunch with me.'

'You never wanted to go out for smart lunches,' said Joe.

'Joe, we met over a smart lunch. And you were in jeans and a half-unravelled jumper.'

'Yes,' he said, smiling at her, his most lopsided smile, 'yes, Caroline, I remember.'

Chloe looked at him, and then at her mother; she was smiling back, half embarrassed, half surprisingly gentle. God, that would be nice, if they were together again.

'Yes, well,' said Caroline briskly, 'that was a lifetime ago. Everything has changed. And Joe is in a suit. Now, shall we have another coffee, and then I must get the bill.'

'I must go to the loo,' said Chloe. 'Excuse me.'

And while she was walking to the loo, there he was, coming through the lobby, looking sleek, smiling at her like a large, well-fed cat.

'Mrs Windsor,' he said, with a half bow. 'How nice to see you.'

Chloe's manners were impeccable, she had never been anything other than perfectly and gently polite in her entire life. But now she looked at him very directly, and said, 'I'm afraid I can't possibly say it's at all nice to see you, Mr Phillips.'

He sighed, smiled at her gently. 'No. I don't suppose it is. And are you better now?'

'I wasn't ill,' said Chloe coldly.

'Oh? I heard you were. A car crash and a miscarriage. That must have been a terrible shock for you.' His eyes moved over her, settled back on her face. 'But you seem to be recovered. I'm so glad.'

He went on, and Chloe went and sat on one of the frilled stools that the Ritz deemed suitable for their Ladies and felt terribly, dreadfully sick. So he knew about the baby; and he had known about Ludovic; was that to appear in this filthy book of his as well? Quite possibly. God, would the power to hurt them that Magnus Phillips possessed ever end?

Much later that afternoon, her phone rang. It was Magnus Phillips. He sounded awkward, almost nervous.

'Chloe, don't ring off. I just wanted to say something. You seemed alarmed by my queries about your miscarriage. Please don't be. It was a purely personal enquiry. Nothing sinister about it whatsoever. I assure you that I see your private life as absolutely no business of mine.'

Chloe slammed the phone down, and then spent the rest of the afternoon thinking what an extraordinary man he was, to be so ruthlessly exposing her husband's life and past, and to be at the same time so clearly concerned about her fears for her own.

Joe had also seen Magnus Phillips at the Ritz that day: as he walked through the lobby towards the cloakroom, he saw him drinking a glass of champagne on the Terrace, his swarthy, rather ferocious face softened with laughter as he raised the glass to his companion, a very pretty, expensively dressed blonde. Joe thought of another woman glasses of champagne had undoubtedly also been raised to, by Magnus Phillips, a tall, beautiful red-headed woman, the great, the only love of his life, lost to him it seemed for ever, and felt briefly so ill with jealousy he thought he might throw up, there and then, on the Ritz's lushly carpeted corridor. Throw up or hit Magnus Phillips again; in the event he did neither but hurried out and away and walked down towards St James's Park where he wandered miserably for over an hour, kicking empty Coke cans and swearing most uncharacteristically at anyone who bumped into him. When he finally got home, there was a message on his answering machine from Caroline: could he ring her?

Because he knew he would be incapable of being anything but hostile towards her, Joe ignored the message; when she rang next day to thank him for coming and for wearing a suit, he was distantly polite.

It was a long time later that he realized it was, for Caroline, a very slender pretext for making a phone call.

What she needed, Fleur decided, was a major distraction. A major one. She wasn't just miserable, she was depressed. Deep down, long-term low. It wasn't just Magnus – although the searing pain she had felt hearing Rose's voice on his phone had still not even begun to ease. It was that she was lonely, remorseful about Reuben – Poppy, who was horribly cold towards her, had said he was still absolutely devastated – and filled with an awful foreboding about everything to do with *Tinsel*, what it might reveal about her father, what might happen to her. Always in the past she had distracted herself from her life by work; but a few freelance commissions, offers of old jobs back, had a staleness about them, a lack of intrigue.

She was lying in bed awake one particularly long night, wondering what on earth she could do with herself (short of casting herself into the Hudson, or going on a round-the-world hike), when she heard her own voice, very clearly, talking to Mick diMaggio.

'Not FitzPatrick and anything. Just FitzPatrick. That's what I want. That's what I'm going to have.'

And that's what I need, she thought, sitting up straight, her mind homing in on what was so clearly an impossibility she knew she had to accomplish it. I'll go solo.

She got up, made herself some coffee and sat down at her desk in the window; light was just drifting over the park; it looked ghostly, grey, enchanted, the trees in 3-D like some theatrical backdrop. God, she loved New York. How could people call it hostile: it was to her family, friend, ally. She loved everything about it, even the dirt, the danger, the noise, the drunks, the muggers, the foul-mouthed yellow cab drivers. They all contributed to it, all made it work, made the adrenaline flow. How could she have even thought of leaving it? For a man?

She made a list. The list read premises, clients, colleagues, money. She ticked off the first three: they were easy, there for the taking. She knew it. Money wasn't. How did she get money?

When Tina came in she was still sitting there; Tina tutted.

'You still not sleeping, Miss Fitz?'

'No, Tina,' said Fleur briefly, and then before Tina could tell her a man would make her sleep, she said, 'I have to make a few phone calls, Tina. Could you hold off on the vacuuming till then?'

Just over an hour later, dressed in a ruinously expensive and very sexy beige T-shirt dress by Halston which managed to combine a certain businesslike cool with a tendency to cling to her nipples every time she moved, her hair brushed free, her eyes made up very dark, very large, her mouth glossy dark plum, she set out for an appointment with a banker she had met at a party with Julian Morell and Mick diMaggio a few days earlier, when they were still both trying to persuade her back into their fold.

He was about the best-looking man she had ever seen in her life, this banker: not her type, but still quite astonishing, very tall, very big, with blond hair and blue eyes and a smile that lit up not just the room, but the whole building, the whole street. He was the heir to the family business, it specialized in the media, he was looking to build up his own area within it, and he had an appalling reputation with women. His name was Baby Praeger.

'Well naturally, Miss FitzPatrick, I would need all kinds of information before I could go any further.' Baby Praeger gave her the smile. 'Cash-flow predictions, letters of intent from possible clients, references, business, professional, all that sort of thing. But if that looked good – well, let's say we could talk. I normally don't invest in something as small as this might be. I'd want guarantees of course. And possibly a share in the equity. But – well, it's our area. And I like the look of it. I like it very much.'

What you mean, you charming bastard, thought Fleur, is you like the look of me. Well, that was all right. A little sexual frisson never did business any harm.

'I'll get all that together for you,' she said, smiling, standing up, aware of his eyes on the clinging jersey, the nipples (the room was cold, he probably did it on purpose, to get all the nipples standing up). 'I hope you don't mind me coming to see you so early in the procedure. But I remembered what you said the other night and –'

'Miss FitzPatrick, I never mind women coming to see me,' said Baby Praeger. 'At any point in any procedure. When you're ready call me. And we'll maybe have lunch.'

'That'd be good,' said Fleur.

Nigel Silk was amused, slightly tetchy, intrigued.

'Well, it's an interesting idea,' he said. 'It's what the Saatchis are doing in London of course. Merging creative with account management.'

'Yes, I know,' said Fleur.

'It'll never work. It can't. Not long-term. The two philosophies have to be side by side. But not one. You'd lose all sorts of things.'

'Like?'

'Well, what creative person could ever think sales? Marketing strategy?' said Nigel.

'I could,' said Fleur firmly. 'Mick does.'

'Mick does no such thing. Mick thinks creative. I pull him around.'

'Yes, and he pulls you around. It's a two-way traffic. And I think it'd be fine. I know I could do it.'

Nigel looked at her. 'Well,' he said finally, 'well, I think for a while you possibly could. At least until your outfit got bigger. You were after all trained at the feet of a master.'

He smiled at her. Fleur smiled back.

'So will you tell Baby Praeger you think I'm worth investing in?'

'I might. On one condition.'

'Oh God,' said Fleur.

'Oh no,' he said. 'It's all right. Lightning never strikes twice in the same place, Fleur. No, on condition you in no way under any pretext try to poach Julian Morell away from us.'

'Nigel!' said Fleur. 'As if I would. Haven't you heard of honour amongst thieves?'

She left him, feeling very cheerful, and made for the next person on her list. Sol Morton.

* * *

Sol Morton bawled her out. He told her she had a nerve and a half, coming to him asking for a reference; he told her Sylvia was still terribly upset about the wedding; he told her she needn't think she was getting any of the Morton's business; he told her she was heartless and ruthless and unworthy of her sex. Then he took her out to lunch, put his hand on her thigh, told her he missed her in more ways than one, and that sure, he'd talk to Baby Praeger about her, and he might even put a very small slice of business her way.

'But you want to watch Baby,' he said, 'he has a terrible reputation with women.'

'Goodness me,' said Fleur, smiling at him sweetly, moving his hand gently from the top of her thigh back down towards her knee. 'And me an innocent, unsullied girl fresh up from Brooklyn. I was wondering, Sol. Do you think Sylvia would like to get involved in this project? Because I'm going to need a really brilliant PA and her organizational ability seems to me absolutely outstanding.'

Sol said he thought Sylvia just might.

'I think,' said Roger Bannerman, 'I'd like you to see someone else about that chest of yours, Piers. I know Winters gave it the all-clear, but you still seem very wheezy to me. How are you doing on the fags?'

'Practically cracked it,' said Piers, 'and when *Othello*'s over, I'll give up for good. I swear.'

'Good man. Now I think you should see Alan Faraday.'

'Good Lord,' said Piers, 'doesn't he at times attend the royal household?'

'He does indeed. Many connections in high places. But he still manages to be an excellent doctor.'

'Good.'

'Are you really worried about Piers?' said Chloe to Bannerman. 'I mean seriously?'

'Good Lord, no. It's just that Winters is a surgeon; Faraday is a physician, looks slightly differently at things. And the old boy doesn't look entirely well.'

'I know,' said Chloe, 'but he's had so much worry lately. And strain. I think that's all it is.'

'I'm sure,' said Bannerman. 'Well, Faraday will sort him out. Don't worry, Chloe.'

Chloe said she wouldn't and thought how terribly badly he would think of her if he knew exactly what she was worrying about.

'I can't possibly tell him yet,' she had said to Ludovic the night before. 'He's under such strain, still hoping against hope some miracle might be worked for his knighthood, and then there's been the book, and –'

'Chloe, there's always something,' said Ludovic. He sounded very strained. 'I want you to act. I want things settled. I want you.'

'All right, Ludo. All right. Just let's see what this doctor says. I can't tell Piers I'm going to leave him if he's seriously ill.'

'No,' said Ludovic, 'no, I suppose you can't. Well, I just pray he isn't. For all our sakes.'

'Yes, all right, Ludovic,' said Chloe, and she was surprised to hear a note of irritation in her voice. 'I'll go to church this afternoon.'

Fleur was working late one night on her cash flow when the phone rang.

She picked it up. 'Fleur FitzPatrick.'

'Fleur, hallo. This is Magnus.'

Fleur sat for several moments staring blankly at the receiver, as if Magnus might emerge from it physically.

'Fuck off,' she said finally, and slammed it down again, very hard. Then she took it off the hook, poured herself a very large bourbon, and continued working as if nothing had happened. Except that in the morning when she checked the figures through she was surprised to see she had made a couple of very silly mistakes, and there were splodges in a couple of places, made by her tears.

Piers saw Faraday on a perfect, windswept morning, late in April; a few hours later Bannerman phoned.

'How did Piers get on with Faraday?'

'I don't know,' said Chloe, 'he's had to go straight back to Stratford. But he was coughing so much last night he was actually sick. And he's hardly sleeping, worrying over this book.'

'I thought it had been stopped.'

'Well, I think it has. But Piers feels it's done the worst damage already.'

'Which is?' said Bannerman.

Greatly to her own surprise and alarm (for Piers would have been enraged had he known), Chloe found herself telling him about Piers's terrible, almost unbearable disappointment over his lost knighthood.

Chapter 37

May – June 1972

'Oh, God,' said Piers. He was very white, the blood drained from his face, standing absolutely motionless, staring at her. There was a strange expression in his eyes, haunted, dark. A letter was in his hand, dangling there.

'Piers, what is it?'

He was silent, looking down again at the letter. Then he lifted his head and held it out to her. 'Look,' he said, 'look, it's come.'

Chloe took the letter from him, still staring at him. Then she glanced down at it. And there it was, unbelievably, the words, the words he had been waiting for all his life, had lost hope of ever seeing: from the Principal Private Secretary, 10 Downing Street, and 'Sir' (she read, skimming frenziedly through it), 'The Prime Minister has asked me to inform you . . . forthcoming list of birthday honours . . . submit your name to the Queen . . . graciously pleased to approve . . . Knight Commander of the British Empire . . .'

But she could read no more, the page blurred, the words lost, and she was in spite of herself crying and Piers was laughing now, slightly hysterically, and banging his fists on the wall, and calling to Pandora, to the other children, and they stood there, in the hall, staring at him, half afraid, half amused by his behaviour; he picked Pandora up and swung her in the air, and said, his voice oddly choked by tears, 'Pandora, your daddy is about to be knighted. I am to be Sir Piers Windsor.'

'Can I be Lady Pandora?' asked Pandora hopefully.

A very few people were told, were entrusted with the secret, sworn to silence, reacted in their individual ways.

'Good God,' said Joe.

'How extraordinary,' said Caroline.

'Marvellous,' said Maria Woolf. 'I'm so thrilled I was able to help.'

'Well done!' said Nicholas Marshall.

'I'm simply delighted,' said Roger Bannerman.

'I never was so thrilled in all my life,' said Michelle Zwirn.

'Christ Almighty,' said Ludovic Ingram. 'Now you'll never leave him.'

'Of course I will,' said Chloe. 'I can easily leave him now.' Her voice sounded hollow, even to her.

The letter was accompanied by a form of acceptance which had to be returned; Piers filled it in and then steamed the envelope open to make sure he'd done it right. 'Lots of people do that,' he said to Chloe defensively when she teased him.

Nicholas Marshall phoned; he said he was cautiously optimistic that their writ had been successful. 'Normally if they were going to go ahead, we would have heard by now. I might add, if they do go ahead now, the damages we get will be greatly increased.'

'I don't care about damages,' said Piers.

'You might,' said Marshall.

Piers was flying, on a wave of excitement and pleasure; his cough eased, his voice sounded better, he put on a couple of pounds in weight. He was exuberant with the children, tender with Chloe, charming to everyone who came within his orbit.

There wasn't long: the official announcement would be made in weeks. On the advice of Faraday, Piers was leaving the cast of *Othello* – to coincide with the investiture: then once the investiture itself was over, he planned a long holiday.

'And hopefully we can get things sorted out,' he said to Chloe. 'Decide what we're going to do. About everything.'

'Yes,' said Chloe. 'Yes, of course.'

He looked at her, and his expression was strange, searching. 'I still need you, you know,' he said, 'desperately. More than ever. I feel so hopeful, so different about everything. There seems to be some justice after all. Even if we can't stop this bloody book, and it looks as if we can, I feel now we can see it through together. I just pray you and I can find some kind of modus vivendi.'

Chloe smiled at him quickly, then went upstairs, shut herself in her room and buried her head in the pillow, so that no one could hear her screaming.

The party was Piers's idea: he sprang it on her, beaming with pride and pleasure.

'It's near enough our wedding anniversary, darling, six years, unbelievable isn't it, and I know, I just know Dream Street is going to win the Derby, and the day of the investiture would be the most perfect occasion for a party. Now although it's not official, I happen to know the date; Maria found out from one of her influential friends. It's the first of the two held in July, July 9th. We shall have the party at Stebbings, a dance in the garden, well, in a marquee; think how wonderful that will be. All our friends there, sharing it with us.'

'But, Piers –'

'Darling, don't, don't be negative, and you don't have to do a thing, just be there, in a ravishing new dress, I've already spoken to Jean and in fact she's going to organize most of it, caterers, band, food, everything, I've drawn up the guest lists. I would have kept it a secret right until the day, only it's getting a bit too complex for that now. But I want to do it, to celebrate and to say thank you for everything, you've been so wonderfully loyal and good. I haven't treated you very well recently, and I'm horribly aware of it. And then in the morning we can go away quietly together and recover from everything.'

'I think he's gone completely mad,' said Chloe to Ludovic. 'It's turned his brain. Honestly, Ludo, you'd think all we'd been worried about over the past months was where we should go for our holidays or whether we should have the drawing room painted. I just don't know what to do with him. I feel like running away.'

'Good idea,' he said, smiling at her. 'The best yet. Just run. To me.'

'You know I can't,' said Chloe irritably, 'not till it's over.'

'God in heaven,' said Ludovic. 'Where have I heard that before?'

He managed to smile at her, but there was a tension behind his eyes. Chloe looked at him miserably. She had thought the knighthood would herald the end of the nightmare; a new one seemed to be just beginning.

'Mrs Windsor, this is the *Sunday Times*. We'd like to come and interview you some time in the next month for a series we're doing on the wife behind the husband. And before you ask, we won't even mention *The Tinsel Underneath*.'

'Mrs Windsor, I wonder if you think we should have tables for ten or twelve at the party?'

'Chloe, I've never heard such nonsense, of course you must go to the palace with Piers. It's a huge honour and will be the most wonderful experience for you.'

'Mama, Mama, why can't I come with you, to see the Queen, why why why? I'll be so good and I know Daddy wants me to. Please, Mama, please.'

'Chloe, honeybunch, of course you must do what seems best, but are you sure this party is a good idea? It just prolongs the agony. Can't you get Piers to cancel it?'

'Chloe, darling darling Chloe, I can see this is a very difficult time for you, but I must, simply must have some kind of definite commitment from you. Otherwise – well, I don't even want to think about the alternative. All right?'

'Chloe, my dear, since I've been so involved in seeing this thing through for Piers, I thought I'd like to give a little surprise dinner for him. Just a few of us, at the London house. On the twelfth, I thought, the day the list is published. Would you help me organize that?'

'Chloe, have you decided what to wear to the palace yet? Because I think you should get something made, and I think you should start on it now. Otherwise you're going to run out of time.'

'Mrs Windsor, I need to finalize the menus for the dinner by the end of this week. Can we have a meeting, perhaps on Wednesday?'

'Mrs Windsor, this is the *Sunday Express*. We understand that your husband has taken out a writ against the publishers of *The Tinsel Underneath*. Would you care to comment on that?'

'Chloe, I know all this is very exciting for Piers, but you simply have to make him calm down a bit, take things more easily. He's still not well, even if he does look better. Can't you get him down to Stebbings for some long weekends? Otherwise he's going to crack up completely, and he won't even get to the palace.'

By way of distraction, she concentrated on the party. It was a measure of her misery that it seemed vastly preferable. She had looked at the guest list and groaned aloud; the great names were all there: Richardson, Olivier, Gielgud, Mills, Morley; the beautiful women: Vanessa Redgrave, Julie Christie, Susannah York, Twiggy, fresh from her triumph in *The Boy Friend*, Annunciata, Tabitha; the gorgeous men: Terence Stamp, Marc Bolan, David Hemmings; on and on it went, no longer quite so terrifying but still daunting in this force, right through to the people she supposed could be called friends, the Woolfs, David and Liza Montague, Damian Lutyens, Ludovic – surely, surely to God Piers must have noticed something, suspected something, was he completely blind, completely stupid or was he playing some hideous Machiavellian game? – Robin Leveret – God Almighty, it got worse and worse – and family, of course, Caroline, Joe, Toby and his terrible new wife Sarah, who was already rather obviously pregnant, Jolyon, who they had seen so sadly little of lately; if there was one thing she hated Piers for over and above the rest, it was what he had done to Jolyon. 'God Almighty,' said Chloe aloud, 'if this doesn't send me into Ludovic's arms nothing will.'

After the investiture, a lunch was being given for Piers at the Garrick Club, hosted by some of the great names of the profession. 'Then I'll come on down to Stebbings after that. I'll be there early evening. It's stag, darling, you won't mind, will you?'

Chloe said she wouldn't mind at all.

Fleur was making her way wearily up the stairs to her loft, after looking at what seemed like the hundredth studio-type office in a week, when she saw a figure sitting on the floor in front of her door. It was Reuben. He looked at her, and his face moved into what no one else would even have recognized as the most distant relative of a smile, and said, 'Hallo.'

'Hallo, Reuben,' said Fleur uncertainly.

'I wanted to see you,' he said.

'Do you want to come in?'

He nodded.

Fleur opened the door. She was frightened of doing anything, anything at all, for fear of it being wrong; she walked in and he followed her, went over to the window, looked out and finally sat down in one of the big Charles Eames chairs.

'Would you like a drink, Reuben?'

'Yes, please.'

She poured him a large bourbon and a smaller one for herself, sat down opposite him.

There was a very long silence. Finally she said, 'Look, Reuben, I know you don't like talking, but I think you should tell me why you're here.'

'I miss you,' he said simply.

'Well, Reuben, darling Reuben, I miss you too. But I don't think we should get back together again.'

'No,' he said, 'no, of course not.'

'Well?'

'I'd like to see you sometimes,' he said.

'Reuben, I really don't think that's a very good idea.'

'I do.'

'But don't you think you'll just get terribly upset, well we both will, and it'll just make things worse?'

'No,' he said, 'no, I don't.'

'But Reuben –'

'I'm feeling fine really,' he said, sounding surprised himself. 'Fine. You know?'

'Not really, Reuben. I don't.'

He leant forward. 'Listen.'

Fleur laughed suddenly. 'Reuben, I never heard you say that word before.'

'I've been in therapy,' he said.

'Really?' said Fleur. 'Well, Reuben, that's great.'

'It was Mother's idea. She's very Jewish you know,' he added as if Mrs Blake's Jewishness had nothing whatsoever to do with him.

'Yes, I suppose she is.'

'And my therapist has done so much for me. I can see it is better without you.'

'I see,' said Fleur, feeling against all logic slightly nettled.

'Even though I miss you so much. You weren't right for me. Too strong. Too overbearing. Dominant.'

'I see,' said Fleur again.

'I have a long way to go. But I told her how much I missed you and she said I should see you. Confront the pain. Learn to accept it.'

'And?'

'And here I am. And I still feel OK. So I'd like to see you sometimes. As a friend. If you agree.'

'Reuben,' said Fleur, 'if you can stand it I can. Of course I agree. I miss you too.'

'We can take it one day at a time,' said Reuben. 'That's what Dorothy says.'

'Dorothy?'

'My therapist.'

'Ah.'

'So I'm going to go and tell her how today went, and then maybe we can meet again. If she thinks it sounds OK.'

'Sure,' said Fleur. She still felt a little dazed. 'Whatever Dorothy says.' She looked at him; he had stood up, was smiling down at her. 'I tell you one thing, Reuben. Whatever else Dorothy's done, she's certainly loosened your tongue.'

She felt enormously cheered by Reuben's visit; she hadn't realized how much she had missed him.

He phoned next day to say that Dorothy was very pleased with what had happened, and would like him to see her again.

'That's excellent,' said Fleur.

Two days later, he took her out for dinner, and Dorothy was pleased with that too. He told Fleur he felt easy, and happy with her, and was not so far at least troubled by any sexual feeling for her. 'I just seem able to love you as a friend. Dorothy says that's excellent.'

Fleur was beginning to feel she could go off Dorothy.

Piers was insisting on having the children at the party, at least for the beginning of the evening; what that meant of course was that Pandora must be there, and the others on sufferance. He told Chloe to get Pandora a dress specially made: 'Something almost fancy dress, darling, nothing little-girly. I see her in the kind of thing perhaps an Infanta would have worn.' Chloe told him briskly that either he saw Pandora in a nice dress from Harrods or Harvey Nichols or not at all.

She found both the girls high-waisted rainbow-coloured silk shifts from Liberty; with their pre-Raphaelite red hair they looked as if they had strayed off the set of the *Dream*.

'Joe? Caroline.'

'Hallo, Caroline.' Joe heard his own voice sounding distant and struggled to nudge it back into warmth. He had hardly spoken to her since the day at the Ritz.

'Joe, is anything the matter?'

'No. No, of course not.'

'Good. I thought we might go to this terrible party together. Would that be all right?'

'Yes. Yes, of course. Good idea. I'd like it. Very much.'

'You don't sound as if you would.'

'Caroline, I'm sorry. I'm a bit – busy, that's all. I'd love to go to the party with you. As your escort. I'll wear my suit.'

'Joe, it's black tie. For heaven's sake.'

'Caroline,' said Joe, all the old pain, the jealousy coming back, 'Caroline, don't boss me about. I'll wear what I like.'

'Oh, for God's sake,' said Caroline, and put the phone down.

Joe rang her back.

'Sorry, Caroline. Of course I'll wear black tie. And I'd like to come with you.'

But his voice still sounded odd and he knew it.

Chloe bought herself a dress from Saint Laurent for the investiture, in navy blue gabardine, with a white and navy straw hat: very simple, very elegant. She felt increasingly as if she was not herself at all, but some actress playing her part. Piers had had a new black morning coat made at Hawes and Curtis; he was also wearing a wing-collar shirt rather than a turn-down, and a silk top hat, more than half a century old, that he had managed to acquire from Herbert Johnson. He was very worried about the whole thing, and spent a great deal of time fretting over whether the trousers looked too loose, made him look too painfully thin, whether the morning coat was just a shade too long, whether the top hat was just too much of an affectation. Chloe, half amused, half irritated, told him at the frequent trying-on sessions that he looked marvellous, and wondered what life would be like if she was as vain as he.

Dream Street did not win the Derby. He came in sixth. Piers was bitterly disappointed and told Chloe it was more frustrating than if he had come in sixteenth. He nevertheless hosted a lavish celebration at the Savoy, made an extravagant speech extolling the brilliance of his trainer, Bill Peterson, and said he knew that next year they would go on to win. The press, who loved the juxtaposition of horsey and theatrical society, took endless photographs of Piers with Dream Street and Pandora, dressed for the Derby in a dress in her father's colours. Chloe told Ned, who was upset not to be included in the fuss, that horses were horrible animals and best stayed away from.

A week later, the birthday honours list was published and a week after that Dream Street won twice at Ascot.

'At last,' said Piers, smiling beatifically at his guests, waving a champagne glass slightly hazily, 'at last my luck has turned.'

In New York, Fleur FitzPatrick heard, over lunch at the Four Seasons with Baby Praeger and Nigel Silk, that Serena Silk's friend, the actor Piers Windsor ('Didn't you meet him once with us, Fleur, I seem to have some recollection') was to be knighted in Queen Elizabeth's birthday honours. Fleur excused herself and went to the Rest Room; the men agreed that she had looked very pale all of a sudden.

'Women's things, I expect,' said Baby Praeger authoritatively, indicating to the wine waiter to pour some more of the Château Lafitte they were so greatly enjoying and to bring a second bottle.

Nigel Silk nodded sagely. 'Probably. So are you going to be able to help her, Baby? She's very talented, you know, and an early protégée of mine.'

'Oh really?' said Praeger. 'I had suspected something of the sort. I wouldn't mind having her as a protégée myself, I have to say.'

'You misunderstand me,' said Nigel pompously.

'I'm quite sure I don't,' said Baby with his radiant grin.

Fleur was very upset that night and cried angrily, furiously on Reuben's shoulder. He held her and soothed her and listened to her and told her she was right to be angry; he suggested she might like to see Dorothy too.

Fleur told him she thought she was probably all right on her own.

A week before the investiture, Magnus Phillips was riding his motorbike up the M1 and had just passed the turn-off for Luton when a Mercedes veered over from the inside lane, and cut sharply in front of him; there was a three-car pile-up, from which Magnus emerged extremely badly cut and bruised, and with an arm fractured in two places, the bone actually protruding through the flesh just below the elbow, and a broken front tooth, which, as he remarked, did nothing for his sex appeal, but otherwise miraculously unscathed. The Mercedes did not stop; witnesses reported it accelerating at at least a hundred and ten up the motorway. An hour later, a London businessman reported his Mercedes stolen from outside his house; the car was found abandoned in a small wood just outside Leicester.

When the police asked Magnus if he had any idea who the driver might have been, he said he hadn't; they asked him if anyone had a grudge against him and he said there were so many it would take a week to list them. The police cautioned him with being flippant and he said he was very sorry, and no, he really couldn't think of anyone in particular.

Three days later, Richard Beauman was phoned in the middle of the night, and told it was the police and he should get down to his office urgently, it was on fire. When he got there, the entire building had gone; mercifully most of the records, manuscripts, and files were stored in a metal safe and survived intact.

Later that day Beauman went to see Magnus Phillips who was still in considerable pain from his arm and said enough was enough and he didn't care about any fucking writ, he was going to publish *The Tinsel Underneath*.

'Only we'll keep that out of the papers. For the time being. I've found a printer who's willing to play ball and who's already at work setting – what was it? Oh, yes.' He smiled. '*A History of Fleet Street*. I really don't think we're going to have any trouble with the distributors after all this. And get the lawyers on the phone, straight away,' he said to the new, very pretty but rather dim new secretary he had hired after Marilyn Chapman had so inconveniently resigned, with no good reason at all that he could see.

Joe Payton heard about the fire, and Magnus's accident, at El Vino's where he was having lunch. He rang Chloe straight away; she asked him to go to the house; Ludovic was there.

'It's horrendous,' she said, looking distraught, 'everyone will think it's something to do with Piers. I don't know what to do.'

'Absolutely nothing,' said Ludovic. 'And if anyone asks you, just keep saying you don't know anything about any of it. Don't elaborate on anything. Thank Christ it's too late to affect Piers's little do.'

'Yes,' said Chloe, 'but it's very nice timing, isn't it? I can see the headlines now.'

'So can I,' said Joe gloomily. 'Have you told Piers, Chloe?'

'Yes,' said Chloe. 'Yes, of course. I have to say,' she added, 'that he seemed extremely uninterested. He's just totally in another world at the moment. And Nicholas says there's still a chance we can stop it. He's hanging on to that.'

'It's not a lot to hang on to,' said Ludovic, 'I'm afraid.'

Three days before the investiture, Fleur FitzPatrick was sitting in reception at Morton's, waiting for Sol Morton to see her, and flicking through the previous day's edition of the London *Times* which Sol always had in the office, together with a lot of other British newspapers and magazines. She was just about to put it down when she saw a small item at the bottom of the third page of Home News about a fire at the offices of Beaumans the successful publishers. Fortunately, most of the manuscripts had survived. By coincidence (*The Times* said) one of Beauman's top authors, Magnus Phillips, had himself been badly injured in a motorbike accident a few days previously.

'Fuck!' said Fleur. 'Holy shit. Fuck me.'

'Now?' said Sol Morton hopefully.

She went home and put in a call to Magnus; an operator said the number was unobtainable, and she had no record of a new one.

'Shit,' said Fleur. She was beginning to sweat. Who else could help her? Beaumans? What was their number? She found it, tried that; after a long delay she was put through.

'May I speak to Mr Beauman, please?'

'Who's calling?' The voice was clipped, rather drawly, a bit like Caroline's.

'My name is Fleur FitzPatrick.'

'Please hold the line, Miss FitzPatrick.'

A male voice came on the line, quicker, clipped, impatient. 'Richard Beauman.'

'Oh, Mr Beauman, you don't know me, but –'

'I've heard a great deal about you.'

'You have?'

'Of course. From Magnus.' He sounded amused; she didn't like him. Arrogant bastard.

'Mr Beauman, how is Magnus?' She struggled to keep her voice calm, heard it, to her irritation, shake slightly.

'He's – just about OK. Shaken, and in a lot of pain, but all right.'

'What happened?'

'He was riding that ridiculous motorbike of his and he got knocked off it. On the M1.'

'Who by?'

'I wish we knew.'

'Was it deliberate?'

'Who could say?'

God she didn't like this man. 'Mr Beauman, where is Magnus?'

'Staying with friends.'

'Where?'

'I can't tell you that, I'm afraid.'

'I see.' The lousy bastard was probably with Rose somewhere.

'Oh. Well. Well, I was just wanting to make sure he was OK. I read about it in the papers.'

'It's reached the American papers?'

'No. No, my boss takes the London *Times*.'

'How very civilized.'

'Er – could you just tell me, Mr Beauman, if you're going ahead with publishing *The Tinsel Underneath*?'

'I'm afraid I just couldn't. I don't know myself. At the moment.'

'Mr Beauman, I really need to talk to Magnus. Could you tell me at least his phone number?'

'I couldn't. He – well, he needs complete peace and quiet. But I will pass your message on. Does he have your number? In case he wants to get back to you?'

'Yes, he does,' said Fleur. 'Thanks.' She slammed the phone down and because she didn't know what else to do, she rang Joe.

'I'm going to London,' she said to Sol. 'To see my sister.'

'You don't have a sister.'

'Yes, I do,' said Fleur. 'I most certainly do.'

Without knowing quite why, she rang Reuben and told him, and told him why. He said fine and rang off; ten minutes later he rang back and said he was going to come with her.

'Reuben, you can't,' said Fleur, thinking how nice it would be if he did come, to have his silent, soothing presence with her.

'I can. It's OK, Fleur, I called Dorothy and she said it was all right. She said it could be very valuable therapy for me.'

'God bless Dorothy,' said Fleur. 'Reuben, I –' she was going to say 'love you' and said, 'really do appreciate it' instead.

'That's OK,' said Reuben.

The day before the investiture, Piers disappeared after breakfast saying rather vaguely he had appointments all morning including getting his hair, which he wore wildly long for *Othello*, at least tidied up. *Othello* had not been on the night before; but he was returning to Stratford that night to appear in it for the last time. His driver would bring him home straight after the performance. Chloe feared for his survival, both physically and emotionally, and had visions about his bursting into tears or collapsing in front of the Queen, but he seemed fairly calm.

Halfway through the morning Jean Potts rang and said she needed to get hold of him urgently; Chloe told her he should be at Truefitt and Hill at some point during the morning. Jean rang back and said Truefitt's had had no appointment with Piers booked at all that morning, and did Chloe have any other ideas. Chloe said more than slightly irritably that she didn't, but that if Piers called, she would tell him to ring Jean immediately. Later, feeling remorseful at her treatment of nice Jean Potts, she rang her back and Jean said, her voice sweet and reasonable as ever, not to worry, and that she had finally tracked him down at Jim Prendergast's office.

'Some very big meeting going on there,' she said. 'They were very reluctant to put me through, but I got him in the end. So it was fine.'

'Good,' said Chloe, slightly surprised that Piers had not told her he was going to see Prendergast. It was not normally the kind of thing he would have kept from her. 'Er – who was it looking for him, Jean?'

'Oh, some big noise in Hollywood,' said Jean. 'About a contract.' She sounded just a little strained, and something seemed wrong about the answer, but Chloe couldn't quite work out what. Much later, she realized what it was: that at eleven in the morning in London, it was three a.m. in Los Angeles, and even in that city perhaps an unusual time to be worrying about an urgent contract: but she shrugged it off and went out to fetch Ned from nursery school. She still liked to do such things if she possibly could.

When she got back at lunch-time, Rosemary said Piers had been home and gone out again. 'He won't be back now until after the performance tonight,' she said. 'He said to tell you to make sure his shoes had arrived from Lobbs. I told him they already had.'

'Good,' said Chloe.

'And Mr Payton rang. Could you ring him at the flat. He said it was very urgent.'

'Oh, God,' said Chloe, and ran up to the bedroom.

But Joe was out, and his answering machine told her he was not to be reached until after seven, when he would get back to her.

'Damn,' she said and rang the *Sunday Times*, who told her he was out on an interview with Annunciata Fallon.

She rang Annunciata. She had gone out, said her machine, and wouldn't be back till 'late, late, late'.

'Silly bitch,' said Chloe and slammed the phone down.

She went back downstairs and into the kitchen, where Rosemary was feeding the children. Ned was wolfing his fish fingers, but Kitty was pushing hers across her plate. It was very unlike her; she was normally greedy, her small mind revolving a great deal around her food. Chloe, worried that she would be a tubby teenager as she had been, fretted disproportionately about it.

'Kitty, are you all right?'

'Got a tummyache,' said Kitty, and promptly threw up all over the kitchen table.

'Oh, God,' said Chloe wearily. 'All I need tomorrow is a sick child. Rosemary, ring Dr Bannerman, would you, ask him to come, just in case. She's very hot.'

Bannerman came in half an hour and said Kitty was fine, had probably picked up a bug at playschool.

'You shouldn't worry so much,' he said.

'I wouldn't normally,' said Chloe untruthfully, 'it's just that – well, tomorrow and everything. I don't want any more anxiety.'

'Oh yes, of course, it's the big day. Piers very nervous?'

'Yes, very.'

'How does he seem?' asked Bannerman. His voice was very casual; he was looking down at his stethoscope, packing it away.

'Oh – better,' said Chloe quickly.

'Good. Well, Faraday's a good chap. Very sound. He'll take good care of him.'

'I suppose he will,' said Chloe. 'Roger, I didn't know he was –' 'still seeing Faraday' she was about to say, when Kitty threw up again all over the bed and Bannerman said, laughing, that he would leave her to it. She and Rosemary spent most of the afternoon changing sheets; at six Kitty fell into a pale, clammy sleep, and Chloe had a long luxurious bath, while reflecting upon the fact that motherhood seemed to consist rather more of clearing up vomit and wringing out smelly nappies than moulding young minds and forging emotional bonds.

She remembered Joe at seven thirty and rang him; he was still not back. She left a message to ring her, ate supper with Rosemary in the kitchen and then, so tired she could hardly move, and with a suspiciously raw-feeling throat, went to bed with a hot toddy and *The Female Eunuch*, and told Rosemary not to disturb her unless Joe called. She switched off the phone by her bed, and thought she heard it ringing once, far below her, but Rosemary did not come up. Probably her boyfriend, an intense young man who was studying architecture at night school. So far it had taken him three years to get through his first-year exams.

In her small self-contained flat on the top floor of the house, Rosemary had just settled Kitty for the third time and for the third time had hauled off her Laura Ashley nightdress and exposed her rather plump limbs to the architectural student, smuggled in under cover of all the excitement, when she heard the phone ringing.

'Bloody hell,' she said, 'I am entitled to some rest. I'm not going to answer that.'

'Good,' said the architectural student.

'No reply,' said Joe. 'Now what do we do?'

'Nothing,' said Caroline. 'I don't know what you thought you would have said to her anyway.'

'We could have warned her.'

'Of what? That Fleur was just possibly on her inexorable way? It would terrify her, I should think. No, it's far better she doesn't know. She'll have enough to worry about tomorrow, without that. Time enough when it's all over.'

'Will it ever be all over?' said Joe.

'Of course. Well, I'd better be getting down to my hotel. Would you call me a taxi, Joe?'

'Why don't I drive you?'

'Because you've had far too much to drink,' said Caroline briskly.

'Sorry,' said Joe humbly and dialled for a taxi.

'Oh, Joe,' said Caroline, 'it's me that should be sorry. I get bossier and bossier, don't I? It's living alone, I'm afraid.'

'No, it isn't,' said Joe. 'I live alone. I'm not bossy.'

'No, you're not,' said Caroline, looking at him fondly.

'But you've always been bossy. I never really minded. There were plenty of other good things.'

'Yes,' she said, 'yes, there were, weren't there? Joe, what's been the matter with you lately? You've been so odd, so hostile. It's upset me.'

'Oh,' he said, at once upset and oddly pleased he could still upset her, 'oh, nothing. Some old wounds reopened, that's all. I'm sorry.'

'What old wounds?'

'Oh,' he said, 'I – well, I saw Magnus Phillips. Just by chance. It knocked me off my perch, that's all. Reminded me how much I hated him.'

'Oh, Joe,' said Caroline, and her face was soft, sad as it seldom was, 'I'm so sorry. So terribly sorry. I should never have done that. Never. It was madness. Total madness. Anyway,' she added more briskly, 'you consoled yourself fairly well, didn't you? Making the gossip columns with a film star.'

'Briefly,' he said.

'What was she like?' she said curiously.

'Self-obsessed,' he said simply. 'In every way.' And laughed.

Caroline laughed too. 'I'm glad to hear it. Joe, what are you staring at?'

'You,' said Joe. 'I always forget how beautiful you are. Much more beautiful than Rose. Than anyone.'

'Oh, Joe,' said Caroline. 'I'm not beautiful. I'm an old woman.'

'Caroline,' said Joe, 'to me you are still the woman who walked into the Coffee House Club that day. So gorgeous, so sexy, you took my breath away. Literally.'

'Well,' said Caroline, 'well, you weren't so bad yourself.' She looked at him and smiled. 'Still aren't. Not really.'

'Not so good either,' said Joe. 'Getting senile. I looked at Chloe this morning and thought this time tomorrow she'd be Lady Windsor and I almost burst into tears.'

'Now, Joe,' said Caroline, 'that is not senility. You've always been like that. That was the first thing I loved about you, the way you cried.' She looked at him closely. 'Joe, you're not crying now, are you? Joe, whatever for? Is it Chloe?'

'No,' he said, blowing his nose hard, 'it isn't Chloe. It's you. I miss you, Caroline, I really do. Sorry,' he added, smiling rather weakly at her.

'I miss you too,' said Caroline. 'Actually. I –' She seemed to be about to say something: then suddenly stood up decisively. 'Well, I'd better be on my way. There's my cab now. We're going to be very late tomorrow. Goodnight, Joe.'

'Goodnight, Caroline.'

He sighed as he shut the door; he felt very bleak.

The day of the investiture was perfect; blue-skied and slightly mistily golden. It was obviously going to stay that way or get even nicer; it was also clearly going to be very hot.

Kitty was much better: a little irritable, but hungry. Pandora went off to school grumbling wildly, after bidding a very sleepy Piers goodbye and good luck. Chloe took Ned to school, rang Stebbings to make sure that everything was all right, that the florists had arrived, that the caterers were on their way (not Browne and Lowe, Piers said Jean had decided against them, which meant he had decided against them; he didn't like her employing them, saying with some justification that she found it even harder than usual to relax), that the chairs and tables were all up, the cloths and napkins in place, and said she would be down immediately after lunch. She wished fervently she was simply staff and not hostess for the evening.

She had set her mind resolutely against anything except the day ahead; so far it seemed to be working. She could think of nothing else.

Her hairdresser arrived at nine thirty to comb her hair out; she suggested he should have a go at Piers's at the same time. Piers was roaming the house, literally, going from room to room, glassy pale; he had been sick twice already, and was sipping iced water neurotically. He seemed far more nervous that he was even before a first night.

'Piers,' said Chloe, 'I'm going to change now. Why don't you let Nicky tidy your hair up? I suppose that meeting at Prendergast's stopped you getting to Truefitt and Hill yesterday?'

'What? Oh yes. Pity.'

'What was it about? Jean said it was terribly high-powered.'

'Oh – nothing much. Tax,' said Piers.

'Oh, right. Well, go on, Nicky's in my room now. And then you should get changed.'

'Yes, all right,' said Piers irritably. 'I'm perfectly capable of telling the time.' He rushed into the bathroom and she heard him retching again; she had been about to ask him why he was still seeing Faraday, but decided this was not the moment.

She was just zipping up her dress when the phone rang. It was Joe. 'Hallo, poppet. Just rang to wish you luck.'

'Oh, Joe, thank you. I did ring you yesterday, twice, but you weren't there. Was it really urgent?'

'Oh – no. No, not really.' He sounded vague. 'Just a couple of things. And I thought I might miss you today. To wish you luck, you know. Both of you,' he added carefully, 'and we'll see you tonight.'

'Yes. I hear you were interviewing Annunciata.'

'Yes,' he said and he sounded very determinedly bright. 'Yes, she seems to have made it at last. Got a proper part in the *Jesus Christ Superstar* film. She's quite good apparently.'

'I'm so glad,' said Chloe, equally determinedly bright.

Piers appeared in the doorway, ashen-faced but calm now, in his wing-collared shirt and nothing else.

'I've just discovered I haven't got any black socks,' he said. 'Could you send Rosemary out quickly to get some? And help me tie this tie, I'm all thumbs.'

Chloe went to his dressing room, found a dozen pairs of black socks, and brought them to him, trying not to look smug; he looked at them and said, 'Really, Chloe, I can't wear those, they're far too thick. I wanted silk.'

'Well, it's either woollen socks or keeping the Queen waiting,' said Chloe. 'Your decision, Piers.'

Piers put on the woollen socks.

He was having a crisis with his cufflinks; Chloe fixed them for him. He was shaking violently; he was also very cold. Chloe felt a sudden, unexpected warmth towards him, reached up on an impulse and kissed him.

'You'll be fine,' she said.

'I hope so,' he said, and then he smiled down at her and said, 'I love you, you know.'

'Do you?' said Chloe, looking at him very directly, feeling the warmth leave her again. 'Do you really?'

'Yes,' he said, clearly surprised by the question. 'Yes, I really do.'

'Piers,' she said, 'Piers, I don't –' 'understand you at all' she had been going to say, but then Kitty ran in and hugged his legs, and he sighed, clearly irritated, and disentangled her a little too firmly, and said, 'I have to finish dressing,' and disappeared into his dressing room.

The car arrived at nine forty-five: the gates of the palace opened at ten. Rosemary and Kitty stood on the steps to see them off, taking endless photographs. There were a couple of journalists there as well. As she stood there, smiling determinedly, Chloe heard the phone ringing and debated telling Rosemary to answer it; then she said, 'Come on, Piers, let's go,' and they were in the car, Piers gripping her hand almost maniacally as they went through Belgrave Square, round Hyde Park Corner and down Constitution Hill to join the long line of other cars making their way into the forecourt of Buckingham Palace, and she looked out of the window, and thought how extraordinary it was that a man who could hold hundreds of people spellbound in a theatre night after night, who could calmly watch himself in the presence of the highest in the land and in his profession, on a screen magnified twenty, a hundred times, every tiny facial gesture under scrutiny, who could make a charming, gracious, amusing speech as he held his Oscar, who could sing in public for the first time in his life together with the chorus of the English National Opera, how extraordinary it was that such a man could be reduced to naked, quivering terror at the prospect of kneeling before one small, rather unremarkable-looking woman and not having to say a single word.

They followed the red carpet into the palace, where they were separated; Piers was taken into a room with the other recipients (where, he told her afterwards, he stood for an hour, with no coffee, nowhere to sit down, no lavatory even, feeling increasingly more dreadful: the only relief being when he was able to practise his kneeling on the kneeling stool – 'The Major Domo kept saying right knee right hand and I was so sure I'd get it wrong) while Chloe went up the Grand Staircase, along the corridor, into the ballroom. She felt more and more as if she was dreaming, as if she was watching some other person, dressed in a stiff navy blue dress, accompanying a man she did not know; she settled on her gilt chair, stared at the pair of thrones ahead of her on the dais and waited. Everything, including the Yeoman of the Guard who flanked the room, seemed to be red and gold. A band was playing in the gallery behind them, a most extraordinary mixture of music, it seemed to her, or was it just her mood, from Elgar to *My Fair Lady*.

At eleven, precisely, the Queen appeared, smiling, walked down towards the dais. Chloe half expected to see the corgis with her. She looked very small, very neat, prettier, less forbidding, than she did in photographs. Piers who had been presented to her once before at premières, and seen her several times, had told Chloe that, but she was still surprised. The band played the national anthem, and the Queen stood listening to it rather intently as if it was a tune she had not heard before; then she smiled and said, 'Ladies and Gentlemen please be seated.'

The recipients began to move, one by one, perfectly choreographed, from the side of the ballroom towards the dais; Chloe watched in the same odd state of detachment, saw Piers pause, bow, walk forward, go down on one knee, looking up at the Queen, watched the blade of the sword flash as it touched first his right shoulder then his left, and wondered why she could not see very well. She realized as he walked backwards away from Her Majesty again, his face still solemn, but softer, easier, and bowed for the second time, that it was because her eyes were filled with tears.

Then it was over and they were outside, besieged by photographers, and he was laughing, relaxed, easy with them, with her, clearly enchanted with everything but most of all himself, and she said, more amused than anything at his patent childlike pleasure and delight, 'Darling, well done, congratulations,' and they drove to the Garrick where he got out of the car after kissing her and saying, 'Goodbye, Lady Windsor, I shall see you later.' Then, limp with relief at being free of him for a few hours, she sank back and watched the centre of London become the rather plain sprawl of the Cromwell Road, the plainer one of the Great West Road, and then the squalid outposts of London Airport; and then it began to soften, change, broaden out, and by half past two they were in the rolling green charm of Berkshire, and at three o'clock she was sitting drinking tea in the kitchen of Stebbings, answering questions about glasses and flowers and microphones and coat rails and Portaloos and wondering if perhaps she had not imagined the entire happenings of the morning.

At four the children arrived in a car with Rosemary; at six Piers arrived, laughing, flushed, still high on pleasure. He kissed them all, said the lunch had been wonderful, marvellous, and first he was going down to the stables to see Dream Street and the other horses and then he was going to have a nap and then a swim, and after that he would feel quite himself again and get ready for the evening. Pandora told him he looked like a prince, and he told her he felt like one, but he was only just a boring old knight, and she said should she curtsy to him, and he said yes, she certainly should; Chloe said, 'Piers really!' and he said, 'Oh darling, don't be so stuffy,' and Pandora jumped off her chair and ran over to him, and dropped the most beautiful curtsy, learnt from Miss Vacani and said, 'I am truly honoured to make your acquaintance, Sir Piers,' and he bowed and kissed her hand. While Chloe was trying to smile, and Ned was jumping up and down trying to win some attention for himself, Jean Potts came in and said Mick McHugh, one of the stable-lads, had just been thrown by Dream Street and that the horse had fallen on him, and could Piers come to the stables straight away.

Mick McHugh suffered some very serious injuries, including a collapsed lung, caused by its being ruptured by two of his ribs and was in intensive care, but declared out of danger by early evening. Dream Street had broken a leg in the fall and had to be shot.

Chloe found Piers weeping in the tack room, a huge tumbler of whisky in his hand placed there by Jean Potts, who had followed him out to the stables and witnessed at first hand his terrible distress.

'Piers, I'm so sorry. So terribly sorry. I –' She raised her hands towards him, and then dropped them again as if aware of how useless she was being.

'I'll leave you,' she said quietly, and went up to their room. The day had darkened; great clouds were rolling up from the west, and the sky was streaked orange and red behind them, dramatic, threatening. Chloe felt chilled as well as sad about Dream Street, anxious about the evening; she felt a sense of great unease, almost of danger; and was even half inclined (while knowing it was impossible, absurd) to cancel the party, to keep her family together, safely about her, the doors closed against intruders. Then she told herself that she was being absurd, that the death of a horse, however upsetting, could hardly rank as a major tragedy and that of course everything should go ahead, it would comfort Piers, restore his happiness. And seized upon the loss of Dream Street as an excuse to ignore the message waiting for her from Jean that her mother had rung and would she ring her back right away. She had enough to deal with; they could both wait.

By the time the first guests came rolling up the drive, the rain had begun: light powdery stuff, more mist than anything. Piers and she stood at the front door with the children, greeting their guests, apologizing for their incompetence at controlling the weather, smiling, accepting congratulations, felicitations, gifts. Piers was laughing, easy again; only the tautness of his jaw told of his pain, his grief over the belated horse.

After half an hour it was raining harder, grey sheets of the stuff, and a driving wind had set in. It was cold; Chloe worried about her women guests, in their summer clothes, fine lawns and silks and floating gauze, sleeveless, strapless (and the younger ones virtually skirtless as well). She phoned the marquee people to tell them to bring some heaters over, but there was no one there; she wished there was some warm food, asked the caterers if they could make some soup, but of course it was too late. She offered shawls, jumpers, wraps, which most people declined, and then stood, some of the women wearing their husbands' dinner jackets, shivering in the marquee, drinking the chilled champagne, the Bellinis, the Bucks Fizz. It was a nightmare, every hostess's nightmare; she felt like sending everyone home, telling them to come back another day.

And then Ludovic arrived, wonderfully handsome in a white dinner jacket, with a pretty girl on his arm who looked young enough to be his daughter ('Just cover,' he whispered in Chloe's ear), and gave her a huge bear-like hug and followed her into the marquee. 'Shit,' he said loudly, audibly, rubbing his hands together, 'it's fucking freezing in here. Maybe we could do some keep-fit or something, Chloe, warm us all up.'

Everyone laughed, made blessedly easier at once; then 'Let's have some music and dancing before dinner,' said Piers. 'It's a good idea, Ludo, get warm that way.'

It worked. The DJ was summoned abruptly from the kitchen and started playing, people started dancing, rather determinedly, and by nine thirty when supper was served, the heat of the bodies had warmed the marquee to such an extent that the men were taking off their jackets voluntarily.

Thank God, thought Chloe, maybe it was going after all to be all right; and everyone seemed very happy, the dancing had mixed the groups as well as warming them, there was a buzz of conversation and laughter louder than supper-level. Piers had relaxed, had enjoyed meeting the challenge, solving the problem; he was sitting at a table with Maria Woolf on one side of him and Pandora on the other, looking very easy, telling jokes, laughing at other people's. It brought back sharply for Chloe that other occasion, more than six years ago, the terrible lunch when she had had no table to sit at, no one to talk to, and she reflected briefly that nothing had really changed so very much. Then she felt an arm round her shoulders and it was Damian. 'Hallo, dear Lady Windsor,' he said and took her hand and kissed it and begged her to join him, and to tell him about the morning; she sat down and the Montagues were at the table, and so was Annunciata, with a young man who looked quite extraordinarily like the boy who played Tadzio in *Death in Venice*, and so was Ludovic with his girlfriend whose name was Candida, and they all told Chloe how lovely she looked, and how much too absurdly young to be the mother of her large family and what a wonderful party she had organized yet again, and how proud of Piers she must be and what a success she had made of the marriage, and she realized things had actually changed a great deal.

She suddenly noticed her mother had still not arrived, or Joe; surely they should be here by now. She hoped nothing had happened to them, that they hadn't had an accident on the road in the torrential rain. Joe was quite likely to be late, but Caroline had promised they would come together.

When she saw Joe and Caroline, standing together in the doorway of the marquee, she was disproportionately pleased; she went over, hugged them both, brushed aside their apologies, fetched them drinks, led them to the buffet table; by then Piers was gone, back to his table, back to his audience, and she concentrated on looking after her mother and Joe. They both seemed slightly strained, but she had been through such intense strain herself that day it seemed almost a natural state of affairs.

'I rang you,' said Caroline, slightly reproachfully, as Chloe led her to a table, followed by Joe. 'Didn't you get the message? It was important, Chloe. I – I wanted to –'

'Yes,' said Chloe, interrupting her, 'yes, Mummy, I did, but we had the most terrible accident here this evening. Dream Street had to be shot.'

'My God, how ghastly,' said Caroline. She was clearly very upset by this; she went white, sat down suddenly, drained her glass, looked round for another drink. 'I'm so sorry, Chloe, how terrible for Piers.'

'Yes, yes, it was,' said Chloe, the irreverent and almost shocking thought entering her head that Caroline was more upset by the death of a horse than she would have been of Piers himself, and the thought made a nervous, hysterical giggle rise in her throat and she crushed it with a great effort. 'It was terrible, but he's all right. For the moment. Tomorrow, it'll really hit him, I think.'

'Chloe,' said Joe, 'Chloe, there's –'

'Oh God,' said Chloe, 'excuse me, both of you, Piers is signalling. I know what it is, there's some problem with the red wine. I'd promised to see the wine waiter before, just as you arrived. I'll be back.'

By the time she had sorted out the problem of the red wine (which was actually impossible to sort, as it was too cold, but had to be poured anyway), listened to Maria Woolf telling a long story about how she had tripped on the red carpet when they had gone to the palace for Jack's MBE, found Rosemary and told her to take Ned, who was crawling around under the tables, away to bed, heard Ludovic's companion tell her that she was so thrilled to be there, and that she thought Piers's *Othello* was just about the most marvellously exciting thing she had ever seen, led Joe over to Annunciata, who was full of excitement at seeing him again, and wanted to tell him all about her new part in *Superstar*, introduced her mother (at Caroline's own request) to Robin Leveret (not sure which of them would hate the other more), listened to Sarah, Toby's wife, tell her at what seemed like immense length about her difficulty in deciding what colour to paint the nursery, enthused over Damian Lutyens's news that he and Liza Montague were to work together on an operetta which was also a children's extravaganza, to be performed at the Coliseum at Christmas, exclaimed dutifully over Tabitha Levine's announcement that she was going to make what she called a tremendously innovative silent film in black and white (while wondering how such a thing could possibly be innovative), kissed Ludovic swiftly, politely, socially, told him she would see him later, that of course she loved him, that of course she could see that Candida was no more than an adornment, a buttonhole, a pair of cufflinks, no sooner had she done all that, than the waiters came round with champagne, and Piers stood up to speak.

'Not a long speech,' he said, 'just a few words.'

There were some catcalls from the guests of 'sure' and 'that'll be the day', some laughter, some slow handclapping; he held up his hand for silence, laughing himself.

'I swear. I only wanted to say this has been the most wonderful day of my life, the crowning of it so to speak: to thank those of you who gave the lunch for me today, to thank all of you for coming tonight, to share it with us, and most important, to thank my lovely wife, Chloe, for being and staying with me through what must have sometimes seemed like a very long six years. Lady Windsor, Chloe, darling, stand up, take a bow.'

Blushing, embarrassed, laughing rather feebly, Chloe stood up, and the whole room clapped, blew her kisses, called out her name. She looked round the room, at the candle-lit tables and the ropes of roses and the faces lifted to her, and knew she had to say something, but her mind was quite blank, she didn't even dare let it think, but just held up her hand, and said simply, 'Thank you all very much for coming. It's been nothing really, I've enjoyed it. All of it.' Everyone laughed and just as she was relievedly sinking back on to her chair, the head waiter appeared in the doorway with a great wedding cake on a trolley, only instead of just the bride and groom, there were three small figures on it with them, and a whole haze of candles, and the DJ put the Anniversary Waltz on and Piers came towards her and said, 'May I have the honour?' and quite suddenly that really was too much, she felt sick at the very sight of it, and of him; she wanted to get it over, make a public announcement, say aloud, there and then, 'This man is a cheat and a liar, and he has had affairs with several men since our marriage,' only of course she didn't, she managed to smile and move into the waltz with him, while flinching from his touch rather as she did when he approached her in bed.

'I love you,' said Piers and bent and kissed her; and then she really couldn't stand it any more; she drew back from him and mumbled that she must check on the children, and ran from the marquee.

* * *

She went to the morning room; it was always her favourite. She sat down in the small chair by the fire and sat hugging herself, staring into the flames, thinking of the first time she had ever been to Stebbings, when all that she had known about Piers had been that she loved him, when their relationship had been innocent and peaceful, and wept, mostly at the dreadful change in herself, and her feelings for him, at love turned to distaste, innocence become darkly carnal knowledge, and suddenly she heard the door open and she turned expecting to see Piers, only it was Ludovic, his face concerned, tender, saying, 'Chloe, darling darling Chloe, don't cry.' He sat down beside her on the floor and said, 'This is insane, Chloe, you have to tell him, tonight, you must, you must.'

She said, 'Oh Ludovic, I don't know what to do.'

Ludovic stared at her; his face white, drawn. 'Chloe, what do you mean, you don't know what to do? You have to leave Piers, and you have to come to me. Of course you know what to do.'

'Yes,' said Chloe, 'yes, of course I know.' She hesitated then, looked at him, her eyes panicky, almost scared. 'Only I don't, really, Ludovic, I don't at all.'

'Chloe,' said Ludovic, 'what are you saying?'

'I'm saying,' said Chloe, 'that I don't know what to do. I've never known what to do, Ludovic, unless someone told me. I've never made up my own mind. I'm a hopeless, mindless creature. I'm not in control of my life at all.'

'Chloe, darling, what are you talking about?' He took her in his arms, started stroking her hair, soothing her. 'Of course you're in control of your life.'

'No, Ludovic, I'm not. Everything that happens to me is because of something somebody else has done or decided. And that awful charade in there just summed it up. I'm only a bit player, Ludovic, a walk-on part. An extra.'

'Darling, you're just upset. Hysterical.'

'No, Ludo, I'm not hysterical. I'm very calm. Actually. Just in despair.' And she burst into tears.

'Darling, darling Chloe, shush. Don't cry, my darling, don't. You've been so brave for such a long time. I – love you so much and I'm so proud of you. There, darling, there.'

And as she lay there against him, in the engulfing warmth and strength and comfort of him, feeling just as panicky, more almost, wanting to stay, but also wanting, needing to go, she looked over his shoulder suddenly and there in the doorway, standing just in front of an embarrassed-looking Jean Potts, was a girl. A tall, extremely beautiful girl, with a cloud of dark hair, and very dark blue eyes. She looked at Chloe, at Ludovic, and then with more than just a suggestion of a smile, she said, 'I presume you're Chloe. I'm Fleur.'

Chapter 38

July 1972

For the rest of her life Chloe, remembering that moment, had thought of all the things she might have said and done: what appropriate, clever, authoritative, sophisticated remark or gesture she might have made; and sometimes laughed, sometimes smiled, sometimes squirmed, according to her mood, at what she actually did and said, which was to stand up, and smile graciously, and offer Fleur a cup of tea.

It wasn't quite like that, of course, quite that bad, quite that (in Fleur's eyes she felt sure) hopelessly predictable. 'You must be very tired,' was what she actually said. 'It's such a horrible night, can I get you anything, a drink, something to eat, maybe even a cup of tea?'

And Fleur had looked at her, taken her in; she could feel her eyes examining her, exploring her, cool, amused (although not hostile) dark blue eyes, and she put up her hand to smooth the hair Ludovic had been stroking, to brush the tears from her still-wet face, looked down quickly to make sure her dress, just slightly perilously low-cut, was still as respectable as it was able to be, and then Fleur said, 'Sure, tea'd be good, thank you.'

'Come this way, then,' she said, leading her across the hall towards the kitchen, adding, over her shoulder to Ludovic who was looking as near to nonplussed as she had ever seen him, 'Ludo, could you go and find Joe, please, and maybe my mother.' She went into the kitchen where various people were sitting about, relaxing now that the food had been served, picking at the dishes themselves, pouring themselves drinks, and said, 'I wonder, could one of you make us a pot of tea please? I'm so sorry to bring you into the kitchen,' she added, feeling even more facile, more absurdly the sort of person she knew Fleur thought her to be, 'but we have a big party going on, it's chaos, we'll find somewhere quiet in a minute.'

'That's OK,' said Fleur and then, looking around her, 'quite a place you have here.'

Chloe started to take in her voice, slightly husky, quite low, that voice, and with quite a strong accent, and then she turned, and saw someone else in the doorway, a very tall, immensely thin young man, with an ugly, bony, hawklike face covered in freckles, wearing jeans and a denim jacket, with a long knitted blue and pink scarf hung around his neck; she looked at him, just stood and stared and had a very strange, strong and plainly absurd feeling that she had known him all her life.

'Oh, my God, I forgot all about you,' said Fleur. 'I'm so sorry. Chloe, this is Reuben Blake, he's a friend of mine. Reuben, this is Chloe. My sister.'

'Hi,' said Reuben, walking forward, holding out his bony hand to Chloe, and she braced herself for it to crush her, and to her great surprise it was gentle, that hand, and very warm; she smiled up at him, noticing that his eyes were the most extraordinary colour, a sort of yellowish brown, flecked with brown, freckled eyes, she thought, how extraordinary, and then the door opened and Caroline came in.

'Oh, for God's sake,' she said, to Fleur, 'what an appalling thing to do. Chloe, surely you can find somewhere more suitable to talk than this, it's absolute bedlam in here.'

They both, her two daughters, looked at her, in silence, equally, albeit briefly, at a loss.

Chloe, to her surprise, recovered first. 'It's absolute bedlam everywhere, Mummy,' she said, 'and Fleur wanted a cup of tea.'

'Well, let's take the tea and move. Maybe Piers's study would be quiet.'

'Yes, all right,' said Chloe, adding, 'Mummy, this is Reuben Blake, a friend of Fleur's. This is my mother, Caroline Hunterton,' she said to Reuben, who bowed slightly at Caroline and said, 'Hi,' again; she nodded at him graciously, indicated to them to follow her and they all obediently filed out into the hall, where Joe was standing, looking impotently, wretchedly miserable, down the corridor, Joe too, and into Piers's study.

Fleur looked around her with a kind of detached interest and sat down on the large, leather-topped desk; Reuben leant, extraordinarily relaxed, Chloe thought, admiring him, liking him for it, against the fireplace, Caroline sat in the swivel chair, Joe in the other chair, by the window. Chloe, mistress of the house, hostess of the evening, stood, feeling awkward, in the middle of the room.

'This is an appalling thing to do,' Caroline said again to Fleur. 'Surely it could have waited. Until tomorrow at least.'

'I specialize in appalling things,' said Fleur, looking at her with an extraordinarily hostile expression in her eyes. 'Maybe it's in my genes.'

'Fleur!' said Reuben. He said it very quietly, very gently; but it seemed to have an effect; she looked down at her hands, was silent.

'Well,' said Chloe, more awkward still, 'we obviously have a lot to talk about. The trouble is, Fleur, I have two hundred and fifty people here. We're – well, we're celebrating something. It's a bit – difficult to talk just now.'

'Oh, don't worry about me,' said Fleur, 'that's fine. We'll just stay here till the two hundred and fifty have gone. Won't we, Reuben? I'm sure you all have much more important things than me to worry about.' 'As always' hung in the air; her face, her eyes were hostile.

'Fleur,' said Joe, 'you surely must see it's not easy for Chloe. Just at the moment.'

'Yeah,' said Fleur, 'I can see that.' She looked at Chloe, her eyes amused, contemptuous. 'In all sorts of ways.'

Chloe flushed, looked down. 'Look,' she said, 'I'm terribly sorry. It must seem so rude. But if you could bear with me – us – for just a little while I'll get you both some food, find you rooms even, if you're tired. And when everyone's gone.' She paused; Piers's voice came down the corridor, calling her.

Well, it had to come, had to happen; he had to know, meet Fleur, find out who she was, what was going on. She took a deep breath, opened the door, called him.

'Piers! We're in here.'

And he walked in, swiftly, impatiently, clearly angry, looked round at them all, and then as he took them in, focused on Fleur, sitting there on his desk, her long legs crossed – long, gorgeous, perfect legs, thought Chloe, irrelevantly envious – her arms folded, her eyes on him coolly interested, his own eyes widened, darkened, into shock, and then, unbelievably, into recognition, and he took a sharp, sudden breath and said, 'What on earth are you doing here?'

Caroline took command with formidable ease; dispatched Joe for drinks, told Chloe to go and see to her guests, ordered Reuben to follow her out to the kitchen, to get some food for himself and Fleur, told Jean Potts, who was clearly in an appalling state, to find the housekeeper and tell her to get two small bedrooms ready. Leaving Piers and Fleur in the study, staring at one another, she with an expression just short of a smile on her face, her long legs swinging, he frozen-faced, ashen, standing almost to attention, his fists clenched at his sides.

Ludovic took over then, took Piers's place, acted as host; in any case the party, sensing somehow, in a corporate way, that things were wrong, out of kilter, was already beginning to break up, people were rising, leaving, shouting farewells at people at other tables, looking round for Piers, for Chloe, kissing her, thanking her, and she was standing there, at the doorway now, with Ludovic at her side, saying goodbye, and she was sorry about Piers, he had had to lie down, he wasn't feeling well suddenly, the strain of the day had been so intense; Maria Woolf offered to go and see him, but Ludovic, smiling, easy, said he really thought Piers was better left to rest, and saw her off; they all went, expressing sympathy, regret, gratitude for a lovely party, the fleet of cars driving endlessly down the drive; it was a clear night now, starry, sweet-smelling after the rain. Horribly different, thought Chloe, looking out into the tranquil darkness of the garden and the meadows beyond, from the seething storm raging inside.

Almost everyone had gone now; Ludovic said to her, 'I'll stay, darling, you need some support, I can send Candida home with someone else,' and she said, desperate to be rid of at least one complication in her life, no, no, she would be fine, Caroline was there, Joe was there, best they were on their own, just the family; he held her for a long time, before kissing her tenderly and then collecting a sulky Candida and driving off very slowly down the drive.

Chloe took a deep breath and went back inside.

They were all in the drawing room now; silently awkward, looking at one another. She went in, asked Joe for a drink.

'I think,' she said, 'perhaps Fleur should tell us why she's here.'

Fleur looked at her, and there was a strange expression in the blue eyes, cautious, wary, but not altogether unfriendly.

'Sure,' she said, 'and I'm sorry it's so inconvenient. I – well, maybe I should have waited. But I was upset. And scared.'

'Scared?' said Chloe. 'Whatever about?' She found it hard to imagine Fleur being scared of anything; she seemed totally invulnerable.

'This book,' said Fleur.

'Oh,' said Chloe, 'the book.'

'Yeah. Did you know – well, I guess you did – that Magnus has been burgled, that the publisher's offices have been burgled, burnt down, and now that Magnus has been knocked off his bike, all that stuff?'

'Yes,' said Chloe. 'Of course we did. I hope you're not implying that's anything to do with us? Mr Phillips is not exactly our favourite person, but we don't have criminal tendencies.'

Fleur looked at her again. 'No, I don't suppose you do. Although you do have very strong reasons for suppressing this book.'

'Possibly,' said Chloe.

'But you might, probably do have theories about who it is doing all this. And why. I wanted to see Magnus, talk to him, but his publisher wouldn't tell me where he is. So – I came to you.'

'I don't quite understand,' said Chloe, 'why you should be so scared. Nobody's going to knock you off your bike or anything.'

'They might,' said Fleur.

'But why? I don't see what it's got to do with you.'

'Well,' said Fleur, 'I'm in the book. And my dad's in the book.'

'Your father?' said Chloe. 'But why? I don't understand. And anyway, how do you know?'

'I know because Magnus Phillips told me.'

'You know Magnus Phillips?' said Caroline. Her face was white suddenly, her eyes very watchful.

'Yes,' said Fleur, 'I know Magnus Phillips. And I may as well tell you, I've been – well, helping him a little. With this book.'

Chloe watched herself, quite detachedly, with a sense of slight surprise, walk forward and slap Fleur very hard across the face. She heard Joe and Caroline and Piers all say her name at once: she watched herself look at them, very calm, very contemptuous, saw herself turn round, walk out of the room, go into the kitchen, bury her head in her arms on the table.

She didn't know how long she had been there, one minute, ten, an hour, when Joe came in. He looked very distressed, sat down, put his arm round her.

'I'm sorry, Chloe,' he said, 'so sorry.'

'Did you know?'

'Did I know what?'

'Well – that she was helping Magnus Phillips. With his enquiries. As they say.'

'No,' he said, 'no of course not. But I did know she'd come to London. I'm sorry. Caroline and I were going to warn you. But we couldn't get hold of you, and we had no idea she would come here.'

'She's awful, Joe. Horrible. So hard, so – angry.'

'Yes,' he said, 'yes, she is. Very angry. But –'

'But what?'

'She does have reason to be angry. Maybe not with you directly. But with all of us. The family. And Piers.'

'Ah, yes,' she said. 'Well she's not alone there.' She was silent for a while; then she said, 'Joe, what is all this about? What possible connection can Fleur's father have with this book?'

'I don't know,' he said, 'but I know what connection Fleur thinks there is.'

'What?'

Joe told her.

Fleur sat looking round the room. Nobody was talking. Her face hurt. She would have died rather than show it, admit it, but it did. It stung and ached, and it felt very hot. Chloe had hit it very hard.

'Maybe,' said Reuben gently, 'maybe we should leave it.'

Caroline looked at him coldly. 'What on earth do you mean, leave it? Leave what?'

He smiled at her, his strange, crumpled smile. 'All of it. For now.'

'Well of course we can't leave it,' said Caroline. 'I never heard of anything so ridiculous.'

Fleur stared at her, and thought how extraordinary it was that in this gathering of her family, her sister, her sister's husband, someone who was to all intents and purposes her stepfather, the one person she knew least, liked least, was her own mother. God, how she didn't like her. Cold, unfeeling bitch. She had been a great deal better off without her all these years. It had been a good day for her when Caroline had handed her over to her father.

She stood up. 'I think Reuben's right. We're all tired. We're not making any sense. We can talk tomorrow.'

Piers looked relieved, just slightly less distraught, yet clearly not wanting to seem as if he was opting out.

'Well, I –'

At which point Jean Potts appeared, looking more distraught, more embarrassed than anyone, and spoke to him very quietly. He looked at her for a long time, then said, 'All right, I'll come. Will you all excuse me? I have to take a phone call.'

Caroline watched him as he left the room; then she too stood up. 'If you come with me,' she said to Fleur and Reuben, 'I'll show you to your rooms.'

They followed her up the stairs; she turned on the first landing and said, 'I'm sorry, but you're on the nursery floor. This one is full.'

'Shit a brick,' said Fleur to Reuben, 'not the nursery floor. Oh my.'

They were in adjacent rooms separated by a large linen cupboard.

'They're all unreal,' said Fleur, walking into Reuben's room. He was already in bed, naked, looking thinner than usual. 'No wonder they behave so badly.'

'They don't all behave badly,' said Reuben. 'Chloe doesn't.'

'Oh, for fuck's sake,' said Fleur. 'She hit me.'

'With good reason,' he said and pulled the blankets up.

'She's exactly what I thought,' said Fleur determinedly, 'a spoilt, ridiculous, pathetic bitch.'

'You don't really think that,' said Reuben.

There was a long silence. Then Fleur said, sounding surprised even to herself, 'No, as a matter of fact, I don't think I do.'

Chloe was lying in bed in the dark when Piers came in. He said, 'Chloe?'

'Go away. Just go away,' she said.

'No,' he said, 'no, I can't.'

'Piers, please!'

'Chloe, I have to talk to you.'

He sat down on the bed. She was grateful for the dark; she didn't have to look at him.

'Chloe,' he said.

'Yes, Piers?'

'Chloe, the father of your baby – was it – was it Ludovic?'

'Yes,' she said, her voice sounding dead, heavy, 'yes, it was.'

'Do you love him?'

'I – God, Piers, I don't know what I feel about anything. I think so. Yes.'

'Has it been going on long?'

'Quite long. Yes.'

'Oh, God,' he said and started to cry.

'Piers, for God's sake. I think that's a little hypocritical. You've been having an affair with my sister.'

'I didn't know she was your sister.'

'And I suppose that makes all the difference?' she said, her voice rising, sitting up in bed, switching on the light suddenly, savagely. His face was tear-stained, he looked odd, not himself.

'A little. I think it makes her behaviour worse than mine.'

'I think we're splitting hairs here,' said Chloe.

'Maybe.'

'Piers, why?'

'Chloe, I don't know why. Why I have affairs with anyone.'

'Men or women?' she asked and saw him wince.

Then, 'Yes,' he said, very low. 'I suppose I want to be needed. Wanted.'

'Oh, really!' she said. 'Well that's a fine excuse, Piers. What if I want to be needed? What then? Do we all go around sleeping with people just because we want to be needed?'

'You had an affair with Ludovic.'

'Yes, I did. After years and years of struggling, of trying to be loyal, of trying to accept your behaviour, of trying to understand you. And then realizing I never could.'

'Ah,' he said, quieter still.

'Piers,' she said, changing the subject, with shocking speed, 'Piers, is it true what Fleur thinks?'

'And what does Fleur think? Does anyone know?'

'She thinks you knew her father in Hollywood. All those years ago. Did you, Piers? Did you?'

'Yes, I did. I knew him quite well.'

'And did you do it, Piers?'

'Do what?'

'What she thought, did you betray him, did you sell his story to the magazine?'

There was a long silence; then he said, 'No, I didn't. Of course I didn't. I would never betray a friend.'

'You betrayed me.'

'That's different.'

'Oh, really.'

'Chloe, please!'

'Well, then, do you know who did?'

'Yes,' he said, 'yes, I know who did. At least I think so.'

'Are you going to tell me?'

'Does it matter?'

'Yes, it does. It's obsessed Fleur all her life apparently, so it does, yes, matter to me.'

He stared at her; he seemed about to speak. And then the phone rang sharply by her bed; she picked it up. 'Yes? Chloe Windsor.'

'I have a person-to-person call from Santa Barbara, California,' said the operator, 'for Mr Piers Windsor. Is Mr Windsor there?'

'Yes,' said Chloe, rage stabbing through her, 'yes, he's here.' She handed the phone to Piers, as if it was going to burn her. 'It's for you,' she said, 'it's from Santa Barbara. Your friend Mr Zwirn no doubt. Take it, Piers, I don't want to have anything to do with it. Or you. Any more.'

He looked at her in silence for a long time; then he walked out of the room. She waited until he had picked up the phone in his study, then put the receiver down. She had no wish to hear a single word.

She lay for a while, waiting, praying he wouldn't come back. It was very quiet. She suddenly felt dirty, contaminated. She got up cautiously, went into the bathroom, ran a bath. She lay in it for a long time, for almost an hour, until the water was growing cold. Then she got up and wrapped herself in a bathrobe; she felt desperately tired and very sick. She couldn't begin to think what she might do next, what might happen in the morning. All she wanted now was to sleep, to rest, to recover just a little. She was just going to crawl back into bed when she heard Ned calling her name on the baby alarm; she ran down the corridor to the room where he was sleeping. He had not really woken; he was lying there, tousled, sweetly restless, obviously in the throes of a bad dream. She climbed into the small bed beside him, took him in her arms, and fell almost immediately asleep.

And so she did not hear Piers knocking quite loudly on her door, did not find the note he pushed underneath it, until just before seven the next morning, when the sun was already rising in the sky, and the day hot and still again, after the storm, and Jean Potts was standing in the doorway of Ned's room, her face contorted with grief, telling her she must come downstairs at once because Piers had been found dead, down at the stables, lying in Dream Street's stall, an empty bottle of whisky and another of sleeping pills in the straw beside him.

Chapter 39

July – August 1972

'Now listen,' said Joe, 'you did not kill him. He killed himself.'

'No, but you don't understand.' She was twisting and turning in her chair, shredding tissues endlessly. 'He killed himself because I was so horrible to him. I told him about Ludovic, I was so angry with him about Fleur, I asked him about – about, you know, about Brendan. I shouldn't have done it, Joe, it was terrible, you know he's unstable, he's done it twice before, I should have been more careful –'

'Darling Chloe,' said Joe, and his voice was very firm, very tender, 'he didn't do it twice before, he went through the motions, under very carefully controlled conditions. Which he did again this time. It was always the same pattern, the notes, or the positioning, so someone was bound to find him. And the method, pills and alcohol which are slow. If he really wanted to die, he would have shot himself –' He stopped suddenly, aware that he was making matters worse.

Chloe stared at him, her eyes huge in her white face. 'Exactly. He did not want to die. He wrote me a note, I should have found it, should have done something.'

'But you didn't find it, because you were with Ned. You didn't ignore it, darling, you just didn't find it.'

'I know. But I shouldn't have done it in the first place, Joe, I shouldn't. It was such a terrible thing to do, I should have shut up, kept quiet, it was so wrong, but – but –'

'Chloe, you've kept quiet for a very long time. He drove you to it. In the end. He had behaved appallingly to you.'

'No, he hadn't, Joe, he hadn't, not really. He told me often, just these last few weeks, he loved me, he wanted us to sort things out, and then – then last night, when it all seemed so terrible, I wanted to hurt him, to pay him back for – well, for things. Oh, Joe –'

Her voice rose to a wail; she looked dreadful, sitting there, her face ravaged, her hair wild, shaking violently. Joe felt totally helpless. Jean Potts came in. She was white-faced but very calm.

'Mr Payton, is there anything I can do?'

'Yes,' said Joe, 'yes, there is. Could you call Bannerman, get him down. I think we need him . . .'

'No, we don't,' said Chloe fretfully, pushing him away. 'I don't want to be sedated, or soothed, I have to see this through, I have to,' and she started crying again, loudly, shockingly.

'I'll get some tea,' said Jean hastily.

'I'll come and fetch it,' said Joe and followed her out to the kitchen. 'Call Dr Bannerman,' he said to her quietly. 'She's in a dreadful state.'

'Yes, all right, Mr Payton. I'm so sorry. Er – Mr Windsor – that is, I mean, the – the body . . .' Her voice tailed off.

'I think he's still Mr Windsor for now,' said Joe gently. 'What about it?'

'The doctor said there would have to be an inquest. He's – been taken away to the hospital. I told Mrs – Lady – oh God. I told Chloe but I don't think she took it in. And the police came, and they took the note. She was very upset about that.'

'Do you . . .' Joe hesitated. 'Do you know what it said? The note? It's all right, you can tell me. I'm family.'

'Yes, I know. I did see it. I actually found it, when I opened the bedroom door. It was very – short. It just said, "I can't take any more. I'm sorry." And it said "I do love you." ' Her voice shook again. 'It's so sad, Mr Payton. After a day like yesterday.'

'Yes, it is dreadful,' said Joe, 'quite dreadful.' Thinking, and trying to suppress the thought, that Piers had always had a wonderful sense of timing, that this whole thing was superb theatre. 'Jean, why don't you go and lie down for a while. You look terrible.'

'No, it's very kind of you, Mr Payton, but I'd really rather not. It helps to be doing things. I'll carry on, there are so many calls to make, and I'll get Dr Bannerman to come down if I can.'

'Fine. Anything urgent, Jean, you can ask me. Where are the children?'

'In the nursery with Rosemary. And Lady Hunterton.'

'How's Pandora?'

'She's fairly calm. Shocked, I suppose. Poor little girl. She loved her father so much. More than anything in the world, he was the person she most cared about, she worshipped him.'

Jesus Christ, thought Joe, where have I heard all this before, and he thought of Fleur, who had undoubtedly helped to bring all this about, and he thought that if he could have got hold of her at the moment, he would easily have killed her.

'Jesus,' said Fleur. 'Sweet Jesus, Reuben, what have I done?'

'You haven't done anything,' said Reuben. 'He did it.'

'Reuben, that's not true. I have done something. First I seduced him, then I came here last night, tore into the family. Don't tell me I haven't done anything, Reuben, I've been the catalyst in this whole thing.'

'Fleur, that is absolutely not true.' Reuben was very distressed, his face pale and anguished, his large hands holding Fleur's small ones. 'Listen, the guy was not stable. He killed himself. He probably didn't mean to die. It was probably a cry for help. It usually is.'

'Don't practise your fucking psychiatry on me, Reuben. I don't need it right now.'

'Maybe you do,' said Reuben calmly.

Fleur raised her hand and hit him. Then she burst into tears.

'Oh, Reuben, darling Reuben, I didn't mean that, really I didn't. I'm so glad you're here. So terribly glad. I'm so sorry. Please forgive me.'

'Sure,' he said. 'I may go for a walk for a little while.'

She watched him loping down the drive, and thought she had never in her entire life felt so near to running away.

Caroline came down the stairs; she looked exhausted.

'Oh,' she said. 'It's you.'

'Yeah,' said Fleur. 'Sorry. I wish I wasn't here, but I have to be, I understand. Anyway, I want to see Chloe.'

'I'm sure she doesn't want to see you.'

'No, I don't suppose she does.'

'Well then, leave her alone. For now.'

'But Caroline, I want to say I'm sorry and –'

'Fleur, in the first place saying you're sorry really won't help at all at the moment. Probably make things worse. In the second Chloe is in an appalling state, feels it's all her fault and –'

'Yes, well, so do I. I feel it's all my fault. That's why I have to see her. You don't understand.'

'Well of course, the simple fact is that it's not your fault. Or Chloe's,' said Caroline. 'Piers was not only an unbalanced personality, he was under appalling strain for a great many reasons, and he killed himself. He's tried to do it before and –'

'He has?'

'Yes, he has. Twice.'

'Oh God,' said Fleur. 'I didn't know.'

'I don't think you knew much about him at all, Fleur, actually. And I don't think it's relevant.'

'Yes, it is. Of course it is. He was a neurotic personality. Which is what Reuben was saying. I should have been more – careful.' Her eyes were blue, very wide, very frightened-looking. 'Shit, Caroline, what have I done?'

'Listen,' said Caroline. She reached out for Fleur, took her hand, led her into the morning room. 'Listen, Fleur. Now I am not a psychiatrist, and know a great deal less about it, I am sure, than your rather odd friend Mr Blake.'

'He's not odd,' said Fleur.

'I'm sorry. I shouldn't criticize your friends. Is that what he is? A friend?'

'Yes. A friend. A good friend.'

'Well, anyway. I know nothing at all about psychiatry. I would go so far as to say I'm deeply suspicious of it. I believe in letting sleeping dogs lie, getting on with things, all that sort of thing. But maybe I'm not the person to pontificate on such matters. I made a fair old hash of motherhood.'

Fleur said nothing. Caroline looked at her steadily.

'But, Fleur, you are not responsible for Piers's death. Absolutely not. Any more than Chloe is, and she is saying much the same as you, at this moment. Of course you shouldn't have had an affair with him, it was an appalling thing to do, whatever your motives. And it was not very wise of you to come here last night. Or to tell Chloe you'd been in cahoots with Magnus. Which, I have to say, makes me personally feel – well, a little odd. To say the least.'

'Yes,' said Fleur, 'yes, I thought it might. It is a little – odd.'

'This is altogether a most outrageous affair,' said Caroline suddenly. Her eyes were almost amused as she looked at Fleur. 'In the very best – what shall we say – family tradition. Anyway, we had better not get on to the subject of Magnus Phillips. But Fleur, you have to be very sure of one thing. Piers is dead because he wanted to be dead. He obviously couldn't cope any longer. Being confronted by his affair with you might not have helped him feel better, but it couldn't possibly have driven him to suicide had he been a stable, well-adjusted person. Or even if he hadn't been stable or well adjusted. There is very seldom one reason for suicide, as I understand it. The person sees everything in a distorted way, and simply can't cope.'

Fleur stared at her. 'I thought you said you knew nothing about psychiatry.'

'I don't. I have a certain amount of common sense. Not enough, I would say, looking back on my life, but quite a lot. And I had a depressive mother. Your grandmother.' She looked at Fleur. 'I don't know what she'd have made of you.'

'Thanks,' said Fleur.

'But my father would have liked you. Very much.'

'Oh, really? Well –' She stood up. 'I think I might go for a walk now.'

'All right,' said Caroline with a sigh.

'And Caroline –'

'Yes, Fleur?'

'Thank you.'

'That's all right.'

Fleur went out into the garden, and stood breathing in the warm summer air, feeling soothed, calmed. For the first time in her entire life, she felt she might know how it felt to have a mother.

Bannerman arrived in less than two hours; Chloe received him in the bedroom, dead-eyed.

'Chloe, I'm so sorry,' he said, 'so terribly sorry.'

'Roger, I feel so bad. It was my fault, you know, my fault.'

'Chloe, it was not your fault.'

'It was, it was, I said some terrible things to him, we'd had a ghastly family row, all of us –'

'What about? Or can't you tell me?'

'Oh, Roger, I couldn't begin. It's so complex. But there had been something – well, quite bad he'd done. Not terrible, no worse than some other things. But I found out last night and I was horrible to him. He was trying and trying to apologize, to get me to understand, to forgive him, and I wouldn't. I was so awful. You just don't know, Roger – oh God, I wish, I wish I was dead too, I think I might –' Her voice rose in a wail; her face was swollen and ugly, her eyes almost closed with crying.

'Chloe,' said Bannerman, 'Chloe, listen to me. Stop crying and listen to me.'

'Look,' said Chloe, 'don't, Roger, don't start telling me he was unstable and he'd have done it anyway, I don't believe it, and besides, I should have been more careful, kinder, should have remembered. I killed him, and I'm wicked and I deserve to die too.'

'Chloe,' said Bannerman, and he sounded angry suddenly, his voice rough. 'Chloe, stop it. At once. Now listen. And think. Now what about his illness. Don't you think that might have been a factor? A BIG FACTOR?'

Chloe stared at him. 'What illness? I don't understand.'

'Didn't he tell you?'

'Tell me what?' She was silent, now, holding her breath, afraid almost to move.

Bannerman stared at her in silence; then he stood up and walked over to the window, looking out. Then he said, without turning round, 'Chloe, Piers had cancer. Lung cancer. He was very ill. That's why he was seeing Faraday.' He came back, sat down beside her again, smiled at her gently. 'I'm so sorry.'

'Oh,' she said, and put out her hand, reached for his. 'Oh God. I had no idea. No idea at all. Tell me about it, Roger. How long had he known, how long had he got?' She could hear the fear in her voice; she felt very weak.

'There isn't much to tell. Farady did some further tests, and they revealed he had cancer. It was – well, inoperable. You'd have to talk to him. There had been discussion about radiotherapy. At best, at very best, it was months of very painful unpleasant treatment. And then he would almost certainly have died in a short while. I can't believe he didn't tell you. He insisted on knowing, Faraday said.'

'Oh,' said Chloe again. She stared at him for a long time, and then she said, with a heavy, pain-racked sigh, 'I'm sorry, Roger, but that doesn't make me feel any better. Worse if anything. All that, knowing that, and he didn't tell me, kept it to himself. He must have been so frightened, so wretched. I can't have been much of a wife. We might have fought it together, tried other things – oh God.' She dropped her head into her hands. 'I failed him. He needed me and I failed him. God, Roger, how am I going to bear this, what am I going to do?'

Joe was sitting in the drawing room when Bannerman came downstairs.

'She's very upset,' he said, 'as you know. I told her Piers was very ill, that he had lung cancer, that it was inoperable. Did you know?'

'No,' said Joe. He swallowed; he felt very sick.

'He must have kept it to himself. I suppose he wanted to wait until after the investiture.' He looked at Joe, slightly awkwardly. 'I don't think there's any need for anyone to know this, but I did tell Faraday how desperate Piers was for this knighthood. I happen to know he put in a good word for him. Given that there was very little hope of him living to see the next honours.'

'Good God,' said Joe. 'Do you mean –'

'Oh, I don't mean anything really,' said Bannerman. 'Except that I told him. Very influential chap, Faraday. Now, I've tried to calm Chloe, stressed that suicides very rarely do it for one single reason. That they are damaged personalities. Which I have to say Piers undoubtedly was.'

'Do you think so?' said Joe. 'Unstable maybe, I'd have thought, a bit over-emotional, but damaged?'

'Oh, undoubtedly,' said Bannerman. 'I've been trying to get him to see someone for years. I don't mean he was actually crazy, of course, but he was, as you say, extremely unstable. I only hope I can bring Chloe round to that view in time. And I have no doubt that other reasons will evolve, other than some ridiculous row they may have had.'

'What sort of other reasons?' said Joe, intrigued.

'Oh – this and that,' said Bannerman vaguely. 'They usually do. I think he had money worries. Chloe denied it when I asked her, but Piers was very secretive, he would have kept that from her. It would help Chloe in a funny way if we could establish that.'

'Maybe,' said Joe. He found it hard to believe that Piers had money worries, the way he threw the stuff around, and the kind of profits the *Dream* had made. 'I have to say if she has to worry about money as well, it's hardly going to help her.'

'You'd be surprised,' said Bannerman, 'what helps on these occasions. Anyway, I've promised not to start doping Chloe, but equally, she's promised to take a couple of pills tonight. Would you be kind enough to see she does that, Joe?'

'Yes, yes of course,' said Joe.

'Meanwhile, I think the best thing she can do is start planning the funeral. It will give her something to do, and channel some of her guilt and whatever. I should encourage her to make it as lavish as possible if I were you.' His lips twitched slightly and his eyes met Joe's in total duplicity. 'It will absorb far more of her energies, and Piers would have liked something pretty spectacular, I think, don't you? You could tell Chloe that, even.'

'Absolutely,' said Joe.

There was, mercifully, a great deal to be done. The company at Stratford had to be notified, and Piers's agent, his press officer briefed, the endless calls taken. All the newspapers phoned, several reporters arrived at the house, and so towards evening did a television crew. They all wanted to speak to Chloe, 'just a short statement' and nothing would deter them, neither Jean Potts's polite requests that they should go away, nor Joe's slightly less polite instruction that they should fuck off.

In the end Chloe came out, and said she would give them a statement; she was startlingly composed, although her voice was shaky. She said that

Piers had taken an overdose but that she could not give them any more information until after the inquest.

'Did you find your husband, Lady Windsor?'

'No, no, I didn't. One of the grooms did.'

'Did he leave a note, Lady Windsor?'

'Yes, he did.'

'Did it give any information as to why he should have done such a thing?'

'I can't answer that, I'm sorry.'

'This is a terrible shock after yesterday, isn't it?'

'Yes, of course it is.'

'Where was he, Lady Windsor? Is it true he was in the stables?'

'Yes, that is correct.'

'How are your children?'

'My children are naturally very upset.'

'How are you feeling yourself, Lady Windsor?'

'She's naturally feeling great,' said Joe, sickened, deeply ashamed of his profession, stepping forward, his arm round Chloe's shoulders. 'Now would you please go away, all of you.'

'Joe, don't,' said Chloe. 'It's all right. I'm feeling pretty horrendous,' she added to the crowd at the door. 'I'd really appreciate some peace and quiet.'

Greatly to Joe's surprise, most of them moved off.

Chloe was sitting in the drawing room, having a drink, when Reuben came in. He looked at her and smiled awkwardly. She smiled back. He had an extraordinary soothing, sweet smile. It made her feel better.

'Hi,' he said, 'how are you doing?'

'Oh – I'm all right, Reuben. Thank you.'

'Not good, huh?' he said.

'No,' said Chloe, 'not good.'

He sat there, looking at her, smiling gently; there was a long silence. She was surprised to find it was not in the least embarrassing or awkward, just rather restful.

'I'm sorry you have to stay here,' she said, 'but I understand you can go tomorrow.'

'Yeah. Well, it's OK. I like it here.'

Chloe laughed for the first time that day. 'You couldn't like it.'

'I do. It's beautiful.'

Another silence. 'Would you like a drink?' said Chloe.

'That'd be good.'

She waved in the direction of the drinks tray; he poured himself a whisky, sat down, smiled at her again.

'Er – is – that is, where is Fleur?'

'Upstairs,' he said and nodded, smiling. Then he added, 'She's very upset.'

'Oh really?' said Chloe. She heard her voice sounding bitter, angry.

'Yeah really. She blames herself. I said she shouldn't. Nor should you,' he added.

'Reuben, I'm sorry, but I must ask you not to talk about this. It's terribly complex and personal and you really don't know anything about it.'

'OK,' he said reasonably.

Chloe looked at him. He was the most extraordinary person she had ever seen, or had anything to do with, so ugly, yet so extraordinarily attractive, so abrupt, yet so extremely engaging, so silent, yet so oddly congenial.

He looked at her, and smiled his sweet smile again.

'I'll go if you want me to,' he said. 'Just say.'

'No, don't go,' said Chloe, realizing that was the last thing she wanted.

'I think you're being wonderful,' he said, picked up a magazine and became instantly engrossed in it.

Ludovic rang her several times. He was sweet, concerned, anxious to help. Should he come down? Could he make phone calls for her? Did she want to be alone? How were the children?

Chloe was pleased to hear from him, talked to him for a while, pouring out her litany of guilt, of despair. He said what everyone had said, that it wasn't her fault, she mustn't blame herself, Piers was clearly under immense strain: in the end, hearing her own voice becoming hysterical, she said goodbye abruptly and put the phone down. She didn't tell him about the cancer. She didn't want to tell anyone about it. It seemed to make everything worse.

She started to think about the funeral; that seemed to make her feel better. There had to be some delay in view of the autopsy, but the police had told her that ten days or so ahead would be all right. She decided it should be in London, rather than the country, and took Joe's advice that it should be a large affair, so that everyone could come. 'You're right, he would have liked that, and it's the last thing I can do for him.'

She phoned the rector of the actors' church, St Paul's in Covent Garden, and started discussing music, readings, hymns, and drawing up a list of people to invite. It was very long. Suddenly she looked up at Joe. 'All I really have to do is duplicate the party list,' she said, and giggled slightly guiltily.

Joe grinned back at her. 'Sure,' he said.

'I thought we might ask Ivor Branwen to do a reading, maybe that lovely thing by Henry Scott Holland, you know, "Death is Nothing". It was one of Piers's favourites. And maybe Tabitha could read something. And then David Montague has already offered to do a tribute.'

'Fine. I'm sure he'll do it brilliantly.'

'Now for the music. I think some Bach, he so loved Bach, and the Mendelssohn *Dream* music, that would be appropriate, don't you think? Or do you think that would be too frivolous?'

'No, not at all,' said Joe. He was beginning to feel very tired.

'Or maybe, Joe, this is all wrong, and we should have just a tiny family service, and then a big memorial in a few weeks' time. What do you think about that?'

'No, I think you should have a big funeral,' said Joe, hastily.

Her eyes were fever bright; she was flushed. Well, at least she was no longer crying. Bannerman had been right about this. There was something just slightly strange about this reaction now; she seemed almost excited. Shock probably; he supposed she could hardly be expected to be behaving entirely rationally.

'And what about the children? Are they too little, do you think? To come?'

'Too little for what? Come to what?' It was Pandora, standing in the doorway, her small face white and oddly misshapen from crying.

Chloe took a deep breath. 'To Daddy's funeral, darling. Well, I think the others are really too little. But I expect you'd want to be there, wouldn't you? To say goodbye to him? Or would you rather stay with the others and Rosemary?'

Pandora gave her a look and there was immense scorn in it, beneath the grief. 'Of course I want to come. Of course I have to be there. Can you go to the nursery? Kitty's crying, she wants you.'

'Oh, all right, darling. I'll go up. Do you want to come with me, or stay and talk to Joe for a bit?'

Joe didn't often pray but he prayed now. Please, God, he said silently, please let Pandora go up with her mother.

God, as He had done so often in the past, ignored his request.

'I'd like to stay and talk to Joe,' said Pandora.

He sat on the sofa with her, and cuddled her. She was oddly composed now, although her small body felt delicate and fragile, literally shaky.

'I'm sorry,' he said, 'so sorry about your daddy. He was –' he made the supreme effort – 'he was a very wonderful man.'

'Yes, he was. I loved him so much. And he loved me so much back, you know. Best in the world, he said. Better than anyone. That was our secret.'

'Oh really?'

'I'm trying to be brave,' she said, almost chattily, 'trying not to cry. Daddy said the most important thing in the world was to be brave. He was very brave, you know.'

'Oh, I know,' said Joe, raking his brain for examples of Piers's courage.

'Sometimes, you know, he felt really ill lately. He had a sore chest. But he always went on. He didn't let people down. And when he broke his ankle, it hurt so much and he didn't complain about it at all.'

'I know,' said Joe again.

'And when we were on holiday together, he was quite scared to do the waterskiing, but he did. We dared each other.'

'Did you?'

'Yes. And even if he had to do things he really didn't want to do, like see his money men, he did it.'

'My goodness, he told you a lot,' said Joe, his mind sharpening at the mention of Piers's money men.

'Yes, he did. We were best friends,' she said simply, and then started to cry, and he watched, deeply touched, as she struggled to control herself and stop again.

'When Granny died,' she went on, 'he was so sad. But he still went and smiled at her funeral, he said, and said lovely things about her, so everyone could remember her happily. Afterwards he was ill, he was so upset.'

'Was he?'

'Yes, but then he was very brave again. I thought I might like to say something lovely at his funeral, so people could remember him happily. What do you think?'

'Well,' said Joe, and the lump in his throat was so large he could hardly speak, 'well I think you should ask Mummy about that. She has to decide.'

'But do you think it's a nice idea?'

'I think it is, yes,' said Joe.

After supper that night, Chloe was sitting in Piers's study, rather helplessly going through the chaos on its surface, trying not to think about what lay within, when she heard someone behind her; she looked round. It was Fleur.

'We have to talk,' she said. She looked interestingly nervous.

'I don't see why,' said Chloe. 'What about?'

'About everything. I feel so terrible about Piers's death –'

'Yes, well, you certainly didn't help last night,' said Chloe. 'But I don't think you should blame yourself.' She sighed, looked coldly at Fleur. 'If any one person was to blame it was me.'

'No,' said Fleur, 'Chloe, that isn't right. I know it isn't.'

'I don't think,' said Chloe more coldly still, 'you know anything about it.'

'Oh all right,' said Fleur. 'Have it your own way. I just wanted to talk about it. That's all.'

'Yes, well, I don't want to talk about it. Not to you,' said Chloe. She looked at Fleur and said suddenly, 'I just don't know how you could do it. Have an affair with my husband. Knowing who he was.'

'Well – I know it sounds terrible. But –'

'Fleur, it *was* terrible. Absolutely terrible. I can't even begin to conceive of how anyone could do such a thing. As far as I can make out, you deliberately seduced him, with some extraordinary end in view.'

'It was not extraordinary,' said Fleur, and Chloe could hear the tremor in her voice, see her trying to control it. 'It mattered desperately to me.'

'Yes, well, a lot of things matter desperately,' said Chloe, 'but we don't have to behave as badly as you did.'

'Chloe,' said Fleur, 'don't you understand? I accept it was terrible. I'm here to say I'm sorry. That I feel terrible about it. Truly deeply terrible.'

'Oh, do you?' said Chloe and suddenly anger ripped through her, hot, violent anger. 'You feel terrible, do you? Well, that's awfully sad, Fleur, but how do you think I feel? My husband has killed himself, God knows why, but certainly all this appalling family feuding hasn't helped. How do you think my children feel? Pandora loved her father more than anyone in the world. She is never going to get over this, never. How do you think we're all going to start living again? It's nice of you to say you're sorry, and I really don't blame you for any of it, but I don't believe you have the faintest idea how we're all feeling and I find it faintly insulting that you should imply that you do, imply that you're part of it even. I understand you're leaving in the morning, and I think that's a very good thing. And then I hope I never see you again,' she added. She heard the words with some surprise, and even regret: words she would never normally use, coming out of her mouth seemingly of their own volition. She felt annoyed with herself; it seemed so important to keep calm.

'I'd echo that,' said Fleur. 'Well, I certainly will go. I shall go back home and try to forget any of this ever happened.'

'How fortunate for you that you can. Sadly, my family will have to live with it for the rest of our lives. Which I can't expect you to care about very much. Although you should. Blood being thicker than water and all that.'

'Now why the fuck should I be concerned about your family?' said Fleur. The tension in the room was mounting now; a lifetime of suspicion, jealousy, hatred, heating it. 'What has your family ever done for me?'

'It certainly hasn't done you any harm,' said Chloe.

Fleur was silent.

Point to me, thought Chloe. She found greatly to her surprise that she was rather enjoying herself, that she felt better suddenly.

'I'll tell you what harm it's done,' said Fleur, and her voice was very low. 'It's pretended I wasn't there. Your mother – my mother – gave me away when I was born, sent me to the other side of the world –'

'With your father.'

'OK. But could you do that? Give away one of your children?'

Chloe hesitated.

Fleur tore into her. 'You see. And then she never came near me again. For years and years, all the time I was growing up, she never wrote, never visited, never even sent a Christmas card.'

'Fleur,' said Chloe, touched for the first time by this terrible raw anger and pain, 'Fleur, I don't know a lot about it, but I think that was the whole point. She had to cut you out of her life in order to be able to cope with it.'

'Cope with you, you mean. You and your brothers and your father. You grew up with a father and a mother and I grew up with no one. Except my grandmother. And even she died.'

Chloe was silent.

'That's what you did to me,' said Fleur and her voice was rising now. 'And do you know what Joe Payton said to me when I found you'd been married? Which I might say I had to read about in a magazine. Nobody thought I might like to know, would need to know even. I asked him what your precious husband thought about me, about my existence as part of your extended family. He said, "Well of course we didn't tell him." ' She paused and her face was flushed, ugly with rage. "Of course." That's what he said. "Of course we didn't tell him." How do you think that made me feel about you? About all of you? That of course I was so unimportant, so of course your husband, my sister's husband, didn't need to be told about me. Don't expect me to feel any remorse, any loyalty to any of you. I owe you nothing, absolutely nothing.'

'Well, there's clearly no future in this discussion,' said Chloe rather wearily. 'It's like the angels on the head of the pin. We could carry on indefinitely. Maybe we should change the subject altogether.'

Fleur stared at her. 'I always knew you'd be a bitch,' she said conversationally. 'A spoilt, superior bitch. It's good to know I was right. I really wanted to try to talk to you this evening. Let you know how sorry I was. How bad I felt. But I shouldn't have bothered. It was just a waste of time and effort.'

Chloe stared at Fleur. I don't like this girl, she thought. She was just as dislikeable, just as hard and tough as she had expected. She didn't like the thought that she was her sister. She didn't like it at all.

Fleur stared back at her, her dark blue eyes blank.

Beautiful eyes, in an exhausted white face. Idly Chloe wondered where they came from, those eyes. From Fleur's father, she supposed. The man her mother had loved. Who had fathered the daughter her mother had loved. She sighed, impatiently, and stood up, signalling to Fleur that she had had enough. And then something happened, as she stood there, waiting, looking at her; they became darker, larger, those eyes, and then they filled with tears. Large brilliant tears, that rolled down the white face with a strange precision. Fleur brushed the tears away impatiently, looked down, turned; walked towards the door. As she did so, Chloe heard a new sound, a strange, distressing sound. It was a sob; a painful, difficult sob. It was followed by another. And another. Chloe stepped forward; she felt deeply, horribly distressed. She cursed her distress, but she couldn't help it.

'Fleur,' she said, 'I'm sorry. If I upset you. Don't cry.'

Fleur turned on her, her face so distorted with rage that Chloe was quite frightened.

'So now you're sorry,' she said. 'Your turn to say it. And what are you sorry for, Chloe? For being born, being loved, having a mother and a father who loved you?'

'Oh, please,' said Chloe, 'not again, please, Fleur, not again. That particular record is beginning to sound a little cracked.'

She turned away, to the window; she did not see Fleur moving towards her, raising her arm, but she felt the blow, felt it on her shoulders, turned, felt the second, on her face. She sat down abruptly on the sofa, shielding her head as Fleur continued to hit her, to punch her, hurting her hands, her arms; looked up again, caught a flailing fist in her eye. She was frightened, felt utterly helpless, unable to move; and then she heard footsteps in the corridor and Fleur's name being called, and then the door opened and Reuben came in.

He stood staring, taking in the extraordinary scene, Chloe being hit about the head by Fleur, her face covered in tears and blood, one eye swollen, warding off the blows.

He walked in, grabbed Fleur by the shoulders. 'Shall I get someone?' he said to Chloe.

To her own immense amazement, staring at Fleur as she did so, at her contorted, desperate face, Chloe said, 'No, no, Reuben, don't. It's not nearly as bad as it looks. Fleur, if you'll just sit down and – and leave me alone, Reuben, maybe you could fetch us some tea, and we can try – try to sort this out.'

Fleur sat down, abruptly, and buried her head in her arms; Chloe fished a handkerchief out of her pocket, handed it to her, waited for Reuben to return. He came in, set down the tray, and said, 'Should I stay?'

'No,' said Fleur and Chloe in unison, and 'OK' he said easily and went out again, closing the door behind him.

'He's nice,' said Chloe slightly distractedly. She couldn't make out why she didn't hurt more, why the eye Fleur had been punching, her jaw weren't agony; it seemed very strange.

'He is. I was going to marry him, but I'm not now.'

'Why not?' She suddenly wanted to know a lot about Fleur, to understand her.

'I didn't love him enough.'

'Ah,' said Chloe. She handed Fleur a cup of tea. 'I seem to have spent the last twenty-four hours giving you cups of tea,' she said slightly irrelevantly.

'You look terrible,' said Fleur suddenly. 'You should get some ice for that eye. I'll go. Chloe, I'm – I'm sorry I went for you.'

'It's all right,' said Chloe, surprisingly cheerful. 'I didn't seem to mind. I hit you yesterday, after all. Maybe we're making up for all the fighting we would have done, if we'd grown up together.'

'Hey,' said Fleur, smiling slightly reluctantly, 'hey, that's a neat thought. I like it.'

Chloe looked at her. 'All my life, or anyway, all the part of my life I've known about you, I've hated you. Now, suddenly, it's not quite so easy. I'm not sure why.'

'I don't see why you should have hated me,' said Fleur truculently.

'Fleur, don't be ridiculous. You've got this all wrong. You were there first. My mother loved your father. She didn't love mine. She never liked me. She still doesn't. She puts up with me. And I suppose it would not take a psychiatrist to tell us why.'

'If your mother – our mother – loves me,' said Fleur, 'she has a strange way of showing it.'

'She is a strange woman,' said Chloe. 'She never told me about you, you know. I found out quite by accident. When I was fifteen years old. Hard to understand, quite such stupidity.'

And 'Silly bitch,' they said as one, and then stared at each other in amazement that they should have come so close in so short a time, and then both smiled, and relaxed, lay back on the sofa together, talking, talking about their mother, who had been so little use to either of them, in such completely different ways, proffering reasons, theories, explanations as to why and how she had behaved as she did, and they felt the first tender, cautious roots of friendship beginning to form between them.

'Could you tell me about your father?' Chloe said suddenly. 'I used to think about him such a lot, wondering what he was like, wondering why she had loved him, done what she did,' and Fleur, falteringly, reluctantly at first, then more surely, began, wishing Chloe to understand about him, to explain that anyone, anyone at all would have fallen in love with him, and as she talked, she became a child again, a fiercely loyal, adoring child, describing the handsome, charming, amusing, wonderful man who had been her father, and the dreadful pain and grief she had known when he had gone away and left her alone, telling her it was only for a few months when actually it had been for ever.

They exchanged many things, that night, putting together things they had been told and had found out for themselves, pieces of fact, half-formed stories, theories, fantasies, and at the end of it, they each understood at least something of what the other had endured and felt the seeds of sympathy for it, and when Chloe finally said, exhausted, that she must go to bed, she lay awake for a while, soothed from her raw misery, and then fell asleep with comparative ease, without having to take the pills Roger Bannerman had prescribed for her.

'Holy shit,' said Magnus Phillips.

He had been watching a six o'clock news magazine on television, in an effort to distract himself from his boredom and discomfort; after the usual predictable items about crime increases, lonely old ladies, inflation record highs, interviews with disgruntled miners and a couple of stories about beauty queens and the final of the Miss Great Britain contest, the announcer said, 'And finally today, the funeral of the actor Piers Windsor who died last week on the very day after his investiture by the Queen at Buckingham Palace as a Knight Commander. The funeral took place at St Paul's in Covent Garden. All the great names of the theatre were there, and of course Sir Piers's family. His young widow, Chloe, led the mourners with her small daughter Pandora, who spoke her own small tribute to her father, along with some of the finest actors on the British stage.'

What had elicited Magnus's expletive, however, was not the sight of Chloe, dressed in black (and looking extremely beautiful), nor Caroline (who still, he noted, looked wonderful, and was clutching Joe Payton's hand very tightly in an interesting way), nor the great clutch of famous faces, following her out of the church, not even little Pandora, gravely, exquisitely pale, wearing a black dress with a white collar, her red hair tied back with a black Alice band, but the person standing beside Chloe as she stood in the sunlight, looking very frail, very vulnerable, waiting for her car. A female person, very tall, with dark hair slicked back, wearing a black dress, soberly long, and a sombre expression; a person whose body language told him very clearly that she and Chloe were (however briefly) surprisingly close; a person he had imagined to be in New York (although he had put in several calls to her, without success); the person he wanted to see more than anyone in the world, the person he cared about more than anyone in the world, the person he knew for a fact could never belong to him, was going to marry some idiot with an idiotic name – and the person he found it imperative that he should see once more, just once more, however fruitless it might prove to be.

'How was the funeral?'

Fleur looked at Reuben; her head ached, she felt exhausted and sick. How was the funeral? How was any funeral? Especially any funeral such as this, hugely attended, beautifully staged: a theatrical event, a happening. A blend of emotion, of shock and grief matched with pride and love. Exquisite music, perfectly trained voices, wonderful words; a lovely young wife widowed, a beautiful young family orphaned. Friends, so many friends, filling the church, grieving, shocked; even Guinevere had come, sweetly sad, even Piers's teachers at RADA, people who had worked for him, dressers, voice coaches, cleaners, stable-lads. All knowing they would be welcome, all a tribute to his greatest gift, to make people feel (however falsely) he cared. And a little girl, in love with her father, standing staunchly before them all at the lectern, reading the last verse of the 23rd Psalm in a clear, steady voice, and saying at the end of it, 'My father was clever and brave and he made us all happy. We shall miss him, but we shall remember him always and love him. Please try not to be sad.'

None of them had cried until then not even Chloe; she had stood, dry-eyed, Joe on one side of her, Ludovic on the other. She had been immensely brave, very strong. Fleur, standing behind her, had seen the tremor go through her as the coffin was carried in, but after that she had stood, rock still, dry-eyed. Until Pandora had spoken, had walked so bravely, so tiny she was, up to the lectern; scarcely visible over it, she had stood there, had demonstrated true grief, true courage, and then Chloe had cried, wept, biting her lip, fighting back the sobs, struggling to keep the sobs silent; and Joe had cried, too, and so had Fleur, partly for the child in the church that day, partly for another little girl, at a smaller, shabbier funeral, experiencing exactly the same loss, precisely the same grief, for a father, the most important, best loved figure in her world, gone, lost for ever.

'Oh,' she said to Reuben, 'oh, it was beautiful. Very sad, but beautiful. You should have come. Chloe would have liked you to come.'

'No,' he said, looking very sad, 'no, I shouldn't have come.'

'That was terrible,' said Caroline. Her face was drawn, her eyes sad. 'I felt so bad.'

'Now why, on God's earth, should you feel bad?'

'Oh Joe, I don't know. If I'd been a better mother to Chloe, made her more secure, feel more loved, would she have married him? Maybe not. And then it might not have happened.'

'Caroline, the man was a wreck. He had cancer, he would have died anyway. He had countless other problems, God knows what. You cannot take that on yourself.'

'Well.' She sighed. 'I've been a terrible mother anyway. To both those girls. I can't pretend otherwise. I've made a hash of it all, Joe. Of everything. Including our relationship.'

'Our relationship was fine,' he said, 'wonderful. Until that bastard Phillips came along.'

'Yes, I know. That's my point. I threw it away, our wonderful relationship. For a little – well, frisson. And was responsible for all this mess, with the book.'

'Nonsense,' said Joe easily. 'He'd have written that book anyway. Nothing to do with you. Don't flatter yourself, Caroline.'

'I'm not flattering myself,' said Caroline indignantly. 'I'm insulting myself if anything. You haven't been listening.'

'Sorry,' said Joe humbly. Then he grinned at her. 'That's better. You sound more yourself.'

'Yes, well I'm going to sound even more myself now. I have to get back. Cameo is about to foal, I don't want to miss it.'

'Dear God,' he said, 'I spend my life coming second to a horse. That's what was wrong with our relationship, Caroline. Not Magnus Phillips.'

'That's untrue. And unfair. You just weren't prepared to spend time in the country.'

'And you weren't prepared to spend time in London.'

'That's different.'

'Why?'

'Well –' She laughed suddenly, put her arm through his. 'I was going to say because the country is nice and London is horrible. But that's not very fair, is it?'

'No.' They were walking towards her car which was parked in a car park near Tottenham Court Road. He looked at her suddenly, stood still, turned her to him, pushed back her red hair. 'You're still so beautiful, you know. More beautiful than either of those daughters of yours.'

'Oh Joe, don't. Of course I'm not.'

'You are to me,' he said, 'and that's saying a lot because I fancy both of them.'

'You don't.'

'I most certainly do. Especially –'

'Especially who?'

'I was going to say Fleur, but that's not true. Since she grew up, Chloe is gorgeous.'

'Do you know,' said Caroline, staring at him, 'I never even thought of that. I can't imagine why. How stupid, how naïve of me. You had Chloe living in your flat, Fleur in a hotel room in Los Angeles. Dear God, how dangerous.'

'Not really,' he said. 'After all, I always had you, waiting at home. You seemed a better bet to me.'

Caroline was silent for a moment, looking at him, exploring his eyes. 'And then I wasn't there. God, I'm a bitch.'

'Well,' he said lightly, 'I've always had a penchant for bitches. They turn me on. In fact I'm having a little trouble with a certain portion of my anatomy even now.'

Caroline looked at him; then she leant forward very gently, so that her body was against his. She opened his raincoat, and moved herself inside it. She moved tentatively again, frowning with concentration. Then she smiled; the old glorious, confident, sensuous grin.

'Joe,' she said, 'Joe, I can't leave you like this. Can I come back to your place? Straight away now?'

'What about the foal?' he said.

'Oh, Jack can look after the foal,' she said.

'Caroline, this has to be love. Or something.'

'Not something,' she said, reaching up, kissing him, pushing her hands through his untidy hair. 'But there is one condition.'

'Yes?'

'In the morning, we go shopping. Together. And buy you a new raincoat, this one is truly disgusting. And some new shirts. And right now, we stop off at Heals and get some new sheets. I'm not sleeping in your old ones.'

'Who said anything about sleeping?' said Joe.

Chloe invited Fleur and Reuben to supper in Montpelier Square that night. They were flying back to New York in the morning.

She cooked a meal herself, and they ate in the kitchen very late: Rosemary was out with her architectural student, taking a long-overdue break, and Pandora had taken a long time to settle.

'Now I have to get on with my life,' she said, as they sat drinking coffee, 'whatever that might mean.'

'Whatever you want,' said Reuben.

'That's what I don't know,' she said. 'I've never really known. I thought I wanted love and marriage and a family, but –'

'You got that,' said Fleur, 'you got all of that.'

'Not really a marriage.'

'What's a marriage?' said Reuben.

Chloe stared at him. 'What do you mean?'

He shrugged, fiddling with his wine glass. 'It doesn't have to be what everyone thinks.'

'Reuben, don't start on all that,' said Fleur sharply. 'We shall be hearing what Dorothy thinks in a minute.'

Reuben looked hurt.

'Who's Dorothy?' said Chloe. 'Is she your girlfriend?'

'My therapist,' said Reuben.

'Ah. And what would she say about marriage?'

'She'd say,' he said, 'that it should be a support system. That's all. I think.'

'I see. Well – that's a very good definition. And if –' she stopped.

'If what?' said Fleur.

'If I married – someone else, I'd certainly be looking for support. So far I've done all the supporting.'

'That's tough,' said Reuben.

'Yes it is.' She was silent.

Then he said, 'Don't rush anything. That's important.'

Chloe looked at him and smiled, a small scared smile. 'Is that also what Dorothy would say?'

'Yes, it is.'

'I'm sure she's right. I'll – try not to.'

'Good.'

During the evening, Jean Potts phoned. 'I forgot to tell you, Chloe. That man rang. Magnus Phillips.'

'Oh, for God's sake,' said Chloe. 'Why can't he just leave us alone? Bastard.'

'He wanted Miss FitzPatrick.'

'Tough shit,' said Miss FitzPatrick. 'What did you tell him?'

'I told him I'd tell you he'd called, and that you and Mr Blake were flying back to New York in the morning. I have a number for him. If you want it.'

'I don't,' said Fleur.

They left soon after that. Chloe saw them off with mixed feelings. She was still uneasy with Fleur, wary of her; the emotional conditioning of ten years was very strong. And she was still angry with her, without being sure why: she supposed for collaborating with Magnus Phillips. For seducing Piers. And for simply existing, being the daughter her mother had wanted, cared about, loved. But there was something else there, something growing with a kind of tentative determination: a liking. She just couldn't help liking her. She liked her honesty, her toughness, her courage; and she trusted her. It was a very strange thing to feel about someone who had done to her what Fleur had done, but feel it she did. She knew that from now on, Fleur was absolutely on her side, with her all the way. And she was a powerful person to have on your side. There was no doubt about that. A bad enemy: but a very good friend.

And Reuben; she would miss Reuben. Several times during the past awful week, she had actually thought it would have been a lot more awful if he hadn't been there. Which was ridiculous, for someone she had only just met, who knew nothing of her, of her marriage, of her problems. But every so often, through those terrible days, he would say something, make an observation, which was so straightforward, so true, so absolutely right, she could hardly believe she hadn't thought of it herself; and yet she hadn't, and it had needed saying, needed thinking, and she would feel immediately better for it.

She thought suddenly, sharply, of Ludovic; he had been so wonderful ever since, loving, caring, supporting, there when she needed him, understanding when she didn't. She should have asked him this evening; he had wanted to be with her, and she had wanted him, of course she had. But it was Fleur and Reuben's last evening, and she had needed to be on her own with them. Which he would probably have understood. It had just been simpler to pretend that she was going to be quite alone. That was all.

She went and looked at Pandora; she was sleeping, but she was restless. Poor little girl. She had been so wonderfully brave and good. God knows how far into her future the tentacles of this were going to reach. Probably until she died. Chloe shivered for her, went and checked on the other two. They were absolutely fine. Ned was still of an age when death was an excitement, something dramatic, something temporary, lifting life out of its everyday dullness. In due course, he would expect his father to return, and then slowly, surely, grief would strike him; meanwhile he was comparatively cheerful. And Kitty understood almost none of it, only knew that Daddy had gone away; he had hardly touched on her small life, and his passing from it hardly touched her either.

Chloe got into bed, picked up a magazine and flicked through it, her head aching. She was still completely unsure of how she felt: how unhappy, how bereft, how frightened of what lay ahead. Only guilt stalked her, relentlessly, cruelly; like some great dark bird of prey. The more she thought of Piers's problems and difficulties, of whatever it was that had driven him to kill himself, the greater the guilt became.

The cancer, Magnus Phillips's book, her affair with Ludovic: on and on it went, wearing a groove in her weary brain. Tomorrow she had to have a meeting with Jim Prendergast; God knew what that would reveal. More problems, no doubt: debts that Piers was unable to tell her about, difficult decisions that he had felt unable to share with her. She had been a useless, lousy, selfish wife; and she had to live with the fact for the rest of her life.

Fleur, lying awake as usual, reliving the day, thought about Chloe: considered the swift reversal of hatred into liking, of suspicion into trust, of envy into sympathy. It was very strange, all of it. She would never have believed it possible. Maybe it was true, all that stuff about blood being thicker than water. If only Caroline had been a little more skilful, a little less – what – scared? they could have met, come together, discovered one another years earlier. Or could they? Thinking about it, with her usual fierce honesty, Fleur decided that actually they couldn't. It wouldn't have worked. Their situation had been so tortuous, so complex as to need a crisis of the proportion they had just been through to overcome it, to draw them along.

Well, it was a terrible thing to say, to think even, but if Piers had had to die, then enormous good had come of it. She tried to stifle the thought, and then thought maybe she shouldn't. She wasn't good at stifling thoughts anyway. Better to be honest, even with yourself.

She was sure that was what Dorothy would have said.

She was getting more than a little tired of Dorothy, and she hadn't even met her. But it had been very nice, having Reuben there through it all. And

Chloe had obviously liked him. He could hardly be more different from that boyfriend of hers, the beautiful barrister. He was nice; very nice. But – Fleur decided she really didn't want to get into that particular but, and thought instead of the very last thing Reuben had said to her that night before they finally went into their rooms.

'Chloe's beautiful,' he had said.

Fleur had looked at him with some foreboding; she knew what that meant, and it could mean trouble.

Well, she was going back now. Back to New York, back to real life, back to her consultancy, back to work. Leaving Chloe and Caroline and the mystery of Piers's death – and it was still a mystery, she was sure of it, she was sure none of them really knew why he had done it – behind. There was still a lot of unfinished business to resolve: the burglaries, the motor accident, Magnus's fears for her; all the reasons she had come to London, all faded into unimportance suddenly, somehow, just for a while. All no nearer resolution. Piers's death, taking with him so many sad, terrible secrets, had increased her need to know, to understand, to solve her father's own mystery, his own sad secrets. Only Magnus could tell her, only Magnus could help. She had to see him, had to confront him: and yet she shrank from it, from what it would do to her. She would get back to New York, back in control of her life, and then she would see him. Over there, on her own ground. She could deal with it better over there. Fleur wrenched her mind away from Magnus with immense effort. It was over, it had never begun, it was nothing: and in time, she would learn to accept that and the thought of him would cease to filter into everything she did and thought and felt and knew. He was a lousy, two-timing bastard, and she hated him. She had to get over him, forget his occupation of her body, and her heart and her head, and get on with her life.

There was nothing else she could possibly do.

In the bedroom of his friend's house in Brighton, Magnus Phillips lay awake and thought about Fleur. Seeing her on television that day had shocked him: the strength of what he felt for her. He wanted to see her now more than he had ever wanted anything: to be with her, near her; to touch her, feel her, tell her he loved her.

But – it was much better that he didn't. If anything was not to be it was him and her. She was in love with someone else, and he had no right to disturb that. He loved her so much he could do that for her at least. She was probably even married already; he had come over here with her, after all. All he could do was stay away, and learn to stop thinking about her. It was going to take all his concentration, all his powerful energies; but he was going to have to do it, drive her out of his head. Somehow. For her sake.

Magnus wasn't used to unselfish thoughts, unselfish emotions; so alien were they to him, he managed to find them quite interesting. Examining them, he finally fell asleep.

Chapter 40

August – October 1972

'Well, now what do we do?' Richard Beauman looked at Magnus across his desk.

Magnus shrugged. 'We can publish if we want to. You can't libel the dead.'

'True. There's the other matter of course.'

'Yes, but we have the affidavit there. No problem. And no injunction to worry about either.'

'Sure. On the other hand –'

'I know what you're going to say. On the other hand, it would be a terrible thing to do. To publish now. With the tragedy. The young widow. The tiny children –'

'Magnus, really! You sound not entirely sincere.'

'Of course I'm sincere. People would hate it. We'd quite possibly even be blamed for being a factor in his death. There'd be a backlash – and,' he grinned, 'we wouldn't sell nearly so many copies.'

'Ah,' said Beauman, 'now we're coming to it. Absolutely right. Even with the – other matter.'

'So probably,' said Magnus, 'we should shelve it for six months, and then hit 'em with it. The story will then seem doubly tragic, doubly sweet. Well, Windsor's story at any rate.'

'Right,' said Beauman, 'let's do that. I'll put out a press release that we're not publishing. Just to the trade of course.'

'Of course,' said Magnus. 'I might even be able to rest easy on my motorbike. For a while.'

'So now what do we do?' Chloe sat looking at Jim Prendergast, her eyes rather wide and anxious.

'Well, you'll have to sell both the houses, I'm afraid. The horses. He'd already sold all his shares.'

'It's that bad?'

'It's that bad. I'm sorry, Chloe. I really thought he'd told you?'

'He didn't tell me anything,' said Chloe briefly. She sighed, heavily. 'Where's it all gone, Jim? I don't understand.'

'He was immensely extravagant. That was the main thing. He lived far beyond his means. Always robbing Peter to pay Paul. Over-extended. Both houses mortgaged twice. He'd lost a lot of money in a couple of his ventures. That play *The Kingdom*, for instance. And he put a lot of money into the *Dream*.'

'Yes, but that made a fortune.'

'It didn't actually, Chloe. It won three Oscars, and great critical acclaim as they say, but it didn't do very well at the box-office. And running two large households and things like lavish parties and racehorses don't come cheap. As I'm sure you must realize.'

'Yes, of course.'

'I think as long as he was up and running, he felt he could win. Next time, next film, next race, it would be all right. And of course while he was so successful, people were patient. They'd wait. He has an enormous number of unpaid bills. Stables, tailors, builders, you name it. And then all these good works of his, donations here, there and everywhere, he was insanely generous . . .'

'Yes,' said Chloe, 'yes, I know.'

'So now what do we do?' Ludovic's face was kind, concerned, but at the same time cheerful. 'You let me help you, that's what we do. In all kinds of ways. Financially first and foremost: I don't want any nonsense, Chloe darling, I'm not exactly on the breadline. I can't save Stebbings, of course, or the stables, but I would like to buy you a little house – think of it as buying us a little house – somewhere in London, and pick up the school fees for now, so you don't have any immediate worries. I can't bear to see you looking like that. It must be such a nightmare for you, as if you didn't have enough to cope with, and it doesn't bear thinking about what a nightmare it must have been for Piers, but I do think, darling, you have to face the fact that it must have been a very big factor in tipping him over the edge. It might even make you feel better. Less guilty. Because –'

'Ludovic,' said Chloe, 'Ludovic, you don't understand. It makes me feel far far worse. That he couldn't tell me about it, share all this with me. Everything I find out, I feel more and more guilty. Every day.'

'So what do we do now?' Caroline looked at Joe, her eyes alarmed. 'She seems to be close to bankruptcy. Everything has to go. The houses, the cars, the lot. God, that man –'

'Caroline, don't. It doesn't help.'

'I know. But I could – I was going to say kill him. Leaving his affairs in this mess, no will, appalling debts. Poor little Chloe. With all that grief and guilt, and now this to cope with as well. Thank God, thank God, that book isn't going to be published now.'

'Yes, good for God. Caroline, can't you help? With the money.'

'Of course I can help. I've offered to buy her a house, set up a trust fund for the children's education, everything. She just keeps saying no, no, she wants to manage on her own. She seems to think she has to, that she doesn't deserve any help, can't take it. She looks terrible, Joe, I just don't know what to do with her.'

'What about Ludovic?'

'He's made the same sort of offers. She won't hear of them either. I don't know why she can't just marry him, straight away. He adores her, and he's waited a long time.'

'Caroline, for God's sake,' said Joe, 'she obviously doesn't feel she wants to. Or that she can. Piers only died a few weeks ago.'

'Yes, but it wasn't any sort of a marriage.'

'I know, but she can't admit that.'

'Well, I can't think why.'

'Then you're a lot more stupid than I thought,' said Joe calmly.

Joe went to see Chloe. She was in the middle of a particularly miserable day sorting through Piers's things, approving house agents' particulars, trying to work out which staff she could get rid of immediately without letting the relevant household fall into disarray before its sale, making appointments with racing stables and trainers, and ploughing her way through a still-huge pile of letters of condolence. She made Joe a cup of coffee and led him upstairs to the drawing room.

'I thought I couldn't feel worse than when Piers first died,' she said, 'and then every day I think I can't feel worse, and then the next day, it gets even more terrible. I don't know what to do, Joe. I feel like – well, of course I don't, but I was going to say I feel like bumping myself off as well.' She smiled at him: a wobbly, brave little smile.

Joe took her hand. 'Look, honeybunch. You can't go on like this. You've got to accept there were a great many reasons for Piers to have killed himself, each of them absolutely valid on its own, and allied with the others, intolerable. And he had a fatal, and potentially horrible illness. None of that is your fault, Chloe. You struggled long and hard, you were loyal –'

'I wasn't loyal. I had an affair with Ludovic, I told Piers about it, I made a fuss about his affairs, I was the opposite of loyal and supportive. Don't try to make me feel better, Joe, it isn't possible. I killed Piers as surely as if I'd put the pills into his whisky and made him drink it. He didn't feel he could talk to me and that's exactly what he should have been able to do.'

Joe gave up.

Fleur phoned Chloe every few days.

'She's in a terrible state,' she said to Reuben, when he asked about her. 'She says it's all her fault, that if she'd been a good wife Piers could have turned to her and because he couldn't he killed himself. Did you ever hear such a load of horse manure?'

'That isn't horse manure,' said Reuben.

Reuben called Chloe. She was touchingly grateful for his interest, and started to explain how she felt. Reuben interrupted her.

'I know. Fleur told me. Listen, Chloe, what you're feeling is right. You have to blame yourself. Accept the guilt. It's part of the healing process.'

'Really?' said Chloe.

'Yes. I asked Dorothy. I hope you don't mind.'

'Of course I don't mind.'

'Right. Goodbye, Chloe.'

'Goodbye, Reuben.'

Two days later he called back.

'Dorothy said to tell you that the only person who has any control over your life is yourself. Only you are in a position to change it. Which went for Piers too. Think about it.'

'I'll think about it. Reuben, you're so sweet. Thank you. Thank you so much.'

'That's OK.'

Of all the hundreds of thousands of words that poured into Chloe's ears, telling her how to feel better, Reuben's were the ones that helped her the most.

Until the letter arrived.

It came at the end of September: on her wedding anniversary. She was feeling particularly low.

She had a buyer for Montpelier Square: a low offer, but one which the agent had urged her to take. Ludovic and her mother urged her to hang on for a better one, but she was dithering, wanting to get it settled. Anything to get it settled.

For Stebbings, things were more complicated. She had an offer for that too: a good offer. But she also had an idea. It was a brave idea, but would be difficult to implement and it was one which she knew Prendergast and Ludovic and, she thought, her mother would all disapprove of. She knew it would be better to give in, take the offer, avoid the disapproval. But for some reason she couldn't quite give in, give up.

She wanted to talk to someone about it, and she couldn't think who, someone who would stand and cheer her on from the sidelines, someone with no vested interest, someone who would applaud courage and discount foolishness. But such a person did not exist. And then she remembered they did. Or rather she did. It was her sister. It was Fleur.

She rang Fleur in New York and rather haltingly outlined her idea.

Fleur was ecstatic about it. 'Yeah,' she said, 'go for it. It's great. Do it, Chloe, do it.'

But Fleur was strong, and she was not weighed down with guilt and she didn't have a family to support or a would-be husband urging her to drop everything and marry him. It was easy for Fleur. She said so.

'Chloe,' said Fleur, 'that's a load of shit.'

'I know,' said Chloe humbly.

She admired Fleur and she longed to take her advice; but she still lacked the confidence and she couldn't find the strength.

Fleur's dream of a creative consultancy was becoming reality; Chloe listened to her stories of a loan from the bank of unimaginable size, of offices found, of staff hired, of accounts promised, in awe. And a degree of shame. If Fleur could do this, Fleur who had started from nothing, who had no rich parents, rich lovers, status, why, in the name of heaven, why couldn't she? The thought depressed her still further, made her feel worse. She put the phone down, feeling small, hopeless, more confused than ever.

There was a ring at the door. A messenger stood there with a vast bouquet of white roses.

'Oh God,' said Chloe. She looked at the card.

'My darling Chloe, from Ludovic, with all my love, on a difficult day.'

Greatly to her surprise, Chloe threw the card on the floor and burst into tears.

'Shit,' she shouted at it. 'Why do you have to be so fucking perfect?'

God, she thought, I'm getting just like Fleur.

And then she saw the letter, lying in the letter-box. An airmail letter, with a Californian postmark. A Santa Barbara postmark to be precise. Addressed to her. Slightly oddly, Lady Piers Windsor, 75 Montpelier Square, London, England. And on the back, Michelle Zwirn, Voluntario Street, Santa Barbara, Ca.'

She turned it over, her heart thudding. It must be a mistake. It must be for Piers. But no. It was for her.

Chloe went into the kitchen, sat down, pulled the letter out of the envelope, and read it. She read it once, very hard, felt her cheeks burn, tears start behind her eyes, and then she read it again, very slowly; and then she put it in her pocket and went for a walk, and every so often she sat down on a seat or some grass and read it again. When she got home, she got a bottle of champagne out of the fridge, poured herself a glass and drank it, and then poured herself another and went upstairs to the drawing room and just sat, staring at the letter, smiling, and feeling as if she had been let out into the sunlight, where she could join other people again, after a long time alone in an airless darkness.

Dear Lady Windsor,

This is a very hard letter for me to write and anyway I'm not very good at expressing myself on paper, but I thought you ought to know what I have to say. Maybe you know anyway. If you do, please forgive me.

I wasn't even sure whether to write it at all, which is why I've taken so long. I hope you won't be too upset with me for that. I don't know if you ever knew about Gerard and me. Piers told us he had decided to tell you in his own good time, and maybe that time had come and maybe not.

Gerard and Piers were very close, long ago. Back in the 1950s. Gerard had a tap dancing studio in Santa Monica, and they met at some party. Piers used to come here, spent a lot of time with us. (Again, Lady

Windsor, you have to forgive me if I am telling you a lot of things you already know.) There was a whole crowd of us, we all had a lot of fun.

And then one night, something happened, there was an accident, down at the pier; I don't want to get into all the details now, but a girl fell and Gerard was trying to save her, and he fell and broke his back, in several places. He was paralysed from the neck down. Piers took him to hospital. He was in hospital for months and then in Rehab; then they said he could come home. He was never going to walk again. I didn't have any money; I didn't know where to turn. Piers just looked after him, after both of us, from then on, for the rest of Gerard's life. He found us somewhere to live, first down in Playa del Rey, and then later when he could, he moved us up here. He paid for nursing, for our homes, he sent us money every month. And he came to see us, to see Gerard, whenever he could, just a few days here and there, sometimes just a few hours. It wasn't that often, but he came. And he wrote and he phoned, and Gerard never felt for one day that he'd forgotten him.

I know, Lady Windsor, if you would forgive me for saying this, that Piers loved Gerard, very much. He felt responsible, because he felt he hadn't done enough, soon enough, after the accident, but he also wanted to take care of Gerard because he loved him. Gerard said of course that was nonsense, but that's what Piers felt. Whatever the facts of the matter, Piers faced his responsibilities, as he saw them. He was the best, the most faithful, the most generous friend anyone could ever have. Without him, I don't know what would have happened to Gerard. He would have lived in an institution. I couldn't have cared for him. It can't have been easy for Piers, specially in the beginning, he had no money, but he always gave us whatever he could. He was a very special person, and at the risk of distressing you, I wanted to make sure you knew that. I guess you do anyway.

Gerard died, just two months ago; you'll know when it was, because it was the day before Piers died. He went very peacefully; he got pneumonia, something that's common in paraplegics, I expect you know. I told Piers he was ill, but of course he couldn't come, he was doing *Othello*, and he promised to come and see him as soon as it was over. But Gerard was getting worse, and I didn't know what to do, I knew Piers would want to say goodbye. And then, the day he was really going, sinking, I knew, but it was the day Piers was going to be honoured by Queen Elizabeth. Gerard was so thrilled about that, so terribly proud; Piers sent us a copy of the letter and we have it framed here. I hope you will see it. In the end I did phone, but we missed you, and Gerard died, very peacefully, at the end of that day. Well, it must have been early morning in England. I phoned, then, to tell Piers, I had to; I knew he would want to know.

I miss Gerard so much, but I couldn't wish him back. It was such a hard life, and he was so brave, and so cheerful. He never complained. Having Piers there, in the background, made his life bearable. Reading about him, following his successes, and he was so proud. I hope Piers knew that.

I was very relieved that that book wasn't published. I really was very angry with myself for talking to Mr Phillips. I don't know why I did it really. I think I wanted everyone to know how good Piers had been to Gerard. Then of course I was worried about what people might think. Anyway, after Piers asked us not to talk to him again, of course we didn't.

When I read in the papers that he had killed himself, I did think I understood why. Of course we knew he had cancer. He wrote to us, and said to Gerard how strange it was that after everything he would probably die first. He even made some joke about Gerard looking after him now, that the balance would even up. When I told him Gerard had gone, he cried, I could hear him, even down the telephone, and then he said, 'Michelle, well, maybe we can be together soon. I don't want to stay on in a world without Gerard.'

Of course I thought he was just talking, was just terribly upset, but he wasn't. I think under the circumstances, he did want to go too. I hope you don't find this too hurtful, Lady Windsor. Please forgive me if it shocks you. Piers has been in our life so long, I find it hard to remember that you don't know us.

I think so much of you and your children. That little Pandora is so beautiful. She must miss her daddy so dreadfully. I hope one day when she is old enough to understand she can hear what he did for his friend.

I would so much like to meet you, and tell you more about us and what Piers did for us. If you ever felt you could come out here, I would welcome you with all my heart. Gerard has a beautiful grave in the churchyard, and I would like you to see that.

Yrs sincerely,
Michelle Zwirn

'Piers Windsor,' said Chloe cheerfully, looking quite fondly at the large photograph of Piers as Hamlet that stood on the mantelpiece, 'you were a devious, manipulative old bugger, but I forgive you.'

She made three phone calls that evening. First she rang Michelle Zwirn, and thanked her for her letter.

'You'll never know how wonderful it was to get it. And I would so much like to come and see you. As soon as possible, if I may. I wonder if it would be all right if I brought my sister. Yes, well, I know, we never talked about her, Piers and I. But her father was out there, with them all then, Brendan FitzPatrick his name was. I wonder if you knew him. Oh, you did? Well, there you are then. May I let you know exactly when we're coming? Thank you. And thank you again for writing. Goodbye, Michelle.'

Then she rang Ludovic.

'Ludo, I've had an idea. About Stebbings. I want to keep it, and turn it into a hotel. No, I know I don't have to, but I want to. Well, I've been thinking about it for a while, but suddenly today I feel much better and I know that's what I want to do. What? Well I just do. I'll tell you about it next time I see you. Ludovic, I don't need to think about it any more. I've thought about it a lot, and I know I want to do it. I'm going to talk to Jim Prendergast tomorrow. Yes, all right, Ludovic. Tomorrow night would be lovely. But I'm not going to change my mind.'

Finally she rang Fleur.

'Fleur, I know you're launching your empire, but could you take a few days off and come to California with me? What? Well, soon. To visit a very nice lady called Michelle Zwirn. I had a letter from her today, and – yes, I will tell you all about it, but maybe I'd better write, I can't afford these huge phone bills any more. Oh, all right then, call me back. The point is, Fleur, she knew your father. Yes, all right, I'll ring off straight away. Oh and Fleur, guess what? I'm launching my empire over here. Not quite your standard, but it's a start. OK, Fleur. Bye.'

Jim Prendergast nodded sagely over Chloe's plans to turn Stebbings into a hotel, and then told her he didn't think she could possibly make it pay. 'And there's no money anywhere to put into it. I'm sorry, Chloe, but that's the bottom line. It's a lovely idea but –'

Chloe was very disappointed. 'I so wanted to do it,' she wailed to Ludovic. 'It would have been something of my very own. I had such plans. To run it not as a hotel, but as close to a country house as it would be. With no bar even, just people in the drawing room, able to get their own drinks, and lots of games after dinner. And have horses in the stables, hacking horses, not those awful thoroughbreds, and tennis parties, and bridge fours and –'

Ludovic kissed her tenderly and said he was very impressed by her ideas, although he felt slightly cynical about letting people get their own drinks, but he thought she would be very sad to see her home turned over to other people. Chloe said she would be seeing it turned over anyway, and her way it would still have belonged to her. Ludovic said if she married him, she could have her own home in the country, and not have to worry about making it pay. Chloe said she wanted to worry about making something pay, and he didn't understand, and not for the first time since Piers's death they parted on rather strained terms.

* * *

Chloe told Joe about her idea for the hotel; Joe told Caroline and Caroline told Chloe she would put some money into it, as much as she needed to make it viable. Chloe said she didn't want to just take Caroline's money and Caroline said she was being stubborn and cutting off her nose to spite her face, but if it would make her feel any better she didn't have to just take it, she could make over a share in the hotel to her, and put it on a proper business footing. Chloe told Jim Prendergast, who said he would need to see some cash projections, and Chloe told him cash projections were his job and why didn't he do some for Caroline, and that he was her first employee, albeit only on a consultancy basis.

When she told Fleur, Fleur said her investment banker, Baby Praeger, had a sister called Virginia who lived in England and was an interior designer, and why didn't Chloe get on to her to talk about doing some work on Stebbings.

Fleur also said she had told Reuben Chloe was going to run a hotel and he was very impressed that she was taking charge of her life.

Chloe felt absurdly flattered.

Fleur was very excited. FitzPatrick Creative was to launch in November, from a studio office in the village. She had a slice of Morton's to see her on her way, and Julian Morell had given her a small project to work on, for his glorious store, Circe, on Fifth Avenue 'so no one can accuse you of walking off with Juliana'. She was also hopeful that she was going to win a pitch she was making for a new charity for the homeless; no money, but it was high-profile: 'And that will be quite enough for now,' she said to Poppy, 'until I have someone to help me.'

One of the best things about her restored friendship with Reuben was that she had Poppy back as a friend.

She had asked Reuben to join her, and initially he had seemed enthusiastic, but he had since then talked to Dorothy about it, and Dorothy had said she didn't think it was the best idea.

'She said it would be straining the new basis of our relationship,' he said, 'and I really have to do what she says.'

'Of course,' said Fleur. She was still having difficulty coming to terms with Reuben's new capacity for conversation.

'So here I am,' she remarked to Samson, her Burmese cat and new life-companion one evening in late September, 'I've done it all, all the things I swore I would. I have my own agency, and I've done Bella Buchanan down, and I've even kind of beaten Nigel Silk to a pitch. Well, I got a bit of Morell business. I did it, Samson, I really did.' Samson looked at her and she could see she wasn't fooling him at all. Very often, when she couldn't sleep, lying awake, trying to divert her mind with some creative or copy problem, or even with some blip in her cash flow, it returned with inexorable, inevitable determination to Magnus Phillips and the heavy, hungry loss she felt for him, and she would hear again and again his voice telling her he loved her, see his eyes as he said it, and then she would hear Rose Sharon's voice on his phone, and feel rage and betrayal rising in her and tell herself that she was better, far better on her own, conducting her own life; some time towards the dawn, sometimes with the help of a sleeping pill, sometimes a mug of hot milk with bourbon, she would finally manage to persuade herself that she believed it, and fall asleep and dream about him.

It was early October when Chloe called her; she had arranged for them to go and stay with Michelle Zwirn for a couple of days in the middle of the month, was that all right?

Sure, said Fleur, absolutely all right, and if they could synchronize their flights into LA they could hire a car and drive up to Santa Barbara together.

'It's a beautiful drive up the coast, you'll really like it.'

* * *

Magnus Phillips's arm was still extremely painful. It haunted his sleep at night and wrecked his concentration during the day; it made him bad-tempered, miserable and spoilt his appetite. He felt, he realized, glaring at his reflection in the bathroom mirror one morning, totally wretched: there seemed little to rejoice about. He had no new project to work on, nothing had captured his interest in the sparky, almost sexual way *Tinsel* or *Dancers* or *The House* had done; nobody seemed even worth profiling for a newspaper or a magazine; there was no part of the world he wished to visit, no friends he wanted to see, no woman he wanted to pursue. Except one: and she was out of bounds. Magnus did not often regard a woman as out of bounds; he was slightly unsure why he felt it so strongly about Fleur. He had in his time with the most efficient ruthlessness broken into marriages, disturbed love affairs, come between friends. But he was not prepared to do that for Fleur. He had spent long hours wrestling with the reasons, and was forced (feeling slightly foolish) to admit it was because he loved her. Love had done the impossible and made him careful, considerate, unselfish. Love, he thought, staring at his gaunt, grey face, was powerful stuff. It was also a bitch.

It was October now: many months since he had seen her, fucked her, told her he loved her. Almost as many since she had told him, in her rather individualistic way, to – well, to leave her alone. Magnus half smiled, thinking of Fleur, the strength of her feelings, the power of her language. And then stopped smiling abruptly, struggling to drag his mind away from her, angry at the extent to which she had monopolized his emotions, his sexual concentration. How the hell had she done it, on one sexual encounter, however savagely, wonderfully powerful it had been? And for that matter what right did she have, when he had trusted her enough to tell her he loved her, to turn hostile, angry, aggressive? What the hell had he done, that she should feel she could reject him so contemptuously? When he had, after all, been phoning as a friend? His anger grew, as it so often did when he allowed his mind to trail down this particular avenue: she had no right to his consideration, his concern; she did not deserve it.

Unless – and he could never think afterwards quite why this thought had not occurred to him before, except that the welter of powerful and dangerous events that had taken place had rendered his sense of time and place oddly impotent – unless she had called him. When Rose Sharon had been there. It was just possible. He had expressly forbidden Rose to answer the phone, had stressed the danger of such a course, had kept the answering machine on at all times: but it was a possibility. That would have hurt Fleur badly. It suddenly seemed important to try to reach her, to set the record straight. It was probably fruitless, and in any case she was probably married by now, married to her eccentrically silent boyfriend.

The more he thought about it that morning, whether because he was particularly exhausted, or the pain in his arm was exceptionally wretched, the angrier he became. What right did she have, whatever her feelings, to quite so harsh a response? Surely the baring of a soul, the revelation of a tenderness, deserved some consideration, some courtesy even. Arrogant, harsh little bitch; he wanted to communicate the fact, to show her what she was. Magnus looked at his watch. Nine. Four in New York. Too early: not that he would greatly mind waking her. But it would hardly be appropriate, to drag her from sleep at dawn and berate her with a lack of common courtesy. He waited: his rage, his sense of outrage unabated, until twelve. Seven o'clock; she should be ready for him now. He was certainly ready for her.

But she was apparently not: Tina answered the phone.

'Miss FitzPatrick's residence.'

'Is that you, Tina? This is Magnus Phillips. You may not remember me –'

'Mr Phillips, I certainly do.' In spite of his anger, Magnus smiled at the bridling voice. 'How could I forget you, Mr Phillips? Are you in New York? We have plenty of your marmalade here, why don't you come on over and I'll give you breakfast?'

'No, Tina, I'm not in New York, I'm afraid. Is Miss FitzPatrick there?'

'She is not, Mr Phillips. She's gone to California.'

'California? Really? Well –' He really had no right to start quizzing Tina about Fleur's whereabouts. On the other hand, having no right had never stopped him doing anything before. 'Whereabouts in California? Do you know?'

'I do, Mr Phillips, yes. She left a number, because she's starting this creating thing of hers very soon, and she didn't want any calls to go astray. She's gone to – let me see, yes, here it is, Santa Barbara. Santa Barbara 785–68943.'

Dear God in heaven: the Zwirns. What on earth was she up to now? 'Er – has she gone with – with her husband, Tina?' he said, gripping the edge of his desk with fingers that he noticed to his immense irritation had become slippery with sweat.

'Her husband? Mr Phillips, she got no husband. I think she's ab-so-lute-ly crazy.' Tina's voice was dark with disapproval. 'She had that beaut-i-ful Mr Blake, just about mad in love with her, the wedding all lined up, the dress still hanging in the closet here, the reception booked, everything fixed, and what does she do, she cancels the lot.'

'Well,' said Magnus. His mind was racing, he couldn't think of anything else to say.

'She needs a man, Mr Phillips. She needs keeping company and looking after. We all do, but her more 'n most. She's all mouth, Miss FitzPatrick is, all mouth. Nowhere near as tough as she thinks.' There was a long silence, then Tina said, 'You should come over here, Mr Phillips. Come over here, see her again. You married yet, Mr Phillips?'

'No,' said Magnus, 'no, I'm not married, Tina. Not the marrying kind.'

'Mr Phillips, we're all the marrying kind. My man thought he wasn't the marrying kind, till he fell over me in the dark.' She laughed. Magnus could almost hear her bulk heaving. 'You got that number, Mr Phillips?'

'Yes,' said Magnus, 'I've got the number. Thank you, Tina.'

* * *

Fleur and Chloe both arrived at LAX within an hour of one another mid afternoon one golden October day. They looked at each other, awkwardly, oddly shy; then Fleur said, 'You must be a lot tireder than I am. Let's go and sort out a car.'

She took charge: took Chloe's bag, threw it on a trolley, led her out to the street, hailed a Hertz bus, climbed on to it. Chloe followed her in silence.

'I never had to do anything like this for myself,' she said, rather soberly. 'I'm only just beginning to realize how hopeless I am.'

'Not hopeless,' said Fleur with a grin, 'just untrained. Spoiled, you could say.'

'I suppose you could.'

They pulled into the Hertz offices; Fleur said they'd take anything, as long as it was convertible. The girl offered them a small T-bird: 'Perfect,' said Fleur, taking out her Gold Amex card, signing for the car.

'It's over there, in H 17. The red one. Here are the keys.'

'Great.'

They got into the car. 'I'll drive, shall I?' said Fleur. 'I'm used to this side of the road. You OK?'

Chloe nodded. 'Fine. I'll settle up with you later, Fleur.'

'Don't worry,' said Fleur. She looked at Chloe. 'You've no idea what a perverse pleasure it gives me to be in charge in this particular situation. Paying for it even. Let me enjoy it.'

'All right,' said Chloe. 'You enjoy it.'

It was already four thirty; but the air was gloriously warm.

'We'll keep the lid up for now,' said Fleur, 'let it down when we hit the highway. It's a bit polluted round here.'

They drove through the suburbs in silence; Chloe was half asleep. As they reached Santa Monica, tipped down the hill on to the Pacific Coast Highway, Fleur pressed the button that sent the roof down. The rush-hour traffic was heavy, thudding along by the brilliant sea.

'How long will it take to Santa Barbara?' asked Chloe.

'Oh – I don't know. A couple of hours. We could have gone on the 101, but this way along the coast is so beautiful, especially at sunset. I thought you should see it.'

'You seem to know it very well.'

'Not really. But I came here a few times. Once with Joe.'

'With Joe?'

'Yeah, when I wasn't much more than a child,' she said and sighed at the memory.

'Do you like Joe?' said Chloe interestedly, with a sudden thud of jealousy.

'I did love Joe. I probably could again. But he – well, we had a huge fight at one point. And I got really really angry with him. My fault as much as his I expect.'

'I expect so too,' said Chloe briskly.

Fleur looked at her. 'I think we could be quite good for each other, in time,' she said and laughed.

They drove on; the sun gave its glorious nightly exhibition, and sank into the brilliant dark turquoise of the Pacific in a series of colour changes, red, orange, pink, as the mountains to their left grew darker, larger. They swung on to the 101 as darkness fell, the sudden, soft California darkness; Fleur had put the top back on the car. Chloe was asleep. She turned the radio on: George Harrison was singing 'My Sweet Lord'. It seemed to go with her mood: hypnotic, powerful, almost mystic. She felt very close to her father suddenly; so close she felt almost scared. She was about to find him, who he had really been, what he had really been doing, maybe how it had all ended; and looking at that, down fifteen years, was heady, heart-stopping stuff.

'Hi, Dad,' she said suddenly, involuntarily, and then felt very foolish, as she saw Chloe turn her head, open her eyes, look at her.

But Chloe only smiled, a soft, sleepy smile.

It was after seven thirty when they finally reached Santa Barbara; a friendly gas station attendant directed them to Voluntario Street.

'You'll love it here,' said Fleur. 'It's terribly peaceful. Kind of a time warp. Not a bit like LA.'

She parked the car outside the house, and they sat looking at it, suddenly both of them scared to go in. It was small, but pretty, slightly Spanish in style, with a path up to the door between two lawns. Fleur took a deep breath, grabbed Chloe's hand.

'Come on. Let's go for it.'

And then the front door opened, the porch light went on and a woman stood framed in it: a stout, rather dumpy figure, wearing Bermudas and espadrilles. She came down the path, rather slowly: Fleur got out first. Michelle Zwirn looked up at her.

'You're very like your father,' she said.

She had cooked them a wonderful American meal, of fried chicken and sweet potatoes and apple pie: she sat watching them eat, smiling at them.

'Aren't you going to have any?' said Chloe anxiously.

'I don't eat too much,' said Michelle Zwirn.

She didn't look like someone who didn't eat much; she was very plump indeed with round cheeks and little fat hands, bedecked with rings. She was blonde, bright blonde, her hair dressed in a style reminiscent of Rita Hayworth, caught back with bright pink combs, and she wore flamboyant wing-framed glasses that matched the combs. The eyes behind them were faded blue, and very sweet.

'I just can't believe you're here,' she said, 'I just can't believe it. Times I said to Gerard, too bad we'll never meet Piers's wife. But I don't think he saw it quite that way. No offence,' she added apologetically.

'Of course not,' said Chloe, and then because it was important, so important that Michelle should understand how she felt, she said, 'Michelle, I do want you to know that I really feel so happy about all this. I mean it's a little strange of course, but Piers was – well, very complex.' She paused, carefully looking for the right words. A discovery of unfaithfulness, as the Zwirns might perceive it, would be very hurtful, damaging. To them Piers was a perfect, almost a saintly figure; it would be cruel to disabuse them of that. 'I think I always knew there was someone else. And finding out who it was made me feel so much better. I hope you can understand that.'

Michelle nodded. 'I do. I'm glad you do, that's the thing. Fleur, you're not eating. Have some more apple pie.'

'I couldn't,' said Fleur, and then said, gently, 'so, Michelle, tell us about Gerard.'

'Well, he was very brave. Very good. He lay on his back for fifteen years in pain and couldn't move and only complained once in a very rare while. He lived in there' – she pointed to a room off the dining room – 'and in the garden, of course. We had a bed on wheels for him, and he had a wheelchair. But that was difficult for him, because he couldn't control his head; he was better on the bed. Would you like to see some pictures of him?'

'Yes, please,' said Chloe.

Michelle stood up, got a large album, sat down beside her, pushed the dishes aside. Chloe started turning the pages and watched the story of the love of her husband's life unfolding and thought what a strange and powerful thing that love had been and wondered at the extraordinary blend of sheer, blind selfishness and self-obsession and absolute generosity and unselfishness that Piers had been.

'Here he is, a little boy, dancing even then you see; he won all the prizes going: went to Hollywood High, and then here he is on graduation day, and here the day he opened his dancing school. Tip Top Tap it was called; don't you like that? Oh, he was so excited, so proud. "I did it, Chelle," he kept saying, "no, we did it." I saw to the paperwork, you know, the bookings and the bills.'

They looked at Gerard: he was small, boyish, with floppy dark hair, big eyes, and a wonderful, wide smile. He had obviously been a snappy dresser; when he wasn't in his dance gear, he wore slacks, two-tone shoes, proper shirts rather than Ts, sweaters tied loosely round his shoulders. 'He's very good-looking,' said Chloe carefully.

'Well, he was very sweet-looking,' said Michelle. 'But there were a lot of lookers around. You had to be very special to stand out. Now look, here are some of the kids –'

'Shit,' said Fleur sharply, 'shit, there's my dad.' And there he was, tall, graceful, leaning on the barre in the studio, a cigarette in his mouth, smiling through the smoke. 'Did Gerard know him well?'

'Pretty well. He came to classes, that's how they met, then joined in the crowd. When he was allowed. Later on when Naomi got her claws into him, we didn't see him very often. Such a handsome man, he was. Couldn't dance of course, but he liked to try.'

'I remember him dancing rather well,' said Fleur defensively.

'Well, dear, he could dance all right for a person,' said Michelle, stressing the word, 'but he was not a dancer. No way was he a dancer.'

'Well, he didn't want to be a dancer,' said Fleur.

Michelle looked at her and smiled, a sweet, tender smile. 'Of course he didn't. He wanted to be an actor. And oh, he was a charmer. Such a charmer. Too charming, I guess. For his own good. Now here they are, on the beach, look, all of them, all that crowd, Gerard, and there's Piers, and look, that's Rose Sharon, she was nobody then –'

'Rose?' said Fleur. 'I don't understand. Rose said Piers wasn't in Hollywood then, that she never met him until he was a big name. Or –'

'Of course she met him. I always thought she rather liked him. But of course she was still in love with your father then, Fleur. Even though Naomi had broken them up. She never did get over him. Never, never.'

Fleur was silent, staring at the album.

'Who's this then?' said Chloe, pointing to a girl in a bikini, with a blonde pony-tail, in between Gerard and another man, an arm round each of their waists.

'That's Kirstie,' said Michelle. 'Kirstie Fairfax. Gerard would still be here today, if it hadn't been for Kirstie.'

'Why?' said Chloe.

Michelle told them.

Excerpt from Sudden Death, chapter of *The Tinsel Underneath*.

Nobody knew who the father of Kirstie's baby was. It could have been one of a dozen people. But she told Brendan it was his, and it was certainly possible. Possible enough for him to be unable to ignore her.

Kirstie was gorgeous: fun, pretty, sexually ambivalent – and absolutely ruthless. And she fell in love with Brendan. Brendan wasn't like most of the men she went around with, men she despised. She admired Brendan; he had a quality she hadn't known before. He seemed to her to be a gentleman. And Kirstie came as near to falling in love with Brendan as she had ever done in her seventeen years.

She got carried away, in fact, on a tide of romanticism and excitement. Brendan, equally carried away on the same tide, the heady excitement of deceiving Naomi, of disobeying orders, flattered by Kirstie's attachment to him, grew careless. He saw Kirstie night after night. They made love in his car, on the beach, in parks, in cinemas. It was part of the game. Then Naomi heard of the affair, and called him back to heel. And Kirstie wanted revenge.

Brendan was scared. He'd talked too much. She knew everything about him. She was dangerous.

She had become pregnant quite deliberately; she had known it was the one way she could get him. When she told him, told him she would talk, he panicked, promised to get her a part, to pay for an abortion, if only she would keep quiet.

It wasn't enough for Kirstie. She wanted blood. She wanted acknowledgement. She wanted Brendan.

Brendan was terrified. He knew she could destroy him. And he couldn't deliver what she wanted. He failed to get her a part. He refused to leave Naomi. And Kirstie became very angry. She threatened to come to the studio, come on to the set, make a scene. He didn't know what to do.

* * *

He agreed to meet her on Santa Monica Pier, late one evening, to plead with her for one last time. And he asked Piers and Gerard to go with him.

Piers and Gerard were by then an item, in the jargon of the town: lovers – and true and devoted friends. And concerned for their other friend, Brendan. They'd seen Brendan through a lot. They didn't want to see him go down.

They walked along the pier. It was a very clear night, the moon was full. Kirstie was hysterical: crying, shouting, threatening. She was furious that Brendan had come with his friends; furious he had not been able to help her get a part, furious he was not prepared to leave Naomi and be with her. She told him she was going to tell: everything. Everything she knew about him. Tell Naomi, the studio, the publicity people. Brendan was desperate. He begged her to be reasonable, to understand his position, to let him pay for an abortion for her. She refused. She started yelling at him; he told her to shut up. She ignored him, shouted louder. He turned and tried to walk away back down the pier; Piers and Gerard were at a discreet distance behind them, not knowing what to do.

Kirstie ran after him, shouting, punching his back with her fists. She came at him, pushing him against the railings of the pier. He pushed her off, she came after him again. He raised his arm, to avoid her, and caught her instead; she toppled back, then flew at him. He ducked: she fell sprawled against the railings. Brendan went and picked her up; she was flailing, screaming, biting him. Suddenly she caught him a blow between the eyes; he staggered against the railings, and Kirstie fell over, on to the wrong side.

She went over, just caught the bottom of the railings with her hands; she hung there, screaming, slowly slipping. Brendan, still dazed, watched her hanging there, and Gerard ran forward, climbed over the rail, desperately trying to reach her. He had just touched her hand, was just taking her fingers, when she finally slipped, and fell; he fell too. Down, down, on to the structure beneath the pier, screaming, breaking as he fell. Kirstie was dead, lying there on the beach; Gerard, and it was perhaps his tragedy, was still alive.

Chapter 41

October 1972

'Come and see his room,' said Michelle quietly. 'I'd like you to see it. Then you must go to bed. Chloe, you look so tired, dear.'

Chloe shook her head, smiled rather confusedly at her. 'I'm all right. Really.'

They followed Michelle into Gerard's room; stood in the doorway.

Chloe gasped aloud.

It was a shrine to Piers. Every surface, every inch of wall space was covered with photographs of him. In every film; every play; pictures of him with his horses, with his cars, outside Stebbings; pictures of him at premières, at charity parties, at award ceremonies, arriving at airports. Reviews were also framed: endless adulatory reviews. And there were other pictures too: of Piers with Gerard, sitting by his bed, in his wheelchair, in the garden, Piers and Gerard gradually growing older, always smiling, laughing, holding hands, looking happy. The only thing missing was any pictures of Chloe. Chloe and the children.

'I – I think I am a little tired,' she said, finally, after walking round and round the room, studying the pictures, the articles, her husband's extraordinary other marriage, other life. 'I think I might go to bed. If you don't mind.'

'Of course not,' said Michelle. 'You look just terrible. I'm sorry, it must have been such a strain for you, the whole day. Let me show you to your room. You're sharing, is that all right?'

'Of course,' said Chloe.

'Chloe, if you don't mind I'm going to stay up, talk to Michelle a little longer,' said Fleur. 'I'll be along in a while. Is that OK?'

'Of course,' said Chloe again.

She walked out of the room after Michelle, very slowly and heavily, looking rather like an old lady.

Fleur settled by the fire with Michelle. Michelle made her a cup of tea. She also looked tired and rather strained.

'So – my dad wasn't exactly a hero. It seems.'

Michelle shrugged. 'Who is? He was a nice guy. And he loved you. Boy, did he love you. The times we all had to sit and look at your pictures, have your letters read to us. "Oh my God," Gerard would say, when he came in, "he has another letter from Fleur." '

'Well,' said Fleur, briskly bright, 'he never wrote back. Or hardly ever. The odd postcard.'

'Life was very difficult for him, Fleur. You have to understand that.'

'Yes. Yes, I do.' But she didn't.

'And you don't have to feel badly about what happened with Kirstie. It was an accident. He wanted to report it. They all did. They intended to. But Gerard was – well, Gerard was screaming with agony, they had to get him off the pier, it took ages, and into the car. Piers took him to the hospital, and by then Kirstie was quite quite gone, gone into the sea. It was such an understandable decision. Such a scandal there would have been, if he'd told everyone, and what good would it have done? It was nobody's fault. She was dead, nothing was going to bring her back.'

'No. No, I suppose not.'

'And then he had such a terrible time. With everything. The clouds were stacking up by then, you know. You have to understand that too. It was an impossible situation for him.'

'He should have come home,' said Fleur. 'We'd have looked after him.'

'Yes, maybe he should. But – well, it was a spider's web he was in. Really. Growing all the time. He was scared, Fleur. Really scared.'

'Yes,' said Fleur absently. She looked at Michelle. 'Michelle?'

'Yes, dear? Would you like some more tea, dear? Maybe some cookies?'

'No. I'm fine.' She paused, gathering her courage, feeling it almost physically, a great force, pulling it around her, hanging on to it.

'Michelle, do you know who – who it was who – who –'

'Sold his story to the paper? Yes, dear, of course I do. It was Rose. Rose Sharon.'

Magnus Phillips had flown into LA the night before and booked into the Beverly Hills Hotel. He had always liked it there; it was so conspicuously, hopelessly vulgar. Magnus liked vulgarity.

He still wasn't quite sure what he was doing, chasing Fleur across the globe like a lovesick boy. He just knew he had to see her; to find out why she had cancelled her wedding to Reuben; to find out why she had been so angry with him.

And anyway, he just knew he had to see her.

He slept badly; he was exhausted and his arm hurt. Around three he took a sleeping pill, washed it down with brandy, and finally slept. The cooked English breakfast he had ordered for eight, complete with toast and Cooper's Oxford marmalade, grew cold. He finally woke after ten with a very thick head, and went out for a swim, before going back to his bungalow and calling the Zwirns.

Michelle answered the phone. Her voice was cool, cautious.

Yes, Fleur was staying there, with Chloe Windsor. She hoped he didn't want to talk to her any more about the book. She thanked him for his letter and the flowers he had sent for Gerard's funeral.

Magnus said that was OK; that he hoped she was feeling better, and that he didn't want to talk to her about the book, the book was anyway not going to be published for a long time. If ever. Could he speak with Fleur?

Fleur was out. She'd gone out in the car. Michelle didn't know where. Could Chloe help?

Magnus said he didn't think Chloe would talk to him but could she ask.

Chloe came to the phone surprisingly quickly.

'Magnus, please go away. I don't know what you're doing here, but I can assure you we don't want to see you. Either of us.'

'I can understand that. So you finally found the truth about Piers?' His voice was gentle.

'Yes, I did. I suppose you had all that in your book?'

'Yes, I did.'

'You are disgusting, Magnus. Absolutely disgusting.'

'Chloe, I'm not disgusting. If you ever read the book, you'll find out. It was a very sympathetic picture of Piers. More sympathetic, I might add, than he deserved. Given the way he treated you.'

'Magnus, just . . .' She hesitated, and then said, rather quickly, like a child saying something it knew it shouldn't, 'Just fuck off. Please.'

He laughed. 'You sound just like your sister. She's obviously having a bad influence on you. I need to find her. When will she be back?'

'I really don't know. I think she'll be quite a while. She's driven down to LA.'

'What for?' He could hear the fear in his voice, making it sharp, urgent.

'Magnus, does it matter?'

'Yes, it bloody well does matter.'

'Magnus, she doesn't want to see you.'

'Chloe, please, for the love of God tell me where she is. She could be in danger.'

'In danger? Oh, Magnus, really! She's gone to see a friend, that's all. A friend in LA.'

'A friend? Who?'

'Rose. Rose Sharon. She –'

'Good God Almighty, Chloe, when did she go?'

'Oh – hours ago. She'll be there by now. She –'

'Where was she meeting her? At the house? Chloe, for the love of God you have to tell me. It's terribly important.'

'Yes, at her house. But why, Magnus, why? I don't understand. Why is it so important? You'd better not just turn up there. She'll –'

'Chloe, Brendan FitzPatrick wasn't just run down by a passing car. Don't you understand? He was murdered.'

Rose Sharon passed Fleur a glass of champagne.

She smiled at her, her sweetest, saddest smile. They were sitting by the pool; she was wearing a white towelling robe, and very large dark glasses that blanked out any expression from her face.

'Yes,' she said, 'yes, I did it. I am more ashamed of it than anything I have ever done. I've spent my life trying to get away from it, get away from the memory.' She sighed. 'I failed.'

Fleur took the champagne, sipped at it. She felt very sick and she thought it might help.

'I'm not surprised,' she said. Her voice, even to her, sounded harsh, bitter. 'It was a terrible thing to do. It killed him. Really. You killed him.'

'Fleur, don't!' Rose put down her glass, put her head in her hands. 'Don't you think I know that? Don't you think that thought haunts me, every day of my life?'

'Good,' said Fleur. 'It should.'

'Fleur, you sound so bitter, so angry. Still.'

'I am bitter, I am angry. I loved my father so much, and you – you took him away from me. For ever. And you didn't just take him away, you ended his life. So he died in dreadful circumstances.'

'I loved him too,' said Rose. She took the glasses off and the eyes looking at Fleur were very wide, almost pleading. 'Try to think how I felt. How I suffered. I loved him more than I could have believed possible. And I thought he loved me. He told me he did. He told me he wanted to marry me, did you know that? No of course not. He wouldn't have told you. We were all the world to each other, Fleur. I gave up a lot for him. I even gave up my first part, because it meant going away filming in Mexico for three months. I couldn't bear to leave him. Can you imagine that? I gave up the first chance I got of a future. For him. And then, then Naomi MacNeice came along, just snapped her fingers and he went. Gave me up, just like that. Oh, he said he was sorry. Of course. He said he would come back for me. When he'd made it, made his name. But he said he had to go. He moved out, and hardly ever spoke to me again. Until he was finished. Then he did, of course. Then he couldn't say enough. How he'd loved me so desperately, how he'd only meant to go for a short while. Think of the hurt of that, Fleur. Just think.'

Fleur was silent: tears were rolling down Rose's face.

'And do you know why he kept telling me he had to go, Fleur? For you. "I'm only doing it for my little girl, Rose," he said, "That's the only reason I'm here at all. When I've made it, we can all live together, the three of us." ' She looked at Fleur, and her face was distorted, ugly. 'Unless you've felt pain like that, Fleur, lost someone you loved so much you'd have died for them, you couldn't begin to understand.'

'I did,' said Fleur. 'Actually.'

She finished her champagne, held out her glass for more. Rose filled the glass, filled her own. She looked at her.

'And the humiliation. Everyone was so sorry for me. That was almost the worst thing. Terrible humiliation. As well as the pain.'

'I see,' said Fleur.

'And, Fleur, when I heard he'd – died, been run over like that, I wanted to die. I was so unhappy, so ashamed. It was like a terrible cross I was going to have to bear for the rest of my life. Brendan had died, and it was my fault. You're right. I did, I killed him. I accept that. It haunts me, Fleur, haunts my dreams.'

Fleur was silent. Rose looked at her.

'I know you can't ever, ever forgive me. But you could try, just try to understand. I did it because I loved him. I loved him too much.'

Fleur stared at her. Then she said, 'No. I don't think I could ever understand. Putting lies, filthy lies out about someone. Just for revenge.'

Rose laughed, gently. 'Not lies, Fleur. Not lies at all. He did have a homosexual relationship. I think he probably had several. Trying to get contracts, to get parts. They all did it, you know. Even Clark Gable, so they say. I didn't really care about that. I understood. In the end, I was so angry, so hurt, it was more than I could stand. All right, it was foolish, it was a foolish and terrible thing to do. Haven't you ever done something foolish, Fleur? If not terrible?'

Fleur looked at her. 'Yes,' she said quietly, 'very foolish and fairly terrible.'

'Well, then. You will understand. One day. I know you will. And forgive me. Fleur, I did it because I loved him. That was the only reason. I loved him and I was jealous and angry and hurt. And I can only keep on and on telling you, I'm so ashamed.'

Fleur finished the champagne. It was helping somehow. Easing the pain. Rose gave her some more; there was only half a glassful.

'I'll get you some more. It's Sue's day off. Wait there.'

Fleur sat in the hot sun, her head swimming slightly with the champagne, trying to sort out her feelings, trying to put herself in Rose's place, to imagine doing what she had done. She felt very confused, very shocked: shocked at the new information about her father as well, about Kirstie, about her death. And tired. She was terribly tired.

Rose reappeared, smiling, with a second bottle of champagne. She opened it, filled Fleur's glass to the top.

'Will you stay for lunch?' she said suddenly.

Fleur stared at her. Here was this woman, who had done this terrible thing to her father, asking her to stay for lunch as if they had had some trifling disagreement and now were friends again.

'No,' she said, 'no, I don't think so.'

'Oh Fleur, please.' Rose sat down again; there was a sob in her voice. 'There's something else. Something I haven't told you. I – was pregnant. I wanted to have that baby so much. So very much. I was so happy about it. And your father said – he said – "Rose, you'll just have to get rid of it. I'm sorry." I can hear his voice now. As if he was talking about a car or a piece of jewellery. Our baby, Fleur. Can you imagine that? I thought, because he loved *you* so much, he'd understand. But he didn't.'

Fleur felt more sick than ever. She stood up. The whole garden seemed to sway, the ground rocked beneath her. She stared at Rose. Somewhere inside the house the phone was ringing. It rang, on and on; Rose ignored it for a while, then she said, 'Excuse me, I'd better go. Ricardo and Marcie are out as well. I sent them to do some marketing.'

She came back. She had put the glasses back on.

'It was nothing. Nobody. Fleur, do you feel all right, darling? You look terrible. Sit down for a little while, put your head between your knees.'

Magnus put the phone down and swore. Not there. Just that cool little piece of a housekeeper, saying that Rose was away for the day, that Miss FitzPatrick had indeed called but had left again. Now where was she? Anywhere in the hills, by the ocean, anywhere really between here and Santa Barbara. Driving and horribly upset. He rang the Zwirns. Fleur hadn't been in touch. Chloe was anxious, fearful. Should he, should she, ring the police?

'Christ,' said Magnus, 'No. No, I don't think so. What do we tell them? I – shit!'

'Magnus, are you all right?' Chloe sounded almost concerned.

'Yes, I'm all right. I have this lousy arm, and it hurts like hell and I knocked it on the table. Oh God – look, Chloe, all we can do is wait, really. At least she's in no danger, if Rose is out of town. If she calls call me here, and tell her to ring me and then get back up to Santa Barbara fast, OK?'

'Yes,' said Chloe. 'OK.'

God, his arm hurt. It really needed strapping up again. That always eased it. Who the hell would do it? He wondered if the tennis pro might know a physio who could help. That'd be an idea. He went out down to the courts, asked for the pro; he was having an early lunch, they said, but he'd be back in ten minutes. Magnus decided to wait. The pain was distracting him; he couldn't think clearly. If it was strapped up, it would ease. He knew it would.

Twenty minutes later the pro hadn't come back; Magnus swore, and asked in reception; they said they had a doctor on call, would Mr Phillips like to wait. Mr Phillips said he'd see the doctor later, and decided to take some more pain-killers for now. He went to his bag, and found he was out of the things; the pharmacy in the hotel only sold aspirin. Christ, he was in bloody agony. He'd have to go out and buy some something really strong like Distalgesic. They'd at least take the edge off the pain. And he wouldn't be long. He left a message for Fleur at the desk, saying he'd be back in half an hour if she rang, and please to come to the hotel and wait for him, and went out to the Mercedes he'd hired. Thank God it was an automatic. Gritting his teeth, he set out on his journey.

'Fleur, please! Stay a little while longer. I feel so terrible still, so guilty. I suppose I'm hoping I can make you understand even now. And you don't look very well, darling. Stay and rest.'

'No, really, I think I should go,' said Fleur. 'Could I just go and get a glass of water, I'm so hot, it's so terribly hot.'

'I'll get you some water, darling. You just stay there. Why don't you get into the pool for a minute or two, cool down, take a costume from the poolhouse, and I'll bring the water out.'

'Well – I–'

Fleur looked at the water. It might just do the trick. Not just cool her down, but clear her head. She felt very strange. She went into the poolhouse, picked out a black costume which was about two sizes too big for her, put it on and got into the water. It sagged loosely around her body. What did it matter?

She did feel better; just a little. Still woozy, but better. She swam up and down, slowly, trying not to think, just concentrating on her strokes and keeping her mind blank.

'Fleur!'

It was Rose. Fleur swam to the side, looked up, squinting slightly; Rose was silhouetted against the sun. She had put her glasses back on: she looked strangely sinister.

'Fleur,' she said, 'I've been thinking. I've decided to tell you a bit more.'

'Honestly, Rose,' said Fleur, 'honestly, I don't want to hear any more.'

'Maybe,' said Rose, 'but you're going to.'

'Rose,' said Fleur, trying to keep her voice calm, 'Rose, I don't . . .'

Her voice trailed off. Rose had picked up the long pole with the short net on the end that she used to clear the odd leaf from the surface of the pool; she was holding it just above her.

It was ridiculous, Fleur knew, but she felt oddly threatened. She swam away, pushed off the side with her feet, and turned in the other direction to climb out. Rose was there, waiting for her, above her, with the pole. She pushed Fleur with it very gently, away from the side.

'Sorry,' she said, 'I don't want to hurt you. But I would like you to stay there.'

'Rose, please!' said Fleur. She fought to keep her voice calm and firm.

'Fleur, this won't take long. Just listen to me, please. I really think you should know. It would be best.'

'Know what, Rose? You've told me about my father and you, about how much he hurt you. I don't think there's anything else.'

'There is, Fleur. There is. Quite a lot more. You see, I didn't feel I'd done enough, selling his story to the magazine. Oh, did I tell you, I got quite a lot of money for it? Very satisfactory. I felt better for a while, and then I started getting angry again. It was very bad. Very bad.'

'Rose, please. I'm getting cold now. Let me get out. I'll stay and listen to you.'

Fleur struggled to get out on to the side. Rose pushed her back in with the pole. She turned and swam to the steps but Rose was waiting for her. Panic began to rise in her: hot, heady panic. She fought it down: taking deep breaths, trying to be calm. If she listened to Rose she'd be all right. Of course she would.

'All right,' she said quietly. 'I'll stay here, and you can tell me whatever it is. Go on.'

Rose stood there holding the pole, watching her.

'Well, you see, I decided in the end I actually hated him enough, felt he'd hurt me enough, to do more. I couldn't wait for ever for him to drink himself to death. I knew he was living on the beach, knew none of his friends was helping him. Well, most of them weren't his friends at all, and Piers was totally occupied with Gerard. Maybe he'd even gone home by then. I don't remember. I went to see him, Fleur. He was living on the beach, with the other down-and-outs. He looked in pretty bad shape. I said I'd like to buy him a meal. If he wouldn't take my offer of a job – I'd offered him a job as my driver, you know – then he could at least let me feed him. After a while he agreed. So I took him out for a meal in some dive in Venice. I didn't want anyone to recognize us. And I bought him a lot of liquor. He was pretty low, pretty upset.'

Fleur didn't think she could take much more of this. Any of it. She struggled again to get out; again Rose pushed her back in. She wondered if she should shout for help, but Sue was out for the day, she knew, and she had seen Ricardo and Marcie leave herself. It was pointless. Rose's voice went on.

'So then I got him back into the car, put a bottle of bourbon in his hands – he always liked bourbon, Fleur, could never get enough of it – and started to drive him out along the highway. He was sitting there, getting drunker and drunker; I did a circuit, we went right along to Malibu, turned round and came back again. It was pretty late; very few cars. Just as we reached the road up to Santa Monica, where the highway hits the hill, I stopped, opened the door and told him to get out.'

Don't think, Fleur, don't think about anything, not this, not your dad, just concentrate on keeping calm. She swam up and down hard, to keep warmer; the pool was very cold.

Rose smiled. 'It is cold, isn't it? I turned the heating off. Well, I'm sure you can guess the rest of the story. He was stumbling up the hill; I turned at the top, and drove down and hit him. It was a wonderful moment.' She smiled at the memory, the sweet wistful smile she was famous for. 'I felt soothed, healed. Fleur, don't cry, darling, you mustn't cry, it's so long ago.'

Magnus went into a pharmacy in the mall in Rodeo Drive. They must have been the most expensive pain-killers in the whole of California, he thought, handing over ten dollars for a packet of Dista. The packet told him to take two; he asked for some water, took four. He decided to go and have a coffee and wait for them to take effect before driving back to the hotel. He wandered into the café on the ground floor of the mall, ordered some iced tea and sat staring moodily in front of him. And then he saw Sue Robinson.

He waved at her.

'Mr Phillips. What are you doing in here? On vacation?'

It seemed a slightly odd remark to make to someone she'd spoken to an hour or so ago, but still. They were a funny lot, the Californians. 'Sort of. What you are doing? Shopping?'

'Yeah,' she said, smiling, 'treating myself. It's my day off.'

'What happened just now then? Did you forget something?'

'I'm sorry?'

'When you were at the house. About an hour ago?'

'I wasn't at the house, Mr Phillips. I haven't been at the house since very early this morning.'

'But –' His mind was racing. 'Didn't I speak to you? Just now? Didn't you tell me Rose was away?'

'No.' She looked puzzled. 'She isn't away anyway. She's at the house. She starts rehearsing her new movie tomorrow, said she wanted some peace today to look at the script.'

'Shit,' said Magnus. 'Dear God. Dear Mother of God. Sue, will you call the police, please. Tell them to get up to Rose's house. Immediately. Immediately.'

He ran faster than he would have believed possible into the car park, flung himself into the Merc, threw a twenty-dollar bill at the attendant and screamed up the street. His heart was banging, beating, bursting; fear rose in his throat like vomit. He shot a red light, then another; good. If any cops started after him so much the better. Shit, it was a long way: fifteen minutes at least. And even then he might be too late.

* * *

'Anyway, that was the end of it, I suppose. Except that it wasn't, because your friend Magnus Phillips started snooping about. I don't know quite how much he knows, but too much, I suspect. If he publishes that book – well, they're not going to now, are they? After Mr Windsor's, I mean Sir Piers's sad demise. What a tragedy. And how sweet. Him and that scrawny little friend of his going the same day.'

Fleur swam harder. She had given up hope of getting out: just wanted to keep from freezing to death.

'Anyway, Fleur, you know much too much now. I thought I'd like to tell you. Where was I? Oh, yes. Mr Phillips. He phoned just now. I pretended to be Sue and said I was out, that you'd left. I'm a very good mimic. As you may know. Mr Phillips. Now there is a sexy man. My type absolutely. Unfortunately it wasn't quite reciprocated. He seems to be in love with you. I even tried again in London, quite recently; doing a little extra checking on him and his book at the same time. You rang up one day, didn't you? I recognized your voice. I couldn't resist answering. I knew you'd know it was me. For some reason, I rather liked hurting you, Fleur. Probably because you manage to be more important to the men I want than I am.'

'Rose, I think you should stop this,' said Fleur. 'I think I should go home now. You have told me everything, and I'm glad you have. As you say it's a long time ago, and it's all over. I certainly won't be mentioning any of it. Please let me get out.'

'Oh, no,' said Rose. She had got the pole now, and was beginning to push

Fleur under the water. Fleur was getting weaker, with the cold, fear, exhaustion. She fought up again, looked up at Rose's face, still unreadable, still masked by her glasses.

'It was all your fault really, wasn't it?' said Rose. 'He left me for you. Not Naomi. So he could make some money, make a home for you. Have you down there. He loved you more than he loved anyone, Fleur. Much more than he loved me. I find that a little hard, Fleur, even now.'

Push again. Under the water. Longer this time. She wriggled, tried to get clear, come up, but Rose was there, with her pole, holding her down. Suddenly she released her; she came up again into the sunlight, gasping, fighting for breath.

'Rose, please, please let me out.'

'No, darling. I'm sorry. I can't. Not now. Goodbye, Fleur darling. What a terrible accident you've had today. Too much champagne, those sleeping pills you always carry with you, me having a nap inside, not hearing you call for help. So sad. So very sad. Goodbye.'

She pushed again. Somewhere deep in the darkness that was engulfing her Fleur could hear a police siren. How ironic. How very ironic. If only they knew what was happening to her, here, now.

Her last thought was of Magnus Phillips, and how much she loved him and how terrible it was that he would never know it.

Epilogue

October – November 1972

'I love you,' said Fleur.

'I know you do,' said Magnus.

She kept saying it. It seemed terribly important; that she did, that she could.

It had been a long day: she had woken up in hospital with Magnus sitting beside her, grey with pain and exhaustion.

'You look terrible,' she said.

'I feel terrible. You look all right.'

'I feel all right,' she said with some surprise. 'Really all right.'

'Well, that's good,' he said, 'because I have to have this arm reset. They're coming for me quite soon. I broke it again. Well, Rose broke it for me. It's bloody agony.'

'What happened to Rose?'

'They took her away. For a long time, I think.'

'Oh God,' said Fleur. The horror came rushing back. 'God, Magnus, that was bad.'

He stroked her hair back.

'You knew, didn't you?'

'Yes,' he said, 'I knew.'

'You should have told the police.'

'Maybe.'

'But you wanted to publish the book. Didn't you?'

'Yes,' he said with a sigh. 'Yes, I did. It seemed worth the risk.'

'Arrogant bastard,' said Fleur good-naturedly. 'Nearly got me killed.'

'And myself,' he said, 'don't forget me. Rose's thugs, knocking me off my bike.'

'You deserved it.' She smiled at him, slightly warily. 'Magnus, how did you know? Who told you?'

'Her hairdresser. Always very close to their employers, hairdressers are. In Hollywood.'

'Her hairdresser!' She was silent, remembering the apparently irrelevant questions about Rose's hairdresser by the pool that day.

'Yes. Not her current one, a pathetic old biddy Rose dismissed years ago.

She'd bought her off. But not quite enough. She had obviously adored her, idolized her. She heard her on the phone to the reporter. And then of course she wasn't sure about the murder. But she heard her coming back late, and next morning she saw – well, she saw signs on the car. Rose told her she'd hit a dog. Sorry, Fleur – Fleur darling, don't look like that. It's all right. It's over. All right, darling, cry. Have a good yell. It'll do you good.'

Fleur yelled. She yelled and sobbed for quite a while. Magnus was right: it did help.

'Incidentally,' he said, as she lay back on her pillows, calmer now, holding his hand, 'did she tell you she was pregnant by your dad?'

'Yes, she did.'

'She told me too. It wasn't true. The hairdresser told me that too. Sympathy bid. Not pregnant at all.'

'Oh,' said Fleur quietly. 'Oh, I see. That's – that's nice. I'm glad about that.'

A nurse came in. 'Time to get you ready for your surgery, Mr Phillips.'

'Can we have just a minute?' said Fleur.

'Just one,' said the nurse.

Fleur sat up, took Magnus's head in her hands and kissed him very hard on the mouth.

'I love you,' she said, 'and we have a lot of ground to make up.'

'I look forward to that. Christ, I hope that nurse doesn't come back just yet. I'm sure people don't usually go into surgery with gigantic erections.'

'Well,' said Fleur, after a while, after reaching out, caressing the bulge in his trousers, looking at it hungrily, 'I guess the nurse would probably quite like it. Actually. Although not as much as I would.' She lay back again with a sigh, taking the hand that was attached to his good arm. 'Well, Rose did one wonderful thing. Before she tried to kill me.'

'Which was?'

'She managed to convince me my dad was one of the good guys. That he did love me best. After all.'

'In that case,' said Magnus, 'it was all worth it.'

Fleur looked at him very solemnly for a long time. 'The reason I love you,' she said, 'is that you always get it right.'

That night Fleur and Chloe took up occupation in Magnus's bungalow at the Beverly Hills Hotel.

'What a day,' said Chloe.

'You could say that,' said Fleur cheerfully.

Chloe looked at her. 'You're very brave, I think,' she said.

'I didn't have a lot of choice. I was shitting myself in that water.'

'You were brave to go at all.'

'Well,' said Fleur, 'actually it was worth it. In all sorts of ways.'

They phoned Michelle, to tell her they were all right. She told them Caroline had called, had been terribly worried.

'Let's call her,' said Fleur, 'we can put it on Magnus's bill.'

She spoke to Caroline; she was shaken, almost tearful at the story. Fleur played it down, told her she was fine, absolutely fine.

'She really seemed upset,' she said to Chloe, her voice surprised.

'Of course she was upset,' said Chloe, 'she loves you.'

'So do you think you'll marry Magnus?' said Chloe.

'God, I don't know,' said Fleur. 'I'll let you know. Do you think you'll marry Ludovic?'

'I'll let you know. I – don't think so.'

'Why?'

'I don't seem to love him any more.'

'Do you know why?'

'Yes,' said Chloe. 'He's another man wanting a devoted wife. I want a man who doesn't.'

'Good for you,' said Fleur. 'Or maybe no man at all?'

There was a silence.

Then Fleur said, 'That would be brave, Chloe. That would really be brave. Much braver than me taking on Rose Sharon.'

'What would?'

'Getting rid of Ludovic. For no good reason.'

'I'm a good reason,' said Chloe, 'but, yes, it would.'

Reception rang through: it was Reuben. For Chloe.

'How do they all know where we are?' she said, going pink.

'Hallo?' she said. 'Yes, this is me. I'm fine. We're both fine. Yes, thank you, Reuben. Oh, well, I don't know. I'll have to ask Fleur.'

She looked at Fleur, her eyes very bright.

'Reuben says can I come back to New York for a few days. He'd like to see me.'

'It's OK with me,' said Fleur, 'but I really don't know what Dorothy will have to say about it.'

Another call: it was the hospital. Mr Phillips was fine. He'd like Miss FitzPatrick to go over and see him.

'Bloody hell,' said Fleur. 'It's midnight. Inconsiderate bastard. Yes, all right.' She looked at Chloe. 'Do you mind? If I go?'

'Of course not,' said Chloe.

'I suppose,' said Fleur thoughtfully, 'this must be love.' She smiled. 'You know, I can think of one very good reason why I shouldn't spend the rest of my life with Magnus Phillips. I'd have to start every single day looking at that filthy marmalade.'